The God *of*
Small Things

The God *of* Small Things

ARUNDHATI ROY

Flamingo
An Imprint of HarperCollins*Publishers*

This is a work of fiction. The characters in it are
all fictional. Liberties have been taken with the locations of
rivers, level crossings, churches and crematoria.

Flamingo
An Imprint of HarperCollins*Publishers*
77–85 Fulham Palace Road,
Hammersmith, London w6 8jb

Published by Flamingo 1997
1 3 5 7 9 8 6 4 2

A catalogue record for this book
is available from the British Library

ISBN 0 00 225586 3

Set in Monotype Baskerville by
Rowland Phototypesetting Ltd,
Bury St Edmunds, Suffolk

Printed and bound in Great Britain by
Caledonian International Book Manufacturing Ltd, Glasgow

ACKNOWLEDGEMENTS

Pradip Krishen, my most exacting critic, my closest friend, my love. Without you this book wouldn't have been *this* book.

Pia and Mithva for being mine.

Aradhana, Arjun, Bete, Chandu, Carlo, Golak, Indu, Joanna, Naheed, Philip, Sanju, Veena and Viveka, for seeing me through the years it took me to write this book.

Pankaj Mishra for flagging it off on its journey into the world.

Alok Rai and Shomit Mitter, for being the kind of readers that writers dream about.

David Godwin, flying agent, guide and friend. For taking that impulsive trip to India. For making the waters part.

Neelu, Sushma & Krishnan for keeping my spirits up and my hamstrings in working order.

And finally but immensely, Dadi and Dada. For their love and support.

Thank you.

For Mary Roy who grew me up.
Who taught me to say 'excuse me' before
interrupting her in Public.
Who loved me enough to let me go.

For LKC, who, like me, survived.

Never again will a single story be told as though it's the only one.

JOHN BERGER

CONTENTS

Paradise Pickles & Preserves

May in Ayemenem is a hot, brooding month. The days are long and humid. The river shrinks and black crows gorge on bright mangoes in still, dustgreen trees. Red bananas ripen. Jackfruits burst. Dissolute bluebottles hum vacuously in the fruity air. Then they stun themselves against clear windowpanes and die, fatly baffled in the sun.

The nights are clear but suffused with sloth and sullen expectation.

But by early June the south-west monsoon breaks and there are three months of wind and water with short spells of sharp, glittering sunshine that thrilled children snatch to play with. The countryside turns an immodest green. Boundaries blur as tapioca fences take root and bloom. Brick walls turn mossgreen. Pepper vines snake up electric poles. Wild creepers burst through laterite banks and spill across the flooded roads. Boats ply in the bazaars. And small fish appear in the puddles that fill the PWD potholes on the highways.

It was raining when Rahel came back to Ayemenem. Slanting silver ropes slammed into loose earth, ploughing it up like gunfire. The old house on the hill wore its steep, gabled roof pulled over its ears like a low hat. The walls, streaked with moss, had grown soft, and bulged a little with dampness that seeped up from the ground. The wild, overgrown garden was full of the whisper and scurry of small lives. In the undergrowth a rat snake rubbed itself against a glistening stone. Hopeful yellow bullfrogs cruised the scummy pond for mates. A drenched mongoose flashed across the leaf-strewn driveway.

The house itself looked empty. The doors and windows were locked. The front verandah bare. Unfurnished. But the skyblue Plymouth with chrome tailfins was still parked outside, and inside, Baby Kochamma was still alive.

She was Rahel's baby grand aunt, her grandfather's younger sister. Her name was really Navomi, Navomi Ipe, but everybody called her Baby. She became Baby Kochamma when she was old enough to be an aunt. Rahel hadn't come to see her, though. Neither niece nor baby grand aunt laboured under any illusions on that account. Rahel had come to see her brother, Estha. They were two-egg twins. 'Dizygotic' doctors called them. Born from separate but simultaneously fertilized eggs. Estha – Esthappen – was the older by eighteen minutes.

They never did look much like each other, Estha and Rahel, and even when they were thin-armed children, flat-chested, worm-ridden and Elvis Presley-puffed, there was none of the usual 'Who is who?' and 'Which is which?' from oversmiling relatives or the Syrian Orthodox Bishops who frequently visited the Ayemenem house for donations.

The confusion lay in a deeper, more secret place.

In those early amorphous years when memory had only just begun, when life was full of Beginnings and no Ends, and Everything was For Ever, Esthappen and Rahel thought of themselves together as Me, and separately, individually, as We or Us. As though they were a rare breed of Siamese twins, physically separate, but with joint identities.

Now, these years later, Rahel has a memory of waking up one night giggling at Estha's funny dream.

She has other memories too that she has no right to have.

She remembers, for instance (though she hadn't been there), what the Orangedrink Lemondrink Man did to Estha in

Abhilash Talkies. She remembers the taste of the tomato sandwiches – *Estha's* sandwiches, that *Estha* ate – on the Madras Mail to Madras.

And these are only the small things.

Anyway, now she thinks of Estha and Rahel as *Them*, because separately, the two of them are no longer what *They* were or ever thought *They'd* be.

Ever.

Their lives have a size and a shape now. Estha has his and Rahel hers.

Edges, Borders, Boundaries, Brinks and Limits have appeared like a team of trolls on their separate horizons. Short creatures with long shadows, patrolling the Blurry End. Gentle half-moons have gathered under their eyes and they are as old as Ammu was when she died. Thirty-one.

Not old.

Not young.

But a viable die-able age.

They were nearly born on a bus, Estha and Rahel. The car in which Baba, their father, was taking Ammu, their mother, to hospital in Shillong to have them, broke down on the winding tea estate road in Assam. They abandoned the car and flagged down a crowded State Transport bus. With the queer compassion of the very poor for the comparatively well off, or perhaps only because they saw how hugely pregnant Ammu was, seated passengers made room for the couple and for the rest of the journey Estha and Rahel's father had to hold their mother's stomach (with them in it) to prevent it from wobbling. That was before they were divorced and Ammu came back to live in Kerala.

According to Estha, if they'd been born on the bus, they'd have got free bus rides for the rest of their lives. It wasn't clear

3

where he'd got this information from, or how he knew these things, but for years the twins harboured a faint resentment against their parents for having diddled them out of a lifetime of free bus rides.

They also believed that if they were killed on a zebra crossing, the Government would pay for their funerals. They had the definite impression that that was what zebra crossings were meant for. Free funerals. Of course there were no zebra crossings to get killed on in Ayemenem, or, for that matter, even in Kottayam, which was the nearest town, but they'd seen some from the car window when they went to Cochin, which was a two hour drive away.

The Government never paid for Sophie Mol's funeral because she wasn't killed on a zebra crossing. She had hers in Ayemenem in the old church with the new paint. She was Estha and Rahel's cousin, their uncle Chacko's daughter. She was visiting from England. Estha and Rahel were seven years old when she died. Sophie Mol was almost nine. She had a special child-sized coffin.

Satin-lined.

Brass handle shined.

She lay in it in her yellow Crimplene bellbottoms with her hair in a ribbon and her Made-in-England go-go bag that she loved. Her face was pale and as wrinkled as a dhobi's thumb from being in water for too long. The congregation gathered around the coffin, and the yellow church swelled like a throat with the sound of sad singing. The priests with curly beards swung pots of frankincense on chains and never smiled at babies the way they did on usual Sundays.

The long candles on the altar were bent. The short ones weren't.

An old lady masquerading as a distant relative (whom nobody recognized), but who often surfaced next to bodies at funerals (a funeral junkie? a latent necrophiliac?) put cologne on a wad of cotton wool and with a devout and gently challenging air, dabbed it on Sophie Mol's forehead. Sophie Mol smelled of cologne and coffinwood.

Margaret Kochamma, Sophie Mol's English mother, wouldn't let Chacko, Sophie Mol's biological father, put his arm around her to comfort her.

The family stood huddled together. Margaret Kochamma, Chacko, Baby Kochamma, and next to her, her sister-in-law, Mammachi – Estha and Rahel's (and Sophie Mol's) grandmother. Mammachi was almost blind and always wore dark glasses when she went out of the house. Her tears trickled down from behind them and trembled along her jaw like raindrops on the edge of a roof. She looked small and ill in her crisp off-white sari. Chacko was Mammachi's only son. Her own grief grieved her. His devastated her.

Though Ammu, Estha and Rahel were allowed to attend the funeral, they were made to stand separately, not with the rest of the family. Nobody would look at them.

It was hot in the church, and the white edges of the arum lilies crisped and curled. A bee died in a coffin flower. Ammu's hands shook and her hymnbook with it. Her skin was cold. Estha stood close to her, barely awake, his aching eyes glittering like glass, his burning cheek against the bare skin of Ammu's trembling, hymnbook-holding arm.

Rahel, on the other hand, was wide awake, fiercely vigilant and brittle with exhaustion from her battle against Real Life.

She noticed that Sophie Mol was awake for her funeral. She showed Rahel Two Things.

Thing One was the newly painted high dome of the yellow church that Rahel hadn't ever looked at from the inside. It was painted blue like the sky, with drifting clouds and tiny whizzing jet planes with white trails that crisscrossed in the clouds. It's true (and must be said) that it would have been easier to notice

5

these things lying in a coffin looking up than standing in the pews, hemmed in by sad hips and hymnbooks.

Rahel thought of the someone who had taken the trouble to go up there with cans of paint, white for the clouds, blue for the sky, silver for the jets, and brushes, and thinner. She imagined him up there, someone like Velutha, bare bodied and shining, sitting on a plank, swinging from the scaffolding in the high dome of the church, painting silver jets in a blue church sky.

She thought of what would happen if the rope snapped. She imagined him dropping like a dark star out of the sky that he had made. Lying broken on the hot church floor, dark blood spilling from his skull like a secret.

By then Esthappen and Rahel had learned that the world had other ways of breaking men. They were already familiar with the smell. Sicksweet. Like old roses on a breeze.

Thing Two that Sophie Mol showed Rahel was the bat baby.

During the funeral service, Rahel watched a small black bat climb up Baby Kochamma's expensive funeral sari with gently clinging curled claws. When it reached the place between her sari and her blouse, her roll of sadness, her bare midriff, Baby Kochamma screamed and hit the air with her hymnbook. The singing stopped for a 'Whatisit? Whathappened?' and for a furrywhirring and a sariflapping.

The sad priests dusted out their curly beards with goldringed fingers as though hidden spiders had spun sudden cobwebs in them.

The baby bat flew up into the sky and turned into a jet plane without a crisscrossed trail.

Only Rahel noticed Sophie Mol's secret cartwheel in her coffin.

The sad singing started again and they sang the same sad verse twice. And once more the yellow church swelled like a throat with voices.

When they lowered Sophie Mol's coffin into the ground in the little cemetery behind the church, Rahel knew that she still wasn't dead. She heard (on Sophie Mol's behalf), the softsounds of the red mud and the hardsounds of the orange laterite that spoiled the shining coffin polish. She heard the dullthudding through the polished coffin wood, through the satin coffin lining. The sad priests' voices muffled by mud and wood.

> *We entrust into thy hands, most merciful Father,*
> *The soul of this our child departed,*
> *And we commit her body to the ground,*
> *Earth to earth, ashes to ashes, dust to dust.*

Inside the earth Sophie Mol screamed, and shredded satin with her teeth. But you can't hear screams through earth and stone.

Sophie Mol died because she couldn't breathe.

Her funeral killed her. *Dus to dus to dus to dus to dus.* On her tombstone it said *A Sunbeam Lent To Us Too Briefly*.

Ammu explained later that Too Briefly meant For Too Short a While.

After the funeral Ammu took the twins back to the Kottayam police station. They were familiar with the place. They had spent a good part of the previous day there. Anticipating the sharp, smoky stink of old urine that permeated the walls and furniture, they clamped their nostrils shut well before the smell began.

Ammu asked for the Station House Officer and when she was shown into his office, she told him that there had been a terrible mistake and that she wanted to make a statement. She asked to see Velutha.

Inspector Thomas Mathew's moustaches bustled like the friendly Air India Maharajah's, but his eyes were sly and greedy.

'It's a little too late for all this, don't you think?' he said. He

7

spoke the coarse Kottayam dialect of Malayalam. He stared at
Ammu's breasts as he spoke. He said the police knew all they
needed to know and that the Kottayam Police didn't take statements from *veshyas* or their illegitimate children. Ammu said
she'd see about that. Inspector Thomas Mathew came around
his desk and approached Ammu with his baton.

'If I were you,' he said, 'I'd go home quietly.' Then he tapped
her breasts with his baton. Gently. *Tap, tap.* As though he was
choosing mangoes from a basket. Pointing out the ones that
he wanted packed and delivered. Inspector Thomas Mathew
seemed to know whom he could pick on and whom he couldn't.
Policemen have that instinct.

Behind him a red and blue board said:

> **P** oliteness
> **O** bedience
> **L** oyalty
> **I** ntelligence
> **C** ourtesy
> **E** fficiency

When they left the police station Ammu was crying, so Estha
and Rahel didn't ask her what *veshya* meant. Or for that matter,
illegitimate. It was the first time they'd seen their mother cry. She
wasn't sobbing. Her face was set like stone, but the tears welled
up in her eyes and ran down her rigid cheeks. It made the twins
sick with fear. Ammu's tears made everything that had so far
seemed unreal, real. They went back to Ayemenem by bus. The
conductor, a narrow man in khaki, slid towards them on the
bus rails. He balanced his bony hips against the back of a seat
and clicked his ticket-puncher at Ammu. *Where to?* the click was
meant to mean. Rahel could smell the sheaf of bus tickets and
the sourness of the steel bus-rails on the conductor's hands.

'He's dead,' Ammu whispered to him. 'I've killed him.'

'Ayemenem,' Estha said quickly, before the conductor lost his temper.

He took the money out of Ammu's purse. The conductor gave him the tickets. Estha folded them carefully and put them in his pocket. Then he put his little arms around his rigid, weeping mother.

Two weeks later, Estha was Returned. Ammu was made to send him back to their father, who had by then resigned his lonely tea estate job in Assam and moved to Calcutta to work for a company that made carbon black. He had remarried, stopped drinking (more or less), and suffered only occasional relapses.

Estha and Rahel hadn't seen each other since.

And now, twenty-three years later, their father had re-Returned Estha. He had sent him back to Ayemenem with a suitcase and a letter. The suitcase was full of smart new clothes. Baby Kochamma showed Rahel the letter. It was written in a slanting, feminine, convent school hand, but the signature underneath was their father's. Or at least the name was. Rahel wouldn't have recognized the signature. The letter said that he, their father, had retired from his carbon black job and was emigrating to Australia where he had got a job as Chief of Security at a ceramics factory, and that he couldn't take Estha with him. He wished everybody in Ayemenem the very best and said that he would look in on Estha if he ever came back to India, which, he went on to say, was a bit unlikely.

Baby Kochamma told Rahel that she could keep the letter if she wanted to. Rahel put it back into its envelope. The paper had grown soft, and folded like cloth.

She had forgotten just how damp the monsoon air in Ayemenem could be. Swollen cupboards creaked. Locked windows burst open. Books got soft and wavy between their covers. Strange insects appeared like ideas in the evenings and burned

9

themselves on Baby Kochamma's dim 40-watt bulbs. In the daytime their crisp, incinerated corpses littered the floor and windowsills, and until Kochu Maria swept them away in her plastic dustpan, the air smelled of Something Burning.

It hadn't changed, the June Rain.

Heaven opened and the water hammered down, reviving the reluctant old well, greenmossing the pigless pigsty, carpet bombing still, tea-coloured puddles the way memory bombs still, tea-coloured minds. The grass looked wetgreen and pleased. Happy earthworms frolicked purple in the slush. Green nettles nodded. Trees bent.

Further away, in the wind and rain, on the banks of the river, in the sudden thunderdarkness of the day, Estha was walking. He was wearing a crushed-strawberry-pink T-shirt, drenched darker now, and he knew that Rahel had come.

Estha had always been a quiet child, so no one could pinpoint with any degree of accuracy exactly when (the year, if not the month or day) he had stopped talking. Stopped talking altogether, that is. The fact is that there wasn't an 'exactly when'. It had been a gradual winding down and closing shop. A barely noticeable quietening. As though he had simply run out of conversation and had nothing left to say. Yet Estha's silence was never awkward. Never intrusive. Never noisy. It wasn't an accusing, protesting silence as much as a sort of aestivation, a dormancy, the psychological equivalent of what lungfish do to get themselves through the dry season, except that in Estha's case the dry season looked as though it would last for ever.

Over time he had acquired the ability to blend into the background of wherever he was – into bookshelves, gardens, curtains, doorways, streets – to appear inanimate, almost invisible to the untrained eye. It usually took strangers a while to notice him even when they were in the same room with him.

It took them even longer to notice that he never spoke. Some never noticed at all.

Estha occupied very little space in the world.

After Sophie Mol's funeral, when Estha was Returned, their father sent him to a boys' school in Calcutta. He was not an exceptional student, but neither was he backward, nor particularly bad at anything. *An average student,* or *Satisfactory work* were the usual comments that his teachers wrote in his Annual Progress Reports. *Does not participate in Group Activities* was another recurring complaint. Though what exactly they meant by 'Group Activities' they never said.

Estha finished school with mediocre results, but refused to go to college. Instead, much to the initial embarrassment of his father and stepmother, he began to do the housework. As though in his own way he was trying to earn his keep. He did the sweeping, swabbing and all the laundry. He learned to cook and shop for vegetables. Vendors in the bazaar, sitting behind pyramids of oiled, shining vegetables, grew to recognize him and would attend to him amidst the clamouring of their other customers. They gave him rusted film cans in which to put the vegetables he picked. He never bargained. They never cheated him. When the vegetables had been weighed and paid for, they would transfer them to his red plastic shopping basket (onions at the bottom, brinjal and tomatoes on the top) and always a sprig of coriander and a fistful of green chillies for free. Estha carried them home in the crowded tram. A quiet bubble floating on a sea of noise.

At meal times when he wanted something, he got up and helped himself.

Once the quietness arrived, it stayed and spread in Estha. It reached out of his head and enfolded him in its swampy arms. It rocked him to the rhythm of an ancient, foetal heartbeat. It sent its stealthy, suckered tentacles inching along the insides of his skull, hoovering the knolls and dells of his memory, dislodging old sentences, whisking them off the tip of his tongue. It stripped his thoughts of the words that described them and left them pared and naked. Unspeakable. Numb. And to an observer therefore, perhaps barely there. Slowly, over the years, Estha withdrew from the world. He grew accustomed to the uneasy octopus that lived inside him and squirted its inky tranquillizer on his past. Gradually the reason for his silence was hidden away, entombed somewhere deep in the soothing folds of the fact of it.

When Khubchand, his beloved, blind, bald, incontinent seventeen-year-old mongrel, decided to stage a miserable, long-drawn-out death, Estha nursed him through his final ordeal as though his own life somehow depended on it. In the last months of his life, Khubchand, who had the best of intentions but the most unreliable of bladders, would drag himself to the top-hinged dog-flap built into the bottom of the door that led out into the back garden, push his head through it and urinate unsteadily, bright yellowly, *inside*. Then with bladder empty and conscience clear he would look up at Estha with opaque green eyes that stood in his grizzled skull like scummy pools and weave his way back to his damp cushion, leaving wet footprints on the floor. As Khubchand lay dying on his cushion, Estha could see the bedroom window reflected in his smooth, purple balls. And the sky beyond. And once a bird that flew across. To Estha – steeped in the smell of old roses, blooded on memories of a broken man – the fact that something so fragile, so unbearably tender had survived, had been *allowed* to exist, was a miracle. A bird in flight reflected in an old dog's balls. It made him smile out loud.

After Khubchand died Estha started his walking. He walked for hours on end. Initially he patrolled only the neighbourhood, but gradually went further and further afield.

People got used to seeing him on the road. A well-dressed

man with a quiet walk. His face grew dark and outdoorsy. Rugged. Wrinkled by the sun. He began to look wiser than he really was. Like a fisherman in a city. With sea-secrets in him.

Now that he'd been re-Returned, Estha walked all over Ayemenem.

Some days he walked along the banks of the river that smelled of shit, and pesticides bought with World Bank loans. Most of the fish had died. The ones that survived suffered from fin-rot and had broken out in boils.

Other days he walked down the road. Past the new, freshly baked, iced, Gulf-money houses built by nurses, masons, wire-benders and bank clerks who worked hard and unhappily in faraway places. Past the resentful older houses tinged green with envy, cowering in their private driveways among their private rubber trees. Each a tottering fiefdom with an epic of its own.

He walked past the village school that his great-grandfather built for Untouchable children.

Past Sophie Mol's yellow church. Past the Ayemenem Youth Kung Fu Club. Past the Tender Buds Nursery School (for Touchables), past the ration shop that sold rice, sugar, and bananas that hung in yellow bunches from the roof. Cheap soft-porn magazines about fictitious South Indian sex fiends were clipped with clothes pegs to ropes that hung from the ceiling. They spun lazily in the warm breeze, tempting honest ration buyers with glimpses of ripe, naked women lying in pools of fake blood.

Sometimes Estha walked past Lucky Press – old Comrade K. N. M. Pillai's printing press, once the Ayemenem office of the Communist Party, where midnight study meetings were held, and pamphlets with rousing lyrics of Marxist Party songs were printed and distributed. The flag that fluttered on the roof had grown limp and old. The red had bled away.

Comrade Pillai himself came out in the mornings in a greying

Aertex vest, his balls silhouetted against his soft white mundu. He oiled himself with warm, peppered coconut oil, kneading his old, loose flesh that stretched willingly off his bones, like chewing gum. He lived alone now. His wife, Kalyani, had died of ovarian cancer. His son, Lenin, had moved to Delhi, where he worked as a services contractor for foreign embassies.

If Comrade Pillai was outside his house oiling himself when Estha walked past, he made it a point to greet him.

'Estha Mon!' he would call out, in his high, piping voice, frayed and fibrous now, like sugarcane stripped of its bark. 'Good morning! Your daily constitutional?'

Estha would walk past, not rude, not polite. Just quiet.

Comrade Pillai would slap himself all over to get his circulation going. He couldn't tell whether Estha recognized him after all those years or not. Not that he particularly cared. Though his part in the whole thing had by no means been a small one, Comrade Pillai didn't hold himself in any way personally responsible for what had happened. He dismissed the whole business as the Inevitable Consequence of Necessary Politics. The old omelette and eggs thing. But then, Comrade K. N. M. Pillai was essentially a political man. A professional omeletteer. He walked through the world like a chameleon. Never revealing himself, never appearing not to. Emerging through chaos unscathed.

He was the first person in Ayemenem to hear of Rahel's return. The news didn't perturb him as much as excite his curiosity. Estha was almost a complete stranger to Comrade Pillai. His expulsion from Ayemenem had been so sudden and unceremonious, and so very long ago. But Rahel Comrade Pillai knew well. He had watched her grow up. He wondered what had brought her back. After all these years.

It had been quiet in Estha's head until Rahel came. But with her she had brought the sound of passing trains, and the light and shade that falls on you if you have a window seat. The world, locked out for years, suddenly flooded in, and now Estha couldn't hear himself for the noise. Trains. Traffic. Music. The Stock Market. A dam had burst and savage waters swept everything up in a swirling. Comets, violins, parades, loneliness, clouds, beards, bigots, lists, flags, earthquakes, despair were all swept up in a scrambled swirling.

And Estha, walking on the riverbank, couldn't feel the wetness of the rain, or the suddenshudder of the cold puppy that had temporarily adopted him and squelched at his side. He walked past the old mangosteen tree and up to the edge of a laterite spur that jutted out into the river. He squatted on his haunches and rocked himself in the rain. The wet mud under his shoes made rude, sucking sounds. The cold puppy shivered – and watched.

Baby Kochamma and Kochu Maria, the vinegar-hearted, short-tempered, midget cook, were the only people left in the Ayemenem house when Estha was re-Returned. Mammachi, their grandmother, was dead. Chacko lived in Canada now, and ran an unsuccessful antiques business.

As for Rahel.

After Ammu died (after the last time she came back to Ayemenem, swollen with cortisone and a rattle in her chest that sounded like a faraway man shouting), Rahel drifted. From school to school. She spent her holidays in Ayemenem, largely ignored by Chacko and Mammachi (grown soft with sorrow, slumped in their bereavement like a pair of drunks in a toddy bar) and largely ignoring Baby Kochamma. In matters related to the raising of Rahel, Chacko and Mammachi tried, but couldn't. They provided the care (food, clothes, fees), but withdrew the concern.

The Loss of Sophie Mol stepped softly around the Ayemenem House like a quiet thing in socks. It hid in books and food. In

Mammachi's violin case. In the scabs of the sores on Chacko's shins that he constantly worried. In his slack, womanish legs.

It is curious how sometimes the memory of death lives on for so much longer than the memory of the life that it purloined. Over the years, as the memory of Sophie Mol (the seeker of small wisdoms: *Where do old birds go to die? Why don't dead ones fall like stones from the sky?* The harbinger of harsh reality: *You're both whole wogs and I'm a half one.* The guru of gore: *I've seen a man in an accident with his eyeball swinging on the end of a nerve, like a yo-yo*) slowly faded, the Loss of Sophie Mol grew robust and alive. It was always there. Like a fruit in season. Every season. As permanent as a Government job. It ushered Rahel through childhood (from school to school) into womanhood.

Rahel was first blacklisted in Nazareth Convent at the age of eleven, when she was caught outside her Housemistress's garden gate decorating a knob of fresh cowdung with small flowers. At Assembly the next morning she was made to look up *depravity* in the Oxford Dictionary and read aloud its meaning. '*The quality or condition of being depraved or corrupt,*' Rahel read, with a row of stern-mouthed nuns seated behind her and a sea of sniggering schoolgirl faces in front. '*Perverted quality: Moral perversion; The innate corruption of human nature due to original sin; Both the elect and the non-elect come into the world in a state of total d. and alienation from God, and can, of themselves do nothing but sin. J. H. Blunt.*'

Six months later she was expelled after repeated complaints from senior girls. She was accused (quite rightly) of hiding behind doors and deliberately colliding with her seniors. When she was questioned by the Principal about her behaviour (cajoled, caned, starved), she eventually admitted that she had done it to find out whether breasts hurt. In that Christian institution, breasts were not acknowledged. They weren't supposed to exist, and if they didn't could they hurt?

That was the first of three expulsions. The second for

smoking. The third for setting fire to her Housemistress's false hair bun which, under duress, Rahel confessed to having stolen.

In each of the schools she went to, the teachers noted that she:

(a) Was an extremely polite child.

(b) Had no friends.

It appeared to be a civil, solitary form of corruption. And for this very reason, they all agreed (savouring their teacherly disapproval, touching it with their tongues, sucking it like a sweet) – all the more serious.

It was, they whispered to each other, *as though she didn't know how to be a girl.*

They weren't far off the mark.

Oddly, neglect seemed to have resulted in an accidental release of the spirit.

Rahel grew up without a brief. Without anybody to arrange a marriage for her. Without anybody who would pay her a dowry and therefore without an obligatory husband looming on her horizon.

So as long as she wasn't noisy about it, she remained free to make her own enquiries: into breasts and how much they hurt. Into false hair buns and how well they burned. Into life and how it ought to be lived.

When she finished school, she won admission into a mediocre college of Architecture in Delhi. It wasn't the outcome of any serious interest in Architecture. Nor even, in fact, of a superficial one. She just happened to take the entrance exam, and happened to get through. The staff were impressed by the size (enormous), rather than the skill, of her charcoal still-life sketches. The careless, reckless lines were mistaken for artistic confidence, though in truth, their creator was no artist.

She spent eight years in college without finishing the five-year undergraduate course and taking her degree. The fees were low and it wasn't hard to scratch out a living, staying in the hostel, eating in the subsidized student mess, rarely going to class, working instead as a draughtsman in gloomy architectural firms that exploited cheap student labour to render their presentation drawings and to blame when things went wrong. The other students, particularly the boys, were intimidated by Rahel's waywardness and almost fierce lack of ambition. They left her alone. She was never invited to their nice homes or noisy parties. Even her professors were a little wary of her – her bizarre, impractical building plans, presented on cheap brown paper, her indifference to their passionate critiques.

She occasionally wrote to Chacko and Mammachi, but never returned to Ayemenem. Not when Mammachi died. Not when Chacko emigrated to Canada.

It was while she was at the School of Architecture that she met Larry McCaslin who was in Delhi collecting material for his doctoral thesis on *Energy Efficiency in Vernacular Architecture*. He first noticed Rahel in the School library and then again, a few days later, in Khan Market. She was in jeans and a white T-shirt. Part of an old patchwork bedspread was buttoned around her neck and trailed behind her like a cape. Her wild hair was tied back to look straight though it wasn't. A tiny diamond gleamed in one nostril. She had absurdly beautiful collarbones and a nice athletic run.

There goes a jazz tune, Larry McCaslin thought to himself, and followed her into a bookshop where neither of them looked at books.

Rahel drifted into marriage like a passenger drifts towards an unoccupied chair in an airport lounge. With a Sitting Down sense. She returned with him to Boston.

When Larry held his wife in his arms, her cheek against his heart, he was tall enough to see the top of her head, the dark tumble of her hair. When he put his finger near the corner of her mouth he could feel a tiny pulse. He loved its location. And that faint, uncertain jumping, just under her skin. He would touch it, listening with his eyes, like an expectant father feeling his unborn baby kick inside its mother's womb.

He held her as though she was a gift. Given to him in love. Something still and small. Unbearably precious.

But when they made love he was offended by her eyes. They behaved as though they belonged to someone else. Someone watching. Looking out of the window at the sea. At a boat in the river. Or a passer-by in the mist in a hat.

He was exasperated because he didn't know what that look *meant*. He put it somewhere between indifference and despair. He didn't know that in some places, like the country that Rahel came from, various kinds of despair competed for primacy. And that *personal* despair could never be desperate enough. That something happened when personal turmoil dropped by at the wayside shrine of the vast, violent, circling, driving, ridiculous, insane, unfeasible, public turmoil of a nation. That Big God howled like a hot wind, and demanded obeisance. Then Small God (cosy and contained, private and limited) came away cauterized, laughing numbly at his own temerity. Inured by the confirmation of his own inconsequence, he became resilient and truly indifferent. Nothing mattered much. Nothing much mattered. And the less it mattered, the less it mattered. It was never important enough. Because Worse Things had happened. In the country that she came from, poised forever between the terror of war and the horror of peace, Worse Things kept happening.

So Small God laughed a hollow laugh, and skipped away cheerfully. Like a rich boy in shorts. He whistled, kicked stones. The source of his brittle elation was the relative smallness of his misfortune. He climbed into people's eyes and became an exasperating expression.

What Larry McCaslin saw in Rahel's eyes was not despair at all, but a sort of enforced optimism. And a hollow where

Estha's words had been. He couldn't be expected to understand that. That the emptiness in one twin was only a version of the quietness in the other. That the two things fitted together. Like stacked spoons. Like familiar lovers' bodies.

After they were divorced, Rahel worked for a few months as a waitress in an Indian restaurant in New York. And then for several years as a night clerk in a bullet-proof cabin at a gas station outside Washington, where drunks occasionally vomited into the money tray, and pimps propositioned her with more lucrative job offers. Twice she saw men being shot through their car windows. And once a man who had been stabbed, ejected from a moving car with a knife in his back.

Then Baby Kochamma wrote to say that Estha had been re-Returned. Rahel gave up her job at the gas station and left America gladly. To return to Ayemenem. To Estha in the rain.

In the old house on the hill, Baby Kochamma sat at the dining table rubbing the thick, frothy bitterness out of an elderly cucumber. She was wearing a limp, checked, seersucker night-gown with puffed sleeves and yellow turmeric stains. Under the table she swung her tiny, manicured feet, like a small child on a high chair. They were puffy with oedema, like little foot-shaped air cushions. In the old days whenever anybody visited Ayemenem, Baby Kochamma made it a point to call attention to their large feet. She would ask to try on their slippers and say, 'Look how big for me they are!' Then she would walk around the house in them, lifting her sari a little so that every-body could marvel at her tiny feet.

She worked on the cucumber with an air of barely concealed triumph. She was delighted that Estha had not spoken to Rahel. That he had looked at her and walked straight past. Into the rain. As he did with everyone else.

She was eighty-three. Her eyes spread like butter behind her thick glasses.

'I told you, didn't I?' she said to Rahel. 'What did you expect?
Special treatment? He's lost his mind, I'm telling you! He doesn't
recognize people any more! What did you think?'

Rahel said nothing.

She could feel the rhythm of Estha's rocking, and the wetness
of rain on his skin. She could hear the raucous, scrambled world
inside his head.

Baby Kochamma looked up at Rahel uneasily. Already she
regretted having written to her about Estha's return. But then,
what else could she have done? Had him on her hands for the
rest of her life? Why *should* she? He wasn't her responsibility.

Or was he?

The silence sat between grand-niece and baby grand aunt like
a third person. A stranger. Swollen. Noxious. Baby Kochamma
reminded herself to lock her bedroom door at night. She tried
to think of something to say.

'How d'you like my bob?'

With her cucumber hand she touched her new haircut. She
left a riveting bitter blob of cucumber froth behind.

Rahel could think of nothing to say. She watched Baby
Kochamma peel her cucumber. Yellow slivers of cucumber skin
flecked her bosom. Her hair, dyed jetblack, was arranged across
her scalp like unspooled thread. The dye had stained the skin
of her forehead a pale grey, giving her a shadowy second
hairline. Rahel noticed that she had started wearing make-
up. Lipstick. Kohl. A sly touch of rouge. And because the
house was locked and dark, and because she only believed in
40-watt bulbs, her lipstick mouth had shifted slightly off her
real mouth.

She had lost weight on her face and shoulders, which had
turned her from being a round person into a conical person.
But sitting at the dining table with her enormous hips concealed,
she managed to look almost fragile. The dim, dining-room light
had rubbed the wrinkles off her face leaving it looking – in a

21

strange, sunken way – younger. She was wearing a lot of jewellery. Rahel's dead grandmother's jewellery. All of it. Winking rings. Diamond earrings. Gold bangles and a beautifully crafted flat gold chain that she touched from time to time reassuring herself that it was there and that it was hers. Like a young bride who couldn't believe her good fortune.

She's living her life backwards, Rahel thought.

It was a curiously apt observation. Baby Kochamma *had* lived her life backwards. As a young woman she had renounced the material world, and now, as an old one, she seemed to embrace it. She hugged it and it hugged her back.

When she was eighteen, Baby Kochamma fell in love with a handsome young Irish monk, Father Mulligan, who was in Kerala for a year on deputation from his seminary in Madras. He was studying Hindu scriptures, in order to be able to denounce them intelligently.

Every Thursday morning Father Mulligan came to Ayemenem to visit Baby Kochamma's father, Reverend E. John Ipe, who was a priest of the Mar Thoma church. Reverend Ipe was well known in the Christian community as the man who had been blessed personally by the Patriarch of Antioch, the sovereign head of the Syrian Christian Church – an episode which had become part of Ayemenem's folklore.

In 1876, when Baby Kochamma's father was seven years old, his father had taken him to see the Patriarch who was visiting the Syrian Christians of Kerala. They found themselves right in front of a group of people whom the Patriarch was addressing in the westernmost verandah of the Kalleny house, in Cochin. Seizing his opportunity, his father whispered in his young son's ear and propelled the little fellow forward. The future Reverend, skidding on his heels, rigid with fear, applied his terrified lips to the ring on the Patriarch's middle finger, leaving it wet with spit. The patriarch wiped his ring on his sleeve, and blessed the little boy. Long after he grew up and became a priest, Reverend

Ipe continued to be known as *Punnyan Kunju* – Little Blessed One – and people came down the river in boats all the way from Alleppey and Ernakulam, with children to be blessed by him.

Though there was a considerable age difference between Father Mulligan and Reverend Ipe, and though they belonged to different denominations of the Church (whose only common sentiment was their mutual disaffection), both men enjoyed each other's company, and more often than not, Father Mulligan would be invited to stay for lunch. Of the two men, only one recognized the sexual excitement that rose like a tide in the slender girl who hovered around the table long after lunch had been cleared away.

At first Baby Kochamma tried to seduce Father Mulligan with weekly exhibitions of staged charity. Every Thursday morning, just when Father Mulligan was due to arrive, Baby Kochamma force-bathed a poor village child at the well with hard red soap that hurt its protruding ribs.

'Morning, Father!' Baby Kochamma would call out when she saw him, with a smile on her lips that completely belied the vice-like grip that she had on the thin child's soapslippery arm.

'Morning to you, Baby!' Father Mulligan would say, stopping and folding his umbrella.

'There's something I wanted to ask you, Father,' Baby Kochamma would say. 'In First Corinthians, chapter ten, verse twenty-three, it says . . . "All things are lawful for me, but all things are not expedient". Father, how can *all* things be lawful unto Him? I mean I can understand if *some* things are lawful for Him, but –'

Father Mulligan was more than merely flattered by the emotion he aroused in the attractive young girl who stood before him with a trembling, kissable mouth and blazing, coal-black eyes. For he was young too, and perhaps not wholly unaware that the solemn explanations with which he dispelled her bogus biblical doubts were completely at odds with the thrilling promise he held out in his effulgent emerald eyes.

Every Thursday, undaunted by the merciless midday sun, they would stand there by the well. The young girl and the intrepid Jesuit, both quaking with unchristian passion. Using the Bible as a ruse to be with each other.

Invariably, in the middle of their conversation, the unfortunate soapy child that was being force-bathed would manage to slip away, and Father Mulligan would snap back to his senses and say, 'Oops! We'd better catch him before a cold does.'

Then he would reopen his umbrella and walk away in chocolate robes and comfortable sandals, like a high-stepping camel with an appointment to keep. He had young Baby Kochamma's aching heart on a leash, bumping behind him, lurching over leaves and small stones. Bruised and almost broken.

A whole year of Thursdays went by. Eventually the time came for Father Mulligan to return to Madras. Since charity had not produced any tangible results, the distraught young Baby Kochamma invested all her hope in faith.

Displaying a stubborn single-mindedness (which in a young girl in those days was considered as bad as a physical deformity – a harelip perhaps, or a club foot), Baby Kochamma defied her father's wishes and became a Roman Catholic. With special dispensation from the Vatican, she took her vows and entered a convent in Madras as a trainee novice. She hoped somehow that this would provide her with legitimate occasion to be with Father Mulligan. She pictured them together, in dark sepulchral rooms with heavy velvet drapes, discussing Theology. That was all she wanted. All she ever dared to hope for. Just to be near him. Close enough to smell his beard. To see the coarse weave of his cassock. To love him just by looking at him.

Very quickly she realized the futility of this endeavour. She found that the Senior Sisters monopolized the priests and bishops with biblical doubts more sophisticated than hers would ever be, and that it might be years before she got anywhere near Father Mulligan. She grew restless and unhappy in the convent. She developed a stubborn allergic rash on her scalp from the constant chafing of her wimple. She felt she spoke much better English than everybody else. This made her lonelier than ever.

Within a year of her joining the convent, her father began to receive puzzling letters from her in the mail. *My dearest Papa, I am well and happy in the service of Our Lady. But Koh-i-noor appears to be unhappy and homesick. My dearest Papa, Today Koh-i-noor vomited after lunch and is running a temperature. My dearest Papa, Convent food does not seem to suit Koh-i-noor, though I like it well enough. My dearest Papa, Koh-i-noor is upset because her family seems to neither understand nor care about her wellbeing . . .*

Other than the fact that it was (at the time) the name of the world's biggest diamond, Reverend E. John Ipe knew of no other Koh-i-noor. He wondered how a girl with a Muslim name had ended up in a Catholic Convent.

It was Baby Kochamma's mother who eventually realized that Koh-i-noor was none other than Baby Kochamma herself. She remembered that long ago she had shown Baby Kochamma a copy of her father's (Baby Kochamma's grandfather's) will in which, describing his grandchildren he had written: *I have seven jewels one of which is my Koh-i-noor.* He went on to bequeath little bits of money and jewellery to each of them, never clarifying which one he considered his Koh-i-noor. Baby Kochamma's mother realized that Baby Kochamma, for no reason that she could think of, had assumed that he had meant *her* – and all those years later at the convent, knowing that all her letters were read by the Mother Superior before they were posted, had resurrected Koh-i-noor to communicate her troubles to her family.

Reverend Ipe went to Madras and withdrew his daughter from the convent. She was glad to leave, but insisted that she would not reconvert, and for the rest of her days remained a Roman Catholic. Reverend Ipe realized that his daughter had by now developed a 'reputation' and was unlikely to find a husband. He decided that since she couldn't have a husband there was no harm in her having an education. So he made arrangements for her to attend a course of study at the University of Rochester in America.

Two years later, Baby Kochamma returned from Rochester with a diploma in Ornamental Gardening, but more in love with Father Mulligan than ever. There was no trace of the slim, attractive girl that she had been. In her years at Rochester, Baby Kochamma had grown extremely large. In fact, let it be said, obese. Even timid little Chellappen Tailor at Chungam Bridge insisted on charging bush-shirt rates for her sari blouses.

To keep her from brooding, her father gave Baby Kochamma charge of the front garden of the Ayemenem House, where she raised a fierce, bitter garden that people came all the way from Kottayam to see.

It was a circular, sloping patch of ground, with a steep gravel driveway looping around it. Baby Kochamma turned it into a lush maze of dwarf hedges, rocks and gargoyles. The flower she loved the most was the anthurium. Anthurium *andraeanum*. She had a collection of them, the 'Rubrum', the 'Honeymoon' and a host of Japanese varieties. Their single succulent spathes ranged from shades of mottled black to blood red and glistening orange. Their prominent, stippled spadices always yellow. In the centre of Baby Kochamma's garden, surrounded by beds of canna and phlox, a marble cherub peed an endless silver arc into a shallow pool in which a single blue lotus bloomed. At each corner of the pool lolled a pink plaster-of-Paris gnome with rosy cheeks and a peaked red cap.

Baby Kochamma spent her afternoons in her garden. In sari and gumboots. She wielded an enormous pair of hedge shears in her bright orange gardening gloves. Like a lion-tamer she tamed twisting vines and nurtured bristling cacti. She limited bonsai plants and pampered rare orchids. She waged war on the weather. She tried to grow edelweiss and chinese guava.

Every night she creamed her feet with real cream and pushed back the cuticles on her toe-nails.

Recently, after enduring more than half a century of relentless, pernickety attention, the ornamental garden had been abandoned. Left to its own devices, it had grown knotted and wild, like a circus whose animals had forgotten their tricks. The weed that people call communist patcha (because it flourished in Kerala like communism) smothered the more exotic plants. Only the vines kept growing, like toe-nails on a corpse. They reached through the nostrils of the pink plaster gnomes and blossomed in their hollow heads, giving them an expression half surprised, half sneeze-coming.

The reason for this sudden, unceremonious dumping was a new love. Baby Kochamma had installed a dish antenna on the roof of the Ayemenem house. She presided over the World in her drawing room on satellite TV. The impossible excitement that this engendered in Baby Kochamma wasn't hard to understand. It wasn't something that happened gradually. It happened overnight. Blondes, wars, famines, football, sex, music, coups d'état – they all arrived on the same train. They unpacked together. They stayed at the same hotel. And in Ayemenem, where once the loudest sound had been a musical bus horn, now whole wars, famines, picturesque massacres and Bill Clinton could be summoned up like servants. And so, while her ornamental garden wilted and died, Baby Kochamma followed American NBA league games, one-day cricket and all the Grand Slam tennis tournaments. On weekdays she watched *The Bold and The Beautiful* and *Santa Barbara*, where brittle blondes with lipstick and hairstyles rigid with spray seduced androids and defended their sexual empires. Baby Kochamma loved their shiny clothes and the smart, bitchy repartee. During the day disconnected snatches of it came back to her and made her chuckle.

Kochu Maria, the cook, still wore the thick gold earrings that had disfigured her earlobes for ever. She enjoyed the WWF *Wrestling Mania* shows, where Hulk Hogan and Mr Perfect, whose necks were wider than their heads, wore spangled Lycra leggings and beat each other up brutally. Kochu Maria's laugh had that slightly cruel ring to it that young children's sometimes have.

All day they sat in the drawing room, Baby Kochamma on the long-armed planter's chair or the chaise longue (depending on the condition of her feet), Kochu Maria next to her on the floor (channel surfing when she could), locked together in a noisy Television silence. One's hair snow white, the other's dyed coal black. They entered all the contests, availed themselves of all the discounts that were advertised and had, on two occasions, won a T-shirt and a Thermos flask that Baby Kochamma kept locked away in her cupboard.

Baby Kochamma loved the Ayemenem house and cherished the furniture that she had inherited by outliving everybody else. Mammachi's violin and violin stand, the Ooty cupboards, the plastic basket chairs, the Delhi beds, the dressing table from Vienna with cracked ivory knobs. The rosewood dining table that Velutha made.

She was frightened by the BBC famines and Television wars that she encountered while she channel surfed. Her old fears of the Revolution and the Marxist-Leninist menace had been rekindled by new television worries about the growing numbers of desperate and dispossessed people. She viewed ethnic cleansing, famine and genocide as direct threats to her furniture.

She kept her doors and windows locked, unless she was using them. She used her windows for specific purposes. For a Breath of Fresh Air. To Pay for the Milk. To Let Out a Trapped Wasp (which Kochu Maria was made to chase around the house with a towel).

She even locked her sad, paint-flaking fridge where she kept her week's supply of cream buns that Kochu Maria brought her from Bestbakery in Kottayam. And the two bottles of rice-water that she drank instead of ordinary water. In the shelf below the baffle tray, she kept what was left of Mammachi's willow-pattern dinner service.

She put the dozen or so bottles of insulin that Rahel brought her in the cheese and butter compartment. She suspected that these days, even the innocent and the round-eyed could be crockery crooks, or cream-bun cravers, or thieving diabetics cruising Ayemenem for imported insulin.

She didn't even trust the twins. She deemed them Capable of Anything. Anything at all. *They might even steal their present back*, she thought, and realized with a pang how quickly she had reverted to thinking of them as though they were a single unit once again. After all those years. Determined not to let the past creep up on her she altered her thought at once. *She. She might steal her present back.*

She looked at Rahel standing at the dining table and noticed the same eerie stealth, the ability to keep very still and very quiet that Estha seemed to have mastered. Baby Kochamma was a little intimidated by Rahel's quietness.

'So!' she said. Her voice shrill, faltering. 'What are your plans? How long will you be staying? Have you decided?'

Rahel tried to say something. It came out jagged. Like a piece of tin. She walked to the window and opened it. For a Breath of Fresh Air.

'Shut it when you've finished with it,' Baby Kochamma said, and closed her face like a cupboard.

You couldn't see the river from the window any more.

You could, until Mammachi had had the back verandah closed in with Ayemenem's first sliding-folding door. The oil portraits of Reverend E. John Ipe and Aleyooty Ammachi (Estha and Rahel's great-grandparents), were taken down from the back verandah and put up in the front one.

They hung there now, the Little Blessed One and his wife, on either side of the stuffed, mounted bison head.

Reverend Ipe smiled his confident-ancestor smile out across the road instead of the river.

Aleyooty Ammachi looked more hesitant. As though she would have liked to turn around but couldn't. Perhaps it wasn't as easy for her to abandon the river. With her eyes she looked in the direction that her husband looked. With her heart she looked away. Her heavy, dull gold kunukku earrings (tokens of the Little Blessed One's Goodness) had stretched her earlobes and hung all the way down to her shoulders. Through the holes in her ears you could see the hot river and the dark trees that bent into it. And the fishermen in their boats. And the fish.

Though you couldn't see the river from the house any more, like a seashell always has a sea-sense, the Ayemenem house still had a river-sense.

A rushing, rolling, fishswimming sense.

From the dining-room window where she stood, with the wind in her hair, Rahel could see the rain drum down on the rusted tin roof of what used to be their grandmother's pickle factory.

Paradise Pickles & Preserves.

It lay between the house and the river.

They used to make pickles, squashes, jams, curry powders and canned pineapples. And banana jam (illegally) after the FPO (Food Products Organization) banned it because according to their specifications it was neither jam nor jelly. Too thin for jelly and too thick for jam. An ambiguous, unclassifiable consistency, they said.

As per their books.

Looking back now, to Rahel it seemed as though this difficulty that their family had with classification ran much deeper than the jam-jelly question.

Perhaps, Ammu, Estha and she were the worst transgressors. But it wasn't just them. It was the others too. They all broke the rules. They all crossed into forbidden territory. They all tampered with the laws that lay down who should be loved and how. And how much. The laws that make grandmothers grandmothers, uncles uncles, mothers mothers, cousins cousins, jam jam, and jelly jelly.

It was a time when uncles became fathers, mothers lovers, and cousins died and had funerals.

It was a time when the unthinkable became thinkable and the impossible really happened.

Even before Sophie Mol's funeral, the police found Velutha.

His arms had goosebumps where the handcuffs touched his skin. Cold handcuffs with a sourmetal smell. Like steel bus rails and the smell of the bus conductor's hands from holding them.

After it was all over, Baby Kochamma said, 'As ye sow, so shall ye reap.' As though *she* had had nothing to do with the Sowing and the Reaping. She returned on her small feet to her cross-stitch embroidery. Her little toes never touched the floor. It was her idea that Estha be Returned.

Margaret Kochamma's grief and bitterness at her daughter's death coiled inside her like an angry spring. She said nothing, but slapped Estha whenever she could in the days she was there before she returned to England.

Rahel watched Ammu pack Estha's little trunk.

'Maybe they're right,' Ammu's whisper said. 'Maybe a boy does need a Baba.'

Rahel saw that her eyes were a redly dead.

They consulted a Twin Expert in Hyderabad. She wrote back to say that it was not advisable to separate monozygotic twins, but that two-egg twins were no different from ordinary siblings and that while they would certainly suffer the natural distress that children from broken homes underwent, it would be nothing more than that. Nothing out of the ordinary.

And so Estha was Returned in a train with his tin trunk and his beige and pointy shoes rolled into his khaki holdall. First class, overnight on the Madras Mail to Madras and then with a friend of their father's from Madras to Calcutta.

He had a tiffin carrier with tomato sandwiches. And an Eagle flask with an eagle. He had terrible pictures in his head.

Rain. Rushing, inky water. And a smell. Sicksweet. Like old roses on a breeze.

But worst of all, he carried inside him the memory of a young man with an old man's mouth. The memory of a swollen face and a smashed, upside-down smile. Of a spreading pool of clear liquid with a bare bulb reflected in it. Of a bloodshot eye that had opened, wandered and then fixed its gaze on him. Estha. And what had Estha done? He had looked into that beloved face and said: Yes.

Yes, it was him.

The word Estha's octopus couldn't get at: *Yes*. Hoovering didn't seem to help. It was lodged there, deep inside some fold or furrow, like a mango hair between molars. That couldn't be worried loose.

In a purely practical sense it would probably be correct to say that it all began when Sophie Mol came to Ayemenem. Perhaps it's true that things can change in a day. That a few dozen hours can affect the outcome of whole lifetimes. And that when they do, those few dozen hours, like the salvaged remains of a burned house – the charred clock, the singed photograph, the scorched furniture – must be resurrected from the ruins and examined. Preserved. Accounted for.

Little events, ordinary things, smashed and reconstituted.

Imbued with new meaning. Suddenly they become the bleached bones of a story.

Still, to say that it all began when Sophie Mol came to Aye-menem is only one way of looking at it.

Equally, it could be argued that it actually began thousands of years ago. Long before the Marxists came. Before the British took Malabar, before the Dutch Ascendency, before Vasco da Gama arrived, before the Zamorin's conquest of Calicut. Before three purple-robed Syrian Bishops murdered by the Portuguese were found floating in the sea, with coiled sea serpents riding on their chests and oysters knotted in their tangled beards. It could be argued that it began long before Christianity arrived in a boat and seeped into Kerala like tea from a teabag.

That it really began in the days when the Love Laws were made. The laws that lay down who should be loved, and how. And how much.

HOWEVER, for practical purposes, in a hopelessly practical world . . .

2

Pappachi's Moth

... it was a skyblue day in December sixty-nine (the nineteen silent). It was the kind of time in the life of a family when something happens to nudge its hidden morality from its resting place and make it bubble to the surface and float for a while. In clear view. For everyone to see.

A skyblue Plymouth, with the sun in its tailfins, sped past young rice-fields and old rubber trees, on its way to Cochin. Further east, in a small country with similar landscape (jungles, rivers, rice-fields, communists), enough bombs were being dropped to cover all of it in six inches of steel. Here, however, it was peacetime and the family in the Plymouth travelled without fear or foreboding.

The Plymouth used to belong to Pappachi, Rahel and Estha's grandfather. Now that he was dead, it belonged to Mammachi, their grandmother, and Rahel and Estha were on their way to Cochin to see *The Sound of Music* for the third time. They knew all the songs.

After that they were all going to stay at Hotel Sea Queen with the oldfood smell. Bookings had been made. Early next morning they would go to Cochin Airport to pick up Chacko's ex-wife – their English aunt, Margaret Kochamma – and their cousin, Sophie Mol, who were coming from London to spend Christmas at Ayemenem. Earlier that year, Margaret Kochamma's second husband, Joe, had been killed in a car accident.

When Chacko heard about the accident he invited them to Ayemenem. He said that he couldn't bear to think of them spending a lonely, desolate Christmas in England. In a house full of memories.

Ammu said that Chacko had never stopped loving Margaret Kochamma. Mammachi disagreed. She liked to believe that he had never loved her in the first place.

Rahel and Estha had never met Sophie Mol. They'd heard a lot about her, though, that last week. From Baby Kochamma, from Kochu Maria, and even Mammachi. None of them had met her either, but they all behaved as though they already knew her. It had been the *What Will Sophie Mol Think?* week.

That whole week Baby Kochamma eavesdropped relentlessly on the twins' private conversations, and whenever she caught them speaking in Malayalam, she levied a small fine which was deducted at source. From their pocket money. She made them write lines – 'impositions' she called them – *I will always speak in English, I will always speak in English.* A hundred times each. When they were done, she scored them out with her red pen to make sure that old lines were not recycled for new punishments.

She had made them practise an English car song for the way back. They had to form the words properly, and be particularly careful about their pronunciation. Prer *NUN* sea ayshun.

> *Rej-Oice in the Lo-Ord Or-Orlways*
> *And again I say rej-Oice,*
> *RejOice,*
> *RejOice,*
> *And again I say rej-Oice.*

Estha's full name was Esthappen Yako. Rahel's was Rahel. For the Time Being they had no surname because Ammu was considering reverting to her maiden name, though she said that choosing between her husband's name and her father's name didn't give a woman much of a choice.

Estha was wearing his beige and pointy shoes and his Elvis puff. His Special Outing Puff. His favourite Elvis song was 'Party'. *'Some people like to rock, some people like to roll,'* he would croon, when nobody was watching, strumming a badminton racquet, curling his lip like Elvis. *'But moonin' an' a-groonin' gonna satisfy mah soul, less have a pardy . . . '*

Estha had slanting, sleepy eyes and his new front teeth were still uneven on the ends. Rahel's new teeth were waiting inside her gums, like words in a pen. It puzzled everybody that an eighteen-minute age difference could cause such a discrepancy in front-tooth timing.

Most of Rahel's hair sat on top of her head like a fountain. It was held together by a Love-in-Tokyo – two beads on a rubber band, nothing to do with Love or Tokyo. In Kerala Love-in-Tokyos have withstood the test of time, and even today if you were to ask for one at any respectable A-1 Ladies' Store, that's what you'd get. Two beads on a rubber band.

Rahel's toy wristwatch had the time painted on it. Ten to two. One of her ambitions was to own a watch on which she could change the time whenever she wanted to (which according to her was what Time was meant for in the first place). Her yellow-rimmed red plastic sunglasses made the world look red. Ammu said that they were bad for her eyes and had advised her to wear them as seldom as possible.

Her Airport Frock was in Ammu's suitcase. It had special matching knickers.

Chacko was driving. He was four years older than Ammu. Rahel and Estha couldn't call him Chachen because when they did, he called them Chetan and Cheduthi. If they called him Ammaven he called them Appoi and Ammai. If they called him Uncle he called them Aunty, which was embarrassing in Public. So they called him Chacko.

Chacko's room was stacked from floor to ceiling with books. He had read them all and quoted long passages from them for no apparent reason. Or at least none that anyone else could fathom. For instance, that morning, as they drove out through the gate, shouting their goodbyes to Mammachi in the verandah, Chacko suddenly said: '*Gatsby turned out all right at the end; it is what preyed on Gatsby, what foul dust floated in the wake of his dreams that temporarily closed out my interest in the abortive sorrows and short-winded elations of men.*'

Everyone was so used to it that they didn't bother to nudge each other or exchange glances. Chacko had been a Rhodes Scholar at Oxford and was permitted excesses and eccentricities nobody else was.

He claimed to be writing a Family Biography that the Family would have to pay him not to publish. Ammu said that there was only one person in the family who was a fit candidate for biographical blackmail and that was Chacko himself.

Of course that was then. Before the Terror.

In the Plymouth, Ammu was sitting in front, next to Chacko. She was twenty-seven that year, and in the pit of her stomach she carried the cold knowledge that for her, life had been lived. She had had one chance. She made a mistake. She married the wrong man.

Ammu finished her schooling the same year that her father retired from his job in Delhi and moved to Ayemenem. Pappachi insisted that a college education was an unnecessary expense for a girl, so Ammu had no choice but to leave Delhi and move with them. There was very little for a young girl to do in Ayemenem other than to wait for marriage proposals while she helped her mother with the housework. Since her father did not have enough money to raise a suitable dowry, no proposals came Ammu's way. Two years went by. Her eighteenth birthday came and went. Unnoticed, or at least unremarked upon by her parents. Ammu grew desperate. All day she dreamed of escaping from Ayemenem and the clutches of her ill-tempered father and bitter, long-suffering mother. She hatched several wretched little plans. Eventually, one worked. Pappachi agreed to let her spend the summer with a distant aunt who lived in Calcutta.

There, at someone else's wedding reception, Ammu met her future husband.

He was on vacation from his job in Assam where he worked as an assistant manager of a tea estate. His family were once-wealthy zamindars who had migrated to Calcutta from East Bengal after Partition.

He was a small man, but well-built. Pleasant-looking. He wore old-fashioned spectacles that made him look earnest and completely belied his easy-going charm and juvenile but totally disarming sense of humour. He was twenty-five and had already been working on the tea estates for six years. He hadn't been to college, which accounted for his schoolboy humour. He proposed to Ammu five days after they first met. Ammu didn't pretend to be in love with him. She just weighed the odds and accepted. She thought that *anything*, anyone at all, would be better than returning to Ayemenem. She wrote to her parents informing them of her decision. They didn't reply.

Ammu had an elaborate Calcutta wedding. Later, looking back on the day, Ammu realized that the slightly feverish glitter in her bridegroom's eyes had not been love, or even excitement at the prospect of carnal bliss, but approximately eight large pegs of whisky. Straight. Neat.

Ammu's father-in-law was Chairman of the Railway Board and had a Boxing Blue from Cambridge. He was the Secretary of the BABA – the Bengal Amateur Boxing Association. He gave the young couple a custom-painted, powder-pink Fiat as a present which after the wedding he drove off in himself, with all the jewellery and most of the other presents that they had been given. He died before the twins were born – on the operating table while his gall bladder was being removed. His cremation was attended by all the boxers in Bengal. A congregation of mourners with lantern jaws and broken noses.

When Ammu and her husband moved to Assam, Ammu, beautiful, young and cheeky, became the toast of the Planters' Club. She wore backless blouses with her saris and carried a silver lamé purse on a chain. She smoked long cigarettes in a silver cigarette holder and learned to blow perfect smoke rings. Her husband turned out to be not just a heavy drinker but a full-blown alcoholic with all of an alcoholic's deviousness and tragic charm. There were things about him that Ammu never understood. Long after she left him, she never stopped wondering why he lied so outrageously when he didn't need to. *Particularly* when he didn't need to. In a conversation with friends he would talk about how much he loved smoked salmon when Ammu knew he hated it. Or he would come home from the club and tell Ammu that he saw *Meet Me in St Louis* when they'd actually screened *The Bronze Buckaroo*. When she confronted him about these things, he never explained or apologized. He just giggled, exasperating Ammu to a degree she never thought herself capable of.

Ammu was eight months pregnant when war broke out with China. It was October of 1962. Planters' wives and children were evacuated from Assam. Ammu, too pregnant to travel, remained on the estate. In November, after a hair-raising, bumpy bus ride to Shillong, amidst rumours of Chinese occupation and India's impending defeat, Estha and Rahel were born. By candlelight. In a hospital with the windows blacked out. They emerged without much fuss, within eighteen minutes of each other. Two little ones, instead of one big one. Twin seals, slick with their mother's juices. Wrinkled with the effort of being born. Ammu checked them for deformities before she closed her eyes and slept.

She counted four eyes, four ears, two mouths, two noses, twenty fingers and twenty perfect toe-nails.

She didn't notice the single Siamese soul. She was glad to have them. Their father, stretched out on a hard bench in the hospital corridor, was drunk.

By the time the twins were two years old their father's drinking, aggravated by the loneliness of tea estate life, had driven him into an alcoholic stupor. Whole days went by during which he just lay in bed and didn't go to work. Eventually, his English manager, Mr Hollick, summoned him to his bungalow for a 'serious chat'.

Ammu sat in the verandah of her home waiting anxiously for her husband to return. She was sure the only reason that Hollick wanted to see him was to sack him. She was surprised when he returned looking despondent but not devastated. Mr Hollick had proposed something, he told Ammu, that he needed to discuss with her. He began a little diffidently, avoiding her gaze, but he gathered courage as he went along. Viewed practically, in the long run it was a proposition that would benefit both of them, he said. In fact *all* of them, if they considered the children's education.

Mr Hollick had been frank with his young assistant. He informed him of the complaints he had received from the labour as well as from the other assistant managers.

'I'm afraid I have no option,' he said, 'but to ask for your resignation.'

He allowed the silence to take its toll. He allowed the pitiful man sitting across the table to begin to shake. To weep. Then Hollick spoke again.

'Well, actually there *may* be an option . . . perhaps we could work something out. Think positive, is what I always say. Count your blessings.' Hollick paused to order a pot of black coffee. 'You're a very lucky man, you know, wonderful family, beautiful children, such an attractive wife . . .' He lit a cigarette and allowed the match to burn until he couldn't hold it any more. 'An *extremely* attractive wife . . .'

The weeping stopped. Puzzled brown eyes looked into lurid, red-veined, green ones. Over coffee, Mr Hollick proposed that Baba go away for a while. For a holiday. To a clinic perhaps, for treatment. For as long as it took him to get better. And for the period of time that he was away, Mr Hollick suggested that Ammu be sent to his bungalow to be 'looked after'.

Already there were a number of ragged, lightskinned children on the estate that Hollick had bequeathed on tea-pickers whom he fancied. This was his first incursion into management circles.

Ammu watched her husband's mouth move as it formed words. She said nothing. He grew uncomfortable and then infuriated by her silence. Suddenly he lunged at her, grabbed her hair, punched her and then passed out from the effort. Ammu took down the heaviest book she could find in the bookshelf – *The Reader's Digest World Atlas* – and hit him with it as hard as she could. On his head. His legs. His back and shoulders. When he regained consciousness, he was puzzled by his bruises. He apologized abjectly for the violence, but immediately began to badger her about helping with his transfer. This fell into a pattern. Drunken violence followed by post-drunken badgering. Ammu was repelled by the medicinal smell of stale alcohol that seeped through his skin, and the dry, caked vomit that encrusted his mouth like a pie every morning. When his bouts of violence began to include the children, and the war with Pakistan began, Ammu left her husband and returned, unwelcomed, to her parents in Ayemenem. To everything that she had fled from only a few years ago. Except that now she had two young children. And no more dreams.

Pappachi would not believe her story – not because he thought well of her husband, but simply because he didn't believe that an Englishman, *any* Englishman, would covet another man's wife.

Ammu loved her children (of course), but their wide-eyed vulnerability, and their willingness to love people who didn't really love them, exasperated her and sometimes made her want to hurt them – just as an education, a protection.

It was as though the window through which their father disappeared had been kept open for anyone to walk in and be welcomed.

To Ammu her twins seemed like a pair of small bewildered frogs engrossed in each other's company, lolloping arm in arm down a highway full of hurtling traffic. Entirely oblivious of what trucks can do to frogs. Ammu watched over them fiercely. Her watchfulness stretched her, made her taut and tense. She was quick to reprimand her children, but even quicker to take offence on their behalf.

For herself she knew that there would be no more chances. There was only Ayemenem now. A front verandah and a back verandah. A hot river and a pickle factory.

And in the background, the constant, high, whining mewl of local disapproval.

Within the first few months of her return to her parents' home, Ammu quickly learned to recognize and despise the ugly face of sympathy. Old female relations with incipient beards and several wobbling chins made overnight trips to Ayemenem to commiserate with her about her divorce. They squeezed her knee and gloated. She fought off the urge to slap them. Or twiddle their nipples. With a spanner. Like Chaplin in *Modern Times*.

When she looked at herself in her wedding photographs, Ammu felt the woman that looked back at her was someone else. A foolish jewelled bride. Her silk sunset-coloured sari shot with gold. Rings on every finger. White dots of sandalwood paste over her arched eyebrows. Looking at herself like this, Ammu's soft mouth would twist into a small, bitter smile at the memory – not of the wedding itself so much as the fact that she had permitted herself to be so painstakingly decorated before being led to the gallows. It seemed so absurd. So futile.

Like polishing firewood.

She went to the village goldsmith and had her heavy wedding ring melted down and made into a thin bangle with snakeheads that she put away for Rahel.

Ammu knew that weddings were not something that could be avoided altogether. At least not practically speaking. But for the rest of her life she advocated *small* weddings in *ordinary* clothes. It made them less ghoulish, she thought.

Occasionally, when Ammu listened to songs that she loved on the radio, something stirred inside her. A liquid ache spread under her skin, and she walked out of the world like a witch, to a better, happier place. On days like this, there was something restless and untamed about her. As though she had temporarily set aside the morality of motherhood and divorceehood. Even her walk changed from a safe mother-walk to another wilder sort of walk. She wore flowers in her hair and carried magic secrets in her eyes. She spoke to no one. She spent hours on the riverbank with her little plastic transistor shaped like a tangerine. She smoked cigarettes and had midnight swims.

What was it that gave Ammu this Unsafe Edge? This air of unpredictability? It was what she had battling inside her. An unmixable mix. The infinite tenderness of motherhood and the reckless rage of a suicide bomber. It was this that grew inside her, and eventually led her to love by night the man her children loved by day. To use by night the boat that her children used by day. The boat that Estha sat on, and Rahel found.

On the days that the radio played Ammu's songs, everyone was a little wary of her. They sensed somehow that she lived in the penumbral shadows between two worlds, just beyond the grasp of their power. That a woman that they had already damned, now had little left to lose, and could therefore be dangerous. So on the days that the radio played Ammu's songs, people avoided her, made little loops around her, because every-body agreed that it was best to just Let Her Be.

On other days she had deep dimples when she smiled.

She had a delicate, chiselled face, black eyebrows angled like a soaring seagull's wings, a small straight nose and luminous nutbrown skin. On that skyblue December day, her wild, curly hair had escaped in wisps in the car wind. Her shoulders in her sleeveless sari blouse shone as though they had been polished with a high-wax shoulder polish. Sometimes she was the most beautiful woman that Estha and Rahel had ever seen. And sometimes she wasn't.

On the back seat of the Plymouth, between Estha and Rahel, sat Baby Kochamma. Ex-nun, and incumbent baby grand aunt. In the way that the unfortunate sometimes dislike the co-unfortunate, Baby Kochamma disliked the twins, for she con-sidered them doomed, fatherless waifs. Worse still, they were Half-Hindu Hybrids whom no self-respecting Syrian Christian would ever marry. She was keen for them to realize that they (like herself) lived on sufferance in the Ayemenem House, their maternal grandmother's house, where they really had no right to be. Baby Kochamma resented Ammu, because she saw her quarrelling with a fate that she, Baby Kochamma herself, felt she had graciously accepted. The fate of the wretched Man-less woman. The sad, Father Mulligan-less Baby Kochamma. She had managed to persuade herself over the years that her uncon-summated love for Father Mulligan had been entirely due to *her* restraint and *her* determination to do the right thing.

She subscribed wholeheartedly to the commonly held view that a married daughter had no position in her parents' home. As for a *divorced* daughter – according to Baby Kochamma, she had no position anywhere at all. And as for a *divorced* daughter from a *love* marriage, well, words could not describe Baby Koch-amma's outrage. As for a *divorced* daughter from a *intercommunity love* marriage – Baby Kochamma chose to remain quiveringly silent on the subject.

The twins were too young to understand all this, so Baby Kochamma grudged them their moments of high happiness when a dragonfly they'd caught lifted a small stone off their palms with its legs, or when they had permission to bathe the pigs, or they found an egg – hot from a hen. But most of all, she grudged them the comfort they drew from each other. She expected from them some token unhappiness. At the very least.

On the way back from the airport, Margaret Kochamma would sit in front with Chacko because she used to be his wife. Sophie Mol would sit between them. Ammu would move to the back.

There would be two flasks of water. Boiled water for Margaret Kochamma and Sophie Mol, tap water for everybody else.

The luggage would be in the boot.

Rahel thought that *boot* was a lovely word. A much better word, at any rate, than *sturdy*. *Sturdy* was a terrible word. Like a dwarf's name. *Sturdy Koshy Oommen* – a pleasant, middle-class, God-fearing dwarf with low knees and a side parting.

On the Plymouth roof rack there was a four-sided tin-lined, plywood billboard that said, on all four sides, in elaborate writing, *Paradise Pickles & Preserves*. Below the writing there were painted bottles of mixed-fruit jam and hot-lime pickle in edible oil, with labels that said, in elaborate writing, *Paradise Pickles & Preserves*. Next to the bottles there was a list of all the Paradise products and a kathakali dancer with his face green and skirts swirling. Along the bottom of the S-shaped swirl of his billowing skirt, it said, in an S-shaped swirl, *Emperors of the Realm of Taste* – which was Comrade K. N. M. Pillai's unsolicited contribution. It was a literal translation of *Ruchi lokathinde Rajavu*, which sounded a little less ludicrous than *Emperors of the Realm of Taste*. But since Comrade Pillai had already printed them, no one had the heart to ask him to re-do the whole print order. So, unhappily, *Emperors of the Realm of Taste* became a permanent feature on the Paradise Pickle labels.

Ammu said that the kathakali dancer was a Red Herring and had nothing to do with anything. Chacko said that it gave the products a Regional Flavour and would stand them in good stead when they entered the Overseas Market.

Ammu said that the billboard made them look ridiculous. Like a travelling circus. With tailfins.

Mammachi had started making pickles commercially soon after Pappachi retired from Government service in Delhi and came to live in Ayemenem. The Kottayam Bible Society was having a fair and asked Mammachi to make some of her famous banana jam and tender mango pickle. It sold quickly, and Mammachi found that she had more orders than she could cope with. Thrilled with her success, she decided to persist with the pickles and jam, and soon found herself busy all year round. Pappachi, for his part, was having trouble coping with the ignominy of retirement. He was seventeen years older than Mammachi, and realized with a shock that he was an old man when his wife was still in her prime.

Though Mammachi had conical corneas and was already practically blind, Pappachi would not help her with the pickle-making, because he did not consider pickle-making a suitable job for a high-ranking ex-Government official. He had always been a jealous man, so he greatly resented the attention his wife was suddenly getting. He slouched around the compound in his immaculately tailored suits, weaving sullen circles around mounds of red chillies and freshly powdered yellow turmeric, watching Mammachi supervise the buying, the weighing, the salting and drying, of limes and tender mangoes. Every night he beat her with a brass flower vase. The beatings weren't new. What was new was only the frequency with which they took place. One night Pappachi broke the bow of Mammachi's violin and threw it in the river.

Then Chacko came home for a summer vacation from Oxford. He had grown to be a big man, and was, in those days, strong from rowing for Balliol. A week after he arrived he found Pappachi beating Mammachi in the study. Chacko strode into the room, caught Pappachi's vase-hand and twisted it around his back.

'I never want this to happen again,' he told his father. 'Ever.'

For the rest of that day Pappachi sat in the verandah and stared stonily out at the ornamental garden, ignoring the plates of food that Kochu Maria brought him. Late at night he went into his study and brought out his favourite mahogany rocking chair. He put it down in the middle of the driveway and smashed it into little bits with a plumber's monkey wrench. He left it there in the moonlight, a heap of varnished wicker and splintered wood. He never touched Mammachi again. But he never spoke to her either as long as he lived. When he needed anything he used Kochu Maria or Baby Kochamma as intermediaries.

In the evenings, when he knew visitors were expected, he would sit on the verandah and sew buttons that weren't missing onto his shirts, to create the impression that Mammachi neglected him. To some small degree he did succeed in further corroding Ayemenem's view of working wives.

He bought the skyblue Plymouth from an old Englishman in Munnar. He became a familiar sight in Ayemenem, coasting importantly down the narrow road in his wide car, looking outwardly elegant but sweating freely inside his woollen suits. He wouldn't allow Mammachi or anyone else in the family to use it, or even to sit in it. The Plymouth was Pappachi's revenge.

Pappachi had been an Imperial Entomologist at the Pusa Institute. After Independence, when the British left, his designation was changed from Imperial Entomologist to Joint

Director, Entomology. The year he retired, he had risen to a rank equivalent to Director.

His life's greatest setback was not having had the moth that *he* had discovered named after him.

It fell into his drink one evening while he was sitting in the verandah of a rest house after a long day in the field. As he picked it out he noticed its unusually dense dorsal tufts. He took a closer look. With growing excitement he mounted it, measured it and the next morning placed it in the sun for a few hours for the alcohol to evaporate. Then he caught the first train back to Delhi. To taxonomic attention and, he hoped, fame. After six unbearable months of anxiety, to Pappachi's intense disappointment he was told that his moth had finally been identified as a slightly unusual race of a well-known species that belonged to the tropical family Lymantriidae.

The real blow came twelve years later, when, as a consequence of a radical taxonomic reshuffle, lepidopterists decided that Pappachi's moth *was* in fact a separate species and genus hitherto unknown to science. By then, of course, Pappachi had retired and moved to Ayemenem. It was too late for him to assert his claim to the discovery. His moth was named after the Acting Director of the Department of Entomology, a junior officer whom Pappachi had always disliked.

In the years to come, even though he had been ill-humoured long before he discovered the moth, Pappachi's Moth was held responsible for his black moods and sudden bouts of temper. Its pernicious ghost – grey, furry and with unusually dense dorsal tufts – haunted every house that he ever lived in. It tormented him and his children and his children's children.

Until the day he died, even in the stifling Ayemenem heat, every single day, Pappachi wore a well-pressed three-piece suit and his gold pocket watch. On his dressing table, next to his cologne and silver hairbrush, he kept a picture of himself as a young man, with his hair slicked down, taken in a photographer's studio in Vienna where he had done the six-month diploma course that had qualified him to apply for the post of Imperial Entomologist. It was during those few months they spent in Vienna that Mammachi took her first lessons on the violin. The lessons were abruptly discontinued when Mammachi's teacher, Launsky-Tieffenthal, made the mistake of telling Pappachi that his wife was exceptionally talented and, in his opinion, potentially concert class.

Mammachi pasted, in the family photograph album, the clipping from the *Indian Express* that reported Pappachi's death. It said:

> Noted entomologist, Shri Benaan John Ipe, son of late Rev. E. John Ipe of Ayemenem (popularly known as *Punnyan Kunju*), suffered a massive heart attack and passed away at the Kottayam General Hospital last night. He developed chest pains around 1.05 a.m. and was rushed to hospital. The end came at 2.45 a.m. Shri Ipe had been keeping indifferent health since last six months. He is survived by his wife Soshamma and two children.

At Pappachi's funeral, Mammachi cried and her contact lenses slid around in her eyes. Ammu told the twins that Mammachi was crying more because she was used to him than because she loved him. She was used to having him slouching around the pickle factory, and was used to being beaten from time to time. Ammu said that human beings were creatures of habit, and it was amazing the kind of things they could get used to. You only had to look around you, Ammu said, to see that beatings with brass vases were the least of them.

After the funeral Mammachi asked Rahel to help her to locate and remove her contact lenses with the little orange pipette that came in its own case. Rahel asked Mammachi whether, after Mammachi died, she could inherit the pipette. Ammu took her out of the room and smacked her.

'I never want to hear you discussing people's deaths with them again,' she said.

Estha said Rahel deserved it for being so insensitive.

The photograph of Pappachi in Vienna, with his hair slicked down, was reframed and put up in the drawing room.

He was a photogenic man, dapper and carefully groomed, with a little man's largeish head. He had an incipient second chin that would have been emphasized had he looked down or nodded. In the photograph he had taken care to hold his head high enough to hide his double chin, yet not so high as to appear haughty. His light brown eyes were polite, yet maleficent, as though he was making an effort to be civil to the photographer while plotting to murder his wife. He had a little fleshy knob on the centre of his upper lip that dropped down over his lower lip in a sort of effeminate pout – the kind that children who suck their thumbs develop. He had an elongated dimple on his chin which only served to underline the threat of a lurking manic violence. A sort of contained cruelty. He wore khaki jodhpurs though he had never ridden a horse in his life. His riding boots reflected the photographer's studio lights. An ivory-handled riding crop lay neatly across his lap.

There was a watchful stillness to the photograph that lent an underlying chill to the warm room in which it hung.

When he died, Pappachi left trunks full of expensive suits and a chocolate tin full of cuff-links that Chacko distributed among the taxi drivers in Kottayam. They were separated and made into rings and pendants for unmarried daughters' dowries.

When the twins asked what cuff-links were for – 'To link cuffs together,' Ammu told them – they were thrilled by this morsel of logic in what had so far seemed an illogical language. *Cuff*+ *link* = *Cuff-link*. This, to them, rivalled the precision and logic of mathematics. *Cuff-links* gave them an inordinate (if exaggerated) satisfaction, and a real affection for the English language.

Ammu said that Pappachi was an incurable British CCP, which was short for *chhi-chhi poach* and in Hindi meant shit-wiper.

Chacko said that the correct word for people like Pappachi was *Anglophile*. He made Rahel and Estha look up *Anglophile* in the *Reader's Digest Great Encyclopaedic Dictionary*. It said *Person well disposed to the English*. Then Estha and Rahel had to look up *disposed*.
   It said:

(1) *Place suitably in particular order.*
(2) *Bring mind into certain state.*
(3) *Do what one will with, get off one's hands, stow away, demolish, finish, settle, consume (food), kill, sell.*

Chacko said that in Pappachi's case it meant (2) *Bring mind into certain state*. Which, Chacko said, meant that Pappachi's mind had been *brought into a state* which made him like the English.
   Chacko told the twins that though he hated to admit it, they were all Anglophiles. They were a *family* of Anglophiles. Pointed in the wrong direction, trapped outside their own history, and unable to retrace their steps because their footprints had been swept away. He explained to them that history was like an old house at night. With all the lamps lit. And ancestors whispering inside.
   'To understand history,' Chacko said, 'we have to go inside and listen to what they're saying. And look at the books and the pictures on the wall. And smell the smells.'
   Estha and Rahel had no doubt that the house Chacko meant was the house on the other side of the river, in the middle of the abandoned rubber estate where they had never been. Kari Saipu's house. The Black Sahib. The Englishman who had 'gone native'. Who spoke Malayalam and wore mundus. Ayemenem's own Kurtz. Ayemenem his private Heart of Darkness. He had shot himself through the head ten years ago when his young lover's parents had taken the boy away from him and sent him to school. After the suicide, the property had become

the subject of extensive litigation between Kari Saipu's cook and his secretary. The house had lain empty for years. Very few people had seen it. But the twins could picture it.

The History House.

With cool stone floors and dim walls and billowing ship-shaped shadows. Plump, translucent lizards lived behind old pictures, and waxy, crumbling ancestors with tough toe-nails and breath that smelled of yellow maps gossiped in sibilant, papery whispers.

'But we can't go in,' Chacko explained, 'because we've been locked out. And when we look in through the windows, all we see are shadows. And when we try and listen, all we hear is a whispering. And we cannot understand the whispering, because our minds have been invaded by a war. A war that we have won and lost. The very worst sort of war. A war that captures dreams and re-dreams them. A war that has made us adore our conquerors and despise ourselves.'

'*Marry* our conquerors, is more like it,' Ammu said drily, referring to Margaret Kochamma. Chacko ignored her. He made the twins look up *Despise*. It said: *To look down upon; to view with contempt; to scorn or disdain.*

Chacko said that in the context of the war he was talking about – the War of Dreams – *Despise* meant all those things.

'We're Prisoners of War,' Chacko said. 'Our dreams have been doctored. We belong nowhere. We sail unanchored on troubled seas. We may never be allowed ashore. Our sorrows will never be sad enough. Our joys never happy enough. Our dreams never big enough. Our lives never important enough. To matter.'

Then, to give Estha and Rahel a sense of historical perspective (though perspective was something which, in the weeks to follow, Chacko himself would sorely lack), he told them about the Earth Woman. He made them imagine that the earth – four thousand six hundred million years old – was a forty-six-year-old woman

– as old, say, as Aleyamma Teacher, who gave them Malayalam lessons. It had taken the whole of the Earth Woman's life for the earth to become what it was. For the oceans to part. For the mountains to rise. The Earth Woman was eleven years old, Chacko said, when the first single-celled organisms appeared. The first animals, creatures like worms and jellyfish, appeared only when she was forty. She was over forty-five – just eight months ago – when dinosaurs roamed the earth.

'The whole of human civilization as we know it,' Chacko told the twins, 'began only *two hours* ago in the Earth Woman's life. As long as it takes us to drive from Ayemenem to Cochin.'

It was an awe-inspiring and humbling thought, Chacko said (*Humbling* was a nice word, Rahel thought. *Humbling along without a care in the world*), that the whole of contemporary history, the World Wars, the War of Dreams, the Man on the Moon, science, literature, philosophy, the pursuit of knowledge – was no more than a blink of the Earth Woman's eye.

'And we, my dears, everything we are and ever will be – are just a twinkle in her eye,' Chacko said grandly, lying on his bed, staring at the ceiling.

When he was in this sort of mood, Chacko used his Reading Aloud voice. His room had a church-feeling. He didn't care whether anyone was listening to him or not. And if they were, he didn't care whether or not they had understood what he was saying. Ammu called them his Oxford Moods.

Later, in the light of all that happened, *twinkle* seemed completely the wrong word to describe the expression in the Earth Woman's eye. Twinkle was a word with crinkled, happy edges.

Though the Earth Woman made a lasting impression on the twins, it was the History House – so much closer at hand – that really fascinated them. They thought about it often. The house on the other side of the river.

Looming in the Heart of Darkness.

A house they couldn't enter, full of whispers they couldn't understand.

They didn't know then, that soon they *would* go in. That they would cross the river and be where they weren't supposed to be, with a man they weren't supposed to love. That they would watch with dinner-plate eyes as history revealed itself to them in the back verandah.

While other children of their age learned other things, Estha and Rahel learned how history negotiates its terms and collects its dues from those who break its laws. They heard its sickening thud. They smelled its smell and never forgot it.

History's smell.

Like old roses on a breeze.

It would lurk for ever in ordinary things. In coat-hangers. Tomatoes. In the tar on the roads. In certain colours. In the plates at a restaurant. In the absence of words. And the emptiness in eyes.

They would grow up grappling with ways of living with what happened. They would try to tell themselves that in terms of geological time it was an insignificant event. Just a blink of the Earth Woman's eye. That Worse Things had happened. That Worse Things kept happening. But they would find no comfort in the thought.

Chacko said that going to see *The Sound of Music* was an extended exercise in Anglophilia.

Ammu said, 'Oh come on, the whole world goes to see *The Sound of Music*. It's a World Hit.'

'Nevertheless, my dear,' Chacko said in his Reading Aloud voice. 'Never. The. Less.'

Mammachi often said that Chacko was easily one of the cleverest men in India. 'According to whom?' Ammu would say. 'On *what* basis?' Mammachi loved to tell the story (Chacko's story) of how one of the dons at Oxford had said that in his opinion, Chacko was brilliant, and made of prime ministerial material.

To this, Ammu always said, 'Ha! Ha! Ha!' like people in the comics.

She said:

(a) Going to Oxford didn't necessarily make a person clever.

(b) Cleverness didn't necessarily make a good prime minister.

(c) If a person couldn't even run a pickle factory profitably, how was that person going to run a whole country?

And, most important of all:

(d) All Indian mothers are obsessed with their sons and are therefore poor judges of their abilities.

Chacko said:

(a) You don't *go* to Oxford. You *read* at Oxford.

And

(b) After *reading* at Oxford you *come down.*

'Down to earth, d'you mean?' Ammu would ask. '*That* you definitely do. Like your famous airplanes.'

Ammu said that the sad but entirely predictable fate of Chacko's airplanes was an impartial measure of his abilities.

Once a month (except during the monsoons), a parcel would arrive for Chacko by VPP. It always contained a balsa aero-modelling kit. It usually took Chacko between eight and ten days to assemble the aircraft with its tiny fuel tank and motorized propellor. When it was ready, he would take Estha and Rahel to the rice-fields in Nattakom to help him fly it. It never flew for more than a minute. Month after month, Chako's carefully constructed planes crashed in the slushgreen paddy fields into which Estha and Rahel would spurt, like trained retrievers, to salvage the remains.

A tail, a tank, a wing.

A wounded machine.

Chacko's room was cluttered with broken wooden planes.

And every month, another kit would arrive. Chacko never blamed the crashes on the kit.

It was only after Pappachi died that Chacko resigned his job as lecturer at the Madras Christian College, and came to Ayemenem with his Balliol Oar and his Pickle Baron dreams. He commuted his pension and provident fund to buy a Bharat bottle-sealing machine. His oar (with his team mates' names inscribed in gold) hung from iron hoops on the factory wall.

Up to the time Chacko arrived, the factory had been a small but profitable enterprise. Mammachi just ran it like a large kitchen. Chacko had it registered as a partnership and informed Mammachi that she was the sleeping partner. He invested in equipment (canning machines, cauldrons, cookers) and expanded the labour force. Almost immediately, the financial slide began, but was artificially buoyed by extravagant bank loans that Chacko raised by mortgaging the family's rice-fields around the Ayemenem House. Though Ammu did as much work in the factory as Chacko, whenever he was dealing with food inspectors or sanitary engineers, he always referred to it as *my* factory, *my* pineapples, *my* pickles. Legally, this was the case because Ammu, as a daughter, had no claim to the property.

Chacko told Rahel and Estha that Ammu had no Locusts Stand I.

'Thanks to our wonderful male chauvinist society,' Ammu said.

Chacko said, 'What's yours is mine and what's mine is also mine.'

He had a surprisingly high laugh for a man of his size and fatness. And when he laughed, he shook all over without appearing to move.

Until Chacko arrived in Ayemenem, Mammachi's factory had no name. Everybody just referred to her pickles and jams as Sosha's Tender Mango, or Sosha's Banana Jam. Sosha was Mammachi's first name. Soshamma.

It was Chacko who christened the factory Paradise Pickles & Preserves and had labels designed and printed at Comrade K. N. M. Pillai's press. At first he had wanted to call it Zeus Pickles & Preserves, but that idea was vetoed because everybody said that Zeus was too obscure and had no local relevance, whereas Paradise did. (Comrade Pillai's suggestion – Parashuram Pickles – was vetoed for the opposite reason: too *much* local relevance.)

It was Chacko's idea to have a billboard painted and installed on the Plymouth's roof rack.

On the way to Cochin now, it rattled and made fallingoff noises.

Near Vaikom they had to stop to buy some rope to secure it more firmly. That delayed them by another twenty minutes. Rahel began to worry about being late for *The Sound of Music*.

Then, as they approached the outskirts of Cochin, the red and white arm of the railway level-crossing gate went down. Rahel knew that this had happened because she had been hoping that it wouldn't.

She hadn't learned to control her Hopes yet. Estha said that that was a Bad Sign.

So now they were going to miss the beginning of the picture. When Julie Andrews starts off as a speck on the hill and gets bigger and bigger till she bursts on to the screen with her voice like cold water and her breath like peppermint.

The red sign on the red and white arm said STOP in white. 'POTS,' Rahel said.

A yellow hoarding said BE INDIAN, BUY INDIAN in red. 'NAIDNI YUB, NAIDNI EB,' Estha said.

The twins were precocious with their reading. They had raced through *Old Dog Tom*, *Janet and John* and their *Ronald Ridout*

58

Workbooks. At night Ammu read to them from Kipling's *Jungle Book.*

> *Now Chil the Kite brings home the night*
> *That Mang the Bat sets free –*

The down on their arms would stand on end, golden in the light of the bedside lamp. As she read, Ammu could make her voice gravelly, like Shere Khan's. Or whining, like Tabaqui's.

'Ye choose and ye do not choose! What talk is this of choosing? By the bull that I killed, am I to stand nosing into your dog's den for my fair dues? It is I Shere Khan, who speak!'

'And it is I, Raksha [The Demon], who answer,' the twins would shout in high voices. Not together, but almost.

'The man's cub is mine Lungri – mine to me! He shall not be killed. He shall live to run with the Pack and to hunt with the Pack; and in the end, look you, hunter of little naked cubs – frog eater – fish killer – he shall hunt thee!'

Baby Kochamma, who had been put in charge of their formal education, had read them a version of *The Tempest* abridged by Charles and Mary Lamb.

'Where the bee sucks, there suck I,' Estha and Rahel would go about saying. *'In a cowslip's bell I lie.'*

So when Baby Kochamma's Australian missionary friend, Miss Mitten, gave Estha and Rahel a baby book – *The Adventures of Susie Squirrel* – as a present when she visited Ayemenem, they were deeply offended. First they read it forwards. Miss Mitten, who belonged to a sect of born-again Christians, said that she was a Little Disappointed in them when they read it aloud to her, backwards.

'*ehT serutnevdA fo eisuS lerriuqS. enO gnirps gninrom eisuS lerriuqS ekow pu.*'

They showed Miss Mitten how it was possible to read both *Malayalam* and *Madam I'm Adam* backwards as well as forwards. She wasn't amused and it turned out that she didn't even know what Malayalam was. They told her it was the language everyone spoke in Kerala. She said she had been under the impression that it was called Keralese. Estha, who had by then taken an active dislike to Miss Mitten, told her that as far as he was concerned it was a Highly Stupid Impression.

Miss Mitten complained to Baby Kochamma about Estha's rudeness, and about their reading backwards. She told Baby Kochamma that she had seen Satan in their eyes. *nataS in their seye.*

They were made to write *In future we will not read backwards. In future we will not read backwards.* A hundred times. Forwards.

A few months later Miss Mitten was killed by a milk van in Hobart, across the road from a cricket oval. To the twins there was hidden justice in the fact that the milk van had been *reversing.*

More buses and cars had stopped on either side of the level crossing. An ambulance that said *Sacred Heart Hospital* was full of a party of people on their way to a wedding. The bride was staring out of the back window, her face partially obscured by the flaking paint of the huge red cross.

The buses all had girls' names. Lucykutty, Mollykutty, Beena Mol. In Malayalam, Mol is Little Girl and Mon is Little Boy. Beena Mol was full of pilgrims who'd had their heads shaved at Tirupati. Rahel could see a row of bald heads at the bus window, above evenly spaced vomit streaks. She was more than a little curious about vomiting. She had never vomited. Not once. Estha had, and when he did, his skin grew hot and shiny, and his eyes helpless and beautiful, and Ammu loved him more than usual. Chacko said that Estha and Rahel were indecently healthy. And so was Sophie Mol. He said it was because they didn't suffer from Inbreeding like most Syrian Christians. And Parsees.

Mammachi said that what her grandchildren suffered from was far worse than Inbreeding. She meant having parents who were divorced. As though these were the only choices available to people: Inbreeding or Divorce.

Rahel wasn't sure what she suffered from, but occasionally she practised sad faces, and sighing in the mirror.

'*It is a far, far better thing that I do, than I have ever done*,' she would say to herself sadly. That was Rahel being Sydney Carton being Charles Darnay, as he stood on the steps, waiting to be guillotined, in the Classics Illustrated comic's version of *A Tale of Two Cities*.

She wondered what had caused the bald pilgrims to vomit so uniformly, and whether they had vomited together in a single, well-orchestrated heave (to music perhaps, to the rhythm of a bus bhajan), or separately, one at a time.

Initially, when the level crossing had just closed, the Air was full of the impatient sound of idling engines. But when the man that manned the crossing came out of his booth, on his backward bending legs and signalled with his limp, flapping walk to the tea stall that they were in for a long wait, drivers switched off their engines and milled about, stretching their legs.

With a desultory nod of his bored and sleepy head, the Level Crossing Divinity conjured up beggars with bandages, men with trays selling pieces of fresh coconut, parippu vadas on banana leaves. And cold drinks. Coca-Cola, Fanta, Rosemilk.

A leper with soiled bandages begged at the car window.

'That looks like Mercurochrome to me,' Ammu said, of his inordinately bright blood.

'Congratulations,' Chacko said. 'Spoken like a true bourgeoise.'

Ammu smiled and they shook hands, as though she really was being awarded a Certificate of Merit for being an honest-to-goodness Genuine Bourgeoise. Moments like these, the twins treasured and threaded like precious beads on a (somewhat scanty) necklace.

Rahel and Estha squashed their noses against the Plymouth's quarter-windows. Yearning marshmallows with cloudy children behind them. Ammu said, 'No,' firmly, and with conviction.

Chacko lit a Charminar. He inhaled deeply and then removed a little flake of tobacco that had stayed behind on his tongue.

Inside the Plymouth, it wasn't easy for Rahel to see Estha, because Baby Kochamma rose between them like a hill. Ammu had insisted that they sit separately to prevent them from fighting. When they fought, Estha called Rahel a Refugee Stick Insect. Rahel called him Elvis the Pelvis and did a twisty, funny kind of dance that infuriated Estha. When they had serious physical fights, they were so evenly matched that the fights went on for ever, and things that came in their way – table lamps, ashtrays and water jugs – were smashed or irreparably damaged.

Baby Kochamma was holding on to the back of the front seat with her arms. When the car moved, her armfat swung like heavy washing in the wind. Now it hung down like a fleshy curtain, blocking Estha from Rahel.

On Estha's side of the road was the tea shack that sold tea and stale glucose biscuits in dim glass cases with flies. There was lemon soda in thick bottles with blue marble stoppers to keep the fizz in. And a red ice-box that said rather sadly *Things go better with Coca-Cola.*

Murlidharan, the level-crossing lunatic, perched cross-legged and perfectly balanced on the milestone. His balls and penis dangled down, pointing towards the sign which said:

COCHIN

23

Murlidharan was naked except for the tall plastic bag that somebody had fitted onto his head like a transparent chef's cap through which the view of the landscape continued – dimmed, chef-shaped, but uninterrupted. He couldn't remove his cap even if had wanted to because he had no arms. They had been blown off in Singapore in '42, within the first week of his running away from home to join the fighting ranks of the Indian National Army. After Independence he had himself registered as a Grade I Freedom Fighter and had been allotted a free first-class railway pass for life. This too he had lost (along with his mind), so he could no longer live on trains or in refreshment rooms in railway stations. Murlidharan had no home, no doors to lock, but he had his old keys tied carefully around his waist. In a shining bunch. His mind was full of cupboards, cluttered with secret pleasures.

An alarm clock. A red car with a musical horn. A red mug for the bathroom. A wife with a diamond. A briefcase with important papers. A coming home from the office. An *I'm sorry, Colonel Sabhapathy, but I'm afraid I've said my say*. And crisp banana chips for the children.

He watched the trains come and go. He counted his keys.

He watched governments rise and fall. He counted his keys.

He watched cloudy children at car windows with yearning marshmallow noses.

The homeless, the helpless, the sick, the small and lost, all filed past his window. Still he counted his keys.

He was never sure which cupboard he might have to open, or when. He sat on the burning milestone with his matted hair and eyes like windows, and was glad to be able to look away sometimes. To have his keys to count and countercheck.

Numbers would do.

Numbness would be fine.

Murlidharan moved his mouth when he counted, and made well-formed words.

Onner.
Runder.
Moonner.

Estha noticed that the hair on his head was curly grey, the hair in his windy, armless armpits was wispy black, and the hair in his crotch was black and springy. One man with three kinds of hair. Estha wondered how that could be. He tried to think of whom to ask.

The Waiting filled Rahel until she was ready to burst. She looked at her watch. It was ten to two. She thought of Julie Andrews and Christopher Plummer kissing each other sideways so that their noses didn't collide. She wondered whether people always kissed each other sideways. She tried to think of whom to ask.

Then, from a distance, a hum approached the held-up traffic and covered it like a cloak. The drivers who'd been stretching their legs got back into their vehicles and slammed doors. The beggars and vendors disappeared. Within minutes there was no one on the road. Except Murlidharan. Perched with his bum on the burning milestone. Unperturbed and only mildly curious.

There was hustle-bustle. And police whistles.

From behind the line of waiting, oncoming traffic, a column of men appeared, with red flags and banners and a hum that grew and grew.

'Put up your windows,' Chacko said. 'And stay calm. They're not going to hurt us.'

'Why not join them, comrade?' Ammu said to Chacko. 'I'll drive.'

Chacko said nothing. A muscle tensed below the wad of fat on his jaw. He tossed away his cigarette and rolled up his window.

Chacko was a self-proclaimed Marxist. He would call pretty women who worked in the factory to his room, and on the pretext of lecturing them on labour rights and trade union law, flirt with them outrageously. He would call them Comrade, and insist that they call him Comrade back (which made them giggle). Much to their embarrassment and Mammachi's dismay, he forced them to sit at table with him and drink tea.

Once he even took a group of them to attend Trade Union classes that were held in Alleppey. They went by bus and returned by boat. They came back happy, with glass bangles and flowers in their hair.

Ammu said it was all hogwash. Just a case of a spoiled princeling playing *Comrade! Comrade!* An Oxford avatar of the old zamindar mentality – a landlord forcing his attentions on women who depended on him for their livelihood.

As the marchers approached, Ammu put up her window. Estha his. Rahel hers. (Effortfully, because the black knob on the handle had fallen off.)

Suddenly the skyblue Plymouth looked absurdly opulent on the narrow, pitted road. Like a wide lady squeezing down a narrow corridor. Like Baby Kochamma in church, on her way to the bread and wine.

'Look down!' Baby Kochamma said, as the front ranks of the procession approached the car. 'Avoid eye contact. That's what really provokes them.'

On the side of her neck, her pulse was pounding.

Within minutes, the road was swamped by thousands of marching people. Automobile islands in a river of people. The air was red with flags, which dipped and lifted as the marchers ducked under the level-crossing gate and swept across the railway tracks in a red wave.

The sound of a thousand voices spread over the frozen traffic like a Noise Umbrella.

'Inquilab Zindabad!
Thozhilali Ekta Zindabad!'

'Long Live the Revolution!' they shouted. 'Workers of the World Unite!'

Even Chacko had no really complete explanation for why the Communist Party was so much more successful in Kerala than it had been almost anywhere else in India, except perhaps in Bengal.

There were several competing theories. One was that it had to do with the large population of Christians in the state. Twenty per cent of Kerala's population were Syrian Christians, who believed that they were descendants of the one hundred Brahmins whom Saint Thomas the Apostle converted to Christianity when he travelled east after the Resurrection. Structurally – this somewhat rudimentary argument went – Marxism was a simple substitute for Christianity. Replace God with Marx, Satan with the bourgeoisie, Heaven with a classless society, the Church with the Party, and the form and purpose of the journey remained similar. An obstacle race, with a prize at the end. Whereas the Hindu mind had to make more complex adjustments.

The trouble with this theory was that in Kerala the Syrian Christians were, by and large, the wealthy, estate-owning (pickle-factory-running) feudal lords, for whom communism represented a fate worse than death. They had always voted for the Congress Party.

A second theory claimed that it had to do with the comparatively high level of literacy in the state. Perhaps. Except that the high literacy level was largely *because* of the communist movement.

The real secret was that communism crept into Kerala insidiously. As a reformist movement that never overtly questioned the traditional values of a caste-ridden, extremely traditional community. The Marxists worked from *within* the communal divides, never challenging them, never appearing not to. They offered a cocktail revolution. A heady mix of Eastern Marxism and orthodox Hinduism, spiked with a shot of democracy.

Though Chacko was not a card-holding member of the Party, he had been converted early and had remained, through all its travails, a committed supporter.

He was an undergraduate at Delhi University during the euphoria of 1957, when the Communists won the State Assembly elections and Nehru invited them to form a government. Chacko's hero, Comrade E. M. S. Namboodiripad, the flamboyant Brahmin high priest of Marxism in Kerala, became Chief Minister of the first ever democratically elected communist government in the world. Suddenly the communists found themselves in the extraordinary – critics said absurd – position of having to govern a people and foment revolution simultaneously. Comrade E. M. S. Namboodiripad evolved his own theory about how he would do this. Chacko studied his treatise on *The Peaceful Transition to Communism* with an adolescent's obsessive diligence and an ardent fan's unquestioning approval. It set out in detail how Comrade E. M. S. Namboodiripad's government intended to enforce land reforms, neutralize the police, subvert the judiciary and 'Restrain the Hand of the Reactionary Anti-People Congress Government at the Centre'.

Unfortunately, before the year was out, the Peaceful part of the Peaceful Transition came to an end.

Every morning at breakfast the Imperial Entomologist derided his argumentative Marxist son by reading out newspaper reports of the riots, strikes and incidents of police brutality that convulsed Kerala.

'So, Karl Marx!' Pappachi would sneer when Chacko came to the table. 'What shall we do with these bloody students now? The stupid goons are agitating against our People's Government. Shall we annihilate them? Surely students aren't People any more?'

Over the next two years the political discord, fuelled by the Congress Party and the Church, slid into anarchy. By the time Chacko finished his BA and left for Oxford to do another one, Kerala was on the brink of civil war. Nehru dismissed the Communist Government and announced fresh elections. The Congress Party returned to power.

It was only in 1967 – almost exactly ten years after they first came to power – that Comrade E. M. S. Namboodiripad's party was re-elected. This time as part of a coalition between what had now become two separate parties – the Communist Party of India, and the Communist Party of India (Marxist). The CPI and the CPI(M).

Pappachi was dead by then. Chacko divorced. Paradise Pickles was seven years old.

Kerala was reeling in the aftermath of famine and a failed monsoon. People were dying. Hunger had to be very high up on any government list of priorities.

During his second term in office, Comrade E. M. S. went about implementing the Peaceful Transition more soberly. This earned him the wrath of the Chinese Communist Party. They denounced him for his 'Parliamentary Cretinism' and accused him of 'providing relief to the people and thereby blunting the People's Consciousness and diverting them from the Revolution'.

Peking switched its patronage to the newest, most militant faction of the CPI(M) – the Naxalites – who had staged an armed insurrection in Naxalbari, a village in Bengal. They organized peasants into fighting cadres, seized land, expelled the owners and established People's Courts to try Class Enemies. The Naxalite movement spread across the country and struck terror in every bourgeois heart.

In Kerala, they breathed a plume of excitement and fear into the already frightened air. Killings had begun in the north. That May there was a blurred photograph in the papers of a landlord in Palghat who had been tied to a lamp post and beheaded.

His head lay on its side, some distance away from his body, in a dark puddle that could have been water, could have been blood. It was hard to tell in black and white. In the grey pre-dawn light.

His surprised eyes were open.

Comrade E. M. S. Namboodiripad (*Running Dog, Soviet Stooge*) expelled the Naxalites from his party and went on with the business of harnessing anger for parliamentary purposes.

The march that surged around the skyblue Plymouth on that skyblue December day was a part of that process. It had been organized by the Travancore-Cochin Marxist Labour Union. Their comrades in Trivandrum would march to the Secretariat and present the Charter of People's Demands to Comrade E. M. S. himself. The orchestra petitioning its conductor. Their demands were that paddy workers, who were made to work in the fields for eleven and a half hours a day – from seven in the morning to six-thirty in the evening – be permitted to take a one-hour lunch break. That women's wages be increased from one rupee twenty-five paisa a day, to three rupees, and men's from two rupees fifty paisa to four rupees fifty paisa a day. They were also demanding that Untouchables no longer be addressed by their caste names. They demanded *not* to be addressed as Achoo *Parayan*, or Kelan *Paravan*, or Kuttan *Pulayan*, but just as Achoo, or Kelan, or Kuttan.

Cardamom Kings, Coffee Counts and Rubber Barons – old boarding school buddies – came down from their lonely, far-flung estates and sipped chilled beer at the Sailing Club. They raised their glasses. '*A rose by any other name . . .*' they said, and sniggered to hide their rising panic.

The marchers that day were party workers, students, and the labourers themselves. Touchables and Untouchables. On their shoulders they carried a keg of ancient anger, lit with a recent fuse. There was an edge to this anger that was Naxalite, and new.

Through the Plymouth window, Rahel could see that the loudest word they said was *Zindabad*. And that the veins stood out in their necks when they said it. And that the arms that held the flags and banners were knotted and hard.

Inside the Plymouth it was still and hot.

Baby Kochamma's fear lay rolled up on the car floor like a damp, clammy cheroot. This was just the beginning of it. The fear that over the years would grow to consume her. That would make her lock her doors and windows. That would give her two hairlines and both her mouths. Hers, too, was an ancient, age-old fear. The fear of being dispossessed.

She tried to count the green beads on her rosary, but couldn't concentrate. An open hand slammed against the car window.

A balled fist banged down on the burning skyblue bonnet. It sprang open. The Plymouth looked like an angular blue animal in a zoo asking to be fed.

A bun.

A banana.

Another balled fist slammed down on it, and the bonnet closed. Chacko rolled down his window and called out to the man who had done it.

'Thanks, *keto!*' he said. '*Valarey* thanks!'

'Don't be so ingratiating, comrade,' Ammu said. 'It was an accident. He didn't really mean to help. How could he *possibly* know that in this old car there beats a truly Marxist heart?'

'Ammu,' Chacko said, his voice steady and deliberately casual, 'is it at all possible for you to prevent your washed-up cynicism from completely colouring everything?'

Silence filled the car like a saturated sponge. *Washed-up* cut like a knife through a soft thing. The sun shone with a shuddering sigh. This was the trouble with families. Like invidious doctors, they knew just where it hurt.

Just then Rahel saw Velutha. Vellya Paapen's son, Velutha. Her most beloved friend Velutha. Velutha marching with a red flag. In a white shirt and mundu with angry veins in his neck. He never usually wore a shirt.

Rahel rolled down her window in a flash.

'Velutha! Velutha!' she called to him.

He froze for a moment, and listened with his flag. What he heard was a familiar voice in a most unfamiliar circumstance. Rahel, standing on the car seat, had grown out of the Plymouth window like the loose, flailing horn of a car-shaped herbivore. With a fountain in a Love-in-Tokyo and yellow-rimmed red plastic sunglasses.

'Velutha! *Ividay!* Velutha!' And she too had veins in her neck.

He stepped sideways and disappeared deftly into the angriness around him.

Inside the car Ammu whirled around, and her eyes were angry. She slapped at Rahel's calves, which were the only part of her left in the car to slap. Calves and brown feet in Bata sandals.

'Behave yourself!' Ammu said.

Baby Kochamma pulled Rahel down, and she landed on the seat with a surprised thump. She thought there'd been a misunderstanding.

'It was Velutha!' she explained with a smile. 'And he had a flag!'

The flag had seemed to her a most impressive piece of equipment. The right thing for a friend to have.

'You're a stupid silly little girl!' Ammu said.

Her sudden, fierce anger pinned Rahel against the car seat. Rahel was puzzled. Why was Ammu so angry? About what?

'But it *was* him!' Rahel said.

'Shut up!' Ammu said.

Rahel saw that Ammu had a film of perspiration on her forehead and upper lip, and that her eyes had become hard, like marbles. Like Pappachi's in the Vienna studio photograph. (How Pappachi's Moth whispered in his children's veins!)

Baby Kochamma rolled up Rahel's window.

Years later, on a crisp fall morning in upstate New York, on a Sunday train from Grand Central to Croton Harmon, it suddenly came back to Rahel. That expression on Ammu's face. Like a rogue piece in a puzzle. Like a question mark that drifted through the pages of a book and never settled at the end of a sentence.

That hard marble look in Ammu's eyes. The glisten of perspiration on her upper lip. And the chill of that sudden, hurt silence.

What had it all meant?

The Sunday train was almost empty. Across the aisle from Rahel a woman with chapped cheeks and a moustache coughed up phlegm and wrapped it in twists of newspaper that she tore off the pile of Sunday papers on her lap. She arranged the little packages in neat rows on the empty seat in front of her as though she was setting up a phlegm stall. As she worked she chatted to herself in a pleasant, soothing voice.

Memory was that woman on the train. Insane in the way she sifted through dark things in a closet and emerged with the most unlikely ones – a fleeting look, a feeling. The smell of smoke. A windscreen wiper. A mother's marble eyes. Quite sane in the way she left huge tracts of darkness veiled. Unremembered.

Her co-passenger's madness comforted Rahel. It drew her closer into New York's deranged womb. Away from the other, more terrible thing that haunted her. *A sourmetal smell, like steel bus-rails, and the smell of the bus conductor's hands from holding them. A young man with an old man's mouth.*

Outside the train, the Hudson shimmered, and the trees were the redbrown colours of fall. It was just a little cold.

'There's a nipple in the air,' Larry McCaslin said to Rahel, and laid his palm gently against the suggestion of protest from a chilly nipple through her cotton T-shirt. He wondered why she didn't smile.

She wondered why it was that when she thought of home, it was always in the colours of the dark, oiled wood of boats, and the empty cores of the tongues of flame that flickered in brass lamps.

It *was* Velutha.

That much Rahel was sure of. She'd seen him. He'd seen her. She'd have known him anywhere, any time. And if he hadn't been wearing a shirt, she would have recognized him from behind. She knew his back. She'd been carried on it. More times than she could count. It had a light brown birthmark, shaped like a pointed dry leaf. He said it was a lucky leaf, that made the monsoons come on time. A brown leaf on a black back. An autumn leaf at night.

A lucky leaf that wasn't lucky enough.

Velutha wasn't supposed to be a carpenter.

He was called Velutha – which means White in Malayalam – because he was so black. His father, Vellya Paapen, was a Paravan. A toddy tapper. He had a glass eye. He had been shaping a block of granite with a hammer when a chip flew into his left eye and sliced right through it.

As a young boy, Velutha would come with Vellya Paapen to the back entrance of the Ayemenem House to deliver the coconuts they had plucked from the trees in the compound. Pappachi would not allow Paravans into the house. Nobody would. They were not allowed to touch anything that Touchables touched. Caste Hindus and Caste Christians. Mammachi told Estha and Rahel that she could remember a time, in her girlhood, when Paravans were expected to crawl backwards with a broom, sweeping away their footprints so that Brahmins or Syrian Christians would not defile themselves by accidentally stepping into a Paravan's footprint. In Mammachi's time, Paravans, like other Untouchables, were not allowed to walk on public roads, not allowed to cover their upper bodies, not allowed to carry umbrellas. They had to put their hands over their mouths when they spoke, to divert their polluted breath away from those whom they addressed.

When the British came to Malabar, a number of Paravans, Pelayas and Pulayas (among them Velutha's grandfather, Kelan) converted to Christianity and joined the Anglican Church to escape the scourge of Untouchability. As added incentive they were given a little food and money. They were known as the Rice-Christians. It didn't take them long to realize that they had jumped from the frying pan into the fire. They were made to have separate churches, with separate services, and separate priests. As a special favour they were even given their own separate Pariah Bishop. After Independence they found they were not entitled to any Government benefits like job reservations or bank loans at low interest rates, because officially, on paper, they were Christians, and therefore casteless. It was a little like having to sweep away your footprints without a broom. Or worse, not being *allowed* to leave footprints at all.

It was Mammachi, on vacation from Delhi and Imperial Entomology, who first noticed little Velutha's remarkable facility with his hands. Velutha was eleven then, about three years younger than Ammu. He was like a little magician. He could make intricate toys – tiny windmills, rattles, minute jewel boxes out of dried palm reeds; he could carve perfect boats out of tapioca stems and figurines on cashew nuts. He would bring them for Ammu, holding them out on his palm (as he had been taught) so she wouldn't have to touch him to take them. Though he was younger than she was, he called her Ammukutty – Little Ammu. Mammachi persuaded Vellya Paapen to send him to the Untouchables' School that her father-in-law, Punnyan Kunju, had founded.

Velutha was fourteen when Johann Klein, a carpenter from a carpenters' guild in Bavaria, came to Kottayam and spent three years with the Christian Mission Society, conducting a workshop with local carpenters. Every afternoon, after school, Velutha caught a bus to Kottayam where he worked with Klein till dusk. By the time he was sixteen, Velutha had finished high school and was an accomplished carpenter. He had his own set of carpentry tools and a distinctly German design sensibility. He built Mammachi a Bauhaus dining table with twelve dining chairs in rosewood and a traditional Bavarian chaise longue in lighter jack. For Baby Kochamma's annual Nativity plays he made her a stack of wire-framed angels' wings that fitted onto children's backs like knapsacks, cardboard clouds for the Angel Gabriel to appear between, and a dismantleable manger for Christ to be born in. When her garden cherub's silver arc dried up inexplicably, it was Dr Velutha who fixed its bladder for her.

Apart from his carpentry skills, Velutha had a way with machines. Mammachi (with impenetrable Touchable logic) often said that if only he hadn't been a Paravan, he might have become an engineer. He mended radios, clocks, water-pumps. He looked after the plumbing and all the electrical gadgets in the house.

When Mammachi decided to enclose the back verandah, it was Velutha who designed and built the sliding-folding door that later became all the rage in Ayemenem.

Velutha knew more about the machines in the factory than anyone else.

When Chacko resigned his job in Madras and returned to Ayemenem with a Bharat bottle-sealing machine, it was Velutha who reassembled it and set it up. It was Velutha who maintained the new canning machine and the automatic pineapple slicer.

Velutha who oiled the water-pump and the small diesel generator. Velutha who built the aluminium sheet-lined, easy-to-clean cutting surfaces, and the ground-level furnaces for boiling fruit.

Velutha's father, Vellya Paapen, however, was an Old World Paravan. He had seen the Crawling Backwards Days and his gratitude to Mammachi and her family for all that they had done for him, was as wide and deep as a river in spate. When he had his accident with the stone chip, Mammachi organized and paid for his glass eye. He hadn't worked off his debt yet, and though he knew he wasn't expected to, that he wouldn't ever be able to – he felt that his eye was not his own. His gratitude widened his smile and bent his back.

Vellya Paapen feared for his younger son. He couldn't say what it was that frightened him. It was nothing that he had said. Or done. It was not *what* he said, but the *way* he said it. Not *what* he did, but the *way* he did it.

Perhaps it was just a lack of hesitation. An unwarranted assurance. In the way he walked. The way he held his head. The quiet way he offered suggestions without being asked. Or the quiet way in which he disregarded suggestions without appearing to rebel.

While these were qualities that were perfectly acceptable, perhaps even desirable in Touchables, Vellya Paapen thought that in a Paravan they could (and would, and indeed, *should*) be construed as insolence.

Vellya Paapen tried to caution Velutha. But since he couldn't put his finger on what it was that bothered him, Velutha misunderstood his muddled concern. To him it appeared as though his father grudged him his brief training and his natural skills. Vellya Paapen's good intentions quickly degenerated into nagging and bickering and a general air of unpleasantness between father and son. Much to his mother's dismay, Velutha began to avoid going home. He worked late. He caught fish in the river and cooked it on an open fire. He slept outdoors, on the banks of the river.

Then one day he disappeared. For four years nobody knew where he was. There was a rumour that he was working on a building site for the Department of Welfare and Housing in Trivandrum. And more recently, the inevitable rumour that he had become a Naxalite. That he had been to prison. Somebody said they had seen him in Quilon.

There was no way of reaching him when his mother, Chella, died of tuberculosis. Then Kuttappen, his older brother, fell off a coconut tree and damaged his spine. He was paralysed and unable to work. Velutha heard of the accident a whole year after it happened.

It had been five months since he returned to Ayemenem. He never talked about where he had been, or what he had done.

Mammachi rehired Velutha as the factory carpenter and put him in charge of general maintenance. It caused a great deal of resentment among the other Touchable factory workers because, according to them, Paravans were not *meant* to be carpenters. And certainly, prodigal Paravans were not meant to be rehired.

To keep the others happy, and since she knew that nobody else would hire him as a carpenter, Mammachi paid Velutha less than she would a Touchable carpenter but more than she would a Paravan. Mammachi didn't encourage him to enter the house (except when she needed something mended or installed). She thought that he ought to be grateful that he was allowed on the factory premises at all, and allowed to touch things that Touchables touched. She said that it was a big step for a Paravan.

When he returned to Ayemenem after his years away from home, Velutha still had about him the same quickness. The sureness. And Vellya Paapen feared for him now more than ever. But this time he held his peace. He said nothing.

77

At least not until the Terror took hold of him. Not until he saw, night after night, a little boat being rowed across the river. Not until he saw it return at dawn. Not until he saw what his Untouchable son had touched. More than touched.

Entered.

Loved.

When the Terror took hold of him, Vellya Paapen went to Mammachi. He stared straight ahead with his mortgaged eye. He wept with his own one. One cheek glistened with tears. The other stayed dry. He shook his own head from side to side to side till Mammachi ordered him to stop. He trembled his own body like a man with malaria. Mammachi ordered him to stop it but he couldn't, because you can't order fear around. Not even a Paravan's. Vellya Paapen told Mammachi what he had seen. He asked God's forgiveness for having spawned a monster. He offered to kill his son with his own bare hands. To destroy what he had created.

In the next room Baby Kochamma heard the noise and came to find out what it was all about. She saw Grief and Trouble ahead, and secretly, in her heart of hearts, she exulted.

She said (among other things) – '*How could she stand the smell? Haven't you noticed, they have a particular smell, these Paravans?*'

And she shuddered theatrically, like a child being force-fed spinach. She preferred an Irish-Jesuit smell to a particular Paravan smell.

By far. By far.

Velutha, Vellya Paapen and Kuttappen lived in a little laterite hut, downriver from the Ayemenem house. A three-minute run through the coconut trees for Esthappen and Rahel. They had only just arrived at Ayemenem with Ammu and were too young to remember Velutha when he left. But in the months since he had returned, they had grown to be the best of friends. They were forbidden from visiting his house, but they did. They would sit with him for hours, on their haunches – hunched punctuation marks in a pool of wood shavings – and wonder how he always seemed to know what smooth shapes waited inside the wood for him. They loved the way wood, in Velutha's hands, seemed to soften and become as pliable as Plasticine. He was teaching them to use a planer. His house (on a good day) smelled of fresh wood shavings and the sun. Of red fish curry cooked with black tamarind. The best fish curry, according to Estha, in the whole world.

It was Velutha who made Rahel her luckiest ever fishing rod and taught her and Estha to fish.

And on that skyblue December day, it *was* him that she saw through her red sunglasses, marching with a red flag at the level crossing outside Cochin.

Steelshrill police whistles pierced holes in the Noise Umbrella. Through the jagged umbrella holes Rahel could see pieces of red sky. And in the red sky, hot red kites wheeled, looking for rats. In their hooded yellow eyes there was a road and red flags marching. And a white shirt over a black back with a birthmark.

Marching.

Terror, sweat and talcum powder blended into a mauve paste between Baby Kochamma's rings of neckfat. Spit coagulated into little white gobs at the corners of her mouth. She imagined she saw a man in the procession who looked like the photograph in the newspapers of the Naxalite called Rajan, who was rumoured to have moved south from Palghat. She imagined he had looked straight at her.

A man with a red flag and a face like a knot opened Rahel's door because it wasn't locked. The doorway was full of men who'd stopped to stare.

'Feeling hot, baby?' the man like a knot asked Rahel kindly in Malayalam. Then unkindly, 'Ask your daddy to buy you an Air Condition!' and he hooted with delight at his own wit and timing. Rahel smiled back at him, pleased to have Chacko mistaken for her father. Like a normal family.

79

'Don't answer!' Baby Kochamma whispered hoarsely. 'Look down! Just look down!'

The man with the flag turned his attention to her. She was looking down at the floor of the car. Like a coy, frightened bride who had been married off to a stranger.

'Hello, sister,' the man said carefully in English. 'What is your name please?'

When Baby Kochamma didn't answer, he looked back at his co-hecklers.

'She has no name.'

'What about Modalali Mariakutty?' someone suggested with a giggle. Modalali in Malayalam means landlord.

'A, B, C, D, X, Y, Z,' somebody else said, irrelevantly.

More students crowded around. They all wore handkerchiefs or printed Bombay Dyeing hand towels on their heads to stave off the sun. They looked like extras who had wandered off the sets of the Malayalam version of *Sinbad: The Last Voyage*.

The man like a knot gave Baby Kochamma his red flag as a present. 'Here,' he said. 'Hold it.'

Baby Kochamma held it, still not looking at him.

'Wave it,' he ordered.

She had to wave it. She had no choice. It smelled of new cloth and a shop. Crisp and dusty. She tried to wave it as though she wasn't waving it.

'Now say *Inquilab Zindabad*!'

'*Inquilab Zindabad*,' Baby Kochamma whispered.

'Good girl.'

The crowd roared with laughter. A shrill whistle blew.

'Okay then,' the man said to Baby Kochamma in English, as though they had successfully concluded a business deal. 'Bye-bye!'

He slammed the skyblue door shut. Baby Kochamma wobbled. The crowd around the car unclotted and went on with its march.

Baby Kochamma rolled the red flag up and put it on the ledge behind the back seat. She put her rosary back into her blouse where she kept it with her melons. She busied herself with this and that, trying to salvage some dignity.

After the last few men walked past, Chacko said it was all right now to roll down the windows.

'Are you sure it was him?' Chacko asked Rahel.

'Who?' Rahel said, suddenly cautious.

'Are you sure it was Velutha?'

'Hmmm . . . ?' Rahel said, playing for time, trying to decipher Estha's frantic thought signals.

'I said, are you sure that the man you saw was Velutha?' Chacko said for the third time.

'Mmm . . . nyes . . . nn . . . nnalmost,' Rahel said.

'You're almost sure?' Chacko said.

'No . . . it was almost Velutha,' Rahel said. 'It almost looked like him . . .'

'So you're *not* sure then?'

'Almost not.' Rahel slid a look at Estha for approval.

'It must have been him,' Baby Kochamma said. 'It's Trivandrum that's done this to him. They all go there and come back thinking they're some great politicos.'

Nobody seemed particularly impressed by her insight.

'We should keep an eye on him,' Baby Kochamma said. 'If he starts this union business in the factory . . . I've noticed some signs, some rudeness, some ingratitude . . . The other day I asked him to help me with the rocks for my scree bed and he –'

'I saw Velutha at home before we left,' Estha said brightly. 'So how could it be him?'

'For his own sake,' Baby Kochamma said, darkly, 'I hope it wasn't. And next time, Esthappen, don't interrupt.'

She was annoyed that nobody asked her what a scree bed was.

In the days that followed, Baby Kochamma focused all her fury at her public humiliation on Velutha. She sharpened it like a pencil. In her mind he grew to represent the march. And the man who had forced her to wave the Marxist Party flag. And the man who christened her Modalali Mariakutty. And all the men who had laughed at her.

She began to hate him.

From the way Ammu held her head, Rahel could tell that she was still angry. Rahel looked at her watch. Ten to two. Still no train. She put her chin on the window sill. She could feel the grey gristle of the felt that cushioned the window glass pressing into her chinskin. She took off her sunglasses to get a better look at the dead frog squashed on the road. It was so dead and squashed so flat that it looked more like a frog-shaped stain on the road than a frog. Rahel wondered if Miss Mitten had been squashed into a Miss Mitten-shaped stain by the milk truck that killed her.

With the certitude of a true believer, Vellya Paapen had assured the twins that there was no such thing in the world as a black cat. He said that there were only black cat-shaped holes in the Universe.

There were so many stains on the road.

Squashed Miss Mitten-shaped stains in the Universe.

Squashed frog-shaped stains in the Universe.

Squashed crows that had tried to eat the squashed frog-shaped stains in the Universe.

Squashed dogs that ate the squashed crow-shaped stains in the Universe.

Feathers. Mangoes. Spit.

All the way to Cochin.

The sun shone through the Plymouth window directly down at Rahel. She closed her eyes and shone back at it. Even behind her eyelids the light was bright and hot. The sky was orange, and the coconut trees were sea anemones waving their tentacles, hoping to trap and eat an unsuspecting cloud. A transparent spotted snake with a forked tongue floated across the sky. Then a transparent Roman soldier on a spotted horse. The strange thing about Roman soldiers in the comics, according to Rahel, was the amount of trouble they took over their armour and their helmets, and then, after all that, they left their legs bare. It didn't make any sense at all. Weatherwise or otherwise.

Ammu had told them the story of Julius Caesar and how he was stabbed by Brutus, his best friend, in the Senate. And how he fell to the floor with knives in his back and said, '*Et tu? Brute? – Then fall Caesar.*'

'It just goes to show,' Ammu said, 'that you can't trust anybody. Mother, father, brother, husband, bestfriend. Nobody.'

With children, she said (when they asked), it remained to be seen. She said it was entirely possible, for instance, that Estha could grow up to be a Male Chauvinist Pig.

At night, Estha would stand on his bed with his sheet wrapped around him and say, '"*Et tu? Brute? – Then fall Caesar!*"' and crash into bed without bending his knees, like a stabbed corpse. Kochu Maria, who slept on the floor on a mat, said that she would complain to Mammachi.

'Tell your mother to take you to your father's house,' she said. 'There you can break as many beds as you like. These aren't your beds. This isn't *your* house.'

Estha would rise from the dead, stand on his bed and say, '*Et tu? Kochu Maria? – Then fall Estha!*' and die again.

Kochu Maria was sure that *Et tu* was an obscenity in English and was waiting for a suitable opportunity to complain about Estha to Mammachi.

The woman in the neighbouring car had biscuit crumbs on her mouth. Her husband lit a bent after-biscuit cigarette. He exhaled two tusks of smoke through his nostrils and for a fleeting moment looked like a wild boar. Mrs Boar asked Rahel her name in a Baby Voice.

Rahel ignored her and blew an inadvertent spit-bubble.

Ammu hated them blowing spit-bubbles. She said it reminded her of Baba. Their father. She said that he used to blow spit-bubbles and shiver his leg. According to Ammu, only clerks behaved like that, not aristocrats.

Aristocrats were people who didn't blow spit-bubbles or shiver their legs. Or gobble.

Though Baba wasn't a clerk, Ammu said he often behaved like one.

When they were alone, Estha and Rahel sometimes pretended that they were clerks. They would blow spit-bubbles and shiver their legs and gobble like turkeys. They remembered their father whom they had known between wars. He once gave them puffs from his cigarette and got annoyed because they had sucked it and wet the filter with spit.

'It's not a ruddy sweet!' he said, genuinely angry.

They remembered his anger. And Ammu's. They remembered being pushed around a room once, from Ammu to Baba to Ammu to Baba like billiard balls. Ammu pushing Estha away: 'Here, you keep one of them. I can't look after them both.' Later, when Estha asked Ammu about that, she hugged him and said he mustn't imagine things.

In the only photograph they had seen of him (which Ammu allowed them to look at once), he was wearing a white shirt and glasses. He looked like a handsome, studious cricketer. With one arm he held Estha on his shoulders. Estha was smiling, with his chin resting on his father's head. Rahel was held against his body with his other arm. She looked grumpy and bad-tempered, with her babylegs dangling. Someone had painted rosy blobs on to their cheeks.

Ammu said that he had only carried them for the photograph

and even then had been so drunk that she was scared he'd drop them. Ammu said she'd been standing just outside the photograph, ready to catch them if he did. Still, except for their cheeks, Estha and Rahel thought it was a nice photograph.

'Will you stop that!' Ammu said, so loudly that Murlidharan, who had hopped off the milestone to stare into the Plymouth, backed off, his stumps jerking in alarm.

'What?' Rahel said, but knew immediately what. Her spit-bubble. 'Sorry, Ammu.'

'Sorry doesn't make a dead man alive,' Estha said.

'Oh come on!' Chacko said. 'You can't dictate what she does with her own *spit!*'

'Mind your own business,' Ammu snapped.

'It brings back memories,' Estha, in his wisdom, explained to Chacko.

Rahel put on her sunglasses. The World became angry-coloured.

'Take off those ridiculous glasses!' Ammu said.

Rahel took off her ridiculous glasses.

'It's fascist, the way you deal with them,' Chacko said. 'Even children have some rights, for God's sake!'

'Don't use the name of the Lord in vain,' Baby Kochamma said.

'I'm not,' Chacko said. 'I'm using it for a very good reason.'

'Stop posing as the children's Great Saviour!' Ammu said. 'When it comes down to brass tacks, you don't give a damn about them. Or me.'

'Should I?' Chacko said. 'Are they *my* responsibility?' He said that Ammu and Estha and Rahel were millstones around his neck.

The backs of Rahel's legs went wet and sweaty. Her skin slipped on the foamleather upholstery of the car seat. She and Estha knew about millstones. In *Mutiny on the Bounty*, when people died at sea, they were wrapped in white sheets and thrown overboard with millstones around their necks so that the corpses wouldn't float. Estha wasn't sure how they decided how many millstones to take with them before they set off on their voyage.

Estha put his head in his lap.

His puff was spoiled.

A distant train rumble seeped upwards from the frog-stained road. The yam leaves on either side of the railway track began to nod in mass consent. *Yesyesyesyesyes.*

The bald pilgrims in Beena Mol began another bhajan.

'I tell you, these Hindus,' Baby Kochamma said piously. 'They have no sense of *privacy*.'

'They have horns and scaly skins,' Chacko said sarcastically. 'And I've heard that their babies hatch from eggs.'

Rahel had two bumps on her forehead that Estha said would grow into horns. At least one of them would because she was half-Hindu. She hadn't been quick enough to ask him about *his* horns. Because whatever She was, He was too.

The train slammed past under a column of dense black smoke. There were thirty-two bogies, and the doorways were full of young men with helmety haircuts who were on their way to the Edge of the World to see what happened to the people who fell off. Those of them who craned too far fell off the edge themselves. Into the flailing darkness, their haircuts turned inside out.

The train was gone so quickly that it was hard to imagine that everybody had waited so long for so little. The yam leaves continued to nod long after the train had gone, as though they agreed with it entirely and had no doubts at all.

A gossamer blanket of coaldust floated down like a dirty blessing and gently smothered the traffic.

Chacko started the Plymouth. Baby Kochamma tried to be jolly. She started a song.

'There's a sad sort of clanging
From the clock in the Hall
And the bells in the stee-ple too.
And up in the nursery
An abs-urd
Litt-le Bird
Is popping out to say —'

She looked at Estha and Rahel, waiting for them to say *Cu-ckoo*. They didn't.

A carbreeze blew. Greentrees and telephone poles flew past the windows. Still birds slid by on moving wires, like unclaimed baggage at the airport.

A pale daymoon hung hugely in the sky and went where they went. As big as the belly of a beer-drinking man.

3

Big Man the Laltain,
Small Man the Mombatti

Filth had laid siege to the Ayemenem house like a medieval army advancing on an enemy castle. It clotted every crevice and clung to the windowpanes.

Midges whizzed in teapots. Dead insects lay in empty vases. The floor was sticky. White walls had turned an uneven grey. Brass hinges and doorhandles were dull and greasy to the touch. Infrequently used plug points were clogged with grime. Light-bulbs had a film of oil on them. The only things that shone were the giant cockroaches that scurried around like varnished gofers on a film set.

Baby Kochamma had stopped noticing these things long ago. Kochu Maria, who noticed everything, had stopped caring.

The chaise longue on which Baby Kochamma reclined had crushed peanut shells stuffed into the crevices of its rotting upholstery.

In an unconscious gesture of television-enforced democracy, mistress and servant both scrabbled unseeingly in the same bowl of nuts. Kochu Maria tossed nuts into her mouth. Baby Kochamma *placed* them decorously in hers.

On the *Best of Donahue* the studio audience watched a clip from a film in which a black busker was singing *Somewhere Over the Rainbow* in a subway station. He sang sincerely, as though he really believed the words of the song. Baby Kochamma sang with him, her thin, quavering voice thickened with peanut paste. She smiled as the lyrics came back to her. Kochu Maria looked at her as though she had gone mad, and grabbed more than her fair share of nuts. The busker threw his head back when he hit the high notes (the *where* of *somewhere*), and the ridged, pink roof of his mouth filled the television screen. He was as ragged as a rock star, but his missing teeth and the unhealthy pallor of his skin spoke eloquently of a life of privation and despair. He had to stop singing each time a train arrived or left, which was often.

Then the lights went up in the studio and Donahue presented the man himself, who, on a prearranged cue, started the song from exactly the point that he had had to stop (for a train) – cleverly achieving a touching victory of Song over Subway.

The next time the busker was interrupted mid-song was only when Phil Donahue put his arm around him and said, 'Thank you. Thank you very much.'

Being interrupted by Phil Donahue was of course entirely different from being interrupted by a subway rumble. It was a pleasure. An honour.

The studio audience clapped and looked compassionate.

The busker glowed with Prime-Time Happiness, and for a few moments, deprivation took a back seat. It had been his dream to sing on the Donahue show, he said, not realizing that he had just been robbed of that too.

There are big dreams and little ones. 'Big Man the Laltain sahib, Small Man the Mombatti,' an old Bihari coolie, who met Estha's school excursion party at the railway station (unfailingly, year after year) used to say of dreams.

Big Man the Lantern. Small man the Tallow-stick.

Huge man the Strobe Lights, he omitted to say. And *Small Man the Subway Station.*

The Masters would haggle with him as he trudged behind them with the boys' luggage, his bowed legs further bowed, cruel schoolboys imitating his gait. Balls-in-Brackets they used to call him.

Smallest Man the Varicose Veins, he clean forgot to mention, as he wobbled off with less than half the money he had asked for and less than a tenth of what he deserved.

Outside, the rain had stopped. The grey sky curdled and the clouds resolved themselves into little lumps, like substandard mattress-stuffing.

Esthappen appeared at the kitchen door, wet (and wiser than he really was). Behind him the long grass sparkled. The puppy stood on the steps beside him. Raindrops slid across the curved bottom of the rusted gutter on the edge of the roof, like shining beads on an abacus.

Baby Kochamma looked up from the television.

'Here he comes,' she announced to Rahel, not bothering to lower her voice. 'Now watch. He won't say anything. He'll walk *straight* to his room. Just watch!'

The puppy seized the opportunity and tried to stage a combined entry. Kochu Maria hit the floor fiercely with her palms and said, 'Hup! Hup! *Poda Patti!*'

So the puppy, wisely, desisted. It appeared to be familiar with this routine.

'Watch!' Baby Kochamma said. She seemed excited. 'He'll walk *straight* to his room and wash his clothes. He's very overclean . . . he won't say a *word!*'

She had the air of a game warden pointing out an animal in the grass. Taking pride in her ability to predict its movements. Her superior knowledge of its habits and predilections.

Estha's hair was plastered down in clumps, like the inverted petals of a flower. Slivers of white scalp shone through. Rivulets of water ran down his face and neck. He walked to his room.

A gloating halo appeared around Baby Kochamma's head. 'See?' she said.

Kochu Maria used the opportunity to switch channels and watch a bit of *Prime Bodies*.

Rahel followed Estha to his room. Ammu's room. Once.

The room had kept his secrets. It gave nothing away. Not in the disarray of rumpled sheets, nor the untidiness of a kicked off shoe, or a wet towel hung over the back of a chair. Or a half-read book. It was like a room in a hospital after the nurse had just been. The floor was clean, the walls white. The cupboard closed. Shoes arranged. The dustbin empty.

The obsessive cleanliness of the room was the only positive sign of volition from Estha. The only faint suggestion that he had, perhaps, some Design for Life. Just the whisper of an unwillingness to subsist on scraps offered by others. On the wall by the window, an iron stood on an ironing board. A pile of folded, crumpled clothes waited to be ironed.

Silence hung in the air like secret loss.

The terrible ghosts of impossible-to-forget toys clustered on the blades of the ceiling fan. A catapult. A Qantas koala (from Miss Mitten) with loosened button eyes. An inflatable goose (that had been burst with a policeman's cigarette). Two ballpoint pens with silent streetscapes and red London buses that floated up and down in them.

Estha put on the tap and water drummed into a plastic bucket. He undressed in the gleaming bathroom. He stepped out of his sodden jeans. Stiff. Dark blue. Difficult to get out of. He pulled his crushed-strawberry T-shirt over his head, smooth, slim, muscular arms crossed over his body. He didn't hear his sister at the door.

Rahel watched his stomach suck inwards and his ribcage rise as his wet T-shirt peeled away from his skin, leaving it wet and honey-coloured. His face and neck and a V-shaped triangle at the base of his throat were darker than the rest of him. His arms too were double-coloured. Paler where his shirtsleeves ended. A dark brown man in pale honey clothes. Chocolate with a twist of coffee. High cheekbones and hunted eyes. A fisherman in a white-tiled bathroom, with sea-secrets in his eyes.

Had he seen her? Was he really mad? Did he know that she was there?

They had never been shy of each other's bodies, but they had never been old enough (together) to know what shyness was.

Now they were. Old enough.

Old.

A viable die-able age.

What a funny word *old* was on its own, Rahel thought, and said it to herself: *Old.*

Rahel at the bathroom door. Slim-hipped. ('Tell her she'll need a Caesarean!' a drunk gynaecologist had said to her husband while they waited for their change at the gas station.) A lizard on a map on her faded T-shirt. Long wild hair with a glint of deep henna-red, sent unruly fingers down into the small of her back. The diamond in her nostril flashed. Sometimes. And sometimes not. A thin, gold, serpent-headed bangle glowed like a circle of orange light around her wrist. Slim snakes whispering to each other, head to head. Her mother's melted wedding ring. Down softened the sharp lines of her thin, angular arms.

At first glance she appeared to have grown into the skin of her mother. High cheekbones. Deep dimples when she smiled. But she was longer, harder, flatter, more angular than Ammu had been. Less lovely perhaps to those who liked roundness and softness in women. Only her eyes were incontestably more beautiful. Large. Luminous. *Drownable in,* as Larry McCaslin had said and discovered to his cost.

Rahel searched her brother's nakedness for signs of herself. In the shape of his knees. The arch of his instep. The slope of his shoulders. The angle at which the rest of his arm met his elbow. The way his toe-nails tipped upwards at the ends. The sculpted hollows on either side of his taut, beautiful buns. Tight plums. Men's bums never grow up. Like school satchels, they evoke in an instant memories of childhood. Two vaccination marks on his arm gleamed like coins. Hers were on her thigh.

Girls always have them on their thighs, Ammu used to say.

Rahel watched Estha with the curiosity of a mother watching her wet child. A sister a brother. A woman a man. A twin a twin.

She flew these several kites at once.

He was a naked stranger met in a chance encounter. He was the one that she had known before Life began. The one who had once led her (swimming) through their lovely mother's cunt.

Both things unbearable in their polarity. In their irreconcilable far-apartness.

A raindrop glistened on the end of Estha's earlobe. Thick, silver in the light, like a heavy bead of mercury. She reached out. Touched it. Took it away.

Estha didn't look at her. He retreated into further stillness. As though his body had the power to snatch its senses inwards (knotted, egg-shaped), away from the surface of his skin, into some deeper more inaccessible recess.

The silence gathered its skirts and slid, like Spiderwoman, up the slippery bathroom wall.

Estha put his wet clothes in a bucket and began to wash them with crumbling, bright blue soap.

4

Abhilash Talkies

Abhilash Talkies advertised itself as the first cinema hall in Kerala with a 70mm CinemaScope screen. To drive home the point, its façade had been designed as a cement replica of a curved cinemascope screen. On top (cement writing, neon lighting) it said *Abhilash Talkies* in English and Malayalam.

The toilets were called HIS and HERS. HERS for Ammu, Rahel and Baby Kochamma. HIS for Estha alone, because Chacko had gone to see about the bookings at the Hotel Sea Queen.

'Will you be okay?' Ammu said, worried.

Estha nodded.

Through the red Formica door that closed slowly on its own, Rahel followed Ammu and Baby Kochamma into HERS. She turned to wave across the slipperoily marble floor at Estha Alone (with a comb), in his beige and pointy shoes. Estha waited in the dirty marble lobby with the lonely, watching mirrors till the red door took his sister away. Then he turned and padded off to HIS.

In HERS, Ammu suggested that Rahel balance in the air to piss. She said that Public Pots were Dirty. Like Money was. You never knew who'd touched it. Lepers. Butchers. Car Mechanics. (Pus. Blood. Grease.)

Once when Kochu Maria took her to the butcher's shop, Rahel noticed that the green five-rupee note that he gave them had a tiny blob of red meat on it. Kochu Maria wiped the blob away with her thumb. The juice left a red smear. She put the money into her bodice. Meat-smelling blood money.

Rahel was too short to balance in the air above the pot, so Ammu and Baby Kochamma held her up, her legs hooked over their arms. Her feet pigeon-toed in Bata sandals. High in the air with her knickers down. For a moment nothing happened, and Rahel looked up at her mother and baby grand aunt with naughty (now what?) question marks in her eyes.

'Come on,' Ammu said. 'Sssss . . .'

Sssss for the sound of Soo-soo. Mmmmm for the Sound of Myooozick.

Rahel giggled. Ammu giggled. Baby Kochamma giggled. When the trickle started they adjusted her aerial position. Rahel was unembarrassed. She finished and Ammu had the toilet paper.

'Shall you or shall I?' Baby Kochamma said to Ammu.

'Either way,' Ammu said. 'Go ahead. You.'

Rahel held her handbag. Baby Kochamma lifted her rumpled sari. Rahel studied her baby grand aunt's enormous legs. (Years later during a history lesson being read out in school – *The Emperor Babur had a wheatish complexion and pillar-like thighs* – this scene would flash before her. Baby Kochamma balanced like a big bird over a public pot. Blue veins like lumpy knitting running up her translucent shins. Fat knees dimpled. Hair on them. Poor little tiny feet to carry such a load!) Baby Kochamma waited for half of half a moment. Head thrust forward. Silly smile. Bosom swinging low. Melons in a blouse. Bottom up and out. When the gurgling, bubbling sound came, she listened with her eyes. A yellow brook burbled through a mountain pass.

Rahel liked all this. Holding the handbag. Everyone pissing in front of everyone. Like friends. She knew nothing then, of how precious a feeling this was. *Like friends.* They would never be together like this again. Ammu, Baby Kochamma and she.

When Baby Kochamma finished, Rahel looked at her watch. 'So long you took, Baby Kochamma,' she said. 'It's ten to two.'

> *Rubadub dub* (Rahel thought),
> *Three women in a tub,*
> *Tarry a while said Slow.*

She thought of Slow being a person. Slow Kurien. Slow Kutty. Slow Mol. Slow Kochamma.

Slow Kutty. Fast Verghese. And Kuriakose. Three brothers with dandruff.

Ammu did hers in a whisper. Against the side of the pot so you couldn't hear. Her father's hardness had left her eyes and they were Ammu-eyes again. She had deep dimples in her smile and didn't seem angry any more. About Velutha or the spit-bubble.

That was a Good Sign.

Estha Alone in HIS had to piss onto naphthalene balls and cigarette stubs in the urinal. To piss in the pot would be Defeat. To piss in the urinal, he was too short. He needed Height. He searched for Height, and in a corner of HIS, he found it. A dirty broom, a squash bottle half-full of a milky liquid (phenyl) with floaty black things in it. A limp floorswab, and two rusty tin cans of nothing. They could have been Paradise Pickle products. Pineapple chunks in syrup. Or slices. Pineapple slices. His honour redeemed by his grandmother's cans, Estha Alone organized the rusty cans of nothing in front of the urinal. He stood on them, one foot on each, and pissed carefully, with minimal wobble. Like a Man. The cigarette stubs, soggy then, were wet now, and swirly. Hard to light. When he finished, Estha moved the cans to the basin in front of the mirror. He washed his hands and wet his hair. Then, dwarfed by the size of Ammu's comb that was too big for him, he reconstructed his puff carefully. Slicked back, then pushed forward and swivelled sideways at the very end. He returned the comb to his pocket, stepped off the tins and put them back with the bottle and swab and broom. He bowed to them all. The whole shooting match. The bottle, the broom, the cans, the limp floorswab.

'Bow,' he said, and smiled, because when he was younger, he had been under the impression that you had to say 'Bow' when you bowed. That you had to *say* it to do it. 'Bow, Estha,' they'd say. And he'd bow and say, 'Bow,' and they'd look at each other and laugh, and he'd worry.

Estha Alone of the uneven teeth.

Outside, he waited for his mother, his sister and his baby grand aunt. When they came out, Ammu said 'Okay, Est-happen?'

Estha said, 'Okay,' and shook his head carefully to preserve his puff.

Okay? Okay. He put the comb back into her handbag. Ammu felt a sudden clutch of love for her reserved, dignified little son in his beige and pointy shoes, who had just completed his first adult assignment. She ran loving fingers through his hair. She spoiled his puff.

The Man with the steel Eveready Torch said that the picture had started, so to hurry. They had to rush up the red steps with the old red carpet. Red staircase with red spit stains in the red corner. The Man with the Torch scrunched up his mundu and held it tucked under his balls, in his left hand. As he climbed, his calf muscles hardened under his climbing skin like hairy cannonballs. He held the torch in his right hand. He hurried with his mind.

'It started longago,' he said.

So they'd missed the beginning. Missed the rippled velvet curtain going up, with lightbulbs in the clustered yellow tassels. Slowly up, and the music would have been *Baby Elephant Walk* from *Hatari.* Or *Colonel Bogey's March.*

Ammu held Estha's hand. Baby Kochamma, heaving up the steps, held Rahel's. Baby Kochamma, weighed down by her melons, would not admit to herself that she was looking forward to the picture. She preferred to feel that she was only doing it for the children's sake. In her mind she kept an organized, careful account of Things She'd Done For People, and Things People Hadn't Done For Her.

She liked the early nun-bits best, and hoped they hadn't missed them. Ammu explained to Estha and Rahel that people always loved best what they *Identified* most with. Rahel supposed she Identified most with Christopher Plummer who acted as Captain von Trapp. Chacko didn't Identify with him at all and called him Captain von Clapp Trapp.

Rahel was like an excited mosquito on a leash. Flying. Weightless. Up two steps. Down two. Up one. She climbed five flights of red stairs for Baby Kochamma's one.

I'm Popeye the sailor man   dum dum
I live in a cara-van   dum dum
I op-en the door

And Fall-on the floor

I'm Popeye the sailor man   dum dum

Up two. Down two. Up one. Jump, jump.

'Rahel,' Ammu said, 'you haven't learned your Lesson yet. Have you?'

Rahel had: *Excitement Always Leads to Tears.* Dum dum.

They arrived at the Princess Circle lobby. They walked past the Refreshment Counter where the orangedrinks were waiting. And the lemondrinks were waiting. The orange too orange. The lemon too lemon. The chocolates too melty.

The Torch Man opened the heavy Princess Circle door into the fan-whirring, peanut-crunching darkness. It smelled of breathing people and hairoil. And old carpets. A magical, *Sound of Music* smell that Rahel remembered and treasured. Smells, like music, hold memories. She breathed deep, and bottled it up for posterity.

Estha had the tickets. Little Man. He lived in a cara-van. Dum dum.

The Torch Man shone his light on the pink tickets. Row J. Numbers 17, 18, 19, 20. Estha, Ammu, Rahel, Baby Kochamma. They squeezed past irritated people who moved their legs this way and that to make space. The seats of the chairs had to be pulled down. Baby Kochamma held Rahel's seat down while she climbed on. She wasn't heavy enough, so the chair folded her into itself like sandwich stuffing, and she watched from between her knees. Two knees and a fountain. Estha, with more dignity that that, sat on the edge of his chair.

The shadows of the fans were on the sides of the screen where the picture wasn't.

Off with the torch. On with the World Hit.

The camera soared up in the skyblue (car-coloured) Austrian sky with the clear, sad sound of church bells.

Far below, on the ground, in the courtyard of the abbey, the cobblestones were shining. Nuns walked across it. Like slow cigars. Quiet nuns clustered quietly around their Reverend Mother, who never read their letters. They gathered like ants around a crumb of toast. Cigars around a Queen Cigar. No hair on their knees. No melons in their blouses. And their breath like peppermint. They had complaints to make to their Reverend Mother. Sweetsinging complaints. About Julie Andrews, who was still up in the hills, singing *The Hills Are Alive with the Sound of Music* and was, once again, late for mass.

She climbs a tree and scrapes her knee

the nuns sneaked musically.

99

Her dress has got a tear.
She waltzes on her way to Mass
And whistles on the stair . . .

People in the audience were turning around.
'Shhh!' they said.
Shh! Shh! Shh!

And underneath her wimple
she has curlers in her hair!

There was a voice from outside the picture. It was clear and true, cutting through the fan-whirring, peanut-crunching darkness. There was a nun in the audience. Heads twisted around like bottle caps. Black-haired backs of heads became faces with mouths and moustaches. Hissing mouths with teeth like sharks. Many of them. Like stickers on a card.

'Shhh!' they said together.

It was Estha who was singing. A nun with a puff. An Elvis Pelvis Nun. He couldn't help it.

'Get him out of here!' the Audience said, when they found him.

Shutup or Getout. Getout or Shutup.

The Audience was a Big Man. Estha was a Little Man, with the tickets.

'Estha, for heaven's sake, shut UP!' Ammu's fierce whisper said.

So Estha shut UP. The mouths and moustaches turned away. But then, without warning, the song came back, and Estha couldn't stop it.

'Ammu, can I go and sing it outside?' Estha said (before Ammu smacked him). 'I'll come back after the song.'

'But don't ever expect me to bring you out again,' Ammu said. 'You're embarrassing *all* of us.'

But Estha couldn't help it. He got up to go. Past angry Ammu. Past Rahel concentrating through her knees. Past Baby Kochamma. Past the Audience that had to move its legs again. Thiswayandthat. The red sign over the door said EXIT in a red light. Estha EXITed.

In the lobby, the orangedrinks were waiting. The lemondrinks were waiting. The melty chocolates were waiting. The electric blue foamleather car-sofas were waiting. The *Coming Soon!* posters were waiting.

Estha Alone sat on the electric blue foamleather car-sofa, in the Abhilash Talkies Princess Circle lobby, and sang. In a nun's voice, as clear as clean water.

> *But how do you make her stay*
> *And listen to all you say?*

The man behind the Refreshments Counter, who'd been asleep on a row of stools, waiting for the interval, woke up. He saw, with gummy eyes, Estha Alone in his beige and pointy shoes. And his spoiled puff. The Man wiped his marble counter with a dirtcoloured rag. And he waited. And waiting he wiped. And wiping he waited. And watched Estha sing.

> *How do you keep a wave upon the sand?*
> *Oh, how do you solve a problem like Maree . . . yah?*

'Ay! *Eda cherukka!*' the Orangedrink Lemondrink Man said, in a gravelley voice thick with sleep. 'What the hell d'you think you're doing?'

> *How do you hold a*
> *moonbeam*
> *in your hand?*

Estha sang.

'Ay!' the Orangedrink Lemondrink Man said. 'Look, this is my Resting Time. Soon I'll have to wake up and work. So I can't have you singing English songs here. Stop it.' His gold wristwatch was almost hidden by his curly forearm hair. His gold chain was almost hidden by his chest hair. His white Terylene shirt was unbuttoned to where the swell of his belly began. He looked like an unfriendly jewelled bear. Behind him there were mirrors for people to look at themselves in while they bought cold drinks and refreshments. To reorganize their puffs and settle their buns. The mirrors watched Estha.

'I could file a Written Complaint against you,' the Man said to Estha. 'How would you like that? A Written Complaint?'

Estha stopped singing and got up to go back in.

'Now that I'm up,' the Orangedrink Lemondrink Man said. 'now that you've woken me up from my Resting Time, now that you've *disturbed* me, at least come and have a drink. It's the least you can do.'

He had an unshaven, jowly face. His teeth, like yellow piano keys, watched little Elvis the Pelvis.

'No thank you,' Elvis said politely. 'My family will be expecting me. And I've finished my pocket money.'

'*Porketmunny?*' the Orangedrink Lemondrink Man said with his teeth still watching. 'First English songs, and now *Porketmunny*! Where d'you live? On the moon?'

Estha turned to go.

'Wait a minute!' the Orangedrink Lemondrink Man said sharply. 'Just a minute!' he said again, more gently. 'I thought I asked you a question.'

His yellow teeth were magnets. They saw, they smiled, they sang, they smelled, they moved. They mesmerized.

'I asked you where you lived,' he said, spinning his nasty web.

'Ayemenem,' Estha said. 'I live in Ayemenem. My grandmother owns Paradise Pickles & Preserves. She's the Sleeping Partner.'

'Is she, now?' the Orangedrink Lemondrink Man said. 'And who does she sleep with?' He laughed a nasty laugh that Estha couldn't understand. 'Never mind. You wouldn't understand.'

'Come and have a drink,' he said. 'A Free Cold Drink. Come. Come here and tell me all about your grandmother.'

Estha went. Drawn by yellow teeth.

'Here. Behind the counter,' the Orangedrink Lemondrink Man said. He dropped his voice to a whisper. 'It has to be a secret because drinks are not allowed before the interval. It's a Theatre Offence.'

'Cognizable,' he added after a pause.

Estha went behind the Refreshments Counter for his Free Cold Drink. He saw the three high stools arranged in a row for the Orangedrink Lemondrink Man to sleep on. The wood shiny from his sitting.

'Now if you'll kindly hold this for me,' the Orangedrink Lemondrink Man said, handing Estha his penis through his soft white muslin dhoti, 'I'll get you your drink. Orange? Lemon?'

Estha held it because he had to.

'Orange? Lemon?' the Man said. 'Lemonorange?'

'Lemon, please,' Estha said politely.

He got a cold bottle and a straw. So he held a bottle in one hand and a penis in the other. Hard, hot, veiny. Not a moonbeam.

The Orangedrink Lemondrink Man's hand closed over Estha's. His thumbnail was long like a woman's. He moved Estha's hand up and down. First slowly. Then fastly.

The lemondrink was cold and sweet. The penis hot and hard.

The piano keys were watching.

'So your grandmother runs a factory?' the Orangedrink Lemondrink Man said. 'What kind of factory?'

'Many products,' Estha said, not looking, with the straw in

his mouth. 'Squashes, pickles, jams, curry powders. Pineapple slices.'

'Good,' the Orangedrink Lemondrink Man said. 'Excellent.'

His hand closed tighter over Estha's. Tight and sweaty. And faster still.

> *Fast faster fest*
> *Never let it rest*
> *Until the fast is faster,*
> *And the faster's fest.*

Through the soggy paper straw (almost flattened with spit and fear), the liquid lemon sweetness rose. Blowing through the straw (while his other hand moved), Estha blew bubbles into the bottle. Stickysweet lemon bubbles of the drink he couldn't drink. In his head he listed his grandmother's produce.

PICKLES	SQUASHES	JAMS
Mango	*Orange*	*Banana*
Green pepper	*Grape*	*Mixed fruit*
Bitter gourd	*Pineapple*	*Grapefruit marmalade*
Garlic	*Mango*	
Salted lime		

Then the gristly-bristly face contorted, and Estha's hand was wet and hot and sticky. It had egg white on it. White egg white. Quarter-boiled.

The lemondrink was cold and sweet. The penis was soft and shrivelled like an empty leather change-purse. With his dirtcoloured rag, the man wiped Estha's other hand.

'Now finish your drink,' he said, and affectionately squished a cheek of Estha's bottom. Tight plums in drainpipes. And beige and pointy shoes. 'You mustn't waste it,' he said. 'Think of all the poor people who have nothing to eat or drink. You're a lucky rich boy, with porketmunny and a grandmother's factory to inherit. You should Thank God that you have no worries. Now finish your drink.'

And so, behind the Refreshments Counter, in the Abhilash Talkies Princess Circle lobby, in the hall with Kerala's first 70mm CinemaScope screen, Esthappen Yako finished his free bottle of fizzed, lemon-flavoured fear. His lemontoolemon, too cold. Too sweet. The fizz came up his nose. He would be given another bottle soon (free, fizzed fear). But he didn't know that yet. He held his sticky Other Hand away from his body.

It wasn't supposed to touch anything.

When Estha finished his drink, the Orangedrink Lemondrink Man said, 'Finished? Goodboy.'

He took the empty bottle and the flattened straw, and sent Estha back into *The Sound of Music*.

Back inside the hairoil darkness, Estha held his Other Hand carefully (upwards, as though he was holding an imagined orange). He slid past the Audience (their legs moving thiswayandthat), past Baby Kochamma, past Rahel (still tilted back), past Ammu (still annoyed). Estha sat down, still holding his sticky orange.

And there was Captain von Clapp-Trapp. Christopher Plummer. Arrogant. Hardhearted. With a mouth like a slit. And a steelshrill police whistle. A captain with seven children. Clean children, like a packet of peppermints. He pretended not to love them, but he did. He loved them. He loved her (Julie Andrews), she loved him, they loved the children, the children loved them. They all loved each other. They were clean, white children, and their beds were soft with Ei. Der. Downs.

The house they lived in had a lake and gardens, a wide staircase, white doors and windows, and curtains with flowers.

The clean white children, even the big ones, were scared of the thunder. To comfort them, Julie Andrews put them all in her clean bed, and sang them a clean song about a few of her favourite things. These were a few of her favourite things:

(1) Girls in white dresses with blue satin sashes.
(2) Wild geese that flew with the moon on their wings.
(3) Bright copper kettles.
(4) Doorbells and sleighbells and schnitzel with noodles.
(5) Etc.

And then, in the minds of certain two-egg twin members of the audience in Abhilash Talkies, some questions arose, that needed answers, i.e.:

(a) *Did Captain von Clapp-Trapp shiver his leg?*
He did not.
(b) *Did Captain von Clapp-Trapp blow spit-bubbles? Did he?*
He did most certainly not.
(c) *Did he gobble?*
He did not.

Oh Captain von Trapp, Captain von Trapp, could you love the little fellow with the orange in the smelly auditorium?

He's just held the Orangedrink Lemondrink Man's soo-soo in his hand, but could you love him still?

And his twin sister? Tilting upwards with her fountain in a Love-in-Tokyo? Could you love her too?

Captain von Trapp had some questions of his own.

(a) *Are they clean white children?*
No. (*But Sophie Mol is.*)
(b) *Do they blow spit-bubbles?*
Yes. (*But Sophie Mol doesn't.*)
(c) *Do they shiver their legs? Like clerks?*
Yes. (*But Sophie Mol doesn't.*)
(d) *Have they, either or both, ever held strangers' soo-soos?*
N . . . Nyes. (*But Sophie Mol hasn't.*)

'Then I'm sorry,' Captain von Clapp-Trapp said. 'It's out of the question. I cannot love them. I cannot be their Baba. Oh no.'
Captain von Clapp-Trapp couldn't.

Estha put his head in his lap.
'What's the matter?' Ammu said. 'If you're sulking again, I'm taking you straight home. Sit up please. And watch. That's what you've been brought here for.'
Finish the drink.
Watch the picture.
Think of all the poor people.
Lucky rich boy with porketmunny. No worries.
Estha sat up and watched. His stomach heaved. He had a greenwavy, thick-watery, lumpy, seaweedy, floaty, bottomless-bottomful feeling.
'Ammu?' he said.
'Now WHAT?' The *WHAT* snapped, barked, spat out.
'Feeling vomity,' Estha said.
'Just feeling or d'you want to?' Ammu's voice was worried.
'Don't know.'
'Shall we go and try?' Ammu said. 'It'll make you feel better.'
'Okay,' Estha said.
Okay? Okay.
'Where're you going?' Baby Kochamma wanted to know.
'Estha's going to try and vomit,' Ammu said.
'Where're you going?' Rahel asked.
'Feeling vomity,' Estha said.
'Can I come and watch?'
'No,' Ammu said.
Past the Audience again (legs thiswayandthat). Last time to sing. This time to try and vomit. Exit through the EXIT. Outside in the marble lobby, the Orangedrink Lemondrink man was eating a sweet. His cheek was bulging with a moving sweet. He made soft, sucking sounds like water draining from a basin.

There was a green Parry's wrapper on the counter. Sweets were free for this man. He had a row of free sweets in dim bottles. He wiped the marble counter with his dirt-coloured rag that he held in his hairy watch hand. When he saw the luminous woman with polished shoulders and the little boy, a shadow slipped across his face. Then he smiled his portable piano smile.

'Out again sosoon?' he said.

Estha was already retching. Ammu moonwalked him to the Princess Circle bathroom. HERS.

He was held up, wedged between the notclean basin and Ammu's body. Legs dangling. The basin had steel taps, and rust stains. And a brownwebbed mesh of hairline cracks, like the roadmap of some great, intricate city.

Estha convulsed, but nothing came. Just thoughts. And they floated out and floated back in. Ammu couldn't see them. They hovered like storm clouds over the Basin City. But the basin men and basin women went about their usual basin business. Basin cars, and basin buses, still whizzed around. Basin Life went on.

'No?' Ammu said.

'No,' Estha said.

No? No.

'Then wash your face,' Ammu said. 'Water always helps. Wash your face and let's go and have a fizzy lemondrink.'

Estha washed his face and hands and face and hands. His eyelashes were wet and bunched together.

The Orangedrink Lemondrink Man folded the green sweet wrapper and fixed the fold with his painted thumbnail. He stunned a fly with a rolled magazine. Delicately, he flicked it over the edge of the counter onto the floor. It lay on its back and waved its feeble legs.

'Sweetboy this,' he said to Ammu. 'Sings nicely.'

'He's my son,' Ammu said.

'Really?' the Orangedrink Lemondrink Man said, and looked

at Ammu with his teeth. 'Really? You don't look old enough!'

'He's not feeling well,' Ammu said. 'I thought a cold drink would make him feel better.'

'Of course,' the Man said. 'Ofcourseofcourse. Orangelemon? Lemonorange?'

Dreadful, dreaded question.

'No thank you.' Estha looked at Ammu. Greenwavy, sea-weedy, bottomless-bottomful.

'What about you?' the Orangedrink Lemondrink Man asked Ammu.

'Coca-ColaFanta? IcecreamRosemilk?'

'No. Not for me. Thank you,' Ammu said. Deep-dimpled, luminous woman.

'Here,' the Man said, with a fistful of sweets, like a generous air hostess. 'These are for your little Mon.'

'No thank you,' Estha said, looking at Ammu.

'Take them, Estha,' Ammu said. 'Don't be rude.'

Estha took them.

'Say Thank you,' Ammu said.

'Thank you,' Estha said. (For the sweets, for the white egg white.)

'No mention,' the Orangedrink Lemondrink Man said in English.

'So!' he said. 'Mon says you're from Ayemenem?'

'Yes,' Ammu said.

'I come there often,' the Orangedrink Lemondrink Man said. 'My wife's people are Ayemenem people. I know where your factory is. Paradise Pickles, isn't it? He told me. Your Mon.'

He knew where to find Estha. That was what he was trying to say. It was a warning.

Ammu saw her son's bright feverbutton eyes.

'We must go,' she said. 'Mustn't risk a fever. Their cousin is coming tomorrow,' she explained to Uncle. And then, added casually, 'From London.'

'From London?' A new respect gleamed in Uncle's eyes. For a family with London connections.

'Estha, you stay here with Uncle. I'll get Baby Kochamma and Rahel,' Ammu said.

'Come,' Uncle said. 'Come and sit with me on a high stool.'

'No, Ammu! No, Ammu, no! I want to come with you!'

Ammu, surprised at the unusually shrill insistence from her usually quiet son, apologized to the Orangedrink Lemondrink Uncle.

'He's not usually like this. Come on then, Esthappen.'

The back-inside smell. Fan shadows. Backs of heads. Necks. Collars. Hair. Buns. Plaits. Ponytails.

A fountain in a Love-in-Tokyo. A little girl and an ex-nun.

Captain von Trapp's seven peppermint children had had their peppermint baths, and were standing in a peppermint line with their hair slicked down, singing in obedient peppermint voices to the woman the Captain nearly married. The blonde Baroness who shone like a diamond.

The hills are alive
with the sound of music.

'We have to go,' Ammu said to Baby Kochamma and Rahel.

'But, Ammu!' Rahel said. 'The Main Things haven't even happened yet! He hasn't even *kissed* her! He hasn't even torn up the Hitler flag yet! They haven't even been *betrayed* by Rolf the Postman!'

'Estha's sick,' Ammu said. 'Come on!'

'The Nazi soldiers haven't even come!'

'Come on,' Ammu said. 'Get up!'

'They haven't even done "*High on a hill was a lonely goatherd*"!'

'Estha has to be well for Sophie Mol, doesn't he?' Baby Kochamma said.

'He doesn't,' Rahel said, but mostly to herself.

'What did you say?' Baby Kochamma said, getting the general drift, but not what was actually said.

'Nothing,' Rahel said.

'I *heard* you,' Baby Kochamma said.

Outside, Uncle was reorganizing his dim bottles. Wiping with his dirtcoloured rag the ring-shaped water-stains they had left on his marble Refreshments Counter. Preparing for the Interval. He was a Clean Orangedrink Lemondrink Uncle. He had an air hostess's heart trapped in a bear's body.

'Going then?' he said.

'Yes,' Ammu said. 'Where can we get a taxi?'

'Out the gate, up the road, on your left,' he said, looking at Rahel. 'You never told me you had a little Mol too.' And holding out another sweet 'Here, Mol – for you.'

'Take mine!' Estha said quickly, not wanting Rahel to go near the man.

But Rahel had already started towards him. As she approached him, he smiled at her and something about that portable piano smile, something about the steady gaze in which he held her, made her shrink from him. It was the most hideous thing she had ever seen. She spun around to look at Estha.

She backed away from the hairy man.

Estha pressed his Parry's sweets into her hand and she felt his fever hot fingers whose tips were as cold as death.

''Bye, Mon,' Uncle said to Estha. 'I'll see you in Ayemenem sometime.'

So, the redsteps once again. This time Rahel lagging. Slow. No I don't want to go. A ton of bricks on a leash.

'Sweet chap, that Orangedrink Lemondrink fellow,' Ammu said.

'Chhi!' Baby Kochamma said.

'He doesn't look it, but he was surprisingly sweet with Estha,' Ammu said.

'So why don't you marry him then?' Rahel said petulantly.

Time stopped on the red staircase. Estha stopped. Baby Kochamma stopped.

'Rahel,' Ammu said.

Rahel froze. She was desperately sorry for what she had said. She didn't know where those words had come from. She didn't know that she'd had them in her. But they were out now, and wouldn't go back in. They hung about that red staircase like clerks in a Government office. Some stood, some sat and shivered their legs.

'Rahel,' Ammu said. 'Do you realize what you have just done?'

Frightened eyes and a fountain looked back at Ammu.

'It's all right. Don't be scared,' Ammu said. 'Just answer me. Do you?'

'What?' Rahel said in the smallest voice she had.

'Realize what you've just done?' Ammu said.

Frightened eyes and a fountain looked back at Ammu.

'D'you know what happens when you hurt people?' Ammu said. 'When you hurt people, they begin to love you less. That's what careless words do. They make people love you a little less.'

A cold moth with unusually dense dorsal tufts landed lightly on Rahel's heart. Where its icy legs touched her, she got goose bumps. Six goose bumps on her careless heart.

A little less her Ammu loved her.

And so, out the gate, up the road, and to the left. The taxi stand. A hurt mother, an ex-nun, a hot child and a cold one. Six goose bumps and a moth.

The taxi smelled of sleep. Old clothes rolled up. Damp towels. Armpits. It was, after all, the taxi driver's home. He lived in it. It was the only place he had to store his smells. The seats had been killed. Ripped. A swathe of dirty yellow sponge spilled out and shivered on the back seat like an immense jaundiced liver. The driver had the ferrety alertness of a small rodent. He had a hooked Roman nose and a Little Richard moustache. He was so small that he watched the road through the steering wheel. To passing traffic it looked like a taxi with passengers but no driver. He drove fast, pugnaciously, darting into empty spaces, nudging other cars out of their lanes. Accelerating at zebra crossings. Jumping lights.

'Why not use a cushion or a pillow or something?' Baby Kochamma suggested in her friendly voice. 'You'll be able to see better.'

'Why not mind your own business, sister?' the driver suggested in his unfriendly one.

Driving past the inky sea, Estha put his head out of the window. He could taste the hot, salt breeze in his mouth. He could feel it lift his hair. He knew that if Ammu found out about what he had done with the Orangedrink Lemondrink Man, she'd love him less as well. Very much less. He felt the shaming churning heaving turning sickness in his stomach. He longed for the river. Because water always helps.

The sticky neon night rushed past the taxi window. It was hot inside the taxi, and quiet. Baby Kochamma looked flushed and excited. She loved not being the cause of ill feeling. Every time a pye-dog strayed onto the road, the driver made a sincere effort to kill it.

The moth on Rahel's heart spread its velvet wings, and the chill crept into her bones.

In the Hotel Sea Queen car park, the skyblue Plymouth gossiped with other, smaller cars. *Hslip Hslip Hsnooh-snah.* A big lady at a small ladies' party. Tailfins aflutter.

'Room numbers 313 and 327,' the man at the reception said. 'Non-airconditioned. Twin beds. Lift is closed for repair.'

The bellboy who took them up wasn't a boy and hadn't a bell. He had dim eyes and two buttons missing on his frayed maroon coat. His greyed undershirt showed. He had to wear his silly bellhop's cap tilted sideways, its tight plastic strap sunk into his sagging dewlap. It seemed unnecessarily cruel to make an old man wear a cap sideways like that and arbitrarily reorder the way in which age chose to hang from his chin.

There were more red steps to climb. The same red carpet from the cinema hall was following them around. Magic flying carpet.

Chacko was in his room. Caught feasting. Roast chicken, finger chips, sweetcorn and chicken soup, two parathas and vanilla ice cream with chocolate sauce. Sauce in a sauceboat. Chacko often said that his ambition was to die of overeating. Mammachi said it was a sure sign of suppressed unhappiness. Chacko said it was no such thing. He said it was Sheer Greed.

Chacko was puzzled to see everybody back so early, but pretended otherwise. He kept eating.

The original plan had been that Estha would sleep with Chacko, and Rahel with Ammu and Baby Kochamma. But now that Estha wasn't well and Love had been reapportioned (Ammu loved her a little less), Rahel would have to sleep with Chacko, and Estha with Ammu and Baby Kochamma.

Ammu took Rahel's pyjamas and toothbrush out of the suitcase and put them on the bed.

'Here,' Ammu said.

Two clicks to close the suitcase.

Click. And click.

'Ammu,' Rahel said, 'shall I miss dinner as my punishment?'

She was keen to exchange punishments. No dinner, in exchange for Ammu loving her the same as before.

'As you please,' Ammu said. 'But I advise you to eat. If you want to grow, that is. Maybe you could share some of Chacko's chicken.'

'Maybe and maybe not,' Chacko said.

'But what about my punishment?' Rahel said. 'You haven't given me my punishment!'

'Some things come with their own punishments,' Baby Kochamma said. As though she was explaining a sum that Rahel couldn't understand.

Some things come with their own punishments. Like bedrooms with built-in cupboards. They would all learn more about punishments soon. That they came in different sizes. That some were so big they were like cupboards with built-in bedrooms. You could spend your whole life in them, wandering through dark shelving.

Baby Kochamma's goodnight kiss left a little spit on Rahel's cheek. She wiped it off with her shoulder.

'Goodnight Godbless,' Ammu said. But she said it with her back. She was already gone.

'Goodnight,' Estha said, too sick to love his sister.

Rahel Alone watched them walk down the hotel corridor like silent but substantial ghosts. Two big, one small, in beige and pointy shoes. The red carpet took away their feet sounds.

Rahel stood in the hotel room doorway, full of sadness.

She had in her the sadness of Sophie Mol coming. The sadness of Ammu's loving her a little less. And the sadness of whatever the Orangedrink Lemondrink Man had done to Estha in Abhilash Talkies.

A stinging wind blew across her dry, aching eyes.

Chacko put a leg of chicken and some finger chips onto a quarter plate for Rahel.

'No thank you,' Rahel said, hoping that if she could somehow effect her own punishment, Ammu would rescind hers.

'What about some ice cream with chocolate sauce?' Chacko said.

'No thank you,' Rahel said.

'Fine,' Chacko said. 'But you don't know what you're missing.'

He finished all the chicken and then all the ice cream.

Rahel changed into her pyjamas.

'Please don't tell me what it is you're being punished for,' Chacko said. 'I can't bear to hear about it.' He was mopping the last of the chocolate sauce from the sauceboat with a piece of paratha. His disgusting, after-sweet sweet. 'What was it? Scratching your mosquito bites till they bled? Not saying "Thankyou" to the taxi driver?'

'Something much worse than that,' Rahel said, loyal to Ammu.

'Don't tell me,' Chacko said. 'I don't want to know.'

He rang for room service, and a tired bearer came to take away the plates and bones. He tried to catch the dinner smells, but they escaped and climbed into the limp brown hotel curtains.

A dinnerless niece and her dinnerfull uncle brushed their teeth together in the Hotel Sea Queen bathroom. She, a forlorn, stubby convict in striped pyjamas and a Fountain in a Love-in-Tokyo. He, in his cotton vest and underpants. His vest, taut and stretched over his round stomach like a second skin, went slack over the depression of his belly-button.

When Rahel held her frothing toothbrush still and moved her teeth instead, he didn't say she mustn't.

He wasn't a fascist.

They took it in turns to spit. Rahel carefully examined her white Binaca froth as it dribbled down the side of the basin carefully, to see what she could see.

What colours and strange creatures had been ejected from the spaces between her teeth?

None tonight. Nothing unusual. Just Binaca bubbles.

Chacko put off the Big Light.

In bed, Rahel took off her Love-in-Tokyo and put it by her sunglasses. Her fountain slumped a little, but stayed standing.

Chacko lay in bed in the pool of light from his bedside lamp. A fat man on a dark stage. He reached over to his shirt lying crumpled at the foot of his bed. He took his wallet out of the pocket, and looked at the photograph of Sophie Mol that Margaret Kochamma had sent him two years ago.

Rahel watched him and her cold moth spread its wings again. Slow out. Slow in. A predator's lazy blink.

The sheets were coarse, but clean.

Chacko closed his wallet and put out the light. Into the night he lit a Charminar and wondered what his daughter looked like now. Nine years old. Last seen when she was red and wrinkled. Barely human. Three weeks later, Margaret his wife, his only love, had cried and told him about Joe.

Margaret told Chacko that she couldn't live with him any more. She told him that she needed her own space. As though Chacko had been using *her* shelves for *his* clothes. Which, knowing him, he probably had.

She asked him for a divorce.

Those last few tortured nights before he left her, Chacko would slip out of bed with a torch and look at his sleeping child. To learn her. Imprint her on his memory. To ensure that when he thought of her, the child that he invoked would be accurate. He memorized the brown down on her soft skull. The shape of her puckered, constantly moving mouth. The spaces between her toes. The suggestion of a mole. And then, without meaning to, he found himself searching his baby for signs of Joe. The baby clutched his index finger while he conducted his insane, broken, envious, torchlit study. Her belly button protruded from her satiated satin stomach like a domed monument on a hill. Chacko laid his ear against it and listened with wonder at the rumblings from within. Messages being sent from here to there. New organs getting used to each other. A new government setting up its systems. Organizing the division of labour, deciding who would do what.

She smelled of milk and urine. Chacko marvelled at how someone so small and undefined, so vague in her resemblances, could so completely command the attention, the love, the *sanity*, of a grown man.

When he left, he felt that something had been torn out of him. Something big.

But Joe was dead now. Killed in a car crash. Dead as a doorknob. A Joe-shaped hole in the universe.

In Chacko's photograph, Sophie Mol was seven years old. White and blue. Rose-lipped, and Syrian Christian nowhere. Though Mammachi, peering at the photograph, insisted she had Pappachi's nose.

'Chacko?' Rahel said, from her darkened bed. 'Can I ask you a question?'

'Ask me two,' Chacko said.

'Chacko, do you love Sophie Mol Most in the World?'

'She's my daughter,' Chacko said.

Rahel considered this.

'Chacko? Is it *necessary* that people HAVE to love their own children Most in the World?'

'There are no rules,' Chacko said. 'But people usually do.'

'Chacko, for example,' Rahel said. 'Just for *example*, is it possible that Ammu can love Sophie Mol more than me and Estha? Or for you to love me more than Sophie Mol, for *example*?'

'Anything's possible in Human Nature,' Chacko said in his Reading Aloud voice. Talking to the darkness now, suddenly insensitive to his little fountain-haired niece. 'Love. Madness. Hope. Infinite joy.'

Of the four things that were Possible in Human Nature, Rahel thought that *Infinnate Joy* sounded the saddest. Perhaps because of the way Chacko said it.

Infinnate Joy. With a church sound to it. Like a sad fish with fins all over.

A cold moth lifted a cold leg.

The cigarette smoke curled into the night. And the fat man and the little girl lay awake in silence.

A few rooms away, while his baby grand aunt snored, Estha awoke.

Ammu was asleep and looked beautiful in the barred-blue streetlight that came in through the barred-blue window. She smiled a sleepsmile that dreamed of dolphins and a deep barred blue. It was a smile that gave no indication that the person who belonged to it was a bomb waiting to go off.

Estha Alone walked weavily to the bathroom. He vomited a clear, bitter, lemony, sparkling, fizzy liquid. The acrid aftertaste of a Little Man's first encounter with Fear. Dum dum.

He felt a little better. He put on his shoes and walked out of his room, laces trailing, down the corridor, and stood quietly outside Rahel's door.

Rahel stood on a chair and unlatched the door for him.

Chacko didn't bother to wonder how she could possibly have known that Estha was at the door. He was used to their sometimes strangeness.

He lay like a beached whale on the narrow hotel bed and wondered idly if it had indeed been Velutha that Rahel saw. He didn't think it likely. Velutha had too much going for him. He was a Paravan with a future. He wondered whether Velutha had become a card-holding member of the Marxist Party. And whether he had been seeing Comrade K. N. M. Pillai lately.

Earlier in the year, Comrade Pillai's political ambitions had been given an unexpected boost. Two local Party members, Comrade J. Kattukaran and Comrade Guhan Menon had been expelled from the Party as suspected Naxalites. One of them – Comrade Guhan Menon – was tipped to be the Party's candidate for the Kottayam by-elections to the Legislative Assembly due next March. His expulsion from the Party created a vacuum that a number of hopefuls were jockeying to fill. Among them Comrade K. N. M. Pillai.

Comrade Pillai had begun to watch the goings-on at Paradise Pickles with the keenness of a substitute at a soccer match. To bring in a new labour union, however small, in what he hoped would be his future constituency, would be an excellent beginning for a journey to the Legislative Assembly.

Until then, at Paradise Pickles, *Comrade! Comrade!* (as Ammu put it) had been no more than a harmless game played outside working hours. But if the stakes were raised, and the conductor's baton wrested from Chacko's hands, everybody (except Chacko) knew that the factory, already steeped in debt, would be in trouble.

Since things were not going well financially, the labour was paid less than the minimum rates specified by the trade union. Of course it was Chacko himself who pointed this out to them and promised that as soon as things picked up, their wages would be revised. He believed that they trusted him and knew that he had their best interests at heart.

But there was someone who thought otherwise. In the evenings, after the factory shift was over, Comrade K. N. M. Pillai waylaid the workers of Paradise Pickles and shepherded them into his printing press. In his reedy, piping voice he urged them on to revolution. In his speeches he managed a clever mix of pertinent local issues and grand Maoist rhetoric which sounded even grander in Malayalam.

'People of the World,' he would chirrup, 'be courageous, *dare* to fight, *defy* difficulties and advance wave upon wave. Then the whole world will belong to the People. Monsters of all kinds shall be destroyed. You must demand what is rightfully yours. Yearly bonus. Provident fund. Accident insurance.' Since these speeches were in part rehearsal for when, as the local Member of the Legislative Assembly, Comrade Pillai would address thronging millions, there was something odd about their pitch and cadence. His voice was full of green rice-fields and red banners that arced across blue skies instead of a small hot room and the smell of printer's ink.

Comrade K. N. M. Pillai never came out openly against Chacko. Whenever he referred to him in his speeches he was careful to strip him of any human attributes and present him as an abstract functionary in some larger scheme. A theoretical construct. A pawn in the monstrous bourgeois plot to subvert the Revolution. He never referred to him by name, but always as 'the Management'. As though Chacko was many people. Apart from it being tactically the right thing to do, this disjunction between the man and his job helped Comrade Pillai to keep his conscience clear about his own private business dealings with Chacko. His contract for printing the Paradise Pickles labels gave him an income that he badly needed. He told himself that Chacko-the-client and Chacko-the-Management were two different people. Quite separate of course from Chacko-the-Comrade.

The only snag in Comrade K. N. M. Pillai's plans was Velutha. Of all the workers at Paradise Pickles, he was the only card-holding member of the Party, and that gave Comrade Pillai an ally he would rather have done without. He knew that all the other Touchable workers in the factory resented Velutha for ancient reasons of their own. Comrade Pillai stepped carefully around this wrinkle, waiting for a suitable opportunity to iron it out.

He stayed in constant touch with the workers. He made it his business to know exactly what went on at the factory. He ridiculed them for accepting the wages they did, when their *own* government, the People's Government, was in power.

When Punnachen the accountant, who read Mammachi the papers every morning, brought news that there had been talk among the workers of demanding a raise, Mammachi was furious. 'Tell them to read the papers. There's a famine on. There are no jobs. People are starving to death. They should be grateful they have any work *at all.*'

Whenever anything serious happened in the factory, it was always to Mammachi and not Chacko that the news was brought. Perhaps this was because Mammachi fitted properly into the conventional scheme of things. She was the Modalali. She played her part. Her responses, however harsh, were straightforward and predictable. Chacko, on the other hand, though he was the Man of the House, though he said, '*My* pickles, *my* jam, *my* curry powders,' was so busy trying on different costumes that he blurred the battle lines.

Mammachi tried to caution Chacko. He heard her out, but didn't really listen to what she was saying. So despite the early rumblings of discontent on the premises of Paradise Pickles, Chacko, in rehearsal for the Revolution, continued to play *Comrade! Comrade!*

That night, on his narrow hotel bed, he thought sleepily about pre-empting Comrade Pillai by organizing his workers into a sort of private labour union. He would hold elections for them. Make them vote. They could take turns at being elected representatives. He smiled at the idea of holding round-table negotiations with Comrade Sumathi, or, better still, Comrade Lucykutty, who had much the nicer hair.

His thoughts returned to Margaret Kochamma and Sophie Mol. Fierce bands of love tightened around his chest until he could barely breathe. He lay awake and counted the hours for them to leave for the airport.

On the next bed, his niece and nephew slept with their arms around each other. A hot twin and a cold one. He and She. We and Us. Somehow, not wholly unaware of the hint of doom and all that waited in the wings for them.

They dreamed of their river.

Of the coconut trees that bent into it and watched, with

coconut eyes, the boats slide by. Upstream in the mornings. Downstream in the evenings. And the dull, sullen sound of the boatmen's bamboo poles as they thudded against the dark, oiled boatwood.

It was warm, the water. Greygreen. Like rippled silk.
With fish in it.
With the sky and trees in it.
And at night, the broken yellow moon in it.

When they grew tired of waiting, the dinner smells climbed off the curtains and drifted through the Sea Queen windows to dance the night away on the dinner-smelling sea.

The time was ten to two.

5

God's Own Country

Years later, when Rahel returned to the river, it greeted her with a ghastly skull's smile, with holes where teeth had been, and a limp hand raised from a hospital bed.

Both things had happened.

It had shrunk. And she had grown.

Downriver, a saltwater barrage had been built, in exchange for votes from the influential paddy-farmer lobby. The barrage regulated the inflow of saltwater from the backwaters that opened into the Arabian Sea. So now they had two harvests a year instead of one. More rice, for the price of a river.

Despite the fact that it was June, and raining, the river was no more than a swollen drain now. A thin ribbon of thick water that lapped wearily at the mud banks on either side, sequinned with the occasional silver slant of a dead fish. It was choked with a succulent weed, whose furred brown roots waved like thin tentacles under water. Bronze-winged lily-trotters walked across it. Splay-footed, cautious.

Once it had had the power to evoke fear. To change lives. But now its teeth were drawn, its spirit spent. It was just a slow, sludging green ribbon lawn that ferried fetid garbage to the sea. Bright plastic bags blew across its viscous, weedy surface like subtropical flying-flowers.

The stone steps that had once led bathers right down to the water, and Fisher People to the fish, were entirely exposed and led from nowhere to nowhere, like an absurd corbelled monument that commemorated nothing. Ferns pushed through the cracks.

On the other side of the river, the steep mud banks changed abruptly into low mud walls of shanty hutments. Children hung their bottoms over the edge and defecated directly onto the squelchy, sucking mud of the exposed river bed. The smaller ones left their dribbling mustard streaks to find their own way down. Eventually, by evening, the river would rouse itself to accept the day's offerings and sludge off to the sea, leaving wavy lines of thick white scum in its wake. Upstream, clean mothers washed clothes and pots in unadulterated factory effluents. People bathed. Severed torsos soaping themselves, arranged like dark busts on a thin, rocking, ribbon lawn.

On warm days the smell of shit lifted off the river and hovered over Ayemenem like a hat.

Further inland, and still across, a five-star hotel chain had bought the Heart of Darkness.

The History House (where map-breath'd ancestors with tough toe-nails once whispered) could no longer be approached from the river. It had turned its back on Ayemenem. The hotel guests were ferried across the backwaters, straight from Cochin. They arrived by speedboat, opening up a V of foam on the water, leaving behind a rainbow film of gasoline.

The view from the hotel was beautiful, but here too the water was thick and toxic. *No Swimming* signs had been put up in stylish calligraphy. They had built a tall wall to screen off the slum and prevent it from encroaching on Kari Saipu's estate. There wasn't much they could do about the smell.

But they had a swimming pool for swimming. And fresh tandoori pomfret and crêpe suzette on their menu.

The trees were still green, the sky still blue, which counted for something. So they went ahead and plugged their smelly paradise – 'God's Own Country' they called it in their brochures

– because they knew, those clever Hotel People, that smelliness, like other people's poverty, was merely a matter of getting used to. A question of discipline. Of Rigour and Air-conditioning. Nothing more.

Kari Saipu's house had been renovated and painted. It had become the centrepiece of an elaborate complex, crisscrossed with artificial canals and connecting bridges. Small boats bobbed in the water. The old colonial bungalow with its deep verandah and Doric columns, was surrounded by smaller, older, wooden houses – ancestral homes – that the hotel chain had bought from old families and transplanted in the Heart of Darkness. Toy Histories for rich tourists to play in. Like the sheaves of rice in Joseph's dream, like a press of eager natives petitioning an English magistrate, the old houses had been arranged around the History House in attitudes of deference. 'Heritage', the hotel was called.

The Hotel People liked to tell their guests that the oldest of the wooden houses, with its air-tight, panelled storeroom which could hold enough rice to feed an army for a year, had been the ancestral home of Comrade E. M. S. Namboodiripad, 'Kerala's Mao Tse-tung,' they explained to the uninitiated. The furniture and knick-knacks that came with the house were on display. A reed umbrella, a wicker couch. A wooden dowry box. They were labelled with edifying placards which said *Traditional Kerala Umbrella* and *Traditional Bridal Dowry Box*.

So there it was then, History and Literature enlisted by commerce. Kurtz and Karl Marx joining palms to greet rich guests as they stepped off the boat.

Comrade Namboodiripad's house functioned as the hotel's dining room, where semi-suntanned tourists in bathing suits sipped tender coconut water (served in the shell), and old communists, who now worked as fawning bearers in colourful ethnic clothes, stooped slightly behind their trays of drinks.

In the evenings (for that Regional Flavour) the tourists were treated to truncated kathakali performances ('Small attention spans,' the Hotel People explained to the dancers). So ancient stories were collapsed and amputated. Six-hour classics were slashed to twenty-minute cameos.

The performances were staged by the swimming pool. While the drummers drummed and the dancers danced, hotel guests frolicked with their children in the water. While Kunti revealed her secret to Karna on the river bank, courting couples rubbed suntan oil on each other. While fathers played sublimated sexual games with their nubile teenaged daughters, Poothana suckled young Krishna at her poisoned breast. Bhima disembowelled Dushasana and bathed Draupadi's hair in his blood.

The back verandah of the History House (where a posse of Touchable policemen converged, where an inflatable goose was burst) had been enclosed and converted into the airy hotel kitchen. Nothing worse than kebabs and caramel custard happened there now. The Terror was past. Overcome by the smell of food. Silenced by the humming of cooks. The cheerful chop-chop-chopping of ginger and garlic. The disembowelling of lesser mammals – pigs, goats. The dicing of meat. The scaling of fish.

Something lay buried in the ground. Under grass. Under twenty-three years of June rain.

A small forgotten thing.

Nothing that the world would miss.

A child's plastic wristwatch with the time painted on it.

Ten to two it said.

A band of children followed Rahel on her walk.

'Hello, hippie,' they said, twenty-five years too late. 'Whatis-yourname?'

Then someone threw a small stone at her, and her childhood fled, flailing its thin arms.

On her way back, looping around the Ayemenem House, Rahel emerged onto the main road. Here too, houses had mushroomed, and it was only the fact that they nestled under trees, and that the narrow paths that branched off the main road and led to them were not motorable, that gave Ayemenem the semblance of rural quietness. In truth, its population had swelled to the size of a little town. Behind the fragile façade of greenery lived a press of people who could gather at a moment's notice. To beat to death a careless bus driver. To smash the windscreen of a car that dared to venture out on the day of an Opposition bandh. To steal Baby Kochamma's imported insulin and her cream buns that came all the way from Bestbakery in Kottayam.

Outside Lucky Press, Comrade K. N. M. Pillai was standing at his boundary wall talking to a man on the other side. Comrade Pillai's arms were crossed over his chest, and he clasped his own armpits possessively, as though someone had asked to borrow them and he had just refused. The man across the wall shuffled through a bunch of photographs in a plastic sachet, with an air of contrived interest. The photographs were mostly pictures of Comrade K. N. M. Pillai's son, Lenin, who lived and worked in Delhi – he took care of the painting, plumbing, and any electrical work – for the Dutch and German embassies. In order to allay any fears his clients might have about his political leanings, he had altered his name slightly. Levin he called himself now. P. Levin.

Rahel tried to walk past unnoticed. It was absurd of her to have imagined that she could.

'*Aiyyo*, Rahel Mol!' Comrade K. N. M. Pillai said, recognizing her instantly. '*Orkunnilley?* Comrade Uncle?'

'*Oower*,' Rahel said.

Did she remember him? She did indeed.

Neither question nor answer was meant as anything more than a polite preamble to conversation. Both she and he knew that there are things that can be forgotten. And things that cannot – that sit on dusty shelves like stuffed birds with baleful, sideways staring eyes.

'So!' Comrade Pillai said. 'I think so you are in Amayrica now?'

'No,' Rahel said. 'I'm here.'

'Yes yes,' he sounded a little impatient, 'but otherwise in Amayrica, I suppose?'

Comrade Pillai uncrossed his arms. His nipples peeped at Rahel over the top of the boundary wall like a sad St Bernard's eyes.

'Recognized?' Comrade Pillai asked the man with the photographs, indicating Rahel with his chin.

The man hadn't.

'The Old Paradise Pickle Kochamma's daughter's daughter,' Comrade Pillai said.

The man looked puzzled. He was clearly a stranger. And not a pickle-eater. Comrade Pillai tried a different tack.

'Punnyan Kunju?' he asked. The Patriarch of Antioch appeared briefly in the sky – and waved his withered hand.

Things began to fall into place for the man with the photographs. He nodded enthusiastically.

'Punnyan Kunju's son? Benaan John Ipe? Who used to be in Delhi?' Comrade Pillai said.

'*Oower, oower, oower,*' the man said.

'His daughter's daughter is this. In Amayrica now.'

The nodder nodded as Rahel's ancestral lineage fell into place for him.

'*Oower, oower, oower.* In Amayrica now, isn't it.' It wasn't a question. It was sheer admiration.

He remembered vaguely a whiff of scandal. He had forgotten the details, but remembered that it had involved sex and death. It had been in the papers. After a brief silence and another series of small nods, the man handed Comrade Pillai the sachet of photographs.

'Okaythen, comrade, I'll be off.'

He had a bus to catch.

'So!' Comrade Pillai's smile broadened as he turned all his attention like a searchlight on Rahel. His gums were startlingly pink, the reward for a lifetime's uncompromising vegetarianism. He was the kind of man whom it was hard to imagine had once been a boy. Or a baby. He looked as though he had been *born* middle-aged. With a receding hairline.

'Mol's husband?' he wanted to know.

'Hasn't come.'

'Any photos?'

'No.'

'Name?'

'Larry. Lawrence.'

'*Oower*. Lawrence.' Comrade Pillai nodded as though he agreed with it. As though given a choice, it was the very one he would have picked.

'Any issues?'

'No,' Rahel said.

'Still in planning stages, I suppose? Or expecting?'

'No.'

'One is must. Boy girl. Anyone,' Comrade Pillai said. 'Two is of course your choice.'

'We're divorced.' Rahel hoped to shock him into silence.

'Die-vorced?' His voice rose to such a high register that it cracked on the question mark. He even pronounced the word as though it were a form of death.

'That is most unfortunate,' he said, when he had recovered. For some reason resorting to uncharacteristic, bookish language. 'Mo-stunfortunate.'

It occurred to Comrade Pillai that this generation was perhaps paying for its forefathers' bourgeois decadence.

One was mad. The other die-vorced. Probably barren.

Perhaps *this* was the real revolution. The Christian bourgeoisie had begun to self-destruct.

Comrade Pillai lowered his voice as though there were people
listening, though there was no one about.

'And Mon?' he whispered confidentially. 'How is he?'

'Fine,' Rahel said. 'He's fine.'

*Fine. Flat and honey-coloured. He washes his clothes with crumbling
soap.*

'*Aiyyo paavam*,' Comrade Pillai whispered, and his nipples
drooped in mock dismay. 'Poor fellow.'

Rahel wondered what he gained by questioning her so closely
and then completely disregarding her answers. Clearly he didn't
expect the truth from her, but why didn't he at least bother to
pretend otherwise?

'Lenin is in Delhi now,' Comrade Pillai came out with it
finally, unable to hide his pride. 'Working with foreign embassies. See!'

He handed Rahel the Cellophane sachet. They were mostly
photographs of Lenin and his family. His wife, his child, his
new Bajaj scooter. There was one of Lenin shaking hands with
a very well-dressed, very pink man.

'German First Secretary,' Comrade Pillai said.

They looked cheerful in the photographs, Lenin and his wife.
As though they had a new refrigerator in their drawing room,
and a down payment on a DDA flat.

Rahel remembered the incident that made Lenin swim into
focus as a Real Person for her and Estha, when they stopped
regarding him as just another pleat in his mother's sari. She
and Estha were five, Lenin perhaps three or four years old.
They met in the clinic of Dr Verghese Verghese (Kottayam's
leading Paediatrician and Feeler-up of Mothers). Rahel was with
Ammu and Estha (who had insisted that he go along). Lenin
was with his mother, Kalyani. Both Rahel and Lenin had the

same complaint – Foreign Objects Lodged up their Noses. It seemed an extraordinary coincidence now, but somehow hadn't then. It was curious how politics lurked even in what children chose to stuff up their noses. She, the granddaughter of an Imperial Entomologist, he the son of a grass-roots Marxist Party worker. So, she a glass bead, and he a green gram.

The waiting room was full.

From behind the doctor's curtain, sinister voices murmured, interrupted by howls from savaged children. There was a clink of glass on metal, and the whisper and bubble of boiling water. A boy played with the wooden *Doctor is IN Doctor is OUT* sign on the wall, sliding the brass panel up and down. A feverish baby hiccupped on its mother's breast. The slow ceiling fan sliced the thick, frightened air into an unending spiral that spun slowly to the floor like the peeled skin of an endless potato.

No one read the magazines.

From below the scanty curtain that was stretched across the doorway that led directly onto the street came the relentless slip-slap of disembodied feet in slippers. The noisy, carefree world of Those with Nothing Up Their Noses.

Ammu and Kalyani exchanged children. Noses were pushed up, heads bent back, and turned towards the light to see if one mother could see what the other had missed. When that didn't work, Lenin, dressed like a taxi – yellow shirt, black stretchlon shorts – regained his mother's nylon lap (*and* his packet of chiclets). He sat on sari flowers and from that unassailable position of strength surveyed the scene impassively. He inserted his left forefinger deep into his unoccupied nostril and breathed noisily through his mouth. He had a neat side-parting. His hair was slicked down with Ayurvedic oil. The chiclets were his to *hold* before the doctor saw him, and to consume after. All was well with the world. Perhaps he was a little too young to know that Atmosphere in Waiting Room, plus Screams from Behind Curtain, ought logically to add up to a Healthy Fear of Dr V. V.

A rat with bristly shoulders made several busy journeys between the doctor's room and the bottom of the cupboard in the waiting room.

A nurse appeared and disappeared through the tattered-curtained doctor's door. She wielded strange weapons. A tiny vial. A rectangle of glass with blood smeared on it. A test tube of sparkling, back-lit urine. A stainless-steel tray of boiled needles. The hairs on her leg were pressed like coiled wires against her translucent white stockings. The box heels of her scuffed white sandals were worn away on the insides, and caused her feet to slope in, towards each other. Shiny black hairpins, like straightened snakes, clamped her starched nurse's cap to her oily head.

She appeared to have rat-filters on her glasses. She didn't seem to notice the bristly shouldered rat even when it scuttled right past her feet. She called out names in a deep voice, like a man's: 'A. Ninan . . . S. Kusumalatha . . . B. V. Roshini . . . N. Ambady.' She ignored the alarmed, spiralling air.

Estha's eyes were frightened saucers. He was mesmerized by the *Doctor is IN Doctor is OUT* sign.

A tide of panic rose in Rahel.

'Ammu, once again let's try.'

Ammu held the back of Rahel's head with one hand. With her thumb in her handkerchief she blocked the beadless nostril. All eyes in the waiting room were on Rahel. It was to be the performance of her life. Estha's expression prepared to blow its nose. Furrows gathered on his forehead and he took a deep breath.

Rahel summoned all her strength. *Please God, please make it come out.* From the soles of her feet, from the bottom of her heart, she blew into her mother's handkerchief.

And in a rush of snot and relief, it emerged. A little mauve bead in a glistening bed of slime. As proud as a pearl in an oyster. Children gathered around to admire it. The boy that was playing with the sign was scornful.

'I could easily do that!' he announced.

'Try it and see what a slap you'll get,' his mother said.

'Miss Rahel!' the nurse shouted and looked around.

'It's out!' Ammu said to the nurse. 'It's come out.' She held up her crumpled handkerchief.

The nurse had no idea what she meant.

'It's all right. We're leaving,' Ammu said. 'The bead's out.'

'Next,' the nurse said, and closed her eyes behind her rat-filters. ('It takes all kinds,' she told herself.) 'S. V. S. Kurup!'

The scornful boy set up a howl as his mother pushed him into the doctor's room.

Rahel and Estha left the clinic triumphantly. Little Lenin remained behind to have his nostril probed by Dr Verghese Verghese's cold steel implements, and his mother probed by other, softer ones.

That was Lenin then.

Now he had a house and a Bajaj scooter. A wife and an *issue*.

Rahel handed Comrade Pillai back the sachet of photographs and tried to leave.

'One mint,' Comrade Pillai said. He was like a flasher in a hedge. Enticing people with his nipples and then forcing pictures of his son on them. He flipped through the pack of photographs (a pictorial guide to Lenin's Life-in-a-Minute) to the last one. '*Orkunnundo?*'

It was an old black and white picture. One that Chacko took with the Rolleiflex camera that Margaret Kochamma had brought him as a Christmas present. All four of them were in it. Lenin, Estha, Sophie Mol and herself, standing in the front verandah of the Ayemenem House. Behind them Baby Koch-amma's Christmas trimmings hung in loops from the ceiling. A cardboard star was tied to a bulb. Lenin, Rahel and Estha looked like frightened animals that had been caught in the headlights of a car. Knees pressed together, smiles frozen on their faces, arms pinned to their sides, chests swivelled to face the photograph. As though standing sideways was a sin.

Only Sophie Mol, with First World panache, had prepared herself, for her biological father's photo, a face. She had turned her eyelids inside out so that her eyes looked like pink-veined flesh petals (grey in a black and white photograph). She wore a set of protruding false teeth cut from the yellow rind of a sweetlime. Her tongue pushed through the trap of teeth and had Mammachi's silver thimble fitted on the end of it. (She had hijacked it the day she arrived, and vowed to spend her holidays drinking only from a thimble.) She held out a lit candle in each hand. One leg of her denim bellbottoms was rolled up to expose a white, bony knee on which a face had been drawn. Minutes before that picture was taken, she had finished explaining patiently to Estha and Rahel (arguing away any evidence to the contrary, photographs, memories) how there was a pretty good chance that they were bastards, and what bastard really meant. This had entailed an involved, though somewhat inaccurate description of sex. 'See what they do is . . .'

That was only days before she died.

Sophie Mol.

Thimble-drinker.

Coffin-cartwheeler.

She arrived on the Bombay–Cochin flight. Hatted, bell-bottomed and Loved from the Beginning.

6

Cochin Kangaroos

At Cochin Airport, Rahel's new knickers were polka-dotted and still crisp. The rehearsals had been rehearsed. It was the Day of the Play. The culmination of the *What Will Sophie Mol Think?* week.

In the morning at the Hotel Sea Queen, Ammu – who had dreamed at night of dolphins and a deep blue – helped Rahel to put on her frothy Airport Frock. It was one of those baffling aberrations in Ammu's taste, a cloud of stiff yellow lace with tiny silver sequins and a bow on each shoulder. The frilled skirt was underpinned with buckram to make it flare. Rahel worried that it didn't really match her sunglasses.

Ammu held out the crisp matching knickers for her. Rahel, with her hands on Ammu's shoulders, climbed into her new knickers (left leg, right leg) and gave Ammu a kiss on each dimple (left cheek, right cheek). The elastic snapped softly against her stomach.

'Thank you, Ammu,' Rahel said.

'Thank you?' Ammu said.

'For my new frock and knickers,' Rahel said.

Ammu smiled. 'You're welcome, my sweetheart,' she said, but sadly.

You're welcome, my sweetheart.

The moth on Rahel's heart lifted a downy leg. Then put it back. Its little leg was cold. *A little less her mother loved her.*

The Sea Queen room smelled of eggs and filter coffee.

On the way to the car, Estha carried the Eagle vacuum flask with the tap water. Rahel carried the Eagle vacuum flask with the boiled water. Eagle vacuum flasks had Vacuum Eagles on them, with their wings spread, and a globe in their talons. Vacuum Eagles, the twins believed, watched the world all day and flew around their flasks all night. As silently as owls they flew, with the moon on their wings.

Estha was wearing a long-sleeved red shirt with a pointed collar and black drainpipe trousers. His puff looked crisp and surprised. Like well-whipped eggwhite.

Estha – with some basis, it must be admitted – said that Rahel looked stupid in her airport frock. Rahel slapped him, and he slapped her back.

They weren't speaking to each other at the airport.

Chacko, who usually wore a mundu, was wearing a funny tight suit and a shining smile. Ammu straightened his tie, which was odd and sideways. It had had its breakfast and was satisfied.

Ammu said, 'What's happened suddenly – to our Man of the Masses?'

But she said it with her dimples, because Chacko was so bursty. So very happy.

Chacko didn't slap her.

So she didn't slap him back.

From the Sea Queen florist Chacko had bought two red roses which he held carefully.

Fatly.

Fondly.

The airport shop, run by the Kerala Tourism Development Corporation, was crammed with Air India Maharajahs (small medium large), sandalwood elephants (small medium large) and papier-mâché masks of kathakali dancers (small medium large).

The smell of cloying sandalwood and terrycotton armpits (small medium large) hung in the air.

In the Arrivals Lounge, there were four life-sized cement kangaroos with cement pouches that said USE ME. In their pouches, instead of cement joeys, they had cigarette stubs, used matchsticks, bottle-caps, peanut shells, crumpled paper cups and cockroaches.

Red betel spit stains spattered their kangaroo stomachs like fresh wounds.

Red-mouthed smiles the Airport Kangaroos had.

And pink-edged ears.

They looked as though if you pressed them they might say 'Ma-ma' in empty battery voices.

When Sophie Mol's plane appeared in the skyblue Bombay–Cochin sky, the crowd pushed against the iron railing to see more of everything.

The Arrivals Lounge was a press of love and eagerness, because the Bombay–Cochin flight was the flight that all the Foreign Returnees came home on.

Their families had come to meet them. From all over Kerala. On long bus journeys. From Ranni, from Kumili, from Vizhinjam, from Uzhavoor. Some of them had camped at the airport overnight, and had brought their food with them. And tapioca chips and chakka velaichathu for the way back.

They were all there – the deaf ammoomas, the cantankerous, arthritic appoopans, the pining wives, scheming uncles, children with the runs. The fiancées to be reassessed. The teacher's husband still waiting for his Saudi visa. The teacher's husband's sisters waiting for their dowries. The wire-bender's pregnant wife.

'Mostly sweeper class,' Baby Kochamma said grimly, and looked away while a mother, not wanting to give up her Good Place near the railing, aimed her distracted baby's penis into an empty bottle while he smiled and waved at the people around him.

'Sssss . . .' his mother hissed. First persuasively, then savagely. But her baby thought he was the Pope. He smiled and waved and smiled and waved. With his penis in a bottle.

'Don't forget that you are Ambassadors of India,' Baby Kochamma told Rahel and Estha. 'You're going to form their First Impression of your country.'

Two-egg Twin Ambassadors. Their Excellencies Ambassador E(lvis). Pelvis, and Ambassador S(tick). Insect.

In her stiff lace dress and her fountain in a Love-in-Tokyo, Rahel looked like an Airport Fairy with appalling taste. She was hemmed in by humid hips (as she would be once again, at a funeral in a yellow church) and grim eagerness. She had her grandfather's moth on her heart. She turned away from the screaming steel bird in the skyblue sky that had her cousin in it, and what she saw was this: red-mouthed roos with ruby smiles moved cemently across the airport floor.

Heel and Toe
Heel and Toe

Long flatfeet.

Airport garbage in their baby bins.

The smallest one stretched its neck like people in English films who loosen their ties after office. The middle one rummaged in her pouch for a long cigarette stub to smoke. She found an old cashew nut in a dim plastic bag. She gnawed it with her front teeth like a rodent. The large one wobbled the standing up sign that said *Kerala Tourism Development Corporation Welcomes You* with a kathakali dancer doing a namasté. Another sign, unwobbled by a kangaroo, said: *emocleW ot eht ecipS tsaoC fo aidnI.*

Urgently, Ambassador Rahel burrowed through the press of people to her brother and co-Ambassador.

Estha look! Look Estha look!

Ambassador Estha wouldn't. Didn't want to. He watched the bumpy landing with his tap-water Eagle flask slung around him, and a bottomless-bottomful feeling: the Orangedrink Lemondrink Man knew where to find him. In the factory in Ayemenem. On the banks of the Meenachal.

Ammu watched with her handbag.

Chacko with his roses.

Baby Kochamma with her sticking out neckmole.

Then the Bombay–Cochin people came out. From the cool air into the hot air. Crumpled people uncrumpled on their way to the Arrivals Lounge.

And there they were, the Foreign Returnees, in wash'n'wear suits and rainbow sunglasses. With an end to grinding poverty in their Aristocrat suitcases. With cement roofs for their thatched houses, and geysers for their parents' bathrooms. With sewage systems and septic tanks. Maxis and high heels. Puff sleeves and lipstick. Mixy-grinders and automatic flashes for their cameras. With keys to count, and cupboards to lock. With a hunger for kappa and meen vevichathu that they hadn't eaten for so long. With love and a lick of shame that their families who had come to meet them were so ... so ... gawkish. *Look at the way they dressed! Surely they had more suitable airport wear! Why did Malayalees have such awful teeth?*

And the airport itself! More like the local bus depot! The birdshit on the building! Oh the spitstains on the kangeroos!

Oho! Going to the dogs India is.

When long bus journeys, and overnight stays at the airport, were met by love and a lick of shame, small cracks appeared, which would grow and grow, and before they knew it, the

Foreign Returnees would be trapped outside the History House, and have their dreams redreamed.

Then, there, among the wash'n'wear suits and shiny suitcases, Sophie Mol.

Thimble-drinker.

Coffin-cartwheeler.

She walked down the runway, the smell of London in her hair. Yellow bottoms of bells flapped backwards around her ankles. Long hair floated out from under her straw hat. One hand in her mother's. The other swinging like a soldier's (lef, lef, lefrightlef).

> *There was*
> *A girl*
> *Tall and*
> *Thin and*
> *Fair*
> *Her hair*
> *Her hair*
> *Was the delicate colourov*
> *Gin—nnn—ger (leftleft, right)*
> *There was*
> *A girl —*

Margaret Kochamma told her to Stoppit.

So she Stoppited.

Ammu said, 'Can you see her, Rahel?'

She turned around to find her crisp-knickered daughter communing with cement marsupials. She went and fetched her, scoldingly. Chacko said he couldn't take Rahel on his shoulders because he was already carrying something. Two roses red.

Fatly.

Fondly.

When Sophie Mol walked into the Arrivals Lounge, Rahel, overcome by excitement and resentment, pinched Estha hard. His skin between her nails. Estha gave her a Chinese Bangle, twisting the skin on her wrist different ways with each of his hands. Her skin became a welt and hurt. When she licked it, it tasted of salt. The spit on her wrist was cool and comfortable.

Ammu never noticed.

Across the tall iron railing that separated Meeters from the Met, and Greeters from the Gret, Chacko, beaming, bursting through his suit and sideways tie, bowed to his new daughter and ex-wife.

In his mind, Estha said, 'Bow.'

'Hello, ladies,' Chacko said in his Reading Aloud voice (last night's voice in which he said, *Love. Madness. Hope. Infinnate Joy*). 'And how was your journey?'

And the Air was full of Thoughts and Things to Say. But at times like these, only the Small Things are ever said. The Big Things lurk unsaid inside.

'Say Hello and How d'you do?' Margaret Kochamma said to Sophie Mol.

'Hello and How d'you do?' Sophie Mol said through the iron railing, to everyone in particular.

'One for you and one for you,' Chacko said with his roses.

'And Thank you?' Margaret Kochamma said to Sophie Mol.

'And Thank you?' Sophie Mol said to Chacko, mimicking her mother's question mark.

Margaret Kochamma shook her a little for her impertinence.

'You're welcome,' Chacko said. 'Now let me introduce everybody.' Then, more for the benefit of onlookers and eavesdroppers, because Margaret Kochamma needed no introduction really, 'My wife, Margaret.'

Margaret Kochamma smiled and wagged her rose at him. *Ex-wife, Chacko!* Her lips formed the words, though her voice never spoke them.

Anybody could see that Chacko was a proud and happy man to have had a wife like Margaret. White. In a flowered, printed frock with legs underneath. And brown back-freckles on her back. And arm-freckles on her arms.

But around her, the air was sad, somehow. And behind the smile in her eyes, the Grief was a fresh, shining blue. Because of a calamitous car crash. Because of a Joe-shaped hole in the Universe.

'Hello, all,' she said. 'I feel I've known you for years.'

Hello wall.

'My daughter, Sophie,' Chacko said, and laughed a small, nervous laugh that was worried, in case Margaret Kochamma said, 'Ex-daughter.' But she didn't. It was an easy-to-understand laugh. Not like the Orangedrink Lemondrink Man's laugh that Estha hadn't understood.

''llo,' Sophie Mol said.

She was taller than Estha. And bigger. Her eyes were blue-greyblue. Her pale skin was the colour of beach sand. But her hatted hair was beautiful, deep red-brown. And yes (oh yes!) she had Pappachi's nose waiting inside hers. An Imperial Entomologist's nose-within-a-nose. A moth-lover's nose. She carried her Made-in-England go-go bag that she loved.

'Ammu, my sister,' Chacko said.

Ammu said a grown-up's Hello to Margaret Kochamma and a children's Hell-oh to Sophie Mol. Rahel watched hawk-eyed to try and gauge how much Ammu loved Sophie Mol, but couldn't.

Laughter rambled through the Arrivals Lounge like a sudden breeze. Adoor Basi, the most popular, best-loved comedian in Malayalam cinema, had just arrived (Bombay–Cochin). Burdened with a number of small unmanageable packages and unabashed public adulation, he felt obliged to perform. He kept dropping his packages and saying, '*Ende Deivomay! Eee sadhanangal!*'

Estha laughed a high, delighted laugh.

'Ammu look! Adoor Basi's dropping his things!' Estha said. 'He can't even carry his things!'

'He's doing it deliberately,' Baby Kochamma said in a strange new British accent. 'Just *ignore* him.'

'He's a filmactor,' she explained to Margaret Kochamma and Sophie Mol, making Adoor Basi sound like a Mactor who did occasionally Fil. 'Just trying to attract attention,' Baby Kochamma said, and resolutely refused to have her attention attracted.

But Baby Kochamma was wrong. Adoor Basi *wasn't* trying to attract attention. He was only trying to deserve the attention that he had already attracted.

'My aunt, Baby,' Chacko said.

Sophie Mol was puzzled. She regarded Baby Kochamma with a beady-eyed interest. She knew of cow babies and dog babies. Bear babies – yes. (She would soon point out to Rahel a bat baby.) But *aunt* babies confounded her.

Baby Kochamma said, 'Hello, Margaret,' and 'Hello, Sophie Mol.' She said Sophie Mol was so beautiful that she reminded her of a wood-sprite. Of Ariel.

'D'you know who Ariel was?' Baby Kochamma asked Sophie Mol. 'Ariel in *The Tempest*?'

Sophie Mol said she didn't.

' "Where the bee sucks there suck I?" ' Baby Kochamma said.

Sophie Mol said she didn't.

' "In a cowslip's bell I lie"?'

Sophie Mol said she didn't.

'Shakespeare's *The Tempest*?' Baby Kochamma persisted.

All this was of course primarily to announce her credentials to Margaret Kochamma. To set herself apart from the Sweeper Class.

'She's trying to boast,' Ambassador E. Pelvis whispered in Ambassador S. Insect's ear. Ambassador Rahel's giggle escaped in a blue-green bubble (the colour of a jackfruit fly) and burst in the hot airport air. Pffft! was the sound it made.

Baby Kochamma saw it, and knew that it was Estha who had started it.

'And now for the VIPs,' Chacko said (still using his Reading Aloud voice).

'My nephew, Esthappen.'

'Elvis Presley,' Baby Kochamma said for revenge. 'I'm afraid we're a little behind the times here.' Everyone looked at Estha and laughed.

From the soles of Ambassador Estha's beige and pointy shoes an angry feeling rose and stopped around his heart.

'How d'you do, Esthappen?' Margaret Kochamma said.

'Finethankyou.' Estha's voice was sullen.

'Estha,' Ammu said affectionately, 'when someone says How d'you do? You're supposed to say How d'you do? back. Not "Fine, thank you." Come on, say How do YOU do?'

Ambassador Estha looked at Ammu.

'Go on,' Ammu said to Estha. 'How do YOU do?'

Estha's sleepy eyes were stubborn.

In Malayalam Ammu said, 'Did you hear what I said?'

Ambassador Estha felt bluegreyblue eyes on him, and an Imperial Entomologist's nose. He didn't have a How do YOU do? in him.

'Esthappen!' Ammu said. And an angry feeling rose in her and stopped around her heart. A Far More Angry Than Necessary feeling. She felt somehow humiliated by this public revolt in her area of jurisdiction. She had wanted a smooth performance. A prize for her children in the Indo-British Behaviour Competition.

Chacko said to Ammu in Malayalam, 'Please. Later. Not now.'

And Ammu's angry eyes on Estha said, *All right. Later.*

And Later became a horrible, menacing, goose-bumpy word.

Lay.Ter.

Like a deep-sounding bell in a mossy well. Shivery, and furred. Like moth's feet.

The Play had gone bad. Like pickle in the monsoon.

'And my niece,' Chacko said. 'Where's Rahel?' He looked around and couldn't find her. Ambassador Rahel, unable to cope with see-sawing changes in her life, had ravelled herself like a sausage into the dirty airport curtain, and wouldn't unravel. A sausage with Bata sandals.

'Just ignore her,' Ammu said. 'She's just trying to attract attention.'

Ammu too was wrong. Rahel was only trying to not attract the attention that she deserved.

'Hello, Rahel,' Margaret Kochamma said to the dirty airport curtain.

'How do YOU do?' the dirty curtain replied in a mumble.

'Aren't you going to come out and say Hello?' Margaret Kochamma said in a kind-schoolteacher voice. (Like Miss Mitten's before she saw Satan in their eyes.)

Ambassador Rahel wouldn't come out of the curtain because she couldn't. She couldn't because she couldn't. Because Everything was wrong. And soon there would be a Lay Ter for both her and Estha.

Full of furred moths and icy butterflies. And deep-sounding bells. And moss.

And a Nowl.

The dirty airport curtain was a great comfort and a darkness and a shield.

'Just ignore her,' Ammu said, and smiled tightly.

Rahel's mind was full of millstones with bluegreyblue eyes.

Ammu loved her even less now. And it had come down to Brass Tacks with Chacko.

'Here comes the baggage!' Chacko said brightly. Glad to get away.

'Come, Sophiekins, let's get your bags.'

Sophiekins.

Estha watched as they walked along the railing, pushing through the crowds that moved aside, intimidated by Chacko's suit and sideways tie and his generally bursty demeanour. Because of the size of his stomach, Chacko carried himself in a way that made him appear to be walking uphill all the time. Negotiating optimistically the steep, slippery slopes of life. He walked on this side of the railing, Margaret Kochamma and Sophie Mol on that.

Sophiekins.

The Sitting Man with the cap and epaulettes, also intimidated by Chacko's suit and sideways tie, allowed him in to the baggage claim section.

When there was no railing left between them, Chacko kissed Margaret Kochamma, and then picked Sophie Mol up.

'The last time I did this I got a wet shirt for my pains,' Chacko said and laughed. He hugged her and hugged her and hugged her. He kissed her bluegreyblue eyes, her entomologist's nose, her hatted redbrown hair.

Then Sophie Mol said to Chacko, 'Ummm . . . excuse me? D'you think you could put me down now? I'm ummm . . . not really used to being carried.'

So Chacko put her down.

Ambassador Estha saw (with stubborn eyes) that Chacko's suit was suddenly looser, less bursty.

And while Chacko got the bags, at the dirty-curtained window Lay Ter became Now.

Estha saw how Baby Kochamma's neckmole licked its chops and throbbed with delicious anticipation. *Der-dhoom, der-dhoom.* It changed colour like a chameleon, Der-green, der-blueblack, der-mustardyellow.

Twins for tea
It would bea

'All right,' Ammu said. 'That's enough. Both of you. Come *out* of there, Rahel!'

Inside the curtain, Rahel closed her eyes and thought of the green river, of the quiet deep-swimming fish, and the gossamer wings of the dragonflies (that could see behind them) in the sun. She thought of her luckiest fishing rod that Velutha had made for her. Yellow bamboo with a float that dipped every time a foolish fish enquired. She thought of Velutha and wished she was with him.

Then Estha unravelled her. The cement kangaroos were watching.

Ammu looked at them. The Air was quiet except for the sound of Baby Kochamma's throbbing neckmole.

'So,' Ammu said.

And it was really a question. So?

And it hadn't an answer.

Ambassador Estha looked down, and saw that his shoes (from where the angry feelings rose) were beige and pointy. Ambassador Rahel looked down and saw that in her Bata sandals her toes were trying to disconnect themselves. Twitching to join someone else's feet. And that she couldn't stop them. Soon she'd be without toes and have a bandage like the leper at the level crossing.

'If you ever,' Ammu said, 'and I *mean* this, EVER, ever again disobey me in Public, I will see to it that you are sent away to somewhere where you will jolly well learn to behave. Is that clear?'

When Ammu was really angry, she said Jolly Well. Jolly Well was a deeply well with larfing dead people in it.

'Is. That. Clear?' Ammu said again.

Frightened eyes and a fountain looked back at Ammu.

Sleepy eyes and a surprised puff looked back at Ammu.

Two heads nodded three times.

Yes. It's. Clear.

But Baby Kochamma was dissatisfied with the fizzling out of a situation that had been so full of potential. She tossed her head.

'As if!' she said.

As if!

Ammu turned to her, and the turn of her head was a question.

'It's useless,' Baby Kochamma said. 'They're sly. They're uncouth. Deceitful. They're growing wild. You can't manage them.'

Ammu turned back to Estha and Rahel and her eyes were blurred jewels.

'Everybody says that children need a Baba. And I say no. Not *my* children. D'you know why?'

Two heads nodded.

'Why. Tell me,' Ammu said.

And not together, but almost, Esthappen and Rahel said: 'Because you're our Ammu and our Baba and you love us Double.'

'More than Double,' Ammu said. 'So remember what I told you. People's feelings are precious. And when you disobey me in Public, *every*body gets the wrong impression.'

'What Ambassadors and a half you've been!' Baby Kochamma said.

Ambassador E. Pelvis and Ambassador S. Insect hung their heads.

'And the other thing, Rahel,' Ammu said, 'I think it's high time that you learned the difference between CLEAN and DIRTY. Especially in this country.'

Ambassador Rahel looked down.

'Your dress is – was – CLEAN,' Ammu said. 'That curtain is DIRTY. Those kangaroos are DIRTY. Your hands are DIRTY.'

Rahel was frightened by the way Ammu said CLEAN and DIRTY so loudly. As though she was talking to a deaf person.

'Now, I want you to go and say Hello *properly*,' Ammu said. 'Are you going to do that or not?'

Two heads nodded twice.

Ambassador Estha and Ambassador Rahel walked towards Sophie Mol.

'Where d'you think people are sent to Jolly Well Behave?' Estha asked Rahel in a whisper.

'To the Government,' Rahel whispered back, because she knew.

'How do you do?' Estha said to Sophie Mol loud enough for Ammu to hear.

'Just like a laddoo one pice two,' Sophie Mol whispered to Estha. She had learned this in school from a Pakistani classmate.

Estha looked at Ammu.

Ammu's look said, *Never Mind Her As Long As You've Done The Right Thing.*

On their way across the airport car park, Hotweather crept into their clothes and dampened crisp knickers. The children lagged behind, weaving through parked cars and taxis.

'Does Yours hit you?' Sophie Mol asked.

Rahel and Estha, unsure of the politics of this, said nothing.

'Mine does,' Sophie Mol said invitingly. 'Mine even Slaps.'

'Ours doesn't,' Estha said loyally.

'Lucky,' Sophie Mol said.

Lucky rich boy with porketmunny. And a grandmother's factory to inherit. No worries.

They walked past the Class III Airport Workers' Union token one-day hunger strike. And past the people watching the Class III Airport Workers' Union token one-day hunger strike.

And past the people watching the people watching the people.
A small tin sign on a big banyan tree said *For VD Sex Complaints
contact Dr O. K. Joy.*

'Who d'you love Most in the World?' Rahel asked Sophie
Mol.

'Joe,' Sophie Mol said without hesitation. 'My dad. He
died two months ago. We've come here to Recover from the
Shock.'

'But Chacko's your dad,' Estha said.

'He's just my *real* dad,' Sophie Mol said. 'Joe's my dad. He
never hits. Hardly ever.'

'How can he hit if he's dead?' Estha asked reasonably.

'Where's *your* dad?' Sophie Mol wanted to know.

'He's . . .' and Rahel looked at Estha for help.

'. . . not here.' Estha said.

'Shall I tell you my list?' Rahel asked Sophie Mol.

'If you like,' Sophie Mol said.

Rahel's 'list' was an attempt to order chaos. She revised it
constantly, torn forever between love and duty. It was by no
means a true gauge of her feelings.

'First Ammu and Chacko,' Rahel said. 'Then Mammachi – '

'Our grandmother,' Estha clarified.

'*More* than your brother?' Sophie Mol asked.

'We don't count,' Rahel said. 'And anyway he might change.
Ammu says.'

'How d'you mean? Change into what?' Sophie Mol asked.

'Into a Male Chauvinist Pig,' Rahel said.

'Very unlikely,' Estha said.

'Anyway, after Mammachi, Velutha, and then – '

'Who's Velutha?' Sophie Mol wanted to know.

'A man we love,' Rahel said. 'And after Velutha, you,' Rahel
said.

'Me? What d'you love me for?' Sophie Mol said.

'Because we're firstcousins. So I have to,' Rahel said piously.

'But you don't even know me,' Sophie Mol said. 'And anyway, I don't love you.'

'But you will, when you come to know me,' Rahel said confidently.

'I doubt it,' Estha said.

'Why not?' Sophie Mol said.

'Because,' Estha said. 'And anyway she's most probably going to be a dwarf.'

As though loving a dwarf was completely out of the question.

'I'm not,' Rahel said.

'You are,' Estha said.

'I'm not.'

'You are.'

'I'm not.'

'You are. We're twins,' Estha explained to Sophie Mol, 'and just see how much shorter she is.'

Rahel obligingly took a deep breath, threw her chest out and stood back to back with Estha in the airport car park, for Sophie Mol to see just how much shorter she was.

'Maybe you'll be a midget,' Sophie Mol suggested. 'That's taller than a dwarf and shorter than a . . . Human Being.'

The silence was unsure of this compromise.

In the doorway of the Arrivals Lounge, a shadowy, red-mouthed roo-shaped silhouette waved a cemently paw only at Rahel. Cement kisses whirred through the air like small helicopters.

'D'you know how to sashay?' Sophie Mol wanted to know.

'No. We don't sashay in India,' Ambassador Estha said.

'Well in England we do,' Sophie Mol said. 'All the models do. On television. Look – it's easy.'

And the three of them, led by Sophie Mol, sashayed across the airport car park, swaying like fashion models, Eagle flasks and Made-in-England go-go bags bumping around their hips. Damp dwarves walking tall.

Shadows followed them. Silver jets in a blue church sky, like moths in a beam of light.

The skyblue Plymouth with tailfins had a smile for Sophie Mol. A chromebumpered sharksmile.

A Paradise Pickles carsmile.

When she saw the carrier with the painted pickle bottles and the list of Paradise products, Margaret Kochamma said, 'Oh dear! I feel as though I'm in an advertisement!' She said Oh dear! a lot.

Oh dear! Oh dearohdear!

'I didn't know you did pineapple slices!' she said. 'Sophie loves pineapple, don't you, Soph?'

'Sometimes,' Soph said. 'And sometimes not.'

Margaret Kochamma climbed into the advertisement with her brown back-freckles and her arm-freckles and her flowered dress with legs underneath.

Sophie Mol sat in front between Chacko and Margaret Kochamma, just her hat peeping over the car seat. Because she was their daughter.

Rahel and Estha sat at the back.

The luggage was in the boot.

Boot was a lovely word. *Sturdy* was a terrible word.

Near Ettumanoor they passed a dead temple elephant, electrocuted by a high tension wire that had fallen on the road. An engineer from the Ettumanoor municipality was supervising the disposal of the carcass. They had to be careful because the decision would serve as precedent for all future Government Pachyderm Carcass Disposals. Not a matter to be treated lightly. There was a fire engine and some confused firemen. The municipal officer had a file and was shouting a lot. There was a Joy Ice Cream cart and a man selling peanuts in narrow cones of paper cleverly designed to hold not more than eight or nine nuts.

Sophie Mol said, 'Look, a dead elephant.'

Chacko stopped to ask whether it was by any chance Kochu Thomban (Little Tusker), the Ayemenem temple elephant who came to the Ayemenem House once a month for a coconut. They said it wasn't.

Relieved that it was a stranger, and not an elephant they knew, they drove on.

'Thang God,' Estha said.

'Thank God, Estha,' Baby Kochamma corrected him.

On the way, Sophie Mol learned to recognize the first whiff of the approaching stench of unprocessed rubber and to clamp her nostrils shut until long after the truck carrying it had driven past.

Baby Kochamma suggested a car song.

Estha and Rahel had to sing in English in obedient voices. Breezily. As though they hadn't been made to rehearse it all week long. Ambassador E. Pelvis and Ambassador S. Insect.

> *RejOice in the Lo-Ord Or-Orlways*
> *And again I say re-jOice.*

Their Prer NUN sea ayshun was perfect.

The Plymouth rushed through the green midday heat, promoting pickles on its roof, and the skyblue sky in its tailfins.

Just outside Ayemenem they drove into a cabbage-green butterfly (or perhaps it drove into them).

7

Wisdom Exercise Notebooks

In Pappachi's study, mounted butterflies and moths had disintegrated into small heaps of iridescent dust that powdered the bottom of their glass display cases, leaving the pins that had impaled them naked. Cruel. The room was rank with fungus and disuse. An old neon-green hula hoop hung from a wooden peg on the wall, a huge saint's discarded halo. A column of shining black ants walked across a windowsill, their bottoms tilted upwards, like a line of mincing chorus girls in a Busby Berkeley musical. Silhouetted against the sun. Buffed and beautiful.

Rahel (on a stool, on top of a table) rummaged in a book cupboard with dull, dirty glass panes. Her bare footprints were clear in the dust on the floor. They led from the door to the table (dragged to the bookshelf), to the stool (dragged to the table and lifted onto it). She was looking for something. Her life had a size and a shape now. She had half-moons under her eyes and a team of trolls on her horizon.

On the top shelf, the leather binding on Pappachi's set of *The Insect Wealth of India* had lifted off each book and buckled like corrugated asbestos. Silverfish tunnelled through the pages, burrowing arbitrarily from species to species, turning organized information into yellow lace.

Rahel groped behind the row of books and brought out hidden things.

A smooth seashell and a spiky one.

A plastic case for contact lenses. An orange pipette.

A silver crucifix on a string of beads. Baby Kochamma's rosary.

She held it up against the light. Each greedy bead grabbed its share of sun.

A shadow fell across the sunlit rectangle on the study floor. Rahel turned towards the door with her string of light.

'Imagine. It's still here. I stole it. After you were Returned.'

That word slipped out easily. *Returned.* As though that was what twins were meant for. To be borrowed and returned. Like library books.

Estha wouldn't look up. His mind was full of trains. He blocked the light from the door. An Estha-shaped hole in the Universe.

Behind the books, Rahel's puzzled fingers encountered something else. Another magpie had had the same idea. She brought it out and wiped the dust off with the sleeve of her shirt. It was a flat packet wrapped in clear plastic and stuck with Sellotape. A scrap of white paper inside it said *Esthappen and Rahel.* In Ammu's writing.

There were four tattered notebooks in it. On their covers they said *Wisdom Exercise Notebooks* with a place for *Name, School/ College, Class, Subject.* Two had her name on them, and two Estha's.

Inside the back cover of one, something had been written in a child's handwriting. The laboured form of each letter and the irregular space between words was full of the struggle for control over the errant, self-willed pencil. The sentiment, in contrast, was lucid: *I Hate Miss Mitten and I Think Her gnickers are TORN.*

On the front of the book, Estha had rubbed out his surname with spit, and taken half the paper with it. Over the whole mess, he had written in pencil *Un-known.* Esthappen Un-known. (His surname postponed for the Time Being, while Ammu chose between her husband's name and her father's.) Next to *Class* it said: *6 years.* Next to *Subject* it said: *Story-writing.*

Rahel sat cross-legged (on the stool on the table).

'Esthappen Un-known,' she said. She opened the book and read aloud.

'When Ulyesses came home his son came and said father I thought you would not come back. many princes came and each wanted to marry Pen Lope, but Pen Lope said that the man who can stoot through the twelve rings can mary me. and everyone failed. and ulyesses came to the palace dressed liked a beggar and asked if he could try. the men all laughed at him and said if we cant do it you cant. ulyesses son stopped them and said let himtry and he took the bow and shot right through the twelve rings.'

Below this there were corrections from a previous lesson.

Ferus	Learned	Neither	Carriages	Bridge	Bearer	Fastened
Ferus	*Learned*	*Niether*	*Carriages*	*Bridge*	*Bearer*	*Fastened*
Ferus	*Learned*	*niether*				
Ferus	*Learned*	*Nieter*				

Laughter curled around the edges of Rahel's voice. '"Safety First,"' she announced. Ammu had drawn a wavy line down the length of the page with a red pen and written, *Margin? And joint handwriting in future, please!*

'When we walk on the road in the town,' cautious Estha's story went, *'we should always walk on the <u>pavement</u>. If you go on the pavement there is no traffic to cause accidnts, but on the main road there is so much dangerouse traffic that they can easily knock you down and make you <u>senseless</u> or a <u>criple</u>. If you break your head or back-bone you will be very <u>unfortunate</u>. policemen can direct the traffic so that there won't be too many <u>invalids</u> to go to hospitil. When we get out of the bus we should do so only after asking the <u>conductor</u> or we will be <u>injured</u> and make the doctors have*

a busy time. The job of a driver is very _fatle_ His famly should be very angshios because the driver could easily be dead.'

'Morbid kid,' Rahel said to Estha. As she turned the page something reached into her throat, plucked her voice out, shook it down, and returned it without its laughing edges. Estha's next story was called *Little Ammu.*

In joint handwriting. The tails of the Ys and Gs were curled and looped. The shadow in the doorway stood very still.

'On Saturday we went to a bookshop in Kottayam to buy Ammu a present because her birthday is in 17th of novembre. We bote her a diary. We hid it in the coberd and then it began to be night. Then we said do you want to see your present she said yes I would like to see it. and we wrote on the paper For a Little Ammu with Love from Estha and Rahel and we gave it to Ammu and she said what a lovely present its just what I whanted and then we talked for a little while and we talked about the diary then we gave her a kiss and went to bed.

We talked with each other and went of to sleep. We had a little dream.

After some time I got up and I was very thirsty and I went to Ammu's room and said I am thirsty. Ammu gave me water and I was just going to my bed when Ammu called me and said come and sleep with me. and I lay at the back of Ammu and talked to Ammu and went of to sleep. After a little while I got up and we talked again and after that we had a mid-night feest. we had orange coffee bananana. afterwards Rahel came and we ate two more bananas and we gave a kiss to Ammu because it was her birthday afterwards we sang happy birthday. Then in the morning we had new cloths from Ammu as a back-present Rahel was a maharani and I was Little Nehru.'

Ammu had corrected the spelling mistakes, and below the essay had written: *If I am Talking to somebody, you may interrupt me only if it is very urgent. When you do, please say 'Excuse me'. I will punish you very severely if you disobey these instructions. Please complete your corrections.*

Little Ammu.

Who never completed *her* corrections.

Who had to pack her bags and leave. Because she had no Locusts Stand I. Because Chacko said she had destroyed enough already.

Who came back to Ayemenem with asthma and a rattle in her chest that sounded like a faraway man shouting.

Estha never saw her like that.

Wild. Sick. Sad.

The last time Ammu came back to Ayemenem, Rahel had just been expelled from Nazareth Convent (for decorating dung and slamming into seniors). Ammu had lost the latest of her succession of jobs – as a receptionist in a cheap hotel – because she had been ill and had missed too many days of work. The hotel couldn't afford that, they told her. They needed a healthier receptionist.

On that last visit, Ammu spent the morning with Rahel in her room. With the last of her meagre salary she had bought her daughter small presents wrapped in brown paper with coloured paper hearts pasted on. A packet of cigarette sweets, a tin Phantom pencil box and *Paul Bunyan* -- a Junior Classics Illustrated comic. They were presents for a seven-year-old; Rahel was nearly eleven. It was as though Ammu believed that if she refused to acknowledge the passage of time, if she willed it to stand still in the lives of her twins, it would. As though sheer willpower was enough to suspend her children's childhoods until she could afford to have them living with her. Then they could take up from where they left off. Start again from seven. Ammu told Rahel that she had bought Estha a comic too, but that she'd kept it away for him until she got another job and could earn enough to rent a room for the three of them to stay together in. Then she'd go to Calcutta and fetch Estha, and he could have his comic. That day was not far off, Ammu said. It could happen *any* day. Soon rent would be no problem. She said she had applied for a UN job and they would all live in The Hague with a Dutch ayah to look after them. Or on the other hand, Ammu said, she might stay on in India and do what she had been planning to do all along – start a school. Choosing between a career in Education and a UN job wasn't easy, she said – but the thing to remember was that the very fact that she had a choice was a great privilege.

But for the Time Being, she said, until she made her decision, she was keeping Estha's presents away for him.

That whole morning Ammu talked incessantly. She asked Rahel questions, but never let her answer them. If Rahel tried to say something, Ammu would interrupt with a new thought or query. She seemed terrified of what adult thing her daughter might say and thaw Frozen Time. Fear made her garrulous. She kept it at bay with her babble.

She was swollen with cortisone, moonfaced, not the slender mother Rahel knew. Her skin was stretched over her puffy cheeks like shiny scar tissue that covers old vaccination marks. When she smiled, her dimples looked as though they hurt. Her curly hair had lost its sheen and hung around her swollen face like a dull curtain. She carried her breath in a glass inhaler in her tattered handbag. Brown Brovon fumes. Each breath she took was like a war won against the steely fist that was trying to squeeze the air from her lungs. Rahel watched her mother breathe. Each time she inhaled, the hollows near her collarbones grew steep and filled with shadows.

Ammu coughed up a wad of phlegm into her handkerchief and showed it to Rahel.

'You must always check it,' she whispered hoarsely, as though phlegm was an Arithmetic answer sheet that had to be revised before it was handed in. 'When it's white, it means it isn't ripe. When it's yellow and has a rotten smell, it's ripe and ready to be coughed out. Phlegm is like fruit. Ripe or raw. You have to be able to tell.'

Over lunch she belched like a truck-driver and said, 'Excuse me,' in a deep, unnatural voice. Rahel noticed that she had new, thick hairs in her eyebrows, long – like palps. Ammu smiled at the silence around the table as she picked fried emperor fish off the bone. She said that she felt like a road sign with birds shitting on her. She had an odd, feverish glitter in her eyes.

Mammachi asked her if she'd been drinking and suggested that she visit Rahel as seldom as possible.

Ammu got up from the table and left without saying a word. Not even goodbye. 'Go and see her off,' Chacko said to Rahel.

Rahel pretended she hadn't heard him. She went on with her fish. She thought of the phlegm and nearly retched. She hated her mother then. *Hated* her.

She never saw her again.

Ammu died in a grimy room in the Bharat Lodge in Alleppey, where she had gone for a job interview as someone's secretary. She died alone. With a noisy ceiling fan for company and no Estha to lie at the back of her and talk to her. She was thirty-one. Not old, not young, but a viable, die-able age.

She had woken up at night to escape from a familiar, recurrent dream in which policemen approached her with snicking scissors, wanting to hack off her hair. They did that in Kottayam to prostitutes whom they'd caught in the bazaar – branded them so that everybody would know them for what they were. *Veshyas*. So that new policemen on the beat would have no trouble identifying whom to harass. Ammu always noticed them in the market, the women with vacant eyes and forcibly shaved heads in the land where long, oiled hair was only for the morally upright.

That night in the lodge, Ammu sat up in the strange bed in the strange room in the strange town. She didn't know where she was, she recognized nothing around her. Only her fear was familiar. The faraway man inside her began to shout. This time the steely fist never loosened its grip. Shadows gathered like bats in the steep hollows near her collarbone.

The sweeper found her in the morning. He switched off the fan.

She had a deep blue sac under one eye that was bloated like a bubble. As though her eye had tried to do what her lungs couldn't. Some time close to midnight, the faraway man who lived in her chest had stopped shouting. A platoon of ants carried a dead cockroach sedately through the door, demonstrating what should be done with corpses.

The church refused to bury Ammu. On several counts. So Chacko hired a van to transport the body to the electric crematorium. He had her wrapped in a dirty bedsheet and laid out on a stretcher. Rahel thought she looked like a Roman Senator. *Et tu, Ammu!* she thought and smiled, remembering Estha.

It was odd driving through bright, busy streets with a dead Roman senator on the floor of the van. It made the blue sky bluer. Outside the van windows, people, like cut-out paper puppets, went on with their paper-puppet lives. Real life was inside the van. Where real death was. Over the jarring bumps and potholes in the road, Ammu's body jiggled and slid off the stretcher. Her head hit an iron bolt on the floor. She didn't wince or wake up. There was a hum in Rahel's head, and for the rest of the day Chacko had to shout at her if he wanted to be heard.

The crematorium had the same rotten, run-down air of a railway station, except that it was deserted. No trains, no crowds. Nobody except beggars, derelicts and the police-custody dead were cremated there. People who died with nobody to lie at the back of them and talk to them. When Ammu's turn came, Chacko held Rahel's hand tightly. She didn't want her hand held. She used the slickness of crematorium sweat to slither out of his grip. No one else from the family was there.

The steel door of the incinerator went up and the muted hum of the eternal fire became a red roaring. The heat lunged out at them like a famished beast. Then Rahel's Ammu was fed to it. Her hair, her skin, her smile. Her voice. The way she used Kipling to love her children before putting them to bed: *We be of one blood, ye and I.* Her good night kiss. The way she held their faces steady with one hand (squashed-cheeked, fish-mouthed) while she parted and combed their hair with the other. The way she held knickers out for Rahel to climb into. *Left leg, right leg.* All this was fed to the beast, and it was satisfied.

She was their Ammu *and* their Baba and she had loved them Double.

The door of the furnace clanged shut. There were no tears.

The crematorium 'In-charge' had gone down the road for a cup of tea and didn't come back for twenty minutes. That's how long Chacko and Rahel had to wait for the pink receipt that would entitle them to collect Ammu's remains. Her ashes. The grit from her bones. The teeth from her smile. The whole of her crammed into a little clay pot. Receipt No. Q498673.

Rahel asked Chacko how the crematorium management knew which ashes were whose. Chacko said they must have a system.

Had Estha been with them, he would have kept the receipt. He was the Keeper of Records. The natural custodian of bus tickets, bank receipts, cash memos, cheque book stubs. Little Man. He lived in a Cara-van. Dum dum.

But Estha wasn't with them. Everybody decided it was better this way. They wrote to him instead. Mammachi said Rahel should write too. Write what? *My dear Estha, How are you? I am well. Ammu died yesterday.*

Rahel never wrote to him. There are things that you can't

do – like writing letters to a part of yourself. To your feet or hair. Or heart.

In Pappachi's study, Rahel (not old, not young), with floor-dust on her feet, looked up from the Wisdom Exercise Notebook and saw that Esthappen Un-known was gone.

She climbed down (off the stool, off the table) and walked out to the verandah.

She saw Estha's back disappearing through the gate.

It was midmorning and about to rain again. The green – in the last moments of that strange, glowing, preshower light – was fierce.

A cock crowed in the distance and its voice separated into two. Like a sole peeling off an old shoe.

Rahel stood there with her tattered Wisdom notebooks. In the front verandah of an old house, below a button-eyed bison head, where years ago, on the day that Sophie Mol came, *Welcome Home, Our Sophie Mol* was performed.

Things can change in a day.

8

Welcome Home, Our Sophie Mol

It was a grand old house, the Ayemenem House, but aloof-looking. As though it had little to do with the people that lived in it. Like an old man with rheumy eyes watching children play, seeing only transience in their shrill elation and their whole-hearted commitment to life.

The steep, tiled roof had grown dark and mossy with age and rain. The triangular wooden frames fitted into the gables were intricately carved, the light that slanted through them and fell in patterns on the floor was full of secrets. Wolves. Flowers. Iguanas. Changing shape as the sun moved through the sky. Dying punctually, at dusk.

The doors had not two, but four shutters of panelled teak so that in the old days, ladies could keep the bottom half closed, lean their elbows on the ledge and bargain with visiting vendors without betraying themselves below the waist. Technically, they could buy carpets, or bangles, with their breasts covered and their bottoms bare. Technically.

Nine steep steps led from the driveway up to the front veran-dah. The elevation gave it the dignity of a stage and everything that happened there took on the aura and significance of per-formance. It overlooked Baby Kochamma's ornamental garden, the gravel driveway looped around it, sloping down towards the bottom of the slight hill that the house stood on.

It was a deep verandah, cool even at midday, when the sun was at its scorching best.

When the red cement floor was laid, the egg white from nearly nine hundred eggs went into it. It took a high polish.

Below the stuffed, button-eyed bison head, with the portraits of her father-in-law and mother-in-law on either side, Mammachi sat in a low wicker chair at a wicker table on which stood a green glass vase with a single stem of purple orchids curving from it.

The afternoon was still and hot. The Air was waiting.

Mammachi held a gleaming violin under her chin. Her opaque fifties sunglasses were black and slanty-eyed, with rhinestones on the corners of the frames. Her sari was starched and perfumed. Off-white and gold. Her diamond earrings shone in her ears like tiny chandeliers. Her ruby rings were loose. Her pale, fine skin was creased like cream on cooling milk and dusted with tiny red moles. She was beautiful. Old, unusual, regal.

Blind Mother Widow with a violin.

In her younger years with prescience, and good management, Mammachi had collected all her falling hair in a small, embroidered purse that she kept on her dressing table. When there was enough of it, she made it into a netted bun which she kept hidden in a locker with her jewellery. A few years earlier, when her hair began to thin and silver, to give it body, she wore her jet-black bun pinned to her small, silver head. In her book this was perfectly acceptable, since all the hair was hers. At night, when she took off her bun, she allowed her grandchildren to plait her remaining hair into a tight, oiled, grey rat's tail with a rubber band at the end. One plaited her hair, while the other counted her uncountable moles. They took turns.

On her scalp, carefully hidden by her scanty hair, Mammachi had raised, crescent-shaped ridges. Scars of old beatings from an old marriage. Her brass vase scars.

She played *Lentement* – a movement from the Suite 1 in D/G of

Handel's *Water Music*. Behind her slanted sunglasses, her useless eyes were closed, but she could see the music as it left her violin and lifted into the afternoon like smoke.

Inside her head, it was like a room with dark drapes drawn across a bright day.

As she played, her mind wandered back over the years to her first batch of professional pickles. How beautiful they had looked! Bottled and sealed, standing on a table near the head of her bed, so they'd be the first thing she would touch in the morning when she woke up. She had gone to bed early that night, but woke a little after midnight. She groped for them, and her anxious fingers came away with a film of oil. The pickle bottles stood in a pool of oil. There was oil everywhere. In a ring under her vacuum flask. Under her Bible. All over her bedside table. The pickled mangoes had absorbed oil and expanded, making the bottles leak.

Mammachi consulted the book that Chacko bought her, *Homescale Preservations*, but it offered no solutions. Then she dictated a letter to Annamma Chandy's brother-in-law, who was the Regional Manager of Padma Pickles in Bombay. He suggested that she increase the proportion of preservative that she used. And the salt. That had helped, but didn't solve the problem entirely. Even now, after all those years, Paradise Pickles' bottles still leaked a little. It was imperceptible, but they did still leak, and on long journeys their labels became oily and transparent. The pickles themselves continued to be a little on the salty side.

Mammachi wondered whether she would ever master the art of perfect preservation, and whether Sophie Mol would like some iced grape crush. Some cold purple juice in a glass.

Then she thought of Margaret Kochamma and the languid, liquid notes of Handel's music grew shrill and angry.

Mammachi had never met Margaret Kochamma. But she despised her anyway. *Shopkeeper's daughter* – was how Margaret

Kochamma was filed away in Mammachi's mind. Mammachi's world was arranged that way. If she was invited to a wedding in Kottayam, she would spend the whole time whispering to whoever she went with, 'The bride's maternal grandfather was my father's carpenter. Kunjukutty Eapen? His great-grandmother's sister was just a midwife in Trivandrum. My husband's family used to own this whole hill.'

Of course Mammachi would have despised Margaret Kochamma even if she had been heir to the throne of England. It wasn't just her working-class background Mammachi resented. She hated Margaret Kochamma for being Chacko's wife. She hated her for leaving him. But would have hated her even more had she stayed.

The day that Chacko prevented Pappachi from beating her (and Pappachi had murdered his chair instead), Mammachi packed her wifely luggage and committed it to Chacko's care. From then onwards he became the repository of all her womanly feelings. Her Man. Her only Love.

She was aware of his libertine relationships with the women in the factory, but had ceased to be hurt by them. When Baby Kochamma brought up the subject, Mammachi became tense and tight-lipped.

'He can't help having a Man's Needs,' she said primly.

Surprisingly, Baby Kochamma accepted this explanation, and the enigmatic, secretly thrilling notion of Men's Needs gained implicit sanction in the Ayemenem House. Neither Mammachi nor Baby Kochamma saw any contradiction between Chacko's Marxist mind and feudal libido. They only worried about the Naxalites, who had been known to force men from Good Families to marry servant girls whom they had made pregnant. Of course they did not even remotely suspect that the missile, when it *was* fired, the one that would annihilate the family's Good Name for ever, would come from a completely unexpected quarter.

Mammachi had a separate entrance built for Chacko's room, which was at the eastern end of the house, so that the objects of his 'Needs' wouldn't have to go traipsing *through* the house. She secretly slipped them money to keep them happy. They took it because they needed it. They had young children and old parents. Or husbands who spent all their earnings in toddy bars. The arrangement suited Mammachi, because in her mind, a fee *clarified* things. Disjuncted sex from love. Needs from Feelings.

Margaret Kochamma, however, was a different kettle of fish altogether. Since she had no means of finding out (though she did once try to get Kochu Maria to examine the bedsheets for stains), Mammachi could only hope that Margaret Kochamma was not intending to resume her sexual relationship with Chacko. While Margaret Kochamma was in Ayemenem Mammachi managed her otherwise unmanageable feelings by slipping money into the pockets of the dresses that Margaret Kochamma left in the laundry bin. Margaret Kochamma never returned the money simply because she never found it. Her pockets were emptied as a matter of routine by Aniyan the dhobi. Mammachi knew this, but preferred to construe Margaret Kochamma's silence as a tacit acceptance of payment for the favours Mammachi imagined she bestowed on her son.

So Mammachi had the satisfaction of regarding Margaret Kochamma as just another whore, Aniyan the dhobi was happy with his daily gratuity, and of course Margaret Kochamma remained blissfully unaware of the whole arrangement.

From its perch on the well, an untidy coucal called *Hwoop Hwoop* and shuffled its rust-red wings.

A crow stole some soap that bubbled in its beak.

In the dark, smoky kitchen, short Kochu Maria stood on her toes and iced the tall, double-deckered WELCOME HOME OUR SOPHIE MOL cake. Though even in those days most Syrian

Christian women had started wearing saris, Kochu Maria still wore her spotless half-sleeved white chatta with a V-neck and her white mundu, which folded into a crisp cloth fan on her behind. Kochu Maria's fan was more or less hidden by the blue and white checked, frilled, absurdly incongruous housemaid's apron that Mammachi insisted she wear inside the house.

She had short, thick forearms, fingers like cocktail sausages, and a broad fleshy nose with flared nostrils. Deep folds of skin connected her nose to either side of her chin, and separated that section of her face from the rest of it, like a snout. Her head was too large for her body. She looked like a bottled foetus that had escaped from its jar of formaldehyde in a Biology lab and unshrivelled and thickened with age.

She kept damp cash in her bodice which she tied tightly around her chest to flatten her unchristian breasts. Her kunukku earrings were thick and gold. Her earlobes had been distended into weighted loops that swung around her neck, her earrings sitting in them like gleeful children in a merry-go-(not all the way)round. Her right lobe had split open once and was sewn together again by Dr Verghese Verghese. Kochu Maria couldn't stop wearing her kunukku because if she did, how would people know that despite her lowly cook's job (seventy-five rupees a month) she was a Syrian Christian, Mar Thomite? Not a Pelaya, or a Pulaya, or a Paravan. But a Touchable, upper-caste Christian (into whom Christianity had seeped like tea from a teabag). Split lobes stitched back were a better option by far.

Kochu Maria hadn't yet made her acquaintance with the television addict waiting inside her. The Hulk Hogan addict. She hadn't yet seen a television set. She wouldn't have believed television existed. Had someone suggested that it did, Kochu Maria would have assumed that he or she was insulting her intelligence. Kochu Maria was wary of other people's versions of the outside world. More often than not, she took them to be a deliberate affront to her lack of education and (earlier) gullibility. In a determined reversal of her inherent nature, Kochu Maria now, as a policy, hardly ever believed anything that anybody said. A few months ago, in July, when Rahel told her that an American astronaut called Neil Armstrong had walked on the moon, she laughed sarcastically and said that a Malayali acrobat called O. Muthachen had done handsprings on the sun. With pencils up his nose. She was prepared to concede that Americans *existed* though she'd never seen one. She was even prepared to believe that Neil Armstrong might conceivably even be some absurd kind of name. But the walking on the moon bit? No sir. Nor did she trust the vague grey pictures that had appeared in the *Malayala Manorama* that she couldn't read.

She remained certain that Estha, when he said, '*Et tu, Kochu Maria!*' was insulting her in English. She thought it meant something like *Kochu Maria, you ugly black dwarf.* She bided her time, waiting for a suitable opportunity to complain about him.

She finished icing the tall cake. Then she tipped her head back and squeezed the leftover icing on to her tongue. Endless coils of chocolate toothpaste on a pink Kochu Maria tongue. When Mammachi called from the verandah ('Kochu Mariye! I hear the car!') her mouth was full of icing and she couldn't answer. When she finished, she ran her tongue over her teeth and then made a series of short smacking sounds with her tongue against her palate as though she'd just eaten something sour.

Distant skyblue carsounds (past the bus stop, past the school, past the yellow church and up the bumpy red road through the rubber trees) sent a murmur through the dim, sooty premises of Paradise Pickles.

The pickling (and the squashing, the slicing, boiling and stirring, the grating, salting, drying, the weighing and bottle sealing) stopped.

'*Chacko Saar vannu,*' the travelling whisper went. Chopping knives were put down. Vegetables were abandoned, half cut, on huge steel platters. Desolate bitter gourds, incomplete pine-apples. Coloured rubber finger-guards (bright, like cheerful, thick condoms) were taken off. Pickled hands were washed and wiped on cobalt-blue aprons. Escaped wisps of hair were recaptured and returned to white headscarves. Mundus tucked up under aprons were let down. The gauze doors of the factory had sprung hinges, and closed noisily on their own.

And on one side of the driveway, beside the old well, in the shade of the kodam puli tree, a silent blue-aproned army gathered in the greenheat to watch.

Blue-aproned, white-capped, like a clot of smart blue and white flags.

Achoo, Jose, Yako, Anian, Elayan, Kuttan, Vijayan, Vawa, Joy, Sumathi, Ammal, Annamma, Kanakamma, Latha, Sushila, Vijayamma, Jollykutty, Mollykuty, Lucykutty, Beena Mol (girls with bus names). The early rumblings of discontent, concealed under a thick layer of loyalty.

The skyblue Plymouth turned in at the gate and crunched over the gravel driveway crushing small shells and shattering little red and yellow pebbles. Children tumbled out.

Collapsed fountains.

Flattened puffs.

Crumpled yellow bellbottoms and a go-go bag that was loved. Jet-lagged and barely awake. Then the swollen-ankled adults. Slow from too much sitting.

'Have you arrived?' Mammachi asked, turning her slanty dark glasses towards the new sounds: car doors slamming, getting-outedness. She lowered her violin.

'Mammachi!' Rahel said to her beautiful blind grandmother. 'Estha vomited! In the middle of *The Sound of Music*! And . . .'

Ammu touched her daughter gently. On her shoulder. And her touch meant *Shhhh* . . . Rahel looked around her and saw that she was in a Play. But she had only a small part.

She was just the landscape. A flower perhaps. Or a tree.

A face in the crowd. A townspeople.

Nobody said Hello to Rahel. Not even the Blue Army in the greenheat.

'Where is she?' Mammachi asked the car sounds. 'Where is my Sophie Mol? Come here and let me see you.'

As she spoke, the Waiting Melody that hung over her like a shimmering temple elephant's umbrella crumbled and gently fell about like dust.

Chacko, in his *What Happened to Our Man of the Masses?* suit and well-fed tie, led Margaret Kochamma and Sophie Mol triumphantly up the nine red steps like a pair of tennis trophies that he had recently won.

And once again, only the Small Things were said. The Big Things lurked unsaid inside. 'Hello, Mammachi,' Margaret Kochamma said in her kind-schoolteacher (that sometimes slapped) voice. 'Thank you for having us. We needed so much to get away.'

Mammachi caught a whiff of inexpensive perfume soured at the edges by airline sweat. (She herself had a bottle of Dior in its soft green leather pouch locked away in her safe.)

Margaret Kochamma took Mammachi's hand. The fingers were soft, the ruby rings were hard.

'Hello, Margaret,' Mammachi said (not rude, not polite), her dark glasses still on. 'Welcome to Ayemenem. I'm sorry I can't see you. As you must know, I am almost blind.' She spoke in a slow deliberate manner.

'Oh that's all right,' Margaret Kochamma said. 'I'm sure I look terrible anyway.' She laughed uncertainly, not sure if it was the right response.

'Wrong,' Chacko said. He turned to Mammachi, smiling a proud smile that his mother couldn't see. 'She's as lovely as ever.'

'I was very sorry to hear about . . . Joe,' Mammachi said. She sounded only a little sorry. Not very sorry.

There was a short, Sad-About-Joe silence.

'Where's my Sophie Mol?' Mammachi said. 'Come here and let your grandmother look at you.'

Sophie Mol was led to Mammachi. Mammachi pushed her dark sunglasses up into her hair. They looked up like slanting cat's eyes at the mouldy bison head. The mouldy bison said, '*No. Absolutely Not.*' In Mouldy Bisonese.

Even after her cornea transplant, Mammachi could only see light and shadow. If somebody was standing in the doorway, she could tell that someone was standing in the doorway. But not who it was. She could read a cheque, or a receipt, or a bank note only if it was close enough for her eyelashes to touch it. She would then hold it steady, and move her eye along it. Wheeling it from word to word.

The Townspeople (in her fairy frock) saw Mammachi draw Sophie Mol close to her eyes to look at her. To read her like a cheque. To check her like a bank note. Mammachi (with her better eye) saw redbrown hair (N . . . Nalmost blond), the curve of two fatfreckled cheeks (Nnnn . . . almost rosy), bluegreyblue eyes.

'Pappachi's nose,' Mammachi said. 'Tell me, are you a pretty girl?' she asked Sophie Mol.

'Yes,' Sophie Mol said.

'And tall?'

'Tall for my age,' Sophie Mol said.

'Very tall,' Baby Kochamma said. 'Much taller than Estha.'

'She's older,' Ammu said.

'Still . . .' Baby Kochamma said.

A little way away, Velutha walked up the shortcut through the rubber trees. Barebodied. A coil of insulated electrical wire was looped over one shoulder. He wore his printed dark blue and black mundu loosely folded up above his knees. On his back, his lucky leaf from the birthmark tree (that made the monsoons come on time). His autumn leaf at night.

Before he emerged through the trees and stepped into the driveway, Rahel saw him and slipped out of the Play and went to him.

Ammu saw her go.

Off stage, she watched them perform their elaborate Official Greeting. Velutha curtsied as he had been taught to, his mundu spread like a skirt, like the English dairymaid in *The King's Breakfast*. Rahel bowed (and said 'Bow'). Then they hooked little fingers and shook hands gravely with the mien of bankers at a convention.

In the dappled sunlight filtering through the dark green trees, Ammu watched Velutha lift her daughter effortlessly as though she was an inflatable child, made of air. As he tossed her up and she landed in his arms, Ammu saw on Rahel's face the high delight of the airborne young.

She saw the ridges of muscle on Velutha's stomach grow taught and rise under his skin like the divisions on a slab of chocolate. She wondered at how his body had changed – so quietly, from a flatmuscled boy's body into a man's body. Contoured and hard. A swimmer's body. A swimmer-carpenter's body. Polished with a high-wax body polish.

He had high cheekbones and a white, sudden smile.

It was his smile that reminded Ammu of Velutha as a little boy. Helping Vellya Paapen to count coconuts. Holding out little gifts he had made for her, flat on the palm of his hand so that she could take them without touching him. Boats, boxes, small windmills. Calling her Ammukutty. Little Ammu. Though she was so much less little than he was. When she looked at him now, she couldn't help thinking that the man he had become bore so little resemblance to the boy he had been. His smile was the only piece of baggage he had carried with him from boyhood into manhood.

Suddenly Ammu hoped that it *had* been him that Rahel saw in the march. She hoped it had been him that had raised his flag and knotted arm in anger. She hoped that under his careful cloak of cheerfulness, he housed a living, breathing anger against the smug, ordered world that she so raged against.

She hoped it had been him.

She was surprised at the extent of her daughter's physical ease with him. Surprised that her child seemed to have a sub-world that excluded *her* entirely. A tactile world of smiles and laughter that she, her mother, had no part in. Ammu recognized vaguely that her thoughts were shot with a delicate, purple tinge of envy. She didn't allow herself to consider whom it was that she envied. The man or her own child. Or just their world of hooked fingers and sudden smiles.

The man standing in the shade of the rubber trees with coins of sunshine dancing on his body, holding her daughter in his arms, glanced up and caught Ammu's gaze. Centuries tele-scoped into one evanescent moment. History was wrong-footed, caught off guard. Sloughed off like an old snakeskin. Its marks, its scars, its wounds from old wars and the walking backwards days all fell away. In its absence it left an aura, a palpable shimmering that was as plain to see as the water in a river or the sun in the sky. As plain to feel as the heat on a hot day, or the tug of a fish on a taut line. So obvious that no one noticed.

In that brief moment, Velutha looked up and saw things that he hadn't seen before. Things that had been out of bounds so far, obscured by history's blinkers.

Simple things.

For instance, he saw that Rahel's mother was a woman.

That she had deep dimples when she smiled and that they stayed on long after her smile left her eyes. He saw that her brown arms were round and firm and perfect. That her shoul-ders shone, but her eyes were somewhere else. He saw that when he gave her gifts they no longer needed to be offered flat on the palms of his hands so that she wouldn't have to touch him. His boats and boxes. His little windmills. He saw too that he was not necessarily the only giver of gifts. That *she* had gifts to give him too.

This knowing slid into him cleanly, like the sharp edge of a knife. Cold and hot at once. It only took a moment.

Ammu saw that he saw. She looked away. He did too. History's fiends returned to claim them. To rewrap them in its old, scarred pelt and drag them back to where they really lived. Where the Love Laws lay down who should be loved. And how. And how much.

Ammu walked up to the verandah, back into the Play. Shaking.

Velutha looked down at Ambassador S. Insect in his arms. He put her down. Shaking too.

'And look at you!' he said, looking at her ridiculous frothy frock. 'So beautiful! Getting married?'

Rahel lunged at his armpits and tickled him mercilessly. *Ickilee ickilee ickilee!*

'I *saw* you yesterday,' she said.

'Where?' Velutha made his voice high and surprised.

'Liar,' Rahel said. 'Liar and pretender. I did see you. You were a communist and had a shirt and a flag. *And* you ignored me.'

'*Aiyyo kashtam*,' Velutha said. 'Would I do that? *You* tell me, would Velutha *ever* do that? It must've been my Long-lost Twin brother.'

'Which Long-lost Twin brother?'

'Urumban silly . . . The one who lives in Kochi.'

'Who Urumban?' Then she saw the twinkle. 'Liar! You haven't got a twin brother! It wasn't Urumban! It was *you*!'

Velutha laughed. He had a lovely laugh that he really meant.

'Wasn't me,' he said. 'I was sick in bed.'

'See, you're smiling!' Rahel said. 'That means it was you. Smiling means, "It was you."'

'That's only in English!' Velutha said. 'In Malayalam my teacher always said, "Smiling means it wasn't me." '

It took Rahel a moment to sort that one out. She lunged at him once again. *Ickilee ickilee ickilee!*

Still laughing, Velutha looked into the Play for Sophie. 'Where's our Sophie Mol? Let's take a look at her. Did you remember to bring her, or did you leave her behind?'

'Don't look there,' Rahel said urgently.

She stood up on the cement parapet that separated the rubber trees from the driveway, and clapped her hands over Velutha's eyes.

'Why?' Velutha said.

'Because,' Rahel said, 'I don't want you to.'

'Where's Estha Mon?' Velutha said, with an Ambassador (disguised as a Stick Insect disguised as an Airport Fairy) hanging down his back with her legs wrapped around his waist, blindfolding him with her sticky little hands. 'I haven't seen him.'

'Oh we sold him in Cochin,' Rahel said airily. 'For a bag of rice. And a torch.'

The froth of her stiff frock pressed rough lace flowers into Velutha's back. Lace flowers and a lucky leaf bloomed on a black back.

But when Rahel searched the Play for Estha, she saw that he wasn't there.

Back inside the Play, Kochu Maria arrived, short, behind her tall cake.

'Cake's come,' she said, a little loudly, to Mammachi.

Kochu Maria always spoke a little loudly to Mammachi because she assumed that poor eyesight automatically affected the other senses.

'*Kando*, Kochu Mariye?' Mammachi said. 'Can you see our Sophie Mol?'

'*Kandoo*, Kochamma,' Kochu Maria said extra loud. 'I can see her.'

She smiled at Sophie, extra wide. She was exactly Sophie's height. More short than Syrian Christian, despite her best efforts.

'She has her mother's colour,' Kochu Maria said.

'Pappachi's nose,' Mammachi insisted.

'I don't know about that, but she's very beautiful,' Kochu Maria shouted. '*Sundarikutty*. She's a little angel.'

Littleangels were beach-coloured and wore bellbottoms.

Littledemons were mudbrown in Airport Fairy frocks with forehead bumps that might turn into horns. With Fountains in Love-in-Tokyos. And backward-reading habits.

And if you cared to look, you could see Satan in their eyes.

Kochu Maria took both Sophie's hands in hers, palms upward, raised them to her face and inhaled deeply.

'What's she doing?' Sophie wanted to know, tender London hands clasped in calloused Ayemenem ones. 'Who's she and why's she smelling my hands?'

'She's the cook,' Chacko said. 'That's her way of kissing you.'

'Kissing?' Sophie Mol was unconvinced, but interested.

'How marvellous!' Margaret Kochamma said. 'It's a sort of sniffing! Do the men and women do it to each other too?'

She hadn't meant it to sound quite like that, and she blushed. An embarrassed schoolteacher-shaped hole in the Universe.

'Oh, all the time!' Ammu said, and it came out a little louder than the sarcastic mumble that she had intended. 'That's how we make babies.'

Chacko didn't slap her.

So she didn't slap him back.

But the Waiting Air grew Angry.

'I think you owe my wife an apology, Ammu,' Chacko said, with a protective, proprietorial air, (hoping that Margaret Kochamma wouldn't say, '*Ex-wife, Chacko!*' and wag a rose at him).

'Oh no!' Margaret Kochamma said. 'It was my fault! I never meant it to sound quite like that . . . what I meant was – I mean it is fascinating to think that –'

'It was a perfectly legitimate question,' Chacko said. 'And I think Ammu ought to apologize.'

'Must we behave like some damn godforsaken tribe that's just been discovered?' Ammu asked.

'Oh dear!' Margaret Kochamma said.

In the angry quietness of the Play (the Blue Army in the greenheat still watching), Ammu walked back to the Plymouth, took out her suitcase, slammed the door, and walked away to her room, her shoulders shining. Leaving everybody to wonder where she had learned her effrontery from.

And truth be told, it was no small wondering matter.

Because Ammu had not had the kind of education, nor read the sorts of books, nor met the sorts of people, that might have influenced her to think the way she did.

She was just that sort of animal.

As a child, she had learned very quickly to disregard the Father Bear Mother Bear stories she was given to read. In her version, Father Bear beat Mother Bear with brass vases. Mother Bear suffered those beatings with mute resignation.

In her growing years, Ammu had watched her father weave his hideous web. He was charming and urbane with visitors, and stopped just short of fawning on them if they happened to be white. He donated money to orphanages and leprosy clinics. He worked hard on his public profile as a sophisticated, generous, moral man. But alone with his wife and children he turned into a monstrous, suspicious bully, with a streak of vicious cunning. They were beaten, humiliated and then made to suffer the envy of friends and relations for having such a wonderful husband and father.

Ammu had endured cold winter nights in Delhi hiding in the

mehndi hedge around their house (in case people from Good Families saw them) because Pappachi had come back from work out of sorts, and beaten her and Mammachi and driven them out of their home.

On one such night, Ammu, aged nine, hiding with her mother in the hedge, watched Pappachi's natty silhouette in the lit windows as he flitted from room to room. Not content with having beaten his wife and daughter (Chacko was away at school), he tore down curtains, kicked furniture and smashed a table lamp. An hour after the lights went out, disdaining Mammachi's frightened pleading, little Ammu crept back into the house through a ventilator to rescue her new gumboots that she loved more than anything else. She put them in a paper bag and crept back into the drawing room when the lights were suddenly switched on.

Pappachi had been sitting in his mahogany rocking chair all along, rocking himself silently in the dark. When he caught her, he didn't say a word. He flogged her with his ivory-handled riding crop (the one that he had held across his lap in his studio photograph). Ammu didn't cry. When he finished beating her he made her bring him Mammachi's pinking shears from her sewing cupboard. While Ammu watched, the Imperial Entomologist shred her new gumboots with her mother's pinking shears. The strips of black rubber fell to the floor. The scissors made snicking scissor-sounds. Ammu ignored her mother's drawn, frightened face that appeared at the window. It took ten minutes for her beloved gumboots to be completely shredded. When the last strip of rubber had rippled to the floor, her father looked at her with cold, flat eyes, and rocked and rocked and rocked. Surrounded by a sea of twisting, rubber snakes.

As she grew older, Ammu learned to live with this cold, calculating cruelty. She developed a lofty sense of injustice and the mulish, reckless streak that develops in Someone Small who has been bullied all their lives by Someone Big. She did exactly nothing to avoid quarrels and confrontations. In fact, it could be argued that she sought them out, perhaps even enjoyed them.

'Has she gone?' Mammachi asked the silence around her.

'She's gone,' Kochu Maria said loudly.

'Are you allowed to say "damn" in India?' Sophie Mol asked.

'Who said "damn"?' Chacko asked.

'She did,' Sophie Mol said. 'Aunty Ammu. She said, "some damn godforsaken tribe".'

'Cut the cake and give everybody a piece,' Mammachi said.

'Because in England, we're not,' Sophie Mol said to Chacko.

'Not what?' Chacko said.

'Allowed to say Dee Ay Em En,' Sophie Mol said.

Mammachi looked sightlessly out into the shining afternoon. 'Is everyone here?' she asked.

'*Oower*, Kochamma,' the Blue Army in the greenheat said. 'We're all here.'

Outside the Play, Rahel said to Velutha: '*We're* not here, are we? We're not even Playing.'

'That is Exactly Right,' Velutha said. 'We're not even Playing. But what I would like to know is, where is our Esthappappy-chachen Kuttappen Peter Mon?'

And that became a delighted, breathless, Rumplestiltskin-like dance among the rubber trees.

> *Oh Esthapappychachen Kuttappen Peter Mon,*
> *Where, oh where have you gon?*

And from Rumplestiltskin it graduated to the Scarlet Pimpernel.

> *We seek him here, we seek him there,*
> *Those Frenchies seek him everywhere.*

Is he in heaven? Is he in hell?
That demmedel-usive Estha – Pen?

Kochu Maria cut a sample piece of cake for Mammachi's approval.

'One piece each,' Mammachi confirmed to Kochu Maria, touching the piece lightly with rubyringed fingers to see if it was small enough.

Kochu Maria sawed up the rest of the cake messily, laboriously, breathing through her mouth, as though she was carving a hunk of roast lamb. She put the pieces on a large silver tray. Mammachi played a *Welcome Home, Our Sophie Mol* melody on her violin. A cloying, chocolate melody. Stickysweet, and meltybrown. Chocolate waves on a chocolate shore.

In the middle of the melody, Chacko raised his voice over the chocolate sound. 'Mamma!' he said (in his Reading Aloud voice). 'Mamma! That's enough! Enough violin!'

Mammachi stopped playing and looked in Chacko's direction, the bow poised in midair.

'Enough? D'you think that's enough, Chacko?'

'More than enough,' Chacko said.

'Enough's enough,' Mammachi murmured to herself. 'I think I'll stop now.' As though the idea had suddenly occurred to her.

She put her violin away into its black, violin-shaped box. It closed like a suitcase. And the music closed with it.

Click. And click.

Mammachi put her dark glasses on again. And drew the drapes across the hot day.

Ammu emerged from the house and called to Rahel.

'Rahel! I want you to have your afternoon nap! Come in after you've had your cake!'

Rahel's heart sank. Afternoon Gnap. She hated those.

Ammu went back indoors.

Velutha put Rahel down, and she stood forlornly at the edge of the driveway, on the periphery of the Play, a Gnap looming large and nasty on her horizon.

'And please stop being so over-familiar with that man!' Baby Kochamma said to Rahel.

'Over-familiar?' Mammachi said. 'Who is it, Chacko? Who's being over-familiar?'

'Rahel,' Baby Kochamma said.

'Over-familiar with *who?*'

'With whom,' Chacko corrected his mother.

'All right, with *whom* is she being over-familiar?' Mammachi asked.

'Your Beloved Velutha – whom else?' Baby Kochamma said, and to Chacko – 'Ask him where he was yesterday. Let's bell the cat once and for all.'

'Not now,' Chacko said.

'What's over-familiar?' Sophie Mol asked Margaret Kochamma, who didn't answer.

'Velutha? Is Velutha here? Are you here?' Mammachi asked the Afternoon.

'*Oower*, Kochamma.' He stepped through the trees into the Play.

'Did you find out what it was?' Mammachi asked.

'The washer in the foot-valve,' Velutha said. 'I've changed it. It's working now.'

'Then switch it on,' Mammachi said. 'The tank is empty.'

'That man will be our Nemesis,' Baby Kochamma said. Not because she was clairvoyant and had had a sudden flash of prophetic vision. Just to get him into trouble. Nobody paid her any attention.

'Mark my words,' she said bitterly.

'See her?' Kochu Maria said when she got to Rahel with her tray of cake. She meant Sophie Mol. 'When she grows up, she'll be our Kochamma, and she'll raise our salaries, and give us nylon saris for Onam.' Kochu Maria collected saris, though she hadn't ever worn one, and probably never would.

'So what?' Rahel said. 'By then I'll be living in Africa.'

'Africa?' Kochu Maria sniggered. 'Africa's full of ugly black people and mosquitoes.'

'You're the only one who's ugly,' Rahel said, and added (in English) 'Stupid dwarf!'

'What did you say?' Kochu Maria said threateningly. 'Don't tell me. I know. I heard. I'll tell Mammachi. Just wait!'

Rahel walked across to the old well where there were usually some ants to kill. Red ants that had a sour farty smell when they were squashed. Kochu Maria followed her with the tray of cake.

Rahel said she didn't want any of the stupid cake.

'*Kushumbi*,' Kochu Maria said. 'Jealous people go straight to hell.'

'Who's jealous?'

'I don't know. You tell me,' Kochu Maria said, with a frilly apron and a vinegar heart.

Rahel put on her sunglasses and looked back into the Play. Everything was Angry-coloured. Sophie Mol, standing between Margaret Kochamma and Chacko, looked as though she ought to be slapped. Rahel found a whole column of juicy ants. They were on their way to church. All dressed in red. They had to be killed before they got there. Squished and squashed with a stone. You can't have smelly ants in church.

The ants made a faint crunchy sound as life left them. Like an elf eating toast, or a crisp biscuit.

The Antly Church would be empty and the Antly Bishop would wait in his funny Antly Bishop clothes, swinging Frankincense in a silver pot. And nobody would arrive.

After he had waited for a reasonably Antly amount of time, he would get a funny Antly Bishop frown on his forehead, and shake his head sadly.

He would look at the glowing Antly stained-glass windows and when he finished looking at them, he would lock the church with an enormous key and make it dark. Then he'd go home to his wife, and (if she wasn't dead) they'd have an Antly Afternoon Gnap.

Sophie Mol, hatted, bellbottomed and Loved from the Beginning, walked out of the Play to see what Rahel was doing behind the well. But the Play went with her. Walked when she walked, stopped when she stopped. Fond smiles followed her. Kochu Maria moved the caketray out of the way of her adoring downwards smile as Sophie squatted down in the well-squelch (yellow bottoms of bells muddy wet now).

Sophie Mol inspected the smelly mayhem with clinical detachment. The stone was coated with crushed red carcasses and a few feebly waving legs.

Kochu Maria watched with her cake-crumbs.

The Fond Smiles watched Fondly.

Little Girls Playing.

Sweet.

One beach-coloured.

One brown.

One Loved.

One Loved a Little Less.

'Let's leave one alive so that it can be lonely,' Sophie Mol suggested.

Rahel ignored her and killed them all. Then in her frothy Airport Frock with matching knickers (no longer crisp) and unmatching sunglasses, she ran away. Disappeared into the green heat.

The Fond Smiles stayed on Sophie Mol, like a spotlight, thinking perhaps, that the sweet cousins were playing hide-and-seek, like sweet cousins often do.

9

Mrs Pillai, Mrs Eapen,
Mrs Rajagopalan

The green-for-the-day had seeped from the trees. Dark palm leaves were splayed like drooping combs against the monsoon sky. The orange sun slid through their bent, grasping teeth.

A squadron of fruit bats sped across the gloom.

In the abandoned ornamental garden, Rahel, watched by lolling dwarves and a forsaken cherub, squatted by the stagnant pond and watched toads hop from stone to scummy stone. Beautiful Ugly Toads.

Slimy. Warty. Croaking.

Yearning, unkissed princes trapped inside them. Food for snakes that lurked in the long June grass. Rustle. Lunge. No more toad to hop from stone to scummy stone. No more prince to kiss.

It was the first night since she'd come that it hadn't rained.

Around now, Rahel thought, *if this were Washington, I would be on my way to work. The bus ride. The streetlights. The gas fumes. The shapes of people's breath on the bulletproof glass of my cabin. The clatter of coins pushed towards me in the metal tray. The smell of money on my fingers. The punctual drunk with sober eyes who arrives exactly at 10 p.m.: 'Hey, you! Black bitch! Suck my dick!'*

She owned seven hundred dollars. And a gold bangle with snakeheads. But Baby Kochamma had already asked her how much longer she planned to stay. And what she planned to do about Estha.

She had no plans.

No plans.

No Locusts Stand I.

She looked back at the looming, gabled, house-shaped hole in the Universe and imagined living in the silver bowl that Baby Kochamma had installed on the roof. It *looked* large enough for people to live in. Certainly it was bigger than a lot of people's homes. Bigger, for instance, than Kochu Maria's cramped quarters.

If they slept there, she and Estha, curled together like foetuses in a shallow steel womb, what would Hulk Hogan and Bam Bam Bigelow do? If the dish were occupied, where would *they* go? Would they slip through the chimney into Baby Kochamma's life and TV? Would they land on the old stove with a *Heeaagh!*, in their muscles and spangled clothes? Would the Thin People – the famine victims and refugees – slip through the cracks in the doors? Would Genocide slide between the tiles?

The sky was thick with TV. If you wore special glasses you could see them spinning through the sky among the bats and homing birds – blondes, wars, famines, football, food shows, coups d'état, hairstyles stiff with hairspray. Designer pectorals. Gliding towards Ayemenem like skydivers. Making patterns in the sky. Wheels. Windmills. Flowers blooming and unblooming.

Heeaagh!

Rahel returned to contemplating toads.

Fat. Yellow. From stone to scummy stone. She touched one gently. It moved its eyelids upwards. Funnily self-assured.

Nictitating membrane, she remembered she and Estha once spent a whole day saying. She and Estha and Sophie Mol.

Nictitating
ictitating
titating
itating
tating
ating
ting
ing

They were, all three of them, wearing saris (old ones, torn in half) that day, Estha was the draping expert. He pleated Sophie Mol's pleats. Organized Rahel's pallu and settled his own. They had red bindis on their foreheads. In the process of trying to wash out Ammu's forbidden kohl, they had smudged it all over their eyes, and on the whole looked like three raccoons trying to pass off as Hindu ladies. It was about a week after Sophie Mol arrived. A week before she died. By then she had performed unfalteringly under the twins' perspicacious scrutiny and had confounded all their expectations.

She had:

(a) Informed Chacko that even though he was her Real Father, she loved him less than Joe – (which left him available – even if not inclined – to be the surrogate father of certain two-egg persons greedy for his affection).

(b) Turned down Mammachi's offer that she replace Estha and Rahel as the privileged plaiter of Mammachi's nightly rat's tail and counter of moles.

(c) (& Most Important) – Astutely gauged the prevailing temper, and not just rejected, but rejected outright and extremely rudely, all of Baby Kochamma's advances and small seductions.

As if this were not enough, she also revealed herself to be human. One day the twins returned from a clandestine trip to the river (which had excluded Sophie Mol), and found her in the garden in tears, perched on the highest point of Baby

Kochamma's Herb Curl, 'Being Lonely,' as she put it. The next day Estha and Rahel took her with them to visit Velutha.

They visited him in saris, clumping gracelessly through red mud and long grass (*Nictitating ictitating tating ating ting ing*) and introduced themselves as Mrs Pillai, Mrs Eapen and Mrs Rajagopalan. Velutha introduced himself and his paralysed brother, Kuttappen (although he was fast asleep). He greeted them with the utmost courtesy. He addressed them all as Kochamma and gave them fresh coconut water to drink. He chatted to them about the weather. The river. The fact that in his opinion coconut trees were getting shorter by the year. As were the ladies in Ayemenem. He introduced them to his surly hen. He showed them his carpentry tools, and whittled them each a little wooden spoon.

It is only now, these years later, that Rahel with adult hindsight, recognized the sweetness of that gesture. A grown man entertaining three raccoons, treating them like real ladies. Instinctively colluding in the conspiracy of their fiction, taking care not to decimate it with adult carelessness. Or affection.

It is after all so easy to shatter a story. To break a chain of thought. To ruin a fragment of a dream being carried around carefully like a piece of porcelain.

To let it be, to travel with it, as Velutha did, is much the harder thing to do.

Three days before the Terror, he had let them paint his nails with red Cutex that Ammu had discarded. That's the way he was the day History visited them in the back verandah. A carpenter with gaudy nails. The posse of Touchable Policemen had looked at them and laughed.

'What's this?' one had said. 'AC-DC?'

Another lifted his boot with a millipede curled into the ridges of its sole. Deep rust brown. A million legs.

The last strap of light slipped from the cherub's shoulder. Gloom swallowed the garden. Whole. Like a python. Lights came on in the house.

Rahel could see Estha in his room, sitting on his neat bed. He was looking out through the barred window at the darkness. He couldn't see her, sitting outside in the darkness, looking in at the light.

A pair of actors trapped in a recondite play with no hint of plot or narrative. Stumbling through their parts, nursing someone else's sorrow. Grieving someone else's grief.

Unable, somehow, to change plays. Or purchase, for a fee, some cheap brand of exorcism from a counsellor with a fancy degree, who would sit them down and say, in one of many ways: 'You're not the Sinners. You're the Sinned Against. You were only children. You had no control. You are the *victims*, not the perpetrators.'

It would have helped if they could have made that crossing. If only they could have worn, even temporarily, the tragic hood of victimhood. Then they would have been able to put a face on it, and conjure up fury at what had happened. Or seek redress. And eventually, perhaps, exorcize the memories that haunted them.

But anger wasn't available to them and there was no face to put on this Other Thing that they held in their sticky Other Hands, like an imaginary orange. There was nowhere to lay it down. It wasn't theirs to give away. It would have to be held. Carefully and for ever.

Esthappen and Rahel both knew that there were several perpetrators (besides themselves) that day. But only one victim. And he had blood-red nails and a brown leaf on his back that made the monsoons come on time.

He left behind a hole in the Universe through which darkness poured like liquid tar. Through which their mother followed without even turning to wave goodbye. She left them behind, spinning in the dark, with no moorings, in a place with no foundation.

Hours later, the moon rose and made the gloomy python surrender what it had swallowed. The garden reappeared. Regurgitated whole. With Rahel sitting in it.

The direction of the breeze changed and brought her the sound of drums. A gift. The promise of a story. *Once upon a time,* they said, *there lived a*

Rahel lifted her head and listened.

On clear nights the sound of the chenda travelled up to a kilometre from the Ayemenem temple, announcing a kathakali performance.

Rahel went. Drawn by the memory of steep roofs and white walls. Of brass lamps lit and dark, oiled wood. She went in the hope of meeting an old elephant who wasn't electrocuted on the Kottayam–Cochin highway. She stopped by the kitchen for a coconut.

On her way out, she noticed that one of the gauze doors of the factory had come off its hinges and was propped against the doorway. She moved it aside and stepped in. The air was heavy with moisture, wet enough for fish to swim in.

The floor under her shoes was slick with monsoon scum. A small, anxious bat flitted between the roof beams.

The low cement pickle vats silhouetted in the gloom made the factory floor look like an indoor cemetery for the cylindrical dead.

The earthly remains of Paradise Pickles & Preserves.

Where long ago, on the day that Sophie Mol came, Ambassador E. Pelvis stirred a pot of scarlet jam and thought Two Thoughts. Where a red, tender-mango-shaped secret was pickled, sealed and put away.

It's true. Things can change in a day.

10

The River in the Boat

While the *Welcome Home, Our Sophie Mol* Play was being performed in the front verandah and Kochu Maria distributed cake to a Blue Army in the green heat, Ambassador E. Pelvis/S. Pimpernel (with a puff) of the beige and pointy shoes, pushed open the gauze doors to the dank and pickle-smelling premises of Paradise Pickles. He walked among the giant cement pickle vats to find a place to Think in. Ousa, the Bar Nowl, who lived on a blackened beam near the skylight (and contributed occasionally to the flavour of certain Paradise products), watched him walk.

Past floating yellow limes in brine that needed prodding from time to time (or else islands of black fungus formed like frilled mushrooms in a clear soup).

Past green mangoes, cut and stuffed with turmeric and chilli powder and tied together with twine. (They needed no attention for a while.)

Past glass casks of vinegar with corks.

Past shelves of pectin and preservatives.

Past trays of bitter gourd, with knives and coloured finger-guards.

Past gunny bags bulging with garlic and small onions.

Past mounds of fresh green peppercorns.

Past a heap of banana peels on the floor (preserved for the pigs' dinner).

Past the label cupboard full of labels.

Past the glue.

Past the glue-brush.

Past an iron tub of empty bottles floating in soapbubbled water.

Past the lemon squash.

The grape-crush.

And back.

It was dark inside, lit only by the light that filtered through the clotted gauze doors, and a beam of dusty sunlight (that Ousa didn't use) from the skylight. The smell of vinegar and asafoetida stung his nostrils, but Estha was used to it, loved it. The place that he found to Think in was between the wall and the black iron cauldron in which a batch of freshly boiled (illegal) banana jam was slowly cooling.

The jam was still hot and on its sticky scarlet surface, thick pink froth was dying slowly. Little banana bubbles drowning deep in jam and nobody to help them.

The Orangedrink Lemondrink Man could walk in any minute. Catch a Cochin–Kottayam bus and be there. And Ammu would offer him a cup of tea. Or pineapple squash perhaps. With ice. Yellow in a glass.

With the long iron stirrer. Estha stirred the thick, fresh jam. The dying froth made dying frothly shapes.

A crow with a crushed wing.

A clenched chicken's claw.

A Nowl (not Ousa) mired in sickly jam.

A sadly swirl.

And nobody to help.

As Estha stirred the thick jam he thought Two Thoughts, and the Two Thoughts he thought, were these:

(a) *Anything can happen to Anyone.*

And

(b) *It's best to be prepared.*

Having thought these thoughts, Estha Alone was happy with his bit of wisdom.

As the hot magenta jam went round, Estha became a Stirring Wizard with a spoiled puff and uneven teeth, and then the Witches of Macbeth.

Fire burn, banana bubble.

Ammu had allowed Estha to copy Mammachi's recipe for banana jam into her new recipe book, black with a white spine.

Acutely aware of the honour that Ammu had bestowed on him, Estha had used both his best handwritings.

Banana Jam (in his *old* best writing)

Crush ripe banana. Add water to cover and cook on a <u>very</u> hot fire till fruit is soft.
Sqweeze out juice by straining through course muslin.
Weigh equal quantity of sugar and <u>keep by</u>.
Cook fruit juice till it turns scarlet and about half the quantity evapourates.

Prepare the gelatin (pectin) thus:
Proportion 1:5
ie: 4 teaspoons Pectin: 20 teaspoons sugar.

Estha always thought of Pectin as the youngest of three brothers with hammers, Pectin, Hectin and Abednego. He imagined them building a wooden ship in failing light and a drizzle. Like Noah's sons. He could see them clearly in his mind. Racing against time. The sound of their hammering echoing dully under the brooding, storm-coming sky. And nearby in the jungle, in the eerie, storm-coming light, animals queued up in pairs:

Girlboy.
Girlboy.
Girlboy.

Girlboy.
Twins were not allowed.

The rest of the recipe was in Estha's new best handwriting. Angular, spiky. It leaned backwards as though the letters were reluctant to form words, and the words reluctant to be in sentences:

> *Add the Pectin to concenterated juice. Cook for a few (5) minutes.*
> *Use a strong fire, burning heavily all around.*
> *Add the sugar. Cook until sheeting consistency is obtained.*
> *Cool slowly.*
> *Hope you will enjoy this recipe.*

Apart from the spelling mistakes, the last line – *Hope you will enjoy this recipe* – was Estha's only augmentation of the original text.

Gradually, as Estha stirred, the banana jam thickened and cooled, and Thought Number Three rose unbidden from his beige and pointy shoes.

Thought Number Three was:

(c) *A boat.*

A boat to row across the river. Akkara. The Other Side. A boat to carry Provisions. Matches. Clothes. Pots and pans. Things they would need and couldn't swim with.

Estha's arm hairs stood on end. The jam-stirring became a boat-rowing. The round and round became a back and forth. Across a sticky scarlet river. A song from the Onam boatrace filled the factory. *'Thaiy thaiy thaka thaiy thaiy thome!'*

> *Enda da korangacha, chandi ithra thenjadu?*
> (Hey Mr Monkey man, why's your bum so red?)
> *Pandyill thooran poyappol nerakkamuthiri nerangi njan.*
> (I went for a shit to Madras, and scraped it till it bled.)

Over the somewhat discourteous questions and answers of the boatsong, Rahel's voice floated into the factory.

'Estha! Estha! Estha!'

Estha didn't answer. The chorus of the boatsong was whispered into the thick jam.

Theeyome
Thithome
Tharaka
Thithome
Theem

A gauze door creaked, and an Airport Fairy with hornbumps and yellow-rimmed red plastic sunglasses looked in with the sun behind her. The factory was Angry-coloured. The salted limes were red. The tender mangoes were red. The label cupboard was red. The dusty sunbeam (that Ousa never used) was red.

The gauze door closed.

Rahel stood in the empty factory with her Fountain in a Love-in-Tokyo. She heard a nun's voice singing the boatsong. A clear soprano wafting over vinegar fumes and pickle vats.

She turned to Estha bent over the scarlet broth in the black cauldron.

'What d'you want?' Estha asked without looking up.

'Nothing,' Rahel said.

'Then why have you come here?'

Rahel didn't reply. There was a brief, hostile silence.

'Why're you rowing the jam?' Rahel asked.

'India's a Free Country,' Estha said.

No one could argue with that.

India was a Free Country.

You could make salt. Row jam, if you wanted to.

The Orangedrink Lemondrink Man could just walk in through the gauze doors.

If he wanted to.

And Ammu would offer him pineapple juice. With ice.

Rahel sat on the edge of a cement vat (frothy ends of buckram and lace, delicately dipped in tender mango pickle) and tried on the rubber finger-guards. Three bluebottles fiercely fought the gauze doors, wanting to be let in. And Ousa the Bar Nowl watched the pickle-smelling silence that lay between the twins like a bruise.

Rahel's fingers were Yellow Green Blue Red Yellow.

Estha's jam was stirred.

Rahel got up to go. For her Afternoon Gnap.

'Where're you going?'

'Somewhere.'

Rahel took off her new fingers, and had her old finger-coloured fingers back. Not yellow, not green, not blue, not red. Not yellow.

'I'm going Akkara,' Estha said. Not looking up. 'To the History House.'

Rahel stopped and turned around, and on her heart a drab moth with unusually dense dorsal tufts unfurled its predatory wings.

Slow out.

Slow in.

'Why?' Rahel said.

'Because Anything can Happen to Anyone,' Estha said. 'It's Best to be Prepared.'

You couldn't argue with that.

Nobody went to Kari Saipu's house any more. Vellya Paapen claimed to be the last human being to have set eyes on it. He said that it was haunted. He had told the twins the story of his encounter with Kari Saipu's ghost. It happened two years ago, he said. He had gone across the river, hunting for a nutmeg tree to make a paste of nutmeg and fresh garlic for Chella, his wife, as she lay dying of tuberculosis. Suddenly he smelled cigar smoke (which he recognized at once, because Pappachi used to smoke the same brand). Vellya Paapen whirled around and hurled his sickle at the smell. He pinned the ghost to the trunk of a rubber tree, where, according to Vellya Paapen, it still remained. A sickled smell, that bled clear, amber blood, and begged for cigars.

Vellya Paapen never found the nutmeg tree, and had to buy himself a new sickle. But he had the satisfaction of knowing that his lightning-quick reflexes (despite his mortgaged eye) and his presence of mind had put an end to the bloodthirsty wanderings of a paedophile ghost.

As long as no one succumbed to its artifice and unsickled it with a cigar.

What Vellya Paapen (who knew most things) *didn't* know was that Kari Saipu's house was the History House (whose doors were locked and windows open). And that inside, map-breath'd ancestors with tough toe-nails whispered to the lizards on the wall. That History used the back verandah to negotiate its terms and collect its dues. That default led to dire consequences. That on the day History picked to square its books, Estha would keep the receipt for the dues that Velutha paid.

Vellya Paapen had no idea that Kari Saipu it was who captured dreams and redreamed them. That he plucked them from the minds of passers-by the way children pick currants from a cake. That the ones he craved most of all, the dreams he loved redreaming, were the tender dreams of two-egg twins.

Poor old Vellya Paapen, had he known then that History would choose him for its deputy, that it would be *his* tears that set the Terror rolling, perhaps he would not have strutted like a young cockerel in the Ayemenem bazaar, bragging of how he swam the river with his sickle in his mouth (sour, the taste of iron on his tongue). How he put it down for just one moment while he kneeled to wash the river-grit out of his mortgaged eye (there was grit in the river sometimes, particularly in the rainy months) when he caught the first whiff of cigar smoke. How he picked up his sickle, whirled around and sickled the smell that fixed the ghost for ever. All in a single, fluid, athletic motion.

By the time he understood his part in History's Plans, it was too late to retrace his steps. He had swept his footprints away himself. Crawling backwards with a broom.

In the factory the silence swooped down once more and tightened around the twins. But this time it was a different kind of silence. An old river silence. The silence of Fisher People and waxy mermaids.

'But communists don't believe in ghosts,' Estha said, as though they were continuing a discourse investigating solutions to the ghost problem. Their conversations surfaced and dipped like mountain streams. Sometimes audible to other people. Sometimes not.

'Are we going to become a communist?' Rahel asked.

'Might have to.'

Estha-the-Practical.

Distant cake-crumbled voices and approaching Blue Army footsteps caused the comrades to seal the secret.

It was pickled, sealed and put away. A red, tender mango-shaped secret in a vat. Presided over by a Nowl.

The Red Agenda was worked out and agreed upon:

Comrade Rahel would go for her Afternoon Gnap, then lie awake until Ammu fell asleep.

Comrade Estha would find the flag (that Baby Kochamma had been forced to wave), and wait for her by the river, and there they would:

(b) *Prepare to prepare to be prepared.*

A child's abandoned fairy frock (semi-pickled) stood stiffly on its own in the middle of Ammu's darkened bedroom floor.

Outside, the Air was Alert and Bright and Hot. Rahel lay next to Ammu, wide awake in her matching airport knickers. She could see the pattern of the cross-stitch flowers from the blue cross-stitch counterpane on Ammu's cheek. She could hear the blue cross-stitch afternoon.

The slow ceiling fan. The sun behind the curtains.

The yellow wasp wasping against the windowpane in a dangerous dzzzz.

A disbelieving lizard's blink.

High-stepping chickens in the yard.

The sound of the sun crinkling the washing. Crisping white bedsheets. Stiffening starched saris. Off-white and gold.

Red ants on yellow stones.

A hot cow feeling hot. *Amhoo*. In the distance.

And the smell of a cunning Englishman ghost, sickled to a rubber tree, asking courteously for a cigar.

'Umm . . . excuse me? You wouldn't happen to have an umm . . . cigar, would you?'

In a kind-schoolteacherly voice.

Oh *dear*.

And Estha waiting for her. By the river. Under the mangosteen tree that Reverend E. John Ipe had brought home from his visit to Mandalay.

What was Estha sitting on?

On what they always sat on under the mangosteen tree. Something grey and grizzled. Covered in moss and lichen, smothered in ferns. Something that the earth had claimed. Not a log. Not a rock . . .

Before she completed the thought, Rahel was up and running.

Through the kitchen, past Kochu Maria fast asleep. Thick-wrinkled like a sudden rhinoceros in a frilly apron.

Past the factory.

Tumbling barefoot through the greenheat, followed by a yellow wasp.

Comrade Estha was there. Under the mangosteen tree. With the red flag planted in the earth beside him. A Mobile Republic. A Twin Revolution with a Puff.

And what was he sitting on?

Something covered with moss, hidden by ferns.

Knock on it and it made a hollow knocked-on sound.

The silence dipped and soared and swooped and looped in figures of eight.

Jewelled dragonflies hovered like shrill children's voices in the sun.

Finger-coloured fingers fought the ferns, moved the stones, cleared the way. There was a sweaty grappling for an edge to hold on to. And a One Two and.

Things can change in a day.

It *was* a boat. A tiny wooden vallom.

The boat that Estha sat on and Rahel found.

The boat that Ammu would use to cross the river. To love by night the man her children loved by day.

So old a boat that it had taken root. Almost.

A grey old boatplant with boatflowers and boatfruit. And underneath, a boat-shaped patch of withered grass. A scurrying, hurrying boatworld.

Dark and dry and cool. Unroofed now. And blind.

White termites on their way to work.

White ladybirds on their way home.

White beetles burrowing away from the light.

White grasshoppers with whitewood violins.

Sad white music.

A white wasp. Dead.

A brittlewhite snakeskin, preserved in darkness, crumbled in the sun.

But would it do, that little vallom? Was it perhaps too old? Too dead? Was Akkara too far away for it?

Two-egg twins looked out across their river.

The Meenachal.

Greygreen. With fish in it. The sky and trees in it. And at night, the broken yellow moon in it.

When Pappachi was a boy, an old tamarind tree fell into it in a storm. It was still there. A smooth barkless tree, blackened by a surfeit of green water. Driftless driftwood.

The first third of the river was their friend. Before the Really Deep began. They knew the slippery stone steps (thirteen) before the slimy mud began. They knew the afternoon weed that flowed inwards from the backwaters of Komarakom. They knew the smaller fish. The flat, foolish pallathi, the silver paral, the wily, whiskered koori, the sometimes karimeen.

Here Chacko had taught them to swim (splashing around his ample uncle stomach without help). Here they had discovered for themselves the disconnected delights of underwater farting.

Here they had learned to fish. To thread coiling purple earthworms onto hooks on the fishing rods that Velutha made from slender culms of yellow bamboo.

Here they studied Silence (like the children of the Fisher Peoples), and learned the bright language of dragonflies.

Here they learned to Wait. To Watch. To think thoughts and not voice them. To move like lightning when the bendy yellow bamboo arced downwards.

So this first third of the river they knew well. The next two-thirds less so.

The second third was where the Really Deep began. Where the current was swift and certain (downstream when the tide was out, upstream, pushing up from the backwaters when the tide was in).

The third third was shallow again. The water brown and murky. Full of weeds and darting eels and slow mud that oozed through toes like toothpaste.

The twins could swim like seals and, supervised by Chacko, had crossed the river several times, returning panting and cross-eyed from the effort, with a stone, a twig or a leaf from the Other Side as testimony to their feat. But the middle of a respectable river, or the Other Side, was no place for children to Linger, Loll or Learn Things. Estha and Rahel accorded the second third and the third third of the Meenachal the deference it deserved. Still, swimming across was not the problem. Taking the boat with Things in it (so that they could (*b. Prepare to prepare to be prepared*) was.

They looked across the river with Old Boat eyes. From where they stood they couldn't see the History House. It was just a darkness beyond the swamp, at the heart of the abandoned rubber estate, from which the sound of crickets swelled.

Estha and Rahel lifted the little boat and carried it to the water. It looked surprised, like a grizzled fish that had surfaced from the deep. In dire need of sunlight. It needed scraping, and cleaning, perhaps, but nothing more.

Two happy hearts soared like coloured kites in a skyblue sky. But then, in a slow green whisper, the river (with fish in it, with the sky and trees in it), bubbled in.

Slowly the old boat sank, and settled on the sixth step.

And a pair of two-egg twin hearts sank and settled on the step above the sixth.

The deep-swimming fish covered their mouths with their fins and laughed sideways at the spectacle.

A white boat-spider floated up with the river in the boat, struggled briefly and drowned. Her white egg sac ruptured prematurely, and a hundred baby spiders (too light to drown, too small to swim), stippled the smooth surface of the green water, before being swept out to sea. To Madagascar, to start a new phylum of Malayali Swimming Spiders.

In a while, as though they'd discussed it (though they hadn't), the twins began to wash the boat in the river. The cobwebs, the mud, the moss and lichen floated away. When it was clean, they turned it upside down and hoisted it onto their heads. Like a combined hat that dripped. Estha uprooted the red flag.

A small procession (a flag, a wasp and a boat-on-legs) wended its knowledgeable way down the little path through the under-growth. It avoided the clumps of nettles, and side-stepped known ditches and anthills. It skirted the precipice of the deep pit from which laterite had been quarried, and was now a still lake with steep orange banks, the thick, viscous water covered with a luminous film of green scum. A verdant, treacherous lawn, in which mosquitoes bred and the fish were fat but inaccessible.

The path, which ran parallel to the river, led to a little grassy clearing that was hemmed in by huddled trees: coconut, cashew, mango, bilimbi. On the edge of the clearing, with its back to the river, a low hut with walls of orange laterite plastered with mud and a thatched roof nestled close to the ground, as though it was listening to a whispered subterranean secret. The low walls of the hut were the same colour as the earth they stood on, and seemed to have germinated from a house-seed planted in the ground, from which right-angled ribs of earth had risen and enclosed space. Three untidy banana trees grew in the little front yard that had been fenced off with panels of woven palm leaves.

The boat-on-legs approached the hut. An unlit oil lamp hung on the wall beside the door, the patch of wall behind it was singed soot black. The door was ajar. It was dark inside. A black hen appeared in the doorway. She returned indoors, entirely indifferent to boat visits.

Velutha wasn't home. Nor Vellya Paapen. But someone was.

A man's voice floated out from inside and echoed around the clearing, making him sound lonely.

The voice shouted the same thing, over and over again, and

each time it climbed into a higher, more hysterical register. It was an appeal to an over-ripe guava threatening to fall from its tree and make a mess on the ground.

Pa pera-pera-pera-perakka
(Mr gugga-gug-gug-guava,)
Ende parambil thooralley.
(Don't shit here in my compound.)
Chetende parambil thoorikko,
(You can shit next door in my brother's compound,)
Pa pera-pera-pera-perakka.
(Mr gugga-gug-gug-guava.)

The shouter was Kuttappen, Velutha's older brother. He was paralysed from his chest downwards. Day after day, month after month, while his brother was away and his father went to work, Kuttappen lay flat on his back and watched his youth saunter past without stopping to say hello. All day he lay there listening to the silence of huddled trees with only a domineering black hen for company. He missed his mother, Chella, who had died in the same corner of the room that he lay in now. She had died a coughing, spitting, aching, phlegmy death. Kuttappen remembered noticing how her feet died long before she had. How the skin on them grew grey and lifeless. How fearfully he watched death creep over her from the bottom up. Kuttappen kept vigil on his own numb feet with mounting terror. Occasionally he poked at them hopefully with a stick that he kept propped up in the corner to defend himself against visiting snakes. He had no sensation in his feet at all, and only visual evidence assured him that they were still connected to his body, and were indeed his own.

After Chella died, he was moved into her corner, the corner that Kuttappen imagined was the corner of his home that Death had reserved to administer her deathly affairs. One corner for cooking, one for clothes, one for bedding rolls, one for dying in.

He wondered how long his would take, and what people who had more than four corners in their houses did with the rest of their corners. Did it give them a choice of corners to die in?

He assumed, not without reason, that he would be the first in his family to follow in his mother's wake. He would learn otherwise. Soon. Too soon.

Sometimes (from habit, from missing her), Kuttappen coughed like his mother used to, and his upper body bucked like a just-caught fish. His lower body lay like lead, as though it belonged to someone else. Someone dead whose spirit was trapped and couldn't get away.

Unlike Velutha, Kuttappen was a good, safe Paravan. He could neither read nor write. As he lay there on his hard bed, bits of thatch and grit fell onto him from the ceiling and mingled with his sweat. Sometimes ants and other insects fell with it. On bad days the orange walls held hands and bent over him, inspecting him like malevolent doctors, slowly, deliberately, squeezing the breath out of him and making him scream. Sometimes they receded of their own accord, and the room he lay in grew impossibly large, terrorizing him with the spectre of his own insignificance. That too made him cry out.

Insanity hovered close at hand, like an eager waiter at an expensive restaurant (lighting cigarettes, refilling glasses). Kuttappen thought with envy of mad men who could walk. He had no doubts about the equity of the deal; his sanity, for serviceable legs.

The twins put the boat down, and the clatter was met with a sudden silence from inside.

Kuttappen wasn't expecting anyone.

Estha and Rahel pushed open the door and went in. Small as they were, they had to stoop a little to go in. The wasp waited outside on the lamp.

'It's us.'

The room was dark and clean. It smelled of fish curry and woodsmoke. Heat cleaved to things like a low fever. But the mud floor was cool under Rahel's bare feet. Velutha's and Vellya Paapen's bedding was rolled up and propped against the wall. Clothes hung on a string. There was a low wooden kitchen shelf on which covered terracotta pots, ladles made of coconut shells and three chipped enamel plates with dark blue rims were arranged. A grown man could stand up straight in the centre of the room, but not along its sides. Another low door led to a backyard where there were more banana trees, beyond which the river glimmered through the foliage. A carpenter's work station had been erected in the backyard.

There were no keys or cupboards to lock.

The black hen left through the back door, and scratched abstractedly in the yard where woodshavings blew about like blonde curls. Judging from her personality, she appeared to have been reared on a diet of hardware: hasps and clasps and nails and old screws.

'*Aiyyo, Mon! Mol!* What must you be thinking? That Kuttappen's a basket case!' an embarrassed, disembodied voice said.

It took the twins a while for their eyes to grow accustomed to the dark. Then the darkness dissolved and Kuttappen appeared on his bed, a glistening genie in the gloom. The whites of his eyes were dark yellow. The soles of his feet (soft from so much lying down) stuck out from under the cloth that covered his legs. They were still stained a pale orange from years of walking barefoot on red mud. He had grey callouses on his ankles from the chafing of the rope that Paravans tied around their feet when they climbed coconut trees.

On the wall behind him there was a benign, mouse-haired calendar-Jesus with lipstick and rouge, and a lurid, jewelled heart glowing through his clothes. The bottom quarter of the calendar (the part with the dates on it) frilled out like a skirt. Jesus in a mini. Twelve layers of petticoats for the twelve months of the year. None had been torn out.

There were other things from the Ayemenem House that had either been given to them or salvaged from the rubbish bin. Rich things in a poor house. A clock that didn't work, a flowered tin waste-paper basket. Pappachi's old riding boots (brown, with green mould) with the cobbler's trees still in them. Biscuit tins with sumptuous pictures of English castles and ladies with bustles and ringlets.

A small poster (Baby Kochamma's, given away because of a damp patch) hung next to Jesus. It was a picture of a blonde child writing a letter, with tears falling down her cheeks. Underneath it said: *I'm writing to say I Miss You.* She looked as though she'd had a haircut, and it was her cropped curls that were blowing around Velutha's backyard.

A transparent plastic tube led from under the worn cotton sheet that covered Kuttappen to a bottle of yellow liquid that caught the shaft of light that came in through the door, and quelled a question that had been rising inside Rahel. She fetched him water in a steel tumbler from the clay koojah. She seemed to know her way around. Kuttappen lifted his head and drank. Some water dribbled down his chin.

The twins squatted on their haunches, like professional adult gossips in the Ayemenem market.

They sat in silence for a while. Kuttappen mortified, the twins preoccupied with boat thoughts.

'Has Chacko Saar's Mol come?' Kuttappen asked.

'Must have,' Rahel said laconically.

'Where's she?'

'Who knows? Must be around somewhere. We don't know.'

'Will you bring her here for me to see?'

'Can't,' Rahel said.

'Why not?'

'She has to stay indoors. She's very delicate. If she gets dirty she'll die.'

'I see.'

'We're not allowed to bring her here . . . and anyway, there's nothing to *see*,' Rahel assured Kuttappen. 'She has hair, legs, teeth – you know – the usual . . . only she's a little tall.' And that was the only concession she would make.

'Is that all?' Kuttappen said, getting the point very quickly. 'Then where's the point in seeing her?'

'No point,' Rahel said.

'Kuttappa, if a vallom leaks, is it very hard to mend?' Estha asked.

'Shouldn't be,' Kuttappen said. 'Depends. Why, whose vallom is leaking?'

'Ours – that we found. D'you want to see it?'

They went out and returned with the grizzled boat for the paralysed man to examine. They held it over him like a roof. Water dripped on him.

'First we'll have to find the leaks,' Kuttappen said. 'Then we'll have to plug them.'

'Then sandpaper,' Estha said. 'Then polish.'

'Then oars,' Rahel said.

'Then oars,' Estha agreed.

'Then offity off,' Rahel said.

'Where to?' Kuttappen asked.

'Just here and there,' Estha said airily.

'You must be careful,' Kuttappen said. 'This river of ours – she isn't always what she pretends to be.'

'What does she pretend to be?' Rahel asked.

'Oh . . . a little old church-going ammooma, quiet and clean . . . idi appams for breakfast, kanji and meen for lunch. Minding her own business. Not looking right or left.'

'And she's really a . . . ?'

'Really a wild thing . . . I can hear her at night – rushing past in the moonlight, always in a hurry. You must be careful of her.'

'And what does she really eat?'

'Really eat? Oh ... Stoo ... and ...' He cast about for something English for the evil river to eat.

'Pineapple slices ...' Rahel suggested.

'That's right! Pineapple slices and Stoo. And she drinks. Whisky.'

'And brandy.'

'And brandy. True.'

'And looks right *and* left.'

'True.'

'And minds *other* people's business ...'

Esthappen steadied the little boat on the uneven earth floor with a few blocks of wood that he found in Velutha's workstation in the backyard. He gave Rahel a cooking ladle made of a wooden handle stuck through the polished half of a coconut shell.

The twins climbed into the vallom and rowed across vast, choppy waters.

With a *Thaiy thaiy thaka thaiy thaiy thome*. And a jewelled Jesus watching.

He walked on water. Perhaps. But could He have *swum* on land?

In matching knickers and dark glasses? With His Fountain in a Love-in-Tokyo? In pointy shoes and a puff? Would He have had the imagination?

Velutha returned to see if Kuttappen needed anything. From a distance he heard the raucous singing. Young voices, underlining with delight the scatology.

Hey Mr Monkey Man
Why's your BUM so RED?

I went for a SHIT to Madras
And scraped it till it BLED!

Temporarily, for a few happy moments, the Orangedrink Lemondrink Man shut his yellow smile and went away. Fear sank and settled at the bottom of the deep water. Sleeping a dog's sleep. Ready to rise and murk things at a moment's notice.

Velutha smiled when he saw the Marxist flag blooming like a tree outside his doorway. He had to bend low in order to enter his home. A tropical Eskimo. When he saw the children, something clenched inside him. And he couldn't understand it. He saw them every day. He loved them without knowing it. But it was different suddenly. Now. After History had slipped up so badly. No fist had clenched inside him before.

Her children, an insane whisper whispered to him.

Her eyes, *her* mouth. *Her* teeth.

Her soft, lambent skin.

He drove the thought away angrily. It returned and sat outside his skull. Like a dog.

'Ha!' he said to his young guests. 'And who, may I ask, are these Fisher Peoples?'

'Esthapappychachen Kuttappen Peter Mon. Mr and Mrs Pleasetomeetyou.' Rahel held out her ladle to be shaken in greeting.

It was shaken in greeting. Hers, then Estha's.

'And where, may I ask, are they off to by boat?'

'Off to Africa!' Rahel shouted.

'Stop *shouting*,' Estha said.

Velutha walked around the boat. They told him where they had found it.

'So it doesn't belong to anybody,' Rahel said a little doubtfully, because it suddenly occurred to her that it might. 'Ought we to report it to the police?'

'Don't be stupid,' Estha said.

Velutha knocked on the wood and then scraped a little patch clean with his nail.

'Good wood,' he said.

'It sinks,' Estha said. 'It leaks.'

'Can you mend it for us, Veluthapappychachen Peter Mon?' Rahel asked.

'We'll see about that,' Velutha said. 'I don't want you playing any silly games on this river.'

'We won't. We promise. We'll use it only when you're with us.'

'First we'll have to find the leaks . . .' Velutha said.

'Then we'll have to plug them!' the twins shouted, as though it was the second line of a well-known poem.

'How long will it take?' Estha asked.

'A day,' Velutha said.

'A *day*! I thought you'd say a month!'

Estha, delirious with joy, jumped on Velutha, wrapped his legs around his waist and kissed him.

The sandpaper was divided into exactly equal halves, and the twins fell to work with an eerie concentration that excluded everything else.

Boat-dust flew around the room and settled on hair and eyebrows. On Kuttappen like a cloud, on Jesus like an offering. Velutha had to prise the sandpaper out of their fingers.

'Not here,' he said firmly. 'Outside.'

He picked the boat up and carried it out. The twins followed, eyes fixed on their boat with unwavering concentration, starving puppies expecting to be fed.

Velutha set the boat up for them. The boat that Estha sat on, and Rahel found. He showed them how to follow the grain of the wood. He started them off on the sandpapering. When he returned indoors, the black hen followed him, determined to be wherever the boat wasn't.

Velutha dipped a thin cotton towel in an earthen pot of water. He squeezed the water out of it (savagely, as though it was an unwanted thought) and handed it to Kuttappen to wipe the grit off his face and neck.

'Did they say anything?' Kuttappen asked. 'About seeing you in the march?'

'No,' Velutha said. 'Not yet. They will though. They know.'

'For sure?'

Velutha shrugged and took the towel away to wash. And rinse. And beat. And wring. As though it was his ridiculous, disobedient brain.

He tried to hate her.

She's one of them, he told himself. *Just another one of them.*

He couldn't.

She had deep dimples when she smiled. Her eyes were always somewhere else.

Madness slunk in through a chink in History. It only took a moment.

An hour into the sandpapering, Rahel remembered her Afternoon Gnap. And she was up and running. Tumbling through the green afternoon heat. Followed by her brother and a yellow wasp.

Hoping, praying, that Ammu hadn't woken up and found her gone.

11

The God of Small Things

That afternoon, Ammu travelled upwards through a dream in which a cheerful man with one arm held her close by the light of an oil lamp. He had no other arm with which to fight the shadows that flickered around him on the floor.

Shadows that only he could see.

Ridges of muscle on his stomach rose under his skin like divisions on a slab of chocolate.

He held her close, by the light of an oil lamp, and he shone as though he had been polished with a high-wax body polish.

He could do only one thing at a time.

If he held her, he couldn't kiss her. If he kissed her, he couldn't see her. If he saw her, he couldn't feel her.

She could have touched his body lightly with her fingers, and felt his smooth skin turn to gooseflesh. She could have let her fingers stray to the base of his flat stomach. Carelessly, over those burnished chocolate ridges. And left patterned trails of bumpy gooseflesh on his body, like flat chalk on a blackboard, like a swathe of breeze in a paddyfield, like jet streaks in a blue church-sky. She could so easily have done that, but she didn't.

He could have touched her too. But he didn't, because in the gloom beyond the oil lamp, in the shadows, there were metal folding chairs arranged in a ring and on the chairs there were people, with slanting rhinestone sunglasses, watching. They all held polished violins under their chins, the bows poised at identical angles. They all had their legs crossed, left over right, and all their left legs were shivering.

Some of them had newspapers. Some didn't. Some of them blew spit-bubbles. Some didn't. But they all had the flickering reflection of an oil lamp on each lens.

Beyond the circle of folding chairs was a beach littered with broken blue glass bottles. The silent waves brought new blue bottles to be broken, and dragged the old ones away in the undertow. There were jagged sounds of glass on glass. On a rock, out at sea, in a shaft of purple light, there was a mahogany and wicker rocking chair. Smashed.

The sea was black, the spume vomit green.

Fish fed on shattered glass.

Night's elbows rested on the water, and falling stars glanced off its brittle shards.

Moths lit up the sky. There wasn't a moon.

He could swim, with his one arm. She with her two.

His skin was salty. Hers too.

He left no footprints in sand, no ripples in water, no image in mirrors.

She could have touched him with her fingers, but she didn't. They just stood together.

Still.

Skin to skin.

A powdery, coloured breeze lifted her hair and blew it like a rippled shawl around his armless shoulder, that ended abruptly, like a cliff.

A thin red cow with a protruding pelvic bone appeared and swam straight out to sea without wetting her horns, without looking back.

Ammu flew through her dream on heavy, shuddering wings, and stopped to rest, just under the skin of it.

She had pressed roses from the blue cross-stitch counterpane on her cheek.

She sensed her children's faces hanging over her dream, like two dark, worried moons, waiting to be let in.

'D'you think she's dying?' she heard Rahel whisper to Estha.

'It's an afternoon-mare,' Estha-the-Accurate replied. 'She dreams a lot.'

If he touched her, he couldn't talk to her, if he loved her he couldn't leave, if he spoke he couldn't listen, if he fought he couldn't win.

Who was he, the one-armed man? Who *could* he have been? The God of Loss? The God of Small Things? The God of Goose Bumps and Sudden Smiles? Of Sourmetal Smells – like steel bus-rails and the smell of the bus conductor's hands from holding them?

'Should we wake her up?' Estha said.

Chinks of late afternoon light stole into the room through the curtains and fell on Ammu's tangerine-shaped transistor radio that she always took with her to the river. (Tangerine-shaped too, was the Thing that Estha carried into *The Sound of Music* in his sticky Other Hand.)

Bright bars of sunlight brightened Ammu's tangled hair. She waited, under the skin of her dream, not wanting to let her children in.

'She says you should never wake dreaming people suddenly,' Rahel said. 'She says they could easily have a Heart Attack.'

Between them they decided that it would be best to *disturb* her discreetly, rather than wake her suddenly. So they opened drawers, they cleared their throats, they whispered loudly, they hummed a little tune. They moved shoes. And found a cupboard door that creaked.

Ammu, resting under the skin of her dream, observed them and ached with her love for them.

The one-armed man blew out his lamp and walked across the jagged beach, away into the shadows that only he could see.

He left no footprints on the shore.

The folding chairs were folded. The black sea smoothed. The creased waves ironed. The spume rebottled. The bottle corked.

The night postponed till further notice.

Ammu opened her eyes.

It was a long journey that she made, from the embrace of the one-armed man to her unidentical two-egg twins.

'You were having an afternoon-mare,' her daughter informed her.

'It wasn't a mare,' Ammu said. 'It was a dream.'

'Estha thought you were dying.'

'You looked so sad,' Estha said.

'I was happy,' Ammu said, and realized that she had been.

'If you're happy in a dream, Ammu, does that count?' Estha asked.

'Does what count?'

'The happiness – does it count?'

She knew exactly what he meant, her son with his spoiled puff.

Because the truth is, that only what *counts* counts.

The simple, unswerving wisdom of children.

If you eat fish in a dream, does it count? Does it mean you've eaten fish?

The cheerful man without footprints – did *he* count?

Ammu groped for her tangerine transistor, and switched it on. It played a song from a film called *Chemmeen*.

It was the story of a poor girl who is forced to marry a fisherman from a neighbouring beach, though she loves some-one else. When the fisherman finds out about his new wife's old lover, he sets out to sea in his little boat though he knows that a storm is brewing. It's dark, and the wind rises. A whirlpool spins up from the ocean bed. There is storm music, and the fisherman drowns, sucked to the bottom of the sea in the vortex of the whirlpool.

The lovers make a suicide pact, and are found the next morning, washed up on the beach with their arms around each other. So everybody dies. The fisherman, his wife, her lover, and a shark that has no part in the story, but dies anyway. The sea claims them all.

In the blue cross-stitch darkness laced with edges of light, with cross-stitch roses on her sleepy cheek, Ammu and her twins (one on either side of her), sang softly with the tangerine radio. The song that fisherwomen sang to the sad young bride as they braided her hair and prepared her for her wedding to a man she didn't love.

> *Pandoru mukkuvan muthinu poyi,*
> (Once a fisherman went to sea,)
> *Padinjaran kattathu mungi poyi,*
> (The West Wind blew and swallowed his boat,)

An Airport Fairy frock stood on the floor, supported by its own froth and stiffness. Outside in the mittam, crisp saris lay in rows and crispened in the sun. Off-white and gold. Small pebbles nestled in their starched creases and had to be shaken out before the saris were folded and taken in to be ironed.

> *Arayathi pennu pizhachu poyi,*
> (His wife on the shore went astray,)

The electrocuted elephant (not Kochu Thomban) in Ettumanoor was cremated. A giant burning ghat was erected on the highway. The engineers of the concerned municipality sawed off the tusks and shared them unofficially. Unequally. Eighty tins of pure ghee were poured over the elephant to feed the fire. The smoke rose in dense fumes and arranged itself in complex patterns against the sky. People crowded around at a safe distance, read meanings into them.

There were lots of flies.

Avaney kadalamma kondu poyi.
(So Mother Ocean rose and took him away.)

Pariah kites dropped into nearby trees, to supervise the supervision of the last rites of the dead elephant. They hoped, not without reason, for pickings of giant innards. An enormous gall bladder, perhaps. Or a charred, gigantic spleen.

They weren't disappointed. Nor wholly satisfied.

Ammu noticed that both her children were covered in a fine dust. Like two pieces of lightly sugar-dusted, unidentical cake. Rahel had a blonde curl lodged among her black ones. A curl from Velutha's backyard. Ammu picked it out.

'I've told you before,' she said. 'I don't want you going to his house. It will only cause trouble.'

What trouble, she didn't say. She didn't know.

Somehow, by not mentioning his name, she knew that she had drawn him into the tousled intimacy of that blue cross-stitch afternoon and the song from the tangerine transistor. By not mentioning his name, she sensed that a pact had been forged between her Dream and the World. And that the midwives of that pact, were, or would be, her sawdust coated two-egg twins.

She knew who he was – the God of Loss, the God of Small Things. Of *course* she did.

She switched off the tangerine radio. In the afternoon silence (laced with edges of light), her children curled into the warmth of her. The smell of her. They covered their heads with her hair. They sensed somehow that in her sleep she had travelled away from them. They summoned her back now with the palms of their small hands laid flat against the bare skin of her midriff. Between her petticoat and her blouse. They loved the fact that the brown of the backs of their hands was the exact brown of their mother's stomach skin.

'Estha, look,' Rahel said, plucking at the line of soft down that led southwards from Ammu's bellybutton.

'Here's where we kicked you.' Estha traced a wandering silver stretchmark with his finger.

'Was it in the bus, Ammu?'

'On the winding estate road?'

'When Baba had to hold your tummy?'

'Did you have to buy tickets?'

'Did we hurt you?'

And then, keeping her voice casual, Rahel's question: 'D'you think he may have lost our address?'

Just the hint of a pause in the rhythm of Ammu's breathing made Estha touch Rahel's middle finger with his. And middle finger to middle finger, on their beautiful mother's midriff, they abandoned that line of questioning.

'That's Estha's kick, and that's mine,' Rahel said. '. . . And that's Estha's and that's mine.'

Between them they apportioned their mother's seven silver stretchmarks. Then Rahel put her mouth on Ammu's stomach and sucked at it, pulling the soft flesh into her mouth and drawing her head back to admire the shining oval of spit and the faint red imprint of her teeth on her mother's skin.

Ammu wondered at the transparence of that kiss. It was a clear-as-glass kiss. Unclouded by passion or desire – that pair of dogs that sleeps so soundly inside children, waiting for them to grow up. It was a kiss that demanded no kiss-back.

Not a cloudy kiss full of questions that wanted answers. Like the kisses of cheerful one-armed men in dreams.

Ammu grew tired of their proprietary handling of her. She wanted her body back. It was hers. She shrugged her children off the way a bitch shrugs off her pups when she's had enough of them. She sat up and twisted her hair into a knot at the nape of her neck. Then she swung her legs off the bed, walked to the window and drew back the curtains.

Slanting afternoon light flooded the room and brightened two children on the bed.

The twins heard the lock turning in Ammu's bathroom door. Click.

Ammu looked at herself in the long mirror on the bathroom door and the spectre of her future appeared in it to mock her. Pickled. Grey. Rheumy-eyed. Cross-stitch roses on a slack, sunken cheek. Withered breasts that hung like weighted socks. Dry as a bone between her legs, the hair feather white. Spare. As brittle as a pressed fern.

Skin that flaked and shed like snow.

Ammu shivered.

With that cold feeling on a hot afternoon that Life had been Lived. That her cup was full of dust. That the air, the sky, the trees, the sun, the rain, the light and darkness were all slowly turning to sand. That sand would fill her nostrils, her lungs, her mouth. Would pull her down, leaving on the surface a spinning swirl like crabs leave when they burrow downwards on a beach.

Ammu undressed and put a red toothbrush under a breast to see if it would stay. It didn't. Where she touched herself her flesh was taut and smooth. Under her hands her nipples wrinkled and hardened like dark nuts, pulling at the soft skin on her breasts. The thin line of down from her belly button led over the gentle curve of the base of her belly, to her dark triangle. Like an arrow directing a lost traveller. An inexperienced lover.

She undid her hair and turned around to see how long it had grown. It fell, in waves and curls and disobedient frizzy wisps – soft on the inside, coarser on the outside – to just below where her small, strong waist began its curve out towards her hips. The bathroom was hot. Small beads of sweat studded her skin like diamonds. Then they broke and trickled down. Sweat ran down the recessed line of her spine. She looked a little critically at her round, heavy behind. Not big in itself. Not big *per se* (as Chacko-of-Oxford would no doubt have put it). Big only because the rest of her was so slender. It belonged on another more voluptuous body.

She had to admit that they would happily support a toothbrush apiece. Perhaps two. She laughed out loud at the idea of walking naked down Ayemenem with an array of coloured toothbrushes sticking out from either cheek of her bottom. She silenced herself quickly. She saw a wisp of madness escape from its bottle and caper triumphantly around the bathroom.

Ammu worried about madness.

Mammachi said it ran in their family. That it came on people suddenly and caught them unawares. There was Pathil Ammai, who at the age of sixty-five began to take her clothes off and run naked along the river, singing to the fish. There was Thampi Chachen, who searched his shit every morning with a knitting needle for a gold tooth he had swallowed years ago. And Dr Muthachen, who had to be removed from his own wedding in a sack. Would future generations say, 'There was Ammu – Ammu Ipe. Married a Bengali. Went quite mad. Died young. In a cheap lodge somewhere.'

Chacko said that the high incidence of insanity among Syrian Christians was the price they paid for Inbreeding. Mammachi said it wasn't.

Ammu gathered up her heavy hair, wrapped it around her face, and peered down the road to Age and Death through its parted strands. Like a medieval executioner peering through the tilted eye-slits of his peaked black hood at the executionee. A slender, naked executioner with dark nipples and deep dimples when she smiled. With seven silver stretchmarks from her two-egg twins, born to her by candlelight amidst news of a lost war.

It wasn't what lay at the end of her road that frightened Ammu as much as the nature of the road itself. No milestones marked its progress. No trees grew along it. No dappled shadows shaded it. No mists rolled over it. No birds circled it. No twists, no turns or hairpin bends obscured even momentarily, her clear view of the end. This filled Ammu with an awful dread, because she was not the kind of woman who wanted her future told. She dreaded it too much. So if she were granted one small wish perhaps it would only have been Not to Know. Not to know what each day held in store for her. Not to know where she might be, next month, next year. Ten years on. Not to know which way her road might turn and what lay beyond the bend. And Ammu knew. Or *thought* she knew, which was really just as bad (because if in a dream you've eaten fish, it means you've eaten fish). And what Ammu knew (or thought she knew), smelled of the vapid, vinegary fumes that rose from the cement vats of Paradise Pickles. Fumes that wrinkled youth and pickled futures.

Hooded in her own hair, Ammu leaned against herself in the bathroom mirror and tried to weep.

For herself.

For the God of Small Things.

For the sugar-dusted twin midwives of her dream.

That afternoon – while in the bathroom the fates conspired to alter horribly the course of their mysterious mother's road, while in Velutha's backyard an old boat waited for them, while in a yellow church a young bat waited to be born – in their mother's bedroom, Estha stood on his head on Rahel's bum.

The bedroom with blue curtains and yellow wasps that worried the windowpanes. The bedroom whose walls would soon learn their harrowing secrets.

The bedroom into which Ammu would first be locked and then lock herself. Whose door, Chacko, crazed by grief, four days after Sophie Mol's funeral, would batter down.

'Get out of my house before I break every bone in your body!'

My house, *my* pineapples, *my* pickle.

After that for years Rahel would dream this dream: a fat man, faceless, kneeling beside a woman's corpse. Hacking its hair off. Breaking every bone in its body. Snapping even the little ones. The fingers. The ear bones cracked like twigs. *Snapsnap* the softsound of breaking bones. A pianist killing the piano keys. Even the black ones. And Rahel (though years later, in the Electric Crematorium, she would use the slipperiness of sweat to slither out of Chacko's grasp), loved them both. The player and the piano.

The killer and the corpse.

As the door was slowly battered down, to control the trembling of her hands, Ammu would hem the ends of Rahel's ribbons that didn't need hemming.

'Promise me you'll always love each other,' she'd say, as she drew her children to her.

'Promise,' Estha and Rahel would say. Not finding words with which to tell her that for them there *was* no Each, no Other.

Twin millstones and their mother. Numb millstones. What they had done would return to empty them. But that would be Later.

Lay Ter. A deep-sounding bell in a mossy well. Shivery and furred like moth's feet.

At the time, there would only be incoherence. As though meaning had slunk out of things and left them fragmented. Disconnected. The glint of Ammu's needle. The colour of a ribbon. The weave of the cross-stitch counterpane. A door slowly breaking. Isolated things that didn't *mean* anything. As though the intelligence that decodes life's hidden patterns – that connects reflections to images, glints to light, weaves to fabrics, needles to thread, walls to rooms, love to fear to anger to remorse – was suddenly lost.

'Pack your things and go,' Chacko would say, stepping over the debris. Looming over them. A chrome door handle in his hand. Suddenly strangely calm. Surprised at his own strength. His bigness. His bullying power. The enormity of his own terrible grief.

Red the colour of splintered doorwood.

Ammu, quiet outside, shaking inside, wouldn't look up from her unnecessary hemming. The tin of coloured ribbons would lie open on her lap, in the room where she had lost her Locusts Stand I.

The same room in which (after the Twin Expert from Hyderabad had replied), Ammu would pack Estha's little trunk and khaki holdall: 12 sleeveless cotton vests, 12 half-sleeved cotton vests. *Estha, here's your name on them in ink.* His socks. His drainpipe trousers. His pointy collared shirts. His beige and pointy shoes (from where the Angry Feelings came). His Elvis records. His calcium tablets and Vydalin syrup. His Free Giraffe (that came with the Vydalin). His Books of Knowledge Vols. 1–4. *No, sweetheart, there won't be a river there to fish in.* His white leather zip-up Bible with an Imperial Entomologist's amethyst cuff-link on the zip. His mug. His soap. His Advance Birthday Present that he *mustn't* open. Forty green inland letter forms. *Look, Estha, I've written our address on it. All you have to do is fold it. See if you can fold it yourself.* And Estha would fold the green inland letter neatly along the dotted lines that said *Fold here* and look up at Ammu with a smile that broke her heart.

Promise me you'll write? Even when you don't have any news?

Promise, Estha would say. Not wholly cognizant of his situation. The sharp edge of his apprehensions blunted by this sudden wealth of worldly possessions. They were His. And had his name on them in ink. They were to be packed into the trunk (with his name on it) that lay open on the bedroom floor.

The room to which, years later, Rahel would return and watch a silent stranger bathe. And wash his clothes with crumbling bright blue soap.

Flatmuscled, and honey coloured. Sea-secrets in his eyes. A silver raindrop on his ear.

Esthapappychachen Kuttappen Peter Mon.

12

Kochu Thomban

The sound of the chenda mushroomed over the temple, accentuating the silence of the encompassing night. The lonely, wet road. The watching trees. Rahel, breathless, holding a coconut, stepped into the temple compound through the wooden doorway in the high white boundary wall.

Inside, everything was white-walled, moss-tiled and moonlit. Everything smelled of recent rain. The thin priest was asleep on a mat in the raised stone verandah. A brass platter of coins lay near his pillow like a comic strip illustration of his dreams. The compound was littered with moons, one in each mud puddle. Kochu Thomban had finished his ceremonial rounds, and lay tethered to a wooden stake next to a steaming mound of his own dung. He was asleep, his duty done, his bowels empty, one tusk resting on the earth, the other pointed to the stars. Rahel approached quietly. She saw that his skin was looser than she remembered. He wasn't *Kochu* Thomban any more. His tusks had grown. He was *Vellya* Thomban now. The Big Tusker. She put the coconut on the ground next to him. A leathery wrinkle parted to reveal a liquid glint of elephant eye. Then it closed and long, sweeping lashes resummoned sleep. A tusk towards the stars.

June is low season for kathakali. But there are some temples that a troupe will not pass by without performing in. The Ayemenem temple wasn't one of them, but these days, thanks to its geography, things had changed.

In Ayemenem they danced to jettison their humiliation in the Heart of Darkness. Their truncated swimming pool performances. Their turning to tourism to stave off starvation.

On their way back from the Heart of Darkness, they stopped at the temple to ask pardon of their gods. To apologize for corrupting their stories. For encashing their identities. Misappropriating their lives.

On these occasions, a human audience was welcome, but entirely incidental.

In the broad, covered corridor – the colonnaded kuthambalam abutting the heart of the temple where the Blue God lived with his flute, the drummers drummed and the dancers danced, their colours turning slowly in the night. Rahel sat down cross-legged, resting her back against the roundness of a white pillar. A tall cannister of coconut oil gleamed in the flickering light of the brass lamp. The oil replenished the light. The light lit the tin.

It didn't matter that the story had begun, because kathakali discovered long ago that the secret of the Great Stories is that they *have* no secrets. The Great Stories are the ones you have heard and want to hear again. The ones you can enter anywhere and inhabit comfortably. They don't deceive you with thrills and trick endings. They don't surprise you with the unforeseen. They are as familiar as the house you live in. Or the smell of your lover's skin. You know how they end, yet you listen as though you don't. In the way that although you know that one day you will die, you live as though you won't. In the Great Stories you know who lives, who dies, who finds love, who doesn't. And yet you want to know again.

That is their mystery and their magic.

To the Kathakali Man these stories are his children and his childhood. He has grown up within them. They are the house he was raised in, the meadows he played in. They are his windows and his way of seeing. So when he tells a story, he handles it as he would a child of his own. He teases it. He punishes it. He sends it up like a bubble. He wrestles it to the ground and lets it go again. He laughs at it because he loves it. He can fly you across whole worlds in minutes, he can stop for hours to examine a wilting leaf. Or play with a sleeping monkey's tail. He can turn effortlessly from the carnage of war into the felicity of a woman washing her hair in a mountain stream. From the crafty ebullience of a rakshasa with a new idea into a gossipy Malayali with a scandal to spread. From the sensuousness of a woman with a baby at her breast into the seductive mischief of Krishna's smile. He can reveal the nugget of sorrow that happiness contains. The hidden fish of shame in a sea of glory.

He tells stories of the gods, but his yarn is spun from the ungodly, human heart.

The Kathakali Man is the most beautiful of men. Because his body *is* his soul. His only instrument. From the age of three it has been planed and polished, pared down, harnessed wholly to the task of story-telling. He has magic in him, this man within the painted mask and swirling skirts.

But these days he has become unviable. Unfeasible. Condemned goods. His children deride him. They long to be everything that he is not. He has watched them grow up to become clerks and bus conductors. Class IV non-gazetted officers. With unions of their own.

But he himself, left dangling somewhere between heaven and earth, cannot do what they do. He cannot slide down the aisles of buses, counting change and selling tickets. He cannot answer bells that summon him. He cannot stoop behind trays of tea and Marie biscuits.

In despair he turns to tourism. He enters the market. He hawks the only thing he owns. The stories that his body can tell.

He becomes a Regional Flavour.

In the Heart of Darkness they mock him with their lolling nakedness and their imported attention spans. He checks his rage and dances for them. He collects his fee. He gets drunk. Or smokes a joint. Good Kerala grass. It makes him laugh. Then he stops by the Ayemenem Temple, he and the others with him, and they dance to ask pardon of the gods.

Rahel (no Plans, no Locusts stand I), her back against a pillar, watched Karna praying on the banks of the Ganga. Karna, sheathed in his armour of light. Karna, melancholy son of Surya, God of Day. Karna the Generous. Karna the abandoned child. Karna the most revered warrior of them all.

That night Karna was stoned. His tattered skirt was darned. There were hollows in his crown where jewels used to be. His velvet blouse had grown bald with use. His heels were cracked. Tough. He stubbed his joints out on them.

But if he had had a fleet of make-up men waiting in the wings, an agent, a contract, a percentage of the profits – what then would he be? An impostor. A rich pretender. An actor playing a part. Could he be Karna? Or would he be too *safe* inside his pod of wealth? Would his money grow like a rind between himself and his story? Would he be able to touch its heart, its hidden secrets, in the way that he can now?

Perhaps not.

This man tonight is dangerous. His despair complete. This story is the safety net above which he swoops and dives like a brilliant clown in a bankrupt circus. It's all he has to keep him from crashing through the world like a falling stone. It is his colour and his light. It is the vessel into which he pours himself. It gives him shape. Structure. It harnesses him. It contains him. His Love. His Madness. His Hope. His Infinnate Joy. Ironically, his struggle is the reverse of an actor's struggle – he strives not to *enter* a part but to escape it. But this is what he cannot do. In his abject defeat lies his supreme triumph. He *is* Karna,

whom the world has abandoned. Karna Alone. Condemned
goods. A prince raised in poverty. Born to die unfairly, unarmed
and alone at the hands of his brother. Majestic in his complete
despair. Praying on the banks of the Ganga. Stoned out of his
skull.

Then Kunti appeared. She too was a man, but a man grown
soft and womanly, a man with breasts, from doing female parts
for years. Her movements were fluid. Full of woman. Kunti,
too, was stoned. High on the same shared joints. She had come
to tell Karna a story.

Karna inclined his beautiful head and listened.

Red-eyed, Kunti danced for him. She told him of a young
woman who had been granted a boon. A secret mantra that
she could use to choose a lover from among the gods. Of how,
with the imprudence of youth, the woman decided to test it to
see if it really worked. How she stood alone in an empty field,
turned her face to the heavens and recited the mantra. The
words had scarcely left her foolish lips, Kunti said, when Surya,
the God of Day, appeared before her. The young woman,
bewitched by the beauty of the shimmering young god, gave
herself to him. Nine months later she bore him a son. The baby
was born sheathed in light, with gold earrings in his ears and
a gold breastplate on his chest, engraved with the emblem of
the sun.

The young mother loved her first-born son deeply, Kunti
said, but she was unmarried and couldn't keep him. She put
him in a reed basket and cast him away in a river. The child
was found downriver by Adhirata, a charioteer. And named
Karna.

Karna looked up at Kunti. *Who was she? Who was my mother?
Tell me where she is. Take me to her.*

Kunti bowed her head. *She's here,* she said. *Standing before you.*

Karna's elation and anger at the revelation. His dance of
confusion and despair. *Where were you,* he asked her, *when I needed*

you most? Did you ever hold me in your arms? Did you feed me? Did you ever look for me? Did you wonder where I might be?

In reply Kunti took the regal face in her hands, green the face, red the eyes, and kissed him on his brow. Karna shuddered in delight. A warrior reduced to infancy. The ecstasy of that kiss. He dispatched it to the ends of his body. To his toes. His fingertips. His lovely mother's kiss. *Did you know how much I missed you?* Rahel could see it coursing through his veins, as clearly as an egg travelling down an ostrich's neck.

A travelling kiss whose journey was cut short by dismay when Karna realized that his mother had revealed herself to him only to secure the safety of her five other, more beloved sons – the Pandavas – poised on the brink of their epic battle with their one hundred cousins. It is *them* that Kunti sought to protect by announcing to Karna that she was his mother. She had a promise to extract.

She invoked the Love Laws.

They are your brothers. Your own flesh and blood. Promise me that you will not go to war against them. Promise me that.

Karna the Warrior could not make that promise, for if he did, he would have to revoke another one. Tomorrow he would go to war, and his enemies would be the Pandavas. They were the ones, Arjuna in particular, who had publicly reviled him for being a lowly charioteer's son. And it was Duryodhana, the eldest of the one hundred Kaurava brothers, that came to his rescue by gifting him a kingdom of his own. Karna, in return, had pledged Duryodhana eternal fealty.

But Karna the Generous could not refuse his mother what she asked of him. So he modified the promise. Equivocated. Made a small adjustment, took a somewhat altered oath.

I promise you this, Karna said to Kunti. *You will always have five sons. Yudhishtira I will not harm. Bhima will not die by my hand. The twins – Nakula and Sahadeva – will go untouched by me. But Arjuna –*

him I will make no promises about. I will kill him, or he will kill me. One of us will die.

Something altered in the air. And Rahel knew that Estha had come.

She didn't turn her head, but a glow spread inside her. *He's come,* she thought. *He's here. With me.*

Estha settled against a distant pillar and they sat through the performance like this, separated by the breadth of the kuthambalam, but joined by a story. And the memory of another mother.

The air grew warmer. Less damp.

Perhaps that evening had been a particularly bad one in the Heart of Darkness. In Ayemenem the men danced as though they couldn't stop. Like children in a warm house sheltering from a storm. Refusing to emerge and acknowledge the weather. The wind and thunder. The rats racing across the ruined landscape with dollar signs in their eyes. The world crashing around them.

They emerged from one story only to delve deep into another. From *Karna Shabadam* – Karna's Oath – to *Duryodhana Vadham* – the death of Duryodhana and his brother Dushasana.

It was almost four in the morning when Bhima hunted down vile Dushasana. The man who had tried publicly to undress the Pandavas' wife, Draupadi, after the Kauravas had won her in a game of dice. Draupadi (strangely angry only with the men that won her, not the ones that staked her), has sworn that she will never tie up her hair until it is washed in Dushasana's blood. Bhima has vowed to avenge her honour.

Bhima cornered Dushasana in a battlefield already strewn with corpses. For an hour they fenced with each other. Traded insults. Listed all the wrongs that each had done the other. When the light from the brass lamp began to flicker and die, they called a truce. Bhima poured the oil, Dushasana cleaned the charred wick. Then they went back to war. Their breathless battle spilled out of the kuthambalam and spun around the temple. They chased each other across the compound, twirling their papier-mâché maces. Two men in ballooning skirts and balding velvet blouses, vaulting over littered moons and mounds of dung, circling around the hulk of a sleeping elephant. Dushasana full of bravado one minute. Cringing the next. Bhima toying with him. Both stoned.

The sky was a rose bowl. The grey, elephant-shaped hole in the Universe agitated in his sleep, then slept again. Dawn was just breaking when the brute in Bhima stirred. The drums beat louder, but the air grew quiet and full of menace.

In the early morning light, Esthappen and Rahel watched Bhima fulfil his vow to Draupadi. He clubbed Dushasana to the floor. He pursued every feeble tremor in the dying body with his mace, hammering at it until it was stilled. An ironsmith flattening a sheet of recalcitrant metal. Systematically smoothing every pit and bulge. He continued to kill him long after he was dead. Then, with his bare hands he tore the body open. He ripped its innards out and stooped to lap blood straight from the bowl of the torn carcass, his crazed eyes peeping over the rim, glittering with rage and hate and mad fulfilment. Gurgling blood-bubbles pale pink between his teeth. Dribbling down his painted face, his neck and chin. When he had drunk enough, he stood up, bloody intestines draped around his neck like a scarf and went to find Draupadi and bathe her hair in fresh blood. He still had about him the aura of rage that even murder cannot quell.

There was madness there that morning. Under the rose bowl. It was no performance. Esthappen and Rahel recognized it. They had seen its work before. Another morning. Another stage. Another kind of frenzy (with millipedes on the soles of its shoes). The brutal extravagance of this matched by the savage economy of that.

They sat there, Quietness and Emptiness, frozen two-egg fossils, with hornbumps that hadn't grown into horns. Separated by the breadth of a kuthambalam. Trapped in the bog of a story that was and wasn't theirs. That had set out with the semblance of structure and order, then bolted like a frightened horse into anarchy.

Kochu Thomban woke and delicately cracked open his morning coconut.

The Kathakali Men took off their make-up and went home to beat their wives. Even Kunti, the soft one with breasts.

Outside and around, the little town masquerading as a village stirred and came to life. An old man woke and staggered to the stove to warm his peppered coconut oil.

Comrade Pillai. Ayemenem's egg-breaker and professional omletteer.

Oddly enough, it was he who had introduced the twins to kathakali. Against Baby Kochamma's better judgement, it was he who took them, along with Lenin, for all-night performances at the temple, and sat up with them till dawn, explaining the language and gesture of kathakali. Aged six, they had sat with him through this very story. It was he who had introduced them to Raudra Bhima – crazed, bloodthirsty Bhima in search of death and vengeance. 'He is searching for the beast that lives in him,' Comrade Pillai had told them – frightened, wide-eyed children – when the ordinarily good-natured Bhima began to bay and snarl.

Which beast in particular, Comrade Pillai didn't say. Searching for the *man* who lives in him was perhaps what he really meant, because certainly no beast has essayed the boundless, infinitely inventive art of human hatred. No beast can match its range and power.

The rose bowl dulled and sent down a warm grey drizzle. As Estha and Rahel stepped through the temple gateway, Comrade

K. N. M. Pillai stepped in, slick from his oil bath. He had sandalwood paste on his forehead. Raindrops stood out on his oiled skin like studs. In his cupped palms he carried a small heap of fresh jasmine.

'Oho!' he said in his piping voice 'You are here! So still you are interested in your Indian culture? Goodgood. Very good.'

The twins, not rude, not polite, said nothing. They walked home together. He and She. We and Us.

13

The Pessimist and the Optimist

Chacko had moved out of his room and would sleep in Pappachi's study so that Sophie Mol and Margaret Kochamma could have his room. It was a small room, with a window that overlooked the dwindling, somewhat neglected rubber plantation that Reverend E. John Ipe had bought from a neighbour. One door connected it to the main house and another (the separate entrance that Mammachi had installed for Chacko to pursue his 'Men's Needs' discreetly) led directly out into the side mittam.

Sophie Mol lay asleep on a little camp cot that had been made up for her next to the big bed. The drone of the slow ceiling fan filled her head. Bluegreyblue eyes snapped open.

A Wake

A Live

A Lert

Sleep was summarily dismissed.

For the first time since Joe had died, he was not the first thing that she thought about when she woke up.

She looked around the room. Not moving, just swivelling her eyeballs. A captured spy in enemy territory, plotting her spectacular escape.

A vase of awkwardly arranged hibiscus, already drooping, stood on Chacko's table. The walls were lined with books. A glass-paned cupboard was crammed with damaged balsa air-planes. Broken butterflies with imploring eyes. A wicked king's wooden wives languishing under an evil wooden spell.

Trapped.

Only one, her mother, Margaret, had escaped to England.

The room went round in the calm, chrome centre of the silver ceiling fan. A beige gecko, the colour of an undercooked biscuit, regarded her with interested eyes. She thought of Joe. Something shook inside her. She closed her eyes.

The calm, chrome centre of the silver ceiling fan went round inside her head.

Joe could walk on his hands. And when he cycled downhill, he could put the wind inside his shirt.

On the next bed, Margaret Kochamma was still asleep. She lay on her back with her hands clasped together just below her ribcage. Her fingers were swollen and her wedding band looked uncomfortably tight. The flesh of her cheeks fell away on either side of her face, making her cheekbones look high and promi-nent, and pulling her mouth downwards into a mirthless smile that contained just a glimmer of teeth. She had tweezed her once bushy eyebrows into the currently fashionable, pencil-thin arcs which gave her a slightly surprised expression even in her sleep. The rest of her expressions were growing back in a nascent stubble. Her face was flushed. Her forehead glistened. Under-neath the flush, there was a paleness. A staved-off sadness.

The thin material of her dark blue and white flowered cotton-polyester dress had wilted and clung limply to the contours of her body, rising over her breasts, dipping along the line between her long, strong legs – as though it too was unaccustomed to the heat and needed a nap.

On the bedside table there was a silver-framed black-and-white wedding picture of Chacko and Margaret Kochamma taken outside the church in Oxford. It was snowing a little. The first flakes of fresh snow lay on the street and sidewalk. Chacko was dressed like Nehru. He wore a white churidar and a black shervani. His shoulders were dusted with snow. There was a rose in his buttonhole, and the tip of his handkerchief, folded into a triangle, peeped out of his breast pocket. On his feet he wore polished black Oxfords. He looked as though he was laughing at himself and the way he was dressed. Like someone at a fancy-dress party.

Margaret Kochamma wore a long, foaming gown and a cheap tiara on her cropped, curly hair. Her veil was lifted off her face. She was as tall as he was. They looked happy. Thin and young, scowling from the sun in their eyes. Her thick, dark eyebrows were knitted together and somehow made a lovely contrast to the frothy, bridal white. A scowling cloud with eyebrows. Behind them stood a large matronly woman with thick ankles and all the buttons done up on her long overcoat. Margaret Kochamma's mother. She had her two little granddaughters on either side of her, in pleated tartan skirts, stockings and identical fringes. They were both giggling with their hands over their mouths. Margaret Kochamma's mother was looking away, out of the photograph, as though she would rather not have been there.

Margaret Kochamma's father had refused to attend the wedding. He disliked Indians, he thought of them as sly, dishonest people. He couldn't believe that his daughter was marrying one.

In the right-hand corner of the photograph, a man wheeling his bicycle along the kerb had turned to stare at the couple.

Margaret Kochamma was working as a waitress at a café in Oxford when she first met Chacko. Her family lived in London. Her father owned a bakery. Her mother was a milliner's assistant. Margaret Kochamma had moved out of her parents' home a year ago, for no greater reason than a youthful assertion of independence. She intended to work and save enough money to put herself through a teacher training course, and then look for a job at a school. In Oxford she shared a small flat with a friend. Another waitress in another café.

Having made the move, Margaret Kochamma found herself becoming exactly the kind of girl her parents wanted her to be. Faced with the Real World, she clung nervously to old remembered rules, and had no one but herself to rebel against. So even up at Oxford, other than playing her gramophone a little louder than she was permitted at home, she continued to lead the same small, tight life that she imagined she had escaped.

Until Chacko walked into the café one morning.

It was the summer of his final year at Oxford. He was alone. His rumpled shirt was buttoned up wrong. His shoelaces were untied. His hair, carefully brushed and slicked down in front, stood up in a stiff halo of quills at the back. He looked like an untidy, beatified porcupine. He was tall, and underneath the mess of clothes (inappropriate tie, shabby coat), Margaret Kochamma could see that he was well-built. He had an amused air about him, and a way of narrowing his eyes as though he was trying to read a faraway sign and had forgotten to bring his glasses. His ears stuck out on either side of his head like teapot handles. There was something contradictory about his athletic build and his dishevelled appearance. The only sign that a fat man lurked inside him was his shining, happy cheeks.

He had none of the vagueness or the apologetic awkwardness that one usually associates with untidy, absent-minded men. He looked cheerful, as though he was with an imaginary friend whose company he enjoyed. He took a seat by the window and sat down with an elbow on the table and his face cupped in the palm of his hand, smiling around the empty café as though he was considering striking up a conversation with the furniture. He ordered coffee with that same friendly smile, but without really appearing to notice the tall, bushy eyebrowed waitress who took his order.

She winced when he put two heaped spoons of sugar into his extremely milky coffee.

Then he asked for fried eggs on toast. More coffee, and strawberry jam.

When she returned with his order, he said, as though he was continuing an old conversation, 'Have you heard about the man who had twin sons?'

'No,' she said, setting down his breakfast. For some reason (natural prudence perhaps, and an instinctive reticence with foreigners) she did not evince the keen interest that he seemed to expect from her about the Man with Twin Sons. Chacko didn't seem to mind.

'A man had twin sons,' he told Margaret Kochamma. 'Pete and Stuart. Pete was an Optimist and Stuart was a Pessimist.'

He picked the strawberries out of the jam and put them on one side of his plate. The rest of the jam he spread in a thick layer on his buttered toast.

'On their thirteenth birthday their father gave Stuart – the Pessimist – an expensive watch, a carpentry set and a bicycle.'

Chacko looked up at Margaret Kochamma to see if she was listening.

'And Pete's – the Optimist's – room, he filled with horse dung.'

Chacko lifted the fried eggs onto the toast, broke the brilliant, wobbling yokes and spread them over the strawberry jam with the back of his teaspoon.

'When Stuart opened his presents he grumbled all morning. He hadn't wanted a carpentry set, he didn't like the watch and the bicycle had the wrong kind of tyres.'

Margaret Kochamma had stopped listening because she was riveted by the curious ritual unfolding on his plate. The toast with jam and fried egg was cut into neat little squares. The dejammed strawberries were summoned one by one, and sliced into delicate pieces.

'When the father went to Pete's – the Optimist's – room, he couldn't see Pete, but he could hear the sound of frantic shovelling and heavy breathing. Horse dung was flying all over the room.'

Chacko had begun to shake with silent laughter in anticipation of the end of his joke. With laughing hands, he placed a sliver of strawberry on each bright yellow and red square of toast – making the whole thing look like a lurid snack that an old woman might serve at a bridge party.

'"What in heaven's name are you doing?" the father shouted to Pete.'

Salt and pepper was sprinkled on the squares of toast. Chacko paused before the punch line, laughing up at Margaret Kochamma, who was smiling at his plate.

'A voice came from deep inside the dung. "Well, Father," Pete said, "if there's so much shit around, there has to be a pony somewhere!"'

Chacko, holding a fork and a knife in each hand, leaned back in his chair in the empty café, and laughed his high, hiccupping, infectious, fat man's laugh till the tears poured down his cheeks. Margaret Kochamma, who had missed most of the joke, smiled. Then she began to laugh at his laugh. Their laughs fed each other and climbed to a hysterical pitch. When the owner of the café appeared, he saw a customer (not a particularly desirable one), and a waitress (an only averagely desirable one), locked in a spiral of hooting, helpless laughter.

Meanwhile, another customer (a regular), had arrived unnoticed, and waited to be served.

The owner cleaned some already-clean glasses clinking them together noisily, and clattered crockery on the counter to convey his displeasure to Margaret Kochamma. She tried to compose herself before she went to take the new order. But she had tears in her eyes, and had to stifle a fresh batch of giggles, which made the hungry man whose order she was taking look up from his menu card, his thin lips pursed in silent disapproval.

She stole a glance at Chacko, who looked at her and smiled. It was an insanely friendly smile.

He finished his breakfast, paid, and left.

Margaret Kochamma was reproached by her employer and given a lecture on Café Ethics. She apologized to him. She was truly sorry for the way she had behaved.

That evening, after work, she thought about what had happened and was uncomfortable with herself. She was not usually frivolous, and didn't think it right to have shared such uncontrolled laughter with a complete stranger. It seemed such an over-familiar, intimate thing to have done. She wondered what had made her laugh so much. She knew it wasn't the joke.

She thought of Chacko's laugh, and a smile stayed in her eyes for a long time.

Chacko began to visit the café quite often.

He always came with his invisible companion and his friendly smile. Even when it wasn't Margaret Kochamma who served him, he sought her out with his eyes, and they exchanged secret smiles that invoked the joint memory of their Laugh.

Margaret Kochamma found herself looking forward to the Rumpled Porcupine's visits. Without anxiety, but with a sort of creeping affection. She learned that he was a Rhodes Scholar from India. That he read Classics. And rowed for Balliol.

Until the day she married him she never believed that she would ever consent to be his wife.

A few months after they began to go out together, he began to smuggle her into his rooms, where he lived like a helpless, exiled prince. Despite the best efforts of his scout and cleaning lady, his room was always filthy. Books, empty wine bottles, dirty underwear and cigarette butts littered the floor. Cupboards were dangerous to open because clothes and books and shoes would cascade down and some of his books were heavy enough to inflict real damage. Margaret Kochamma's tiny, ordered life relinquished itself to this truly baroque bedlam with the quiet gasp of a warm body entering a chilly sea.

She discovered that underneath the aspect of the Rumpled Porcupine, a tortured Marxist was at war with an impossible, incurable Romantic – who forgot the candles, who broke the wine glasses, who lost the ring. Who made love to her with a passion that took her breath away. She had always thought of herself as a somewhat uninteresting, thick-waisted, thick-ankled girl. Not bad-looking. Not special. But when she was with Chacko, old limits were pushed back. Horizons expanded.

She had never before met a man who spoke of the world – of what it was, and how it came to be, or what he thought would become of it – in the way in which other men she knew discussed their jobs, their friends or their weekends at the beach.

Being with Chacko made Margaret Kochamma feel as though her soul had escaped from the narrow confines of her island country into the vast, extravagant spaces of his. He made her feel as though the world belonged to them – as though it lay before them like an opened frog on a dissecting table, begging to be examined.

In the year she knew him, before they were married, she discovered a little magic in herself, and for a while felt like a blithe genie released from her lamp. She was perhaps too young to realize that what she assumed was her love for Chacko was actually a tentative, timorous acceptance of herself.

As for Chacko, Margaret Kochamma was the first female friend he had ever had. Not just the first woman that he had slept with, but his first real companion. What Chacko loved most about her was her self-sufficiency. Perhaps it wasn't remarkable in the average English woman, but it was remarkable to Chacko.

He loved the fact that Margaret Kochamma didn't cling to him. That she was uncertain about her feelings for him. That he never knew till the last day whether or not she would marry him. He loved the way she would sit up naked in his bed, her long white back swivelled away from him, look at her watch and say in her practical way – 'Oops, I must be off.' He loved the way she wobbled to work every morning on her bicycle. He encouraged their differences in opinion, and inwardly rejoiced at her occasional outbursts of exasperation at his decadence.

He was grateful to her for not wanting to look after him. For not offering to tidy his room. For not being his cloying mother. He grew to depend on Margaret Kochamma for not depending on him. He adored her for not adoring him.

Of his family Margaret Kochamma knew very little. He seldom spoke of them.

The truth is that in his years at Oxford, Chacko rarely thought of them. Too much was happening in his life and Ayemenem seemed so far away. The river too small. The fish too few.

He had no pressing reasons to stay in touch with his parents. The Rhodes Scholarship was generous. He needed no money. He was deeply in love with his love for Margaret Kochamma and had no room in his heart for anyone else.

Mammachi wrote to him regularly, with detailed descriptions of her sordid squabbles with her husband and her worries about Ammu's future. He hardly ever read a whole letter. Sometimes he never bothered to open them at all. He never wrote back.

Even the one time he did return (when he stopped Pappachi from hitting Mammachi with the brass vase, and a rocking chair was murdered in the moonlight), he was hardly aware of how stung his father had been, or his mother's redoubled adoration of him, or his young sister's sudden beauty. He came and went in a trance, yearning from the moment he arrived to return to the long-backed white girl who waited for him.

The winter after he came down from Balliol (he did badly in his exams), Margaret Kochamma and Chacko were married. Without her family's consent. Without his family's knowledge.

They decided that he should move into Margaret Koch-amma's flat (displacing the Other waitress in the Other café) until he found himself a job.

The timing of the wedding couldn't have been worse.

Along with the pressures of living together came penury. There was no longer any scholarship money, and there was the full rent of the flat to be paid.

With the end to his rowing came a sudden, premature, middle-aged spread. Chacko became a Fat Man, with a body to match his laugh.

A year into the marriage, and the charm of Chacko's studently sloth wore off for Margaret Kochamma. It no longer amused her that while she went to work, the flat remained in the same filthy mess that she had left it in. That it was impossible for him even to consider making the bed, or washing clothes or dishes. That he didn't apologize for the cigarette burns in the new sofa. That he seemed incapable of buttoning up his shirt, knotting his tie *and* tying his shoe laces before presenting himself for a job interview. Within a year she was prepared to exchange the frog on the dissecting table for some small, practical concessions. Such as a job for her husband and a clean home.

Eventually Chacko got a brief, badly paid assignment with the Overseas Sales Department of the India Tea Board. Hoping that this would lead to other things, Chacko and Margaret moved to London. To even smaller, more dismal rooms. Margaret Kochamma's parents refused to see her.

She had just discovered that she was pregnant when she met Joe. He was an old school friend of her brother's. When they met, Margaret Kochamma was physically at her most attractive. Pregnancy had put colour in her cheeks and brought a shine to her thick, dark hair. Despite her marital troubles, she had that air of secret elation, that affection for her own body that pregnant women often have.

Joe was a biologist. He was updating the third edition of a

dictionary of Biology for a small publishing house. Joe was everything that Chacko wasn't.

Steady. Solvent. Thin.

Margaret Kochamma found herself drawn towards him like a plant in a dark room towards a wedge of light.

When Chacko finished his assignment and couldn't find another job, he wrote to Mammachi, telling her of his marriage and asking for money. Mammachi was devastated, but secretly pawned her jewellery and arranged for money to be sent to him in England. It wasn't enough. It was never enough.

By the time Sophie Mol was born, Margaret Kochamma realized that for herself and her daughter's sake, she *had* to leave Chacko. She asked him for a divorce.

Chacko returned to India, where he found a job easily. For a few years he taught at the Madras Christian College, and after Pappachi died, he returned to Ayemenem with his Bharat bottle-sealing machine, his Balliol oar and his broken heart.

Mammachi joyfully welcomed him back into her life. She fed him, she sewed for him, she saw to it that there were fresh flowers in his room every day. Chacko needed his mother's adoration. Indeed, he *demanded* it, yet he despised her for it and punished her in secret ways. He began to cultivate his corpulence and general physical dilapidation. He wore cheap, printed Terylene bush shirts over his white mundus and the ugliest plastic sandals that were available in the market. If Mammachi had guests, relatives, or perhaps an old friend visiting from Delhi, Chacko would appear at her tastefully laid dining table – adorned with her exquisite orchid arrangements and best china – and worry an old scab, or scratch the large, black oblong calluses he had cultivated on his elbows.

His special targets were Baby Kochamma's guests – Catholic bishops or visiting clergy – who often dropped by for a snack.

In their presence Chacko would take off his sandals and air a revolting, pus-filled diabetic boil on his foot.

'Lord have mercy upon this poor leper,' he would say, while Baby Kochamma tried desperately to distract them from the spectacle by picking out the biscuit crumbs and bits of banana chips that littered their beards.

But of all the secret punishments that Chacko tormented Mammachi with, the worst and most mortifying of all, was when he reminisced about Margaret Kochamma. He spoke of her often and with a peculiar pride. As though he admired her for having divorced him.

'She traded me in for a better man,' he would say to Mammachi, and she would flinch as though he had denigrated her instead of himself.

Margaret Kochamma wrote regularly, giving Chacko news of Sophie Mol. She assured him that Joe made a wonderful, caring father and that Sophie Mol loved him dearly – facts that gladdened and saddened Chacko in equal measure.

Margaret Kochamma was happy with Joe. Happier perhaps than she would have been had she not had those wild, precarious years with Chacko. She thought of Chacko fondly, but without regret. It simply did not occur to her that she had hurt him as deeply as she had, because she still thought of herself as an ordinary woman, and him as an extraordinary man. And because Chacko had not then, or since, exhibited any of the usual symptoms of grief and heartbreak, Margaret Kochamma just assumed that he felt it had been as much of a mistake for him as it had been for her. When she told him about Joe he had left sadly, but quietly. With his invisible companion and his friendly smile.

They wrote to each other frequently, and over the years their relationship matured. For Margaret Kochamma it became a comfortable, committed friendship. For Chacko it was a way, the *only* way, of remaining in touch with the mother of his child and the only woman he had ever loved.

When Sophie Mol was old enough to go to school, Margaret Kochamma enrolled herself in a teacher training course, and then got a job as a junior school teacher in Clapham. She was in the staff room when she was told about Joe's accident. The news was delivered by a young policeman who wore a grave expression and carried his helmet in his hands. He had looked strangely comical, like a bad actor auditioning for a solemn part in a play. Margaret Kochamma remembered that her first instinct when she saw him had been to smile.

For Sophie Mol's sake, if not her own, Margaret Kochamma did her best to face the tragedy with equanimity. To *pretend* to face the tragedy with equanimity. She didn't take time off from her job. She saw to it that Sophie Mol's school routine remained unchanged – *Finish your homework. Eat your egg. No, we can't not go to school.*

She concealed her anguish under the brisk, practical mask of a schoolteacher. The stern, schoolteacher-shaped hole in the Universe (who sometimes slapped).

But when Chacko wrote inviting her to Ayemenem, something inside her sighed and sat down. Despite everything that had happened between her and Chacko, there was nobody in the world she would rather spend Christmas with. The more she considered it, the more tempted she was. She persuaded herself that a trip to India would be just the thing for Sophie Mol.

So eventually, though she knew that her friends and colleagues at the school would think it odd – her running back to her first husband just as soon as her second one had died – Margaret Kochamma broke her term deposit and bought two airline tickets. London–Bombay–Cochin.

She was haunted by that decision for as long as she lived.

She took with her to her grave the picture of her little daughter's body laid out on the chaise longue in the drawing room of the Ayemenem House. Even from a distance, it was obvious that she was dead. Not ill or asleep. It was something to do with the way she lay. The angle of her limbs. Something to do with Death's authority. Its terrible stillness.

Green weed and river grime were woven into her beautiful redbrown hair. Her sunken eyelids were raw, nibbled at by fish. (O yes they do, the deepswimming fish. They sample everything.) Her mauve corduroy pinafore said *Holiday!* in a tilting, happy font. She was as wrinkled as a dhobi's thumb from being in water for too long.

A spongy mermaid who had forgotten how to swim.

A silver thimble clenched, for luck, in her little fist.

Thimble-drinker.

Coffin-cartwheeler.

Margaret Kochamma never forgave herself for taking Sophie Mol to Ayemenem. For leaving her there alone over the weekend while she and Chacko went to Cochin to confirm their return tickets.

IT WAS ABOUT NINE in the morning when Mammachi and Baby Kochamma got news of a white child's body found floating downriver where the Meenachal broadens as it approaches the backwaters. Estha and Rahel were still missing.

Earlier that morning the children – all three of them – hadn't appeared for their morning glass of milk. Baby Kochamma and Mammachi thought that they might have gone down to the river for a swim, which was worrying because it had rained heavily the previous day and a good part of the night. They knew that the river could be dangerous. Baby Kochamma sent Kochu Maria to look for them but she returned without them. In the chaos that ensued after Vellya Paapen's visit, nobody could remember when they had actually last seen the children. They hadn't been uppermost on anybody's mind. They could have been missing all night.

Ammu was still locked into her bedroom. Baby Kochamma had the keys. She called through the door to ask Ammu whether she had any idea where the children might be. She tried to keep the panic out of her voice, make it sound like a casual enquiry. Something crashed against the door. Ammu was incoherent with rage and disbelief at what was happening to her – at being locked away like the family lunatic in a medieval household. It was only later, when the world collapsed around them, after Sophie Mol's body was brought to Ayemenem, and Baby Kochamma unlocked her, that Ammu sifted through her rage to try to make sense of what had happened. Fear and apprehension forced her to think clearly, and it was only then that she remembered what she had said to her twins when they came to her bedroom door and asked her why she had been locked up. The careless words she hadn't meant.

'Because of you!' Ammu had screamed. 'If it wasn't for you I wouldn't be here! None of this would have happened! I wouldn't be here! I would have been free! I should have dumped you in an orphanage the day you were born! *You're* the millstones round my neck!'

She couldn't see them crouched against the door. A Surprised Puff and a Fountain in a Love-in-Tokyo. Bewildered Twin Ambassadors of God-knows-what. Their Excellencies Ambassadors E. Pelvis and S. Insect.

'Just go away!' Ammu had said. 'Why can't you just go away and leave me alone?'

So they had.

But when the only answer Baby Kochamma got to her question about the children was something crashing against Ammu's bedroom door, she went away. A slow dread built up inside her as she began to make the obvious, logical and completely mistaken connections between the night's happenings and the missing children.

The rain had started early the previous afternoon. Suddenly the hot day darkened and the sky began to clap and grumble. Kochu Maria, in a bad mood for no particular reason, was in the kitchen standing on her low stool savagely cleaning a large fish, working up a smelly blizzard of fish scales. Her gold earrings swung fiercely. Silver fish scales flew around the kitchen, landing on kettles, walls, vegetable peelers, the fridge handle. She ignored Vellya Paapen when he arrived at the kitchen door, drenched and shaking. His real eye was bloodshot and he looked as though he had been drinking. He stood there for ten minutes waiting to be noticed. When Kochu Maria finished the fish and started on the onions, he cleared his throat and asked for Mammachi. Kochu Maria tried to shoo him away, but he wouldn't go. Each time he opened his mouth to speak, the smell of arrack on his breath hit Kochu Maria like a hammer. She had never seen him like this before, and was a little frightened. She had a pretty good idea of what it was all about, so she eventually decided that it would be best to call Mammachi. She shut the kitchen door, leaving Vellya Paapen outside in the back mittam, weaving drunkenly in the driving rain. Though it was December, it rained as though it was June. *Cyclonic disturbance*, the newspapers called it the next day. But by then nobody was in any condition to read the papers.

Perhaps it was the rain that drove Vellya Paapen to the kitchen door. To a superstitious man, the relentlessness of that unseasonal downpour could have seemed like an omen from an angry god. To a drunk superstitious man, it could have seemed like the beginning of the end of the world. Which, in a way, it was.

When Mammachi arrived in the kitchen, in her petticoat and pale pink dressing gown with rickrack edging, Vellya Paapen climbed up the kitchen steps and offered her his mortgaged eye. He held it out in the palm of his hand. He said he didn't deserve it and wanted her to have it back. His left eyelid drooped over his empty socket in an immutable, monstrous wink. As though everything that he was about to say was part of an elaborate prank.

'What is it?' Mammachi asked, stretching her hand out, thinking perhaps that for some reason Vellya Paapen was returning the kilo of red rice she had given him that morning.

'It's his eye,' Kochu Maria said loudly to Mammachi, her own eyes bright with onion tears. By then Mammachi had already touched the glass eye. She recoiled from its slippery hardness. Its slimy marbleness.

'Are you drunk?' Mammachi said angrily to the sound of the rain. 'How dare you come here in this condition?'

She groped her way to the sink, and soaped away the sodden Paravan's eye-juices. She smelled her hands when she'd finished. Kochu Maria gave Vellya Paapen an old kitchen cloth to wipe himself with, and said nothing when he stood on the topmost step, almost inside her Touchable kitchen, drying himself, sheltered from the rain by the sloping overhang of the roof.

When he was calmer, Vellya Paapen returned his eye to its rightful socket and began to speak. He started by recounting to Mammachi how much her family had done for his. Generation for generation. How, long before the communists thought of it, Reverend E. John Ipe had given his father, Kelan, title to the land on which their hut now stood. How Mammachi had paid for his eye. How she had organized for Velutha to be educated and given him a job . . .

Mammachi, though annoyed at his drunkenness, wasn't averse to listening to bardic stories about herself and her family's Christian munificence. Nothing prepared her for what she was about to hear.

Vellya Paapen began to cry. Half of him wept. Tears welled up in his real eye and shone on his black cheek. With his other eye he stared stonily ahead. An old Paravan, who had seen the Walking Backwards days, torn between Loyalty and Love.

Then the Terror took hold of him and shook the words out of him. He told Mammachi what he had seen. The story of the little boat that crossed the river night after night, and who was in it. The story of a man and woman, standing together in the moonlight. Skin to skin.

They went to Kari Saipu's House, Vellya Paapen said. The white man's demon had entered them. It was Kari Saipu's revenge for what he, Vellya Paapen, had done to him. The boat (that Estha sat on and Rahel found) was tethered to the tree stump next to the steep path that led through the marsh to the abandoned rubber estate. He had seen it there. Every night. Rocking on the water. Empty. Waiting for the lovers to return. For hours it waited. Sometimes they only emerged through the long grass at dawn. Vellya Paapen had seen them with his own eye. Others had seen them too. The whole village knew. It was only a matter of time before Mammachi found out. So Vellya Paapen had come to tell Mammachi himself. As a Paravan and a man with mortgaged body parts, he considered it his duty.

The lovers. Sprung from his loins and hers. His son and her daughter. They had made the unthinkable thinkable and the impossible really happen.

Vellya Paapen kept talking. Weeping. Retching. Moving his mouth. Mammachi couldn't hear what he was saying. The sound of the rain grew louder and exploded in her head. She didn't hear herself shouting.

Suddenly the blind old woman in her rickrack dressing gown and her thin grey hair plaited into a rat's tail stepped forward and pushed Vellya Paapen with all her strength. He stumbled backwards, down the kitchen steps and lay sprawled in the wet mud. He was taken completely by surprise. Part of the taboo of being an Untouchable was expecting not to be touched. At least not in these circumstances. Of being locked into a physically impregnable cocoon.

Baby Kochamma, walking past the kitchen, heard the commotion. She found Mammachi spitting into the rain, THOO! THOO! THOO! and Vellya Paapen lying in the slush, wet, weeping, grovelling. Offering to kill his son. To tear him limb from limb.

Mammachi was shouting, 'Drunken dog! Drunken Paravan liar!'

Over the din Kochu Maria shouted Vellya Paapen's story to Baby Kochamma. Baby Kochamma recognized at once the immense potential of the situation, but immediately anointed her thoughts with unctuous oils. She bloomed. She saw it as God's Way of punishing Ammu for her sins and simultaneously avenging her (Baby Kochamma's) humiliation at the hands of Velutha and the men in the march – the *Modalali Mariakutty* taunts, the forced flag-waving. She set sail at once. A ship of goodness ploughing through a sea of sin.

Baby Kochamma put her heavy arm around Mammachi.

'It must be true,' she said in a quiet voice. 'She's quite capable of it. And so is he. Vellya Paapen would not lie about something like this.'

She asked Kochu Maria to get Mammachi a glass of water and a chair to sit on. She made Vellya Paapen repeat his story, stopping him every now and then for details – Whose boat? How often? How long had it been going on?

When Vellya Paapen finished, Baby Kochamma turned to Mammachi. 'He must go,' she said. 'Tonight. Before it goes any further. Before we are completely ruined.'

Then she shuddered her schoolgirl shudder. That was when she said: *'How could she stand the smell? Haven't you noticed? They have a particular smell, these Paravans.'*

With that olfactory observation, that specific little detail, the Terror unspooled.

Mammachi's rage at the old one-eyed Paravan standing in the rain, drunk, dribbling and covered in mud was redirected into a cold contempt for her daughter and what she had done. She thought of her naked, coupling in the mud with a man who was nothing but a filthy *coolie*. She imagined it in vivid detail: a Paravan's coarse black hand on her daughter's breast. His mouth on hers. His black hips jerking between her parted legs. The sound of their breathing. His particular Paravan smell. *Like animals*, Mammachi thought and nearly vomited. *Like a dog with a bitch on heat.* Her tolerance of 'Men's Needs' as far as her son was concerned, became the fuel for her unmanageable fury at her daughter. She had defiled generations of breeding (The Little Blessed One, blessed personally by the Patriarch of Antioch, an Imperial Entomologist, a Rhodes Scholar from Oxford) and brought the family to its knees. For generations to come, *for ever* now, people would point at them at weddings and funerals. At baptisms and birthday parties. They'd nudge and whisper. It was all finished now.

Mammachi lost control.

They did what they had to do, the two old ladies. Mammachi provided the passion. Baby Kochamma the Plan. Kochu Maria was their midget lieutenant. They locked Ammu up (tricked her into her bedroom) before they sent for Velutha. They knew that they had to get him to leave Ayemenem before Chacko returned. They could neither trust nor predict what Chacko's attitude would be.

It wasn't entirely their fault, though, that the whole thing spun out of control like a deranged top. That it lashed out at those that crossed its path. That by the time Chacko and Margaret Kochamma returned from Cochin, it was too late.

The fisherman had already found Sophie Mol.

Picture him.

Out in his boat at dawn, at the mouth of the river he has known all his life. It is still quick and swollen from the previous night's rain. Something bobs past in the water and the colours catch his eye. Mauve. Red-brown. Beach sand. It moves with the current, swiftly towards the sea. He sends out his bamboo pole to stop it and draw it towards him. It's a wrinkled mermaid. A mer-child. A mere mer-child. With red-brown hair. With an Imperial Entomologist's nose, and a silver thimble clenched for luck in her fist. He pulls her out of the water into his boat. He puts his thin cotton towel under her, she lies at the bottom of his boat with his silver haul of small fish. He rows home – *Thaiy thaiy thakka thaiy thaiy thome* – thinking how wrong it is for a fisherman to believe that he knows his river well. *No one* knows the Meenachal. No one knows what it may snatch or suddenly yield. Or when. That is what makes fishermen pray.

At the Kottayam police station, a shaking Baby Kochamma was ushered into the Station House Officer's room. She told Inspector Thomas Mathew of the circumstances that had led to the sudden dismissal of a factory worker. A Paravan. A few days ago he had tried to, to . . . to force himself on her niece, she said. A divorcée with two children.

Baby Kochamma misrepresented the relationship between Ammu and Velutha, not for Ammu's sake, but to contain the scandal and salvage the family reputation in Inspector Thomas Mathew's eyes. It didn't occur to her that Ammu would later invite shame upon herself – that she would go to the police and try and set the record straight. As Baby Kochamma told her story, she began to believe it.

Why wasn't the matter reported to the police in the first place, the Inspector wanted to know.

'We are an old family,' Baby Kochamma said. 'These are not things we want talked about . . .'

Inspector Thomas Mathew, receding behind his bustling Air India moustache, understood perfectly. He had a Touchable wife, two Touchable daughters – whole Touchable generations waiting in their Touchable wombs . . .

'Where is the molestee now?'

'At home. She doesn't know I've come here. She wouldn't have let me come. Naturally – she's frantic with worry about the children. Hysterical.'

Later, when the real story reached Inspector Thomas Mathew, the fact that what the Paravan had taken from the

Touchable Kingdom had not been snatched but *given*, concerned him deeply. So after Sophie Mol's funeral, when Ammu went to him with the twins to tell him that a mistake had been made and he tapped her breasts with his baton, it was not a policeman's spontaneous brutishness on his part. He knew exactly what he was doing. It was a premeditated gesture, calculated to humiliate and terrorize her. An attempt to instil order into a world gone wrong.

Still later, when the dust had settled and he had had the paperwork organized, Inspector Thomas Mathew congratulated himself for the way it had all turned out.

But now, he listened carefully and courteously as Baby Kochamma constructed her story.

'Last night it was getting dark – about seven in the evening – when he came to the house to threaten us. It was raining very heavily. The lights had gone out and we were lighting the lamps when he came,' she told him. 'He knew that the man of the house, my nephew, Chacko Ipe, was – is – away in Cochin. We were three women alone in the house.' She paused to let the Inspector imagine the horrors that could be visited by a sex-crazed Paravan on three women alone in a house.

'We told him that if he did not leave Ayemenem quietly we would call the police. He started off by saying that my niece had *consented*, can you imagine? He asked us what proof we had of what we were accusing him of. He said that according to the Labour Laws we had no grounds on which to dismiss him. He was very calm. "The days are gone," he told us, "when you can kick us around like dogs . . ."' By now Baby Kochamma sounded utterly convincing. Injured. Incredulous.

Then her imagination took over completely. She didn't describe how Mammachi had lost control. How she had gone up to Velutha and spat right into his face. The things she had said to him. The names she had called him.

Instead she described to Inspector Thomas Mathew how it

was not just *what* Velutha had said that had made her come to the police, but the *way* he said it. His complete lack of remorse, which was what had shocked her most. As though he was actually *proud* of what he had done. Without realizing it herself, she grafted the manner of the man who had humiliated her during the march onto Velutha. She described the sneering fury in his face. The brassy, insolence in his voice that had so frightened her. That made her sure that his dismissal and the children's disappearance were not, could not possibly be, unconnected.

She had known the Paravan since he was a child, Baby Kochamma said. He had been educated by her family, in the Untouchables' school started by her father, Punnyan Kunju (Mr Thomas Mathew must know who he was? Yes, of course) . . . He was trained to be a carpenter by her family, the house he lived in was given to his grandfather by her family. He owed everything to her family.

'You people,' Inspector Thomas Mathew said, 'first you spoil these people, carry them about on your head like trophies, then when they misbehave you come running to us for help.'

Baby Kochamma lowered her eyes like a chastised child. Then she continued her story. She told Inspector Thomas Mathew how in the last few weeks she had noticed some presaging signs, some insolence, some rudeness. She mentioned seeing him in the march on the way to Cochin and the rumours that he was or had been a Naxalite. She didn't notice the faint furrow of worry that this piece of information produced on the Inspector's brow.

She had warned her nephew about him, Baby Kochamma said, but never in her wildest dreams had she thought that it would ever come to this. A beautiful child was dead. Two children were missing.

Baby Kochamma broke down.

Inspector Thomas Mathew gave her a cup of police tea. When she was feeling a little better, he helped her to set down all she had told him in her FIR. He assured Baby Kochamma of the Full Co-operation of the Kottayam Police. The rascal would be caught before the day was out, he said. A Paravan with a pair of two-egg twins, hounded by history – he knew there weren't many places for him to hide.

Inspector Thomas Mathew was a prudent man. He took one precaution. He sent a Jeep to fetch Comrade K. N. M. Pillai to the police station. It was crucial for him to know whether the Paravan had any political support or whether he was operating alone. Though he himself was a Congress man, he did not intend to risk any run-ins with the Marxist Government. When Comrade Pillai arrived, he was ushered into the seat that Baby Kochamma had only recently vacated. Inspector Thomas Mathew showed him Baby Kochamma's FIR. The two men had a conversation. Brief, cryptic, to the point. As though they had exchanged numbers and not words. No explanations seemed necessary. They were not friends, Comrade Pillai and Inspector Thomas Mathew, and they didn't trust each other. But they understood each other perfectly. They were both men whom childhood had abandoned without a trace. Men without curiosity. Without doubt. Both in their own way truly, terrifyingly adult. They looked out at the world and never wondered how it worked, because they knew. *They* worked it. They were mechanics who serviced different parts of the same machine.

Comrade Pillai told Inspector Thomas Mathew that he was acquainted with Velutha, but omitted to mention that Velutha was a member of the Communist Party, or that Velutha had knocked on his door late the previous night, which made Comrade Pillai the last person to have seen Velutha before he disappeared. Nor, though he knew it to be untrue, did Comrade Pillai refute the allegation of attempted rape in Baby Kochamma's FIR. He merely assured Inspector Thomas Mathew that as far as he was concerned Velutha did not have the patronage or the protection of the Communist Party. That he was on his own.

After Comrade Pillai left, Inspector Thomas Mathew went over their conversation in his mind, teasing it, testing its logic, looking for loopholes. When he was satisfied, he instructed his men.

Meanwhile, Baby Kochamma returned to Ayemenem. The Plymouth was parked in the driveway. Margaret Kochamma and Chacko were back from Cochin.

Sophie Mol was laid out on the chaise longue.

When Margaret Kochamma saw her little daughter's body, shock swelled in her like phantom applause in an empty auditorium. It overflowed in a wave of vomit and left her mute and empty-eyed. She mourned two deaths, not one. With the loss of Sophie, Joe died again. And this time there was no homework to finish or egg to eat. She had come to Ayemenem to heal her wounded world, and had lost all of it instead. She shattered like glass.

Her memory of the days that followed was fuzzy. Long, dim hours of thick, furry-tongued serenity (medically administered by Dr Verghese Verghese), lacerated by sharp, steely slashes of hysteria, as keen and cutting as the edge of a new razor blade.

She was vaguely conscious of Chacko – concerned and gentle-voiced when he was by her side – otherwise incensed, blowing like an enraged wind through the Ayemenem House. So different from the amused Rumpled Porcupine she had met that longago Oxford morning at the café.

She remembered faintly the funeral in the yellow church. The sad singing. A bat that had bothered someone. She remembered the sounds of doors being battered down, and frightened women's voices. And how at night the bush crickets had sounded like creaking stairs and amplified the fear and gloom that hung over the Ayemenem House.

She never forgot her irrational rage at the other two younger

children who had for some reason been spared. Her fevered
mind fastened like a limpet onto the notion that Estha was
somehow responsible for Sophie Mol's death. Odd, considering
that Margaret Kochamma didn't know that it was Estha –
Stirring Wizard with a Puff who had rowed jam and thought
Two Thoughts – Estha who had broken rules and rowed Sophie
Mol and Rahel across the river in the afternoons in a little boat,
Estha who had abrogated a sickled smell by waving a Marxist
flag at it. Estha who had made the back verandah of the History
House their home away from home, furnished with a grass mat
and most of their toys – a catapult, an inflatable goose, a Qantas
koala with loosened button eyes. And finally, on that dreadful
night, Estha who had decided that though it was dark and
raining, the Time Had Come for them to run away, because
Ammu didn't want them any more.

Despite not knowing any of this, why did Margaret Kochamma blame Estha for what had happened to Sophie? Perhaps
she had a mother's instinct.

Three or four times, swimming up through thick layers of
drug-induced sleep, she had actually sought Estha out and
slapped him until someone calmed her down and led her away.
Later, she wrote to Ammu to apologize. By the time the letter
arrived, Estha had been Returned and Ammu had had to pack
her bags and leave. Only Rahel remained in Ayemenem to
accept, on Estha's behalf, Margaret Kochamma's apology.
I can't imagine what came over me, she wrote. *I can only put it
down to the effect of the tranquillizers. I had no right to behave the way
I did, and want you to know that I am ashamed and terribly, terribly
sorry.*

Strangely, the person that Margaret Kochamma never thought
about was Velutha. Of him she had no memory at all. Not even
what he looked like.

Perhaps this was because she never really knew him, nor ever heard what happened to him.

The God of Loss.

The God of Small Things.

He left no footprints in sand, no ripples in water, no image in mirrors.

After all, Margaret Kochamma wasn't with the platoon of Touchable policemen when they crossed the swollen river. Their wide khaki shorts rigid with starch.

The metallic clink of handcuffs in someone's heavy pocket.

It is unreasonable to expect a person to remember what she didn't know had happened.

SORROW, HOWEVER, was still two weeks away on that blue cross-stitch afternoon, as Margaret Kochamma lay jet-lagged and still asleep. Chacko, on his way to see Comrade K. N. M. Pillai, drifted past the bedroom window like an anxious, stealthy whale intending to peep in to see whether his wife (*Ex-wife, Chacko!*) and daughter were awake and needed anything. At the last minute his courage failed him and he floated fatly by without looking in. Sophie Mol (A wake, A live, A lert) saw him go.

She sat up on her bed and looked out at the rubber trees. The sun had moved across the sky and cast a deep house-shadow across the plantation, darkening the already dark-leafed trees. Beyond the shadow, the light was flat and gentle. There was a diagonal slash across the mottled bark of each tree through which milky rubber seeped like white blood from a wound, and dripped into the waiting half of a coconut shell that had been tied to the tree.

Sophie Mol got out of bed and rummaged through her sleeping mother's purse. She found what she was looking for – the keys to the large, locked suitcase on the floor, with its airline stickers and baggage tags. She opened it and rooted through the contents with all the delicacy of a dog digging up a flowerbed. She upset stacks of lingerie, ironed skirts and blouses, shampoos, creams, chocolate, Sellotape, umbrellas, soap (and other bottled London smells), quinine, aspirin, broad spectrum

266

antibiotics. 'Take everything,' her colleagues had advised Margaret Kochamma in concerned voices. 'You never know.' Which was their way of saying to a colleague travelling to the Heart of Darkness that:

(a) Anything Can Happen To Anyone.

So

(b) It's Best to be Prepared.

Sophie Mol eventually found what she had been looking for. Presents for her cousins. Triangular towers of Toblerone chocolate (soft and slanting in the heat). Socks with separate multi-coloured toes. And two ballpoint pens – the top halves filled with water in which a cut-out collage of a London streetscape was suspended. Buckingham Palace and Big Ben. Shops and people. A red double-decker bus propelled by an air-bubble floated up and down the silent street. There was something sinister about the absence of noise on the busy ballpoint street.

Sophie Mol put the presents into her go-go bag, and went forth into the world. To drive a hard bargain. To negotiate a friendship.

A friendship that, unfortunately, would be left dangling. Incomplete. Flailing in the air with no foothold. A friendship that never circled around into a story, which is why, far more quickly than ever should have happened, Sophie Mol became a Memory, while The Loss of Sophie Mol grew robust and alive. Like a fruit in season. Every season.

14

Work is Struggle

Chacko took the shortcut through the tilting rubber trees so that he would have to walk only a very short stretch down the main road to Comrade K. N. M. Pillai's house. He looked faintly absurd, stepping over the carpet of dry leaves in his tight airport suit, his tie blown over his shoulder.

Comrade Pillai wasn't in when Chacko arrived. His wife, Kalyani, with fresh sandalwood paste on her forehead, made him sit down on a steel folding chair in their small front room and disappeared through the bright pink, nylon, lace-curtained doorway into a dark adjoining room where the small flame from a large brass oil lamp flickered. The cloying smell of incense drifted through the doorway, over which a small wooden placard said, *Work is Struggle. Struggle is Work.*

Chacko was too big for the room. The blue walls crowded him. He glanced around, tense and a little uneasy. A towel dried on the bars of the small green window. The dining table was covered with a bright flowered plastic tablecloth. Midges whirred around a bunch of small bananas on a blue-rimmed white enamel plate. In one corner of the room there was a pile of green unhusked coconuts. A child's rubber slippers lay pigeon-toed in the bright parallelogram of barred sunlight on the floor. A glass-paned cupboard stood next to the table. It had printed curtains hanging on the inside, hiding its contents.

Comrade Pillai's mother, a minute old lady in a brown blouse

and off-white mundu, sat on the edge of the high wooden bed
that was pushed against the wall, her feet dangling high above
the floor. She wore a thin white towel arranged diagonally over
her chest and slung over one shoulder. A funnel of mosquitoes,
like an inverted dunce cap, whined over her head. She sat with
her cheek resting in the palm of her hand, bunching together
all the wrinkles on that side of her face. Every inch of her, even
her wrists and ankles, were wrinkled. Only the skin on her throat
was taut and smooth, stretched over an enormous goitre. Her
fountain of youth. She stared vacantly at the wall opposite her,
rocking herself gently, grunting regular, rhythmic little grunts,
like a bored passenger on a long bus journey.

Comrade Pillai's SSLC, BA and MA certificates were
framed and hung on the wall behind her head.

On another wall was a framed photograph of Comrade Pillai
garlanding Comrade E. M. S. Namboodiripad. There was a
microphone on a stand, shining in the foreground with a sign
that said *Ajantha*.

The rotating table fan by the bed measured out its mechanical
breeze in exemplary, democratic turns – first lifting what was
left of Old Mrs Pillai's hair, then Chacko's. The mosquitoes
dispersed and reassembled tirelessly.

Through the window Chacko could see the tops of buses,
luggage in their luggage racks, as they thundered by. A Jeep
with a loudspeaker drove past, blaring a Marxist Party song
whose theme was Unemployment. The chorus was in English,
the rest of it in Malayalam.

> No vacancy! No vacancy!
> *Wherever in the world a poor man goes,*
> No no no no no vacancy!

'No' pronounced to rhyme with door.

Kalyani returned with a stainless-steel glass of filter coffee and a stainless-steel plate of banana chips (bright yellow with little black seeds in the centre) for Chacko.

'He has gone to Olassa. He'll be back any time now,' she said. She referred to her husband as *addeham* which was the respectful form of 'he', whereas 'he' called her 'edi' which was, approximately, 'Hey, you!'

She was a lush, beautiful woman with golden brown skin and huge eyes. Her long frizzy hair was damp and hung loose down her back, plaited only at the very end. It had wet the back of her tight, deep red blouse and stained it a tighter, deeper red. From where the sleeves ended, her soft arm-flesh swelled and dropped over her dimpled elbows in a sumptuous bulge. Her white mundu and kavani were crisp and ironed. She smelled of sandalwood and the crushed green gram that she used instead of soap. For the first time in years, Chacko watched her without the faintest stirring of sexual desire. He had a wife (*Ex-wife, Chacko!*) at home. With arm freckles and back freckles. With a blue dress and legs underneath.

Young Lenin appeared at the door in red stretchlon shorts. He stood on one thin leg like a stork and twisted the pink lace curtain into a pole, staring at Chacko with his mother's eyes. He was six now, long past the age of pushing things up his nose.

'Mon, go and call Latha,' Mrs Pillai said to him.

Lenin remained where he was, and still staring at Chacko, screeched effortlessly, in the way only children can.

'Latha! Latha! You're wanted!'

'Our niece from Kottayam. His elder brother's daughter,' Mrs Pillai explained. 'She won the First Prize for Elocution at the Youth Festival in Trivandrum last week.'

A combative-looking young girl of about twelve or thirteen appeared through the lace curtain. She wore a long, printed skirt that reached all the way down to her ankles and a short, waist-length white blouse with darts that made room for future breasts. Her oiled hair was parted into two halves. Each of her tight, shining plaits was looped over and tied with ribbons so that they hung down on either side of her face like the outlines of large, drooping ears that hadn't been coloured in yet.

'D'you know who this is?' Mrs Pillai asked Latha.

Latha shook her head.

'Chacko saar. Our factory Modalali.'

Latha stared at him with a composure and a lack of curiosity unusual in a thirteen-year-old.

'He studied in London Oxford,' Mrs Pillai said. 'Will you do your recitation for him?'

Latha complied without hesitation. She planted her feet slightly apart.

'Respected Chairman,' she bowed to Chacko, 'mydearjudges and . . .' she looked around at the imaginary audience crowded into the small, hot room, 'beloved friends.' She paused theatrically.

'Today I would like to recite to you a poem by Sir Walter Scott entitled "Lochinvar".' She clasped her hands behind her back. A film fell over her eyes. Her gaze was fixed unseeingly just above Chacko's head. She swayed slightly as she spoke. At first Chacko thought it was a Malayalam translation of 'Lochinvar'. The words ran into each other. The last syllable of one word attached itself to the first syllable of the next. It was rendered at remarkable speed.

> '*O, young Lochin varhas scum out of the vest,*
> *Through wall the vide Border his teed was the bes;*
> *Tand savissgood broadsod heweapon sadnun,*
> *Nhe rod all unarmed, and he rod all lalone.*'

The poem was interspersed with grunts from the old lady on the bed, which no one except Chacko seemed to notice.

'Nhe swam the Eske river where ford there was none;
Buttair he alighted at Netherby Gate,
The bridehad cunsended, the gallantcame late.'

Comrade Pillai arrived mid-poem, a sheen of sweat glazed his skin, his mundu was folded up over his knees, dark sweatstains spread under his Terylene armpits. In his late thirties, he was an unathletic, sallow little man. His legs were already spindly and his taut, distended belly, like his tiny mother's goitre, was completely at odds with the rest of his thin, narrow body and alert face. As though something in their family genes had bestowed on them compulsory bumps that appeared randomly in different parts of their bodies.

His neat pencil moustache divided his upper lip horizontally into half and ended exactly in line with the ends of his mouth. His hairline had begun to recede and he made no attempt to hide it. His hair was oiled and combed back off his forehead. Clearly youth was not what he was after. He had the easy authority of the Man of the House. He smiled and nodded a greeting to Chacko, but did not acknowledge the presence of his wife or his mother.

Latha's eyes flicked towards him for permission to continue with the poem. It was granted. Comrade Pillai took off his shirt, rolled it into a ball and wiped his armpits with it. When he finished, Kalyani took it from him and held it as though it was a gift. A bouquet of flowers. Comrade Pillai, in his sleeveless vest, sat on a folding chair and pulled his left foot up onto his right thigh. Through the rest of his niece's recitation, he sat staring meditatively down at the floor, his chin cupped in the palm of his hand, tapping his right foot in time with the metre and cadence of the poem. With his other hand he massaged the exquisitely arched instep of his left foot.

When Latha finished, Chacko applauded with genuine kindness. She did not acknowledge his applause with even a flicker of a smile. She was like an East German swimmer at a local competition. Her eyes were firmly fixed on Olympic Gold. Any lesser achievement she took as her due. She looked at her uncle for permission to leave the room.

Comrade Pillai beckoned to her and whispered in her ear, 'Go and tell Pothachen and Mathukutty that if they want to see me, they should come immediately.'

'No, comrade, really . . . I won't have anything more,' Chacko said, assuming that Comrade Pillai was sending Latha off for more snacks. Comrade Pillai, grateful for the misunderstanding, perpetuated it.

'No no no. Hah! What is this? . . . Edi Kalyani, bring a plate of those avalose oondas.'

As an aspiring politician, it was essential for Comrade Pillai to be seen in his chosen constituency as a man of influence. He wanted to use Chacko's visit to impress local supplicants and Party Workers. Pothachen and Mathukutty, the men he had sent for, were villagers who had asked him to use his connections at the Kottayam hospital to secure nursing jobs for their daughters. Comrade Pillai was keen that they be *seen* waiting outside his house for their appointment with him. The more people that were seen waiting to meet him, the busier he would appear, the better the impression he would make. And if the waiting people saw that the factory Modalali himself had come to see him, on *his* turf, he knew it would give off all sorts of useful signals.

'So! Comrade!' Comrade Pillai said, after Latha had been dispatched and the avalose oondas had arrived. 'What is the news? How is your daughter adjusting?' He insisted on speaking to Chacko in English.

'Oh fine. She's fast asleep right now.'

'Oho. Jet lag, I suppose,' Comrade Pillai said, pleased with himself for knowing a thing or two about international travel.

'What's happening in Olassa? A Party meeting?' Chacko asked.

'Oh, nothing like that. My sister Sudha met with fracture sometime back,' Comrade Pillai said, as though Fracture were a visiting dignitary. 'So I took her to Olassa Moos for some medications. Some oils and all that. Her husband is in Patna, so she is alone at in-laws' place.'

Lenin gave up his post at the doorway, placed himself between his father's knees and picked his nose.

'What about a poem from you, young man?' Chacko said to him. 'Doesn't your father teach you any?'

Lenin stared at Chacko, giving no indication that he had either heard or understood what Chacko said.

'He knows everything,' Comrade Pillai said. 'He is genius. In front of visitors only he's quiet.'

Comrade Pillai jiggled Lenin with his knees.

'Lenin Mon, tell Comrade Uncle the one Pappa taught you. *Friends Romans countrymen . . .*'

Lenin continued his nasal treasure hunt.

'Come on, Mon, it's only our Comrade Uncle –'

Comrade Pillai tried to kick-start Shakespeare. '*Friends, Romans, countrymen, lend me your –*?'

Lenin's unblinking gaze remained on Chacko. Comrade Pillai tried again.

'*. . . lend me your –*?'

Lenin grabbed a handful of banana chips and bolted out of the front door. He began to race up and down the strip of front yard between the house and road, braying with an excitement that he couldn't understand. When he had worked some of it off his run turned into a breathless, high-kneed gallop.

'*lend me yawYERS;*'

Lenin shouted from the yard, over the sound of a passing bus.

'I cometoberry Caeser, not to praise him.
Theevil that mendoo lives after them,
The goodisoft interred with their bones;'

He shouted it fluently, without faltering once. Remarkable, considering he was only six and didn't understand a word of what he was saying. Sitting inside, looking out at the little dust-devil whirling in his yard (future service contractor with a baby and Bajaj scooter), Comrade Pillai smiled proudly.

'He's standing first in class. This year he will be getting double-promotion.'

There was a lot of ambition packed into that little hot room. Whatever Comrade Pillai stored in his curtained cupboard, it wasn't broken balsa airplanes.

Chacko, on the other hand, from the moment he had entered the house, or perhaps from the moment Comrade Pillai had arrived, had undergone a curious process of invalidation. Like a general who had been stripped of his stars, he limited his smile. Contained his expansiveness. Anybody meeting him there for the first time might have thought him reticent. Almost timid.

With a street-fighter's unerring instincts, Comrade Pillai knew that his straitened circumstances (his small, hot house, his grunting mother, his obvious proximity to the toiling masses) gave him a power over Chacko that in those revolutionary times no amount of Oxford education could match.

He held his poverty like a gun to Chacko's head.

Chacko brought out a crumpled piece of paper on which he had tried to sketch the rough layout for a new label that he wanted Comrade K. N. M. Pillai to print. It was for a new product that Paradise Pickles & Preserves planned to launch in the spring. Synthetic Cooking Vinegar. Drawing was not one of Chacko's strengths, but Comrade Pillai got the general gist. He was familiar with the logo of the kathakali dancer, the slogan under his skirt that said *Emperors of the Realm of Taste* (his idea) and the typeface they had chosen for Paradise Pickles & Preserves.

'Design is same. Only difference is in text, I suppose,' Comrade Pillai said.

'And the colour of the border,' Chacko said. 'Mustard instead of red.'

Comrade Pillai pushed his spectacles up into his hair in order to read aloud the text. The lenses immediately grew fogged with hairoil.

'*Synthetic Cooking Vinegar*,' he said. 'This all is in caps, I suppose.'

'Prussian Blue,' Chacko said.

'*Prepared from Acetic Acid*?'

'Royal Blue,' Chacko said. 'Like the one we did for green pepper in brine.'

'*Net Contents. Batch No., Mfg date, Expiry Date, Max Rtl Pr. Rs* . . . same Royal Blue colour but c. and l.c.?'

Chacko nodded.

'*We hereby certify that the vinegar in this bottle is warranted to be of the nature and quality which it purports to be. Ingredients: Water and Acetic Acid*. This will be red colour, I suppose.'

Comrade Pillai used 'I suppose' to disguise questions as statements. He hated asking questions unless they were personal ones. Questions signified a vulgar display of ignorance.

By the time they finished discussing the label for the vinegar, Chacko and Comrade Pillai had each acquired personal mosquito funnels.

They agreed on a delivery date.

'So yesterday's march was a success?' Chacko said, finally broaching the real reason for his visit.

'Unless and until demands are met, comrade, we cannot say it is Success or Non-success.' A pamphleteering inflection crept into Comrade Pillai's voice. 'Until then, struggle must continue.'

'But Response was good,' Chacko prompted, trying to speak in the same idiom.

'That is of course there,' Comrade Pillai said. 'Comrades

have presented Memorandum to Party High Command. Now let us see. We have only to wait and watch.'

'We passed them on the road yesterday,' Chacko said. 'The procession.'

'On the way to Cochin, I suppose,' Comrade Pillai said. 'But according to Party sources Trivandrum Response was much more better.'

'There were thousands of comrades in Cochin too,' Chacko said. 'In fact my niece saw our young Velutha among them.'

'Oho. I see.' Comrade Pillai was caught off guard. Velutha was a topic he had planned to broach with Chacko. Some day. Eventually. But not this straightforwardly. His mind hummed like the table fan. He wondered whether to make use of the opening that was being offered to him, or to leave it for another day. He decided to use it now.

'Yes. He is good worker,' he said thoughtfully. 'Highly intelligent.'

'He is,' Chacko said. 'An excellent carpenter with an engineer's mind. If it wasn't for –'

'Not *that* worker, comrade,' Comrade Pillai said. '*Party* worker.'

Comrade Pillai's mother continued to rock and grunt. There was something reassuring about the rhythm of the grunts. Like the ticking of a clock. A sound you hardly noticed, but would miss if it stopped.

'Ah, I see. So he's a card-holder?'

'Oh yes,' Comrade Pillai said softly. 'Oh yes.'

Perspiration trickled through Chacko's hair. He felt as though a company of ants was touring his scalp. He scratched his head for a long time, with both his hands. Moving his whole scalp up and down.

'*Oru kaaryam parayattey?*' Comrade Pillai switched to Malayalam and a confiding, conspiratorial voice. 'I'm speaking as a friend, *keto*. Off the record.'

Before he continued, Comrade Pillai studied Chacko, trying to gauge his response. Chacko was examining the grey paste of sweat and dandruff lodged under his fingernails.

'That Paravan is going to cause trouble for you,' he said. 'Take it from me . . . get him a job somewhere else. Send him off.'

Chacko was puzzled at the turn the conversation had taken. He had only intended to find out what was happening, where things stood. He had expected to encounter antagonism, even confrontation, and instead was being offered sly, misguided collusion.

'Send him away? But why? I have no objections to him being a card-holder. I was just curious, that's all . . . I thought perhaps you had been speaking to him,' Chacko said. 'But I'm sure he's just experimenting, testing his wings, he's a sensible fellow, Comrade. I trust him . . .'

'Not like that,' Comrade Pillai said. 'He may be very well okay as a person. But other workers are not happy with him. Already they are coming to me with complaints . . . You see, Comrade, from local standpoint, these caste issues are very deep-rooted.'

Kalyani put a steel tumbler of steaming coffee on the table for her husband.

'See her, for example. Mistress of this house. Even she will never allow Paravans and all that into her house. Never. Even *I* cannot persuade her. My own wife. Of course inside the house she is Boss.' He turned to her with an affectionate, naughty smile. '*Allay edi*, Kalyani?'

Kalyani looked down and smiled, coyly acknowledging her bigotry.

'You see?' Comrade Pillai said triumphantly. 'She understands English very well. Only doesn't speak.'

Chacko smiled half-heartedly.

'You say my workers are coming to you with complaints . . .'

'Oh yes, correct,' Comrade Pillai said.

'Anything specific?'

'Nothing specifically as such,' Comrade K. N. M. Pillai said. 'But see, Comrade, any benefits that you give him, naturally others are resenting it. They see it as a partiality. After all, whatever job he does, carpenter or electrician or whateveritis, for them he is just a Paravan. It is a conditioning they have from birth. This I myself have told them is wrong. But frankly speaking, Comrade, Change is one thing. Acceptance is another. You should be cautious. Better for him you send him off . . .'

'My dear fellow,' Chacko said. 'That's impossible. He's invaluable. He practically runs the factory . . . and we can't solve the problem by sending all the Paravans away. Surely we have to learn to deal with this nonsense.'

Comrade Pillai disliked being addressed as My Dear Fellow. It sounded to him like an insult couched in good English, which, of course, made it a double-insult – the insult itself, and the fact that Chacko thought he wouldn't understand it. It spoiled his mood completely.

'That may be,' he said caustically. 'But Rome was not built in a day. Keep it in mind, Comrade, that this is not your Oxford college. For you what is a nonsense, for Masses it is something different.'

Lenin, with his father's thinness and his mother's eyes, appeared at the door, out of breath. He had finished shouting the whole of Mark Antony's speech and most of 'Lochinvar' before he realized that he had lost his audience. He repositioned himself between Comrade Pillai's parted knees.

He clapped his hands over his father's head, creating mayhem in the mosquito funnel. He counted the squashed carcasses on his palms. Some of them bloated with fresh blood. He showed them to his father, who handed him over to his mother to be cleaned up.

Once again the silence between them was appropriated by

old Mrs Pillai's grunts. Latha arrived with Pothachen and Mathukutty. The men were made to wait outside. The door was left ajar. When Comrade Pillai spoke next, he spoke in Malayalam and made sure it was loud enough for his audience outside.

'Of course the proper forum to air workers' grievances is through the Union. And in this case, when Modalali himself is a Comrade, it is a shameful matter for them not to be unionized and join the Party Struggle.'

'I've thought of that,' Chacko said. 'I am going to formally organize them into a union. They will elect their own representatives.'

'But Comrade, you cannot stage their revolution for them. You can only create awareness. Educate them. They must launch their *own* struggle. *They* must overcome their fears.'

'Of whom?' Chacko smiled. 'Me?'

'No, not you, my dear Comrade. Of centuries of oppression.'

Then Comrade Pillai, in a hectoring voice, quoted Chairman Mao. In Malayalam. His expression curiously like his niece's.

'Revolution is not a dinner party. Revolution is an insurrection, an act of violence in which one class overthrows another.'

And so, having bagged the contract for the Synthetic Cooking Vinegar labels, he deftly banished Chacko from the fighting ranks of the Overthrowers to the treacherous ranks of the To Be Overthrown.

They sat beside each other on steel folding chairs, on the afternoon of the Day that Sophie Mol Came, sipping coffee and crunching banana chips. Dislodging with their tongues the sodden yellow mulch that stuck to the roofs of their mouths.

The Small Thin Man and the Big Fat Man. Comic book adversaries in a still-to-come war.

It turned out to be a war which, unfortunately for Comrade Pillai, would end almost before it began. Victory was gifted to him wrapped and be-ribboned, on a silver tray. Only then, when it was too late, and Paradise Pickles slumped softly to the floor without so much as a murmur or even the pretence of resistance – did Comrade Pillai realize that what he really needed was the process of war more than the outcome of victory. War could have been the stallion that he rode, part of, if not all, the way to the Legislative Assembly, whereas victory left him no better off than when he started out.

He broke the eggs but burned the omelette.

Nobody ever learned the precise nature of the role that Comrade Pillai played in the events that followed. Even Chacko – who knew that the fervent, high-pitched speeches about Rights of Untouchables ('Caste is Class, comrades') delivered by Comrade Pillai during the Marxist Party siege of Paradise Pickles, were pharisaic – never learned the whole story. Not that he cared to find out. By then, numbed by the loss of Sophie Mol, he looked out at everything with a vision smudged with grief. Like a child touched by tragedy, who grows up suddenly and abandons his playthings, Chacko dumped his toys. Pickle Baron dreams and the People's War joined the racks of broken airplanes in his glass-paned cupboard. After Paradise Pickles closed down, some rice-fields were sold (along with their mortgages) to pay off the bank loans. More were sold to keep the family in food and clothes. By the time Chacko emigrated to Canada, the family's only income came from the rubber estate that adjoined the Ayemenem House and the few coconut trees in the compound. This was what Baby Kochamma and Kochu Maria lived off after everybody else had died, left, or been Returned.

To be fair to Comrade Pillai, he did not plan the course of events that followed. He merely slipped his ready fingers into History's waiting glove.

It was not entirely his fault that he lived in a society where a man's death could be more profitable than his life had ever been.

Velutha's last visit to Comrade Pillai – after his confrontation with Mammachi and Baby Kochamma – and what had passed between them, remained a secret. The last betrayal that sent Velutha across the river, swimming against the current, in the dark and rain, well in time for his blind date with history.

VELUTHA CAUGHT the last bus back from Kottayam where he was having the canning machine mended. He ran into one of the other factory workers at the bus stop, who told him with a smirk that Mammachi wanted to see him. Velutha had no idea what had happened and was completely unaware of his father's drunken visit to the Ayemenem House. Nor did he know that Vellya Paapen had been sitting for hours at the door of their hut, still drunk, his glass eye and the edge of his axe glittering in the lamplight, waiting for Velutha to return. Nor that poor paralysed Kuttappen, numb with apprehension, had been talking to his father continuously for two hours, trying to calm him down, all the time straining his ears for the sound of a footstep or the rustle of undergrowth so that he could shout a warning to his unsuspecting brother.

Velutha didn't go home. He went straight to the Ayemenem House. Though, on the one hand, he was taken by surprise, on the other, he knew, had known, with an ancient instinct, that one day History's twisted chickens would come home to roost. Through the whole of Mammachi's outburst he remained restrained and strangely composed. It was a composure born of extreme provocation. It stemmed from a lucidity that lies beyond rage.

When Velutha arrived, Mammachi lost her bearings and spewed her blind venom, her crass, insufferable insults, at a

283

panel in the sliding-folding door until Baby Kochamma tactfully swivelled her around and aimed her rage in the right direction, at Velutha standing very still in the gloom. Mammachi continued her tirade, her eyes empty, her face twisted and ugly, her anger propelling her towards Velutha until she was shouting right into his face and he could feel the spray of her spit and smell the stale tea on her breath. Baby Kochamma stayed close to Mammachi. She said nothing, but used her hands to modulate Mammachi's fury, to stoke it anew. An encouraging pat on the back. A reassuring arm around the shoulders. Mammachi was completely unaware of the manipulation.

Just *where* an old lady like her – who wore crisp ironed saris and played the *Nutcracker Suite* on the violin in the evenings – had learned the foul language that Mammachi used that day was a mystery to everybody (Baby Kochamma, Kochu Maria, Ammu in her locked room) who heard her.

'Out!' she had screamed, eventually. 'If I find you on my property tomorrow I'll have you castrated like the pariah dog that you are! I'll have you killed!'

'We'll see about that,' Velutha said quietly.

That was all he said. And that was what Baby Kochamma in Inspector Thomas Mathew's office, enhanced and embroidered into threats of murder and abduction.

Mammachi spat into Velutha's face. Thick spit. It spattered across his skin. His mouth and eyes.

He just stood there. Stunned. Then he turned and left.

As he walked away from the house, he felt his senses had been honed and heightened. As though everything around him had been flattened into a neat illustration. A machine drawing with an instruction manual that told him what to do. His mind, desperately craving some kind of mooring, clung to details. It labelled each thing it encountered.

Gate, he thought as he walked out of the gate. *Gate. Road. Stones. Sky. Rain.*

Gate.
Road.
Stones.
Sky.
Rain.

The rain on his skin was warm. The laterite rock under his feet jagged. He knew where he was going. He noticed everything. Each leaf. Each tree. Each cloud in the starless sky. Each step he took.

> *Koo-koo kookum theevandi*
> *Kooki paadum theevandi*
> *Rapakal odum theevandi*
> *Thalannu nilkum theevandi*

That was the first lesson he had learned in school. A poem about a train.

He began to count. Something. Anything. *One two three four five six seven eight nine ten eleven twelve thirteen fourteen fifteen sixteen seventeen eighteen nineteen twenty twenty-one twenty-two twenty-three twenty-four twenty-five twenty-six twenty-seven twenty-eight twenty-nine . . .*

The machine drawing began to blur. The clear lines to smudge. The instructions no longer made sense. The road rose to meet him and the darkness grew dense. Glutinous. Pushing through it became an effort. Like swimming underwater.

It's happening, a voice informed him. *It has begun.*

His mind, suddenly impossibly old, floated out of his body and hovered high above him in the air, from where it jabbered useless warnings.

It looked down and watched a young man's body walk through the darkness and the driving rain. More than anything else that body wanted to sleep. Sleep and wake up in another world. *With the smell of her skin in the air that he breathed. Her body on his. He might never see her again. Where was she? What had they done to her? Had they hurt her?*

He kept walking. His face was neither lifted towards the rain, nor bent away from it. He neither welcomed it, nor warded it off.

Though the rain washed Mammachi's spit off his face, it didn't stop the feeling that somebody had lifted off his head and vomited into his body. Lumpy vomit dribbling down his insides. Over his heart. His lungs. The slow thick drip into the pit of his stomach. All his organs awash in vomit. There was nothing that rain could do about that.

He knew what he had to do. The instruction manual directed him. He had to get to Comrade Pillai. He no longer knew why. His feet took him to Lucky Press, which was locked, and then across the tiny yard to Comrade Pillai's house.

Just the effort of lifting his arm to knock exhausted him.

Comrade Pillai had finished his avial and was squashing a ripe banana, extruding the sludge through his closed fist into his plate of curd, when Velutha knocked. He sent his wife to open the door. She returned looking sulky, and, Comrade Pillai thought, suddenly sexy. He wanted to touch her breast immediately. But he had curd on his fingers and there was someone at the door. Kalyani sat on the bed and absent-mindedly patted Lenin, who was asleep next to his tiny grandmother, sucking his thumb.

'Who is it?'

'That Paapen Paravan's son. He says it's urgent.'

Comrade Pillai finished his curd unhurriedly. He waggled his fingers over his plate. Kalyani brought water in a little stainless-steel container and poured it out for him. The leftover morsels of food in his plate (a dry red chilli, and stiff angular brushes of sucked and spat-out drumsticks) rose and floated. She brought him a hand-towel. He wiped his hands, belched his appreciation, and went to the door.

'*Enda?* At this time of the night?'

As he replied, Velutha heard his own voice beat back at him as though it had hit a wall. He tried to explain what had happened, but he could hear himself slipping into incoherence. The man he was talking to was small and far away, behind a wall of glass.

'This is a little village,' Comrade Pillai was saying. 'People talk. I listen to what they say. It's not as though I don't know what's been going on.'

Once again Velutha heard himself say something which made no difference to the man he spoke to. His own voice coiled around him like a snake.

'Maybe,' Comrade Pillai said. 'But Comrade, you should know that Party was not constituted to support workers' indiscipline in their private life.'

Velutha watched Comrade Pillai's body fade from the door. His disembodied, piping voice stayed on and sent out slogans. Pennants fluttering in an empty doorway.

It is not in the Party's interests to take up such matters.

Individuals' interest is subordinate to the organization's interest.

Violating Party Discipline means violating Party Unity.

The voice went on. Sentences disaggregated into phrases. Words.

Progress of the Revolution.

Annihilation of the Class Enemy.

Comprador capitalist.

Spring-thunder.

And there it was again. Another religion turned against itself. Another edifice constructed by the human mind, decimated by human nature.

Comrade Pillai shut the door and returned to his wife and dinner. He decided to eat another banana.

'What did he want?' his wife asked, handing him one.

'They've found out. Someone must have told them. They've sacked him.'

'Is that all? He's lucky they haven't had him strung up from the nearest tree.'

'I noticed something strange . . .' Comrade Pillai said as he peeled his banana. 'The fellow had red varnish on his nails . . .'

Standing outside in the rain, in the cold, wet light from the single streetlight, Velutha was suddenly overcome by sleep. He had to force his eyelids to stay open.

Tomorrow, he told himself. *Tomorrow when the rain stops.*

His feet walked him to the river. As though they were the leash and he were the dog.

History walking the dog.

15

The Crossing

It was past midnight. The river had risen, its waters quick and black, snaking towards the sea, carrying with it cloudy night skies, a whole palm frond, part of a thatched fence, and other gifts the wind had given it.

In a while the rain slowed to a drizzle and then stopped. The breeze shook water from the trees and for a while it rained only under trees, where shelter had once been.

A weak, watery moon filtered through the clouds and revealed a young man sitting on the topmost of thirteen stone steps that led into the water. He was very still, very wet. Very young. In a while he stood up, took off the white mundu he was wearing, squeezed the water from it and twisted it around his head like a turban. Naked now, he walked down the thirteen stone steps into the water and further, until the river was chest high. Then he began to swim with easy, powerful strokes, striking out towards where the current was swift and certain, where the Really Deep began. The moonlit river fell from his swimming arms like sleeves of silver. It took him only a few minutes to make the crossing. When he reached the other side he emerged gleaming and pulled himself ashore, black as the night that surrounded him, black as the water he had crossed.

He stepped onto the path that led through the swamp to the History House.

He left no ripples in the water.

No footprints on the shore.

He held his mundu spread above his head to dry. The wind lifted it like a sail. He was suddenly happy. *Things will get worse*, he thought to himself. *Then better*. He was walking swiftly now, towards the Heart of Darkness. As lonely as a wolf.

The God of Loss.

The God of Small Things.

Naked but for his nail varnish.

16

A Few Hours Later

Three children on the river bank. A pair of twins and another, whose mauve corduroy pinafore said *Holiday!* in a tilting, happy font.

Wet leaves in the trees shimmered like beaten metal. Dense clumps of yellow bamboo drooped into the river as though grieving in advance for what they knew was going to happen. The river itself was dark and quiet. An absence rather than a presence, betraying no sign of how high and strong it really was.

Estha and Rahel dragged the boat out of the bushes where they usually hid it. The paddles that Velutha had made were hidden in a hollow tree. They set it down in the water and held it steady for Sophie Mol to climb in. They seemed to trust the darkness and moved up and down the glistening stone steps as surefooted as young goats.

Sophie Mol was more tentative. A little frightened of what lurked in the shadows around her. She had a cloth bag with food purloined from the fridge slung across her chest. Bread, cake, biscuits. The twins, weighed down by their mother's words — *If it weren't for you I would be free. I should have dumped you in an orphanage the day you were born. You're the millstones round my neck* — carried nothing. Thanks to what the Orangedrink Lemondrink Man did to Estha, their Home away from Home was already equipped. In the two weeks since Estha rowed scarlet jam and

Thought Two Thoughts, they had squirrelled away Essential Provisions: matches, potatoes, a battered saucepan, an inflatable goose, socks with multicoloured toes, ballpoint pens with London buses and the Qantas koala with loosened button eyes.

'What if Ammu finds us and *begs* us to come back?'

'Then we will. But only if she begs.'

Estha-the-Compassionate.

Sophie Mol had convinced the twins that it was *essential* that she go along too. That the absence of children, *all* children, would heighten the adults' remorse. It would make them truly sorry, like the grown-ups in Hamelin after the Pied Piper took away all their children. They would search everywhere and just when they were sure that all three of them were dead, they would return home in triumph. Valued, loved, and needed more than ever. Her clinching argument was that if she were left behind she might be tortured and forced to reveal their hiding place.

Estha waited until Rahel got in, then took his place, sitting astride the little boat as though it were a seesaw. He used his legs to push the boat away from the shore. As they lurched into the deeper water they began to row diagonally upstream, against the current, the way Velutha had taught them to. ('If you want to end up there, you must aim *there*.')

In the dark they couldn't see that they were in the wrong lane on a silent highway full of muffled traffic. That branches, logs, parts of trees, were motoring towards them at some speed.

They were past the Really Deep, only yards from the Other Side, when they collided with a floating log and the little boat tipped over. It had happened to them often enough on previous expeditions across the river, and they would swim after the boat and, using it as a float, dog-paddle to the shore. This time, they couldn't see their boat in the dark. It was swept away in the current. They headed for the shore, surprised at how much effort it took them to cover that short distance.

Estha managed to grab a low branch that arched down into the water. He peered downriver through the darkness to see if he could see the boat at all.

'I can't see anything. It's gone.'

Rahel, covered in slush, clambered ashore and held a hand out to help Estha pull himself out of the water. It took them a few minutes to catch their breath and register the loss of the boat. To mourn its passing.

'And all our food is spoiled,' Rahel said to Sophie Mol and was met with silence. A rushing, rolling, fishswimming silence.

'Sophie Mol?' she whispered to the rushing river. 'We're here! Here! Near the Illimba tree!'

Nothing.

On Rahel's heart Pappachi's moth snapped open its sombre wings.

Out.

In.

And lifted its legs.

Up.

Down.

They ran along the bank calling out to her. But she was gone. Carried away on the muffled highway. Greygreen. With fish in it. With the sky and trees in it. And at night the broken yellow moon in it.

There was no storm-music. No whirlpool spun up from the inky depths of the Meenachal. No shark supervised the tragedy.

Just a quiet handing over ceremony. A boat spilling its cargo. A river accepting the offering. One small life. A brief sunbeam. With a silver thimble clenched for luck in its little fist.

It was four in the morning, still dark, when the twins, exhausted, distraught and covered in mud, made their way through the swamp and approached the History House. Hansel and Gretel in a ghastly fairy tale in which their dreams would be captured and redreamed. They lay down in the back verandah

293

on a grass mat with an inflatable goose and a Qantas koala bear. A pair of damp dwarves, numb with fear, waiting for the world to end.

'D'you think she's dead by now?'

Estha didn't answer.

'What's going to happen?'

'We'll go to jail.'

He Jolly Well knew. Little Man. He lived in a cara-van. Dum dum.

They didn't see someone else lying asleep in the shadows. As lonely as a wolf. A brown leaf on his black back. That made the monsoons come on time.

17

Cochin Harbour Terminus

In his clean room in the dirty Ayemenem House, Estha (not old, not young) sat on his bed in the dark. He sat very straight. Shoulders squared. Hands in his lap. As though he was next in line for some sort of inspection. Or waiting to be arrested.

The ironing was done. It sat in a neat pile on the ironing board. He had done Rahel's clothes as well.

It was raining steadily. Night rain. That lonely drummer practising his roll long after the rest of the band has gone to bed.

In the side mittam, by the separate 'Men's Needs' entrance, the chrome tailfins of the old Plymouth gleamed momentarily in the lightning. For years after Chacko left for Canada, Baby Kochamma had had it washed regularly. Twice a week for a small fee, Kochu Maria's brother-in-law who drove the yellow municipal garbage truck in Kottayam would drive into Ayemenem (heralded by the stench of Kottayam's refuse, which lingered long after he had gone) to divest his sister-in-law of her salary and drive the Plymouth around to keep its battery charged. When she took up television, Baby Kochamma dropped the car and the garden simultaneously. Tutti-frutti.

With every monsoon, the old car settled more firmly into the ground. Like an angular, arthritic hen settling stiffly on her clutch of eggs. With no intention of ever getting up. Grass grew around its flat tyres. The Paradise Pickles & Preserves signboard rotted and fell inwards like a collapsed crown.

A creeper stole a look at itself in the remaining mottled half of the cracked driver's mirror.

A sparrow lay dead on the back seat. She had found her way in through a hole in the windscreen, tempted by some seat-sponge for her nest. She never found her way out. No one noticed her panicked car-window appeals. She died on the back seat, with her legs in the air. Like a joke.

Kochu Maria was asleep on the drawing-room floor, curled into a comma in the flickering light of the television that was still on. American policemen were stuffing a hand-cuffed teenaged boy into a police car. There was blood spattered on the pavement. The police car lights flashed and a siren wailed a warning. A wasted woman, the boy's mother perhaps, watched fearfully from the shadows. The boy struggled. They had used a mosaic blur on the upper part of his face so that he couldn't sue them. He had caked blood all over his mouth and down the front of his T-shirt like a red bib. His baby-pink lips were lifted off his teeth in a snarl. He looked like a werewolf. He screamed through the car window at the camera.

'I'm fifteen years old and I wish I were a better person than I am. But I'm not. Do you want to hear my pathetic story?'

He spat at the camera and a missile of spit splattered over the lens and dribbled down.

Baby Kochamma was in her room, sitting up in bed, filling in a Listerine discount coupon that offered a two-rupee rebate on their new 500ml bottle and two-thousand-rupee gift vouchers to the Lucky Winners of their lottery.

Giant shadows of small insects swooped along the walls and ceiling. To get rid of them Baby Kochamma had put out the lights and lit a large candle in a tub of water. The water was already thick with singed carcasses. The candlelight accentuated her rouged cheeks and painted mouth. Her mascara was smudged. Her jewellery gleamed.

She tilted the coupon towards the candle.

Which brand of mouthwash do you usually use?

Listerine, Baby Kochamma wrote in a hand grown spidery with age.

State the reasons for your preference:

She didn't hesitate. *Tangy Taste. Fresh Breath.* She had learned the smart, snappy language of television commercials.

She filled in her name and lied about her age.

Under *Occupation:* she wrote, *Ornamental Gardening (Dip) Roch. USA.*

She put the coupon into an envelope marked RELIABLE MEDICOS, KOTTAYAM. It would go with Kochu Maria in the morning, when she went into town on her Bestbakery cream-bun expedition.

Baby Kochamma picked up her maroon diary which came with its own pen. She turned to 19 June and made a fresh entry. Her manner was routine. She wrote: *I love you I love you.*

Every page in the diary had an identical entry. She had a case full of diaries with identical entries. Some said more than just that. Some had the day's accounts, To-do lists, snatches of favourite dialogue from favourite soaps, But even these entries all began with the same words: *I love you I love you.*

Father Mulligan had died four years ago of viral hepatitis, in an ashram north of Rishikesh. His years of contemplation of Hindu scriptures had led initially to theological curiosity, but eventually to a change of faith. Fifteen years ago, Father Mulligan became a Vaishnava. A devotee of Lord Vishnu. He stayed in touch with Baby Kochamma even after he joined the ashram. He wrote to her every Diwali and sent her a greeting card every New Year. A few years ago he sent her a photograph of himself addressing a gathering of middle-class Punjabi widows at a spiritual camp. The women were all in white with their sari palloos drawn over their heads. Father Mulligan was in saffron. A yolk addressing a sea of boiled eggs. His white beard and hair were long, but combed and groomed. A saffron Santa with votive ash on his forehead. Baby Kochamma couldn't believe it. It was the only thing he ever sent her that she hadn't kept. She was offended by the fact that he had actually, eventually, renounced his vows, but not for her. For other vows. It was like welcoming someone with open arms, only to have him walk straight past into someone else's.

Father Mulligan's death did not alter the text of the entries in Baby Kochamma's diary, simply because as far as she was concerned, it did not alter his availability. If anything, she possessed him in death in a way that she never had while he was alive. At least her memory of him was *hers*. Wholly hers. Savagely, fiercely, hers. Not to be shared with Faith, far less with competing co-nuns, and co-sadhus or whatever it was they called themselves. Co-swamis.

His rejection of her in life (gentle and compassionate though it was) was neutralized by death. In her memory of him, he embraced her. Just her. In the way a man embraces a woman. Once he was dead, Baby Kochamma stripped Father Mulligan of his ridiculous saffron robes and reclothed him in the Coca-Cola cassock she so loved. (Her senses feasted, between changes, on that lean, concave, Christ-like body.) She snatched away his begging bowl, pedicured his horny Hindu soles and gave him back his comfortable sandals. She reconverted him into the high-stepping camel that came to lunch on Thursdays.

And every night, night after night, year after year, in diary after diary after diary, she wrote: *I love you I love you.*

She put the pen back into the pen-loop and shut the diary. She took off her glasses, dislodged her dentures with her tongue, severing the strands of saliva that attached them to her gums like the sagging strings of a harp, and dropped them into a glass of Listerine. They sank to the bottom and sent up little bubbles, like prayers. Her nightcap. A clenched-smile soda. Tangy teeth in the morning.

Baby Kochamma settled back on her pillow and waited to hear Rahel come out of Estha's room. They had begun to make her uneasy, both of them. A few mornings ago she had opened her window (for a Breath of Fresh Air) and caught them red-handed in the act of Returning From Somewhere. Clearly they had spent the whole night out. Together. Where could they have been? What and how much did they remember? When would they leave? What were they doing, sitting together in the dark for so long? She fell asleep propped up against her pillows, thinking that perhaps, over the sound of the rain and the television, she hadn't heard Estha's door open. That Rahel had gone to bed long ago.

She hadn't.

Rahel was lying on Estha's bed. She looked thinner lying down. Younger. Smaller. Her face was turned towards the window beside the bed. Slanting rain hit the bars of the window-grill and shattered into a fine spray over her face and her smooth bare arm. Her soft, sleeveless T-shirt was a glowing yellow in the dark. The bottom half of her, in blue jeans, melted into the darkness.

It was a little cold. A little wet. A little quiet. The Air.

But what was there to say?

From where he sat, at the end of the bed, Estha, without turning his head, could see her. Faintly outlined. The sharp line of her jaw. Her collarbones like wings that spread from the base of her throat to the ends of her shoulders. A bird held down by skin.

She turned her head and looked at him. He sat very straight. Waiting for the inspection. He had finished the ironing.

She was lovely to him. Her hair. Her cheeks. Her small, clever-looking hands.

His sister.

A nagging sound started up in his head. The sound of passing trains. The light and shade and light and shade that falls on you if you have a window seat.

He sat even straighter. Still, he could see her. Grown into their mother's skin. The liquid glint of her eyes in the dark. Her small straight nose. Her mouth, full lipped. Something wounded-looking about it. As though it was flinching from something. As though long ago someone – a man with rings – had hit her across it. A beautiful, hurt mouth.

Their beautiful mother's mouth, Estha thought. Ammu's mouth.

That had kissed his hand through the barred train window. First class, on the Madras Mail to Madras.

'Bye, Estha. Godbless, Ammu's mouth had said. Ammu's trying-not-to-cry mouth.

The last time he had seen her.

She was standing on the platform of the Cochin Harbour Terminus, her face turned up to the train window. Her skin grey, wan, robbed of its luminous sheen by the neon station light. Daylight stopped by trains on either side. Long corks that kept the darkness bottled in. The Madras Mail. The Flying Rani.

Rahel held by Ammu's hand. A mosquito on a leash. A Refugee Stick Insect in Bata sandals. An Airport Fairy at a railway station. Stamping her feet on the platform, unsettling clouds of settled station-filth. Until Ammu shook her and told her to Stoppit and she Stoppited. Around them the hostling-jostling crowd.

Scurrying hurrying buying selling luggage trundling porter paying children shitting people spitting coming going begging bargaining reservation-checking.

Echoing stationsounds.

Hawkers selling coffee. Tea.

Gaunt children, blonde with malnutrition, selling smutty

magazines and food they couldn't afford to eat themselves.

Melted chocolates. Cigarette sweets.

Orangedrinks.

Lemondrinks.

CocaColaFantaicecreamrosemilk.

Pink-skinned dolls. Rattles. Love-in-Tokyos.

Hollow plastic parakeets full of sweets with heads you could unscrew.

Yellow-rimmed red sunglasses.

Toy watches with the time painted on them.

A cartful of defective toothbrushes.

The Cochin Harbour Terminus.

Grey in the stationlight. Hollow people. Homeless. Hungry. Still touched by last year's famine. Their revolution postponed for the Time Being by Comrade E. M. S. Namboodiripad (*Soviet Stooge, Running Dog*). The former apple of Peking's eye.

The air was thick with flies.

A blind man without eyelids and eyes as blue as faded jeans, his skin pitted with smallpox scars, chatted to a leper without fingers, taking dexterous drags from scavenged cigarette stubs that lay beside him in a heap.

'What about you? When did *you* move here?'

As though they had had a choice. As though they had *picked* this for their home from a vast array of posh housing estates listed in a glossy pamphlet.

A man sitting on a red weighing machine unstrapped his artificial leg (knee downwards) with a black boot and nice white sock painted on it. The hollow, knobbled calf was pink, like proper calves should be. (When you recreate the image of man, why repeat God's mistakes?) Inside it he stored his ticket. His towel. His stainless-steel tumbler. His smells. His secrets. His love. His madness. His hope. His infinnate joy. His real foot was bare.

He bought some tea for his tumbler.

An old lady vomited. A lumpy pool. And went on with her life.

The Stationworld. Society's circus. Where, with the rush of commerce, despair came home to roost and hardened slowly into resignation.

But this time, for Ammu and her two-egg twins, there was no Plymouth window to watch it through. No net to save them as they vaulted through the circus air.

Pack your things and leave, Chacko had said. Stepping over a broken door. A handle in his hand. And Ammu, though her hands were trembling, hadn't looked up from her unnecessary hemming. A tin of ribbons lay open on her lap.

But Rahel had. Looked up. And seen that Chacko had disappeared and left a monster in his place.

A thick-lipped man with rings, cool in white, bought Scissors cigarettes from a platform vendor. Three packs. To smoke in the train corridor.

For Men of Action
    SatisfAction.

He was Estha's escort. A Family Friend who happened to be going to Madras. Mr Kurien Maathen.

Since there was going to be a grown-up with Estha anyway, Mammachi said there was no need to waste money on another ticket. Baba was buying Madras–Calcutta. Ammu was buying Time. She too had to pack her things and leave. To start a new life, in which she could afford to keep her children. Until then, it had been decided that one twin could stay in Ayemenem. Not both. Together they were trouble. *nataS ni rieht seye*. They had to be separated.

Maybe they're right, Ammu's whisper said as she packed his trunk and holdall. *Maybe a boy does need a Baba.*

The thick-lipped man was in the coupé next to Estha's. He said he'd try and change seats with someone once the train started.

For now he left the little family alone.

He knew that a hellish angel hovered over them. Went where they went. Stopped where they stopped. Dripping wax from a bent candle.

Everybody knew.

It had been in the papers. The news of Sophie Mol's death, of the police 'Encounter' with a Paravan charged with kidnapping and murder. Of the subsequent Communist Party siege of Paradise Pickles & Preserves, led by Ayemenem's own Crusader for Justice and Spokesman of the Oppressed. Comrade K. N. M. Pillai claimed that the Management had implicated the Paravan in a false police case because he was an active member of the Communist Party. That they wanted to eliminate him for indulging in 'Lawful Union Activities'.

All that had been in the papers. The Official Version.

Of course the thick-lipped man with rings had no idea about the other version.

The one in which a posse of Touchable Policemen crossed the Meenachal river, sluggish and swollen with recent rain, and picked their way through the wet undergrowth, clumping into the Heart of Darkness.

18

The History House

A posse of Touchable Policemen crossed the Meenachal river, sluggish and swollen with recent rain, and picked their way through the wet undergrowth, the clink of handcuffs in someone's heavy pocket.

Their wide khaki shorts were rigid with starch, and bobbed over the tall grass like a row of stiff skirts, quite independent of the limbs that moved inside them.

There were six of them. Servants of the State.

P oliteness
O bedience
L oyalty
I ntelligence
C ourtesy
E fficiency.

The Kottayam Police. A cartoonplatoon. New-Age princes in funny pointed helmets. Cardboard lined with cotton. Hairoil stained. Their shabby khaki crowns.

Dark of Heart.

Deadlypurposed.

They lifted their thin legs high, clumping through tall grass. Ground creepers snagged in their dewdamp leghair. Burrs and grass flowers enhanced their dull socks. Brown millipedes slept in the soles of their steel-tipped, Touchable boots. Rough grass left their legskin raw, crisscrossed with cuts. Wet mud farted under their feet as they squelched through the swamp.

They trudged past darter birds on the tops of trees, drying their sodden wings spread out like laundry against the sky. Past egrets. Cormorants. Adjutant storks. Sarus cranes looking for space to dance. Purple herons with pitiless eyes. Deafening, their *wraark wraark wraark*. Motherbirds and their eggs.

The early morning heat was full of the promise of worse to come.

Beyond the swamp that smelled of still water, they walked past ancient trees cloaked in vines. Gigantic mani plants. Wild pepper. Cascading purple acuminus.

Past a deepblue beetle balanced on an unbending blade of grass.

Past giant spider webs that had withstood the rain and spread like whispered gossip from tree to tree.

A banana flower sheathed in claret bracts hung from a scruffy, torn-leafed tree. A gem held out by a grubby schoolboy. A jewel in the velvet jungle.

Crimson dragonflies mated in the air. Doubledeckered. Deft. One admiring policeman watched and wondered briefly about the dynamics of dragonfly sex, and what went into what. Then his mind clicked to attention and Police Thoughts returned.

Onwards.

Past tall anthills congealed in the rain. Slumped like drugged sentries asleep at the gates of Paradise.

Past butterflies drifting through the air like happy messages.

Huge ferns.

A chameleon.

A startling shoeflower.

The scurry of grey jungle fowl running for cover.

The nutmeg tree that Vellya Paapen hadn't found.

A forked canal. Still. Choked with duckweed. Like a dead

green snake. A tree trunk fallen over it. The Touchable
policemen minced across. Twirling polished bamboo batons.

Hairy fairies with lethal wands.

Then the sunlight was fractured by thin trunks of tilting trees.
Dark of Heartness tiptoed into the Heart of Darkness. The
sound of stridulating crickets swelled.

Grey squirrels streaked down mottled trunks of rubber trees
that slanted towards the sun. Old scars slashed across their bark.
Sealed. Healed. Untapped.

Acres of this, and then, a grassy clearing. A house.

The History House.

Whose doors were locked and windows open.

With cold stone floors and billowing, ship-shaped shadows
on the walls.

Where waxy ancestors with tough toe-nails and breath that
smelled of yellow maps whispered papery whispers.

Where translucent lizards lived behind old paintings.

Where dreams were captured and re-dreamed.

Where an old Englishman ghost, sickled to a tree, was abrogated by a pair of two-egg twins – a Mobile Republic with a
Puff who had planted a Marxist flag in the earth beside him.
As the platoon of policemen minced past they didn't hear him
beg. In his kind-missionary voice. *Excuse me, would you, umm . . .
you wouldn't happen to umm . . . I don't suppose you'd have a cigar on
you? No? . . . No, I didn't think so.*

The History House.

Where, in the years that followed, the Terror (still-to-come)
would be buried in a shallow grave. Hidden under the happy
humming of hotel cooks. The humbling of old communists. The
slow death of dancers. The toy histories that rich tourists came
to play with.

It was a beautiful house.

White-walled once. Red-roofed. But painted in weather-colours now. With brushes dipped in nature's palette. Moss-green. Earthbrown. Crumbleblack. Making it look older than it really was. Like sunken treasure dredged up from the ocean bed. Whale-kissed and barnacled. Swaddled in silence. Breathing bubbles through its broken windows.

A deep verandah ran all around. The rooms themselves were recessed, buried in shadow. The tiled roof swept down like the sides of an immense, upside-down boat. Rotting beams supported on once-white pillars had buckled at the centre, leaving a yawning, gaping hole. A History hole. A History-shaped hole in the Universe through which, at twilight, dense clouds of silent bats billowed like factory smoke and drifted into the night.

They returned at dawn with news of the world. A grey haze in the rosy distance that suddenly coalesced and blackened over the house before it plummeted through the History hole like smoke in a film running backwards.

All day they slept, the bats. Lining the roof like fur. Spattering the floors with shit.

The policemen stopped and fanned out. They didn't really need to, but they liked these Touchable games.

They positioned themselves strategically. Crouching by the broken, low stone boundary wall.

Quick Piss.

Hotfoam on warmstone. Police-piss.

Drowned ants in yellow bubbly.

Deep breaths.

Then together, on their knees and elbows, they crept towards the house. Like Film-policemen. Softly, softly through the grass. Batons in their hands. Machine-guns in their minds. Responsibility for the Touchable future on their thin but able shoulders.

They found their quarry in the back verandah. A Spoiled Puff. A Fountain in a Love-in-Tokyo. And in another corner (as lonely as a wolf) – a carpenter with blood-red nails.

307

Asleep. Making nonsense of all that Touchable cunning.

The Surpriseswoop.

The Headlines in their heads.

DESPERADO CAUGHT IN POLICE DRAGNET.

For this insolence, this spoiling-the-fun, their quarry paid. Oh yes.

They woke Velutha with their boots.

Esthappen and Rahel woke to the shout of sleep surprised by shattered kneecaps.

Screams died in them and floated belly up, like dead fish. Cowering on the floor, rocking between dread and disbelief, they realized that the man being beaten was Velutha. Where had he come from? What had he done? Why had the policemen brought him here?

They heard the thud of wood on flesh. Boot on bone. On teeth. The muffled grunt when a stomach is kicked in. The muted crunch of skull on cement. The gurgle of blood on a man's breath when his lung is torn by the jagged end of a broken rib.

Blue-lipped and dinner-plate-eyed, they watched, mesmerized by something that they sensed but didn't understand: the absence of caprice in what the policemen did. The abyss where anger should have been. The sober, steady brutality, the economy of it all.

They were opening a bottle.

Or shutting a tap.

Cracking an egg to make an omelette.

The twins were too young to know that these were only history's henchmen. Sent to square the books and collect the dues from those who broke its laws. Impelled by feelings that were primal yet paradoxically wholly impersonal. Feelings of contempt born of inchoate, unacknowledged fear – civilization's fear of nature, men's fear of women, power's fear of powerlessness.

Man's subliminal urge to destroy what he could neither subdue nor deify.

Men's Needs.

What Esthappen and Rahel witnessed that morning, though they didn't know it then, was a clinical demonstration in controlled conditions (this was not war after all, or genocide) of human nature's pursuit of ascendancy. Structure. Order. Complete monopoly. It was human history, masquerading as God's Purpose, revealing herself to an under-age audience.

There was nothing accidental about what happened that morning. Nothing *incidental*. It was no stray mugging or personal settling of scores. This was an era imprinting itself on those who lived in it.

History in live performance.

If they hurt Velutha more than they intended to, it was only because any kinship, any connection between themselves and him, any implication that if nothing else, at least biologically he was a fellow creature – had been severed long ago. They were not arresting a man, they were exorcizing fear. They had no instrument to calibrate how much punishment he could take. No means of gauging how much or how permanently they had damaged him.

Unlike the custom of rampaging religious mobs or conquering armies running riot, that morning in the Heart of Darkness the posse of Touchable Policemen acted with economy, not frenzy. Efficiency, not anarchy. Responsibility, not hysteria. They didn't tear out his hair or burn him alive. They didn't hack off his genitals and stuff them in his mouth. They didn't rape him. Or behead him.

After all, they were not battling an epidemic. They were merely inoculating a community against an outbreak.

In the back verandah of the History House, as the man they loved was smashed and broken, Mrs Eapen and Mrs Rajagopalan, Twin Ambassadors of God-knows-what, learned two new lessons.

Lesson Number One:
Blood barely shows on a Black Man. (Dum dum)
And
Lesson Number Two:
It smells, though.
Sicksweet.
Like old roses on a breeze. (Dum dum)

'*Madiyo?*' one of History's Agents asked.
'*Madi aayirikkum,*' another replied.
Enough?
Enough.
They stepped away from him. Craftsmen assessing their work. Seeking aesthetic distance.

Their Work, abandoned by God and History, by Marx, by Man, by Woman and (in the hours to come) by Children, lay folded on the floor. He was semi-conscious, but wasn't moving.

His skull was fractured in three places. His nose and both his cheekbones were smashed, leaving his face pulpy, undefined. The blow to his mouth had split open his upper lip and broken six teeth, three of which were embedded in his lower lip, hideously inverting his beautiful smile. Four of his ribs were splintered, one had pierced his left lung, which was what made him bleed from his mouth. The blood on his breath bright red. Fresh. Frothy. His lower intestine was ruptured and haemorrhaged, the blood collected in his abdominal cavity. His spine was damaged in two places, the concussion had paralysed his right arm and resulted in a loss of control over his bladder and rectum. Both his knee caps were shattered.

Still they brought out the handcuffs.
Cold.
With the sourmetal smell. Like steel bus-rails and the bus conductor's hands from holding them. That was when they noticed his painted nails. One of them held them up and waved

310

the fingers coquettishly at the others. They laughed. 'What's this?' in a high falsetto. 'AC-DC?'

One of them flicked at his penis with his stick. 'Come on, show us your special secret. Show us how big it gets when you blow it up.' Then he lifted his boot (with millipedes curled into its sole) and brought it down with a soft thud.

They locked his arms across his back.

Click.

And click.

Below a Lucky Leaf. An autumn leaf at night. That made the monsoons come on time.

He had goosebumps where the handcuffs touched his skin.

'It isn't him,' Rahel whispered to Estha. 'I can tell. It's his twin brother. Urumban. From Kochi.'

Unwilling to seek refuge in fiction, Estha said nothing.

Someone was speaking to them. A kind Touchable policeman. Kind to his kind.

'Mon, Mol, are you all right? Did he hurt you?'

And not together, but almost, the twins replied in a whisper. 'Yes. No.'

'Don't worry. You're safe with us now.'

Then the policemen looked around and saw the grass mat.

The pots and pans.

The inflatable goose.

The Qantas koala with loosened button eyes.

The ballpoint pens with London's streets in them.

Socks with separate coloured toes.

Yellow-rimmed red plastic sunglasses.

A watch with the time painted on it.

'Whose are these? Where did they come from? Who brought them?' An edge of worry in the voice.

Estha and Rahel, full of fish, stared back at him.

The policemen looked at one another. They knew what they had to do.

The Qantas koala they took for their children.

And the pens and socks. Police children with multi-coloured toes.

They burst the goose with a cigarette. *Bang*. And buried the rubber scraps.

Yooseless goose. Too recognizable.

The glasses one of them wore. The others laughed so he kept them on for a while. The watch they all forgot. It stayed behind in the History House. In the back verandah. A faulty record of the time. Ten to two.

They left.

Six princes, their pockets stuffed with toys.

A pair of two-egg twins.

And the God of Loss.

He couldn't walk. So they dragged him.

Nobody saw them.

Bats, of course, are blind.

19

Saving Ammu

At the police station, Inspector Thomas Mathew sent for two Coca-Colas. With straws. A servile constable brought them on a plastic tray and offered them to the two muddy children sitting across the table from the Inspector, their heads only a little higher than the mess of files and papers on it.

So once again, in the space of two weeks, bottled Fear for Estha. Chilled. Fizzed. Sometimes Things went worse with Coca-Cola.

The fizz went up his nose. He burped. Rahel giggled. She blew through her straw till the drink bubbled over onto her dress. All over the floor. Estha read aloud from the board on the wall.

'ssenetilo**P**,' he said. 'ssenetilo**P**, ecneideb**O**,'

'ytlayo**L**, ecnegilletn**I**,' Rahel said.

'ysetruo**C**.'

'ycneiciff**E**.'

To his credit, Inspector Thomas Mathew remained calm. He sensed the growing incoherence in the children. He noted the dilated pupils. He had seen it all before . . . the human mind's escape valve. Its way of managing trauma. He made allowances for that, and couched his questions cleverly. Innocuously. Between 'When is your birthday, Mon?' and 'What's your favourite colour, Mol?'

Gradually, in a fractured, disjointed fashion, things began to fall into place. His men had briefed him about the pots and pans. The grass mat. The impossible-to-forget toys. They began to make sense now. Inspector Thomas Mathew was not amused. He sent a Jeep for Baby Kochamma. He made sure that the children were not in the room when she arrived. He didn't greet her.

'Have a seat,' he said.

Baby Kochamma sensed that something was terribly wrong. 'Have you found them? Is everything all right?'

'Nothing is all right,' the Inspector assured her.

From the look in his eyes and the tone of his voice, Baby Kochamma realized that she was dealing with a different person this time. Not the accommodating police officer of their previous meeting. She lowered herself into a chair. Inspector Thomas Mathew didn't mince his words.

The Kottayam police had acted on the basis of an FIR filed by *her*. The Paravan had been caught. Unfortunately he had been badly injured in the encounter and in all likelihood would not live through the night. But now the children said that they had gone of their own volition. Their boat had capsized and the English child had drowned by accident. Which left the police saddled with the Death in Custody of a technically innocent man. True, he was a Paravan. True, he had misbehaved. But these were troubled times and technically, as per the law, he was an innocent man. There was no *case*.

'Attempted rape?' Baby Kochamma suggested weakly.

'*Where* is the rape-victim's complaint? Has it been filed? Has she made a statement? Have you brought it with you?' The Inspector's tone was belligerent. Almost hostile.

Baby Kochamma looked as though she had shrunk. Pouches of flesh hung from her eyes and jowls. Fear fermented in her and the spit in her mouth turned sour. The Inspector pushed a glass of water towards her.

'The matter is very simple. Either the rape-victim must file a complaint. Or the children must identify the Paravan as their

abductor in the presence of a police witness. Or.' He waited
for Baby Kochamma to look at him. 'Or I must charge you
with lodging a false FIR. Criminal offence.'

Sweat stained Baby Kochamma's light blue blouse dark blue.
Inspector Thomas Mathew didn't hustle her. He knew that
given the political climate, he himself could be in very serious
trouble. He was aware that Comrade K. N. M. Pillai would
not pass up this opportunity. He kicked himself for acting so
impulsively. He used his printed hand-towel to reach inside his
shirt and wipe his chest and armpits. It was quiet in his office.
The sounds of police-station activity, the clumping of boots, the
occasional howl of pain from somebody being interrogated,
seemed distant, as though they were coming from somewhere
else.

'The children will do as they're told,' Baby Kochamma said.
'If I could have a few moments alone with them?'

'As you wish.' The Inspector rose to leave the office.

'Please give me five minutes before you send them in.'

Inspector Thomas Mathew nodded his assent and left.

Baby Kochamma wiped her shining, sweaty face. She
stretched her neck, looking up at the ceiling in order to wipe
the sweat from crevices between her rolls of neckfat with the
end of her pallu. She kissed her crucifix.

Hail Mary, full of grace . . .

The words of the prayer deserted her.

The door opened. Estha and Rahel were ushered in. Caked
with mud. Drenched in Coca-Cola.

The sight of Baby Kochamma made them suddenly sober.
The moth with unusually dense dorsal tufts spread its wings
over both their hearts. *Why had she come? Where was Ammu? Was
she still locked up?*

Baby Kochamma looked at them sternly. She said nothing
for a long time. When she spoke her voice was hoarse and
unfamiliar.

315

'Whose boat was it? Where did you get it from?'

'Ours. That we found. Velutha mended it for us,' Rahel whispered.

'How long have you had it?'

'We found it the day Sophie Mol came.'

'And you stole things from the house and took them across the river in it?'

'We were only playing . . .'

'*Playing?* Is that what you call it?'

Baby Kochamma looked at them for a long time before she spoke again.

'Your lovely little cousin's body is lying in the drawing room. The fish have eaten out her eyes. Her mother can't stop crying. Is that what you call *playing?*'

A sudden breeze made the flowered window curtain billow. Outside Rahel could see Jeeps parked. And walking people. A man was trying to start his motorcycle. Each time he jumped on the kick-starter lever, his helmet slipped to one side.

Inside the Inspector's room, Pappachi's Moth was on the move.

'It's a terrible thing to take a person's life,' Baby Kochamma said. 'It's the worst thing that anyone can ever do. Even *God* doesn't forgive that. You know that, don't you?'

Two heads nodded twice.

'And yet –' she looked sadly at them, 'you did it.' She looked them in the eye. 'You are murderers.' She waited for this to sink in.

'You know that I know that it wasn't an accident. I know how jealous of her you were. And if the judge asks me in court I'll have to tell him, won't I? I can't tell a lie, can I?' She patted the chair next to her. 'Here, come and sit down –'

Four cheeks of two obedient bottoms squeezed into it.

'I'll have to tell them how it was strictly against the Rules for you to go alone to the river. How you forced her to go with

you although you knew that she couldn't swim. How you pushed
her out of the boat in the middle of the river. It wasn't an
accident, was it?'

Four saucers stared back at her. Fascinated by the story she
was telling them. *Then what happened?*

'So now you'll have to go to jail,' Baby Kochamma said
kindly. 'And your mother will go to jail because of you. Would
you like that?'

Frightened eyes and a fountain looked back at her.

'Three of you in three different jails. Do you know what jails
in India are like?'

Two heads shook twice.

Baby Kochamma built up her case. She drew (from her
imagination) vivid pictures of prison life. The cockroach-crisp
food. The *chhi-chhi* piled in the toilets like soft brown mountains.
The bedbugs. The beatings. She dwelled on the long years
Ammu would be put away because of them. How she would
be an old, sick woman with lice in her hair when she came out
– if she didn't die in jail, that was. Systematically, in her kind,
concerned voice she conjured up the macabre future in store
for them. When she had stamped out every ray of hope,
destroyed their lives completely, like a fairy godmother she presented them with a solution. God would never forgive them for
what they had done, but here on Earth there was a way of
undoing some of the damage. Of saving their mother from
humiliation and suffering on their account. Provided they were
prepared to be practical.

'Luckily,' Baby Kochamma said, 'luckily for you, the police
have made a mistake. A *lucky* mistake.' She paused. 'You know
what it is, don't you?'

There were people trapped in the glass paperweight on the
policeman's desk. Estha could see them. A waltzing man and a
waltzing woman. She wore a white dress with legs underneath.

'Don't you?'

There was paperweight waltz music. Mammachi was playing it on her violin.

Ra-ra-ra-ra-rum.

Parum-parum.

'The thing is,' Baby Kochamma's voice was saying, 'what's done is done. The Inspector says he's going to die anyway. So it won't really matter to him what the police think. What matters is whether you want to go to jail and make Ammu go to jail because of *you*. It's up to you to decide that.'

There were bubbles inside the paperweight which made the man and woman look as though they were waltzing underwater. They looked happy. Maybe they were getting married. She in her white dress. He in his black suit and bow-tie. They were looking deep into each other's eyes.

'If you want to save her, all you have to do, is to go with the Uncle with the big *meeshas*. He'll ask you a question. One question. All you have to do is to say "Yes". Then we can all go home. It's so easy. It's a small price to pay.'

Baby Kochamma followed Estha's gaze. It was all she could do to prevent herself from taking the paperweight and flinging it out of the window. Her heart was hammering.

'So!' she said, with a bright, brittle smile, the strain beginning to tell in her voice. 'What shall I tell the Inspector Uncle? What have we decided? D'you want to save Ammu or shall we send her to jail?'

As though she was offering them a choice of two treats. Fishing or Bathing the pigs? Bathing the pigs or fishing?

The twins looked up at her. Not together (but almost) two frightened voices whispered, 'Save Ammu.'

In the years to come they would replay this scene in their heads. As children. As teenagers. As adults. Had they been deceived into doing what they did? Had they been tricked into condemnation?

In a way, yes. But it wasn't as simple as that. They both knew that they had been given a choice. And how quick they had been in the choosing! They hadn't given it more than a second of thought before they looked up and said (not together, but almost) – 'Save Ammu.' Save us. Save our mother.

Baby Kochamma beamed. Relief worked like a laxative. She needed to go to the bathroom. Urgently. She opened the door and asked for the Inspector.

'They're good little children,' she told him when he came. 'They'll go with you.'

'No need for both. One will serve the purpose,' Inspector Thomas Matthew said. 'Any one. Mon. Mol. Who wants to come with me?'

'Estha.' Baby Kochamma chose. Knowing him to be the more practical of the two. The more tractable. The more far-sighted. The more responsible. 'You go. Goodboy.'

Little Man. He lived in a cara-van. Dum dum.

Estha went.

Ambassador E. Pelvis. With saucer-eyes and a spoiled puff. A short ambassador flanked by tall policemen, on a terrible mission deep into the bowels of the Kottayam police station. Their footsteps echoing on the flagstone floor.

Rahel remained behind in the Inspector's office and listened to the rude sounds of Baby Kochamma's relief dribbling down the sides of the Inspector's pot in his attached toilet. 'The flush doesn't work,' she said when she came out. 'It's so annoying.' Embarrassed that the Inspector would see the colour and consistency of her stool.

The lockup was pitch-dark. Estha could see nothing, but he could hear the sound of rasping, laboured breathing. The smell of shit made him retch. Someone switched on the light. Bright. Blinding. Velutha appeared on the scummy, slippery floor. A mangled genie invoked by a modern lamp. He was naked, his soiled mundu had come undone. Blood spilled from his skull like a secret. His face was swollen and his head look liked a pumpkin, too large and heavy for the slender stem it grew from. A pumpkin with a monstrous upside-down smile. Police boots stepped back from the rim of a pool of urine spreading from him, the bright, bare electric bulb reflected in it.

Dead fish floated up in Estha. One of the policemen prodded Velutha with his foot. There was no response. Inspector Thomas Mathew squatted on his haunches and raked his Jeep key across the sole of Velutha's foot. Swollen eyes opened. Wandered. Then focused through a film of blood on a beloved child. Estha imagined that something in him smiled. Not his mouth, but some other unhurt part of him. His elbow perhaps. Or shoulder.

The Inspector asked his question. Estha's mouth said Yes.

Childhood tiptoed out.

Silence slid in like a bolt.

Someone switched off the light and Velutha disappeared.

On their way back in the police Jeep, Baby Kochamma stopped at Reliable Medicos for some Calmpose. She gave them two each. By the time they reached Chungam Bridge their eyes were beginning to close. Estha whispered something into Rahel's ear.

'You were right. It wasn't him. It was Urumban.'

'Thang god,' Rahel whispered back.

'Where d'you think he is?'

'Escaped to Africa.'

They were handed over to their mother fast asleep, floating on this fiction.

Until the next morning, when Ammu shook it out of them. But by then it was too late.

Inspector Thomas Mathew, a man of experience in these matters, was right. Velutha didn't live through the night.

Half an hour past midnight, Death came for him.

And for the little family curled up and asleep on a blue cross-stitch counterpane? What came for them?

Not death. Just the end of living.

After Sophie Mol's funeral, when Ammu took them back to the police station and the Inspector chose his mangoes (*Tap, tap*), the body had already been removed. Dumped in the *themmady kuzhy* – the pauper's pit – where the police routinely dump their dead.

When Baby Kochamma heard about Ammu's visit to the police station, she was terrified. Everything that she, Baby Kochamma, had done, had been premised on one assumption. She had gambled on the fact that Ammu, whatever else she did, however angry she was, would never publicly admit to her relationship with Velutha. Because, according to Baby Kochamma, that would amount to destroying herself and her children. For ever. But Baby Kochamma hadn't taken into account the Unsafe Edge in Ammu. The Unmixable Mix – the infinite tenderness of motherhood, the reckless rage of a suicide bomber.

Ammu's reaction stunned her. The ground fell away from under her feet. She knew she had an ally in Inspector Thomas Mathew. But how long would that last? What if he were transferred and the case reopened? It was possible – considering the shouting, sloganeering crowd of Party workers that Comrade K. N. M. Pillai had managed to assemble outside the gate. That prevented the labourers from coming to work, and left vast quantities of mangoes, bananas, pineapple, garlic and ginger rotting slowly on the premises of Paradise Pickles.

Baby Kochamma knew she had to get Ammu out of Ayemenem as soon as possible.

She managed that by doing what she was best at. Irrigating her fields, nourishing her crops with other people's passions.

She gnawed like a rat into the godown of Chacko's grief.

Within its walls she planted an easy, accessible target for his insane anger. It wasn't hard for her to portray Ammu as the person actually responsible for Sophie Mol's death. Ammu and her two-egg twins.

Chacko breaking down doors was only the sad bull thrashing at the end of Baby Kochamma's leash. It was *her* idea that Ammu be made to pack her bags and leave. That Estha be Returned.

20

The Madras Mail

And so, at the Cochin Harbour Terminus, Estha Alone at the barred train window. Ambassador E. Pelvis. A millstone with a puff. And a green-wavy, thick-watery, lumpy, seaweedy, floaty, bottomless-bottomful feeling. His trunk with his name on it was under his seat. His tiffin box with tomato sandwiches and his Eagle flask with an eagle was on the little folding table in front of him.

Next to him an eating lady in a green and purple Kanjeeva-ram sari and diamonds clustered like shining bees on each nostril offered him yellow laddoos in a box. Estha shook his head. She smiled and coaxed, her kind eyes disappeared into slits behind her glasses. She made kissing sounds with her mouth.

'Try one. Verrrry sweet,' she said in Tamil. *Rombo maduram.*

'Sweet,' her oldest daughter, who was about Estha's age, said in English.

Estha shook his head again. The lady ruffled his hair and spoiled his puff. Her family (husband and three children) was already eating. Big round yellow laddoo crumbs on the seat. Trainrumbles under their feet. The blue nightlight not yet on.

The eating lady's small son switched it on. The eating lady switched it off. She explained to the child that it was a sleeping light. Not an awake light.

Every First Class train thing was green. The seats green. The

323

berths green. The floor green. The chains green. Darkgreen Lightgreen.

TO STOP TRAIN PULL CHAIN, it said in green.

OT POTS NIART LLUP NIAHC, Estha thought in green.

Through the window bars, Ammu held his hand.

'Keep your ticket carefully,' Ammu's mouth said. Ammu's trying-not-to-cry mouth. 'They'll come and check.'

Estha nodded down at Ammu's face tilted up to the train window. At Rahel, small and smudged with station dirt. All three of them bonded by the certain, separate knowledge that they had loved a man to death.

That wasn't in the papers.

It took the twins years to understand Ammu's part in what had happened. At Sophie Mol's funeral and in the days before Estha was Returned, they saw her swollen eyes, and with the self-centredness of children, held themselves wholly culpable for her grief.

'Eat the sandwiches before they get soggy,' Ammu said. 'And don't forget to write.'

She scanned the fingernails of the little hand she held, and slid a black sickle of dirt from under the thumb-nail.

'And look after my sweetheart for me. Until I come and get him.'

'When, Ammu? When will you come for him?'

'Soon.'

'But when? When eggzackly?'

'Soon, sweetheart. As soon as I can.'

'Month-after-next? Ammu?' Deliberately making it a long time away so that Ammu would say, *Before that, Estha. Be practical. What about your studies?*

'As soon as I get a job. As soon as I can go away from here and get a job,' Ammu said.

'But that will be never!' A wave of panic. A bottomless-bottomful feeling.

The eating lady eavesdropped indulgently.

'See how nicely he speaks English,' she said to her children in Tamil.

'But that will be never,' her oldest daughter said combatively. 'En ee vee ee aar. Never.'

By 'never' Estha had only meant that it would be too far away. That it wouldn't be *now*, wouldn't be *soon*.

By 'never' he hadn't meant Not Ever.

But that's how the words came out.

But that will be never!

For Never they just took the O and T out of Not Ever.

They?

The Government.

Where people were sent to Jolly Well Behave.

And that's how it had all turned out.

Never. Not Ever.

It was *his* fault that the faraway man in Ammu's chest stopped shouting. *His* fault that she died alone in the lodge with no one to lie at the back of her and talk to her.

Because he was the one that had *said* it. *But Ammu that will be never!*

'Don't be silly, Estha. It'll be soon,' Ammu's mouth said. 'I'll be a teacher. I'll start a school. And you and Rahel will be in it.'

'And we'll be able to afford it because it will be ours!' Estha said with his enduring pragmatism. His eye on the main chance. Free bus rides. Free funerals. Free education. Little Man. He lived in a cara-van. Dum dum.

'We'll have our own house,' Ammu said.

'A little house,' Rahel said.

'And in our school we'll have classrooms and blackboards,' Estha said.

'And chalk.'

'And Real Teachers teaching.'

'And proper punishments,' Rahel said.

This was the stuff their dreams were made of. On the day that Estha was Returned. Chalk. Blackboards. Proper punishments.

They didn't ask to be let off lightly. They only asked for punishments that fitted their crimes. Not ones that came like cupboards with built-in bedrooms. Not ones you spent your whole life in, wandering through its maze of shelves.

Without warning the train began to move. Very slowly.

Estha's pupils dilated. His nails dug into Ammu's hand as she walked along the platform. Her walk turning into a run as the Madras Mail picked up speed.

Godbless, my baby. My sweetheart. I'll come for you soon!

'Ammu!' Estha said as she disengaged her hand. Prising loose small finger after finger. 'Ammu! Feeling vomity!' Estha's voice lifted into a wail.

Little Elvis the Pelvis with a spoiled, special-outing puff. And beige and pointy shoes. He left his voice behind.

On the station platform Rahel doubled over and screamed and screamed.

The train pulled out. The light pulled in.

TWENTY-THREE YEARS LATER, Rahel, dark woman in a yellow T-shirt, turns to Estha in the dark.

'Esthapappychachen Kuttappen Peter Mon,' she says.

She whispers.

She moves her mouth.

Their beautiful mother's mouth.

Estha, sitting very straight, waiting to be arrested, takes his fingers to it. To touch the words it makes. To keep the whisper. His fingers follow the shape of it. The touch of teeth. His hand is held and kissed.

Pressed against the coldness of a cheek, wet with shattered rain.

Then she sat up and put her arms around him. Drew him down beside her.

They lay like that for a long time. Awake in the dark. Quietness and Emptiness.

Not old. Not young.

But a viable die-able age.

They were strangers who had met in a chance encounter.

They had known each other before Life began.

There is very little that anyone could say to clarify what happened next. Nothing that (in Mammachi's book) would separate Sex from Love. Or Needs from Feelings.

Except perhaps that no Watcher watched through Rahel's eyes. No one stared out of a window at the sea. Or a boat in the river. Or a passer-by in the mist in a hat.

Except perhaps that it was a little cold. A little wet. But very quiet. The Air.

But what was there to say?

Only that there were tears. Only that Quietness and Emptiness fitted together like stacked spoons. Only that there was a snuffling in the hollows at the base of a lovely throat. Only that a hard honey-coloured shoulder had a semi-circle of teethmarks on it. Only that they held each other close, long after it was over. Only that what they shared that night was not happiness, but hideous grief.

Only that once again they broke the Love Laws. That lay down who should be loved. And how. And how much.

On the roof of the abandoned factory, the lonely drummer drummed. A gauze door slammed. A mouse rushed across the factory floor. Cobwebs sealed old pickle vats. Empty, all but one – in which a small heap of congealed white dust lay. Bone dust from a Bar Nowl. Long dead. Pickledowl.

In answer to Sophie Mol's question: *Chacko, where do old birds go to die? Why don't dead ones fall like stones from the sky?*

Asked on the evening of the day she arrived. She was standing on the edge of Baby Kochamma's ornamental pond looking up at the kites wheeling in the sky.

Sophie Mol. Hatted, bellbottomed and Loved from the Beginning.

Margaret Kochamma (because she knew that when you travel to the Heart of Darkness (b) *Anything can Happen to Anyone*) called her in to have her regimen of pills. Filaria. Malaria. Diarrhoea.

She had no prophylaxis, unfortunately, for Death by Drowning.

Then it was time for dinner.

'Supper, silly,' Sophie Mol said when Estha was sent to call her.

At *supper silly*, the children sat at a separate smaller table. Sophie Mol, with her back to the grown ups, made gruesome faces at the food. Every mouthful she ate was displayed to her admiring younger cousins, half-chewed, mulched, lying on her tongue like fresh vomit.

When Rahel did the same, Ammu saw her and took her to bed.

Ammu tucked her naughty daughter in and switched off the light. Her good-night kiss left no spit on Rahel's cheek and Rahel could tell that she wasn't really angry.

'You're not angry, Ammu.' In a happy whisper. *A little more her mother loved her.*

'No.' Ammu kissed her again. 'Good night, sweetheart. Godbless.'

'Good night, Ammu. Send Estha soon.'

And as Ammu walked away she heard her daughter whisper, 'Ammu!'

'What is it?'

'We be of one blood, ye and I.'

Ammu leaned against the bedroom door in the dark, reluctant to return to the dinner table where the conversation circled like a moth around the white child and her mother as though they were the only source of light. Ammu felt that she would die, wither and die, if she heard another word. If she had to endure another minute of Chacko's proud, tennis-trophy smile. Or the undercurrent of sexual jealousy that emanated from Mammachi. Or Baby Kochamma's conversation that was designed to exclude Ammu and her children, to inform them of their place in the scheme of things.

As she leaned against the door in the darkness, she felt her dream, her afternoon-mare move inside her like a rib of water rising from the ocean, gathering into a wave. The cheerful one-armed man with salty skin and a shoulder that ended abruptly like a cliff emerged from the shadows of the jagged beach and walked towards her.

Who was he?

Who could he have been?

The God of Loss.

The God of Small Things.

The God of Goose Bumps and Sudden Smiles.

He could do only one thing at a time.

If he touched her, he couldn't talk to her, if he loved her he couldn't leave, if he spoke he couldn't listen, if he fought he couldn't win.

Ammu longed for him. Ached for him with the whole of her biology.

She returned to the dinner table.

21

The Cost of Living

When the old house had closed its bleary eyes and settled into sleep, Ammu, wearing one of Chacko's old shirts over a long white petticoat, walked out onto the front verandah. She paced up and down for a while. Restless. Feral. Then she sat on the wicker chair below the mouldy, button-eyed bison head and the portraits of the Little Blessed One and Aleyooty Ammachi that hung on either side of it. Her twins were sleeping the way they did when they were exhausted – with their eyes half open, two small monsters. They got that from their father.

Ammu switched on her tangerine transistor. A man's voice crackled through it. An English song she hadn't heard before.

She sat there in the dark. A lonely, lambent woman looking out at her embittered aunt's ornamental garden, listening to a tangerine. To a voice from far away. Wafting through the night. Sailing over lakes and rivers. Over dense heads of trees. Past the yellow church. Past the school. Bumping up the dirt road. Up the steps of the verandah. To her.

Barely listening to the music, she watched the frenzy of insects flitting around the light, vying to kill themselves.

The words of the song exploded in her head.

> *There's no time to lose*
> *I heard her say*
> *Cash your dreams before*

331

They slip away
Dying all the time
Lose your dreams and you
Will lose your mind.

Ammu drew her knees up and hugged them. She couldn't believe it. The cheap coincidence of those words. She stared fiercely out at the garden. Ousa the Bar Nowl flew past on a silent nocturnal patrol. The fleshy anthuriums gleamed like gunmetal.

She remained sitting for a while. Long after the song had ended. Then suddenly she rose from her chair and walked out of her world like a witch. To a better, happier place.

She moved quickly through the darkness, like an insect following a chemical trail. She knew the path to the river as well as her children did and could have found her way there blindfolded. She didn't know what it was that made her hurry through the undergrowth. That turned her walk into a run. That made her arrive on the banks of the Meenachal breathless. Sobbing. As though she was late for something. As though her life depended on getting there in time. As though she knew he would be there. Waiting. As though *he* knew she would come.

He did.

Know.

That knowledge had slid into him that afternoon. Cleanly. Like the sharp edge of a knife. When history had slipped up. While he had held her little daughter in his arms. When her eyes had told him he was not the only giver of gifts. That she had gifts to give him too, that in return for his boats, his boxes, his small windmills, she would trade her deep dimples when she smiled. Her smooth brown skin. Her shining shoulders. Her eyes that were always somewhere else.

He wasn't there.

Ammu sat on the stone steps that led to the water. She buried

her head in her arms, feeling foolish for having been so sure.
So *certain*.

Further downstream in the middle of the river, Velutha floated
on his back, looking up at the stars. His paralysed brother and
his one-eyed father had eaten the dinner he had cooked them
and were asleep. So he was free to lie in the river and drift
slowly with the current. A log. A serene crocodile. Coconut
trees bent into the river and watched him float by. Yellow
bamboo wept. Small fish took coquettish liberties with him.
Pecked him.

He flipped over and began to swim. Upstream. Against the
current. He turned towards the bank for one last look, treading
water, feeling foolish for having been so sure. So *certain*.

When he saw her the detonation almost drowned him. It
took all his strength to stay afloat. He trod water, standing in
the middle of a dark river.

She didn't see the knob of his head bobbing over the dark
river. He could have been anything. A floating coconut. In any
case she wasn't looking. Her head was buried in her arms.

He watched her. He took his time.

Had he known that he was about to enter a tunnel whose
only egress was his own annihilation, would he have turned
away?

Perhaps.

Perhaps not.

Who can tell?

He began to swim towards her. Quietly. Cutting through the
water with no fuss. He had almost reached the bank when she
looked up and saw him. His feet touched the muddy riverbed.
As he rose from the dark river and walked up the stone steps,
she saw that the world they stood in was his. That he belonged
to it. That it belonged to him. The water. The mud. The trees.

The fish. The stars. He moved so easily through it. As she watched him she understood the quality of his beauty. How his labour had shaped him. How the wood he fashioned had fashioned him. Each plank he planed, each nail he drove, each thing he made, had moulded him. Had left its stamp on him. Had given him his strength, his supple grace.

He wore a thin white cloth around his loins, looped between his dark legs. He shook the water from his hair. She could see his smile in the dark. His white, sudden smile that he had carried with him from boyhood into manhood. His only luggage.

They looked at each other. They weren't thinking any more. The time for that had come and gone. Smashed smiles lay ahead of them. But that would be later.

Lay Ter.

He stood before her with the river dripping from him. She stayed sitting on the steps, watching him. Her face pale in the moonlight. A sudden chill crept over him. His heart hammered. It was all a terrible mistake. He had misunderstood her. The whole thing was a figment of his imagination. This was a trap. There were people in the bushes. Watching. She was the delectable bait. How could it be otherwise? They had seen him in the march. He tried to make his voice casual. Normal. It came out in a croak.

'Ammukutty . . . what is it?'

She went to him and laid the length of her body against his. He just stood there. He didn't touch her. He was shivering. Partly with cold. Partly terror. Partly aching desire. Despite his fear his body was prepared to take the bait. It wanted her. Urgently. His wetness wet her. She put her arms around him.

He tried to be rational: *What's the worst thing that can happen?* *I could lose everything. My job. My family. My livelihood. Everything.* She could hear the wild hammering of his heart.

She held him till it calmed down. Somewhat.

She unbuttoned her shirt. They stood there. Skin to skin.

Her brownness against his blackness. Her softness against his hardness. Her nut-brown breasts (that wouldn't support a toothbrush) against his smooth ebony chest. She smelled the river on him. His Particular Paravan smell that so disgusted Baby Kochamma. Ammu put out her tongue and tasted it, in the hollow of his throat. On the lobe of his ear. She pulled his head down towards her and kissed his mouth. A cloudy kiss. A kiss that demanded a kiss-back. He kissed her back. First cautiously. Then urgently. Slowly his arms came up behind her. He stroked her back. Very gently. She could feel the skin on his palms. Rough. Calloused. Sandpaper. He was careful not to hurt her. She could feel how soft she felt to him. She could feel herself through him. Her skin. The way her body existed only where he touched her. The rest of her was smoke. She felt him shudder against her. His hands were on her haunches (that could support a whole array of toothbrushes), pulling her hips against his, to let her know how much he wanted her.

Biology designed the dance. Terror timed it. Dictated the rhythm with which their bodies answered each other. As though they knew already that for each tremor of pleasure they would pay with an equal measure of pain. As though they knew that how far they went would be measured against how far they would be taken. So they held back. Tormented each other. Gave of each other slowly. But that only made it worse. It only raised the stakes. It only cost them more. Because it smoothed the wrinkles, the fumble and rush of unfamiliar love and roused them to fever pitch.

Behind them the river pulsed through the darkness, shimmering like wild silk. Yellow bamboo wept.

Night's elbows rested on the water and watched them.

They lay under the mangosteen tree, where only recently a grey old boatplant with boatflowers and boatfruit had been uprooted by a Mobile Republic. A wasp. A flag. A surprised puff. A Fountain in a Love-in-Tokyo.

335

The scurrying, hurrying, boatworld was already gone.
The White termites on their way to work.
The White ladybirds on their way home.
The White beetles burrowing away from the light.
The White grasshoppers with whitewood violins.
The sad white music.
All gone.
Leaving a boat-shaped patch of bare dry earth, cleared and ready for love. As though Esthappen and Rahel had prepared the ground for them. Willed this to happen. The twin midwives of Ammu's dream.

Ammu, naked now, crouched over Velutha, her mouth on his. He drew her hair around them like a tent. Like her children did when they wanted to exclude the outside world. She slid further down, introducing herself to the rest of him. His neck. His nipples. His chocolate stomach. She sipped the last of the river from the hollow of his navel. She pressed the heat of his erection against her eyelids. She tasted him, salty, in her mouth. He sat up and drew her back to him. She felt his belly tighten under her, hard as a board. She felt her wetness slipping on his skin. He took her nipple in his mouth and cradled her other breast in his calloused palm. Velvet gloved in sandpaper.

At the moment that she guided him into her, she caught a passing glimpse of his youth, his *youngness*, the wonder in his eyes at the secret he had unearthed and she smiled down at him as though he was her child.

Once he was inside her, fear was derailed and biology took over. The cost of living climbed to unaffordable heights; though later, Baby Kochamma would say it was a Small Price to Pay.

Was it?

Two lives. Two children's childhoods.

And a history lesson for future offenders.

Clouded eyes held clouded eyes in a steady gaze and a luminous woman opened herself to a luminous man. She was as wide and deep as a river in spate. He sailed on her waters. She could feel him moving deeper and deeper into her. Frantic. Frenzied. Asking to be let in further. Further. Stopped only by the shape of her. The shape of him. And when he was refused, when he had touched the deepest depths of her, with a sobbing, shuddering sigh, he drowned.

She lay against him. Their bodies slick with sweat. She felt his body drop away from her. His breath become more regular. She saw his eyes clear. He stroked her hair, sensing that the knot that had eased in him was still tight and quivering in her. Gently he turned her over on her back. He wiped the sweat and grit from her with his wet cloth. He lay over her, careful not to put his weight on her. Small stones pressed into the skin of his forearms. He kissed her eyes. Her ears. Her breasts. Her belly. Her seven silver stretchmarks from her twins. The line of down that led from her navel to her dark triangle, that told him where she wanted him to go. The inside of her legs, where her skin was softest. Then carpenter's hands lifted her hips and an untouchable tongue touched the innermost part of her. Drank long and deep from the bowl of her.

She danced for him. On that boat-shaped piece of earth. She lived.

He held her against him, resting his back against the mangosteen tree, while she cried and laughed at once. Then, for what seemed like an eternity, but was really no more than five minutes, she slept leaning against him, her back against his chest. Seven years of oblivion lifted off her and flew into the shadows on weighty, quaking wings. Like a dull, steel peahen. And on Ammu's Road (to Age and Death) a small, sunny meadow appeared. Copper grass spangled with blue butterflies. Beyond it, an abyss.

Slowly the terror seeped back into him. At what he had done. At what he knew he would do again. And again.

She woke to the sound of his heart knocking against his chest.

337

As though it was searching for a way out. For that movable rib. A secret sliding-folding panel. His arms were still around her, she could feel the muscles move while his hands played with a dry palm frond. Ammu smiled to herself in the dark, thinking how much she loved his arms – the shape and strength of them, how safe she felt resting in them when actually it was the most dangerous place she could be.

He folded his fear into a perfect rose. He held it out in the palm of his hand. She took it from him and put it in her hair.

She moved closer, wanting to be within him, to touch more of him. He gathered her into the cave of his body. A breeze lifted off the river and cooled their warm bodies.

It was a little cold. A little wet. A little quiet. The Air.

But what was there to say?

An hour later Ammu disengaged herself gently.

'I have to go.'

He said nothing, didn't move. He watched her dress.

Only one thing mattered now. They knew that it was all they could ask of each other. The only thing. Ever. They both knew that.

Even later, on the thirteen nights that followed this one, instinctively they stuck to the Small Things. The Big Things ever lurked inside. They knew that there was nowhere for them to go. They had nothing. No future. So they stuck to the small things.

They laughed at ant-bites on each other's bottoms. At clumsy caterpillars sliding off the ends of leaves, at overturned beetles that couldn't right themselves. At the pair of small fish that always sought Velutha out in the river and bit him. At a particularly devout praying mantis. At the minute spider who lived in a crack in the wall of the black verandah of the History House and camouflaged himself by covering his body with bits of rubbish – a sliver of wasp wing. Part of a cobweb. Dust. Leaf rot.

The empty thorax of a dead bee. *Chappu Thamburan*, Velutha called him. Lord Rubbish. One night they contributed to his wardrobe – a flake of garlic skin – and were deeply offended when he rejected it along with the rest of his armour from which he emerged – disgruntled, naked, snot-coloured. As though he deplored their taste in clothes. For a few days he remained in this suicidal state of disdainful undress. The rejected shell of garbage stayed standing, like an outmoded world-view. An antiquated philosophy. Then it crumbled. Gradually *Chappu Thamburan* acquired a new ensemble.

Without admitting it to each other or themselves, they linked their fates, their futures (their Love, their Madness, their Hope, their Infinnate Joy) to his. They checked on him every night (with growing panic as time went by) to see if he had survived the day. They fretted over his frailty. His smallness. The adequacy of his camouflage. His seemingly self-destructive pride. They grew to love his eclectic taste. His shambling dignity.

They chose him because they knew that they had to put their faith in fragility. Stick to Smallness. Each time they parted, they extracted only one small promise from each other.

'*Tomorrow?*'

'*Tomorrow.*'

They knew that things could change in a day. They were right about that.

They were wrong about *Chappu Thamburan*, though. He outlived Velutha. He fathered future generations.

He died of natural causes.

That first night, on the day that Sophie Mol came, Velutha watched his lover dress. When she was ready she squatted facing him. She touched him lightly with her fingers and left a trail of goosebumps on his skin. Like flat chalk on a blackboard. Like breeze in a paddyfield. Like jet-streaks in a blue church sky. He

The God *of*
Small Things

PREFACE

This text is neither a traditional introduction to public relations nor is it the typical campaigns or management text. Rather, it uses both the case method and an analysis of public relations campaigns to help students learn and apply concepts of planning, research, and international or intercultural communication to the field of public relations. It is designed to meet the need for an upper-division course in public relations. We assume that students reading the book will have already had some introduction to the practice and profession of public relations. It is, however, designed for use by students who may have had limited experience with public relations campaigns. We provide a structure for analyzing campaigns that can be applied by any student with a background in communication theory and research, regardless of his or her public relations experience.

The text can be used for a course specifically in intercultural or international public relations cases. It can also be used as the text in a course focusing on the analysis of all types of public relations campaigns, or it could be used for the introductory portion of a class in which students develop their own campaign proposals. We envision two different ways a course could be designed around the text. First, the text could be used in a case methods course. In this pedagogy, introductory lectures based on the text would explain the concepts of research, planning, and application in diverse public relations settings. Students would then be guided through discussions of the cases in the text. Using this approach would help students appreciate and apply concepts of planning, theory, research, and intercultural sensitivity and overcome the oft-held belief that public relations can be accomplished by a "people person" using only intuition or common sense.

Second, the text could be used to lay the basis for a public relations campaign course. In such a course, the ROSTE model presented would be introduced and explained through analysis of the cases provided. After reviewing the ROSTE model, students could be assigned a problem or client and use the principles to develop their own campaign or campaign proposal.

When we refer to the cases or the case method, we simply mean the use of existing real-world situations to provide examples that help illustrate principles. This method also can be used to encourage student discussion. We have found that such discussions help students organize and remember concepts. Our research also shows that this approach improves critical thinking skills.

When we refer to public relations campaigns, we include all structured efforts to influence the behavior, beliefs, or attitudes of any target public. Our approach to campaigns includes the accidental or poorly conceived actions of some clients or organizations as well as successful and well-planned campaigns. We submit that any communication program that impacts the beliefs or actions of a public is worthy of analysis. Analysis of an accidental communication can sometimes demonstrate principles of public relations as effectively as the study of planned public relations efforts. We have also included descriptions of campaigns that failed to meet their objectives. Most public relations texts or case books only include cases that succeeded, either because the authors believe that successful cases are superior teaching aids or because they are the cases most easily acquired. Here we have gone to the trouble to describe unsuccessful cases, sometimes without the cooperation of the organizations that planned and administered the campaigns. We included these "failures" for three reasons. First, we wanted to avoid the impression that all public relations campaigns are successful. Many well-known campaigns administered by famous corporations and public relations agencies simply are not well planned. We want to ensure that students know what poor public relations work looks like. Second, often a student can learn more from identifying mistakes than from critiquing successful work. Finally, we believe it is important to let young public relations professionals know that everyone makes mistakes. Not only is this realization good for students' egos, it also helps encourage them to more aggressively critique the campaigns they review.

The information on international and intercultural communication is not only useful in the analysis of international public relations cases. It is also applicable to very traditional public relations campaigns within the United States. Rarely are clients and their publics from the same ethnic, economic, and age groups. These demographic or socio-economic differences should be addressed with the same knowledge and sensitivity required for an international campaign.

Most public relations casebooks omit the introductory material presented here. Asking students to analyze cases without first introducing a framework for analysis is analogous to asking film students to criticize motion pictures without first exposing them to principles of acting, directing, and lighting. Before students can identify quality work, critique poor work, or even organize their observations, they must first be given a framework and some rules to help them evaluate what they see.

This text begins with four chapters devoted to explaining an approach to public relations campaign analysis. These are followed by one chapter devoted to principles of intercultural and international communication and a final chapter in which we present a model for development or analysis of intercultural public relations cases. We hope that most of the concepts introduced here are not new to the reader. Our intent is only to take concepts presented in most introductory public relations texts and apply them to create a structure that can be used to analyze the campaigns presented later in the text. This same structure can also be used to develop new campaigns.

Following the description of our campaign analysis approach (ROSTE) and the introduction of information on intercultural communication, several campaigns are presented for analysis and to demonstrate principles of international or intercultural communication. We anticipate that a course using this text will begin with a few introductory lectures or discussions that help students understand the ROSTE analytical framework. The bulk of such a course would be devoted to a case method analysis of the cases presented and other timely campaigns found in the news or the students' experiences.

Most of the campaigns we included here involve far more than a simple special event or media placement. We submit that it requires complete research, a complicated plan, and thorough execution to truly change a public. Further, if one only analyzes single events in isolation without taking into account all of the components of a complete public relations campaign, it seems unlikely that even rudimentary principles of international or intercultural communication can be applied.

The application of intercultural communication concepts is important even for students who believe they will spend their entire public relations career in the United States. There are cultural differences and communication differences among groups of different incomes, ages, religions, ethnic identification, and regions within the United States. When old, bald, fat, white men on a corporate board are the clients and young men or women are their target public, the public relations professional must be able to plan and implement an intercultural campaign.

After describing a model for how to plan or analyze international or intercultural public relations campaigns, we provide a series of campaigns for analysis. Public relations cases can be organized or categorized in several ways. Here we have opted not to present these cases in any particular order. Rather, we leave it to the reader or the teacher using this book to determine the order in which the cases will be read. We did this for two reasons. First, many of the cases present issues or concepts from more than one typical category of public relations campaigns. For example, Case 5, dealing with drug patents in Africa, could be included in a set of lessons or discussions about ethics because it raises questions about the conflict between a pharmaceutical company's obligation to produce revenue for its shareholders and that same company's duty to help poor but ill consumers. The same case can be used to discuss lobbying, because it includes conflicts between governmental entities and focuses, in part, on the importance of influencing government regulators. This case can also be used in an instructional block focusing on investor relations, or in a discussion of how to communicate with competing publics.

Our second reason for not imposing our own order on these cases is to give readers or teachers the freedom to organize the cases to place emphasis on the concepts they think important. If, for example, a teacher wants to organize a block of instruction that focuses on ethical issues, those cases that include specific ethical questions can be read together. Below we have tried to anticipate typical categories of public relations instruction and to list under the label of each category those cases that could be included in that area. Of course, the reader is free to create other categories or to place other cases in any of these categories.

Internal Relations

Case 4—Internal Public Relations in the Post-War Balkans

Case 7—Global Public Relations in South Korea: A Case Study of a Multinational Corporation

Case 11—Improved Internal Communications in a Large South African Financial Services Organization

Case 15—Engaging Colombian Coffee Growers in Dialogue: Social Reports Campaign of the Departmental Committee of Antioquia

Community Relations

Case 6—Competing Community Relations Campaigns in Australia: Public Relations Efforts for and against a Biosolids Production Facility

Case 8—The Latvian Naturalization Project

Case 14—One Tambon, One Product: Part of the War against Poverty in Thailand

The ROSTE Model

We have elected to use an unusual acronym as the skeleton of our analytical framework and we want to explain that decision here. Most public relations texts use one of three such acronyms. They are:

RACE (Research, Action, Communication, and Evaluation)
ROPE (Research, Objective, Programming, and Evaluation) or
ROPES (Research, Objective, Programming, Evaluation, and Stewardship)

Each of these acronyms is useful but each omits concepts that are essential, particularly to understanding intercultural public relations campaigns. Therefore, we have opted to combine concepts from RACE and ROPE and organize our analysis around ROSTE— Research, Objective, Strategies, Tactics, and Evaluation. In conversation we have been pronouncing this acronym like "roast" but we admit this pronunciation, at best, requires some creative treatment of language. Despite any difficulty with pronunciation, we believe the acronym has the advantage of including essential elements of public relations analysis omitted in the other more easily pronounced acronyms.

The RACE acronym was described in John Marsdon's *The Nature of Public Relations* in 1963. It is a useful model but it ignores the significance of a clearly identified objective. Without an articulated (and, we would submit, an operationalized) objective, evaluation of a campaign's success is impossible. Our experiences evaluating and judging campaigns from Silver Anvil entries to student papers suggest that the absence of a clear, simple, and measurable objective is a major weakness in many otherwise well-designed public relations campaigns. The fact that many campaigns attempt to demonstrate their success with such nonsensical evaluations as column inches of news copy generated or advertising cost equivalents is evidence of the importance of a campaign objective.

The ROPE model is described by Jerry Hendrix and used for case analysis in his book *Public Relations Cases.* ROPES is a model that differs from ROPE only in the addition of the notion of stewardship. ROPE is also a useful tool for public relations planning but it and ROPES both ignore the facts that public relations requires a strategic plan and must be a management function. Even the most gifted communicator cannot create a campaign that makes his or her client appear culturally sensitive if the client's actions violate cultural norms. We therefore include in all of our campaign analysis framework a strategy step that will guide the planned actions of the client and communications on behalf of the client. Strategic planning must include both action and communication.

RACE, ROPE, and ROPES also seem to ignore the difference between the planned actions and communications and the actual actions of the public relations practitioner needed to implement those plans. In the ROSTE model, strategies include action strategies and communication strategies. Action strategies are the actions recommended by the public relations practitioner and taken by the client. In effect, action strategies describe things to be done by the client so that the public relations practitioner has something to communicate about. In addition to action strategies, we included tactics in our analytic scheme. Tactics are the actions of the public relations practitioner taken to deliver the messages identified in communication strategies.

Following the ROSTE framework, a public relations plan should begin with extensive research, both primary and secondary. After that research, a practitioner should identify a public relations objective. The practitioner should then develop a strategic plan designed to meet that objective. This strategic plan should include both action components (things the client or practitioner must do) and communication message components (ideas or information the practitioner must communicate to target publics). The plan should also include specific tactics. Tactics are the specific actions taken to deliver the communication component of the strategic plan to the target public. Finally, recognizing that public relations is a dynamic and accountable process, a public relations campaign must include evaluation. Evaluation enables practitioners to judge their success and to modify the plan as needed. Although the component terms of this model may not be what the reader has seen elsewhere, the concepts they represent are always part of well-planned and well-managed public relations work. They do provide a useful framework for evaluating or constructing public relations campaigns.

Acknowledgments

We want to acknowledge the contributions and assistance of three groups of people. First, everyone who researched and wrote a case included in this work deserves our gratitude.

Norman E. Youngblood also deserves our special thanks for his work on the tables and graphics included in several of the cases. These documents arrived from many countries and in many very different formats. Making them usable was no small task.

We want specifically to acknowledge the work of L. Brooks Hill. A few months before this book was scheduled for completion, Dr. Ekachai became ill. Despite the very short notice, Dr. Hill was able to research and write the chapter on international and intercultural communications in time for us to complete the work on schedule. For his willingness to help and for his expertise we are truly grateful.

The publisher would like to thank the reviewers of this book: Eric Brown, Canyon College; Michael A. Dickerson, George Mason University; Deborah Menger, University of Texas at San Antonio; Harold C. Shaver, Marshall University; and Sharon S. Smith, Middle Tennessee State University.

LIST OF CONTRIBUTORS

Philip J. Auter received his Ph.D. in Communication from the University of Kentucky. He is now an assistant professor of communication specializing in electronic media and international media communication. His research interests include audience uses of—and effects on—television and the Internet, as well as multicultural representations in media.

Nilanjana Bardhan is an associate professor in the Speech Communication Department at Southern Illinois University–Carbondale. She completed her Ph.D. at Ohio University in 1998. Her research interests include international public relations, intercultural communication, critical media communication, and health communication.

Lynda Dee Dixon, Ph.D., is professor of communication at Bowling Green State University. Her research is in intercultural, health, and organizational communication. Her publications have appeared as book chapters and in several national and international journals.

Daradirek Ekachai (Ph.D., Southern Illinois University–Carbondale) is associate professor in advertising and public relations at Marquette University, Milwaukee, Wisconsin. She has published journal articles and book chapters on public relations in Thailand, PR education and pedagogy, computer-mediated communication, and intercultural communication. Her research has been published in *Public Relations Review, Handbook of Public Relations, Handbook of Media in Asia, International Public Relations, Images of the U.S. Around the World,* and most recently, *Public Relations in Asia.* She recently received a multi-year grant from the Robert Wood Johnson Foundation to plan and conduct a communication campaign on long-term care in Milwaukee County.

Peeraya Hanpongpandh (Ph.D., University of Iowa) is the chair of the Public Relations Department in the School of Communication Arts at Bangkok University, Thailand.

L. Brooks Hill (Ph.D., University of Illinois) is a professor and chair of the Department of Speech and Drama at Trinity University in San Antonio, Texas. He is a former president of the International Association for Intercultural Communication Studies and has taught intercultural communication at all levels. He has also served as a consultant, trainer, and researcher in international and intercultural communication.

Derina R. Holtzhausen, Ph.D., is an associate professor and sequence head of the public relations program in the School of Mass Communications, University of South Florida. She is a native of South Africa with 27 years experience as a communications practitioner and teacher.

Ali M. Kanso is an associate professor in the Department of Communication at the University of Texas at San Antonio. He received his Ph.D. from Ohio University.

Rosechongporn Komolsevin, Ph.D., is an associate professor in communication at Bangkok University, where she has served as chair of the doctoral program in communication. In addition to her teaching and research in advertising and public relations, she has served on a number of advisory committees on government PR and mass media projects.

Virginia Kreimeyer is a retired U.S. Air Force major, who served in the Balkans twice and earned the Air Combat Medal. She is also accredited by the Public Relations Society of America. After retiring from the Pentagon, she taught public relations and has written two public relations handbooks. She also wrote a novel, *Sins of the Father,* in 2003 that is available through amazon.com.

Steve Mackey, Ph.D., is a senior lecturer in public relations at Deakin University in Victoria, Australia. He was previously a journalist and a regional government press officer in London.

Juan-Carlos Molleda received his doctoral degree in Journalism and Mass Communications from the University of South Carolina. He is an assistant professor of public relations at the University of Florida. His research interests are global public relations and practices in Latin America. Molleda's latest publication concerns public relations licensing in Brazil (*Public Relations Review,* 2003).

Bonita Dostal Neff (Ph.D., University of Michigan) is an associate professor in the Department of Communication at Valparaiso University–Indiana and a visiting professor of public relations for Zadar and Zagreb University in Croatia. She has published in *Public Relations Review, The Strategist,* and handbooks on public relations. She also serves on the editorial boards of two journals.

Richard Alan Nelson is a professor and the Public Relations Area Head in the Manship School of Mass Communication, Louisiana State University and A&M College in Baton Rouge. He is accredited by the Public Relations Society of America and received his Ph.D. from Florida State University.

Bolanle A. Olaniran (Ph.D., University of Oklahoma) is a professor in the Department of Communication Studies at Texas Tech University. His research interests include crisis communication, organizational communication, and communication technologies.

Judy B. Oskam, Ed.D., is an associate professor of mass communications at Texas Tech University. Oskam has directed various health, agriculture, and safety public awareness campaigns and grant projects.

Michael G. Parkinson (Ph.D., University of Oklahoma; J.D., Southern Illinois University) is the associate dean for graduate studies in the College of Mass Communications at Texas Tech University. He has published more than 35 research articles and book chapters and made more than 50 presentations at academic and professional conferences. He is accredited by the Public Relations Society of America and has administered public relations campaigns in the United States, Asia, Central America, Europe, and the Middle East.

Padmini Patwardhan (Ph.D., Southern Illinois University) is an assistant professor in the College of Mass Communications at Texas Tech University. She previously taught at the University of Pune, India, and consulted with Indian branches of multinational advertising agencies. Her research interests include international advertising and public relations, individual–Internet dependency relations, and online consumer behavior.

Zenaida Sarabia-Panol is a professor at the School of Journalism, Middle Tennessee State University. She earned a Bachelor of Journalism degree, *magna cum laude,* from Silliman University; a Master of Arts in Communication from the University of the Philippines; and a doctorate in mass communication from Oklahoma State University.

Ana-María Suárez is a professor and researcher of the College of Communication and Corporate Relations at the University of Medellín, Colombia. She received her master's degree from Potificia Universidad Javeriana. Her research interests include organizational communication and public relations practices in Latin America.

MinJung Sung is a Ph.D. student studying public relations at the University of Maryland at College Park. Her research interests include strategic management of public relations and global public relations. Before joining the doctoral program, she worked as a public relations practitioner at Cheil Communications in South Korea, managing international accounts.

Vlado Susac is a senior lecturer in the Department of Information and Communication at the University of Zadar in Croatia. His M.A. is from the University of Zadar and he is doing doctoral work at the Viadrina University. His published research addresses public television and language analysis.

Katerina Tsetsura is an assistant professor in the Department of Communication at the University of Oklahoma. She is the author or co-author of several works on the development of PR in Russia and is co-author of "Composite Index by Country (66 countries) of Variables Related to the Likelihood of the Existence of 'Cash for News Coverage.'"

Wanda Reyes Velázquez is completing her dissertation for a Ph.D. at Pennsylvania State University's College of Communications. Her research focuses on public relations practice targeting Latinos(as) in the United States and mass mediated health communications.

David E. Williams (Ph.D., University of Ohio) is an associate professor in the Department of Communication Studies at Texas Tech University. His areas of research include crisis communication and crisis management.

Norman E. Youngblood, Ph.D., is an assistant professor in the College of Mass Communications at Texas Tech University. His dissertation was on the development of landmine warfare and he is currently under contract with Praeger Publishing to produce a book tracing the evolution of land and sea mines.

1 Introduction to Public Relations Campaign Analysis

The purpose of this chapter is to provide a definition of public relations and to begin introducing the reader to the ROSTE framework for analyzing and critiquing public relations cases. Chapters 2 through 4 provide detailed descriptions of the stages in the ROSTE model and Chapter 5 is an introduction to the concepts of intercultural and international communication. It includes guidelines to help you understand and cope with public relations campaigns with culturally diverse clients or publics. Chapter 6 puts the ROSTE model in an intercultural context and provides a checklist for creating or critiquing international public relations campaigns. Following Chapter 6, nineteen public relations campaign cases are described.

What Is Public Relations?

Of course, to determine how well a public relations campaign was administered, one must first know what public relations is. Only after we agree on a definition of public relations can we move to critique how well a particular public relations project was performed. This task is not as simple as it may seem. There are nearly as many definitions of public relations as there are authors who write about the field. While the phrase "public relations" may have been first used in the United States, the practice of using communication to influence the opinions of publics has developed all over the world. Now many organizations have developed their own definitions. For example, the British Institute of Public Opinion defines public relations as: ". . . the deliberate, planned and sustained effort to establish and maintain mutual understanding between an organization and its publics." The Dansk PR Klub of Denmark states: "PR is the sustained and systematic managerial effort through which private and public organizations seek to establish understanding, sympathy, and support in those public circles with which they have or expect to obtain contact." According to the World Assembly of PR in Mexico City, "Public relations practice is the art and social science of analyzing trends, predicting their consequences, counseling organization leaders, and implementing planned programs of action which serve both the organizations and the public's interest."

Even the U.S. government has made an attempt to define public relations practice. In the Foreign Agents Act, public relations counsel is defined as "any person who engages directly or indirectly in informing, advising or in any way representing a principal in any public relations matter pertaining to political or public interest, policies or relations of such principal." They also define a publicity agent as "any person who engages directly or indirectly in the publication or dissemination of oral, visual, graphic, written or pictorial information or matter of any kind, including publication by means of advertising, books, periodicals, newspapers, lectures, broadcasts, motion pictures or otherwise."

Despite the fact that there is no consistent definition and that there is some disagreement about what public relations really includes, all definitions of public relations include some common elements. In this text we focus on those common elements and offer not a definition of public relations but rather a collection of components that should be included in any analysis of public relations activities.

Specifically, if you read the definitions of public relations presented above, you will find that all include the following components:

> A client and advocacy
> A public or publics
> Research
> Planning
> Counseling
> Communication and media
> Actions by the public relations representative or client
> Evaluation of success

These components can be collapsed further into the five components of Research, Objectives, Strategies (Action and Communication), Tactics, and Evaluation.

In short, we submit that if you find someone who has completed reasonable research, identified a realistic and measurable objective, formulated a strategic plan for action and communication, exercised tactics to implement that plan, and evaluated the effort, they have "done public relations" and they have done it well.

What Is ROSTE?

The ROSTE model used in this text was developed from the components of public relations found in definitions of the profession and practice: Research, Objectives, Strategies, Tactics, and Evaluation. Each of these components is fully introduced here, then discussed in detail in the chapters to come.

Research

Before beginning a public relations campaign or even deciding why one is needed, a good practitioner must gather information. Very simply put, research is gathering information. Chapter 2 describes several techniques for securing information formally or informally. That chapter also describes the kinds of information that must be gathered before a public relations campaign can be designed and implemented. Although several textbooks in public re-

TRUTH-JUSTICE-EQUALITY-PUBLIC RELATIONS

lations focus on research methods, what is critical to public relations campaign design or evaluation is not how the information was gathered but rather the propriety, validity, and reliability of the information obtained.

By propriety of information we simply mean the usefulness and completeness of the information for the present campaign. In other words, did the public relations practitioner have enough information and could he or she actually be sure it was accurate? "Reliability" refers to whether the information is free from biases imposed by the public relations practitioner or the client. "Validity" refers to the accuracy of the information—does it represent what the practitioner thinks it represents? Particularly in campaigns that involve multiple cultures or nations, it is essential that a public relations practitioner take great care to use information that is not tainted by the biases of any one culture or national perspective.

Objectives

Public relations campaigns are conducted for the benefit of the client. Therefore, the campaign objective must support the client's organizational goals. In Chapter 3 we will describe organizational goals, the public relations objective, and how the two are related. Here we also introduce the idea of operationalization and explains why operationalized objectives are critical to both campaign planning and evaluation.

Strategies

Strategies can be divided into action strategies and communications strategies. Action strategies are the things the public relations representative or client will do, and the communication strategies are the things they will say.

Action Strategies.   Some models of public relations campaign design ignore actions altogether. Other models combine action and communication into a single component called programming. After describing public relations objectives, in Chapter 3 we explain why the client's calculated and strategized actions are essential to a good public relations campaign. In that chapter we also introduce the idea of public relations as a management function and explain why the public relations practitioner must be involved in managerial decisions about client actions. We submit that the practitioner must help the client evaluate any proposed actions to avoid problems that could arise from actions that reflect insensitivity to a significant public. Further, we suggest that recommending client actions is an essential part of the public relations campaign because the client's actions both demonstrate the client's attitudes and give the public relations practitioner subjects for communication messages.

Communication Strategies.   While many people seem to believe that public relations is simply creating the correct message or "spin," communication is only one part of the whole public relations campaign. In Chapter 3 we explore systems and theories of communication that can be used to help develop or evaluate message systems aimed at accomplishing the campaign objective. There we discuss how strategies can be chosen to ensure that target publics are aware of client actions. We also provide theories or paradigms that can help guide decisions about what to communicate and what media to select for communication.

Tactics

Tactics are the nuts and bolts of a public relations campaign. They are the tools, techniques, and actions taken to deliver the messages identified by the campaign strategy. For example, if a communication strategy were to inform people in rural Brazil about the importance of a balanced diet, tactics could include writing and placing a news release or planning and implementing home visits. Scheduling, budgeting, message construction, training spokespersons, preparing press conference statements, and even selecting the language are all components of tactics. Chapter 4 includes descriptions of rules that guide tactics.

Evaluation

To demonstrate a campaign's success, one must relate the evaluation to the objective. In Chapter 4 we explain the importance of the relationship between the objective and the evaluation. Further, we explain how the operationalized objectives described in the section on objectives are essential to any realistic or meaningful campaign evaluation. We also identify some common mistakes in campaign evaluation and explain how a program of evaluation can be used to correct or improve a public relations campaign while it is in progress.

REFERENCES AND SUGGESTED READINGS

Hendrix, J. A. (2004). *Public relations cases* (6th ed.). Belmont, CA: Wadsworth.

Marston, J. A. (1963). *The nature of public relations.* New York: McGraw-Hill.

Parkinson, M., & Ekachai, D. (2002). The Socratic method in the introductory PR course: An alternative pedagogy. *Public Relations Review 28*(2), 167–174.

Smith, R. D. (2002). *Strategic planning for public relations.* Mahwah, NJ: Lawrence Erlbaum Associates.

22 USCS § 611 (g) and 22 USCS § 612 (h). United States Foreign Agent Act.

2 Research for Public Relations Campaigns

Clifton Fadiman once said, "[w]hen you travel remember that a foreign country is not designed to make you comfortable. It is designed to make its own people comfortable." Following this principle, when you design a public relations campaign, especially one targeting a diverse public, you must find a way to make your campaign comfortable and effective for the targeted public. Your campaign may or may not be comfortable for you. Because your comfort is irrelevant, you must be able to conduct research to determine what will make the campaign comfortable and effective for its intended publics.

Many students and even some practitioners in public relations believe they can simply intuit the best way to approach a client's problems. Our own research shows that many students think they have all the skills necessary to practice public relations even before they have taken their first public relations course. However, if a public relations campaign is to be based on anything more than guess work, it must begin with thorough research. Further, the research must follow a methodology appropriate to the questions asked or the information sought.

It is not our intent here to teach you how to do research. There are many excellent and extensive works on the subject of research methodology. Our intent is only to remind you of the many research tools and then to summarize the kinds of questions that should be asked before you identify a public relations objective, recommend actions to your client, or plan your communication strategy.

We begin by explaining when and why you do research. We then describe the kinds of questions you should ask. Finally, we explain how to answer those questions through primary and secondary research. We discuss the concepts of reliability and validity and the distinction between qualitative and quantitative research.

When Do You Do Research?

Research in public relations serves several functions and therefore is conducted at many stages of a public relations campaign. Generally, consider research as a tool to influence management and build client relationships before you even begin planning a campaign. Then, use research as a major tool to plan the campaign. Finally, use research to monitor a campaign's effectiveness and evaluate its success.

"What do you think . . . should we get started
on that motivation research or not?"

Source: © 2003 Bob Zahn from cartoonbank.com. All Rights Reserved.

To Influence Management

Before you begin a campaign, or even before you prepare a campaign proposal, you can use research to influence management. A practitioner who has researched the client company, the potential publics, available media, and resources looks more professional to current and potential clients. Many public relations students think they can simply "make up" a public relations campaign as they go. Similarly, many managers think they know the field of public relations better than their public relations counselors. If management has research information you do not have, you add to the impression that you are only functioning intuitively and you make it more likely that management will impose on you unrealistic objectives or impossible campaign strategies. In contrast, if you have the results of thorough research at your command, you will appear more knowledgeable and be better able to defend your ideas and to secure approval for your campaign objectives and strategies. Of course, if your client agrees to adopt objectives you have proposed, then you are more likely to succeed in meeting those goals.

If you are not interested in being retained or in impressing the management team with your skills, you can omit the research stage completely! For example, one of the authors worked for a local humane society that sought public relations representations. One of the agencies bidding for the contract proposed a fundraising campaign. Had the agency done even basic research they would have known this particular humane society was funded by a tax referendum that specifically prohibited independent fundraising. What the client needed was a campaign to encourage residents to neuter pets. Because the agency failed to conduct basic research they proposed a campaign that was actually illegal. Obviously the agency was not retained.

For Campaign Planning

When you are identifying objectives, deciding on actions, or determining tactics, all your decisions must be based on good and thorough research. If you do not have research to support your decisions, you are only guessing. You will be able to make correct decisions only if you base your judgment on facts rather than intuition.

The United States' "Shared Values" campaign targeting the Arab world is an example of a campaign that failed because of poor research. After the September 11, 2001, tragedy, that campaign sought to improve attitudes toward the United States in Arab countries with a series of television advertisements featuring Arab Americans. If its planners had done the required research, they would have learned the campaign was doomed to failure before it began. Television media in most Arab countries are controlled by the government and many of those governments refused to air the "Shared Values" advertisements. Further, even the most basic observations demonstrate that many in the Arab world have strongly held anti-U.S. beliefs and virtually all existing attitude and persuasion research shows that strongly held beliefs cannot be changed with short and impersonal messages presented in television advertisements. After millions of dollars had been spent, the campaign was canceled and its creator was removed.

One component of research for campaign planning that deserves special mention is message testing. After deciding what public to target, what media to use, and what ideas to communicate, a practitioner must decide exactly how to form the appropriate messages. Finding a way to test messages is particularly important if the practitioner does not speak the language of the target public or share their cultural values. Many practitioners rely on their own judgment or prior experiences, but if they do not share the language and culture of the target public they are ill prepared to make those judgments. In such situations, focus groups, surveys, or experimental studies using representatives of the target public are appropriate. All of these techniques can be used to test the impact of message components. Other tools such as readability indices and comprehension scales can be used to gauge whether the target public will even understand the messages.

For Campaign Monitoring and Evaluation

Many campaigns are not evaluated at all, and some are only evaluated at the end. Failing to monitor and evaluate presents two problems for a public relations practitioner. First, the practitioner does not know if the campaign is working and may waste resources on strategies and tactics that do not work. Second, the practitioner does not have an objective way to prove to the client that the campaign was successful. In the business world, which is almost always driven by numbers and hard evidence, the absence of objective proof of success makes it difficult for practitioners to justify their worth and, of course, their fee.

During the campaign, constant research must be used to determine if the strategies and tactics are working. Monitoring research can be as simple and low-tech as counting yard signs or bumper stickers during an election campaign, or as elaborate as periodic surveys or polling to identify attitude and behavior trends in the target publics. Obviously, the technique chosen must actually measure whether the campaign objective is being met.

Many reputable and otherwise competent public relations practitioners attempt to demonstrate their success with measures such as "advertising equivalent values" or measures of news coverage through the use of news clippings. It is a rare client whose objective was simply to secure news coverage. Any truly valuable measure of campaign success must measure whether the public relations objective was met. Usually, that objective involved changing how the target public thinks or acts. Therefore, quality campaign monitoring and evaluation research almost always includes some pre-campaign and post-campaign measures of the target public's knowledge, attitudes, or conduct.

What Kinds of Questions Do You Ask?

The first step in any research is deciding what you want to know. One of the most common mistakes in research is to identify a research method before deciding what to ask. Only after you know what information is needed can you properly select a research technique. To influence management and for campaign planning, the questions asked typically address some measure of the client's needs and resources. Other research questions may involve information about possible target publics' knowledge, attitudes, and behaviors, information on possible campaign resources and restrictions, and information about the culture in which the campaign will be conducted. Figure 2.1 contains a list of research questions that should be asked before any public relations campaign. For campaign monitoring and evaluation the question is much simpler. For campaign evaluation, the question is *always:* "Is the target public doing what my objective said it would do?"

Remember, each question does not necessarily require an extensive research program. Some questions can be answered with the simple technique of asking. Particularly questions about a *client* may be addressed by simply asking the client or by reviewing the client's public records such as annual reports, mission statement, or press clippings. In order to properly represent the client you must understand their business or organizational goals. To do that you have to know the organization's purpose and all its problems. Particularly when planning or evaluating an international or intercultural campaign, you must know if an action by your client in one country will lead to change in the impression of that client in another country or culture. Therefore your understanding of the client organization must include knowledge of its size, the location of its offices and factories, and the client's practices in its global market.

What Resources Are Available?

Knowing how financially successful the client is will help you identify the resources you can use in the campaign. Obviously, a campaign plan for a U.S.-based airline company that is approaching bankruptcy cannot use the same resources as one for a large and financially successful petroleum company. Also, do not forget that much more than money can be used in a public relations campaign. The client's personnel and equipment could contribute to a

FIGURE 2.1   Research Question Checklist

Who is the client?
> What is the business of the client? What do they do?
> Do they have any subsidiaries?
> How successful and how large are they?
> Where are their offices, factories etc?
> How much money can they spend on the campaign?
> Do they have trained personnel who can help?
> What equipment do they have that can be used on the campaign?
> What is their existing reputation?
> Are they credible?
> What campaigns have they conducted in the past? What worked and what did not?

Who are the possible target publics?
> How large is each public?
> How old are the public's members?
> Where do they live?
> Are they wealthy or poor?
> What is their religion?
> What language do they speak?
> Do they identify with any other group?
> Is there animosity between them and any other group?
> What do they think of the client?
> What sources do they see as credible? What do they value or think important?
> What media do they consume and what media influences them?
> Do they have any prior experiences with the client or with other PR campaigns?

What resources and restrictions might apply?
> What media are available and will use your messages?
> What media reach the target publics?
> Are there government restrictions on public relations?
> Do I have to have a government license to run the campaign?

Are there cultural considerations?
> What is the language of the client and target publics?
> What is the history of the area and the publics?
> Are there cultural symbols, icons, or personalities I can use?
> Are there cultural symbols, icons, or personalities I cannot use?
> Are there norms of behavior I must not violate?

---

campaign. Most importantly, it is easiest to design a campaign for a client who already has a good reputation or is well liked by a target public.

Finally, research could tell you what campaigns this client has implemented in the past. Reviewing the records of those campaigns could help you learn what messages were effective or ineffective, what publics were responsive or passive, and what media supported or opposed your client. At the very least, knowing what failed in the past will keep you from proposing the repetition of a prior failure.

What Do You Need to Know about Possible Publics?

Begin your research on target publics by listing all the publics that interact with the client. Then pick the publics that could, if they changed their behavior or attitudes, ameliorate the client's problems or help accomplish the client's goals. Do not assume you have to find a single audience group who can, by itself, solve all the client's problems. Rather, consider all publics who either contribute to the client's problems or who could contribute to a solution. For example, if your client's problem arises from governmental restrictions imposed by the Japanese government, do not assume the only possible target public is the Japanese officials responsible for the restrictions. Target publics might include voters in Japan, U.S. politicians who can influence their counterparts in Japan, Japanese companies with whom your client does business, your client's customers in Japan, or the Japanese companies who supported or opposed the restrictions in the first place.

To secure information about possible target publics you may need a combination of observation, review of existing records, and primary research. To be able to design a campaign targeting any group, you must know both the demographics and the psychographics of the target publics. Demographics are data about the physical or measurable characteristics of the public. Demographics include the size of the group, the age of its members, where they live, and their wealth. This information about the target public can help you determine how susceptible they may be to persuasion and how best to reach them. Opinions, attitudes, and values of the target public are also important because this information can be used to determine what messages, if any, might persuade the public to change in a way that advances the client's objective.

Are There Restrictions on the Resources You Can Use?

Another category of questions you must ask involves identification of the resources and restrictions that will impact your campaign. In addition to the resources of your client and the existing characteristics of the target publics, you must consider what other resources can be used. Are media in place reaching the target publics? If so, can you access those media with news releases or advertising? When considering such resources and media, many practitioners and students confine themselves to traditional mass media. Remember, outside the mainstream culture of the United States, resources can include unconventional media. Public gatherings, church sermons, festivals, storytellers, word-of-mouth, and personal relationships have all been used as resources in public relations campaigns. Also, do not forget secondary publics. Secondary publics are groups of people who, if motivated to do so, can deliver your message to the primary public. Secondary publics might include clergy or missionaries who would explain your client's position to their parishioners. Similarly, physicians, midwives, or herbal healers can be used to deliver messages to their patients.

Many cultures and governments impose restrictions on the flow of information or the conduct of foreigners. In the United States, for example, the Foreign Agent Registration Act requires that public relations practitioners representing governments or corporations from outside the United States register before communicating on behalf of their clients. Outside the United States there are often more significant restrictions. Some countries require a license to practice public relations, and some require government or industry approval for messages. Before beginning a public relations campaign you should explore all such restrictions. Otherwise, your campaign material may never reach the intended public and you or your client may be fined or incarcerated.

What Do You Need to Know about Culture?

Finally, even if you believe you understand the client and target publics, do not forget to thoroughly investigate their cultures. While there are many different definitions and dimensions of "culture," when we refer to culture here we focus on considerations such as language, history, and social norms. The most obvious cultural consideration is language. One would think that everyone knows you cannot simply impose the client's language or the practitioner's language on a target public. However, campaigns have been run in the wrong language or sometimes with embarrassing translation simply because the public relations practitioners did not perform adequate research. Early in campaign planning or in the critique of a campaign, be sure you know what language the target public uses. Language includes dialects, slang, and idiomatic speech. Do not assume that having your messages translated into a generic language will make them understandable or acceptable to your target public. Anyone who has traveled in the southern United States may have noticed that Spanish-speaking Cuban Americans and Spanish-speaking Mexican Americans often cannot understand each other. Always ask yourself (or better still, ask members of your target public) whether your messages are in the correct language. A mistake by General Motors demonstrates the importance of idiomatic speech and slang. In Canada, General Motors marketed the Buick replacement for the mid-sized Regal and Century under the name "LaCrosse." General Motors thought it was naming the car for a popular sport developed by Native Americans. Unfortunately, to many French Canadians LaCrosse is local slang referring to masturbation. Using focus groups of native speakers, rather than individual academic translators, would avoid such problems.

Asking questions about the cultural history of the target public will help you understand what is important to them. If you are not aware that there have been thousands of years of conflict between Greece and what is now Turkey, you may not be aware of the animosity between many older Greeks and Turks. Similar animosity exists between many Japanese and Koreans. Obviously there are many areas of the world where long-standing conflicts over religion, nationalism, or custom result in contemporary friction.

Of course there are rules of polite behavior in every society. We have collapsed these rules under the general rubric of "social norms." Despite what may be valued and polite in your culture, you must know what is appropriate conduct and what is valued in the social system of the target public. There are far too many examples of social norms to list even a representative sample here, so we only admonish you to have people who are intimately familiar with the target public's social norms review all your proposed actions and messages before you launch your campaign.

How Do You Answer These Questions?

There are two major types of research techniques used to answer questions for public relations planning or evaluation. These are primary and secondary research. Before beginning your research or even deciding whether to do your own primary research or to use secondary sources, you need to know some basic criteria for quality research. The most eloquent way to describe the criteria for quality research is to say it must be both reliable and valid. Before you act on any information you must be sure that it is both reliable and valid. This is true whether you conduct the research yourself or gather the results of other people's research. Usually, research and data published in journals or books have been reviewed for reliability and validity before publication, but do not assume that is always true. Even more important, remember that any fool with a computer can put anything online. Before using information gathered from the Internet, be particularly careful to ensure it is both reliable and valid.

Reliability and Validity

Rather than discussing the requirement for reliability and validity with each research method, we will begin by reminding the reader that any research method must be both reliable and valid. Any research technique that does not meet both of these requirements cannot produce usable and credible results. Therefore, before you commit to any research decision, whether it is a decision to conduct your own elaborate and expensive survey or to simply check the Internet for information on a client's business, be sure to determine if the results are both reliable and valid.

Reliability refers to the technique's replicability. Research texts tend to make this concept very complicated, but to measure reliability, simply ask yourself: If you or someone else repeated this research would they get the same results again? The answer to that question must be absolutely yes or you cannot rely on the results. The need for careful assessment of reliability in public relations research is particularly important, because there are many factors that may make PR research unreliable. For example, clients are often asked about their public image, their commitment to the public good, or even about what a target public thinks of them. In each of these situations the client may be motivated not to disclose the truth, or to deceive. Also, the client simply may not have an accurate perception of reality. Especially when asking people for their perceptions or their opinions, be careful to ensure those perceptions or opinions are reliable. In primary research, experienced practitioners control for these variations by asking several subjects or by controlling carefully for intervening variables such as self-interest. But in secondary research or the informal techniques often used in the beginning of public relations research, experienced practitioners use multiple sources to ensure their data is unbiased.

Validity refers to a research method's ability to actually measure what it says it measures. While this may seem the same as reliability, it is not. In public relations research the most common problem with validity comes from assuming that two events that co-occur are causally related. For example, often a communication campaign is followed by an increase in sales of the client's product. This chain of events does not necessarily mean that the communication campaign caused the increase in sales. In experimental research design, control for intervening variables is used to guarantee a valid measure of causality. There are, of course, elaborate techniques for measuring validity in survey instruments, but perhaps the simplest and most accurate technique is to be very careful when describing what was measured in the research. If, for example, a client is asked about his image, do not describe the client's response as a measure of image. Rather, describe it only as the client's *perception* of his image.

Research methods are often divided into categories based on whether they are qualitative or quantitative and whether they are primary or secondary. Many authors treat qualitative research and secondary research as inferior or inappropriate methods, but both have appropriate and valid uses. Here we will describe the two category systems so you can determine which is appropriate for your use and also so you can accurately judge the quality of information when you read research.

Qualitative and Quantitative Measures

Very generally, qualitative research is based on careful but subjective judgments by the researcher. Examples might include the evaluations by judges at a beauty pageant. Of course, one weakness of any research based on judgment is that different people have different judgments. What one judge in a beauty pageant sees as attractive might not be the same as what another judge finds attractive. The major advantage of qualitative research, however, is that many of the questions that interest public relations practitioners have to do with the judgments of our publics. Often we really want to know what our public sees as attractive or what they value. These questions may be most appropriately answered with a qualitative method. In public relations the qualitative research methods most often used are focus groups, interviews, participation, and observation.

Quantitative research, on the other hand, is based on things that can be counted or quantified. These are often empirical. "Empirical" simply refers to the fact that something can be seen, heard, felt, tasted, or smelled with the physical senses. Quantitative data are further divided into nominal, ordinal, interval, and ratio data. Nominal data are numbers that only record the frequency of something. For example, nominal data might show the number of men or women in a sample. Ordinal data are numbers that show the order of something such as first, second, or third. Interval and ratio data are numbers that actually reflect the amount of something, such as 25 points or 1,000 miles. Only interval and ratio data can be manipulated using simple mathematics. Nominal and ordinal data require special statistical treatment. The greatest advantage of quantitative research is that once data are recorded, the system of analysis is governed by mathematical rules and cannot be subjectively influenced.

The quantitative research tool most often associated with public relations is a survey based on a random sample. Such surveys are quantitative because the researcher can count the specific responses of the subjects without making any subjective judgment.

Despite the relative objectivity of quantitative studies, note that purely quantitative research is very rare. There is an element of creativity in all research. Even in a very carefully designed survey of a randomly selected sample, the researcher had to decide what questions to ask. The researcher had to select the population from which to draw the sample, and had to determine how to record answers to the questions. All of these are qualitative judgments that prevent the research from being absolutely quantitative and objective. The goal of all research is to be as reliable and valid as possible. However, some element of subjectivity or judgment enters into everything human beings do. When designing primary research or selecting secondary research in international or intercultural public relations, recognize this fact and do everything you can to ensure that your own nationalistic chauvinism or cultural biases do not taint your research decisions.

Primary and Secondary Research

Most research texts focus on the research tools used in academic research. In academia the goal of research is usually the creation of new knowledge or the testing of existing theoretic constructs. In the professional world of public relations, the goal of research is much more pragmatic. Usually public relations practitioners conduct research only because they need the answer to a question. Because of these different perspectives, academic research tends to be primary research and professional research is more often secondary.

Primary research refers to research which gathers information directly from subjects or the natural world. Primary research methods include experiments, surveys, focus groups, and content analysis. Primary research can be qualitative, quantitative, or some combination of the two. Secondary research (sometimes called "library" research) explores published information, including reports of earlier primary research.

Typically, secondary research is faster and costs less than primary research. These advantages, however, are often offset by the fact that secondary research is not as current or specific as primary research. Also, secondary research sometimes is not as accurate or directly applicable to a target audience as primary research. If you have the time, resources, and research skills, primary research results are almost always superior to what you will learn from secondary research. Despite these advantages, those of us in public relations seldom have the time and resources to conduct our own primary research. We must select the technique that best meets the needs of our client while not exceeding the available time, money, and other resources. Figure 2.2 lists questions that will help determine whether primary or secondary research is appropriate.

FIGURE 2.2   Checklist for Primary and Secondary Research Decision

What questions do I need answered?
What public or publics must I question?
How can I reach the publics I need to question? Do they have e-mail, phones, receive mail, etc.?
How quickly must I have the answers to these questions?
How much money can my client spend on research?
Do I have access to outside consultants or research experts?
Do I have access to e-mail lists, phone banks, contact lists or other research tools?
Is there existing, reliable, and valid research that answers my questions?

Because secondary research is usually less expensive and faster than primary research it is much more attractive to the public relations practitioner who may have a limited research budget and who probably has too little time to complete primary research. The next section begins with a summary of secondary research methods and sources.

Secondary Research.   Secondary research is sometimes called "informal" research. This label implies that secondary research is somehow less rigorous than primary research. Let us begin by dispelling that notion. Secondary research may be faster and it may be less expensive than primary research, but it must be done carefully to be at all useful. Simply because information is in print or online does not make it valid or reliable. A practitioner conducting secondary research must carefully select and evaluate sources, which fall into three major categories—organizational records, databases, and research reports.

Organizational Records.   Virtually every organization keeps some kind of records. Clients have annual reports and other financial records. Even target publics may include interest groups or civic organizations that keep records. Review of these organizational records, sometimes called archival research, can answer questions about size, location, and wealth of organizations or its members. Such research can also help the public relations practitioner identify the publics who interact with the client, the "target" publics.

Locating organizational records for the client should be a simple task accomplished by asking the client representatives for access. However, finding organizational records for target publics, competitors, and other organizations may present more of a challenge. Remember that in the United States, publicly traded corporations are required to file reports with the Securities and Exchange Commission, so financial records are available. Also, most publicly traded companies provide information for shareholders, potential investors, brokers, and investment counselors through their company web page. Such target publics as charitable groups or civic organizations often solicit donations and volunteers and provide information about their membership, finances, and goals through web pages or other recruiting and development material that is readily available.

Any medium of communication to be used in a campaign should be explored. Those media may have morgue files, online archives, or other accessible records. These records can provide insight into how each particular medium has covered the client or similar topics in the past.

Finally, do not overlook the public relations representative's own records. If a large public relations firm is involved in the campaign it should have records of prior experience with the target publics and/or records of similar campaign problems.

Databases.   Databases are simply collections of information. Such collections can be used to identify demographic characteristics of target publics or to locate media. The best known and most frequently used of these databases is the U.S. Census. The Census is available online and is indexed by both geographic area and public characteristics. While the U.S. Census is well known by practitioners in the United States, other countries also produce similar thorough and very useful collections. In particular, the United Kingdom and most former Commonwealth countries have easily searched and thorough censuses. Figure 2.3 lists websites that may be used for public relations campaign research.

**FIGURE 2.3   Recommended Websites for Census, Public
Opinion, International Business, and News Information**

www.aapor.org
American Association for Public Opinion Research (AAPOR)

www.arbitron.com/home/content.stm
Arbitron Inc.; an international media and marketing research firm serving radio broadcasters, cable companies, advertisers, advertising agencies and outdoor advertising companies in the United States, Europe, and Asia.

www.arbitron.com/international/content.stm
Arbitron outside the United States

www.bls.gov
Bureau of Labor Statistics site includes information on economy and labor market

www.brint.com/International.htm#index
This site for Brint Research Directories has links to other sites addressing international business and technology. It is like one stop shopping. It includes world newspapers, U.S. newspapers, international laws, finance and worldwide telephone directories.

www.car.ua.edu
Site for Content Analysis Resources includes information helpful to analysis of texts and messages.

www.census.gov
U.S Census Bureau

www.census.gov/stat_abstract
Site includes abstracts and summaries of United States Census Information

www.cios.org/www/tocs/JPR.htm
Journal of Public Relations Research

www.demographics.com
This site covers U.S. Demographics

www.gallup.com
The Gallup Organization

www.gannett.com/go/newswatch/nwwebtips/business.html
This site is a Web newsroom. It includes links to business news and information.

www.holmesreport.com
The Holmes Report covers the public relations industry with a focus on corporate communications.

www.icahdq.org
International Communication Association

www.ijpor.oupjournals.org
International Journal of Public Opinion Research

http://ilc2.doshisha.ac.jp/users/kkitao/organi/wca
World Communication Association

www.instituteforpr.com
Site includes information on public relations research and education.

(continued)

FIGURE 2.3   Continued

www.ipr.org.uk
  Site includes publications in PR with focus on U.K.

www.ipranet.org
  International Public Relations Association

www.ire.org
  Investigative Reporters and Editors

www.marketingtools.com
  Site includes a trade show directory

http://www.newspapers.com/
  Newspapers online. An easy to use tool for referencing the world's newspapers

http://www.nielsenmedia.com
  Nielsen Media Research, a media ratings company active in more than 40 countries, offers television and radio audience measurement, print readership, and custom media research services.

www.norc.uchicago.edu
  Site of National Public Opinion Research Center. The research is client based but the site does report research summaries

http://www.nova.edu/ssss/QR/web.html
  Qualitative Research Web Site

http://www.online-pr.com/
  Online Public Relations

www.people-press.org
  Pew Center site includes summaries of survey results

www.pollingreport.com
  PollingReport.com—Public Opinion Online

poynteronline.org/default.asp
  This site is designed for journalists. It includes news sources and commentary on journalism and news coverage.

www.prsa.org
  Site is for Public Relations Society of America and includes links to public relations research.

www.publicagenda.org
  Public Agenda Online

www.quirks.com
  Site archives research indexed by topic, research method, and industry.

www.ropercenter.uconn.edu
  Roper Center for public opinion research

www.sims.berkeley.edu/resources/infoecon/International.html
  This site includes several links to international resources.

www.srl.uic.edu
  University of Illinois at Chicago Survey Research Laboratory site. Includes survey instructions.

FIGURE 2.3   Continued

www.usg.edu/galileo/internet/area/areamenu.html

www.usg.edu/cgi-bin/intres.cgi

www.usg.edu/galileo/internet/electronic/etexmenu.html

www.usg.edu/galileo/internet/news/newsmenu.html
   This academic website provides links to numerous topics of interests. Included here are some
   web links relevant to international and intercultural PR World regions and ethnic studies:
   includes excellent country information for all regions. Others cover news, media and
   publishing, and magazines and periodicals.

http://usinfo.state.gov/usa/infousa/media/media.htm
   U.S. Department of State International Information Programs

www.usatoday.com
   USATODAY.com—News & Information Homepage

www.worldopinion.com
   Site includes a link to country watch. That link includes an international news summary.

http://wtfaculty.wtamu.edu/~sanwar.bus/otherlinks.htm#International_Business_Links
   This site, established by a faculty member at West Texas A&M has links to several
   international business sources. It is organized by both country and topic.

Several commercially available databases report information about media. These include Bacon's, Simmon's *Media and Markets,* and *Standard Rate and Data.* Such directories can be used to find media that reach the target public and to identify information as
specific as the name and address of editors who might respond favorably to a news release
with your client's message. Outside the United States there are several media directories that
provide similar information. Countries in Western Europe seem to have the best media directories, but directories for other areas of the world can be found with an online search
using the term "media directory" and the country or area for which information is sought.

Research Reports.   One of the best and most often overlooked sources for secondary research is the published results of other people's research. Commercial organizations like
Gallup's publish information resulting from opinion polls. The results of these polls can be
used to gauge existing opinions, values, or attitudes within a target public. For those doing
work outside of the United States it is important to note that these polls are conducted all
over the world and their results are often published online. Figure 2.4 lists several sources
for such reports. An online search using the term "Gallup Index" can locate the results of
dozens of individual international opinion studies.
   The scholarly research produced by college professors and other academicians is another source of useful research reports. Almost every university requires its faculty to make
some contribution to their field of study in the form of original research. Also, students completing graduate degrees are usually required to complete a thesis or dissertation that is a
report of some original research. Because of the huge number of professors and graduate

FIGURE 2.4   Secondary Research Sources

Asian Communication Handbook, published by Asian Media and Information Center (AMIC); Singapore

Editor & Publisher International Yearbook—mainly directory of media worldwide.

Freedom House in New York issues annual study of press freedom worldwide. *UNESCO Statistical Yearbook*—statistics on media infrastructure, media reach etc.

Gunaratne, S. (Ed.). (2000). *Handbook of media in Asia.* New Delhi, India: Sage Publications.

The Leo Burnett worldwide Advertising Media Fact Book

Sriramesh, K., & Vercic, D. (Eds.). (2003). *The global public relations handbook. Theory, research and practice.* Mahwah, NJ: Lawrence Erlbaum Associates, Inc.

Sriramesh, K. (2004). *Public relations in Asia: An anthology.* Singapore: Thomson Learning Asia.

U.S. Bureau of Democracy, Human Rights and Labor—including information on media in general as well as press freedom.

World Factbook—Central Intelligence Agency—gives info and stats on each country (population, political system, economy, culture, transportation, mass media etc)

World Telecommunication Development Report. International Telecommunication Union, Geneva: ITU.

Yearbook of Statistics, Telecommunication. International Telecommunication Union, Geneva: ITU.

---

students and the requirement that their research be original, they have already conducted and reported studies on a vast array of questions of interest to public relations practitioners. These research reports appear in indices of dissertations and theses and in academic journals. Unfortunately, they are often not well indexed and it may require some creativity to find results of an appropriate study. However, the subjects addressed and the rigor with which this research is reviewed make it a usually reliable source of information. Several public relations organizations do have useful compendia of research indexed for practitioners. The Public Relations Society of America (PRSA) includes reports of public relations campaigns and other professional information through the resources and research services links on its web page. Also linked off the PRSA web page is a site for the Public Relations Educators' Academy. This page, in turn, provides access to reports of research presented at prior conferences of public relations educators. The Institute for Public Relations provides an excellent listing of research. Its web page includes links to both academic research on public relations and some very practical studies on public relations measurement and techniques. Outside the United States, other organizations such as the International Public Relations Association in the United Kingdom also provide very helpful research indices. Another valuable source is the faculty of any university offering a graduate degree in public relations or a related field. These faculties should be aware of current journals and research in their field and usually welcome any opportunity to see academic research applied in the profession.

Primary research is both slower and more expensive than secondary research. However, if planning your campaign requires answers to questions and you cannot locate those answers from reliable and valid secondary sources, you will have to spend the time and money to conduct primary research.

Primary Research. There are as many ways to conduct research as there are creative minds to design that research. What we provide here is a very brief description of some common techniques that public relations practitioners can or should use to gather information to guide campaign planning. We will provide some basic rules for conducting or evaluating surveys, focus groups, and experiments.

Surveys. The most commonly used primary research method in public relations is the survey. Survey research involves asking questions of some sample of a total public (called the population) and then applying the answers to gauge the opinions, behavior, or characteristics of the whole population.

Although surveys are the most common primary research method used in public relations, surveys are not always appropriate. Most basic public relations courses focus on survey methodology and most practitioners are familiar with the techniques of survey research. Perhaps because of this familiarity, too many practitioners see a survey as the appropriate tool to answer every question. Just like any other tool, a survey is only as good as the purpose to which it is put. Surveys can answer questions about the opinions or expressed values of a public. Other questions, like how effective a campaign message will be, may be better addressed with other methods.

Common design mistakes damage the survey method's reliability and validity. The first source of possible error may come in the selection of the sample. The second possible error can arise from the technique used to ask questions of the sample.

To draw a sample, first you must identify the population. The population is the public or group of people about whom you want to answer a question. For example, if you want to know who will vote for your client in a local election, your population is limited to those people who will vote in that election. It does not include people who cannot register because of age or residence and it does not include those people who do not vote. The sample is the group of people you actually ask questions. The sample is a subset of the population. To guarantee that a survey's results can be reliably generalized to the whole population, the sample must be randomly selected from the whole population. There are countless articles and texts that describe techniques for selecting samples from populations, but those techniques can all be evaluated using a single criterion. The sample is randomly selected from a population if every member of the population had an equal chance for being chosen to be in the sample. If this rule of "equal opportunity" or random selection is violated, the survey cannot be a reliable and representative measure of the population.

When designing the questions to ask the sample, be sure you avoid imposing your own biases and do not ask leading questions that encourage any particular answer. Most such sources of error can be identified using common sense, but providing labels for common mistakes may help you find them. Demand questions (or demand effect) refer to questions asked in a way that tends to force one response over another. For example, "Are you going to vote for my client, or his opponent, the idiot?" Or, "You are going to vote for my client, aren't you?" *Courtesy bias* (or courtesy effect) refers to the tendency of the person who is asked a question to provide the answer he or she thinks you want to hear. For example, if you are wearing your client's campaign button while asking respondents who they prefer in an election, just to be polite they may tell you they will vote for your client. People answering surveys also tend to be agreeable. This *agreement bias* means they will fall into patterns of answering questions in the affirmative. To compensate for this bias be sure to change the order or form of questions so that any one point of view is not always represented by the positive response. Finally, when completing printed questionnaires many people have a *right-hand bias*. They tend to mark answers on the right side of the page more often than those on the left. To compensate for this bias be sure answers that represent one point of view are not always on the same side of the page.

Obviously, there is much more to designing and administering a quality survey than choosing the right sample and asking the right questions, but if you conduct a survey and avoid these major pitfalls you are well on the way to gathering information that will be helpful in your campaign planning. If you are critiquing an existing campaign and find that the sample was not random or that the questions asked included some bias, you may assume the information that resulted was not valid and that the practitioner who conducted the research probably made other significant mistakes.

Focus Groups.   One technique often overlooked by public relations practitioners is the focus group. This technique combines one advantage of the survey with low cost and speed. The advantage focus groups share with surveys is that the technique gathers information directly from members of the target public or research population.

A focus group is a collection of people from the population whose opinions or values you seek to explore. The group is usually about 12 individuals. These individuals can be selected randomly from the target public or they can be selected based on their similarity to one another. Groups selected randomly from the population are more representative, but those selected for their internal similarity (or "homophily") are more likely to interact with each other. However selected, this group meets together and while being observed discusses the opinions, values, or behaviors you want to know about.

Advantages of a focus group technique are speed, low cost, and, usually, the absence of demand from questions imposed by the researcher. The speed and low cost are the result of using a small group. Typically such small groups can be quickly identified and scheduled for meeting. The absence of demand from questions results from the group being allowed to interact and discuss the topic among themselves. Of course, the skill of the group facilitator or interviewer is key. The moderator charged with guiding the group must ask some questions and provide some guidance to keep the group on topic, but must not impose an agenda or ideas. One of the significant advantages of the focus group is that the group itself decides what is important and what questions to ask.

Some disadvantages of a focus group result from the same characteristics that created its advantages. The small group that can be quickly and inexpensively gathered may not be as representative of the public or population as the large samples that are usually associated with surveys. This is particularly true for groups whose members were selected because of their similarity to each other. Further, allowing the group to interact may result in the group deviating from the subject of study. One other problem of focus groups results from the necessity to observe and record the group's discussion. In ideal situations the observers are hidden behind two-way mirrors or video systems. However, it may not be ethically possible to conceal the fact that the focus group is being observed. Just as questions in a survey questionnaire can cause response bias, so the simple act of being observed can motivate focus group members to perform for the observer. This tendency to behave differently when being observed is called the Hawthorne Effect.

Also, the observers must find some way to record and analyze their observations. When conducting focus groups a facilitator or public relations practitioner must be very careful to record the results of the focus group and not simply the perceptions or "wishful thinking" of the observers.

Experiments. Surveys and focus groups are excellent tools for learning what a public knows and is willing to share. However, these tools are limited. Because the researcher cannot manipulate variables in a survey or focus group it is impossible to measure causality. Often in public relations we need to know something the members of the target public either do not know about themselves or are unwilling to tell us about themselves. Specifically, we want to know what motivates them to change their attitudes or actions. In these situations an experiment is the only effective primary research tool. If you ask representatives of a public what message characteristic influences them, they may not be willing to tell you because the truth embarrasses them or they may honestly not know what message trait actually causes changes in their beliefs or attitudes. People often are unwilling to admit that they are influenced by racial prejudice, sexual attraction, or tasteless graphics. A well-designed experiment will enable you to identify the characteristics that influence the subject, even if the subject is personally unwilling to share that information. Also, people may think they are influenced by a spokesperson's education or appearance, when it is really the word choice of the message that is most influential. Again, an experiment will allow you to identify the reason for a respondent's reaction even if the respondent is not aware of the reason.

What makes research an experiment is that it measures the effect of some manipulation. While there are more complicated experimental designs, for our purposes we will only describe two—the pre/post test design and the control/treatment group design. Both designs involve measurement of two variables. The attitude, value, or behavior we hope to influence is called the dependent variable. The characteristic of our message or campaign we want to use to influence the dependent variable is called the independent variable. One way to keep these two concepts straight is to remember that changes in the dependent variable depend on changes in the independent variable.

In both the pre/post test and the control/treatment design we first identify a representative or representatives of the public whose characteristics we are studying. These representatives are called subjects. In a pre/post test design the subjects are first tested for the dependent variable. This is the pre-test. They are then exposed to the independent variable and thereafter are tested for the dependent variable again. This second testing for the dependent variable is the post-test. We assume any change in the dependent variable between the pre-test and post-test is the result of the independent variable.

In a control/treatment design the subjects are randomly divided into two groups. One group is exposed to the independent variable, and after this exposure both groups are measured for the dependent variable. We assume that any difference in the dependent variable between the two groups is the result of the independent variable. If we repeat this design with different forms of the independent variable we can learn which of those forms causes the greatest change in the dependent variable.

As an example of the application of a control/treatment experimental design to an international public relations campaign, assume your client wants you to develop a campaign to encourage a public in rural Brazil to have dental examinations. Your secondary research shows that members of this public think English-speaking physicians from the United States are very knowledgeable about health issues. That same secondary research shows that members of the target public are suspicious of all English speakers. When you attempt survey or focus group research you find that members of the public tell English-speaking interviewers they like and trust Americans, but they tell local Portuguese-speaking interviewers that they suspect all Americans are only motivated by financial greed and they do not trust English speakers. Only an experiment will help you discover which language, English or Portuguese, will most effectively deliver your dental health message to the target public. The independent variable is language—specifically English—and the dependent variable is the likelihood of having a dental exam. The likelihood of having a dental examination can be most accurately measured by offering an exam and counting the number of subjects who accept the offer. In this situation you would first randomly select a representative sample of the population (here the target public). This sample would be randomly divided into two groups. The first group (the control) would receive information about dental health and the importance of dental examinations in Portuguese. The second group (the treatment) would receive the same information in English. If you find that a significantly larger number of those who received the information in English accepted the offered dental examinations, you could be reasonably confident that receiving the information in English positively affected their decision. Obviously, if you find that a significantly larger number of those who received the information in Portuguese accepted the offered examinations, then you know that receiving information in English negatively affected the decision. Based on these results you can make an informed decision about the language in which to present your campaign message.

Field Experiments.   Although true experiments may be rare in public relations, it is not uncommon to design a study around naturally occurring events that mimic the design of an experiment. Such studies, often called field experiments, are neither as expensive nor as artificial as laboratory experiments. To conduct a field experiment you first identify two groups of subjects that are as similar as possible in every way except that one group has been exposed to the independent variable you wish to study and the other has not. If you measure the dependent variable in each group, any difference in that measurement should be the result of exposure to the independent variable. Advertisers, for example, use such a research strategy when they conduct an advertising campaign only in one city. They can then compare sales of the advertised product in the city in which they advertised to sales in cities without the advertising campaign. If they select cities that have similar populations and other characteristics, they can be reasonably certain that any difference in sales between the two cities is the product of the advertising campaign's effectiveness. In this situation the advertising is the independent variable and product sales are the dependent variable. Of course, the key to success in such a field experiment is finding two cities or other groups that are identical in every way except their exposure to the independent variable.

REFERENCES AND SUGGESTED READINGS

Babbie, E. (2004). *The practice of social research* (10th ed.). Belmont, CA: Wadsworth.

Barzun, J. (1998). *Modern researcher* (4th ed.). Orlando, FL: Harcourt Brace Jovanovich.

Brody, E. W., & Stone, G. (1989). *Public relations research.* New York: Praeger.

Broom, G. M., & Dozier, D. (1990). *Using research in public relations*. Englewood Cliffs, NJ: Prentice-Hall.

Creamer, M. (March 10, 2003). Beers' resignation unlikely to affect U.S. government's image goals. *PR Week,* p. 1.

Grunig, L. A. (1990). Using focus group research in public relations. *Public Relations Review,* Summer, 36–49.

How to measure relationships? Grunig/Hon study for Institute Measurement Commission lays groundwork. (October 11, 1999). *PR Reporter, 42,* 1–3.

Lopez, E. M. (2003, October 24). How Embarrassing! New Buick's Name Means Masturbation to French Canadians. Retrieved from www.DiversityInc.com.

McGuire, M., Stilborne, L., McAdams, M., & Hyatt, L. (1997). *The Internet handbook for writers, researchers and journalists.* Ontario, Canada: Trifolium Books.

Parkinson, M., & Ekachai, D. (2002). The confident incompetent: Sophomores are alive, well and majoring in public relations. *Proceedings of PRSA Educators' Academy Fifth International, Interdisciplinary PR Research Conference.* Miami, Florida.

Parkinson, M., & Parkinson, L. M. (2003, in press). Constitutional mythology in the United States: The arguments against public relations licensing refuted. *Intercultural Communication Studies Journal.*

Webb, E. J., Campbell, D., Schwartz, R. D., & Sechrest, L. (1996). *Unobtrusive measures: Nonreactive research in the social sciences.* Chicago: Rand McNally.

Wimmer, R. D., & Dominick, J. (2003) *Mass media research* (7th ed.). Belmont, CA: Wadsworth.

3 Public Relations Objectives and Strategies

Crafting an objective, identifying strategies, and selecting tactics are the three steps in actually planning how to accomplish the public relations objective. Research is indispensable because it prepared you for these planning steps. Evaluation is essential because it allows you to determine whether a campaign was successful.

A well-known model or principle that explains how the objective, strategies, and tactics work together is management by objectives (MBO). MBO uses a concrete statement of a management objective as the criterion for making all decisions in any plan. Nager and Allen applied the principles of MBO to public relations in their 1984 book *Public Relations Management by Objectives.* Nager and Allen identified 10 steps for the creation of a public relations plan (Figure 3.1). Each of the steps can be stated as a question. In effect, as you answer each of the 10 questions your answers provide all the decisions necessary to form a public relations plan. Here we reduce those 10 questions to three component concepts. Those concepts are the objective statement, the strategies, and the tactics.

Nager and Allen used MBO to approach public relations planning as a balance between the objectives of the client, the target public, and the media. The ROSTE model focuses on the client's objective in the component called PR Objective. It addresses the target public's objectives under Strategy and it deals with the media's objectives under Tactics. Although we do provide extensive explanations and criteria for each of the three component concepts, this is actually a simpler and more efficient way to ensure a public relations plan does everything possible to advance its objective.

Following the ROSTE model, research is conducted to support formulation of appropriate objectives and to provide the information that permits the planner to select strategies and tactics that will advance the objective. This is based on principles of MBO. However, the planner must realize that neither MBO nor ROSTE is a purely linear planning process. Flexibility is an integral part of public relations research and planning. In other words, the selection of an objective does not mean that research ends. Objectives may be modified if appropriate strategies cannot be found, and strategies may be abandoned or changed if tactics to support them are not available. At each stage of the ROSTE model it may be necessary to make some changes. A client may reject an objective statement or there may be some intervening event that forces the practitioner to adopt a new objective. Crises happen. Airplanes crash, tourists get sick, and governments change. Any of these events and scores of others can force the public relations practitioner to adopt a new objective. But, regardless of how quickly the objective changes, the skillful practitioner always manages to know enough

FIGURE 3.1   MBO—Ten Questions to Guide Public Relations Planning

1. **What are the employer's objectives?**   What does the client want to happen?
2. **Who is the target public?**   What group of people can make the client's objective happen?
3. **What are characteristics of target public?**   What should you know about the target public?
4. **What are the objectives of the target public?**   What do they want or value?
5. **What media channels reach the target public?**   What media of communication can be used to reach the target publics?
6. **What are the objectives of the media channels?**   What do they want or value?
7. **What sources of information are available?**   Where can you get credible information for your messages?
8. **What kind of messages will reach the target publics?**   What other information or messages are competing for the target public's attention or trust?
9. **What kind of messages or communication will influence the target publics?**   Do you only have to inform them, do you have to persuade them or must you instruct them in how to do something?
10. **What kind of non-verbal support is needed?**   Should you use verbal or visual images, charts, motion picture etc?

Source: Norman Nager and Harrell Allen, *Public Relations Management by Objectives* (New York & London: Longman, 1984).

to ensure those changes can work. Research may have to be done very quickly or even intuitively, but it always precedes the selection of an objective.

Later in the campaign development a practitioner may learn that there is no simple strategy that can advance the chosen objective. For example, perhaps the target public identified in the objective simply cannot be motivated to change to meet the objective. In that case the objective should be changed to be realistic. Also, after objectives and strategies are selected the practitioner may find that there are not media available to deliver the required information to the target public. This means there are not available tactics. In this situation the strategy or the objective must be changed.

These examples of change are offered to demonstrate that public relations campaign planning is a dynamic process. It is in constant flux and must be adaptable to change. However, even as it changes, every decision, including the adoption of the current objectives, must be based on research. Any strategy must be evaluated based on its ability to meet the objective, and any tactic used should support the strategies. In other words, every decision should follow the ROSTE model, even those that must be made quickly.

Campaign Objectives

After using research to gather all the needed information, the next step in a public relations campaign is selecting an objective. While this sounds like a very simple task it is both complex and important. Creating a good objective requires careful analysis of the client's goals, problems, resources, and publics. Creation of the objective must also be based on knowledge of appropriate media resources, laws, and culture. An objective is always a very brief and specific statement, but creating a good objective is the most difficult and the most important step in public relations campaign development.

Why Is an Objective So Important?

The objective has three purposes and each of these is critical to a campaign's success. First, the objective guides strategic planning and tactical decisions. When strategies are evaluated, those actions and messages that do not address the target public identified in the objective can be eliminated. Actions or messages that do not specifically advance the objective can be rejected in favor of those that do support the objective. In short, a well-formulated objective keeps the public relations campaign on track and prevents wasting time, thought, and other resources.

Second, a well-written objective is an effective tool for client persuasion. A good objective shows a relationship between the public relations campaign and the client's organizational goals. When pitching a campaign to a potential new client or a client with whom you have an established relationship, showing the relationship between the public relations program and the client's organizational goals increases the chance that management will support your program or a client will retain your agency.

Third, the well-written objective provides a means of evaluation. At the end of the campaign you can, with a well-written objective, very specifically measure your success. That measurement can then be used to prove your value to management or your client. The measurement can also be used to modify the public relations campaign in response to failure or to identify successful techniques for future application.

A good objective followed by a successful campaign keeps you from wasting resources, it persuades the client to support you, and it proves your success. Without a good objective you can do none of these things.

What Is a Public Relations Objective?

A public relations objective can guide strategic planning, serve as a tool for client persuasion, and be the foundation for campaign evaluation. In order to serve these purposes an objective must meet six criteria. All good public relations objectives:

1. Are realistic, short, and simple
2. Support the client's organizational goals
3. Specify a public
4. Specify a change in that public
5. Specify a time of accomplishment
6. Operationalize the public, change, and time

Realistic, Short, Simple.   Most readers have seen organizational goals or mission statements that say the organization does everything for everyone. Colleges and universities are often guilty of this flaw. Many schools have mission statements that go on for a page with multiple statements of commitment or values trying to appeal to every possible constituency. No school can teach everything to everyone and at the same time produce all kinds of research and community service. Likewise, no organization can appeal to everyone or do everything. To have any value an objective must limit the things an organization tries to do; otherwise the organization will simply waste resources trying to do everything. Keeping the objective statement short and simple helps keep it realistic. One rule that helps formulate good objectives is: "If you cannot state your objective in one sentence it may be to complicated to be realistic." To evaluate an objective statement, read it and ask yourself:

1. Will everyone working on this campaign *always* remember this is what we are trying to do?
2. Am I sure we can do this in the time allotted?

If the answer to either of these questions is "no," go back and simplify the objective.

Organizational Goals.   Organizational goals are aims or aspirations of the client organization. For a business organization goals may include increased sales, increased market share, increased profit, or reduced employee turnover. For corporations goals may be increased share price or a larger number of investors. For political organizations goals might include winning election for a client or winning passage of specific legislation. The goals of charitable organizations are typically increasing donations, recruiting volunteers, or motivating people to use the charity's service.

Whether the client is a business, corporation, political organization, or charity, any public relations campaign should advance the client organization's goals. Why would a client retain a public relations practitioner to administer a campaign that did not advance the client's interests? Although it seems incredibly obvious that the public relations objective should advance the organizational goals, it is not always easy to ensure that it does. Occasionally the public relations practitioner does not *know* the organization's goals. Sometimes the organization itself has not identified its goals and quite often the organization seems unwilling to admit what its goals really are.

In a perfect world the public relations practitioner would already be a part of management and would know the organization's goals. Unfortunately this often is not the case. In you are not part of management decisions and do not know the organization's goals they may be identified from business plans, marketing campaigns, or other secondary research. Also, do not forget the simple expedient of asking management what they see as their goals or problems. Often problems are perceived only when goals are not met, so management's perceptions of problems may be an inverse statement of organizational goals.

For organizations that have not formulated their own sense of purpose, secondary research into the organization's industry, political party, or area of charity can identify reasonable organizational goals. If you must use external sources to identify organizational goals it is advisable to confirm those goals with your client's management before assuming your research has produced an accurate statement of their goals.

For reasons known only to them, many clients seem unwilling to admit capitalistic or self-serving goals. Businesses often talk about client service and quality products but may find it difficult to admit their capitalistic goals such as sales and profits. Politicians talk about public service and are reluctant to include election victories in their goal statements. Even charities and universities are reluctant to include fundraising in their goal statements. Because they often do not include all organizational goals or omit the most important organizational goals, do not stop seeking organizational objectives when you locate an organizational mission statement. Look too at practices, reward systems, and reported problems. These will help you identify all of the organization's goals.

Specify a Public, Not "The" Public.   The most common mistake made when formulating a public relations objective is to include the phrase "the public." In public relations there is no such thing as "the public." Public relations depends on relationships between multiple publics, and strategies and tactics must be developed that target a specific group. A good public relations objective always specifies which public is being targeted. The phrase "the public" is simply too vague to provide useful guidance to campaign planning. It seems obvious that you would not use the same strategies and tactics to influence middle-aged subsistence farmers in rural China and young urban professionals in Paris. While these two groups are obviously different, each public has different values and media habits that must be considered when developing a campaign to reach them. If you do not identify a specific public in your public relations objective you risk either delivering the wrong information or delivering the right information to the wrong people.

To select a public, first identify all the stakeholders in the client's organization. Stakeholders can include customers, voters, opponents, competitors, consumer groups, employees, and shareholders. In effect, they are any group that influences or is influenced by the actions of the client organization. Stakeholders are the potential publics. From these groups you will select one to be the target public of your campaign. You must consider all stakeholders when selecting your target public or you risk omitting the one public that could be most easily influenced or that could do the most to help meet your client's organizational objectives.

When considering potential publics or stakeholders, do not forget those groups we call *latent* publics. Publics can be divided into three general categories. They are active publics, passive publics, and latent publics. *Active publics* are already taking action to either support or oppose your client's organizational objectives. Active publics are the ones that most public relations practitioners think of first. However, active publics are usually already committed to a course of action and are, therefore, difficult to influence. Active supporters are either already helping your client and you may waste resources trying to change them, or they are already taking action against your client and may have strong opinions that are impossible to change—regardless of the creativity of the public relations campaign. Public relations efforts directed at these individuals are usually a waste of resources. *Passive publics* are groups that simply do not care about your client's organizational objectives; regardless of the information you give them, they will not act. Again, it is a waste of your client's resources to support a public relations campaign directed to a passive public.

Latent publics are those groups who, if given the right information, can be converted to active supporters or opponents of your client's organizational objective. These groups, who would act if properly motivated, are the best publics for most campaigns.

Specify a Change. The next component of a public relations objective is some change in the target public. To identify this change ask yourself, what is it you want the target public to think or do after the campaign that they do not think or do now? If the target public is not changed by the campaign, then you have not accomplished anything significant and the campaign does not advance the client's goals.

Change can involve inoculation. Inoculation means changing a public's attitude so they resist some new argument or attempt to change their behavior. In other words, the change created by a public relations campaign may not be change at all. The concept of inoculation is drawn from medicine, where an inoculation does not change the health of a well person but does strengthen their immune system so they remain healthy. An application of this concept to public relations can be seen in a political campaign designed to keep the ruling party in power. For example, if you represent a client who is now president of Venezuela and there is a growing opposition political party, you may design a public relations campaign with the objective of keeping your client in office. The change you have created is only strengthening support for your client so that change will *not* occur.

While changes in a target public's *behavior* is most easily seen and measured, changes in knowledge, beliefs, attitudes, or values can also be the part of a public relations objective. Later we will explain the requirement that components of the objective be operationalized (measurable). Remember that if you seek a change in the target public's beliefs, attitudes, or values, you must have some baseline measure of those beliefs, attitudes, or values so you can demonstrate change at the end of the campaign.

Specify a Time Frame. Specifying a time for campaign completion seems obvious. If you do not indicate when you will create and measure the change in the target public your client cannot know when the campaign will end. If they do not know when the campaign will end they cannot know how much to budget for campaign costs. Also, if you have not specified a time for completion *you* cannot know when to demonstrate your success.

Operationalize the Public, Change, and Time. The public, the change to be created, and the time for the campaign should all be *operationalized*. Operationalized means stated or defined in a way that facilitates measurement. For example, a poor objective might say, "Housewives will buy more Thrifty soap." This is not a good public relations objective because it does not tell us how to measure "housewives" and "more soap." It also fails as an objective because it does not specify a time for accomplishment. A quality public relations objective with operationalized terms would say: "Married women between the ages of 20 and 45 in Bangkok will buy 20 percent more Thrifty soap in November 2009 than they bought in November 2008." Using this objective to guide planning we can design a campaign that uses only media that reach the Bangkok area and we can limit our messages to those that will appeal to women between 20 and 45 from Thailand. Specifying exactly how much sales will increase allows us both to measure our success and to show how our success justifies the cost of the campaign.

Of course, not all public relations objectives are as easily operationalized as one that only seeks a sales increase, and some may actually be more easily operationalized. Campaigns that seek to change attitudes, values, or beliefs, or those that seek to inoculate against anticipated change, are more difficult. To measure changes in attitude, for example, one must have a baseline measure of attitude. An operationalized public relations objective in such a situation might say: "Five percent more Texans between the ages of 20 and 50 will indicate a willingness to donate to Muslim charities in December of 2009 than did in December of 2007, where willingness to donate is measured by a poll of 500 randomly selected individuals in the target public." If the change in the target public is to be operationalized based on a poll or survey of the target public then the technique for conducting that poll must be presented in detail. This detail is essential to the whole concept of operationalization. Because changes in beliefs, attitudes, and values are more difficult to operationalize, it is often advisable to find a behavioral change that can be used as a measure of the psychographic change. Willingness to donate to Muslim charities, for example, could be measured by looking at the total actual donations. The objective statement, in this situation, could say: "Donations to Muslim charities from Texas will increase by five percent between 2007 and 2009."

Public relations objectives that seek to prevent change must rest on some assumption that change would have occurred without the public relations campaign. For the sake of simplicity, this assumption should not be included in the objective statement itself, but the assumption must be explained to the client. If you represented the Saudi Royal Family and you anticipated public demonstrations or a popular demand for democratic government you might have a public relations objective that said: "The Saudi Royal Family will remain in power until 2009." Unless you explained the need for inoculation and the anticipated popular campaign for democratic government, a hereditary monarchy would see no reason to devote resources to support your objective or your campaign.

When Is the Target Public Not the Target Public?

Occasionally it is impossible or prohibitively difficult to reach the real target public or to measure the real public relations objective. In these situations we must use secondary publics or secondary objectives. A secondary public is one that we can reach who will, in turn, influence the public whose behavior or thoughts actually can advance the client's organizational goals. The best example of a secondary public is a grassroots lobbying campaign. Grassroots lobbying is used when the primary objective is to influence legislators to vote for a particular bill or law but it is impossible or difficult to deliver messages directly to the legislators. In this situation a secondary public—the constituents of the legislators—is targeted. A campaign is designed whose public relations objective might be: "To have 5,000 constituents of Senator X write letters to the senator supporting our bill during the week before it comes to a vote." The real objective is to have the senator vote for our bill, but we designed a campaign to influence the secondary public to use their status as voters to influence the senator.

A skillfully written public relations objective is essential to a good public relations campaign. When critiquing the campaign work of others you should look for the public relations objective. If it is vague, is not operationalized, or lacks any of the components of a good objective, there is a very good chance the entire public relations campaign will fail. When designing your own public relations campaign, taking the time to craft a good objective will help you sell the campaign to your client, guide your planning, and evaluate your work.

Campaign Strategies

Remember that the ROSTE method of public relations planning or campaign evaluation is not linear. If you cannot identify appropriate strategies it may be necessary to change the campaign's objective in order to keep it realistic. Furthermore, after selecting a strategy it may be necessary to conduct additional research to determine the strategy's probability of success and to identify whether there are available tactics to implement the strategy. Finally, once strategies and tactics are selected for each objective, they must be relevant to the objective. Figure 3.2 graphically shows the relationship between goals, objectives, and tactics.

What Is a Strategy?

Strategies are conceptual. They describe messages, themes, or guidelines for the overall public relations effort. One simple way to think of a strategy is as an expression of an idea or message that will motivate the target public to change to meet the public relations objective. Tactics, which will be covered in the next chapter, describe exactly what will be done by the public relations practitioner to communicate the theme or message to the target public.

For example, suppose your objective is to increase the number of pregnant women in Pakistan who eat high-calcium diets. Your strategy might be to inform those in your target audience that a high-calcium diet increases the health of their children. A tactic might be to have local healthcare workers show comparisons of infant mortality for children whose mothers ate high- and low-calcium diets. The strategy is based on an understanding that the women in the target public value the health of their children and will act on the information about the relationship between diet and health. To evaluate a strategy one must demonstrate an understanding of the relationship between the message or theme and the beliefs and behaviors of

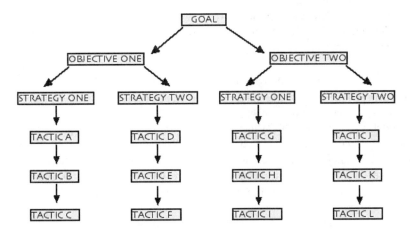

FIGURE 3.2   PR Objectives, Strategies, and Tactics Flow Chart. If you have a second goal it will follow the same model. The number of objectives, strategies, and tactics may differ based on the specific plan.

Source: Artwork by Bridget Krause.

the target public. In other words, you evaluate a strategy based on whether you know that a particular theme or message will motivate the target public identified in the objective. When evaluating a strategy you should ask questions such as:

> Does this information appeal to some value in the target public?
>
> Will the target public's members believe the information is true?
>
> Will the target public resist or distort the information because it conflicts with other beliefs or values?
>
> Will the target public resist or distrust the information because of its source or authority?

You should also ask if this strategy is specifically related to the objective. Will the message or theme motivate the target public identified in the objective in a way that helps meet the objective?

The Relation between Strategy and Communication Theory

Because the evaluation of a strategy is based on an understanding of what motivates the target public, good public relations strategies are almost always based on some model, theory, or paradigm that explains human beliefs, values, habits, and behavior. The public relations representative designing a campaign should be able to defend the strategy and explain why it is appropriate in terms of some tested and proven theory, model, or principle of persuasion or communication. Therefore, the discussion of strategies here will focus on the models, theories, and principles of persuasion and communication that are most often applied to public relations campaigns.

Any theory, model, or principle of persuasion must begin with some understanding of public opinion. In other words, before you can identify messages or themes that will change public opinion you must know what public opinion is.

Public Opinion.   Public opinion is an expression of the combined thoughts, predispositions, and motivations of a group. Since public opinion includes thoughts and predispositions it can lead to action. Those people in a target public are more likely to do something if that action is consistent with their thoughts (values, attitudes, and ideals). If a campaign strategy successfully changes public opinion, it can therefore also change public actions. Because of this, even if your public relations objective is to change the actions or behavior of a target public, a strategy is likely to be successful if it changes the target public's opinions. Of course, the successful strategy must change public opinion in a way that will motivate the desired behavior.

It is important to remember that there is no one public opinion. Rather, there are multiple public opinions. There is one public opinion for each public, and a public's opinion is usually a collective expression of what the members of that public perceive as their self-interest at a specific time. Thus, the concept of self-interest is central both to identifying public opinion and to evaluating strategies designed to change public opinion. Simply put, self-interest is motivating. If you can appeal to the self-interest of a target public you can motivate people to act, but if you cannot appeal to their self-interest it is nearly impossible to motivate people to act or to change.

In should also be noted that perceived self-interest varies from public to public. The more diverse two publics are, the more likely it is that they will perceive very different self-interests. Especially when dealing with groups of a different culture or nationality, a public relations practitioner must be careful to research the values of the target public in order to identify their perceived self-interests. For example, most U.S. citizens find the motivation of suicide terrorist bombers completely unfathomable. Terrorist groups can motivate their members to perform suicide bombings only because those individuals perceive their self-interests very differently. Whereas most U.S. citizens would describe life and religious freedom as central values in their system of self-interest, the suicide terrorist might place a higher self-interest in being recognized as a martyr and receiving a reward in an afterlife. To appeal to any group, a strategy must be based on what they perceive to be their self-interest.

Self-interest is necessary but by itself it is not sufficient to motivate a public to action. Awareness is also required. To be successful, a strategy must make the target public aware not only of the strategic message or theme but also why the desired action is in their self-interest. In the case of suicide bombers, not only must they believe that martyrdom is in their self-interest, but also some authority in which they believe must tell them that they will be rewarded in an afterlife.

To appeal to a public's self-interest, a public relations practitioner can either have his or her client do something that will make the target public aware of a theme or message (this is an action strategy) or the practitioner can communicate a new message to the target public (this is a communication strategy). Of course the practitioner can do both: have the client do something and then talk about that action in a message to the target public. The following sections discuss those strategies.

Action Strategies

Some would argue that all clients have an obligation to the public and that one function of public relations is to ensure the client meets those obligations. In this context, action strategies could be seen as advising the client to engage in conduct that meets the obligation to the public and avoid any actions that violate their public obligation. Even the PRSA code of professional standards, which includes multiple references to the practitioner's obligation to act in the public interest, suggests that this is an appropriate approach to action strategies. However, interpreting action strategies in terms of their contribution to the public interest is unworkably complicated for two reasons. First, there simply is no such thing as the public and therefore no such thing as the public interest. Each of the individual publics with whom the client must maintain a relationship has its own values and interests. These differentiating values and interests are the very characteristics that define a public. Further, each public's perception of the client organization's obligations may not coincide with the client's objectives.

A simpler and more effective way to approach action strategies is to first decide what information, message, or theme must be delivered to the target publics in order to advance the client's objectives, and then to determine what image or message is created by the client's actions. Action strategies are then the selection of client actions that communicate appropriate images or messages to the target publics. This, of course, does not mean that the client is free to ignore the interests of its target publics. It means that the practitioner must consider the perceived interests of each individual target public when advising client actions.

You may ask yourself how a practitioner can simultaneously maintain personal ethical standards while addressing competing interests of a target public and the client's organizational goals. This is done by modifying the client's organizational goals to make them consistent with the target public's expectations. For example, your client's objective may simply be to make money. However, even that simplistic objective can be phrased in a way that acknowledges that publics do not buy from clients who make inferior or unsafe products. A client's goal can be to maximize product quality or safety in order to improve sales and to make money.

We have all heard that public relations is a management function. One interpretation of this phrase is that those of us in public relations should advise the management of our client organizations on proper courses of action. Very simply put, if the client's actions violate a significant target public's perception of their obligations we will either have nothing to talk about in our communication strategy or we have to invest our communication efforts in fixing the disasters and compensating for a bad public image created by the client's actions. In our capacity as boundary spanners, public relations practitioners must focus on the actions that facilitate relationships. We must advise our clients to pursue courses of action that simultaneously advance their organizational goals and meet the reasonable expectations of target publics.

"Our best strategy may be to destigmatize embezzlement."

Source: © The New Yorker Collection 1998, Leo Cullum from cartoonbank.com.
All Rights Reserved.

One approach to advising clients about modifications of their organizational goals is to recognize that all goals are made up of incremental goals or accomplishments. To meet the goal of making money, our client must meet the incremental goals of (1) establishing investor trust in order to secure operating capital, (2) establishing a good reputation with customers to motivate sales, and (3) securing the confidence of regulators to avoid their impositions on our client's operations. To meet these incremental goals the client must act in ways that inspire trust, confidence, and a favorable reputation. With this perspective it is possible to demonstrate to the client that their organizational goal can exist simultaneously with the interests of all target publics.

In addition to actions of the client, it should be noted that many actions are the primary responsibility of the public relations office. For example, the public relations office may be charged with administering an employee picnic. This action, if done properly, communicates the client's concern for and involvement with employees while also helping to meet a more cynical objective of avoiding labor problems. Annual shareholder meetings, donor recognition banquets, and alumni homecoming events all fit a similar pattern.

Communication Strategies

The client's actions are critical to a successful public relations campaign and the evaluation of any public relations program should include a careful analysis of its action strategies. However, do not forget that awareness is an essential part of all public relations strategies. No action, no matter how difficult or noble, can motivate a target public if that public is not aware of the action. Therefore, all public relations campaigns must include communication strategies. We must find ways to make target publics aware of the client's actions and aware of how those actions fulfill the self-interest of the target public. The need for public awareness is met with communication strategies.

Some authors divide objectives into motivational objectives and informational objectives. Motivational objectives specify things you want the target public to do. For example, objective statements that specify increased sales, votes for a particular candidate, or donations to a client charity are motivational objectives. Informational objectives, on the other hand, are objectives that specify information the public relations practitioner wants to ensure the target public receives and understands. Examples of informational objectives include increased awareness of the client among members or the target public, education of the target public, or issue familiarity within a target public. Understanding the distinction between motivational objectives and informational objectives can help you conceptualize communication strategies. While motivational objectives are embedded in the public objectives of the ROSTE model that was discussed earlier, informational objectives are much the same as communication strategies. It may help your understanding of communication strategies to think of them as steps toward accomplishment of the public objective, just as an informational objective is a step toward meeting a motivational objective.

Another way to think of the communication strategies uses the term "positioning." Although the word position is overused and often misused in descriptions of public relations campaigns, the idea is helpful. In this context the client's position is the perception the target public has of the client, as that perception is reflected in descriptive or identifying statements. For example: If your client charity is described by your target public as helpful or concerned about the poor, then your client is positioned as helpful and concerned about the poor. This position helps communicate an image of the client that can advance the accomplishment of the public objective.

You position the client by using descriptive and identifying statements in your communications about the client. The success of such a positioning strategy depends entirely on the target public's reception, understanding, and acceptance of your description as true. Your client is not positioned simply because you have delivered a message or because you, as the client's public relations representative, have decided to position the client.

Deciding what information or positioning statements or what informational objective will help advance your client's objective is the heart of a communication strategy. To be successful, your decision about what positioning statement or informational objective to use must be guided by principles, models, paradigms, or theories of communication. These principles express relations between kinds of information, channels for delivering information, and the impact that information will have on target publics. In effect they provide the roadmap for deciding what information and what media to deliver.

In the rest of this chapter we present a more comprehensive series of models and theories that can be used to analyze public relations case strategies or to guide the development of a strategy for a public relations campaign. First, we describe a simple model of human communication. This model identifies five components of the communication process— source, channel, message, receiver, and response. You can use it to help identify all the important parts of your strategy. Second, we describe two systems for determining why a target public will resist your information or persuasion. Knowing the sources of resistance will help you select appropriate strategies to overcome the resistance. Third, we describe some principles of persuasion or influence that you can use to help overcome the resistance you anticipate. Choosing from these models and theories, you should be able to critique a public relations case to determine if it used an appropriate strategy. You can use the same models and theories to guide your decisions about strategy creation when you are developing your own public relations campaigns.

Model of Human Communication.   Since Aristotle, innumerable scholars have found ways to model the components of human communication in ways that graphically represent the relationship among those components. It would take several academic courses to summarize those models and their evolution. In the introduction to Chapter 5 we also present a contextual approach to the study of human communication and explain how it can be used to guide the practice of international or intercultural public relations. Here we will collapse all the models of human communication into one aggregate model. This model can be used identify the communications variables that should be considered when critiquing a public relations campaign. Those same communications variables should be controlled, if possible, when developing your own public relations campaign. We certainly do not argue that this is the best model or that it is the only acceptable model. It is used here primarily because of its simplicity and the ease with which it can be applied to communication strategies in public relations.

Based on the components in this model one can see that all communication (at least in public relations) involves five components. They are a source of the information, a channel of communication, the message being communicated, the receiver of the information, and the receiver's reaction to the communication.

The source of the information is not the medium of communication but is the person, authority, or organization seen by the receiver as the initiator of the communication. It is important to identify the target public's perceived source of the information in order to assess such things as credibility and similarity between the communicating parties. These concepts will be discussed in more detail later. For now, suffice it to say that the members of the target public are likely to attend to information or to believe information from some sources and are unlikely to pay attention to or trust information from other sources. Therefore it is essential to the evaluation of a communication strategy to know whom or what the target public will perceive as the source of messages directed to them.

The message is the content or information you seek to deliver. It must appeal to some value or belief already held by the target public in order to affect them. The message includes both the ideas you seek to communicate and the actual language you use to deliver that communication. In this context, language is not only the tongue but also includes the dialect, vernacular, and idiomatic expressions used. Further, the language of the message includes the structure or order of the message content. The language of the message must be selected so that the target public has the desired understanding and perception of the information being delivered.

The channel is what many people would call the medium. It is the system for delivering the message to the receiver. Channels or media of communication will be addressed more thoroughly in our discussion of tactics, but for now you should understand that the channel in which a message is delivered influences how a receiver perceives that message. For example, information in a news medium is seen as more credible than information included in advertising, and information delivered in person by a trusted friend is more influential than information delivered in an anonymous poster.

The receiver is usually the individual member of the target public, but there are also inadvertent or accidental receivers. Particularly when you deliver information in public media you must remember that people who were not your intended targets will see, read, or hear the information and they, as well as your intended targets, will form opinions of your client based on that information. Since every target public has different values and beliefs, it is imperative that public relations practitioners target their messages to the individual target recipients and that they anticipate the reactions of those collateral publics who may see and react to information intended for others.

Receivers' reactions, sometimes called feedback, are the messages delivered back to the source. These messages are particularly important in public relations because they provide a measure of the success of the public relations strategy. When assessing reactions it is important to remember that reactions usually are not delivered in the same channels as the original messages. Measuring receivers' reactions may be as simple as placing a news release and then reading responses in the "letters to the editor" section of the same newspaper. Measuring receivers' reactions may also be as complicated as delivering information in a political speech and then testing public reaction through an overnight poll. Receivers may react in any medium, so a sophisticated public relations practitioner constantly monitors all media to accurately gauge how target or latent publics are reacting to messages.

Target Public Resistance.   Careful analysis of the perceived source, message form and content, channel of delivery, target and collateral receivers' characteristics, and receivers' reactions helps public relations practitioners assess the quality of communication strategies. Such analysis also helps explain some typical sources of a public's resistance to the campaign's message. Two models that help predict such resistance are one based on the public's *selectivity* and one based on the public's *reaction to dissonance* or information that is inconsistent with their current beliefs.

Selectivity.   *Selectivity* refers to normal human tendencies to avoid information overload. Everyone, including the members of your target public, is bombarded with stimuli every waking moment of their lives. We all devise strategies to avoid the cacophony of this information. Simply put, we select from our environment a small amount of information and we only think about or act upon that information, which we allow through the filter of our own selection process. This filtering takes place in stages that can be described as selective exposure, selective attention, selective perception, and selective retention.

   Selective exposure refers to the fact that all people only expose themselves to a small amount of available information. Most devout Christians do not attend a mosque, therefore they are not exposed to the teachings of Muhammad. Similarly, most devout Muslims do not attend a church and they are not exposed to the teachings of Jesus. Each group, by its selective exposure, filters out information about the other group. This is not because either group is somehow mentally defective, it is a normal response to a need to protect ourselves from too much information. We simply cannot expose ourselves to all available information, so we select only some information sources and therefore limit the amount of information to which we are exposed.

   Selective attention is only slightly more sophisticated than selective exposure. Selective attention refers to our ability to only pay attention to some events in our environment while ignoring others. Television advertisers are responding to this selective attention when they increase the volume for their messages. They know that the average American has developed the ability to "selectively attend" to the entertainment content and advertising content of television. Most experienced television viewers simply stop paying attention when the advertisements begin. When you drive past billboards without reading their message, read a newspaper and only pay attention to the headlines that "grab your attention," or only "hear" the weather for your hometown while ignoring the weather report for other cities, these are all the product of your selective attention.

   Selective perception is even more complex than selective exposure and attention. Even if we are exposed to a message and pay attention to it, we tend to perceive it in ways that are filtered through our own belief system. A U.S. citizen hearing the North Korean claim that President Kim Jong-il is a great athlete may think something like: "The little butterball is lying to his people again." A loyal North Korean hearing the same claim may think "There is another piece of evidence that we are being led by a great man." Each receiver filtered the message through his or her existing belief system and perceived something different (see Figure 3.3). That is selective perception.

   Selective retention may be the easiest of the filters to understand. Any student who has taken an examination and realized that he or she forgot something said in class has experienced selective retention. Even if we are exposed to a piece of information, paid attention

FIGURE 3.3   Kim Jong-il Perceptions

The "Real" Kim Jong-il

The North Korean government and the United States government paint very different pictures of North Korea's President. Your perception of Kim Jong-il may depend entirely on which public relations service gives you information about him.

North Korean Information	Western Information
When Kim Jong-il was born February 16, 1942 on Korea's sacred Mount Paektu "the iceberg in the pond on Mount Paektu emitted a mysterious sound and a double rainbow rose up."	Kim Jong-il was born February 16, 1942 while his mother was in exile in the Soviet Union.
Kim Jong-il is the composer of six operas and is a skilled engineer who designed the largest tower in Korea.	Kim Jong-il's only academic or intellectual accomplishment is receiving a degree from Kim il-sung University (Kim il-sung is his father).
Kim Jong-il is the commander of all the armed forces in North Korea	Kim Jong-il has never served in the military at all.
Kim Jong-il is the world's greatest athlete. He hit four holes-in-one the first time he played golf.	Kim Jong-il is a five feet three inch tall "butter ball" who wears lifts in his shoes and perms his hair to try to look five feet six inches tall.

Sources: CNN, BBC, and CIA Web pages.

to it, and understood it (perceived it accurately), most of us are not capable of remembering everything. Whether it is the product of competition for our memory by new information or simply memory decay, we all forget some things while we remember others. This perfectly natural tendency to forget some things is called selective retention.

For a public relations communication strategy to be effective it must overcome all the filters of selectivity. (1) The messages must be delivered in a medium to which the target audience is exposed, to overcome selective exposure. (2) The message must be delivered in a way that actually gets the attention of the target public's members, to overcome their selective attention. (3) It must be delivered with adequate clarity to ensure they do not distort it with their selective perception, and (4) it must be delivered with enough force or repetition to ensure it is not forgotten, to overcome selective retention.

Dissonance.   Another model that can help explain why messages may not motivate a target public is *dissonance*. Dissonance is a term popularized by the research of Leon Festinger. Festinger attempted to use dissonance to explain why people are motivated by some messages but not by others. There are some questions about the reliability of his research into motivation, but one area of his research is unquestionably valuable to those of us in public relations. The research on dissonance has identified stages or steps that people usually use to avoid information that is not consistent with their current beliefs. If we seek to motivate a target public to change its values or actions we must overcome each of these steps.

According to dissonance theory, people confronted with information that violates their existing beliefs will—in order—leave the field, derogate the source, distort the message, or change their existing beliefs to be consistent with the new information.

When confronted with information that is not consistent with their existing beliefs, members of the target public will leave the field. In other words, they will simply avoid the information altogether. They may physically leave so they do not have to hear or see the new information, or they will mentally leave. Physically leaving the field is the same as selective exposure and mentally leaving the field is the same as selective attention. In either case, in order to overcome this tendency the public relations practitioner must adopt a strategy that prevents the target public from leaving the field. He or she must adopt a communication strategy that places the client's message inescapably in front of the target public with such force that the members of that public cannot ignore it.

If it is not possible to leave the field, members of the target public may avoid the public relations campaign's message by derogating the source. Derogation of the source is something like selective perception. It refers to the target public's tendency to assume a source that delivers information not consistent with its existing beliefs or values is ill informed, dishonest, or incompetent. If the target public decides the source of the information cannot be trusted its members can reject the information. To be successful, a communication strategy must overcome this tendency by selecting credible sources of information. Credibility will be discussed later in this chapter.

If they are unable to leave the field or to derogate the source, target public members may distort the message to make it seem consistent with their existing beliefs. Distortion of the message is exactly the same concept as selective perception. Even when people in the target public hear the campaign message and understand that it came from a knowledgeable and honest source they will try to find some way to twist the message in their minds to make it consistent with what they already believe. The only way to overcome this tendency is to ensure that messages are absolutely clear and to repeat the message in several forms.

Finally, if the target public's members are not able to leave the field, derogate the source, or distort the message they will have to change their existing values or beliefs to make them consistent with the new information. Of course, this change is the goal of most communication strategies in public relations.

Techniques for Overcoming Communication Resistance.   Obviously the members of a target public will resist many public relations messages. They can use their selective filters and they can use the techniques presented for avoiding dissonance. A public relations practitioner's most valuable skill is the ability to develop a strategy to overcome the target public's resistance. There are several principles, theories, or paradigms that will help you identify such a strategy. These include: uses and gratifications theory, two-step flow of communication, source credibility, homophily, message clarity, and repetition.

Uses and Gratifications Theory.   This is really a pre-theoretic supposition or hypothesis that posits a relationship between motivation and media consumption habits. It is based on the observation that audiences are not passive observers of media, they seek to be entertained or informed and they seek out the information and media content that appeals to them. In effect, they seek information that impacts their self-interest and that is consistent with their existing beliefs, opinions, and predispositions. This idea is important when we evaluate a public relations communication strategy because it tells us we are more likely to overcome selective exposure or field avoidance if we place our campaign messages in media that gratify the needs of our target public. We cannot reach a significant number of conservative Israeli consumers with a message using Aljazeera because the content of that network does not gratify an entertainment or information need of the target public and they therefore do not use it.

Two-Step Flow of Communication.   This describes how information flows from media to the members of a target public. It is referred to as "two-step" or sometimes "multi-step" to acknowledge that the information does not move directly from the media of mass communication directly to individual receivers. Instead, information often moves from the media to individuals who act as opinion leaders and then to the members of the target public. This principle is important when we design or evaluate a public relations campaign communication strategy because it helps determine who should be targeted with the media releases. Since most information flows from the media to opinion leaders and from the opinion leaders to the individuals in the target public, we should place our media releases and/or advertisements in media that are most likely to reach and influence the opinion leaders within our target public. Selecting those media and crafting effective messages are facilitated by an understanding of who opinion leaders may be. Opinion leaders can be generally divided into the categories of formal and informal opinion leaders. Formal opinion leaders are the individuals who hold appointed or elected positions, such as fraternity presidents or college deans. Because of their titles they are usually easy to identify, but often the formal title does not really translate to an ability to influence the opinions of others. Informal opinion leaders may be more difficult to identify but are better able to advance a public relations communication strategy.

Informal opinion leaders usually share some characteristics. For example, relative to those whose opinions they influence, they are active in public life, well educated, high consumers of information, and have many social contacts. When identifying opinion leaders it is imperative to remember that opinion leaders must be part of the group they influence. The characteristics listed for informal opinion leaders must be considered relative to those same characteristics in the public they influence. For example, an opinion leader among subsistence farmers in India will generally be better educated than other subsistence farmers in India but his level of education may still be quite low. All college professors may be well educated but that does not make them opinion leaders, even among other college professors. To be an opinion leader among college professors one must be exceptionally well informed. The best source for identification of opinion leaders in any public is the members of the target public themselves. They, and only they, really know to whom they look for interpretation and evaluation of information. Remember your research tools and do not be afraid to use them.

To overcome the tendency of an audience to derogate the source or to selectively perceive it, it is helpful to use a source that is credible. The phrase "source credibility" refers to people who inspire trust and are able to influence others. To be credible a source must be perceived by the target public as both knowledgeable and honest. Further, the message attributed to the source must be well composed. Credible sources may be thought of as having competence, character, and composure. Competence means that the target public must perceive the source as expert enough on the subject of the message to provide useful and trustworthy information. Character means that the target public must perceive the source as honest. The members of the target public must feel that the source is more concerned about their interests than about his or her own interests. Composure simply refers to the form of the message itself. Most cultures perceive people who are inarticulate as less knowledgeable or less honest. People often transfer this system of evaluation to messages in all media. Many people in your target audience will assume that the person who composed a message was incompetent or dishonest if the message itself contains language errors, is poorly organized, or is factually inconsistent.

Homophily.   This is a bit like credibility, in that it is based on a characteristic of the source, as that characteristic is perceived by the members of the target public. The natural human tendency to be attracted to and to trust people that we perceive as being like ourselves is homophily. The principle of homophily suggests that when public relations practitioners select a source for messages to a target public they should select a source that is similar to the members of the target public. Therefore, a wealthy U.S. politician is not the best source for messages directed to an opium grower in Afghanistan. However, if there is some common characteristic that commonality may be used to make the message attractive to even a very disparate public. For example, even people from different cultures, nations, and socioeconomic groups may appeal to each other based on their common concerns for their families or their environment. When you are developing a public relations communication strategy, find some way to make the target public members feel that the source of information is like them and understands their concerns.

Other techniques for overcoming the target public's tendencies to filter or distort messages include message clarity, repetition, and connection to self-interest. Message clarity can be achieved by keeping the message simple. The less complex a message the more difficult it is for members of the target public to distort it or to use the filter of selective perception to misconstrue it. The best messages, in this context, are those that present one idea with direct and easily understood support that is based on the existing beliefs and self-interest of the target public.

Repetition.   This means exactly what it sounds like. The more often members of the target public are exposed to a message the less likely they are to use selective attention or perception to avoid it and the more likely they are to retain the message. Repetition also makes message distortion and "leaving the field" more difficult. Messages that are slightly restated in several forms are less likely to be distorted by the target public because each restatement requires a new distortion; even the most resistant target public will eventually run out of ways to twist the message's meaning. Repetition in multiple media helps overcome the tendency to "leave the field" to engage in selective exposure.

The Medium Is Part of the Message.   All of the principles we have discussed thus far have dealt with the content of messages delivered to target publics. It is also important to consider the media in which those messages are delivered. Obviously, a message placed in a medium that does not reach the target public is a complete waste of the public relations practitioner's efforts and the client's money. However, media selection is more complicated than simply picking the medium read or seen by those in the target public. Print media, for example, are better able to deliver long or complicated messages. Face-to-face communication is still the most effective for influencing almost all people. In short, always pick the medium of communication that both reaches the target public and is able to deliver the kind of message your research shows will influence those in the public to meet your public relations objective. Also, do not assume people in other cultures follow your culture's norms. There are still illiterate people, people without electricity, and people who cannot access the Internet. Do not use a medium that those in your target public cannot access because they cannot read or do not have a computer or television.

While there is certainly no guarantee that even a well-designed communication strategy can accurately deliver the intended messages to all members of a target public, knowing what makes the members of that public resist new information and using proven principles to design a strategy to overcome their resistance will help. When all else fails, remember that a message tied to the self-interest of the target public is most likely to break through any barriers they may create to your client's objectives.

REFERENCES AND SUGGESTED READINGS

Hon, L. C. (1998). Demonstrating effectiveness in public relations: Goals, objectives and evaluation. *Journal of Public Relations Research, 10*(2), 103–135.

Nager, N. R., & Allen, T. H. (1984). *Public relations management by objectives.* New York & London: Longman.

Rogers, E. M. (2003). *Diffusion of innovation* (5th ed.). New York: Free Press.

Rogers, E. M., & Shoemaker, F. (1971). *Communication of innovation: A cross cultural approach* (2nd ed.). New York: The Free Press.

Smith, R. D. (2002). *Strategic planning for public relations.* Mahwah, NJ: Lawrence Erlbaum Associates.

4 Public Relations Tactics and Evaluation

Public relations campaign strategy uses principles, theories, models, and paradigms to guide decisions about what messages to deliver and what media to use. Campaign tactics are the nuts and bolts decisions about exactly how to get the desired messages into the chosen media. In effect, tactics are what the public relations practitioner must do to make the strategy happen. These nuts and bolts decisions include determining the timing of activities and communications, the exact wording of messages, whether advertising or publicity is best, and whether direct or mediated publicity will be most likely to deliver the intended message. Other, even more detailed components of publicity involve deciding how best to motivate media to use news releases or how best to deliver direct publicity. Tactical options are limited only by your imagination, the available resources, and an honest evaluation of what will influence the target publics.

Campaign Media Tactics

There are as many ways to organize tactical decisions as there are public relations practitioners. Many authors divide public relations media into controlled and uncontrolled media, internal and external media, or mass media and interpersonal media. Others divide media based on channels such as word-of-mouth, print, or electronic. While any of these systems can be useful, here we divide the discussion of tactics into three categories: advertising, mediated publicity, and direct publicity. These labels are unusual but they do simplify some decisions that are necessary to evaluate or create public relations tactics and they cover nearly all the essential decisions. We conclude our discussion of tactics with some brief notes about budgeting.

For use here, we define *advertising* as communication that depends on purchased space or time in existing media. Billboards, radio and television commercials, display or classified ads in newspapers, and banner ads on the Internet are all examples of advertising. *Mediated publicity* is information delivered through existing mass communications media. The vast majority of mediated publicity is delivered as news. Other mediated publicity includes product placements in motion pictures or clients' personal appearances on talk shows. *Direct publicity* is information delivered in media created or controlled by the client or public relations professional for the purpose of reaching a specific target public. Corporate newsletters, annual reports, direct mail pieces, brochures, and agency or client web pages are examples of direct publicity. There is obviously some overlap between these three categories of media. For example, a direct mail flyer or telemarketing message may be seen as advertising if it uses and pays for existing delivery systems but would be direct publicity if the public relations practitioner used his or her own staff to create and deliver the message. Performances or demonstrations at trade shows, fairs, or festivals are mediated publicity if the trade show or fair was an existing medium, but they are direct publicity if the public relations practitioner created the event in order to draw the target public for communication. These small areas of overlap between the categories may lead to some ambiguity when defining certain tactics, but the category system is attractively simple and allows the planner or critic of a public relations campaign to very quickly evaluate media selection tactics. Figure 4.1 presents different media tactics and their advantages and disadvantages.

Advertising

Many agencies and corporate communication structures divide advertising from public relations, and many academic programs separate advertising majors from public relations

FIGURE 4.1   Media Tactics Grid

	Examples	Advantages	Disadvantages
Advertising Communication using purchased space or time in existing media	■ Outdoor-billboards etc. ■ Newspaper and magazine print ads ■ Radio and TV commercials ■ Internet pop ups and banners ■ Telemarketing and spam	■ Control of content ■ Control of placement ■ Control of timing	■ High cost ■ Lower credibility ■ Target public's tendency to filter or ignore message ■ Not able to deliver long or complex messages
Mediated Publicity Communication using existing news or entertainment media	■ News releases ■ Movie product placements ■ Talk show appearances ■ Pseudo-events	■ High credibility of existing news media ■ High visibility of existing entertainment media	■ No control over editing and content ■ No control over placement
Direct Publicity Communication using media created or controlled for the purpose of reaching the target public	■ Newsletters ■ Brochures ■ Speakers' bureaus ■ Corporate web pages	■ Control of content ■ Some control of placement ■ Ability to target very specific public	■ High cost ■ Low credibility ■ Competition for attention by other messages and media

majors. These divisions lead many students and practitioners to believe that advertising is not appropriately a part of public relations. Despite the prejudice against advertising, it is simply a tool or tactic that can be used to deliver a message. Therefore advertising can be subsumed by public relations. You should only reject advertising as a public relations tactic if it exceeds your client's budget or is not the best tactic for delivering the message your strategy identified as most suited for meeting your public relations objective.

Advertising has several advantages over other media more commonly associated with public relations. Because advertising uses purchased time or space the public relations practitioner can control the content of the ads. If you carefully write and review your advertising copy you control the message, unlike a news release where an editor or journalist may edit, reject, or rewrite your copy. Also, when using paid space or time you can determine both when it will be seen or heard and where it will be placed in the delivery medium. The primary disadvantage of advertising is its cost. However, there are other disadvantages that should be considered. Because of selective exposure and attention, those in your target audience may simply not read or listen to an advertising message. Your message also may be lost in the clutter of competing advertisements. A final disadvantage of advertising is its low credibility. Most experienced consumers of information know that advertisements are purchased by someone who seeks to influence their behavior or opinions. Therefore, those in your target public are likely to derogate the source of advertising, or selectively perceive it as one-sided or dishonest. In short, advertising is a good, though expensive, tactic for placing a message in front of your target public, but its ability to influence the public's behavior or opinion may be limited.

To maximize the impact of advertising the sophisticated public relations practitioner will select from several forms and will construct his or her advertisement to ensure members of the target public attend to the message. Advertising is most often conceptualized as a component of product or service marketing. In this context, advertisements simply present information or claims about the quality of some consumer goods or services. However, there are several other forms of advertising that can be more useful in public relations campaigns.

Institutional advertising or issue advertising uses purchased time or space just like consumer advertising, but it uses that time or space to present more complicated ideas, to create an image, or to defend a position. For example, advertisements that look like editorials or that appear to be news copy can be placed in newspapers. Examples of such "news-look" advertisements can often be found in the real estate or automobile section of many major newspapers. These sections often are made up completely of paid advertisements but appear to be financial or lifestyle news. Spring break inserts in college newspapers and broadcast infomercials are other examples of advertisements that have the appearance of news. Of course, these must be labeled as advertising, but using an editorial, news, or "advertorial" format allows for the presentation of longer explanations and more complex information. Although it violates most journalists' sense of ethics, many newspapers even tie the amount of coverage in specialty sections such as business, real estate, or life style, to the amount of advertising space purchased. When confronted with such exchange rules it can be to the public relations practitioner's advantage to purchase large news-look advertisements.

Public service announcements (PSAs) are another advertising variant that can be used to overcome a disadvantage of advertising. Historically, PSAs referred to the free time given to charitable or community service groups by television stations. These announcements were essentially free advertisements and they were given to enhance the appearance that the station acted in the public interest. Action in the public interest was a component of the evaluations for station license renewal. License renewal has become significantly easier for U.S. television stations and the motivation to donate time for PSAs has been reduced. However, most local radio and television stations still do donate advertising time for messages that serve the public interest. Such messages usually encourage charitable donations and volunteering for community projects or encourage practices to improve education or public health. It should also be noted that many newspapers and magazines also donate advertising space for such messages. Because PSAs were encouraged by the FCC licensing requirements in the United States, the tradition of free advertising is stronger in the United States than in other countries. This, of course, does not mean that a persuasive practitioner with a popular client cannot secure free advertising time or space in other countries.

Whether a traditional "marketing" advertisement, a negative advertisement for a politician, or a public service announcement, any advertising message is only as good as its ability to reach and influence the target public. Variables that affect an advertisement's effectiveness include its ability to secure attention, the message form, the perceived source of the advertisement, and the context in which the advertisement is placed.

Before an advertisement can have any impact it must move through two selective filters, selective exposure and selective attention. Choosing a medium that is used by members of the target public should overcome the filter of selective exposure, but even after the message is placed in a medium seen or heard by members of the target public they may still simply ignore it. To be successful, an advertisement must include something that secures the attention of its intended audience. When planning or critiquing public relations campaigns that include advertising tactics, you must be sure to evaluate the advertisements' attention-grabbing ability. In mainstream U.S. culture, attention may be secured with sexual images, humor, or unusual images or sounds. Obviously the advertisement must secure the attention of members of the target public without distracting them from the intended message. Attention devices that offend those in the target public defeat the purpose of the advertisement as a tactic. In particular, advertisements that use humor depend heavily on language and cultural variations, and attention devices using sexual images may easily violate rules of propriety in some cultures.

When designing advertisements for cultures or nationalities other than your own, be sure to test those messages with subjects from the target public to ensure the attention devices do secure attention and are not counterproductive. In addition, studying the commercial speech laws of the country in which you plan to advertise will help you identify what advertising is and is not permitted. Advertising content, format, or design can be legally restricted. For example, comparison advertising that is heavily used in the United States is not allowed in Thailand.

To be effective, an advertising message must be short and simple. With the exception of some news-look advertisements or advertorials, advertisements are usually too small or short to carry long complex messages. In addition, to get past the target public's filters of selective attention and selective retention, short, simple messages are best. Short messages are more likely to be noticed or attended to and they are easier to remember than are long or complex messages.

Particularly when placing cross-cultural or international advertising, the public relations practitioner must be sure the target public will perceive the message's source as credible. If information in an advertisement is not attributed to some specific source, its readers or viewers will usually assume the message came from the client or a paid representative of the client. In an international context, a "slick" or well-produced advertisement may be perceived as American. Even such a vague source as "America" could damage the credibility of the information if it is delivered to a target public who suspects or has had poor relations with U.S. organizations. Advertisements may attribute the information contained in them to celebrities, experts, or neutral persons in order to overcome a bias against large corporations or U.S. interests. If an advertisement is to be based on a celebrity or expert endorsement, that spokesperson or source must be carefully chosen for his or her credibility with the target public. Again, research into the values and beliefs of the target public is essential to making this decision.

Even the most carefully designed advertisement cannot be effective if it is placed in the wrong context. One of the advantages of using paid advertising is the ability to control placement and timing. It is imperative that you take advantage of that control. If you are placing a print, outdoor, or Internet advertisement as part of a public relations campaign, be sure it does not appear next to a competing advertisement. Similarly, when placing a broadcast advertisement, be sure it is not scheduled right before or after another advertisement that will compete with its message. Of course, placing advertisements during times when members of your target public are not reading the paper or watching television also destroys the effectiveness of the advertising tactic. If you are critiquing a campaign, be sure to note the context in which any advertisements were placed.

Mediated Publicity

Advertising may be the first tactic people think of for delivering a message to a large target public. Advertising is a useful tool, but the costs can be high and it is inappropriate for long or complicated messages. The archetype of mediated publicity is the news release. News releases are far less expensive than advertising and can be used to deliver long or complex messages. As we are using the concept here, mediated publicity refers to any public relations tactic that uses existing media to deliver a publicity message. Mediated publicity includes news releases, talk show appearances, press interviews or conferences, movie product placements, and pseudo-events designed to secure news coverage.

The success of mediated publicity depends absolutely on the symbiotic relationship between news media and the public relations practitioner. In this relationship each partner—the journalist and the public relations practitioner—meets some need of the other. The journalist meets the public relations practitioner's need to deliver information to a target public. Further, the journalist lends the credibility of the newspaper, television station, or other medium to the public relations message. The public relations practitioner's contribution to the symbiotic relationship is his or her knowledge, writing skills, and labor. For this relationship to work the public relations practitioner must, in effect, do the journalist's job. Therefore, a successful news release must actually be news, as a journalist would write it.

The majority of public relations practitioners fail to produce news releases that are acceptable to journalists. Most journalists report that they simply discard the vast majority of news releases they are given. To get past this gatekeeping, every news release must be as attractive as possible to the journalist who reviews it. Without trying to demean the journalists with whom public relations practitioners must work, it is helpful to think of journalists as incredibly lazy. The less effort a journalist must expend to use a news release, the more likely it is to be used. A more flattering way to think of journalists is to remember that they will respond to courtesy and honesty. Releases that meet their needs and that are factually accurate are more likely to be used. Regardless of how you conceptualize the relationship with the media, remember that for a news release to have any value at all it must be used by a journalist.

To maximize the chance a news release will be used it must meet the needs of the journalist or editor who reviews it, and those needs vary from medium to medium. Each electronic or print medium has different audiences with different interests. They also have their own deadlines and formats. When writing or placing a news release you should consider the reporter's deadlines, interests, and format. There is little to say about deadlines. Obviously a release that reaches a reporter or editor after their paper is printed or their broadcast completed is useless and cannot be used. Part of the essential research in any public relations campaign is learning when media must receive releases for use. Figures 4.2a and 4.2b show an excerpt from a news release and a clipping of coverage that resulted from the release. As you can see, even successful releases are not used verbatim.

Interests. The first step in securing use of your news release is getting it to a journalist or editor who is interested in the topic. For very large-scale campaigns, those that are national or international in scope, it may be necessary to rely on media directories to identify media people who are interested in your client's message. Certainly for local campaigns, even those set in a local area outside your own country, it is worth the time and effort to make some personal contact with the media. Models and many salesmen use the term "go-sees" to talk about visits to agents, photographers, or customers. A public relations practitioner can use the same kind of visit to discover the needs and interests of local reporters or editors. Other techniques for learning the interests of an individual medium, journalist, or editor is to read or watch the material usually published or broadcast. Many media and media people have patterns in their reporting that reveal biases and interests. If your client's message fits into one of those biases or interests you are more likely to be able to place your message.

When contacting a journalist or editor, even if it is only to send a news release, do not forget to include information on how to contact you. If you have omitted some information or if the reporter wants to know how your release fits with other information, you want to do everything possible to make it easy for him or her to contact you personally. Personal contact and ease of contact add to the symbiotic relationship and increase your chances for placing this and future releases. After-hours availability is particularly important in international public relations, because the practitioner and media representative may live in very different time zones.

National Hispanic Cultural Center Foundation

July 25, 2003

PRESS RELEASE

CONTACT: Stephanie Kozemchak, Marketing & Membership Director
National Hispanic Cultural Center Foundation
1701 4th Street SW, Albuquerque, NM 87102
(505) 766-9858
stephaniek@nhccnm.org

Edna Ruano, Public Relations
Southwest Airlines
2702 Love Field Dr., P.O. Box 36611, HDQ/1PR, Dallas, TX 75208
(214) 792-4309
edna.ruano@wnco.com

-

National Hispanic Cultural Center and Southwest Airlines Unite
First Official Sponsor for the NHCC

The National Hispanic Cultural Center (NHCC) in Albuquerque, New

Mexico, is proud to announce Southwest Airlines as the Official Airline of the

NHCC. "The National Hispanic Cultural Center is proud to begin its first official

sponsorship with our country's most profitable airline. Southwest Airlines'

commitment to reaching out to the national Hispanic community matches the

NHCC's commitment to the cross-cultural appreciation and understanding of

FIGURE 4.2a   Southwest Airlines News Release
Used with permission of Southwest Airlines.

BUSINESSWEEKLY

NEW MEXICO

Cultural center lifts off with Southwest Airlines

Heather Harrison
NMBW Staff

Southwest Airlines announced on Friday that it will be the official airline sponsor of the National Hispanic Cultural Center in Albuquerque. The airline is the first official sponsor for the center, according to center officials.

The airline has signed a one-year agreement with the center. Financial terms of the agreement could not be disclosed.

Southwest will be included in all of the center's print and Web media as the center's official sponsor. In return, Southwest will profile the center in an upcoming issue of the airline's on-board magazine, Spirit, which is displayed in the front seat pocket of passenger seats on airline flights, says Katherine Archuleta, the center foundation's executive director.

Stephanie Kozemchak, marketing and membership director for the center, says Southwest wants to continue to build its marketing efforts to the Hispanic population.

"We're officially honored to have Southwest as our official sponsor," says Kozemchak. "We have the same common mission to reach out to Hispanics through arts and culture projects. Southwest wants to be a part of what the center does and to help us grow.

Southwest Airlines is the Albuquerque International Sunport's largest carrier. The Dallas-based airline reported a total of 300,890 passengers coming in and out of the Sunport for June -- a 1.46% increase over the same period last year.

"Southwest Airlines values its relationships in the community, which have been built over 23

FIGURE 4.2b   Coverage Resulting from News Release at Figure 4.2a

Used with permission of Southwest Airlines.

Format.   If a news release is to be easy for a journalist to use it must be in the format normally written by that journalist. It must be stylistically correct and it must actually be news. Stylistic propriety includes correct spelling and grammar. Remember, if the journalist has to carefully proofread or edit the release it will be easier to just discard it and take the next well-written release. Also, the release must follow the style guide of the medium to which it is submitted. Before submitting a news release, learn what style is used by the target medium. Most newspapers use the Associated Press style guide, but many deviate from standard style, particularly for local names or titles. It is far beyond the scope of this campaign critique model to provide detailed instructions on how to write news releases, but whether you are implementing your own campaign or critiquing the public relations work of others, it is essential that you be familiar with the style used by any medium you target.

Style not only includes the structure of the release itself, it also includes the method of delivery. Current research shows most journalists prefer to receive releases by e-mail. It is not clear whether the preference for e-mail is because it allows journalists to quickly weed out and delete the releases they do not want to use or if it is because having an electronic copy facilitates cut-and-paste editing of the releases they use. Obviously, preferences will vary from medium to medium depending on available equipment and organizational practices. Again, do your research and deliver the release in the way that meets the needs of the individual you hope will publish it.

The most common criticism journalists direct at news releases is that they are not really news. The most efficient way to judge whether a release is really news is to apply the "Si, Lo, Ba, Ti, Un, Fa" test. To apply this test ask yourself if the information contained in the release is significant, local, balanced, timely, unusual, or deals with famous people. Most newsworthy stories are significant, local, balanced, and timely. They often involve unusual events or famous people. Information is significant if it will interest or is seen as important by the readers or viewers of the target medium. It is local if it impacts those readers rather than some distant group. It is balanced if it is presented objectively and does not advance the interest of the public relations client at the expense of honesty or full disclosure. Timely means exactly what it sound like it means. Information that is out of date or has already been reported in other media simply is not news. While not all news releases must deal with unusual events or famous people, including information that is interesting because of its novelty or because it involves people in whom the target public is already interested can add newsworthiness to a release.

When working in an international or intercultural context, a public relations practitioner may find significant cultural variations in what is perceived to be balanced or objective. Some European media, for example, seem to believe that criticism of famous or wealthy people is balanced by their wealth or power. Many Middle-Eastern cultures judge objectivity based on the intent of the message rather than its actual content. Just as you should check a medium's style guide you should also investigate what that medium perceives as news. In order to place a release you have to conform to the culture's values and expectations.

Alternatives to a News Release.   The news release may be the ubiquitous tool of mediated publicity, but often reporters prefer to write their own copy, so the public relations practitioner must do more than just provide a release. These alternative mediated publicity tactics can be divided into two categories. The first such category is information. Essentially the public relations practitioner gives the media representatives information and materials that enable journalists to prepare their own story. The second category is pseudo-events such as press conferences, appearances, interviews, and ceremonies.

The first step in preparing media information or a press kit is to determine exactly what the reporter needs and whether he or she is interested in the story at all. A pitch letter is a communication directed to individual reporters explaining what information is available, detailing why the story is useful or interesting and offering assistance. Even without a specific request from a reporter there are components that should be included in any information provided. For print journalists this information includes fact sheets, photographs, and biographies of significant parties. Fact sheets and biographies are simply references for the reporters that summarize the key points or data the reporter may use to either gain an understanding of the story or to support the article. Photography should be included both to help the reporter's understanding and because photography increases chance of story being used. There is some risk associated with unusual or artistic photography. Such photos may actually decrease the amount of copy used. Therefore, carefully choose photographs if they actually support or carry a message that supports your strategy and objective.

Television reporters, in particular, resist the use of news releases and usually prefer to prepare their own scripts and visual support. However, for all electronic markets, material can be provided by the public relations practitioner who seeks to stimulate coverage of the client's message. Video News Releases (VNR) are rarely used in their entirety but they are often edited for their visual material and do increase the possibility of coverage of their subjects. The expense of producing VNRs is prohibitive for many clients. B-roll footage or stock tape combined with some sound bites from client executives or experts provides a less expensive and useful alternative for distribution to electronic media.

Sometimes even the most creative pitch letter cannot secure coverage for a client's story. In these circumstances, staging an event may make the story appear more significant, timely, or unusual. Names can make news. If celebrities are involved in the event it adds the news element of "famous people." Events staged in order to encourage media coverage are often called pseudo-events. The prefix pseudo means false or spurious. The term pseudo-event may accurately describe events used to encourage news coverage because they are often invented or staged only for the benefit of the media. However, to be effective they must display or represent factual information. When inviting the media to a pseudo-event be sure to explain specifically what will happen and why the event is newsworthy.

The classic pseudo-event is a press conference. Everyone who has paid attention to politics in the United States has seen or heard a press conference at which a candidate announces he or she is running for office or dropping out of a political race. The announcement itself probably would not have been covered if delivered as a news release. However, even when everyone already knows a candidate will run, a press conference is often successful in securing media coverage and it provides the candidate a forum in which to appeal to voters or criticize an opponent.

"We're interested in words, not deeds."

When arranging your own press conference, one task is to carefully select and prepare the speakers. They should be individuals who appear credible both to the media and to the target public. Particularly if the spokespeople are celebrities they should be chosen to consistently appeal to the target public. The stability of the celebrity spokesperson is critical. Recent experiences with professional athletes and actresses show that the popularity or appeal of a spokesperson can change very quickly. Spokespersons should also be able to perform attractively and to answer questions in a way that is both honest and delivers the campaign strategy's message. Even experienced spokespersons should rehearse. Probably the most common and damaging mistake made by speakers at press conferences and in media interviews is to request that some comment be off the record. It would not hurt to remind even experienced speakers that there is no such thing as off the record and that anything said to a reporter can be reported to the target public.

Direct Publicity

Sometimes neither advertising nor mediated publicity can carry the messages required to meet your communication strategy. Advertising may not be available because the client cannot afford that tactic, because there is no existing advertising medium that reaches the target public, or because the client's message is too complex for advertisements. Mediated communication may not be appropriate because the client's message is just not news or because existing media do not reach the target public. In these cases it may be necessary to create a medium to carry the client's message. This tactic of creating a medium is called direct publicity. Media for publicity can be created using print, electronic vehicles, and interpersonal communication or speech.

Printed direct publicity tactics include brochures, in-house publications, newsletters, company magazines, shareholder reports, and annual reports. Each of these communication vehicles must be designed with a specific purpose and public in mind. Because of the convenience and ease of desktop publishing there is no need to have a general-purpose brochure or a generic newsletter. Each document should be designed, written, and delivered to advance a very specific communication strategy with a specific target public. Just as news releases had to meet the interests and stylistic needs of the target media, so the direct publicity print materials must appeal to the interests of the target public and be written in a language and style that captures the attention and understanding of the intended audience. For employee newsletters, these interests and style preferences can be ascertained with employee questionnaires. For other target publics, similar research should be conducted to determine how to produce printed direct publicity materials.

Even the best brochure or newsletter is worthless if it does not overcome the filters of selective exposure and selective attention. Delivery of all these materials must be made from an accurate mailing list or other inventory of target public members.

When selecting material for printed direct publicity, do not forget that not all target publics read. Often where there are multiple languages involved or a public with a low level of literacy, the best print material is not text. Cartoons and posters can be effective ways to deliver simple messages. Even organizational logos or icons can be used to communicate the connection between that organization and some idea. For example, food aid dropped by the United States to refugees in the Iraq in 2003 was carefully packaged in containers marked with a U.S. flag. It was hoped this marking would associate the United States with humanitarian aid in the minds of the food recipients.

Electronic media can be created to reach target publics. Videotapes, CDs, or DVDs can be distributed as part of a political campaign. Employee break rooms can be used to display an institutional motivation or training video, and the client or public relations practitioner's web page and e-mail can be used to distribute messages that advance the campaign's communication strategy. Just as with print tactics, the practitioner who chooses to use electronic media for direct publicity must ensure the content meets the style and interest needs of the target public. Also, the material must be delivered to those in the target audience. One of the most common errors in recent public relations campaigns is too much reliance on web pages. Information on a web page is only useful if members of the target public actually view it. Any campaign using a web page must include some system for drawing members of the target public to the web page. This system must include both information on how to reach the web page and some motivation for those in the target public.

There are significant cultural and national differences in access to electronic media. The more sophisticated a technology, the greater the limitations on its use. Obviously you cannot use electronic media or the Internet for a target public without electricity, but there are additional limitations. For example, a practitioner working on a U.S. senatorial campaign in the rural midwest learned that elderly people are much less likely to view a message delivered via videotape than are younger Americans. He opined that "there is an inverse correlation between the time it takes people to come to the door and the probability they will watch the tape." Older people were both slower to get to the door and less likely to view the tape. They either did not have a video player or were intimidated by the technology.

Face-to-face contact is the most influential tactic. Communication directly from another human being is difficult to avoid. Therefore, it is an effective tool for overcoming selective exposure and selective attention. When the target public has direct contact with a human source of communication audience members are also less likely either to distort the message (engage in selective perception) or derogate the source standing in front of them. Speech and interpersonal communication tactics are also particularly effective ways to reach primitive or nonliterate publics. Even in developed countries there are often social, service, or educational groups who seek speakers for their meetings. A campaign that has available trained speakers in a well-organized speakers' bureau can take advantage of this demand to deliver their campaign messages. The overwhelming disadvantage of interpersonal communication as a public relations tactic is cost—cost both in resources and human energy. However, the high cost is worth paying if the target public is small or if no other tactic can deliver the needed message.

Since speeches or interpersonal interactions cannot be edited, the practitioner who uses such tactics must be very careful to ensure that public address systems work, that the appropriate audience is present, and that the speaker is very well prepared. Any error in delivery or preparation should be noted in a critique of a public relations campaign. If you are the practitioner organizing such a campaign, take every possible precaution to avoid errors in delivery or preparation.

Obviously print, electronic, and interpersonal media are not an exhaustive list of all available direct publicity tactics, and these three categories are not mutually exclusive. Speech can be mixed with electronic media in a tactic where members of the target public are called by telephone. Speech can be mixed with print media by providing a transcript of a spokesperson's speech to newspaper reporters.

Other media include festivals, plays, and ceremonies that can be produced as pseudo-events to stimulate media coverage. These pseudo-events can also be produced with an embedded message directed to an audience that is physically present. Such pseudo-events, like speeches and interpersonal contact, are particularly effective for primitive or nonliterate publics.

Before selecting tactics for implementation, the public relations practitioner must decide whether the client's budget is adequate to fund those tactics. Obviously, tactics beyond the reach of a client's budget must be eliminated.

Budgeting Tactics

The form of a public relations budget depends on the type of practice for which it is prepared. There simply is no one form that fits all situations. For example, practitioners who are in-house counsel and work full time for one public relations client budget very differently than do agency practitioners who represent multiple clients. Here we present one set of terminology and principles that can be applied to any public relations campaign or project.

Indirect Costs. Indirect costs are the expenses of running a public relations office. They typically are not associated with any one campaign or project but are expenses that must be paid in order for the office or agency to operate. Indirect costs include the salaries and fringe benefits of regular office and agency employees. Also included in indirect costs are the expenses associated with keeping the office open, which may include office rent, utility payments, organizational memberships, subscriptions to research services, and office supplies. Depreciation on standard office equipment is also usually treated as an indirect cost.

For an in-house public relations office, these expenses are typically paid by the company served by the public relations office. Since these costs are already paid by the employer, they are not included in a campaign or project budget. A public relations agency must include such costs, indirectly, in its campaign and project budgets as part of a retainer or hourly fees. In many cases, public relations agency employees only receive one-third to one-quarter of the hourly fee billed for their services. The remainder of the hourly fee is used by the agency to pay its indirect costs.

The cost of preparing campaign proposals and bids is also an indirect cost. Agencies usually do not bill clients for the work performed before they were retained, and obviously an agency cannot bill a client for a failed proposal. Some agency directors report that as much as half of their time is invested in preparing proposals that are never funded.

Direct Costs. Direct costs are the expenses that are uniquely associated with one particular campaign or project. Such direct costs may include the expense of hiring extra personnel for a task. For example, if the campaign included a convention display, the fees paid convention models or product demonstrators are a direct cost. Overtime payments required by the project may also be listed as a direct cost. Staff travel expenses including lodging and meals are also often included in direct costs.

Production costs for direct publicity are included as direct costs. These might include printing, video production, graphics design, and reproduction. Project-specific research and evaluation and any equipment that must be purchased exclusively for one campaign or project are also included in this category. Other direct costs include facility rentals such as meeting rooms or exhibit space. Finally, the fees paid for any advertising used in the campaign or project are budgeted as direct costs. Figure 4.3 is a sample budget for a public relations campaign designed to increase awareness of long-term care needs among elderly people in a midwestern U.S. city. It exemplifies how many direct costs are budgeted.

Developing a public relations objective, selecting strategies, and planning tactics are the three steps in actually implementing a public relations campaign. Even before the campaign

FIGURE 4.3   **Sample Budget**

Direct Program Costs in Dollars:	Itemized	Subtotal	Total
Intern			
10 hours/week for 15 weeks @ $8.00/hour			**1,200.00**
Intern assigned to preparation			
of news releases and other tasks			
that are unique to this campaign.			
Database			
41,625 elderly @ 45.00 per CPM			**1,873.13**
Evaluation—Surveys at special event			
¼ sheets on card stock			
500 @ .10	50.00		
Surveys for public hearing			
500 @ 0.7	35.00		**85.00**
Post event survey			
1500 @ .07			**105.00**
Publicity			
Letterheads			
Base printing pricc (10,000)	844.25		
Printer S&H	101.00		**945.25**
Special Event			
Food and Beverage			
1500 people @ 5.00 per plate			**7,500.00**
Announcement News Releases			
Generic News Release			
1,500 sheets @ .07			**105.00**
Television Appearance			
Morning news show appearance w/			
5 minute time slot for interview			N/C
Press kits:			
75 folders @ 1.00	75.00		
525 sheets @ .07	36.75		**111.75**
Informational Advertisements			
¼ page ad, black and white			
in local newspaper			
9 ads @ 3,833.00 each			
(production included)	3,833.00		**34,497.00**
Supplement Advertisements			
¼ page ad in local newspaper supplement edition			
3 ads @ 3,833.00 each	3,833.00		**11,499.00**

FIGURE 4.3   Continued

Direct Program Costs in Dollars:	Itemized	Subtotal	Total
Brochures			
Tri-fold brochure (4-color)			
10,000 @.11	954.00		
Printer S&H	101.00		**1,055.00**
Community Magazine			
Monthly full page, 4 color ad in life style section			**2,550.00**
Radio Commercial			
30 sec spot on morning drive time			
(5:00 A.M.–10:00 A.M.)			
1st Quarter	250.00		
15 ads @ 250.00			**3,750.00**
Public Service Announcement			N/C
Website			
Freelance web developer			**500.00**
Rack Cards	**Itemized**	**Subtotal**	**Total**
Base printing price (41,625)	2,233.44		
+ Aqueous Coating	0.00		
Printing		2,233.44	
Cost each	.06		
+ S&H	481	481.06	
6 sets @ 2,714.50			**16,287.00**
Postage			
249,750 pieces @ .22			**54,945.00**
Newsletter			
Redesign logo			**500.00**
Bus Shelter Ads			
4 one month faces @ 800.00 each for four months	800.00		**$12,800**
Transit Exterior Advertising			
Extra Large Size			
12 ads for one month @ 1,100.00 per ad			**13,200.00**
PR Specialist/Spokesperson			**40,000**
Campaign Subtotal			**198,508.13**
Contingency Fund			
10% contingency fund			**20,354.31**
CAMPAIGN GRAND TOTAL			**218,862.44**

is complete, skilled public relations practitioners begin evaluating their efforts. That evaluation can help guide modification of the strategies and tactics or it can be used to justify the campaign to the client.

Campaign Evaluation

Evaluation is measuring the consequences of your campaign. It is how you determine if the campaign was a success or failure. Other, more complex definitions include assessing the overall effectiveness of the campaign or comparing the relative effectiveness of two or more campaigns. In a 1984 article in *Public Relations Review,* David Dozier identified three forms of public relations evaluation—seat of the pants, scientific dissemination, and scientific impact. At best, seat of the pants evaluations are speculative. They really are not evaluation at all. Dissemination is only one component of communication, so even the most thorough "scientific" measure of dissemination cannot evaluate a public relations campaign's effectiveness. Scientific measures of dissemination only tell you if your message reached a public, not if they believed it or if it affected them.

To realistically evaluate the effectiveness of any campaign or to compare its results to those of another campaign, the measure of effectiveness must be objective, systematic, and empirical. It also must measure impact on the target public. While this may sound difficult or complicated, all you need do to evaluate any public relations campaign is apply the research skills described at the beginning of this chapter to a measurable objective. If you know how to conduct reliable and valid research and you have an operationalized objective statement, evaluation is easy. If you do not know how to conduct reliable and valid research or if you did not have a measurable objective, evaluation is impossible. Campaigns that meet their objectives are successful. Campaigns that do not meet their objective fail. It really is exactly that simple.

For a campaign that was well-designed and implemented, evaluation is very simple. Unfortunately, evaluation is the part of a campaign that is most often omitted or done poorly. Since evaluation can be done easily, why is it so often omitted or done poorly? The explanation could be that practitioners and their clients do not want to know if they failed or that the client does not have the time or resources to evaluate the campaign. However, we suspect that often practitioners do not know how to properly evaluate a campaign.

Real Evaluation versus Selling Snake Oil

Unfortunately, many people who claim to do public relations—many of them well known and representing major public relations firms—are more gifted at selling bad public relations campaigns than they are at producing a good campaign. For these people, vague unreliable measures or measures of invalid data such as message dissemination can be used to make themselves look successful even as they fail. These people are the modern equivalent of the snake oil salesmen of the nineteenth century.

Prior to the Food and Drug Administration regulations, concoctions of little medical value were sold as patent medicines sometimes called snake oil, which often contained alcohol or opium. Salesmen claimed their product could cure everything from fatigue to terminal cancer. Of course, snake oil had no medicinal value, but the alcohol and opium made those who took the concoction feel better. The euphoria created by the intoxicants, coupled with a good sales pitch, made many clients of the snake oil salesmen real advocates of their tonics.

In today's public relations marketplace there are many purported practitioners who sell the public relations equivalent of snake oil in the form of "output evaluation" or "advertising equivalents." These charlatans may tout the artistic quality of a brochure, the number of people who attended a special event, or report the column inches of copy their news releases received. A client CEO may feel good because he was interviewed on a morning talk show and the client may experience euphoria at seeing his or her name in many news releases, but these are the public relations equivalent of an opium-induced high. Just as the snake oil of old made the client feel good while doing nothing to cure him, a public relations campaign that simply creates publicity without advancing the client's organizational goals only feels good—it is not actually good public relations. The evaluations that focus on these feel-good components of the campaign have all the merit of the snake oil salesman's pitch. They are only shams intended to convince the client that their euphoria indicates a public relations cure for their problems.

Many reports of public relations campaigns conclude by calculating the cost of advertising equivalents. These calculations usually involve measuring the number of column inches of print coverage and the number of seconds of broadcast airtime. They then add together how much it would have cost to purchase print advertisements the same size as the column inches of news copy and broadcast advertising the same length as the radio or television news stories. This total number is then compared to the cost of the public relations campaign. When the advertising equivalent cost is lower than the cost of the public relations campaign, the practitioner proudly claims to have saved the client money.

Evaluation of public relations campaigns based on advertising equivalents is fatally flawed for two reasons. First, the advertising industry itself has never produced any evidence that advertising actually changes public behavior or beliefs. More accurately, agenda-setting theory and the research that supports it show that advertising, news coverage, and all media do not influence what people actually think or do. Rather, media only influences what people think about and talk about. So even if the client had purchased the advertising there is no certainty that the money would have facilitated the client's organizational goals. Second, news coverage simply is not equivalent to advertising. Generally, news coverage is perceived as being more credible than advertising so it should have more impact on its auditors. Those who would argue that advertising is more effective than public relations would argue that advertising is controlled. A client purchasing advertising can specify the content, the timing, and the placement of the message. Public relations coverage may be in a more obscure medium or a less desirable location and is usually not limited to the favorable messages that a client would pay an advertiser to place. In short, whether you believe news is more credible or less controlled than advertising, there is no doubt that public relations placements and advertising are not equivalent.

Further arguments against using advertising equivalents as an evaluation of a public relations campaign can be found in *The Fall of Advertising and the Rise of PR* by Al Ries and Laura Ries. These authors describe the advertising industry's infatuation with winning awards. They suggest that one of the major advantages public relations has over advertising is public relations' commitment to actually changing public opinions rather than the production of artistic communications. All of us in public relations welcome the argument that we are superior to advertisers but scrutiny of how many public relations campaigns are evaluated does not support the assertion. Many public relations practitioners still conclude their client reports with "evidence" of success like advertising cost equivalent or number of inches of copy given their press releases. Some even use the fact that their client renewed their contract as the sole evidence of success. In short, none of these measures are evaluation at all. Just as you should reject feel-good evaluations such as amount of coverage, you should reject any campaign evaluation based on advertising equivalent. Just because a client ran an advertising campaign does not mean those advertisements motivated the target public to purchase the client's product, contribute to his charity, or vote for her election. So too, a public relations campaign measured in advertising equivalent is no evaluation of success at all.

The amount of coverage a news release receives only shows that the message was distributed. The message itself may not have been read. Even if the message was read it may not have advanced the client's organizational goals. Consider, for example, the extensive print and electronic coverage of sexual misconduct allegations at the United States Air Force Academy in 2003. The Academy's releases were used. Its commandant even appeared on several national news programs. However, each time the Academy's sources were quoted or their releases were used, that information was coupled with allegations by very credible young women saying they were the victims of rape or other assaults. If we calculate what it would have cost the Academy to purchase the amount of news coverage it received or if we count the minutes of coverage or inches of copy, it would appear they ran a successful campaign. However, the campaign resulted in a massive loss of prestige, removal of major school officials, and a congressional investigation. The campaign hurt virtually every organizational goal of the Air Force Academy.

Evaluation is simple but must be preceded by a carefully crafted and measurable objective. As you critique the campaigns of others be sure to look for an evaluation that actually measures the desired change in the target public. If you notice a campaign that does not measure change in the target public you should see that as a real weakness of the campaign. Also, as you design campaigns yourself always be sure your objective is specific and operationalized so that you can evaluate your own campaign. Occasionally you will learn, to your pain or embarrassment, that your campaign did not succeed. At least you will know what did not work and you can avoid repeating the same mistakes again.

Primary research tools are used to properly evaluate a public relations campaign. Those tools were described in Chapter 2. The descriptions will not be repeated here, but we recommend that you review them for guidance in any evaluation or critique of a campaign evaluation method.

REFERENCES AND SUGGESTED READINGS

Blount, D., & and Cameron, G. T. (1997). VNRs and air checks: A content analysis of on-air use of video news releases. *Journalism and Mass Communication Quarterly, 73*(4), 890–904.

Dozier, D. M. (1984). Program evaluation and the roles of practitioners. *Public Relations Review, 10*(2), 13–21.

Dye, T. R. (2002). *Understanding public policy* (10th ed.). Upper Saddle River, NJ: Prentice Hall.

Elsasser, J. (July, 1997). Escape from Measure-Not Land. *Public Relations Tactics,* 30–31.

Hon, L. C. (1997). What have you done for me lately? Exploring effectiveness in public relations. *Journal of Public Relations Research, 9*(1), 1–30.

Hon, L. C. (1998). Demonstrating effectiveness in public relations: Goals, objectives and evaluation. *Journal of Public Relations Research, 10*(2),103–135.

Ries, A., & Ries, L. (2002). *The fall of advertising and the rise of PR.* New York: Harper Collins.

5

The Intercultural Communication Context: Preparation for International Public Relations

L. BROOKS HILL and LYNDA DEE DIXON

Chapters 2, 3, and 4 described a model for the design and evaluation of public relations campaigns. Each of the five components of that model affects and is affected by the environment in which it is applied. Research must be designed to accommodate the culture of the subjects studied. A campaign objective must be consistent with the culture of the client and of the publics to be changed by the campaign. The theories upon which strategies are based must fit within the culture where the strategies are to be implemented. Tactics can only use the media available in the target culture, and the system of evaluation must be appropriate to the culture in which the campaign was administered. In short, even a public relations campaign based on a thorough understanding of research, objectives, strategies, tactics, and evaluation can only be successful if the client, public relations practitioner, and the target publics all share the same culture. Any successful public relations campaign must be designed with sensitivity for the culture of the client, the practitioner, and the target publics.

While it is easy to say a campaign must accommodate the culture of its participants, it is particularly difficult to make those accommodations when the client, the public relations practitioner, or a target public are from different cultures. To facilitate those accommodations, this chapter examines intercultural communication and fits that emphasis into an international communication and public relations context, providing the tools for developing or critiquing public relations campaigns that cross cultural or national borders.

Intercultural Communication Perspective

Of the several approaches, perspectives, and theories for the study of human communication and its professional applications, a contextual approach is probably most appropriate to discuss at this point. As Figure 5.1 displays, communication can be approached from the standpoint of the distinctive context within which it occurs. These contexts range from

FIGURE 5.1   Contextual Approach for Communication Study

communication with one's self (intra-personal communication) to the most expansive international communication. To conceptualize these varied contexts in terms of concentric circles emphasizes how the more expansive contexts include the less expansive ones they encompass. In other words, no matter how expansive the context, one cannot exclude considerations that originate in the perceptual patterns, self-concept, and other very personal concerns of the intra-personal level. To communicate effectively in any context, one must understand all of the communication events occurring in the smaller circles subsumed by that context's circle. For example, to understand intercultural communication you must also understand the organizational communication, small group communication, interpersonal communication, and intra-personal communication occurring within the cultures involved. Examining communication from this general approach encourages us to consider the interrelationships among branches of communication study, instead of myopically viewing one specific area exclusively.

The contextual approach to communication study surfaced in several places during the 1960s and 1970s. L. Brooks Hill and his colleagues used a version of the contextual approach to reorganize their graduate program at Oklahoma University in the early 1970s. In his basic communication textbook, Keltner (1970) used a contextual approach to organize communication study and added the pie-shaped crossover of different contexts (similar to that in Figure 5.2) with three prominent sets of functions he labeled utilitarian, aesthetic, and therapeutic. More recent works routinely employ the contextual approach, but tend to neglect a model or the inherent limitation that requires some adjustment for the multi-context activities and processes.

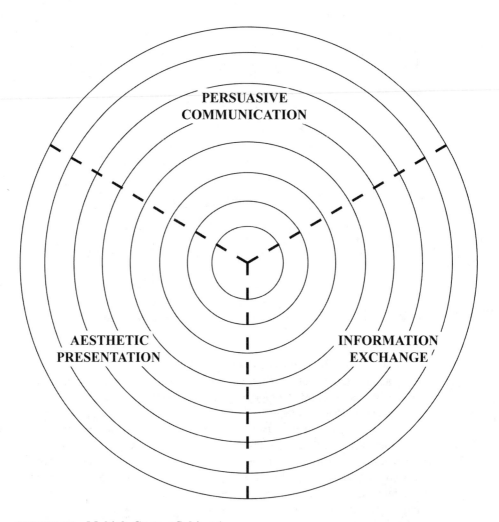

FIGURE 5.2   Multiple Context Subject Area

The contextual approach, like any approach, has limitations. For present purposes, one of the inherent limitations forces us to address the primary concerns of this chapter. Many of the very interesting subject areas of human communication study and applications do not fit neatly within the concentric circles. Consider the general area of persuasion, for example, which seems to cross virtually all contexts. This weakness of the concentric circles calls for the addition of a feature that addresses the challenging variation of persuasion in real situations. A pie-shaped slice of the concentric circles captures the multiple contexts that persuasion cuts across.

Similarly, specific professions can be seen as cutting across these circles and slices. Persuasion and public relations are inextricably related, and public relations also has aesthetic and informative aspects. The pie-shaped slices in Figure 5.3 can be overlapped to

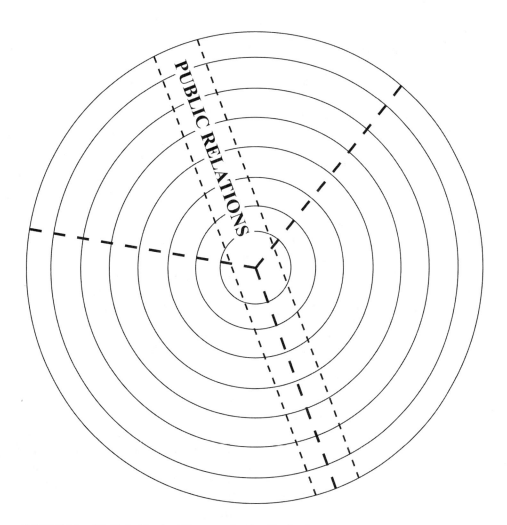

FIGURE 5.3   Multiple Context Communication Professions

indicate the interdependence of persuasion and public relations with many other aspects of human communication. An examination of these simple models reveals the intersection of intercultural communication with the areas of persuasion and international public relations. This chapter pursues this line of analysis and elaborates on the critical relation of intercultural communication and international public relations.

Before going further, we must define several components of these models. *Communication* is the development, adaptation, and transmission of messages between and among people to achieve some desired effect. Communication involves a dynamic set of processes that employ all sorts of symbols to induce meaningful responses. Intercultural communication obviously emphasizes the dimension of culture in the basic communication processes. Like water to a fish, culture is an all-encompassing set of ideas and behaviors that are taken for granted and used as a point of departure for coping with the world. As people from different cultures communicate, intercultural effectiveness is contingent on how well they recognize the limitations of their own culture and adapt to the differing features of other cultures. The primary index of effectiveness centers on how carefully people manage their own tendencies and synchronize them with alternate ways of thinking and acting. International communication deals more with the movement of influence between and among national and supra-national groups, and has historically drawn its distinctiveness from concerns for political decision making and the mass media.

In its most primitive form, public relations can be seen as a response to a client's need for acceptance by a single public. To secure that acceptance, a public relations practitioner must develop, adapt, and transmit messages that advance the interests of the client to the target public. More sophisticated conceptualizations of public relations embrace multiple publics, including the members of the client organization, varied groups of people in society who might determine the success or failure of the client's organization, and individuals who represent the media that foster transmission of the message about the institutions to other publics. Thus contemporary public relations tend to emphasize at least three major publics: in-house internal communication of the organizational message, external communication with people outside the organization, and media relations. International public relations, like international communication, expands to add cultural complications to each cluster of publics. The complexities of cultural variation complicate communication (1) with the internal publics as the organization tries to integrate greater cultural diversity in its work force (Hon & Brunner, 2000), (2) with the external publics as the message must be adapted to a wide variety of cultural perspectives (Berger, 1999), and (3) with the media, who are more culturally heterogeneous than is often presumed.

These preliminary definitions immediately call attention to the central role of culture and intercultural communication in the study and practice of international public relations (Zaharna, 2000). Communication is the essential feature of public relations. With the increase in workplace diversity, globalization, and organizational mergers, cultural concerns have become essential for effective public relations. These major trends not only impose intercultural concerns, but also international concerns as well. Such rapidly increasing emphasis on easily seen international concerns can obscure the relevance of the basic concepts depicted near the center of Figure 5.1. No matter how expansive our focal context might be, the primary concern must be individual people with personal and group needs and pressures. How a public relations practitioner influences their thoughts and actions ultimately determines success in dealing with the so-called mass audience. Some organizations give little emphasis to the internal audience. With increasing use of outsourcing procedures, effective organizations must not only deal with the diversity of their intra-cultural workforce, but also address the unique problems with the relations between and among the primary internal public and the groups that serve as out-sources. Failure to deal effectively with these problems can increase cost, lead to overextension, or even cause infrastructure collapse. On a parallel with this line of reasoning, one can easily determine the implications of intercultural communication for maximum effectiveness with the external public and media representatives.

One weakness of research in this area is the separate perspectives used to study intercultural communication and international communication. Intercultural communication is often studied from an interpersonal perspective, and international communication is usually studied from a mass media orientation. Intercultural communication tends to come out of the more humanistic, rhetorical tradition associated with the social sciences of psychology, sociology, and anthropology, whereas international communication has come from a more professional media orientation associated with journalism and political science. Recent developments, however, are expanding each subject and thus cultivating the areas of overlapping concerns. Even though each area has independent contributions to make, the synergy developed by their combination will make even greater impact on international public relations.

The next section summarizes the salient features of intercultural communication. Many textbooks are available on this topic for the motivated student to pursue beyond this chapter. These texts are often separated by their approach. Some take a primarily social scientific perspective, and others take a more humanistic perspective. Our approach draws from both perspectives as we build a position more closely aligned with an artistic framework devoted to the practical use of what we know for the student of international public relations.

Salient Features of Intercultural Communication

Central to the study of human communication is the recognition of homo sapiens as a symbol-using, information processing system. Figure 5.4 is a summary model of the several processes involved in this human system. This information processing model is based on the nature of human perceptions, and progresses through the cognitive processing of this information to the final stages of using information as they structure and manage it to deal with the world. The following explanation of this model accents the many ways that culture influences the ultimate development of a worldview and coping procedures for dealing with the socially generated world.

Within the perspective of this model, the world is a constant source of accessible information. Think of a person as a funnel; some information gets into the funnel, but most does not. No one knows what they do not get, and they presume that what they get is all there is. Herein lies the first major problem of all human interaction: no one person has exactly the same information as anyone else. This basic problem grows as one further examines how people gather this information. Humans are connected to the world through five senses. As

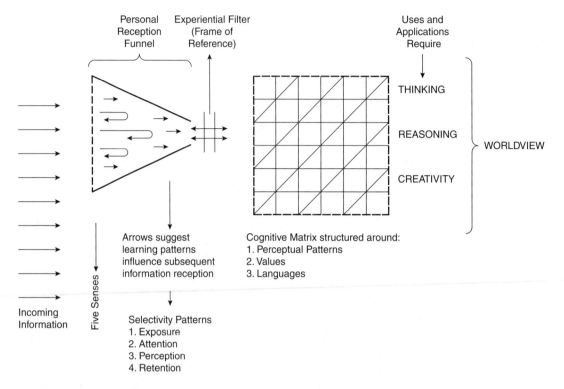

FIGURE 5.4   Information Processing–Worldview Model

people detect information through one or more of their senses, they are simultaneously programming those senses for future operations. The programming of these senses is often referred to as learning selectivity patterns. Selective exposure, attention, retention, and perception were introduced in Chapter 3, in the discussion of a target public's resistance to change. Here those same concepts are applied to intercultural sensitivity. People learn to expose themselves selectively to certain sources of information and tend to neglect others, and selectively pay attention to certain important parts of the information they have selected for exposure. People selectively perceive how this information fits into what they already know as they may need to accent, delete, or modify certain parts. After the initial encounter with this information, people selectively recall only the most useful parts of what they gathered as they try to use the information. To communicate effectively people must first recognize the distance between what is available and what they actually apprehend, and then understand how the resulting differences impede success.

Over time, a developing person combines a wide diversity of information into a cognitive framework that serves as a frame of reference for future acquisition and processing of information, as a storage system for managing the huge quantity of information that will be amassed across a life span, and as the processing network for developing tactics and strategies that apply perceived information to dealing with the people, things, and ideas in the world. No one fully understands this cognitive framework, but some of its components and functions are known. It can help to think of the cognitive framework as a multi-dimensional matrix that includes at least three prominent sets of intersecting lines. Imagine one set of horizontal lines representing perceptual patterns, a vertical set representing values, and a third diagonal set created by language. The spaces created by the intersection of these lines produces a huge matrix with many categories into which information is labeled and stored. Either incoming information or the movement of information within these spaces may serve to intensify certain areas according to their relative importance or how much an individual values them.

The use of information in the cognitive matrix basically involves how people relate the bits and pieces together to develop tactics and strategies for dealing with the world. At the most fundamental level, the acts of taking incoming information and fitting it into the matrix or simply relating pieces of information that are already in the matrix constitute *thinking. Reasoning* is a more systematic form of thinking in predetermined and socially acceptable patterns. If someone says to you that you are being reasonable, what they are saying is that your actions reveal how you have been thinking in predictable and socially acceptable ways, according to what society has determined is a reasonable way of doing anything. *Creativity* is another form of thinking, but it differs from reasoning. In contrast to being reasonable, creativity refers to thinking and acting in unpredictable ways, and social acceptability is less of a concern. In other words, what people do with the information they receive is to work it around in their cognitive matrix and then use it to help them deal with any and all situations they might encounter.

Now that you have a perspective on the person as an information processing system, consider how this perception-based system can be influenced from the beginning to end by features of culture. The environment provides the information from which we might choose. So much of the environment is carefully constructed by fellow members of a culture, people are unaware of what they are not getting, either because the information is simply not there or because it is represented in a culturally distinctive fashion. Through parents, peers, and the rest of society they learn what they should look for and how to perceive it. Social rewards and punishment even encourage them to recall or forget certain information as they process it for decisions. Because this socially constructed filter is so critical for social acceptability, people are gradually led to perceive that this perspective is right, that it is the most accurate and most in harmony with the world. One major result of this presumption of rightness is a strong tendency for people to judge negatively whatever they perceive as different. Humans are unable to eradicate their frame of reference and this tendency to judge, but they can learn to recognize differences as differences and to arrest the tendency to become judgmental. This is far more easily said than done, but continued efforts can develop your skills.

Your cognitive matrix and its use represent your individual worldview. Illustrations that interrelate the dimensions of this matrix into a functional worldview can help you manage its potential more effectively. Humans have five senses and an ability to integrate information derived from one or more of them. This integrative capacity may well be what some people call a sixth sense. Each of our five senses has many patterns, and these patterns variously interweave with each other as well as with values and symbols. Consider one pattern from only one sense, for example. When we learn to read and write a language, we simultaneously develop a visual scanning pattern. Those of us who are primarily literate in English have a predominant left to right, horizontal scanning behavior that will influence how we gather information in any situation. This would be different from the scanning behavior of someone who is literate in Arabic (right to left, horizontal) or Japanese (top to bottom, vertical). This example represents only one pattern for one sense, and we have many patterns with each sense, plus the lesser-known integrative capabilities, that create a perceptual foundation of our cognitive matrix. From a cultural perspective, people literally sense the world differently, resulting in varied worldviews. As you begin to think about this information, you should not be surprised at how cultures vary in how they think and reason and how wildly different their creative tendencies might be.

The second part of this cognitive matrix is values. This simply means the positive, negative, or neutral weight or importance people assign to anything in their worldview. Represented by the vertical lines in the cognitive matrix of Figure 5.4, these values are learned, but variable, depending on their relative importance in a person's life. Some writers identify certain values at the core of our lives, and these central values have little variability. As we move out from this core to less important aspects of our lives, we may vary significantly in the relative weighting of items. To appreciate another culture we must learn what its members value most highly and where their flexibility is most likely situated. Not only will this help us adapt to their priorities, but it will also help us better understand their viewpoints, because the values become inseparable from the perceptual patterns. If we value something highly, our perceptions will reflect that tendency, just as nonchalance may indicate a perceived lack of importance about something peripheral to our lives. Someone from outside our culture may readily detect how our values influence our perceptual patterns, but those inside the culture typically cannot separate them. Especially as we approach our core values, separating values from perceptual patterns is extremely difficult because what seems important is "really that way."

Languages, both verbal and nonverbal, comprise the third major component of the cognitive matrix, represented in Figure 5.4 by the diagonal lines. Languages have two primary functions. One is to label and facilitate the organization and structure of the world. In this regard, human symbols are thoroughly combined with perceptual patterns and values to promote psychological adaptation to the world and to render the cognitive matrix more coherent. The second and more obvious function of languages is to facilitate communication and thus the necessary social adjustment in the world. These two functions appear to be independent, but are actually not so. As people communicate, they are using languages to confirm, disconfirm, and otherwise expand their perceptions and values. Through social interaction people simultaneously engage in what sociologists call the "negotiation of reality." Communication, therefore, involves a psychological as well as a sociological dimension, and both dimensions become inextricably related to the development of each human culture. Learning a second language, for example, not only introduces us to more effective ways to communicate with its primary users, it also helps us to learn the ways they perceive and structure their world. Thus a preferred outcome of learning a language is the partial acquisition of the culture of its users.

Learning how culture molds behavior requires us to examine the function of society. Just as a cognitive matrix helps people structure the psychological aspects of the world, society creates another overlapping matrix of norms, rules, and roles that help people determine how to behave. *Norms* are literally the typical patterns of socially acceptable behavior. More importantly, however, these normal behaviors (1) serve as standards for evaluating acceptable social behavior, (2) reflect how other people in a culture expect people to behave, and (3) entail the consequences of a failure to comply. We can loosely categorize norms into three general types. Some are very formal and codified; we call these *laws* and the consequences of noncompliance are very explicit. Another set is also formal, but has less extensive application and consequences. Sometimes these norms are explicitly codified into manuals, but they tend to apply within subgroups such as the major organizations in a society. The more subtle norms of the third category are implicit with varied consequences for noncompliance. For example, laws may govern traffic patterns around a university, and manuals may govern who reports to whom about what within the university. While no one in our office has ever recorded specific guidance about brewing new coffee, when you take the last cup, everyone knows how to pressure the violator into compliance. To implement these norms, rules are developed that specify how one is supposed to behave and what happens if one does not. In other words, rules are the means for implementing norms. Anyone who visits another culture quickly notices variations in norms and rules, but learning exactly what they are and the levels of tolerance for violations is difficult. Even more challenging is coming to know how violations can affect relationships with people in the culture.

This social matrix of norms and rules is situated within an overarching set of social roles. Simply stated, one prominent view defines society as a structured set of roles or expectations of how people should behave in whatever positions they hold. "How to behave" is best understood as what people expect you to do and what you expect yourself to do when performing the role involved in a position. When, for example, a person is in the position of teacher, students expect this person to act in certain ways and relate more predictably and comfortably within this understood set of behaviors. When that teacher assumes the roles of spouse or parent, then other expectations are imposed, making relations with significant others more predictable and comfortable. Obviously, we learn our roles as we develop within our society. Through the use of rewards and punishments we internalize these roles, and they gradually become a part of the socially constructed world of our culture. Even a casual consideration of another culture will reveal variations in the expectations the members have of each other in various roles and the rigor with which they enforce the consequences of misbehavior. Much of this structure of norms, rules, and roles is like an iceberg, just below the observable surface. Learning how to operate effectively within another culture requires acquisition of its social skills.

Perhaps the most significant aspect of intercultural communication grows out of the categorization tendencies built into the cognitive and social matrix. One way or another, people come to know that the world is far more complicated than they can manage, so they learn to simplify it through the use of categorization. Out of necessity people categorize to organize and make their world predictable, and then impose their categories on reality, often (not surprisingly) finding exactly what they expected. Without some flexibility people will distort and restrict much of what they encounter. Just as hardening of the arteries can become a fatal threat to physical health, hardening of the categories is a fatal threat to intellectual and social health. Not only do people categorize, but they also use their language to label the category, and this tendency gives the illusion of permanence to the categorization. The tendency to categorize can create not only a misleading worldview, but also leads to stereotyping and ethnocentrism. When people stereotype, to use Walter Lippmann's original metaphor, they take a mental snapshot of a group of people or situations and freeze them for consequent application when they encounter another situation with similar features (1922). Rather than learn the individual peculiarities of the specific case, people impose the stereotype for good or ill. When repeatedly used in a negative fashion, stereotypes lead to seriously adverse *prejudice* that can obscure perspectives of the value and potential ability of other people and other features of the world.

As people apply these information-processing skills in the world, they also apply this perspective to themselves. The result of this application is social identity, a crucial dimension of personhood and a major determinant of social behavior and expectations. In other words, people perceive themselves according to social pressures and categorizations. They locate themselves within a social order according to many possibilities, such as gender, age, religion, ethnicity, and occupation. Location in the social order then helps people determine what they can reasonably expect from others, what they can expect of themselves, and how they fit into the vast scheme of social relationships.

As we literally discover ourselves, we also discover how we group with others of similar characteristics. The upshot of this pattern of social grouping is less, rather than more, harmony. Instead of homogenization of groups into a smaller number of broader cultures, we are encountering increasing prominence of subcultures and co-cultures based on ethnic, religious, and other group identities. Whereas this cultural pluralism has some positive features, it has also led to intense conflicts within and between nations all over the globe. One pervasive response to subcultural struggles and conflicts has been an expanding emphasis on human rights. Collectively these personal, group, and cultural developments have created a new dimension of political relations that is often referred to as minority politics. Despite the positive aspects of a strong social identity, it can also seriously complicate social relations. On the one hand, an organization may want to protect human rights and maintain harmony as a social unit, but understanding the varied interpretations of human rights and the best ways to preserve them in light of pressures from diverse groups is a major problem when subcultures and their diverse worldviews are included in the mix.

When we place ourselves at the center of the world, this is called *egocentrism*. Placing our culture at the center is called *ethnocentrism*. Both tendencies are difficult to control, but their significance as obstacles to interpersonal and intercultural communication is major. We can all recognize the problems of a friend who constantly imposes his personal interests on us, but who fails to recognize the imposition. Unfortunately, we have even greater difficulty recognizing the imposition of our culture. Because culture includes our collective values, we have trouble separating this imposition from what is "right." This problem is further exacerbated in U.S. culture by a superiority complex that derives from our international status, power, and affluence. Until we can see ourselves as others see us, we will continue to have trouble recognizing our ethnocentric tendencies. What we have created around the world is a weak version of nineteenth-century imperialism, but this time what we are imposing could be more accurately labeled cultural imperialism. As recent surveys strongly reinforce, our credibility and status around the world is decreasing rapidly, and the explanations accent our superiority complex, cultural imperialism, and ethnocentrism. As representatives of U.S. and Western interests, we must better understand the cultural underpinnings of these attitudes and control our ethnocentrism. To achieve these goals we must develop a plan of action. This chapter concludes by describing how each of us, as individuals, can most successfully function in an intercultural or international setting.

Personal Adaptation for Intercultural Effectiveness

By this point, the relevance of intercultural communication for effectiveness in international public relations should be apparent. How to use this perspective is now the primary focus. Obviously, before you can represent a client or design a public relations campaign targeting a large public from another culture, you must first be able to deal with representatives of that culture as individuals. This section presents guidelines or suggestions to help you understand and communicate more effectively in intercultural or international settings. We begin by suggesting your own mental preparation and then suggest practical skills necessary for success.

Preliminary Guidance and Mental Preparation

If you learned nothing else from the discussion of intercultural communication, you should realize that one essential step toward intercultural sensitivity is to know your own culture as well as possible. This may seem like a very simple task, but the most difficult challenge for intercultural communication students is to discuss their own culture. Because so much of one's own culture is taken for granted, people rarely examine its features. As a result they are often confused by the reactions of people from other cultures. Why, they ask, are "those people" aggravated? What did we do, or not do, to create difficulty? People need to create some sort of cultural mirror into which they can look and discover. Despite the impossibility of such a creation, we can learn from its suggestion. We can ask what others think about us, listen carefully to their responses, and then construct a sketch of our strengths and weaknesses. From this information we can build a more systematic way to adapt and to increase our understanding of others' reactions to our culture and us.

No matter what group the public relations experts may represent, they necessarily deal with individuals in all aspects of their work. When these individuals are from different cultural backgrounds, several preliminary warnings are important. *Do not presume that people from other cultures are similar to you and your culture.* Remember that people find it easier to impose their predispositions onto the world. This holds especially true for other people. If we presume they are similar to us, we begin to seek out confirming information and to suppress disconfirming information. This tendency with people is further complicated because we often attach a moral imperative to our impositions. We like to think that people are basically good in the same way that we are good, sharing our positive motivations, expectations, and versions of success. That way of thinking can be seriously misleading, as what constitutes goodness and success may differ widely. Another complication in our desire to maintain cordial relations is a tendency to manipulate feedback so that we mutually confirm what we want to perceive, regardless of the differences involved. The

"Joe, these people say they want flesh-colored Band-Aids."

Source: © The New Yorker Collection 1963, William O'Brian from cartoonbank.com.
All Rights Reserved.

pleasant smile on the face of an Asian negotiator does not mean that they agree with you or necessarily like you! As we communicate with others we simultaneously convey two messages: the explicit message that seemingly justifies the communication and a more implicit message suggesting how we want the other person to respond to our message and us as individuals. Learning a culture increases our sensitivity to these varied and potentially conflicting messages.

An obvious point of departure for anyone working with people from another culture is this: *Learn cautiously as much as you can about other cultures.* Whereas this preparation may be indispensable, it includes some negative potential as well. The disciplines of anthropology, communication, and political science provide many approaches to the characterization of another culture. Each approach may have its strengths and weaknesses, but they all tend to provide a profile that lends itself to stereotyping. That is to say, people often tend to characterize another culture based on the typical characteristics of its average members, and then use this characterization as the basis for predicting individual behaviors. Between the cultural profile and individual behaviors are several intervening factors that make these predictions dangerous. Individual values, self-concepts, and personalities may vary significantly among members of a culture. This variety will lead to complications in predictions of an individual's behavior. This line of thought strongly confirms another preliminary guideline: *no matter how much you know about another culture, learn to treat its members as individuals.* As you come to know the individuals, your grasp of the culture will improve.

Most people prefer to deal with people similar to themselves. As the old adage contends, "Birds of a feather tend to flock together." This creates a pleasant comfort zone where people are not required to be constantly on guard. When they encounter someone from another culture, the differences push them out of their comfort zone. This discomfort causes an increase in adrenaline flow and causes more anxiety. Thus their defensive system becomes more alert and prepared to cope. On the one hand, this syndrome can be very exciting and prepares people well to deal with the uncertainty they face. If they have the necessary skills to manage this uncertainty, the results can be gratifying. If they lack the necessary skills, the resulting frustration can make them revert to their predispositions and either impose those predispositions or withdraw completely from the interaction. On the other hand, whether exciting or frustrating, the continued exertion of this syndrome can lead to culture fatigue, when people simply grow very tired of the constant need to explain the obvious or to accommodate confusion. Without relief, culture fatigue can worsen into culture shock, a strong disorientation that compromises people's responses and threatens their longer-term potential to deal effectively with people and situations.

Not all of our preliminary guidance has such negative potential. The experience of dealing well with people from other cultures can significantly expand your cognitive and social matrices and enhance your life skills. With this increase in cognitive complexity, you become more cosmopolitan in your outlook and potential. Expressed another way, you enhance your intercultural communication competence. Essentially, the idea of competence refers to the basic human potential for behaving more effectively. The literature suggests intercultural communication competence will include at least knowledge of the culture, motivation to interact successfully, and a repertory of effective skills. These three dimensions of intercultural communication competence are interdependent: The more we come to know about cultures, our own included, the better we can know ourselves and the better we are able to deal with others regardless of how different they might be. From this cultural awareness we can come to understand better our motivations and how they are interrelated with the interaction of other people (Freitag, 2002).

Practical Guidelines and Skills Development

Beyond this preliminary guidance, you need to learn the more specific skills that lead to effectiveness in intercultural communication (Gudykunst and Kim, 2003; Gudykunst, 2004). Some authors argue that these skills are a set of traits within the individual that can be applied when needed. Other authors argue that the skills of intercultural communication effectiveness are observable behaviors confirmed through the interaction between people. We would argue that both positions contribute to an understanding of the skills necessary to deal well with people from other cultures. Among the traits identified are mindfulness, patience, tolerance, self-control, extroversive tendencies, recognizing the value of people, and adaptive sensitivity. Among the observable skills are controlled emotions, display of respect, nonjudgmental reactions, interaction management, performance of roles, and openness. Obviously the skills simply actualize the traits, so we will examine them as they combine.

During the 1960s the Useems presented the idea of a *third culture* to improve understanding of effective international exchange (1967). Their position proposed that international effectiveness involves the negotiation of a zone of shared advantages drawn from the representative's cultures, a zone of mutual benefits they called a third culture. One can easily understand how this international exchange perspective was adapted and expanded by many authors to apply to intercultural relations more generally. Pursuing this analogy, communication between people from different cultures could result from one group simply imposing its perspective and forcing another person or group to comply. In fact, this was historically a major problem with colonialism, wherein one national culture was simply imposed on the subordinate group. The Useems' position suggested a mutually beneficial model wherein genuine intercultural communication results from building rapport and respect between cultures and creating a new ground for interaction. This position was designed to offer an alternative to the imperialistic colonialism that had so devastated much of the world. In a similar vein, a provocative symposium at International Christian University in Tokyo, Japan, addressed the profound question "Communicating Across Cultures for What?" (1976). Their collective answer was a strong confirmation of an intercultural communication perspective built on mutual respect and the long-term cost benefit of building a better world community.

Mindfulness.   Most textbooks about intercultural communication encourage readers to behave more thoughtfully when dealing with people from other cultures. This deceptively simple advice involves two lines of thought. On the one hand, people generally pursue the path of least resistance and often think and act with little thought. The easiest path is to perform as if one is on autopilot, programmed to behave as in the past with minimal adjustment to the unique features of new situations. With so many unknowns involved in intercultural communication, this path is cluttered with accidents waiting to happen. On the other hand, one can be mindful or alert to the differences and adapt to variations encountered. Mindfulness is obviously a necessary aspect of intercultural communication effectiveness, but alone it is insufficient. People must have at their disposal a repertory of skills and the motivation to adapt them to each and every situation. What follows is an introduction to several sets of interrelated skills built around the preferred traits and behaviors that are essential for your repertory.

Patience.   Patience is closely correlated with mindfulness because the first step to becoming more patient is thoughtful consideration of what and why you are doing what you have chosen to do. Patience is also closely correlated with openness and tolerance, our next topics, but patience also has a distinctive temporal dimension, especially in contemporary U.S. culture. Patience primarily involves taking the time to consider your actions, listening carefully to others, and calmly implementing your choice of action. The intercultural communication literature often uses a monochronic/polychronic continuum to illustrate the various cultural orientations to time. The U.S. culture tends toward the monochronic end of the continuum, where people are typically very time conscious, organize their lives around careful segmentation of their time, and generally create a social rhythm that reinforces the efficient use of time. Cultures with a polychronic orientation are much less concerned with such temporal constraints and can appear inefficient to U.S. observers. Consistent with this temporal framework, a monochronic lifestyle adversely impacts a person's patience, as they often do not have the time to "bother" with what appears to be inefficient. The skills of patience must be deliberately cultivated by people in U.S. culture because so much of our culture works against those skills.

Openness.   Patience is an essential aspect of openness, as people cannot consider alternatives well if they are impatient. Openness, however, goes beyond patience to involve the consideration of alternative courses of action and unpredicted reactions to ideas. This is where U.S. tendencies to efficiency complicate people's effectiveness. We may all realize the importance of considering alternatives, but we often take shortcuts to simplify our approach. In this fashion we may choose a solution that deals efficiently and expeditiously with a problem, but may ultimately fail because we neglected something that seemed at the time peripheral or confusing.

Developing openness requires that you examine how you personally cope with violations of your expectations, because people from other cultures often do what seems unpredictable. When you encounter such violations, how should you respond? The first step is to recognize the difference, then control your initial reaction by listening ever more carefully, and thus opening further the set of alternatives for consideration. These simple steps will permit the creativity of all parties to surface and not allow a socially constrained sense of reason to limit your potential. Sounds easy and promising, doesn't it? Rest assured, success with openness requires cultivated skills, especially when you are dealing with the unknowns of other cultural perspectives.

Tolerance for Ambiguity.   Tolerance for ambiguity represents a variant of the openness for alternative courses of action. Although these two aspects overlap, tolerance for ambiguity is sufficiently different to require separate consideration. Ambiguity is most easily treated as a language variable. Because there are a finite number of symbols in human language to deal with an infinite world and because people's personal experiences with symbols and their referents are so varied, the symbols of human languages are inherently ambiguous. Ordinarily, the context in which these symbols are used helps highlight the intended meaning, but even this assistance leaves room for varied interpretation. Adding culture to this situation creates even greater ambiguity, especially in terms of what one can reasonably expect the context to provide. The literature identifies cultures according to whether they are *high context* or *low context,* referring to how dependent people in a culture are on contextual variables to help interpret the language. For example, people in the U.S. culture are explicit in their verbal language use and rely minimally on contextual information to aid the interpretation of their messages. In stark contrast, people from Japanese culture are far less explicit verbally and much more dependent on contextual factors to aid in message interpretation. Such differences create great difficulties interpreting and disambiguating a message. For some people with a low tolerance for ambiguity, this intercultural challenge becomes overwhelming, whereas others with a higher level of tolerance for ambiguity can cope easily. As indicated before, you must first examine your own tendencies, determine your level of tolerance for ambiguity, and apply the skills of mindfulness and patience to reduce the ambiguity to a manageable level. Even with these skills you must learn the behaviors of people in other cultures in order to know how to disambiguate the symbols they provide. A person's social status, indirect reference to social protocol or rituals, and subtle nonverbal expressions may be crucial to understanding what is actually said. So, just being mindful and patient is alone insufficient, one must also know much more about the culture.

Self-Control.   Growing out of the concern for patience, openness, and tolerance is an obvious need for self-control. Although this is easier said than done, you must regulate your emotional reactions. Consider the carefully controlled language diplomats use, sometimes called *diplomatese.* The very guarded, careful use of verbal and nonverbal behavior provides a way to regulate the personal and perhaps more emotional reactions of diplomats in whatever situations they encounter. In this somewhat guarded fashion they can retain their capacity to listen ever more carefully and treat reasonably whatever occurs. They recognize how damaging an off-the-cuff remark or an emotional outburst could easily become.

Most people do not have the diplomats' special training and extensive experience, but do have some personal skills at "keeping cool." What we recommend is a system of cautions that can alert you when you are most likely to "lose it." By knowing these signs, you can then exert additional energy to maintain a more controlled demeanor. In class, we often ask our students to first make a list of what really aggravates them; then we discuss how to recognize when those symptoms surface and develop tactics to meet those demands. Since no two lists are the same and cultural situations will introduce new variations, you must continually update and reassess your tendencies and behaviors. This will minimally require nonjudgmental, mindful responses.

Most people are reasonably perceptive about their extroversive and introversive tendencies and just how shy or outgoing they might be. Intercultural effectiveness does not require any specific amount of outgoing behavior, as people of all types can be very effective interculturally. You do, however, need to have a core value of the importance of other people and a desire to relate effectively with others. If you are so self-centered that you do not have these core values, then the likelihood of interpersonal effectiveness, intercultural or otherwise, is weak. If, however, you can cultivate these core values, then you can begin to adapt your own behavior to the demands of an intercultural context. What is required is recognition of your tendencies, how those tendencies are manifest, and how you can adapt your behavior as necessary. To manage these situations, you need to use the approach we suggested for increased self-control: identify your tendencies and develop a plan to accommodate them.

Adaptive Sensitivity.   A final trait and set of skills concern adaptive sensitivity, sometimes labeled intuitive sensitivity. This refers to your ability to understand a situation and determine a response that is maximally beneficial for everyone involved. Obviously you have your own interests and objectives. Of the many ways to achieve them, you should select options that protect the interest and integrity of everyone possible. Central to this goal is understanding well what others are thinking, how they are presenting their position, and the consequences of various options. To obtain this level of sensitivity requires you to know your own position well, conduct prior research about the positions of others, to listen carefully, when interacting, for multiple messages, and to control your reactions. This trait combines all of the former traits, focuses all of the skills, and adds a touch of extraordinary intuition for the achievement of your goals and objectives. The primary obstacles are to think of your own perspective narrowly and to ignore the cultural and situational influences on yourself as well as other people. Unless you have a good understanding of the varied forces at play and how they are patterning, you will be unable to adapt.

Summary

This chapter speaks directly to any practitioner of public relations, whether you work on the domestic or international scene. The better you know yourself, the better you will represent your client and the better you can adapt to the amazingly varied, kaleidoscopic situations you will encounter. We tried to root our approach in the basic features of human behavior. Within that framework we explained the emergence of many cultural variables, and we provided you several ways to prepare yourself for intercultural encounters, with guidelines to assist with those events. As we suggested at the outset, effectiveness in intercultural communication is an art with few absolutes and wild variety. Knowing yourself and having a constructive framework can set the stage well for your challenges. The next chapter combines these concepts and guidelines for intercultural communication with the ROSTE model for designing and evaluating international public relations campaigns. This combination of a paradigm for campaign analysis and guidelines for intercultural communication will be used to critique the cases that follow and to guide your development of new public relations campaigns within intercultural or international contexts.

REFERENCES AND SUGGESTED READINGS

Berger, B. K. (1999). The Halcion affair: Public relations and the construction of ideological world view. *Journal of Public Relations Research, 11*(3), 185–203.

Condon, J. C., & Saito, M. (1976). (Eds.). *Communicating across cultures for what?* The proceedings of an international symposium on humane responsibility in intercultural communication held at International Christian University, Tokyo, Japan, January 24–25, 1976. Tokyo: The Simul Press.

Freitag, A. (2002). Ascending cultural competence potential: An assessment and profile of U.S. public relations practitioners' preparation for international assignments. *Journal of Public Relations Research, 14*(3), 207–227.

Gudykunst, W. B. (2004). *Bridging differences: Effective intergroup communication* (4th ed.). Thousand Oaks, CA: Sage.

Gudykunst, W. B., & Kim, Y. Y. (2003). *Communicating with strangers: An approach to intercultural communication* (4th ed.). New York: McGraw-Hill.

Hon, L. C., & Brunner, B. (2000). Diversity issues and public relations. *Journal of Public Relations Research, 12*(4), 309–340.

Keltner, J. W. (1970). *Interpersonal speech-communication: Elements and structures.* Belmont, CA: Wadsworth.

Lippmann, W. (1922). *Public opinion.* London: Collier-Macmillan.

Useem, J., & Useem, R. H. (1967). The interfaces of a bi-national third culture: A study of the American community in India. *Journal of Social Issues, 23*(1), 130–143.

Zaharna, R. S. (2000). Intercultural communication and international public relations: Exploring parallels. *Communication Quarterly, 48*(1), 85–100.

6 Guidelines for Successful Intercultural or International Public Relations

Thus far we have detailed a model for analyzing public relations cases that emphasizes careful planning based on research and communication theory. We also introduced guidelines for communication in intercultural and international situations. In this chapter we bring those two constructs together and suggest a model for the creation or analysis of intercultural or international public relations campaigns.

By way of review, you now know there is no universally accepted definition of public relations and that there is some disagreement even about what it means "to do" public relations. But, you know that public relations always includes a practitioner, a client, and at least one target public. You also know that "doing" public relations requires research, objectives, strategies (action and communication), tactics, and evaluation.

Public relations campaigns based in whole, or in part, on intuition are doomed to failure. Any good public relations practitioner begins every campaign with research. The research must answer questions like: (1) What does the client want? (2) What resources are available? (3) What are the demographics and attitudes of the target public? (4) Are there legal or cultural restrictions on the use of any resources or messages? To answer these questions one may conduct primary or secondary research and the choice between these two options depends largely on the time and resources available. Regardless of what research method is chosen, any competent public relations practitioner guarantees the research is both reliable and valid and knows how to assess reliability and validity.

Any campaign that lacks a clear objective cannot succeed. Objectives must support the client's organizational goals. They must also be realistic, and operationalized. The objective must also identify the target public or publics, specify a change in the target public, and specify when that change will occur.

In a public relations campaign strategy, communication theory and practice must come together. A good strategy specifies at least one message and a medium for delivering each message to the target public. The choice of messages and media should be based on a theory, paradigm, or model that predicts how the target public will react to the message and assures the practitioner that the chosen medium will deliver the message to the target public. Action strategies use communication theory to help the practitioner advise the client on how to act or what to do. Communication strategies are used to guide the choice of images, themes, or information directed to the target public.

Tactics are the nuts and bolts of the public relations campaign. Tactical decisions include the selection of advertising, mediated publicity, or direct publicity. The format for information released, the language of a release, and the specific contents of special events are all components of a public relations campaign.

Evaluation is the single most important component of any public relations campaign. Evaluation based on research guides the process of campaign modification and provides a valid measure of campaign success or failure. To be useful, evaluation must reliably and validly measure whether the campaign actually met its stated objective.

When judging whether your research, objectives, strategies, tactics, and evaluation are adequate, you must consider not only your own culture but also the cultures of your client and the target publics. Chapter 5 provided principles and guidelines for intercultural communication. Because public relations is a communications activity these guidelines can be applied to the development or criticism of any public relations campaign.

To successfully evaluate a public relations campaign you should be aware of your own norms, rules, and values. To avoid imposing your ethnocentric prejudices you should also recognize the norms, rules, and values of clients or target publics from cultures different from your own. To improve your ability to implement a public relations campaign in or for another culture, you should know your own culture as well as possible. Also, you must not presume that people from other cultures are similar to you and to your culture, and you must learn cautiously as much as you can about other cultures. Finally, you must remember to treat each member of another culture as an individual not as a stereotypic representative of his or her culture. Specific skills that will help you in intercultural situations include mindfulness, patience, and tolerance, particularly tolerance for ambiguity.

Some Unique Problems for International Public Relations

As public relations campaigns come to represent clients whose interests cross national borders, the practitioner is confronted with two unique problems. These strategic concerns are the need for public diplomacy and corporate foreign policy. Public diplomacy and corporate foreign policy are two interdependent topics of great importance in international public relations (Mannheim, 1994). Public diplomacy refers to the involvement of people outside of government who generate sufficient influence to affect diplomatic activities and negotiations. In our environment of rapid communication and transparency of government activities, diplomats and their governments can no longer easily work in secrecy. As the public discovers something they like or dislike, they can quickly mount public pressures to express this concern. Similar activity may develop in reaction to the work of any organization, thus making public diplomacy a matter of continual concern for any organizations working in another culture.

Foreign policy has traditionally been thought of as a concern of nations, but the supra-national status of so many organizations around the world necessitates consideration of corporate foreign policy. This new way of thinking makes the work of public relations practitioners even more important. In fact, some supra-national organizations use their public relations personnel and others to gather intelligence to assist these serious leadership functions. This certainly raises the bar of competition as the nongovernmental organizations (NGOs) are compelled to study how their foreign policy relates to policies in the nations where they operate, and especially to their primary host nations (Taylor, 2000). Because of the declining image of the United States, some U.S. NGOs are trying to disassociate their corporate foreign policy from that of the United States. In fact, some are making it very difficult to determine where they originate. For example, who can say where Shell calls home?

The increasing concern for corporate foreign policy creates a social expectation that the NGOs will take a more active role in community development where they operate. To be sure, the practitioners of international public relations have known and promoted for many years the value of being a good citizen in the communities where they work. This is an excellent way to associate corporate values with high priorities in the community and thereby enhance the status and credibility of the company. Anymore this has become an expectation, especially in developing countries, and should consequently be made a central part of the foreign policy. To manage this task invites us to consider the expanding literature about community development, a topic of growing concern as the U.S. culture becomes increasingly pluralistic (Gudykunst, 2004). From this literature we offer the following suggestions, most of which directly grow out of the earlier guidelines about intercultural communication.

Community Development

Recognize that community development is essential for peaceful cooperation. Without community cohesion, the interests of the NGO are threatened. Genuine community development requires individual commitment and the continued demonstration of the intercultural communication skills such as mindfulness, patience, tolerance, and others already discussed. People cannot develop community without coming to terms with cultural diversity and the conflict that differences between people will ultimately foster. In his book *The Global Me,* G. Zachary argues that cultural pluralism represents the future for creative solutions to economic and other social problems (2000). People must learn to deal with differences at the local level, and no matter how small the group is people can begin to build the solidarity and support for later confronting larger problems. Finally, no one can buy a community, a lesson learned by many NGOs who deceived themselves into thinking that community development is only about dollars. "Community" is definitely more than money. With increasing urgency a broader conception of community development must be made a central part of corporate foreign policy.

A crucial part of community development is learning to deal constructively with the conflict that will inevitably emerge. Cultures differ widely on how they perceive and deal with conflict. Some cultures avoid any semblance of conflict and deal very indirectly and over long periods of time with the concerns before them. In due time the culture will have dealt with the potential causes of conflict, and no one will be the worse for the lengthy resolution of their concerns. Other cultures, like that in the United States, are very direct and contentious, wanting to define the issue very explicitly and to directly address it. People in the United States tend to objectify the problem, separate it from personalities (if possible), and then collectively take pride in resolving the problem. Such vastly different approaches to conflict make this a potential source of serious strife between and among cultures. At the governmental level, bureaucrats, diplomats, and other formal negotiators have developed a language and approach, albeit primarily a western approach, to deal with conflicts behind the scenes, and they then plot the varied adaptation of the negotiated results to their different constituencies. At lower levels, the luxury of such a shared approach to conflict resolution is unavailable. So, we must try to understand the differences in approach and locate the techniques that permit a mutually useful resolution of the concerns for everyone in the community. To achieve this goal requires the deliberate cultivation of skills, because most people are so set in their problem-solving ways (Ting-Toomey & Oetzel, 2001).

Ultimately, the expert in international public relations must adapt the organizational message to a culturally diverse audience. With declining budgets, the advertising industry has struggled with whether to create one generic message for the global community, multiple messages for regional clusters of nations, or to work more locally on specific cultural variations. Our position is not the least expensive or the simplest, but we recommend the use of all these levels of adaptation for different purposes, with the essential approach anchored at the local level. At the global level, one can establish the NGO's commitment to some universal values as a means to create a transnational ethos. At the regional level, one can demonstrate the NGO's commitment to problems and indicate how they might be resolved for mutual benefit. Consistent with our observation about community development, this level represents the anchor point for the most effective intercultural relations and the creation of a support network to facilitate mutually desirable goals. Granted, this approach may take more time, but the integration of the NGO and its mission into the community can help deal with far greater unanticipated problems much later.

Public relations, especially international public relations, stands at a crucial point in its development and is struggling to overcome some serious obstacles. Public relations is currently growing beyond the constraining perspective of its roots in journalism, but it is still often seen as a vague art with little structure and certainly without any academic or theoretic foundation. We hope the paradigm represented by ROSTE helps overcome the negative perception that our profession is merely an intuitive art. We believe it provides the aspiring practitioner with a model that can be used consistently to create public relations campaigns with demonstrable results. However, even if the ROSTE paradigm could magically produce public relations campaigns with clearly predictable results, it would have to be applied in the real world where variations in perception and values make its application difficult. Simply put, we may have a good model for designing public relations campaigns, but that model is only as good as our ability to adapt it to intercultural situations.

Intercultural/International Public Relations Model

Presuming you can now critique a public relations campaign using the ROSTE model and that you are generally prepared to deal with people from other cultures, we need to combine these two skills into a broader, more strategic perspective about intercultural and international public relations. The model we provide closely follows the public relations campaign steps of research, objective, strategy, tactics, and evaluation, but within each of these five components it includes concepts designed to ensure that each step is completed or implemented with some cultural sensitivity. The model also intersperses some points of adaptation among the five steps. These points of adaptation recognize how culture influences, and is potentially influenced by, the cultures of the practitioner, client, and target public. In our discussion of the ROSTE model we specifically noted that it is not necessarily a linear model. At times it is necessary to repeat a step or to loop backwards to modify earlier steps in the model. The points of adaptation included in our model for intercultural and international public relations are placed where the public relations campaign planner is most likely to make such nonlinear modifications in the model.

Figure 6.1 displays the basic model for intercultural or international public relations. This model is not designed to identify all variables, but rather to suggest features that flag major concerns for those planning or critiquing intercultural or international public relations campaigns. The model is intended to assist a very broad or cursory evaluation of an intercultural public relations campaign. Thorough analysis of any campaign would require using both this model and a careful review of all the component concepts addressed in Chapters 2 through Chapter 5.

The model has three major columns, representing three of the major components of a public relations campaign: Objectives, Strategies, and Tactics. Each of these columns has its own input and output, and each has prominent aspects that serve as input and output to other

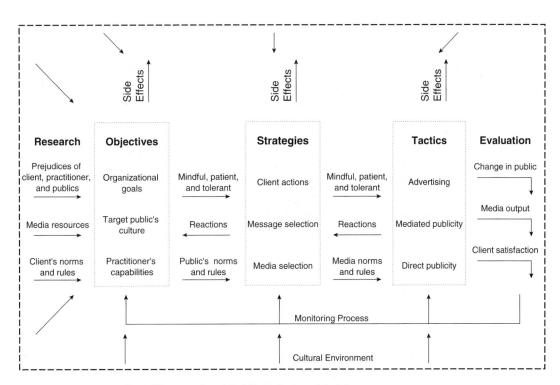

FIGURE 6.1   Intercultural/International Public Relations Model

columns. To the right and left of the three major columns are Research and Evaluation. These are separated from objectives, strategies, and tactics to acknowledge the *process* nature of public relations. In effect, evaluation *is* research, and evaluation research is used both to measure the campaign's output and as input for the modification of the campaign's objectives, strategies, and tactics. Interspersed between the columns representing objectives and strategies and between the columns representing strategies and tactics are points of adaptation. These points should indicate the need to exercise the skills associated with good intercultural communication, to accommodate the different norms and rules of other cultures and to react to any difficulty caused by conflict between the cultures of the practitioner, client, and target publics. The entire model is surrounded by a cultural environment, to indicate that the campaign will be impacted by the environment in which it is implemented. Finally, any successful campaign of public persuasion may influence the cultural environment with unanticipated side effects, shown on the model as moving outward from the three components columns.

The broken lines surrounding the entire model and surrounding the columns labeled Objectives, Strategies, and Tactics suggest a dynamic situation from which influence is constantly pressing on all parts of the model. No matter how carefully any organization might wish to control those influences, they are constant, variable, and cannot be totally suppressed. Instead, one can only monitor these influences and try to manage them. In other words, the development and implementation of a public relations campaign is a *process*. Particularly in the case of international or intercultural public relations campaigns, this process must be subject to constant evaluation and modification.

Many client organizations operate in a highly variable socio-cultural environment. From the outset this indicates a prominent concern for constant research and re-interpretation of the research input from diverse cultures. Initial research must be conducted in a way that acknowledges the prejudices of the client, practitioner, and the target publics. Such research must identify those prejudices so that accommodations can be made. Also, the research itself must be conducted so that prejudices of the practitioner and publics do not damage reliability and validity. Something as simple as a survey of a public's existing attitude toward the client can be rendered unreliable if not completed with sensitivity for the prejudices of the measured public. For example, in many Muslim countries women cannot be used to administer survey protocols to men and men cannot be used to administer those protocols to women. By U.S. norms this may seem sexist, but in fundamentalist Islamic culture, survey results would be rendered useless by violating a culture norm against mixed gender meetings.

Other research must address the identification of media resources available in the culture where the campaign will be implemented and identification of the client's norms and rules. These norms and rules may restrict what actions a client organization can appropriately take and what messages it will be willing to have delivered on its behalf.

Possible scenarios might place the Objectives column in more than one culture. In fact, the selection of a public relations objective might have several possible permutations located in various cultural situations. Consider the possibilities associated with one manufacturing company located in San Antonio, Texas, with production facilities in six different countries around the world, and international sales and marketing. This realistic situation shows that the model may be too simple and only useful to suggest considerations for international public relations. When identifying a public relations objective, public relations practitioners must consider the client's organizational goals, the target public's culture, and the practitioner's capabilities. How we operationalized change, what changes in the target public are realistic, and even how to define the target public—these questions are influenced by the norms, values, and social rules that arise from the culture of that target public. Further, the practitioner's degree of facility in the culture of the target public will limit what can realistically be accomplished. All these limitations, imposed by an intercultural setting, should guide the selection of the public relations objective for any campaign that involves more than one culture or country.

The Strategy column includes selection of both action strategies and communication strategies. Communication strategies are divided into the selection of messages and media. When selecting its actions, a client must have the advice of a public relations practitioner who is sensitive to the cultural expectations of its target publics and who can help predict the response of those in another culture to its actions. For example, when the Japanese decision makers for Bridgestone (Firestone Tire's parent company) decided not to recall tires that were alleged to cause accidents in the United States they ignored a U.S. culture norm that specifically values the safety of U.S. citizens. They opted instead to rely on recommendations from advisors in Japan who blamed the tire failure on driving habits in the United States. In short, their actions were not sensitive to the prejudices or norms of the target public. Likewise, the U.S. companies Union Carbide and Dow expressed similar cultural insensitivity when, after purchasing Union Carbine, Dow disavowed responsibility for deaths in Bhopal, India, caused by a Union Carbide gas leak. Dow simply followed a typical U.S. cultural norm of only acknowledging liability that could be imposed by law, while the families of the Indian victims of the gas leak followed a norm that identified liability with the parent company. Similarly, the selection of messages must be based on an understanding of the culture of the target public. One very primitive example is the selection of a spokesperson to deliver information. While a U.S. football player might be seen as an extraordinarily credible spokesperson to endorse athletic wear in the United States, he would hardly be effective in most of the world's cultures, where football is the game called soccer in the United States. Media must also be selected with sensitivity. As many international advertisers learned when they explored placing messages on Aljazeera, the medium of delivery can become part of the message. In much of the world, Aljazeera is seen as a perfectly reasonable and credible source of information, but consumers in the United States interpreted advertising on Aljazeera as an endorsement of anti–United States terrorism.

Tactics include selection from the three options discussed in Chapter 4. Whether the public relations practitioner opts for advertising, mediated publicity, or direct publicity will depend largely on the available media identified in the Research phase and the observations about the target audience made when selecting strategies. In this context it should also be noted that the internal publics of the client organization are critical in any program using face-to-face direct publicity. The internal publics of the organization, for example its employees, will have a network of family and friends who can impose cultural influences on and can be influenced by the internal public. Media representatives, who are critical to the implementation of any mediated publicity tactic, can also be some of the practitioner's strongest allies or they may be a major obstacle. The practitioner must be sensitive not only to the broad culture in which the media work, but also to the local standards of profession-alism among journalists. For example, in some cultures journalists expect to be paid for re-viewing or using news releases. In other cultures, journalists will be offended by what their norms deem the insult of offered payments.

The Evaluation column includes the very specific campaign evaluation advocated in Chapter 4, which begins with a change in the target public. All good public relations cam-paigns have as their objective some change in the values, attitudes, or actions of a target pub-lic. Therefore all campaign evaluation must focus on a measure of that change. However, evaluation includes more than the measure of the entire campaign's success. Media output must be measured to determine whether the strategic messages are actually being delivered to the target publics and client satisfaction must be measured for the practitioner's hard work to be rewarded.

Finally, Figure 6.1 shows points of internal adjustment between Objectives and Strate-gies and between Strategies and Tactics. After the practitioner and client have agreed on an objective, the practitioner must adjust the chosen strategies for the target public's culture using the skills of mindfulness, patience, and tolerance. The practitioner must also adjust those strategies using an understanding of the target public's norms and rules of appropri-ate behavior. Further, observing the target public's reactions to strategies will help the prac-titioner adjust strategies to maximize success in meeting the public relations objective. The points of adjustment between Strategies and Tactics are similar, but also include adjustment for the norms and rules of the media representatives whose cooperation is necessary for cam-paign success.

Again, it is essential to realize that the model shown in Figure 6.1 does not include every variable that can influence intercultural or international public relations. It does, how-ever, provide a framework that can be used to begin development or evaluation of a public relations campaign in an intercultural or international setting. The following chapters are 19 intercultural and/or intercultural campaign cases. As you read them, you can test their merit by applying this model and the other principles we have discussed. Figure 6.2 includes some very practical suggestions for placing news releases in international media.

REFERENCES AND SUGGESTED READINGS

Gudykunst, W. B. (2004). *Bridging differences: Effective intergroup communication* (4th ed.). Thou-sand Oaks CA: Sage.

Manheim, J. B. (1994). *Strategic public diplomacy and American foreign policy: The evolution of in-fluence.* New York: Oxford University.

Pittman, B. (2003, December 2). Make it personal: International editor reveals ten ways U.S. PR practitioners can build rapport—and score ink—with reporters abroad. *Bulldog Reporter's e-newsletter.* Retrieved from http://www.infocomgroup.com/

Taylor, M. (2000). Toward a public relations approach to nation building. *Journal of Public Relations Research, 12*(2), 179–210.

Ting-Toomey, S., & Oetzel, J. G. (2001). *Managing intercultural conflict effectively.* Thousand Oaks, CA: Sage.

Zachary, G. P. (2000). The global me: New cosmopolitans and the competitive edge-picking global-ism's winners and losers. New York: Public Affairs.

FIGURE 6.2   Make It Personal: International Editor Reveals Ten Ways U.S. PR Practitioners Can Build Rapport—and Score Ink—with Reporters Abroad

"If you asked me what I thought of PR ten years ago, I would have said I didn't think much of it as a trade," claims **Jurriaan Kamp,** editor-in-chief of *ODE* magazine, an eight-year-old international news digest that launched a U.S. version just last month [www.ode magazine.com]. "I didn't think I ever used their stories. But over time, I realized I was wrong," he concedes.

"Looking back, there were many in PR who introduced good stories—and they did it in ways that we [reporters] liked," continues Kamp, whose career as an international journalist and broadcast reporter included a stint as chief economics editor for the *NRC Handelsblad* [the Dutch equivalent to *The London Times* or France's *Le Monde*]. "It was all about relationships. Where there was success, there was also the human touch. Knowing the person allows us to forgive mistakes. For example, if an American PR person calls me and has no clue about the time difference or even where I am located on a map, but we get along—then everything is fine."

Here's his further advice for successfully pitching influential international outlets like *The London Times, Le Monde, ODE* magazine or even the *NRC Handelsblad:*

1. Think high-touch—not high-tech. "In this world of email, it's about establishing a real connection with a person," says Kamp. "People should take the time to meet each other or to reach out—especially if you are a PR person who wants to work with the press. It can be a love-hate relationship between us. That is sometimes even stronger if you come from another culture or country—like a US PR person calling a French reporter. That is because there are those [PR people] who are just selling stories, and there are those who get to know us."

His advice: "Email is so impersonal. A phone call can be better—even if there is a small language barrier," Kamp says. "Even better is to meet—to put a name to a face. For example, there is a PR person with Chiquita Bananas [George Jaksch] who is half-American and who is now based in Brussels. It's not an easy job to represent them—they are international and easy to criticize. But he does a good job because he realizes sensitivities surrounding third-world labor issues—and he invites us to come to the company.

There is no hiding—he puts a face on the company and tries to meet the press personally."

2. Trust is reciprocal—so give a little. "Successful PR people are open and honest whatever happens," Kamp says. "What builds trust is when people are open and tell the truth—even when the story is bad." He offers these additional examples of practices that help build trust with the press—international or otherwise:

- *Respect deadlines.* "It's important not to be too aggressive," continues Kamp. "Understand the importance of introducing an idea—and then leaving time for the reporter to work. For example, don't follow up immediately. It's frustrating to get a release and then a follow-up call the next day. Not doing this shows you respect the [reporter's] time—and you get the same in return."
- *Be available.* "Nothing builds trust more than if you are there whenever a journalist calls," he adds. "If bad news happens, returning phone calls is still important."
- *Provide access.* "As a journalist, you're always after the person behind the PR person. So don't be a [gatekeeper] all the time. Provide access and help us get the information we need."
- *Contribute or step aside.* "It's important for PR people to know when to be there—and when not to be there," according to Kamp. "If you're not saying anything during an interview with [your CEO], don't just sit there. If you're not helping, then leave." Trust is reciprocal, he stresses: "There will be more trust between you and the reporter if you [step aside] and leave it to the reporter."

3. Don't be too U.S.-centric—pull out a map. "If you live in the Netherlands, more than half the newspaper is foreign news," Kamp says. "But in the U.S., it's a lot if your newspapers are ten percent foreign news." What's his point? "There is a lot to be said about the rest of the world—it's a global village. But many Americans don't act that way. For example, they have no clue about maps. If I asked an American PR person where the Netherlands is, he wouldn't know."

(continued)

FIGURE 6.2   Continued

His advice: "Being [U.S.-centric] might be OK if you are an American reading the news. But if you are in PR, it's your job to research us," Kamp stresses. "You might [get away with pitching] different U.S. newspapers the same story, but it will never work here. You must know how our readers will respond—and they're all very different at different outlets. Cultures are very different within five hundred miles here [in Europe]. So I advise getting familiar with world maps and the [regions or countries] you are trying to reach."

4. Brush up on time zones. "We Europeans live with time zones in our minds," Kamp says. "If you're a correspondent here, you deal with time changes all day. We relate to them and know them without [looking them up]."

His advice: "Put more effort toward this. While Europeans wouldn't mind a PR person pitching or leaving a message at the wrong time, it would help show that you did your homework if you can say you are sorry for calling so early or late. Many Americans don't even realize the difference or [acknowledge it]. Again, this shows sensitivity that everybody isn't in America."

5. Localize every story. Kamp also suggests that many stateside PR practitioners fail to find a local spokesperson, source or angle for the readerships they're pitching abroad. "If you are trying to send a story idea to a big Dutch newspaper, for example, you must find a Dutch person to speak [or quote] in the story," he says. "If a story originates about a farmer in Iowa, then try to find the global [angle] and show how it impacts each market [you're pitching]. Show the connection to the people in the Netherlands, for example. It shouldn't be hard—everything is connected these days. In this case, the connection might be how subsidizing farmers in Iowa impacts consumers in the Netherlands because of the ongoing trade dispute between the U.S. and the European Union. Perhaps the story is about how we subsidize steel because you subsidize farmers in Iowa."

Ultimately: "You will not interest a European paper or any other overseas [outlet] if you can't show them how your story can be localized," Kamp warns. "If you represent Wal-Mart and it's opening an outlet here, then show what that means for jobs, pollution—those things. We are much closer together here [in Europe], so a store like this will have different impacts on our communities than in the U.S. Show the impact here—not there [in America]. Many multinationals and U.S. PR people make this mistake—they have no idea how we live and work here. An opening like this might be a negative thing to us, but in South Dakota it's [not a] big deal."

6. Don't lump countries together—be culturally sensitive. "It's important to understand that in a small area, we have very different cultures—and you can't [group] countries together," says Kamp. "If you do that, you will miss very important differences between us that could hurt [your chances] with the press."

He offers these examples: "The Dutch are pretty straightforward—more so even than the British," according to Kamp. "For PR people that means Dutch reporters might be more comfortable getting straight to business. But the French, Italians and British—it might take more time with them. For example, expect to spend more time on pleasantries with reporters from these countries. Or don't be so aggressive—phrase things right. For example, don't be over-sure of yourself. Frame your [email or first contact] with questions to make it softer. Another thing is that the Dutch are more multi-lingual than some other Europeans—most of us speak three languages. It's because we trade worldwide historically. This is different than a German person. Expect some language difficulties—especially with the French." Similarly: "Some stories will go nowhere just because of the country," Kamp elaborates. "Can you imagine taking a French person to a fast food restaurant for a story in New York City? Ridiculous!"

7. Don't cold call—leverage references. "This is another example of being sensitive," says Kamp. "There are many people in Europe who are still very formal. For example, the Germans think in hierarchies. They are very prompt and formal—and often prefer you to say who [referred] you before getting to business."

In addition: "This is changing," Kamp continues. "Many countries are opening up to loose forms of communicating. So be open to different styles."

FIGURE 6.2   Continued

8. Don't be overly familiar.   Presenting a variation on the theme, Kamp warns against assuming an overtly familiar tone with many journalists abroad. "Using first names is acceptable and good in America," he says. "There, nobody wants to be called Mr. So-And-So. It's always Bill or Jack. That is clearly not the case in Europe."

His advice: "Use formal [salutations]—even in email. If [the reporter] starts to use the familiar in response, then feel free. For example, I am not that formal. But if I didn't know the CEO of Barnes & Noble before this week, I would have used his last name. Now after our first introduction, I can use [Marie]."

9. Check out the language—get names right. "It's more likely for a foreign reporter to get your name right than the other way around," Kamp says. "If you can look up the name [in a directory with pronunciations] first, then fine. Whatever you can do helps. But don't be overly sensitive to saying names right. More important is to be aware of the language barrier—maybe that means speaking slowly, for example. Someone in our magazine once said that what really promotes world peace is learning another language. The point is it makes you go more deeply into the other's culture. I think it's the same with PR and the media."

10. Show your thanks—but personalize everything. With the holiday season approaching, the question on a PR person's mind might be whether international [and European, in particular] outlets frown on gift giving as they do here. "We don't mind gift giving or holiday cards," according to Kamp. "Nobody wants to feel like they're being bribed, but most Europeans won't mind a PR person saying thank you or being grateful for a positive story." Of course, that's anathema to a U.S. reporter—and Kamp knows it. "A simple gift or card can't threaten a reporter's objectivity," he counters.

His advice: "Don't send out a formal card in a mass mailing. If we can see that only a few cards were mailed, then we appreciate that a lot. It's dark, rainy and snowy outside—so go ahead," Kamp exhorts. "Send me a card, please. If you want to send a gift about a positive story—do it. But don't make it gratuitous. It must be related to the story or the relationship we have. It can't be a silver wine opener, for example. Make it personal, make it real—and make it sincere."

Cases

The following cases are not presented in categories. The preface contains a list of the cases and the appropriate subfields of intercultural or international public relations they can be used to analyze.

1

Corporate Reputation under Attack: A Case Study of Nike's Public Relations Campaign to Blunt Negative Perceptions of Its Labor Practices

ALI M. KANSO and RICHARD ALAN NELSON

Executive Summary

Every social movement needs a villain. For almost a decade, the sports shoe manufacturer Nike has been under fire for its labor practices in contracted factories in Asia. On the positive side, the firm successfully converted a traditionally narrow-market product into a mainstream necessity. As a global icon, the Nike swoosh provides a sense of identity to millions of young men and women that bridges international boundaries. This case study examines Nike's public relations efforts to change negative public perceptions about its labor practices. Such efforts have been aimed at foreign and domestic employees, shareholders, media, colleges, opinion leaders, the U.S. Labor Department, foreign governments, factory managers and workers, and customers. Nike's primary objectives were (1) to inform the publics of the company's endeavor to handle unjust treatments of factory workers, (2) to shift the negative public opinion of Nike by promoting the company as a positive contributor to the Asian economy, and (3) to encourage target publics to join Nike in patrolling labor abuses.

Nike's public relations efforts had several strengths. First, the company used a knowledgeable spokesperson to deal with the media. Second, Nike implemented a Code of Conduct to fight labor abuses. Third, the company offered factory tours to members of the media, opinion leaders, and college students and professors to view and evaluate the labor conditions for themselves. Fourth, Nike emphasized its economic contributions to Asian countries by providing employment and generating a significant amount of foreign currency.

Along with the positive attributes, the campaign also had some weaknesses. First, the spokesperson was sometimes contradictive. For example, he defended his company and its labor practices to the very end, maintaining that neither Nike nor its subcontractors have ever had abusive labor conditions. However, he initiated dialogue to address the very accusation he was denying. Second, Nike implemented an extensive education program but never fully acknowledged the conditions of each factory or addressed the individual needs of each one. Third, Nike public relations efforts could have been more effective had the company addressed labor abuses sooner. Nike's hesitance to react to violations made its efforts look forced and insincere. For the last few years, Nike has continued to defend its labor practices and has tried to repair its tarnished image. These efforts seem to be having impact, but only time will tell if Nike's reputation can be restored.

Research

Visionary Chairman Phil Knight has made his Nike sports shoe line a household item in 82 countries by leveraging the low-cost labor markets of southeast Asia and attracting top-name "ambassadors with attitude" such as Michael Jordan, Carl Lewis, Pete Sampras, Andre Agassi, Monica Seles, Michael Johnson, and Eric Cantona. But Nike, the most profitable of the global athletic footwear companies, has been under fire for almost a decade about labor practices in its contracted factories. In fact, Nike can be seen as a poster child for both the benefits and risks inherent in globalization (Locke, 2003).

Critics (including international human rights groups, U.S. Congress members, and exploited workers, among others) have long protested low wages, long hours, unsafe conditions, and corporal punishment practiced by some factory managers (Hogan & Manning, 1998). By the mid-1990s, awareness of these conditions led U.S. Labor Secretary Robert Reich to encourage the World Trade Organization to harmonize global labor standards (*Weekly Standard Staff,* 1996). American companies also received pressure to monitor and improve employee treatment in their foreign-contracted factories located in developing countries.

Although these issues have been an ongoing problem, many people first heard about them in connection with Nike when the CBS television news program *48 Hours* aired a program in 1996 about poor conditions in Nike manufacturing sites. Not long after, researcher Dara O'Rourke prompted a front-page story in the *New York Times* in 1997 by releasing an internal Nike audit on the deplorable state of one of the company's subcontracted factories in Vietnam (Cortes, 1997).

These stories led to national news coverage that continues to reverberate today. The reporting painted a picture of thousands of young women, all under the age of 25, laboring 10.5 hours a day, six days a week in excessive heat, noise, and foul air, for slightly more than $10 a week (Cortes, 1997). The *New York Times* story also revealed that workers with skin or breathing problems had not been transferred to departments free of chemicals, and the majority of the workers who dealt with dangerous chemicals did not wear protective masks or gloves. As the leading seller of athletic wear and apparel, Nike was becoming an example of U.S. companies' exploitation of women and children in other countries to save money and boost profits.

The exposé on Nike was published at a time when many other companies were being uncovered for running sweatshops. The previous year, talk show host Kathie Lee Gifford held a weepy press conference after it was revealed that her Kathie Lee clothing line, sold at Wal-Mart, was made by sweatshop workers in Honduras (Elliot, 1996).

The extent of protest against Nike in particular is extraordinary, with many protest groups emerging to fight against the inhumane and unjust treatment of workers in these sweatshops. Organizations such as Amnesty International began to coordinate boycotts and pressure companies that were contracting sweatshops to take responsibility for their actions (Elliot, 1996). Global Exchange (based in San Francisco) was especially successful in implementing its own anti-Nike public relations campaign (Bullet, 2000; Bennett, 2003). In addition, protesters were adding pressure to government officials who were already determined to improve labor conditions and standards. For example, Trim Bissell, coordinator of the Campaign For Labor Rights, called for a boycott of Nike products with a mission to secure "economic justice" for workers around the world" (Plitch, 1996; *Weekly Standard* Staff, 1996). Uniting the anti-Nike organizers was their continued belief that it is immoral for rich U.S. companies to employ foreign workers at low pay for long hours in hot factories.

Cultural Context

Actually, exploitive sweatshops have long been a global issue, if a backburner one. But foreign workers were not the only laborers being affected. In 1996, the U.S. Department of Labor estimated that in more than 10,000 domestic sweatshops women worked 17-hour shifts for less than $2 a day (Elliot, 1996). Many U.S. citizens also were losing their jobs because of the practice of contracting factories abroad in Asia, Latin America, and the Caribbean, where manufacturing costs and labor are less expensive (*Weekly Standard Staff*, 1996).

Nike was a leader in this trend. During the company's first year of operation in 1972, Nike was already outsourcing its manufacturing operations to Japan. When the yen's value became independent of the dollar, the cost of Japanese-made products soared and Nike left Japan to contract with factories in Taiwan and Korea (Nike, Inc., Labor Practices Timeline, 2001). Nike continued to expand operations in the factories that offered the least expensive labor costs. However, in 1978 Nike attempted to establish its own factories in Maine and New Hampshire, but those factories were short-lived, closing in 1985.

By the mid-1990s, the manufacturing move overseas had accelerated. For example, the International Labor Organization (ILO) issued a study in 1996 that showed a dramatic shift of work from Europe and North America to Asia and the developing world (Elliot, 1996). As a result, sweatshops have become a way of life for some people. In Malaysia alone, the number of workers making shoes, clothes, and fabrics increased more than 600% since 1970.

Sweatshops have also been known to use child labor. A second ILO study conducted in 1996 revealed that 61 percent of the world's child workers, nearly 153 million, were working in Asia (Elliot, 1996). Culturally, businesses and governments in poorer countries in Asia were exploiting children while producing cheap labor, primarily for U.S. companies.

Company History and Structure

Bill Bowerman and Phil Knight established Nike in 1972. Although it started as a private company, Nike went public in 1980 with an initial public offering of two million shares of common stock (Nike, Inc., Our Chronology, 2001). Knight is currently the CEO of

Nike and owns about 36 percent of the company. In times of crisis, Knight serves as the official spokesperson of Nike, although the company employs an extensive public relations department. Nike is headquartered in Beaverton, Oregon, and currently employs 21,800 people.

For the past two decades, Nike has been a leader in the athletic shoe and apparel industry. Currently, it is the No. 1 company in its product market, controlling more than 40 percent of the U.S. athletic shoe industry. Nike's primary target market is the pre-teen and teen athlete. The company has become a status symbol and many kids feel they must have their own Nike products with the distinctive swoosh trademark (Plitch, 1996).

Throughout its existence, Nike has contracted a long list of celebrity athletes popular with youth who, for a great deal of money, endorse its products. These celebrities include tennis great John McEnroe, basketball star Michael Jordan, and golf pro Tiger Woods. However, Jordan was the most prominent spokesperson at the time the Nike crisis broke. Jordan, who was paid about $20 million a year as an endorser, took a lot of criticism for his expressed indifference to the labor issues (Elliot, 1996). He "earned more per minute of play than a Nike worker would earn in a decade" (*Weekly Standard* Staff, 1996).

Clarifying the Issue

Nike's early response to growing condemnations of worker exploitation was to deny responsibility for conditions in the contractor companies that have always been the core of Nike's production system. However, in the face of sagging sales and growing protests, Nike's leadership began to take seriously the concern that Nike's brand image and corporate reputation were being tarnished due to the stigma of labor abuses. Although the company remained at the top of the product market, demand for Nike products slowed and stock prices dropped, resulting in layoffs of 1,600 Nike employees following the negative news coverage and organized anti-Nike protests (Read, 1998a). For example, from 1997 to 1998 stock prices plummeted from $66.50 per share to $47.44 (Hogan & Manning, 1998). Investors panic if shares drop precipitously, and Nike needed to address such a potential problem.

A content analysis of news reports clearly shows the heightened interest in the controversy. A Lexis/Nexis General News full-text search of "Nike" and "Indonesia" in the *New York Times* and *The Washington Post* shows the controversy peaked in 1997. A similar analysis of major world newspapers demonstrates consistent findings (see Tables 1 and 2).

TABLE 1   Nike Media Coverage, 1988 to 1999

Number of Articles with Keywords "Nike" and "Indonesia"										
Year	1988–90	1991	1992	1993	1994	1995	1996	1997	1998	1999 (to Oct.)
New York Times	0	3	3	2	5	4	19	31	22	7
Washington Post	0	1	2	2	3	1	5	10	5	4

Source: Bullett (2000). Retrieved from http://depts.washington.edu/gcp/pdf/strategic_public_relations.pdf.

TABLE 2   **Unfavorable Nike Labor Relations Media Mentions**

Media Mentions with Keywords "Nike" and "Sweatshop" in Major World Newspapers										
Year *1992*	*1993*	*1994*	*1995*	*1996*	*1997*	*1998*	*1999*	*2000*	*2001*	*2002*
No. of Articles 4	7	4	3	24	59	43	20	33	26	9

Source: Locke (2003). Retrieved from http://mitsloan.mit.edu/50th/nikepaper.pdf.

Although CEO Knight denied any connection between Nike's labor practices and the declines in sales and stock prices, he clearly recognized that changes had to occur and fences be mended. Nike didn't want to risk losing its high percentage of the market share, especially in such a competitive and changing market as athletic shoes and apparel. So while there was a dip in stock value in the late 1990s (Figure 1), overall the stock has performed spectacularly well against the New York Stock Exchange Average (NYA) (Figure 2). In the year 2002, Nike's sales bounced back—surpassing $9.8 billion.

Today, Nike employs more that 500,000 workers in some 700 factories located in 51 countries—although less than 23,000 are direct employees, mostly in the United States (Locke, 2003). So, what did Nike do and how did its public relations efforts influence public opinion?

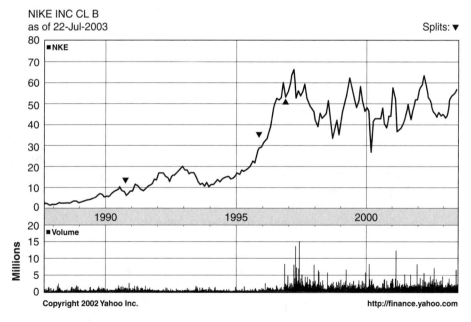

FIGURE 1   **Nike Stock Prices, 1988–2003**

Source: http://finance.yahoo.com

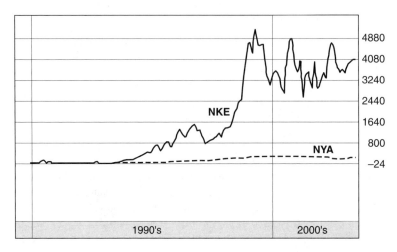

FIGURE 2 **Comparison of Nike Stock Performance vs. the New York Stock Exchange Average**

Source: Compiled from online analytical tools available in the Portfolio Manager section of *Business Week* online, http://www.businessweek.com/, accessed July 23, 2003.

Preliminary Data Gathering

Since Nike's labor practices had become a controversial issue, gathering data on public opinion was not difficult for the company. Nike already had in place several departments that worked with public relations to assist in conducting a situational analysis, including the Nike Environmental Action Team (formed in 1993) and the Labor Practices Department (formed in 1996). Both are now organized under the Corporate Responsibility and Compliance Department.

Nike representatives monitored reported poll data. Also, as a result of the controversy over its labor practices, many organizations and individuals were developing anti-Nike websites. A quick search (May 2001) of Internet sites with either an exclusive or a partial Nike focus (along with themes about international labor, human rights, and environmental abuses, and the need for standards) yielded 58 sites. These sites enabled nongovernmental agencies (NGOs) and other "activist groups to share information, coordinate political goals and protests, and further embarrass the company" (Locke, 2003). Nike employees track these websites, which mainly aim at trying to get consumers to boycott Nike products and persuading government figures to take action to improve working conditions. In addition, the websites attempt to get Nike to assume responsibility for changing its unethical practices.

Nike also gathered information through a conference call with Dartmouth College, allowing students and faculty to ask questions of the Nike spokesperson, Vada Manager, and the Labor Practices Director, Dusty Kidd (Kidd, 1997). This conference gave a chance for Nike representatives to develop an understanding of consumers' concerns and sentiments. In addition, Nike in 1997 requested that a group of MBA students at Dartmouth's Tuck School of Business undertake a study described "as an investigation into whether wages paid by Nike contractors in Indonesia and Vietnam matched the worker's cost of living." The report proved positive, but as Howard (1998) points out, "The study, which found that Nike wages provided not only for basic needs but even for a significant amount of discretionary income, was severely criticized as being methodologically and analytically flawed, and too much under the direction of Nike. It was as embarrassing to the Tuck School as it was to Nike."

In addition to the public opinion research, Nike attempted to find out what other companies were doing to regulate their labor practices in other countries and to investigate competitive public relations campaigns. For example, Nike researched Reebok's labor practices and regulations (Elliot, 1996).

Nike also was forced to more closely research the factories that it contracts with, evaluating the working conditions and labor practices of these facilities. Although Nike had a Code of Conduct for its factories, the code was not always implemented.

Objective

Public Relations Approaches

Nike first employed a reactive approach, but after its reputation got badly damaged CEO Phil Knight decided to shift tactics in 1997. The company adopted a proactive approach by clarifying its target publics and attempting to rebuild relationships with each of them through specific statements and actions.

Rather than specify clear-cut measurable objectives (at least publicly), Nike's management outlined more directional goals. These impact goals were defined on three levels: informational, attitudinal, and behavioral. For example, informational goals were to make the target publics aware of the programs and benefits that the company provides for its workers and publicize the company's effort to patrol any unjust treatment of factory workers. These target publics were identified as:

- Human rights activists/groups
- National and international government/regulatory officials
- Factory managers and workers in Asia
- Nike domestic employees and celebrity endorsers
- College/university administrators and students, especially where Nike had contracts to provide athletic wear
- Shareholders
- Media
- Consumers

The attitudinal goals were to shift the negative public opinion of Nike to a positive one by promoting the company as a constructive contributor to the Asian economy, dedicated to improving factory conditions, and operating as a good corporate citizen.

The behavioral goals were to (1) retain and even increase Nike's market share, (2) maintain and even increase shareholders, and (3) encourage target publics to join Nike in patrolling labor abuses.

Strategies

Nike found itself forced to react to negative publicity and was thus in a crisis communication mode. Nevertheless, management was determined to reshape the debate on its own terms. Following its situation analysis and assessment of the current information climate, Nike's management recognized the need to make changes in the way the company did business. This was a critical decision. In addition, Nike decided that the firm needed to strategically involve key publics (such as selected media representatives) in specific high-profile forums and hands-on activities if opinion was to shift favorably. Holding special events and building alliances with other groups also would prove to be important in blunting negative press coverage and dividing activist critics.

Action Strategies

Knight outlined eight changes the company intended to pursue (Hogan & Manning, 1998). These changes were incorporated into a sophisticated public relations offensive:

- Expanding independent factory monitoring to include nongovernmental organizations, foundations, and educational institutions, and to make summaries of the findings public. This included championing its participation in the "Fair Labor Association," a labor-monitoring program derided by anti-sweatshop activists.
- Hosting industrial tourism visits to Nike production sites.
- Building on its Code of Conduct to participate in a number of other initiatives where Nike can promote itself as a leader in corporate responsibility (such as Business for Social Responsibility).
- Having all Nike shoe factories meet U.S. Occupational Safety and Health Administration indoor air quality standards by the end of 1998.
- Expanding educational programs near the Asian footwear factories.
- Increasing a short-term enterprise loan program to assist 1,000 families each in Vietnam, Indonesia, Pakistan, and Thailand.
- Financing university research on global manufacturing issues such as independent monitoring and air quality standards.
- Raising the minimum age of workers to 18 at shoe factories and 16 at apparel and equipment factories.

Communication Strategies

The companies actions were communicated in several messages. For example, in 1997 Nike made a public declaration through the Fair Labor Association that as a company it respected the right of freedom of association incorporated in Article 23 of the Universal Declaration of Human Rights. Nike CEO Phil Knight then announced in a May 1998 speech before the National Press Club in Washington, DC, the company's plan to improve labor practices in its factories. In that speech, Knight told the audience that "the Nike product had become synonymous with slave wages, forced overtime, and arbitrary abuse." Knight then pledged that Nike would lead efforts to reform working conditions at overseas factories.

Since then, Nike has aggressively marketed an image of new concern for the working conditions in its factories. Easing this transition was the ability of the company to build on its existing Code of Conduct, first established in 1992, to meet the concerns of the target publics. However, Nike critics say that the strategy that Nike appears to be pursuing is to take a number of high-profile initiatives that portray the company in a positive light, while maintaining the core policies that allow it to profit from horribly exploited labor. What clearly has changed is that Nike has turned its marketing prowess toward blunting criticism of its practices (UNITE!, 2000).

Knight further reiterated the company's commitments in July 2000 through high-profile support for the United Nation's Global Compact. By being at the same press conference and appearing with Knight at the Global Compact launch, UN Secretary General Kofi Annan gave credibility to Nike's pledge to conform to these higher standards, even though the promises were not necessarily backed up by action (Connor, 2001).

Tactics

Management knew actions speak louder than words. As a result, Nike conducted an elaborate factory-training program to explain to workers and managers its Code of Conduct and the new initiatives that Knight had presented at the National Press Club (Read, 1998b). In addition, Nike organized a forum, "Leaving Organic Solvents Behind," for all the Asia-based executives from the top five major footwear brands and hygiene officials. The objective was to inform the attendees of Nike's processes. The forum also provided Nike with an opportunity to reiterate its commitment to meet U.S. Occupational Safety and Health Administration permissible exposure limits governing solvents and indoor air quality for its Southeast Asia footwear factories by the end of 1998 (Nike, Inc., 1998).

Critics had argued that "telling the truth will show Nike that the only way to repair its brand image—the company's most important asset—is to dramatically improve the economic and workplace conditions of the people who make Nike products" (UNITE!, 2000). With Nike's new commitment to increasing the quality and conditions of the factories in Asia, a source for enforcing these codes was necessary. In addition to its corporate responsibility and compliance managers, the company formed a staff of 1,000 labor practices managers to carry out a program that Nike calls SHAPE (Safety, Health, Attitude of Management, People, Environment). Nike's Washington lobbyist, Brad Figel, claimed in 1998 that Nike is the only company that has people dedicated exclusively to labor practice enforcement (Saporito, 1998). All Nike personnel responsible for either production or compliance receive training in Nike's Code of Conduct, labor practices, and cross-cultural awareness. In 1998, a spokesperson for Nike also disclosed that the company had fired four factories for violating its Code of Conduct, bringing the total to eight in two years (Read, 1998a).

As Knight had previously promised, Nike held an open forum in November 1998 to increase public disclosure of independent monitoring and test results in its Asian footwear factories. Nike made public the results of certified aid quality tests that indicate its continued improvement of indoor air quality in its footwear factories in Asia (Nike, Inc., 1998).

Former United Nations Ambassador Andrew Young was also retained to undertake an independent assessment of Nike's Code of Conduct in three countries: Vietnam, Indonesia, and China. Mr. Young's report proved useful to the company, although critics quickly labeled it "a whitewash." His findings indicated: "The factories that we visited which produce Nike goods were clean, organized, adequately ventilated and well lit. . . . I found no evidence or pattern of widespread or systematic abuse or mistreatment of workers. . . . It is my sincere belief that Nike is doing a good job in the application of its Code of Conduct. But Nike can and should do better" (Young, 1997, "Findings and Observations" section).

Use of Media

In terms of technique, today's activists operate with a greater degree of sophistication than in the past, so companies also have to be adept at making their communication tools useful and effective. Like many businesses, Nike utilizes various types of uncontrolled and controlled media in its public relations campaigns. In dealing with the anti-Nike controversy, the most obvious type of uncontrolled media involved press releases regularly issued to document positive news about Nike. One major controlled medium proved to be CEO Phil Knight's speech at the National Press Club where he addressed criticism of Nike's labor practices and the company's response. This generated considerable favorable news coverage. However, Knight never admitted wrongdoing and maintained that neither Nike nor its subcontractors had ever abused labor conditions (Hogan & Manning, 1998).

Another controlled medium was leaflets. One leaflet titled "Truth About Nike's Corporate Practices" was given to visitors of Niketown factory stores. This claims that Nike pays attention to issues of concern to its customers and cares about the people who make its products. Another leaflet titled "Code of Conduct" proclaimed that Nike does not tolerate abuses of any kind and supports programs for worker welfare and health (Lampriere, 1998).

Still another controlled medium remains Nike's interlinked websites. Nike's main public affairs website, Nikebiz.com, includes a copy of its Code of Conduct and posts a timeline tracking Nike's improvements, programs in its factories, and news about current events. Featured is an extensive Corporate Responsibility section, with community affairs, diversity, environment, manufacturing practices, and reporting sections. An online factory tour is another highlight. The website also has a link for frequently asked questions about Nike's labor practices. If that link does not answer a question, then the question can be e-mailed directly to Nike. Vada Manager, public relations director for Nike, observes "that while university activism isn't new, the use of new technology prolongs and changes campus demonstrations. The use of cell phones and e-mail allows for more coordination on campus, around the country, and around the globe." Manager further notes that Nike, which built its brand as an activist company using rebel athletes, understands that activists come from every stripe, from hopelessly naive to those who respect the business model. When the media appear to be hearing only one side of a story, Nike uses its Web site to share corporate information with its publics so that they could begin to understand the complexity of the issues at hand. (National Association of State Universities and Land-Grant Colleges, 2001).

Nike also used issue advertisements to reiterate its commitment to fair labor practices. One journalist pointed out that it was not a coincidence that at a time when Nike was most under fire for its labor practices, the company ran an advertisement with "CEO Jordan," referring to endorser Michael Jordan engaged in the very same labor as the workers (Cortes, 1996).

Nike also felt that seeing is believing, wanting opinion leaders to observe factory conditions for themselves and report their findings to the public. While the final news product could not be fully predicted, the company felt the risk of loss of control was worth the effort. Therefore, the company encouraged influential figures (including human rights leaders, journalists, college students, and others) to tour its facilities in Asia. For example, Nike asked health and safety/environment experts who had been extremely critical of the company to review extensive data on one factory's performance against basic standards of worker protection and health issues. The experts also visited the factory to confirm the accuracy of the data. In addition, Nike CEO Knight invited 34 colleges and universities to join the Fair Labor Association and evaluate its factories (Footwear News Staff, 1999).

As part of its proactive approach, the company continually publicizes its numerous other philanthropic contributions to communities in the United States and abroad. For example, Nike provides children with the opportunities and support programs to play sports. It also helps people in low-income countries with small business start-up capital (Nike Inc., 2000). On the national level, Nike also made a $5 million contribution to the Boys and Girls Club of America. The company then forged a three-year partnership with the 100 Black Men of America to help the development and education of African America youth. In addition, Nike runs an annual Rescue a Shoe Program to recycle more than two million athletic shoes.

Evaluation

Critics say "Nike's public relations campaign is an effort to muddy the waters—to show that Nike cares, that oppressive wages aren't Nike's fault, that inhumane work hours aren't Nike's fault. The deplorable conditions in Nike factories *are* Nike's fault. In a global economy with no rules that protect workers, it is [the leaders of] companies such as Nike who direct the global sweatshop in industries such as clothing and footwear. To rescue its brand image, Nike must turn from public relations to paying a living wage, providing humane working conditions, and respecting the right of workers to organize" (UNITE!, 2000).

However, Nike's efforts generally have proved very successful in generating favorable news coverage and separating moderate activists from the more extreme anti-Nike crusaders. Two key examples: Dara O'Rourke, the reporter who wrote the exposé on Nike's factory conditions that appeared in the *New York Times* in November 1997, went back to the factory with full access to records and the 9,000 employees. As one of the most prominent critics, he credited Nike for its improvements in air quality and the loss of harmful chemicals (*New York Times* Staff, 1999). Subsequently, staff from *Time* magazine visited Nike plants in China and Vietnam and found them to be modern, clean, well lighted, and well ventilated (Nike, Inc., 2000).

Critique

Overall, Nike's public relations campaign had many strengths. The first strength was the use of CEO Phil Knight as the company spokesperson to announce the company's new initiatives. The CEO, in most instances, is the most credible spokesperson in the organization (Seeger,

Sellnow & Ullmer, 1998). Another strength was the fact that Nike had an existing Code of Conduct that the firm continued to develop and promote as a symbol of Nike's commitment to fighting labor abuses. Nike's willingness to discontinue contracts with many factories found to violate the code further reiterated the seriousness of the company's commitment.

Still another strength of the campaign was the offering of factory tours to members of the media and college students and professors. These tours helped longtime critics, as well as opinion leaders, to view and evaluate the labor conditions for themselves. Here they learned firsthand the value of Nike's economic contribution to Asian countries. While the region was facing tough economic conditions, Nike provided employment and generated a significant amount of foreign currency. Typical is the contribution Nike shoes made to Vietnam, about 5 percent of total exports (Knight, 1998).

The campaign had also some drawbacks. CEO Knight was sometimes very contradictory. For example, he defended his company and its labor practices to the very end, maintaining that neither Nike nor its subcontractors ever had abusive labor conditions. However, he undertook initiatives to address the very same accusations that he was publicly denying. In retrospect, Nike should have dealt with these issues earlier, conducted its own investigation, made public the findings, and then admitted any wrongdoing right away. By postponing the admission of a problem and even an action plan, the company lost some credibility.

Another drawback was that Nike did not address all factory problems. To Indonesian labor activists, Knight's initiatives appeared convenient for the company and the changes seemed crafted to appeal more to Westerners than workers (Read, 1998b). For example, Nike implemented an extensive education and loan program, yet never addressed the basic issue of the lack of bathrooms in each factory. The company should have acknowledged the conditions of each factory and should have addressed the individual shortcomings of each one.

Knight's attempts to intimidate universities from supporting an anti-sweatshop investigatory organization that would make its findings public, the Worker Rights Consortium (WRC), resulted in negative press. In particular, Knight's threats to cancel Nike sponsorship of Brown University's hockey team and his withdrawal of a large endowment donation to the University of Oregon because of that University's decision to join the WRC gave fodder to those who argued that Nike's leadership was insensitive.

Sometimes Nike's product advertising had unintended blowback. "Its clumsy efforts to appear friendly to women through its 'If you let me play' ad campaign have backfired, with the National Organization for Women and other women's groups mounting a campaign to publicize the exploitation of women and girls in Nike plants in Vietnam, China, and Indonesia" (Reed, 1998).

There were other glitches in the process. A front-page article appearing in the *New York Times* reported that Ernst & Young had produced an inspection report for Nike which found "workers at the factory near Ho Chi Minh City were exposed to carcinogens . . . and that 77 percent of the employees suffered from respiratory problems." This report, apparently leaked by a Nike insider, provided another weapon for critics to use against the company (Howard, 1998).

So, in retrospect, Nike's campaign has contained most of the worst damage but could have been more effective had the labor abuses been addressed sooner. Once the first violation was exposed, the company should have implemented a plan to patrol any labor abuses. Nike's hesitance to react made its efforts seem forced and insincere. For the past decade,

Nike has continued to defend its labor practices and tried to repair its tarnished image, but only time will tell if this goal is achieved.

Research

Nike had the resources to respond to its critics and used them effectively, especially in researching the problems at hand and determining what to do about them. Of greater concern is how the company management failed to anticipate the criticism that would result from the decision to move production to extremely low wage nations with histories of human rights problems. The lack of strategic foresight perhaps stemmed from the drive for profits, but would prove damaging to the Nike reputation in future years.

Objectives

We were forced to impute Nike's goals and objectives from publicly available materials. As a result, we have an incomplete understanding of the company's communication planning. Many internal documents, as well as comments from those with inside knowledge, were not available because Nike considers them proprietary. This is understandable given the competitive nature of its business, but nevertheless the lack of transparency in company actions was one of the contributing factors to Nike's problems. Further, because the objectives were not measurable there was no way to determine if the company achieved its aims. Indeed, the campaign seems to be an open-ended one in that the central issues, while muted, remain on the table.

By focusing on Nike, we also did not look at the communication efforts of the opponents in any depth. Future application of the Heath-Nelson Social Movement Model (in Heath & Nelson, 1986) may prove useful in addressing the issue. The model documents how activist issues can be monitored by examining how they progress through five separable, but interdependent, stages: strain, mobilization, confrontation, negotiation, and resolution. The value of this model is its ability to provide insight into the ways and places corporations can intervene to prevent a movement from achieving a point contrary to their business interests. If corporations understand movements, they can work proactively to solve problems of corporate performance before they mature into regulatory legislation or costly litigation.

Strategies

The actions implemented here were critically important, because the company needed to reassess its own activities and commitments before asking others to endorse them. By clarifying internal policies and emphases, Nike's management was better able to communicate a focused message and to blunt criticism. Never really answered, however, was the disparity issue between Nike's ultimate profit on a pair of sports shoes versus how much the workers who made them actually earned.

Tactics

Focusing on key opinion leaders was an excellent strategy. In this case, Nike was very successful in generating positive news coverage. Special events, plant visits by selected journalists, and other activities also proved effective. Our evidence for this is the favorable shift in news coverage, maintenance of stock prices, and figures documenting product sales. We also pointed out a number of glitches that marred the process. Plus we can't determine with high accuracy how much targeted publics know about the issue or the intensity of their feelings. We also do not have message-testing data to determine if the public relations and issue advertising were at maximum efficiency. As will be described in the addendum to this case, Nike seems to have underestimated the opposition's resourcefulness, especially in turning to the courts.

Evaluation

All in all, Nike has maintained its profitability. So in at least one respect, the campaign has proved a success. However, the company also now knows we live in an era of greater continuing scrutiny with a heightened probability of litigation.

Addendum

In addition to the issue not fully disappearing, Nike faced new challenges because of communication efforts to counteract claims that its workers (1) were paid less than the applicable minimum wage, (2) were required to work overtime, (3) were subjected to physical, verbal, and sexual abuse, and (4) were exposed to toxic chemicals. Nike's public statements, issue ads, and letters all claimed that workers were paid in accordance with local labor laws and, on average, received double the minimum wage plus free meals and health care.

Marc Kasky, who managed a foundation that preserves San Francisco's Ft. Mason, decided to take Nike to court in 1998 after reading an article in the *New York Times* about the company's contract factories. Kasky, a consumer activist, sued Nike under California truth-in-advertising laws (*California Business and Professions Code 17200,*) saying Nike's claims were false, arguing that Nike deliberately issued misleading statements (*Kasky v. Nike* San Francisco Superior Court, filed April 20, 1998). Nike obviously disagreed and left the issue largely to its legal staff to handle.

Although the trial court dismissed the case and the state Appellate Court agreed in 2000, on subsequent appeal in 2002 the California Supreme Court in *Kasky v. Nike* overturned those decisions and remanded the case back to the lower court. The California Supreme Court held that Kasky had a right to sue, since "Communications are subject to government regulation if they are made by a commercial speaker, such as an officer of a company, intended for a commercial audience and contain representations of fact that are commercial in nature." The court concluded that the purpose of company's public relations activities is to "maintain sales and profit" and thus its campaign did qualify as commercial speech. Nike, the court said, could be held liable under California law, regardless of the nature of its public relations communications, for "deceptive advertising" if the firm was found to make misleading public statements about its operations and conduct (Dolan, 2002). So, although the California Supreme Court did not rule on the merits of the case, the state justices refused to throw out the suit and said a trial should take place.

This was a blow to Nike, which appealed to the federal courts, further adding that statements the company made about its overseas factories were protected speech (see, for example, the official corporate statement in a press release, Nike, Inc., May 2, 2002). So the case quickly evolved beyond the specifics of Nike's practices into a broader concern—whether or not the U.S. Constitution's First Amendment free speech protections extend to public relations activities. A host of organizations, including the Public Relations Society of America, the Institute for Public Relations, and the Public Affairs Council, joined Nike in arguing against the California decision—warning it has the potential to blur traditional distinctions between advertising and public relations efforts. For example, Bruce Keller of the U.S. law firm Debevoise & Plimpton issued the following statement in conjunction with the announcement that those and other groups would be filing briefs in support of Nike:

> Because the *Kasky* test covers any utterance where consumers might be present or might be expected to receive the information through media outlets, corporate speech will disappear from every medium of communication with the public. The *Kasky* decision inevitably will stymie public relations professionals' ability to assist corporations maintain an open dialogue with the public and engage in the 'uninhibited, robust and wide-open' public debate that was previously thought to be protected by the First Amendment. . . . In short, because a prudent CEO would no longer be willing to risk speaking about any issue of public importance that also touches upon the 'business operations' or profitability of the company the information flow to the public would be severely circumscribed. Prudent, risk-adverse companies will have no option but to decline speaking in order to avoid the possibility of strike suits. (The Arthur W. Page Society, Public Affairs Council, Public Relations Society of America, Council of Public Relations Firms, and Institute for Public Relations to file U.S. Supreme Court brief, 2002)

The court battle starkly shined a light on that one essential issue: was Nike's public relations campaign refuting claims about working conditions in overseas manufacturing facilities subject to regulation because it was "commercial speech" with only limited constitutional protection; or information entitled to full free-speech protection because such communication is important to a fully informed public.

Because of these sharply edged arguments, the U.S. Supreme Court accepted the case for review (Cunningham & Freeman, 2003). However, in a surprise move, the high court justices changed their mind and on June 26, 2003, sent the case back to the state for another round of adjudication. Nike's management, responding to the potential loss of its case, agreed to an out-of-court settlement two and a half months later (Nike Settles Sweatshop Labor Suit, PR Stays Muted, 2003). Under the agreement, Nike admitted no liability, but agreed to donate $1.5 million to the Fair Labor Association, a Washington, D.C.-based workers' rights group.

One great concern the groups opposing Kasky point to is the potential to chill open communication. For example, after the ruling by the California Supreme Court, Nike suspended much of its communications surrounding corporate social responsibility. The firm also did not file a listing in the Dow Jones Sustainability Report. Following the settlement, Nike said "it still intends to curtail its corporate public relations efforts," *PR Week* reports. "Despite the settlement . . . Nike said it does not plan to ramp up the public relations activities that had been curtailed because of the pending lawsuit. Specifically, because of what the company regards as the California Supreme Court's unfavorable interpretation of a state law regarding transparency, Nike has also decided not to issue its corporate-responsibility report for fiscal year 2002" (Creamer, 2003).

Kirk Stewart, the company's vice president for corporate communications, told *PRWeek* that Nike "will exercise restraint in when and how we communicate in California." He added, "We continue to be chilled by the statute and the interpretation" (Creamer, 2003). However, Jack O'Dwyer (2002), publisher of a number of public relations publications, warns that PRSA and the other organizations are on "the wrong side" of the Nike commercial speech lawsuit. "Instead of siding with Nike, which refuses to defend the truthfulness of its statements about labor practices abroad (see *No Logo* for labor conditions in 18 foreign countries), the public relations groups should be demanding that accuracy be served," he said.

Despite the limitations Nike's management says it will implement in terms of the company's own future communications, we believe O'Dwyer makes a point. Nike and other firms engaging in controversial practices have certainly opened the door to more inspection of corporate actions, including communications. If one honestly dissects the purpose and practice behind media relations and similar public relations activities, they are in fact forms of commercial speech, irrespective of the legal issues surrounding the term. The sky hasn't fallen, nor is advertising speech without robustness, just because advertisers are accountable for what they claim. Why should the public relations field fear for its future?

DISCUSSION QUESTIONS

1. What could Nike have done at an early stage to preempt criticism of its overseas employment and manufacturing practices?

2. If you were Nike's vice president for corporate communications, what recommendations would you give management today?

3. If you were head of strategic planning and public communication for one of the major groups critical of Nike, how would you analyze the situation following Nike's settlement with Kasky?

4. What other sources of information would have proved useful to you in analyzing this case?

5. Do you think corporations must meet a "social responsibility" standard of performance?

6. If you answered no to number 5, why not? What is the harm in asking businesses to do more than provide jobs and pay taxes?

7. If you answered yes to number 5, why so? What criteria should be used to measure whether or not a business is, in fact, "socially responsible?"

8. As a professional communicator, how do you anticipate integrating your personal values and ethics into your work life, particularly when facing issues such as those illustrated by the Nike experience, where both sides have a case to make?

REFERENCES AND SUGGESTED READINGS

Bennett, W. L. (2003, in press). Branded political communication: Lifestyle politics, logo campaigns, and the rise of global citizenship. In M. Micheletti, A. Follesdal, & D. Stolle (Eds.), *Politics, products, and markets: Exploring political consumerism past and present.* New Brunswick, NJ:

Transaction Books. Retrieved from http://depts.washington.edu/ccce/Assets/documents/pdf/NewBrandedPoliticalCommunication(BennettChapterFinal)61002.pdf.

Bullet, B. J. (2000). *Strategic public relations, sweatshops, and the making of a global movement.* Working Paper Series #2000-14. Cambridge, MA: Harvard University. The Joan Shorenstein Center on the Press, Politics and Public Policy. Retrieved from http://depts.washington.edu/gcp/pdf/strategic_public_relations.pdf.

Connor, T. (2001, July 28). Still waiting for Nike to respect the right to organize. *Global Exchang.* Retrieved from www.corpwatch.org/campaigns/PCD.jsp?articleid=619.

Cortes, J. (1997). Star-spangled business: Labor, patriotism, and Michael Jordan in a Nike advertisement. *To The Quick: The Journal Magazine of Media and Cultural Studies and Binghamton University.* Issue No. 1. Binghamton, NY: Binghamton University, State University of New York, Department of English. Retrieved from http://to-the-quick.binghamton.edu/issue%201/nike.html.

Council of Public Relations Firms (2003). Nike vs. Kasky. Retrieved from www.prfirms.org/resources/nike.

Creamer, M. (2003, September 12). Nike talks to PRWeek after Kasky settlement. *PRWeek.* Retrieved from www.prweek.com/news/news_story.cfm?ID=190002&site=3.

Cunningham, A., and Freeman, C. M. (2003). On the wings of Nike: A streamlined approach to the commercial speech doctrine. Unpublished research study. Baton Rouge, LA: Louisiana State University, Manship School of Mass Communication.

Dolan, Maura (2002, May 3). Nike can't just say it, court rules. *Los Angeles Times.* Retrieved from www.wgaeast.org/features/latimes-nike.html.

Elliot, J. (1996). Santa's little sweatshop. *Albion Monitor.* Retrieved from www.monitor.net/monitor/sweatshops/ss-intro.html.

Harris, J. F., & McKay, P. (1996, August 3). Companies agree to meet on sweatshops. *The Washington Post,* p. A10.

Heath, R. L., & Nelson, R. A. (1986). *Issues management: Corporate public policymaking in an information society.* Newbury Park, CA: Sage.

Hogan, D., & Manning, J. (1998, May 13). Nike promises to make improvements in Asian factories' working conditions. *The Oregonian,* 5–15.

Howard, E. (1998, Fall). Swooshed! What activists are teaching Nike. *Public Relations Strategist.* 38.

Kidd, D. (Moderator). (1997, October). Dartmouth professors speak on cost of living study. Retrieved from www.nikebiz.com/media/dartmouth.html.

Knight, P. (1998, August 1). Global manufacturing: The Nike story is just good business. *Vital Speeches, 64*(20), 637.

Lampriere, L. (1998, January). Nike PR blitz on overseas labor. *World Press Review, 45*(37), 32.

Locke, R. M. (2003). *The promise and perils of globalization: The case of Nike.* Case study prepared for the Sloan School of Management's 50th Anniversary. Cambridge, MA: Massachusetts Institute of Technology, Sloan School of Management. Retrieved from http://mitsloan.mit.edu/50th/nikepaper.pdf.

National Association of State Universities and Land-Grant Colleges (2001, November 6). Resurgence of social activism on campuses poses new challenges. *NASULGC Newsline, 11*(1), 6.

Nike, Inc. (1998). Senior Nike officials and industrial health specialists gather in Bangkok to evaluate the impact of the new water-based solutions upon worker health and safety. Retrieved from www.nikebiz.com/media/n_airqulty.shtml.

Nike, Inc. (2000). Labor: Frequently asked questions. Retrieved from www.nikebiz.com/labor/faq.shtml.

Nike, Inc. (2001a). Labor: Practices timeline. Retrieved from www.nikebiz.com/labor/time3.shtml.

Nike, Inc. (2001b). Our chronology. Retrieved from www.nikebiz.com/story/chrono.shtml.

Nike, Inc. (2002, May 2). California Supreme Court remands Kasky v. Nike case to lower court. Press release. Beaverton, OR. Retrieved from www.nike.com/nikebiz/news/pressrelease.jhtml?year=2002&month=05&letter=b.

Nike critic praises gains in air quality at Vietnam factory. (1999, March 12). *New York Times,* p. C3.

Nike invites workplace exams. (1999, March 19). *Footwear News.*

Nike settles sweatshop labor suit, PR stays muted (2003, September 12). *PRWatch.* Retrieved from www.prwatch.org/spin/September_2003.html#1063339201.

Niketown shantytowns. (1996, September 16). *The Weekly Standard.* Retrieved from www.geocities.com/Athens?Acropolis?5232?nikeshantytown.html, 9–16.

O'Dwyer, Jack (2002, November 6). PR groups on wrong side. *PRWatch.* Retrieved from www.prwatch.org/spin/November_2002.html.

Plitch, P. (1996, June 30). Sweatshop issues have very little impact on retail sales. *Dow Jones News Service.*

Read, R. (1998a, June 15). Factories struggle to cope amid Asia's economic crisis. *The Oregonian,* 5–14.

Read, R. (1998b, June 2). Workers wary Nike reforms will fit. *The Oregonian,* 5–14.

Reed, B. (1998, May–June). The business of social responsibility. *Dollars & Sense,* issue #217.

Saporito, B. (1998, March 30). Taking a look inside Nike's factories. *Time, 151*(12), 15.

Seeger, M., Sellnow, T., & Ullmer, R. (1998). Communication, organization, and crisis. *Communication Yearbook, 21,* 231–275.

Solomon, J. (1998, March 20). When cool gets cold. *Newsweek, 131*(13), 36–37.

SriMedia Corporate Governance News. (2002, November 15). The Arthur W. Page Society, Public Affairs Council, Public Relations Society of America, Council of Public Relations Firms, and Institute for Public Relations to file U.S. Supreme Court brief. Retrieved from www.srimedia.com/artman/publish/article_276.shtml

UNITE! Union of Needletrades, Industrial and Textile Employees. (2000, April 25). Sweatshops behind the Swoosh: A report on recent investigations of working conditions in Nike contractor plants in Asia. Retrieved from www.uniteunion.org/pressbox/nike-report.html.

Young, A. (1997, June 24). *The NIKE Code of Conduct by GoodWorks International, LLC: A Report on Conditions in International Manufacturing Facilities for NIKE, Inc.* Atlanta, GA: GoodWorks International, LLC. Retrieved from www.calbaptist.edu/dskubik/young.htm.

Más Que Comida, Es Vida—It's More Than Food, It's Life

WANDA REYES VELÁZQUEZ

Executive Summary

Diabetes is a metabolism disorder that increases the risk of cardiovascular disease and can cause blindness and renal failure. The disease often leads to amputation and death. In fact, in 1992 more than 50,000 people in the United States died of diabetes. In 1995 the U.S. Department of Health and Human Services reported that seven million people were diagnosed with diabetes and another seven million sufferers have not been diagnosed.

Diabetes does not impact all people equally. African Americans, American Indians, Alaska Natives, Hispanics, Asians, Pacific Islanders, elderly persons, and economically disadvantaged persons are all disproportionately affected by diabetes and its complications. Although there is no cure for diabetes, risks of the disease and its long-term effects can be reduced with diet and exercise. Medical treatment is also important for both preventing and controlling diabetes.

To deal with the health problems caused by diabetes and other diseases, the U.S. government, private organizations, and individuals worked together on two health agendas—Healthy People 2000 and Healthy People 2010. The U.S. Department of Health and Human Services served as leader, convener, and facilitator over a period of three years to develop a strategy for significantly improving the health of the nation by the year 2000. Healthy People 2000, as the report has been named, offered a vision to reduce significantly preventable death and disability, enhance quality of life, and reduce disparities in the health status of different populations in the United States. The Healthy People 2010 project followed Healthy People 2000. It was designed to identify the most significant health threats and to establish national goals to reduce them during the first decade of the 21st century. Some of its goals are "to reduce the risk of diabetes, to reduce the economic burden of diabetes, and to improve the quality of life for all persons who have or are at risk for diabetes."

The National Institutes of Diabetes and Digestive and Kidney Diseases (NIDDK) and the Division of Diabetes Translation of the Centers for Disease Control and Prevention created the National Diabetes Education Program) to improve treatment for people with diabetes, to promote early diagnosis, and, ultimately, to prevent the onset of diabetes. A network of more than 200 partner organizations concerned about the health of their constituents jointly sponsors the program. The organization launched the campaign *Más que comida, es*

117

vida (It's more than food, it's life). The campaign began with an announcement at the National Hispanic Medical Association's annual meeting.

Research

The National Diabetes Education Program (NDEP) is a joint initiative of the National Institute of Health (NIH) National Institutes of Diabetes and Kidney Disease (NIDKD) and the Division of Diabetes Translation of the Center for Disease Control (CDC). The initiative involves private industry, community organizations, and diabetes advocates who seek to improve treatment for people with diabetes. The initiative develops and implements ongoing diabetes awareness and education activities and also identifies, develops, and disseminates educational tools and resources for people with diabetes and those at risk for the disease. A network of more than 200 partner organizations jointly sponsors the program. This network has a steering committee of 14 work groups (CDC, 2003). The steering committee collaborates to develop new projects, set priorities, identify program needs, and share information about effective approaches and new ideas.

Partner organizations expand NDEP's capabilities by forming their own networks in their communities that spread program messages to target audiences. They also conduct community-based health programs[1] and encourage other groups to become part of the national program to disseminate NDEP messages and mobilize action to control diabetes. Frequently, partners advise program staff on special needs and are available to lend their expertise in developing materials or programs for specific populations. The program's partners also help develop and disseminate diabetes education and awareness campaign products for specific cultural groups and language communities.

NDEP targets several groups, such as people with diabetes and their families, people at risk for Type II diabetes, people with pre-diabetes, Hispanics, African Americans, Asian Americans, Pacific Islanders, Native Americans, health care providers, and health care payers, purchasers, and policy makers. In 1998, NDEP launched the campaign *Control Your Diabetes. For Life,* which is the first of many diabetes-related campaigns to come from the program. This campaign sought to reach the 16 million people in the United States with diabetes and their families with messages about the seriousness of the disease and ways to control it. *Control Your Diabetes. For Life* is NDEP's principal message. There are four sub-messages, which are: eat a healthy diet, engage in physical activity, monitor your glucose, and take your medications (NDEP Outreach Communication Plan, 2000). To target different groups in the United States, several diabetes media campaigns have been created. This case description concentrates on the nutrition campaign *Más que comida, es vida* (It's more than food, it's life). The campaign targeted Hispanics and their families in the United States.

Cultural Considerations about Hispanics

Hispanics are the fastest growing minority group in the United States (Castillo, 1996). In 2000, the U.S. population was 281.4 million and 35.3 million, or 12.5 percent, of that population was Hispanics (Therrien & Ramirez, 2001). The Hispanic minority is 58.5 percent Mexican, 9.6 percent Puerto Rican, 3.5 percent Cuban, 2.2 percent Dominican, 1.1 percent Guatemalan, 1.9 percent Salvadorian, and 1.3 percent Colombian. Several other South

American countries each contribute less than one percent of the Hispanic population of the United States. Spaniards, who are also considered Hispanic, make up 0.3 percent of the Hispanic population. Despite this diversity, Hispanics do share some characteristics in common. For example, nearly 40 percent of Hispanics under the age of 65 have no health insurance. California, Florida, New York, and Texas, which are the four states with the highest Hispanic population, account for 73 percent of all uninsured Hispanics (Mills, 1999). In 1998, 29 percent of the adult Hispanic population in the United States had less than a ninth-grade education, and only about 11 percent had a bachelor's degree or higher (U.S. Census Bureau, Population Division, Ethnic & Hispanic Statistics Branch, 2000).

Diabetes is also a trait shared by many Hispanics. According to Carter, Pugh, and Monterrosa (1996), the prevalence of Type II diabetes among Hispanics is two to five times greater than in European Americans. Hispanics' diabetes-specific mortality rates are also higher than those of European Americans and are increasing (Carter et al., 1993).

Nutrition Campaign "Más Que Comida, Es Vida"

A research firm was contracted to design and implement a diabetes nutrition media campaign targeting Hispanics in the United States. Formal research was conducted before launching the *Más que comida, es vida* campaign (Inteligencia Qualitative Research, 2000). Fourteen in-depth interviews were conducted in Miami, Florida, and Houston, Texas, before the campaign was launched. Eight of the interviews were conducted in Miami and six were conducted in Houston. Seven interviewees were female and seven were male. There were six Cubans, six Mexicans, one Honduran, and one Guatemalan in the group. All participants had been diagnosed with Type II diabetes. The subjects were also all 40 years of age or older and were of Hispanic origin. Spanish was their predominant language. All had annual household incomes of $30,000 or less, and none had participated in research within the last 12 months.

Print advertising, TV spots, and the poster that would be used in the campaign were shown to the participants. Results showed that for the TV public service announcements to be credible, food portion sizes that were shown had to be correct. Portions should be similar to the ones diabetics are supposed to eat. Results also showed that advertisements produced for the campaign have to emphasize that there is a toll-free number to assist diabetics, and that the recipe book was free. Some of the vocabulary used did not work well in Miami but did work in Houston. The reverse was also noted.

Based on the research, the campaign targeted Hispanic women 40 years of age and older with Type II diabetes, living in either in urban, semi-urban, or rural regions. The campaign focused on women because they are the decision makers when it comes to food preparation. Diabetics' extended families were also targeted. Campaign messages could be delivered via print and by television and radio public service announcements through the Spanish television networks Univision and Telemundo.

Objective

The ultimate goals of the National Diabetes Education Program are to improve treatment for people with diabetes, to promote early diagnosis, and to prevent the onset of diabetes (NDEP, 2003). Four objectives supported the program's goals. Those objectives were (1) to increase public awareness of the seriousness of diabetes, its risk factors, and strategies for preventing diabetes and its complications among at risk groups, (2) to improve understanding about diabetes and its control and to promote better self-management behaviors among people with diabetes, (3) to improve health care providers' understanding of diabetes and its control, and (4) to promote health care policies to improve quality and access to diabetes care. The campaign objective was designed to emphasize, to diabetic Hispanics, the important role nutrition plays in the management and control of the disease.

Strategies

The strategies used to accomplish the campaign's objectives were intended to increase nutrition awareness among Hispanics diagnosed with Type II diabetes. There were two types of strategies—action and communication strategies.

Action Strategies

■ Spanish nutrition material already available and usable for the effort was reviewed and incorporated in the campaign.
■ New materials with a call-to-action for more information were created.

Communication Strategies

Various messages with a hopeful and helpful tone were delivered through different Spanish media outlets to the target public. These media outlets were chosen because they reach the Hispanic community. The following messages were delivered in the campaign:

■ The campaign's key promise was *Si tomo el control de mi diabetes comiendo saludablemente, me sentiré mejor, lo cual es bueno para mi familia.* (If I take control of my diabetes by eating healthy, I will feel better, which is good for my family.)

Support Messages

■ I will do my best to prevent complications of diabetes, such as amputation, blindness, kidney failure, heart disease, and impotence.
■ I will feel more energetic.
■ The quality of my life will be the best it can be.
■ I will help control my blood sugar, which will make me feel better.
■ Substitutes can make healthy food taste good.
■ *Controle su diabetes deliciosamente.* (Control your diabetes deliciously.)

Several considerations guided the design of educational materials. These included literacy levels, language (using Spanish and English), and readability of messages. Other strategies included a call to download information about diabetes, inclusion of the NDEP logo and tag line, and integrating appetite appeal whenever possible.

Tactics

A series of Spanish-language public service announcements about the role nutrition plays in controlling diabetes was developed and placed with Spanish radio stations and two Spanish TV networks (Univision and Telemundo). This same information was also given to Spanish-language newspapers as advertisements and news releases. These announcements included:

- Ten, 20 and 30-second radio public service announcements in both Spanish and English (Figure 1).

FIGURE 1   Live Radio Spanish and English PSAs

10 seconds

*Si es hispano y tiene diabetes, no tiene que vivir sin sus comidas favoritas. Para recibir **su recetas y plan de comidas gratuitas,** llame al 1-877-232-3422. Un mensaje del Programa Nacional de Educación sobre la Diabetes.*

You don't have to give up your favorite foods if you are a Hispanic/Latino living with diabetes. To receive a free meal planner and recipe guide, call 1-877-232-3422. This message is from the National Diabetes Education Program.

20 seconds

*Si es hispano y tiene diabetes, no tiene que vivir sin sus comidas favoritas. Para ayudar a prevenir serias complicaciones, simplemente controle cuánto come, la frecuencia con que come y cómo prepara la comida. Para recibir **sus recetas y plan de comidas gratuitas** llame al 1-877-232-3422. Este mensaje fue traído a usted por el Programa Nacional de Educación sobre la Diabetes.*

You don't have to give up your favorite foods if you are a Hispanic/Latino living with diabetes. By monitoring how much and how often you eat, and how you prepare your food you can help prevent serious complications. To receive a free meal planner and recipe guide, call 1-877-232-3422. This message is brought to you by the National Diabetes Education Program.

30 Seconds

*Si es hispano y tiene diabetes, no tiene que vivir sin sus comidas favoritas. Simplemente controle cudnto come, la frecuencia con que come, cómo prepara la comida y podrá ayudar a prevenir serias complicaciones. Con una rutina regular de ejercicios, medicinas, y monitoreando con regularidad sus niveles de glucosa usted puede controlar su diabetes de por vida. Para recibir **su recetas y plan de comidas gratuitas,** llame al 1-877-232-3422. Este mensaje fue traído a usted por el Programa Nacional de Educación sobre la Diabetes.*

You don't have to give up your favorite foods if you are a Hispanic/Latino living with diabetes. By monitoring how much and how often you eat, and how you prepare your food you can help prevent serious complications and STILL eat your favorite traditional meals. Together with regular exercise, medication and glucose monitoring you can control your diabetes for life. To receive a free meal planner and recipe guide, call 1-877-232-3422. This message is brought to you by the National Diabetes Education Program.

- 30- and 15-second TV public service announcements in both Spanish and English
- Black and white newspaper advertisements in various shapes and sizes with the message that the food diabetics put on their plates can prevent serious complications.

Publications used in the campaign included:

- News releases in English and Spanish (Figure 2).
- Posters that carried the same message as the TV, radio, and print advertisements. They were suitable for hanging in clinics, stores, or homes. According to campaign designers, this poster should serve as a reminder that one positive way of avoiding diabetes complications is by eating wisely and tastefully.
- A meal planner in English and Spanish with recipes for every day of the week and tips to control diabetes.

Evaluation

An independent opinion research company was contracted to evaluate the campaign. The evaluation's goal was to identify how gatekeepers, identified as executives or staff of community-based organizations from the Hispanic community, and consumers used or intended to use the Meal Planner (Evaluation Report, 2004). The evaluation also probed a variety of topics beyond the Meal Planner, such as knowledge, attitudes, behaviors, and beliefs about diabetes. Six focus groups were conducted in Miami, Florida, and Atlanta, Georgia, to evaluate the Meal Planner designed for the campaign.

Because of their close relationship with the target audience, gatekeepers were included in the evaluation. Gatekeepers are executives and staff of community-based organizations who provide health or comprehensive social services to Hispanic audiences. They participated in two focus groups. Potential consumers participated in four focus groups. The results from both types of focus groups are reported below.

Gatekeeper Focus Groups

The participants identified several health issues affecting the Hispanic community. Participants mentioned the following problems: access to health care, lack of culturally appropriate or bilingual health information, lack of affordable health services or programs, lack of bilingual services, and lack of culturally competent health care providers. Poverty, which is another problem for many Hispanics, was also mentioned because of its impact on health care. In addition, it was also noted that due to their citizenship status, some Hispanics are not able to receive health care services.

Regarding health priorities in the Hispanic community, participants listed diet, obesity, access to health care and affordable health programs, cancer, hypertension, HIV/AIDS, and diabetes. Participants were not able to pick a single priority because many problems overlap and some of the problems affect the occurrence of other health issues. For example, poor eating habits cause obesity and exacerbate diabetes. Also, some gatekeepers said that Hispanics identify top priorities according to what they can afford because they face so many economic problems.

FIGURE 2   Media Advisory

Contact: Phyllis McGuire
(770) xxx-xxxx

MEDIA ADVISORY

National Diabetes Education Program to Launch Hispanic/Latino Nutrition Campaign

"Más que comida, es vida" (It's more than food, it's life) Informs Hispanics/Latinos
That They Can Still Enjoy their Favorite Foods While Controlling Their Diabetes

Washington, DC—March 24, 2001. During the National Hispanic Medical Association's (NHMA) fifth annual conference, "Healthy Hispanic Families," on March 23–25, 2001, the National Diabetes Education Program (NDEP), a joint initiative of the Centers for Disease Control and Prevention (CDC) and the National Institutes for Health (NIH), will announce its plan to launch a new media campaign. The campaign targets Hispanics/Latinos with the message that they can help control their diabetes with food.

In the Hispanic/Latino culture, food is an integral part of family gatherings and community celebrations. Food is often a symbol of affection or care for family and friends and a way for mothers to nurture and fathers to provide for their families. However, many people with diabetes believe incorrectly that they need to give up their favorite foods. NDEP has created a public service campaign called "Más que comida, es vida" (It's more than food, it's life) for people with diabetes and their families. The campaign urges Hispanics/Latinos and their families to consider how much and how often they eat and how they prepare their food, but does NOT ask them to forego their favorite foods when making dietary decisions.

"Hispanics/Latinos with diabetes and their families can continue eating the foods they love; we are simply asking them to make some changes in their portion sizes and how they prepare their favorite dishes," explained Dr. Elizabeth Valdéz and Yanira Cruz-González, co-chairs of the Hispanic/Latino work group for NDEP. "For example, cooking with olive oil instead of lard or limiting salt intake by using fresh herbs and spices like cilantro to season foods. These are just two examples of ways that Hispanics can prepare healthier foods without sacrificing taste."

The "Más que comida, es vida" campaign includes a meal planner to help Hispanics/Latinos with diabetes and their families to understand how they can better control their diabetes and still include their favorite food choices. The meal planner includes tips on healthy eating and a recipe guide that offers seven flavorful food recipes, low in added fat, high-fat meats, and salt, that could be enjoyed by the whole family. Radio, television, and print public service announcements target Hispanic/Latino audiences with campaign messages. Viewers and listeners can call a toll-free number to receive the meal planner and recipe guide.

One of the campaign audiences is physicians and other caretakers who work with Hispanics/Latinos with diabetes and their families. Initial campaign research revealed that physicians' advice to Hispanic/Latino patients with diabetes often conflicts with cultural dietary habits. "We are pleased to include NDEP in our Healthy Hispanic Families conference this year," said Dr. Elena Ríos, President of the National Hispanic Medical Association. "We will have hundreds of Hispanic/Latino health professionals in attendance who can take the good news back to patients and colleagues that by controlling portion sizes and cooking with less fat, Hispanics/Latinos with diabetes can continue to eat favorite foods."

— more —

(continued)

FIGURE 2   **Continued**

Page Two/National Diabetes Education Program

Diabetes is a significant concern in Hispanic/Latino populations. According to CDC statistics, six percent of Hispanic/Latino adults in the United States and Puerto Rico have been diagnosed with diabetes. This rate is a staggering 50 percent higher than that of white Americans. Approximately 2.3 percent of Hispanics aged 18–44 have been diagnosed with diabetes, 12 percent of those aged 45–64, and 21.4 percent of those aged 65 and older.

The National Diabetes Education Program (NDEP) is a federally sponsored initiative involving public and private partners, to improve the treatment and outcomes for people with diabetes, to promote early diagnosis, and ultimately, to prevent the onset of diabetes. This healthy eating campaign for Hispanics/Latinos with diabetes and their families will be released in April 2001.

# #

In terms of health information disseminated, participants indicated that they have heard a few general health messages targeting Hispanics with information about the prevention and control of diabetes. Some of the messages were linked with diet, exercise, and obesity. Participants also said that because there are so many different Hispanic populations, education materials and programs must be community-specific and culturally appropriate.

Gatekeepers also mentioned that their organizations perform activities or programs related to diabetes prevention and control. Some participants said they would be more motivated to educate their communities if they had more money and resources such as bilingual materials and diabetes education modules.

Gatekeepers also described a cultural value associated with food in the Hispanic community. Hispanics attach importance to eating in certain ways and eating foods they have consumed their entire lives. It is difficult for Hispanics to change their eating habits because doing so may be insulting to other individuals around them.

Gatekeepers also assessed the Meal Planner. Initial reactions to the Meal Planner were positive. Participants liked the cover, the recipes, and the use of Spanish and English languages. They believed the publication was easy to read and easy to use. Some participants indicated that they could plan activities around the Meal Planner, such as a cooking demonstration.

There were also negative reactions to the Meal Planner. Some of the participants did not like the Meal Planner because they thought its glossy material was hard to read for some people. Some participants thought the food selection was not appropriate because it did not include traditional foods. Participants also worried that some of their elderly constituents would not cook foods featured in the Meal Planner. Moreover, because the recipes seemed to be primarily from the Caribbean region, they indicated that food choices were not appropriate for many communities.

Participants thought the Meal Planner would be more useful if it offered suggestions for gradual changes in food preparation. For instance, adding less cheese to enchiladas or cooking tortillas with vegetable oil instead of lard. Some participants also wondered whether their constituents would be able to afford the ingredients listed in the recipes or would be able to spend their money to try new dishes. One participant mentioned that for the Meal Planner to be effective, it would need to make clear that healthy eating does not have to be expensive. Participants also discussed the specific vocabulary differences of each Hispanic group. One participant suggested creating a fact sheet that gives bulleted information about diabetes risk. Another suggestion was to list a telephone number for people to call to get more recipes specific to their culture.

Consumer Focus Groups

Focus groups provided information on consumers' health concerns, the need for education campaigns, health priorities in the Hispanic community, diabetes beliefs, and what they thought of the Meal Planner. Results showed that most of the consumers' health concerns centered around diabetes, cancer, and cardiovascular problems, including high cholesterol. They said they were concerned about the lack of knowledge about the causes of common illnesses. Participants also said they did not know what causes diabetes. They noted that lack of health care due to cost, and the complexity of the health care system, are also problems for the Hispanic community in the United States. Moreover, the lack of health insurance in this community further restricts access to health care. Due to these factors, they stressed the importance of prevention campaigns.

Participants suggested an education campaign to increase awareness about diabetes. They also offered suggestions for how and what types of messages to carry to their community. These suggestions included using Spanish language television to reach Hispanics, using peak hours to catch different demographic groups, and using radio talk shows and Spanish-language newspapers with health sections to disseminate news releases or educational information. Face-to-face or personal contact was deemed important for reaching the Hispanic community. Participants also stressed the importance of having culturally appropriate materials and messages on diabetes prevention and control. They pointed out that health-related messages must address people's food preferences and traditions, the cost of care, the higher cost of healthier foods such as fruits and vegetables, the lack of education, and the lack of appropriate venues for walking or exercise.

Participants said that the top health priorities in the Hispanic community were cancer, diabetes, and heart conditions. They also mentioned poor nutrition, weight problems, and HIV/AIDS. They also indicated that they ate healthier and got more exercise in their home country than they do in the United States. Participants also noted that poor nutrition, leading to obesity, was one of the most prevalent health problems in the U.S. Hispanic community.

Some participants referred to diabetes as the "silent killer." According to participants, Hispanics are not aware of the symptoms and complications of diabetes. They also do not know that they may be at risk. Some participants thought diabetes was hereditary and incurable. There was also some confusion about different types of diabetes, which led to fatalistic attitudes. Some participants indicated that there are things you cannot change. Therefore, they believe they cannot do anything about diabetes.

Regarding the Meal Planner, participants had positive reactions to it. Some of them indicated that it was easy to use and the information was balanced. They liked the food pyramid shown because it was information that normal recipe books do not have. They liked the fact that it is bilingual. Also, it was suggested that the Meal Planner could be introduced by using cooking demonstrations to attract an audience. Using the Meal Planner in restaurants as a guide for selecting from the menu was also suggested. Most participants commented on the Meal Planner's presentation. They indicated that at first they thought it was something they had to pay for. It was a little intimidating because Hispanics are used to less expensive-looking products.

Critique

NDEP was trying to tailor diabetes education campaigns to accommodate diverse cultures. Unlike some health education providers, NDEP has taken into consideration cultural aspects of different groups. The *Más que comida, es vida* campaign addressed Hispanics' cultural differences from the mainstream society. It also used strategies and tactics relevant to Hispanic beliefs.

According to Airhihenbuwa (1995), culturally different groups respond in a dissimilar way to health and disease. Public relations practitioners should examine health behaviors in minority groups to find out whether they are rooted in the cultural values and beliefs of the people. In addition, practitioners should also examine groups' values, lifestyle, and, particularly, cultural beliefs when designing campaigns targeting at Hispanics. Bartholomew et al. (1990) assert that chronic disease prevention and control interventions designed for the mainstream population have not been effective in reaching the Hispanic community. Likewise, public relations campaigns would not be effective if the factors mentioned above are not considered. The following section offers some recommendations for future health public relations campaigns targeting Hispanics in the United States.

Research

Before launching the campaign, Hispanics' nutrition habits were identified as a problem. In-depth interviews were conducted in Miami, Florida, and Houston, Texas, to learn whether the target audience would be able to understand the information to be disseminated. It is important that individuals from the communities were asked to participate in the study.

For future health campaigns targeting Hispanics in the United States, it is necessary to investigate within-group differences prior designing the campaign. Hispanic individuals have been generically categorized as one ethnic or cultural group. However, the subgroups within this community have both commonalities and differences. Some commonalities are family values, gender roles, fatalism, religious beliefs, and attention to alternative health care. Language use is also more complex than many assume. Some Hispanics speak only Spanish and some speak both Spanish and English. Many also speak only English. There are also differences such as country of origin, food consumption habits, level of acculturation to the mainstream society, generation, and socio-economic status. During the research process, it is extremely important to identify how these factors may influence a campaign's outcome.

The country of origin for each individual in the target public is one of the most important aspects to consider when targeting Hispanics in the United States. This is because individuals may have different beliefs or behaviors based on the country or territory from which they come. For example, food consumption habits are one of the factors among Hispanic groups that influence diabetes. Although Hispanics' food consumption differs from that of the mainstream society, there are some within-group differences that must be considered. For example, Mexicans and Puerto Ricans have different diets and food preferences.

For Mexicans, food-related activities facilitate interactions between family members and help delineate family roles (Goyan-Kittler & Sucher, 1998). The diet is high in complex carbohydrates (Sanjur, 1995). There is a liberal use of added fat in cooking and food preparation. There is also a preference for high-fat meats such as organ meats, *chorizo* or *longanizas* (sausages), *chicharrón* (fried pork skin), and *patitas de cerdo* (pig's feet). Corn, beans, wheat, *chiles, tortillas* (flat corn cakes), *frijoles* (beans), bread, soups, rice, hot sauce, eggs, *burritos,* and chicken are consumed as part of the Mexican diet. For Puerto Ricans, rice and beans are the basic dietary items (Sanjur, 1995). Usually rice is cooked with salt and oil. There are two critical ingredients in the Puerto Rican cooking: a seasoning called *adobo,* and *sofrito,* which is the foundation for many dishes, made of blended onion, garlic, oregano, green or red pepper, cilantro, and *recao* (an herb found in Puerto Rico and Asia) (Novas, 1998). Nutrition campaigns discussing Mexican cooking and eating habits would not be effective in the Puerto Rican community not only because of the differences explained but also because of language nuances. Both cultural groups have different names for food items. For example, for a Mexican, *tortillas* may be used to prepare tacos; for some Puerto Ricans, *tortillas* are omelets.

It is also necessary to recognize that members of ethnic groups may have adopted eating patterns and food choices of the mainstream society (Satia-Abouta et al., 2002). Therefore, in addition to investigating food habit differences, it is important to learn whether individuals from the target audience may have undergone dietary acculturation, which happens when people from minority groups adopt eating patterns and food choices of the host country (Satia-Abouta et al., 2002).

Objective

The *Más que comida, es vida* campaign's objective was to emphasize to diabetic Hispanics the important role nutrition plays in the management and control of the disease. This objective responds to the problem identified by NDEP: diabetic Hispanics' eating habits must be modified in order for them to control diabetes. However, the campaign emphasized that nutrition is not the only way to control diabetes; there are other important factors.

Although *Más que comida, es vida*'s objective addresses the problem identified, it lacks a timeline and a system for measuring success. Therefore, the objective lacks any indication of how the campaign will be evaluated. Since *Más que comida, es vida* is an awareness campaign, it would not be difficult to evaluate the objective. It is imperative to operationalize the objectives so that individuals evaluating the campaign would have criteria to measure the campaign accurately. This is particularly important when an organization different from the one that designed the campaign will evaluate the campaign's success.

For future campaigns targeting Hispanics, the use of attitudinal objectives[2] and behavior objectives[3] is recommended. Further, some indication of a timeline and how meeting the objective will be measured or evaluated must be included. It should be noted that evaluating these types of objectives is relatively complex and, according to the objective, either pre- and post-tests or both might be required. For these objectives it is also necessary to consider Hispanic family values, gender roles, fatalism, religious beliefs, alternative health care seeking, language, country of origin, food consumption habits, level of acculturation to the mainstream society, generation individuals belong to, and political and socio-economic status.

Strategy

The action strategies implemented seem appropriate to achieve the campaign's objective. These strategies included: keeping in mind literacy levels, using generic Spanish-cross-cultural language, disseminating information in both Spanish and English, and including a call to action to motivate those in the public to seek information on diabetes. These strategies were wisely chosen to reach the audience. In addition, choosing Spanish media outlets was appropriate.

However, there were no strategies addressing family members who, according to the news release published before launching the campaign, were also targeted. Strategies to stimulate familial support for diabetics should have been included.

Furthermore, the campaign designers should investigate whether the use of the slogan *Control Your Diabetes. For Life* is effective in the Hispanic community. Most individuals from this community have a low socio-economic status,[4] which affects their health and disease conditions because they may not have access to health care services or lack health insurance coverage. Thus, these individuals may not have appropriate means to control their disease. As a result, they might not do what the campaign is asking because they may think that nothing effective can be done. Moreover, due to cultural beliefs, some Hispanic groups may have fatalistic views, which, along with a low socio-economic status, impact how individuals manage diabetes.

Rotter (1966) affirms that fatalism is a generalized expectation that outcomes of situations are determined by forces external to one's self, such as powerful others, luck, fate, or chance. Those external forces may be malicious, benign, or beneficial (Joiner Jr. et al., 2001). Fatalism is a cognitive orientation learned through social interaction. It is a belief in an external locus of control over the events of one's life (Ross, Mirowsky, & Cockerham, 1983). Parker and Kleiner (1966) note that fatalism has also been interpreted as a potentially adaptive response to an uncontrollable life situation often experienced by minorities. For example, the Mexican culture is imbued with fatalism (Ross, Mirowsky & Cockerham, 1983; Neff, Hoppe & Perea, 1993; Joiner Jr. et al., 2001). Social class also influences fatalism because individuals from lower social classes learn through recurrent experiences that they have limited opportunities and that powerful others and unpredictable forces control their lives (Ross, Mirowsky & Cockerham, 1983). No matter how hard these individuals try, they cannot get ahead. Examining fatalism among Hispanic groups is worthwhile to help campaign planners better strategize their health messages.

Tactics

Spanish and English diabetes public service announcements were placed in Spanish television networks, which reach the target audience. The recipe book was published in both Spanish and English. This book provided important information for diabetes management. It used simple vocabulary to explain what diabetes is, how to determine if one is at risk for the disease, and suggestions about what to do to cook and eat healthy food. The language used should be understood across Hispanic groups.

For future campaigns targeting Hispanics in the United States, it is recommended that the English-language television networks and newspapers should be included because there are Hispanics who select those media because they only speak English, or who select English language media because they are trying to learn the language.

Evaluation

Evaluating whether a campaign has achieved its objectives is fundamental. To determine whether a campaign has been successful, practitioners have to assess the campaign's objectives. As mentioned before, an independent opinion research company, which had nothing to do with planning the campaign, conducted the evaluation.

The *Más que comida, es vida* campaign's objective was to emphasize to diabetic Hispanics the important role nutrition plays in the management and control of the disease. Not operationalizing the objective made it impossible to evaluate the campaign's success in meeting a specific objective. However, the opinion research evaluating the Meal Planner did shed light on the strengths of this product and identified areas for improvement (Evaluation report, 2004). Although evaluating the strengths of the Meal Planner was important, some aspects of the campaign were not assessed. For instance, evaluation findings do not show whether the messages disseminated in the public services announcements were accurate, how many individuals the announcements reached, or whether the messages affected behavior.

ENDNOTES

1. Windsor et al. (1994) define health intervention as a planned and systematically implemented combination of standardized health promotion and education content, procedures, and methods designed to produce change in cognitive, affective, skill, behavior, or health status objectives for a defined at risk population, at a specified site, and during a defined period of time.

2. Hendrix (1995) states that attitudinal objectives aim at modifying the way an audience feels about the organization and its products, or services. Attitude modification forms new attitudes where none exist, reinforces existing attitudes, or changes existing attitudes (p. 23).

3. Behavioral objectives involve behavior modification (Hendrix, 1995). Basically, this type of objective consists of the creation or stimulation of a new behavior, the enhancement or intensification of existing favorable behavior, or the reversal of negative behaviors on the part of an audience. It is difficult to measure it because one may need to measure before exposing the audience to the

campaign and after it has been exposed to it. Even if the tests were conducted, one may not find out whether or not there was a behavioral change because individuals may give socially desirable answers.

4. Socio-economic status is a broad concept. Individuals' financial, occupational, and educational influences have been used to measure this concept (Winkleby, Gardner, & Taylor, 1996). Even though these dimensions of socio-economic status are interrelated, it has been proposed that each reflects different individual and societal forces associated with health and disease (Susser, Watson, & Hopper, 1985). For example, occupation measures prestige, responsibility, and work exposure. Education indicates skills necessary for acquiring positive social, psychological, and economic resources. Income shows individuals' spending power, housing, diet, and medical care.

DISCUSSION QUESTIONS

1. The National Diabetes Education Program is made up of 200 partner organizations. Does the size and complexity of the organization make it difficult to identify organizational goals? How can such a large and complex organization be coordinated in a single public relations campaign?

2. The National Diabetes Education Program identifies four public relations objectives.
   a. Are these really public relations objectives? Why or why not?
   b. Please identify **one** public relations objective that would help meet the goals of NDEP.

3. The campaign primarily targeted women.
   a. Do you agree with this decision? Why or why not?
   b. What research would you do to determine whether the campaigns should specifically target women?

4. This campaign used Univision and Telemundo to deliver messages to Hispanics over 40.
   a. Describe the research you would do to determine how many people in the target public are reached by Telemundo and Univision.
   b. What other media effectively reach the target public?

5. The research conducted by Inteligencia Qualitative Research was used to design the TV public service announcements.
   a. Was the sample size for that research adequate?
   b. Can research conducted in Miami and Houston be generalized to all Hispanics in the United States? Present one argument for and one against such generalization.

6. Several support messages are listed under "Communication Strategies" in this campaign.
   a. For each message, what theory, model, or paradigm explains why it should or should not work?
   b. What research would you conduct to determine whether each of these messages would help meet any of the four public relations objectives?

7. Many of the campaign messages were delivered in Spanish.
   a. Are there different Spanish dialects used by members of the target public?
   b. What research would you conduct to determine what Spanish dialect should be used in each medium selected for this campaign?

8. Evaluation of this campaign had not been completed as of this writing. Describe how you would evaluate the campaign's success.

REFERENCES AND SUGGESTED READINGS

Airhihenbuwa, C. O. (1995). *Health and culture: Beyond the Western paradigm.* Thousand Oaks, CA: Sage.

Bartholomew, A. M., et al., (1990). Food frequency intakes and sociodemographic factors of elderly Mexican Americans and non-Hispanic whites. *Journal of American Dietetic Association, 90,* 1693–1696.

Bellenir, K. (1999). *Health reference series: Diabetes sourcebook* (2nd ed.). Omnigraphics, Inc.: Detroit.

Carter, J. S., Wiggins, C. L., Becker, T. M., Key, C. R., & Samet, J. M. (1993). Diabetes mortality among New Mexico's American Indian, Hispanic, and non-Hispanic white populations, 1958–1987. *Diabetes Care, 16,* 306–309.

Carter, J. S., Pugh, J. A., & Monterrosa, A. (1996). Non-insulin dependent diabetes mellitus in minorities in the United States. *Annals of International Medicine, 125,* 221–232.

Castillo, H. M. (1996). Cultural diversity: Implications for nursing. In S. Torres (Ed.). *Hispanic voices: Hispanic health educators speak out* (pp. 1–12). New York: NLN Press.

CDC at www.cdc.gov/team-ndep/partners-info.htm, accessed July 21, 2003.

Evaluation Report (2004). Meal Planner Final Report provided via e-mail by Dr. Jane Kelly, Director National Diabetes Education Program, January, 2004.

Glasgow, R. E., et al. (1999). If diabetes is a public health problem, why not treat it as one? A population-based approach to chronic illness. *Annals of Behavioral Medicine, 21*(2), 159–170.

Goyan-Kittler, P., & Sucher, K. P. (1998). *Food and culture in America: A nutrition handbook* (2nd ed.). Belmont, CA: Wadsworth.

Hendrix, J. A. (1992). *Public relations cases* (2nd ed.). Belmont, CA: Wadsworth.

Inteligencia Qualitative Research. (2000). *A Qualitative Concept Pre-Test Conducted Among Hispanic Males and Females for NDEP.*

Joiner, T. E., Jr., et al. (2001). On fatalism, pessimism, and depressive symptoms among Mexican-Americans and other adolescents attending an obstetrics-gynecology clinic. *Behavior Research and Therapy, 39,* 887–896.

McGuire, P. (2001) *Media advisory.* National Diabetes Education Program to Launch Hispanic/Latino Nutrition Campaign.

National Diabetes Advisory Board. (1983). *The prevention and treatment of five complications of diabetes: A guide for primary care.* The U.S. Department of Health and Human Services.

NDEP Outreach Communication Plan. (2000). Provided via e-mail by Roberto Noriega of the National Diabetes Education Program, 2003. See also, http://ndep.nih.gov/materials/pubs/ndep, accessed June 22, 2003.

National Institute of Diabetes and Digestive and Kidney Diseases (1998). *Diabetes special report.* United States Department of Health and Human Services.

Neff, J. A., Hoppe, K., & Perea, P. (1993). Acculturation and alcohol use: Drinking patterns and problems among Anglo and Mexican-American male drinkers. *Hispanic Journal of Behavioral Sciences, 9,* 151–181.

Novas, H. (1998). *Everything you need to know about Latino history* (2nd ed.). Penguin Putnam Inc: New York.

Parker, S. & Kleiner, R. (1966). *Mental illness in the urban Negro community.* New York: Free Press.

Ross, C. E., Mirowsky, J., & Cockerham, W. C. (1983). Social class, Mexican culture, and fatalism: Their effects on psychological distress. *American Journal of Community Psychology, 11,* 383–399.

Rotter, J. B. (1966). Generalized expectations for internal vs. external control of reinforcement. *Psychological Monographs, 80,* 1–28.

Satia-Abouta et al. (2002). Dietary acculturation: Applications to nutrition research and dietetics. *Journal of the American Dietetic Association, 102*(8), 1105–1118.

Susser, M. W., Watson, W., & Hopper, K. (1985). *Sociology in Medicine.* New York: Oxford University Press.

Therrien, M., & Ramirez, R. (2001, March). *The Hispanic population characteristics in the United States: Current population reports P20–535.* Washington, DC: U.S. Census Bureau.

U.S. Department of Health and Human Services. (1990). *Healthy People: National Health Promotion and Disease Prevention Objectives.* U.S. Government Printing Office. DHHS Publication No. (PHS) 91-50212.

U.S. Department of Health and Human Services. (1996). *Healthy People 2000: Midcourse Review and 1995 Revisions.* Boston: Jones & Bartlett Publishers.

U.S. Department of Health and Human Services. (2000). *Healthy People 1992 National Health Promotion and Disease Prevention Objectives.* Boston: Johns & Barlet Publishers.

U.S. Department of Health and Human Services. (2001). *Healthy People 2010. Vol. 1 & 2.* Boston: Jones & Bartlett Publishers.

Wilcox, D. L., Ault, P. H., & Agee, W. K. (2001). *Essentials of public relations.* New York: Addison Wesley Longman.

Winkleby, M. A., Gardner, C. D., & Taylor, C. B. (1996). The influence of gender and socioeconomic factors on Hispanic/White differences in body mass index. *Preventive Medicine, 25,* 203–211.

The International Campaign to Ban Landmines and the 1997 Ban Bus Campaign

NORMAN E. YOUNGBLOOD

In addition to the sources cited in the bibliography, much of the information for this case study was obtained from interviews conducted by the author in 2003 with Mary Wareham and Barbara Ayotte. Wareham is currently a Senior Advocate in the Arms Division at Human Rights Watch and was the Campaign Coordinator for the U.S. Committee to Ban Landmines (USCBL) during the 1990s, as well as one of the principal organizers of the 1997 Ban Bus Campaign. Ayotte is currently the Director of Communications for Physicians for Human Rights, the lead organization for USCBL. She also managed media relations for the International Campaign to Ban Landmines at the Nobel Peace Prize Ceremonies in Oslo, Norway, and participated in Ban Bus activities in Boston. *Landmines* and *land mines* are both correct spellings for the weapon discussed in the chapter. The former is the more common today.

Executive Summary

The movement to ban antipersonnel (AP) landmines began in the 1970s when the International Committee of the Red Cross and other nongovernmental organizations (NGOs) began pressuring governments to reexamine their landmine use policies in light of the devastating effects of landmines on both soldiers and civilians during the Vietnam War. The International Campaign to Ban Landmines (ICBL) was founded two decades later in October 1992 by a group of six NGOs. In October 1996, representatives from more than 70 countries and from dozens of NGOs met in Ottawa at the "Towards a Global Ban on Anti-Personnel Landmines" Conference. Fifty of the countries represented at the conference signed a declaration recognizing the need for a total ban on AP landmines, and the Canadian government called for a treaty-signing conference to be held in December the following year in Ottawa.

Two events occurred between the two Ottawa conferences that helped bring international attention to the landmine issue. In January 1997, Diana, Princess of Wales, spoke out in favor of the upcoming treaty and spent the next seven months campaigning for it and talking with landmine survivors. Her death in an automobile accident that August further highlighted the landmine issue. Two months later, in October 1997, the Nobel Committee announced that ICBL and its coordinator, Jodie Williams, would share the 1997 Nobel Peace Prize. Despite the international attention drawn by the upcoming treaty conference, it was clear to members of ICBL that U.S. president Bill Clinton would not sign the treaty on behalf of the United States.

In an effort to educate the U.S. public about the problem of landmines and garner support for the treaty, ICBL and other NGOs organized the Ban Bus campaign. The campaign sent a group of experienced anti-landmine advocates from around the world on a trip across the United States. The group traveled by bus from San Francisco to Ottawa between October 23 and December 1, 1997, stopping in 24 U.S. cities along the way to conduct landmine-awareness events and encourage people to write to their government officials in support of the Ottawa treaty. By the time the group reached Ottawa, the trip had drawn considerable media attention and their arrival there was met by both the press and government officials, including the Prime Minister of Canada. While the United States did not sign the Ottawa treaty, the trip was remarkably successful in drawing media attention to the upcoming treaty and in building grassroots support for the anti-landmine movement in the United States. It also provided a model for future landmine awareness campaigns.

Research

The Ban Bus campaign was based in large part on past efforts at political organizing. Ban Bus organizer and chair of the United States Campaign to Ban Landmines (USCBL), Mary Wareham, recalled that the genesis for the idea came about during after-hours discussions at a conference in Mozambique. During these discussions, landmine advocates were looking for a way to educate the U.S. public about the landmine issue and to draw attention to the upcoming treaty signing in Ottawa. ICBL already had a model in place for educating publics and frequently sent representatives on speaking tours. It was at one of ICBL organizer Jody Williams's 1993 talks in New Zealand that Mary Wareham first became involved in the movement. In 1996, ICBL began using mobile advocacy offices, sending representatives on speaking tours based out of vans equipped with cellular phones and computers. Despite the group's experience with these mobile advocacy offices, putting together the Ban Bus tour was a daunting process. By the time the decision was made to organize the trip in September, the Ottawa treaty-signing conference was less than three months away and the projected starting date for the trip was at the end of October, barely a month away.

One of the first issues that had to be addressed was where the Ban Bus should stop. Cities were selected by working backwards on the map from Ottawa to San Francisco, and locations were chosen in part because of an existing support base in the area. Second, organizers had to decide who should go on the tour. Based on past experience with putting together educational events, Ban Bus organizers selected a diverse group of participants to accompany Mary Wareham on the trip. John Rodsted, an Australian photographer, had come to visually document the landmine issue after working as a freelance photographer in landmine-affected areas and had photographed landmine victims in a number of countries including Cambodia, Bosnia, and Mozambique. Usman Fitrat, an Afghani landmine survivor, had lost both hands and most of his family to landmines and had proven to be a powerful speaker. Petter Quande, a Norwegian landmine activist, had worked for Norwegian People's Aid in Angola. Mette Sophie Eliseussen, also from Norway, had spent several years conducting landmine awareness programs for children in Kabul, Afghanistan. Dalma Foldes, from Hungary, had created numerous anti-landmine exhibits, including exhibits at many of the conferences and meetings that led to the Ottawa treaty signing. Michael Hands of the United Kingdom was a mine clearance specialist and 15-year veteran of the British Army. His experience in demining provided him with a way to teach people about the problems posed by landmines, and his experience as a soldier made him good with veterans groups. The combined talents and experience of the group members set the tone for the general format of a Ban Bus event—an exhibit of black and white photographs documenting the damage caused by AP landmines, a display of postcards written by children in Afghanistan, a display of mine clearance techniques, and, when possible, meetings with public officials.

The target public for the Ban Bus campaign was multifold: the U.S. public at large, U.S. government officials, and the national and international media. Many of the events were held on college campuses, in part because many of the cooperating groups had existing support bases at colleges. This allowed them access to a free speech area, as well as a population that have traditionally been viewed as more likely to be open to new ideas, and as good candidates for a call-to-action campaign at college. Events were also frequently held at public and private elementary and secondary schools. As at all events, students were encouraged to write letters to government officials asking why the United States was not going to sign the treaty. In addition to the benefits the organizers gained from the emotional appeal of children writing letters, teaching children about the problems posed by landmines also provided organizers with a future cadre of activists and helped them reach the children's parents.

One of ICBL's more innovative techniques for promoting the event was coordinating the Ban Bus trip with a website that provided visitors with a running update of the trip's progress, as well as contact names for upcoming events. The website address was included in promotional materials and painted on the side of the bus. While this technique is commonplace today, it was still relatively rare in 1997, a scant seven years after the invention of the World Wide Web. In addition, Wareham transmitted many of the updates directly to the Web while she was traveling in the van, using a computer and mobile phone, a practice which is still relatively uncommon. In addition to taking advantage of new technology such as the Web, organizers also relied on the traditional print and broadcast media to publicize the campaign, sending out printed press releases and making phone calls to coordinate press coverage of Ban Bus events. Area activists handled much of the local promotion for events.

Objectives

An ICBL/USCBL brochure about the Ban Bus campaign included a three-part call for action by the U.S. public: contact the White House and urge the president to sign the treaty, contact members of Congress to support the *Landmines Elimination* bill introduced by Senators Chuck Hagel and Patrick Leahy, and "urge the American government to support international programs for humanitarian mine clearance and mine victim assistance." This call for action illustrates several of the stated main objectives of the Ban Bus campaign—to raise public awareness in the United States about the landmine issue and the upcoming treaty signing in Ottawa, and to encourage the U.S. government to sign the Ottawa treaty.

Organizers also hoped that the campaign would leave a strong anti-landmine grassroots organization in its wake as well as provide ICBL and USCBL with contacts for future campaigns. Ban Bus efforts to influence government officials in the United States to support the ban and related issues were not limited to meetings with members of the federal government, but also included meetings with state and local government officials. In many cases, local officials proved willing to call for action on the treaty at the national level. While the stated objectives included convincing President Clinton to sign the Ottawa treaty, Ban Bus organizer and then USCBL coordinator Mary Wareham stated that when they were organizing the campaign they had no illusions that the United States was likely to sign the treaty; however, they hoped to use the campaign to draw national and international attention to the landmine issue, particularly the upcoming treaty signing in Ottawa. Finally, organizers planned to use the event to draw the attention of the U.S. and international press to the Ottawa Accords and the United States' refusal to sign the treaty.

Strategies

Ban Bus organizers had roughly a month to plan a one-month, 24-city trip across the United States. One of their challenges was to involve the public at each stop in a way that would personalize the landmine issue. This challenge not only set the stage for the events held at each stop, but helped shape the composition of the bus crew so that it included not only speakers, but people with the skills needed to set up exhibits and communicate with the press.

Action Strategies

ICBL is by its nature a cooperative effort, having been formed out of a coalition of six NGOs—the Vietnam Veterans of America Foundation, Physicians for Human Rights, Human Rights Watch, Mines Advisory Group, Handicap International, and Medico International. By 1997, it included more than 1,000 NGOs. USCBL was formed in a similar manner, and by 1997 included more than 250 member organizations. At the time of the Ban Bus campaign, Vietnam Veterans of America was in the forefront of these groups, and their participation helped lend credibility to the movement among veterans and military personnel. Given the coalition nature of the landmine movement, it was only logical that the Ban Bus campaign forged alliances along the way with local groups sympathetic to the landmine issue. Among the groups were women's groups, religious-based organizations, and human rights groups. These alliances proved invaluable in setting up events, as local groups were able to find suitable sites to hold events, help apply for appropriate permits, and assist in publicizing events.

Communication Strategies

One of the challenges ICBL faced in organizing the Ban Bus campaign was to find a way to personalize the landmine issue. This was of paramount importance in getting the U.S. public behind the treaty. To accomplish this, ICBL took a two-pronged approach. First, they communicated the human cost of the landmine problem, particularly the pain and suffering caused by the weapon. Second, they explained the financial cost of landmine clearance operations and how long it takes to effectively clear an area of landmines.

Ban Bus organizers sought to communicate using a variety of means. These included demonstrations of landmine clearance techniques, displays of photographs of landmine victims, and public talks by landmine survivors, landmine clearance specialists, and other landmine activists. They produced a brochure (Figures 1 and 2) that explained the project and provided information for people to donate money to the project. In addition, organizers took full advantage of both the broadcast and print media, including appearing on local talk

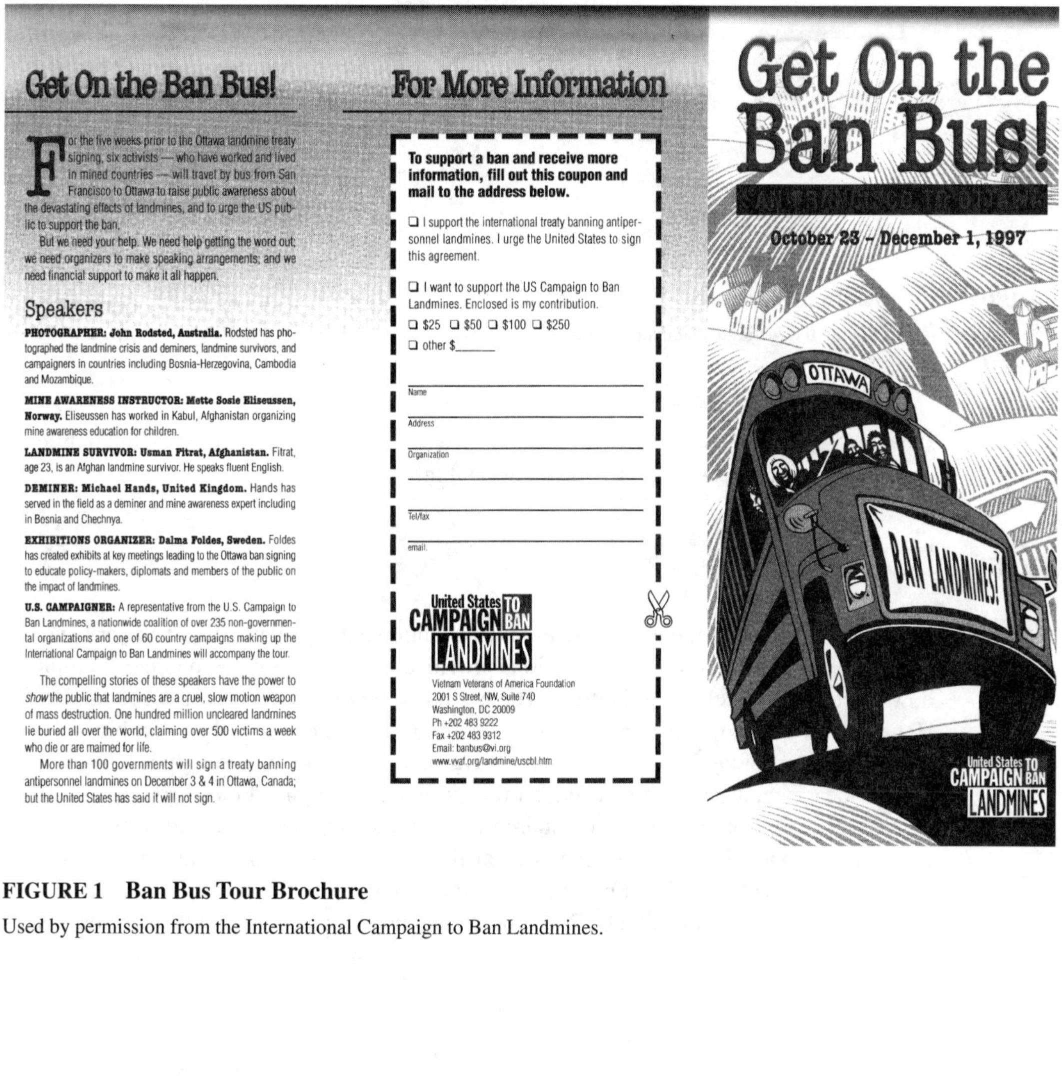

Get On the Ban Bus!

For the five weeks prior to the Ottawa landmine treaty signing, six activists — who have worked and lived in mined countries — will travel by bus from San Francisco to Ottawa to raise public awareness about the devastating effects of landmines, and to urge the US public to support the ban.

But we need your help. We need help getting the word out; we need organizers to make speaking arrangements; and we need financial support to make it all happen.

Speakers

PHOTOGRAPHER: John Rodsted, Australia. Rodsted has photographed the landmine crisis and deminers, landmine survivors, and campaigners in countries including Bosnia-Herzegovina, Cambodia and Mozambique.

MINE AWARENESS INSTRUCTOR: Mette Sosie Eliseussen, Norway. Eliseussen has worked in Kabul, Afghanistan organizing mine awareness education for children.

LANDMINE SURVIVOR: Usman Fitrat, Afghanistan. Fitrat, age 23, is an Afghan landmine survivor. He speaks fluent English.

DEMINER: Michael Hands, United Kingdom. Hands has served in the field as a deminer and mine awareness expert including in Bosnia and Chechnya.

EXHIBITIONS ORGANIZER: Dalma Foldes, Sweden. Foldes has created exhibits at key meetings leading to the Ottawa ban signing to educate policy-makers, diplomats and members of the public on the impact of landmines.

U.S. CAMPAIGNER: A representative from the U.S. Campaign to Ban Landmines, a nationwide coalition of over 235 non-governmental organizations and one of 60 country campaigns making up the International Campaign to Ban Landmines will accompany the tour.

The compelling stories of these speakers have the power to *show* the public that landmines are a cruel, slow motion weapon of mass destruction. One hundred million uncleared landmines lie buried all over the world, claiming over 500 victims a week who die or are maimed for life.

More than 100 governments will sign a treaty banning antipersonnel landmines on December 3 & 4 in Ottawa, Canada; but the United States has said it will not sign.

For More Information

To support a ban and receive more information, fill out this coupon and mail to the address below.

❑ I support the international treaty banning antipersonnel landmines. I urge the United States to sign this agreement.

❑ I want to support the US Campaign to Ban Landmines. Enclosed is my contribution.

❑ $25 ❑ $50 ❑ $100 ❑ $250

❑ other $______

Name

Address

Organization

Tel/fax

email

United States CAMPAIGN TO BAN LANDMINES

Vietnam Veterans of America Foundation
2001 S Street, NW, Suite 740
Washington, DC 20009
Ph +202 483 9222
Fax +202 483 9312
Email: banbus@vi.org
www.vvaf.org/landmine/uscbl.htm

Get On the Ban Bus!

October 23 – December 1, 1997

United States CAMPAIGN TO BAN LANDMINES

FIGURE 1 Ban Bus Tour Brochure

Used by permission from the International Campaign to Ban Landmines.

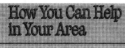

How You Can Help in Your Area

We need your help prior to the Ottawa land-mine treaty signing in December! This tour is an opportunity to spread our message on a grassroots level nation-wide. We need committed individuals like yourself who recognize the horrors of landmines to work with us during the Ban Bus Tour to change US policy. There are many ways you can help — it depends on your imagination, your resources and your talents. Here are a few suggestions:

SPEAKERS: Organize speaking events in your community in connection with visits of the Ban Bus. Contact schools, places of worship, community centers, or other public venues to arrange speaking engagements. Collaborate with peace, human rights, religious, and other grassroots groups to get the word out.

ACCOMMODATIONS: Open your hearts and your home to the campaigners during their visits so that they don't have to sleep on the Ban Bus.

MONEY: Please donate toward the cost of the Ban Bus tour. And use your contacts to provide support, financial or in-kind donations in the areas visited.

MEDIA: Notify the press in your community about the arrival of the Ban Bus, the speakers, and the importance of the ban treaty. Press releases are available for your use from our campaign headquarters.

Call the US Campaign to Ban Landmines in Washington, DC at 202-483-9222 or email at banbus@vi.org.

Ban Bus Itinerary

The Ban Bus will stop in 24 cities across the US during its five week tour. During scheduled stops, the campaigners will speak about their experiences living and working in mined countries, and show photographs, posters, videos and slides. They will also participate in events ranging from talks at high schools and colleges to public rallies, and protests at land-mine producing companies in Janesville and Minneapolis.

Monday–Wednesday
Oct. 20–22
San Francisco, CA

Thursday, Oct. 23
Berkeley, CA

Friday, Oct. 24
Davis, CA

Saturday, Oct. 25
Sacramento, CA

Sunday, Oct. 26
Reno, NV

Tuesday, Oct. 28
Salt Lake City, UT

Thursday, Oct. 30
Grand Junction, CO

Friday, Oct. 31
Boulder, CO

Saturday, Nov. 1
Ogallala, NE

Sunday, Nov. 2
Omaha, NE

Monday–Wednesday
Nov. 3–5
Minneapolis, MN

Thursday, Nov. 6
Iowa City, IA

Friday, Nov. 7
Davenport, IA

Saturday & Sunday
Nov. 8 & 9
Janesville, WI

Monday & Tuesday
Nov. 10 & 11
Chicago, IL

Wednesday, Nov. 12
South Bend, IN

Thursday, Nov. 13
Ann Arbor, MI

Friday, Nov. 14
Cleveland, OH

Saturday, Nov. 15
Youngstown, OH

Monday, Nov. 16
Morgantown, WV

Monday, Nov. 17
Pittsburgh, PA

Tuesday & Wednesday
Nov. 18 & 19
Washington DC

Thursday, Nov. 20
Philadelphia, PA

Friday–Sunday
Nov. 21–23
New York, NY

Monday, Nov. 24
New Haven, CT

Tuesday, Nov. 25
Boston, MA

Wednesday, Nov. 26
Concord/Nashua, NH

Thursday & Friday
Nov. 27 & 28
Burlington, VT

Saturday & Sunday
Nov. 29 & 30
Montreal, QB

Monday, Dec. 1
Ottawa, ONT

Demand a Change in U.S. Landmine Policy

On September 18, 1997, a historic treaty banning the use, production, stockpiling and transfer of antiper-sonnel landmines was adopted at a diplomatic confer-ence in Oslo, Norway. The US insisted on the incorpo-ration of demands that would undermine the treaty: that their so-called 'smart mines' should be an exception; use of smart and dumb mines in Korea, a nine-year delay of the treaty's effective date, and a withdrawal of the treaty during times of armed conflict. All of these proposals failed to find support in Oslo, the US then indicated it would not sign.

President Clinton can show true leadership by banning antipersonnel landmines do-mestically and joining 100-plus nations, including key NATO allies such as France, Germany, Italy and the United Kingdom, for the signing of the comprehen-sive ban treaty in Ottawa.

Official signing of the Oslo treaty will occur in Ottawa December 3 & 4. We must insist that the United States not abandon the world: we must heed the cry of citizens from all over the world — *landmines must be banned.*

Here's what you can do:

- Urge President Clinton to sign the ban treaty in Ottawa. Contact the White House at 202-456-1111.
- Urge your Senators to support the Landmines Elimination Bill, and your Representative to support similar House leg-islation. Contact members of Congress through the Capital Switchboard at 202-224-3121 (House) or 202-225-3121 (Senate).
- Urge the US government to support international programs for humanitarian mine clearance and mine victim assistance.

Demand a complete ban on antipersonnel landmines now!

FIGURE 2   Ban Bus Tour Brochure
Used by permission from the International Campaign to Ban Landmines.

shows. The group also made use of the World Wide Web as a means to keep the public up to date on their progress and provide additional information.

Tactics

Finding events that would attract the public's attention and sympathy was a major concern. Michael Hands' demining demonstrations provided onlookers with a concrete example of how difficult it is to clear a minefield. The normal scenario for one of these events was for Hands to lay out a grid pattern used in a demining operations and then don his working attire—bulletproof clothing and protective headgear—and then go through the tedious pro-cess of locating a dummy mine using a mine probe, a pencil-sized metal rod that is gently pushed into the ground every two-square inches in the area being cleared. Upon locating the dummy mine, Hands would gently clear the area around the mine using a trowel and brush, hook up a cord to the mine and detonate it—setting off a small explosive charge that sent baby powder into the air. Hands would then explain that while an AP landmine cost as little as $3 to produce, removing the mine costs up to $1,000 and that it takes up to eight hours to clear a 30-square yard area. In Boston, organizers coupled the demining demonstration with an invitation to the public to walk through a mock minefield in Copley Square, helping them better understand the challenges facing people in mine-affected countries.

Another program that drew the media's attention was John Rodsted's exhibit of his black and white photographs illustrating the human cost of landmines. These photographs of landmine victims from around the world vividly illustrated the damage caused by AP landmines, particularly among women and children. The sight of a young child who has had both legs amputated after accidentally stepping on a mine sends a strong message about the weapon to the viewer and puts a human face on the 70 casualties caused daily by landmines. Talks by 23-year-old Afghani Usman Fitrat also helped put a human face on the figures. Fitrat related to audiences how he lost both hands and his left eye to an AP landmine he found near his house, and that a scant ten days before his accident, his mother and a cousin were killed when they accidentally set off a mine while walking home from a health clinic. Mette Eliseussen relied on her work with children in Afghanistan to drive the landmine problem home to audiences. She did this not only by describing the destruction caused by landmines, but also by drawing comparisons between the lives of children in Afghanistan to the lives of children in the United States, pointing out that while in the United States parents teach children not to play in the streets, in Afghanistan she had to teach children not to play in areas that might be mined.

At all the events, audience members were encouraged to write letters to President Clinton and Congress supporting the upcoming landmine treaty. This call to action was included in the ICBL/USCBL brochure distributed at each event. In many cases anti-landmine activists also provided the public with petitions to sign, as well as pre-stamped postcards to send to officials. At some events, organizers suggested that audience members send a single shoe to the president, representing one of the many amputations that occur because of landmines. At the University of Notre Dame, Ban Bus members successfully encouraged students to stage a protest at the upcoming West Virginia football game. As the national anthem was played, an estimated 5,000 students stood at attention, hand over their heart, and held a single shoe above their head in memory of the victims of landmines. The protest was covered from coast-to-coast and was even discussed in the *Journal of Higher Education*. The Ban Bus also staged protests at local industries which were or had been involved with the production of landmines, including Accudyne in Wisconsin, CAPCO in Utah, and Alliant Techsystems in Minnesota.

Evaluation

The Ban Bus campaign was largely successful in meeting many of its objectives. While there is little quantifiable data about the effects of the trip, the group conducted over 100 presentations, received air time on numerous local television and radio programs, and their protests were covered by newspapers across the country. In addition, the trip, one of the first major efforts at grassroots organizing in the United States, helped identify sympathetic groups and local organizers for future programs. As of 2003, ICBL and USCBL were still using updated versions of these lists. ICBL has used the idea of the Ban Bus in other countries since the original 1997 trip through the United States, most notably Belgium. The trip was also relatively successful in getting state and local officials involved in the anti-landmine movement. In Milwaukee, the city council recognized ICBL and Jody Williams for "their commitment to freeing the world of landmines." In Philadelphia, the city council unanimously passed a resolution calling for the U.S. government to sign the Ottawa Treaty. In Massachusetts, Governor Paul Cellucci declared November 25, 1997 "Ban Landmines Day." The group also met with some success with companies which had previously been involved in the manufacture of landmines. Unitrode, which previously produced landmine components, pledged that it would not "knowingly design, produce, or sell parts intended for [the production of landmines]." The group secured a similar pledge from Dyno Nobel.

While the Ban Bus campaign received a good deal of local press, it is questionable how much success they had with news story placement at the national level. A search of the Vanderbilt Television News Archive reveals no coverage of Ban Bus events on any of the evening national news programs. Similar results are found when looking for coverage of Ban Bus events by the *New York Times*. The campaign had better success, however, in news placement in other large cities including Pittsburg and Boston.

In the end, the United States did not sign the Ottawa Treaty, nor has it done so as of this writing. While convincing the United States to sign the treaty was certainly one of the campaign's objectives, this should by no means suggest that the campaign was a failure. Ban Bus organizer Mary Wareham stated that the group had no illusions that the United States was likely to sign the treaty, Ban Bus campaign or not. The successes of the trip seem to outweigh any of the trip's shortcomings—the Ban Bus Campaign left in its wake a stronger, more galvanized cadre of landmine advocates, ready to continue the effort to gain U.S. accession to the treaty and encourage the United States to support international demining efforts.

Critique

Research

While there is no doubt that the individuals who orchestrated this campaign were deeply dedicated to the control or elimination of anti-personnel landmines, there are major flaws in the case. Most of these flaws are the result of the almost total absence of valid and reliable research. For example, there was apparently no research at all to identify the pre-campaign values and beliefs of the target audiences. The campaign was begun without even knowing whom, if anyone, in the target publics already supported encouraging the U.S. government to sign the Ottawa treaty to ban landmines. Further, there appears to be no research to identify the reasons why Bill Clinton and the U.S. government opposed the landmine ban. Without information on the values and beliefs of the target publics it is virtually impossible to select messages that may influence those publics.

Those administering the campaign opted to select the route for the Bus Ban Tour working backwards from Ottawa to San Francisco, picking points of existing support. Those points of support were usually college campuses. Although the campaign planners selected college campuses because campuses usually housed some supporters of the anti-landmine movement, there was no research to determine if those supporters could influence others to join the movement. One weakness of using college campuses becomes particularly obvious when one notes that the tour sites also included elementary and secondary schools. While students from elementary to college may be active and may be easily motivated by new information, research conducted for other campaigns shows that students have historically been ineffective in political influence. College students have one of the lowest rates of voter registration of any demographic, and obviously elementary students cannot vote because of their age. Without some research showing that younger students could influence others, such as their parents, site visits to elementary and secondary schools seem a potential waste of campaign resources.

Other decisions that should have been preceded by research include the commitment to a website and the decision to include the distribution of news releases. While campaigns today often successfully integrate an online presence into their message distribution, this campaign was conducted only seven years after the introduction of the Internet. Here there was no research to show that either the intended audience used the website or that the website was effective. News release distribution, if not preceded by media research, may be a waste of campaign resources. The description of this campaign does not indicate that any research was done to identify sympathetic or receptive media. A simple review of secondary sources such as media guides, or a content analysis of news coverage, could have been used to identify media outlets and representatives most likely to use the news releases. Further, content analysis could have been used to guide message construction of the news releases, to maximize the probability of their use.

Finally, the decision to include multiple speakers representing several diverse groups and perspectives would have benefited from some research. For example, the campaign designers appeared to assume that if they included a British Army veteran landmine expert, this would improve their credibility and their ability to reach U.S. veterans groups. Some research should have been conducted to determine if a "foreign" veteran was as influential as a U.S. veteran. Since the Bus Ban tour was jointly sponsored by a Vietnam veterans' group, it should have been possible to procure a veteran of the U.S. armed forces who shared the campaign organizers' opposition to anti-personnel mines.

In sum, there appears to have been no empirical research and most decisions seem to have been based on the intuition and prior experience of the organizers. Certainly, prior experience is one source of research, but it often lacks validity and almost always lacks reliability. Other campaign weaknesses that resulted from this lack of research will be detailed in the discussions of objectives, strategies, tactics, and evaluation.

Objectives

The single greatest weakness of the objectives is their ambiguity. From reading a description of the campaign objectives it is nearly impossible to determine what the campaign really hopes to accomplish. Without the identification of a clear objective it is nearly impossible to select strategies and tactics calculated to advance those objectives.

Under call to action the campaign's authors identify three separate goals. They wanted to have people contact the White House. They also wanted people to contact the U.S. Congress to urge support of the Hagel-Leahy bill, and they wanted to "urge the government to support international programs for mine clearance." Possibly because the organizational goals were obfuscated, the public relations objectives also are not clear.

When describing specific objectives, two are identified:

- Raise awareness
- Encourage the U.S. government to sign the Ottawa Treaty

Neither public relations objective is operationalized. In other words, neither we, as readers of the campaign description, nor the campaign organizers can know how to measure their success. Raising awareness is almost never an appropriate public relations objective. In this case we do not have a pre-campaign measure of awareness, so we have no way to know if we succeeded and even more important, because of a lack of pre-campaign research we do not even know if increased awareness will increase or decrease the likelihood of a ban on anti-personnel landmines. Encouraging the U.S. government to sign a treaty is also too vague to be useful. One can "urge" virtually any course of action in any number of completely ineffective ways.

It would appear the public relations objective of this campaign was to have the United States sign the Ottawa ban on anti-personnel landmines. However, a statement in the objective section of the campaign description may explain why that objective is never articulated. The Ban Bus organizer said that she "had no illusions that the United States was likely to sign the treaty." It may well be that the organizers knew the campaign could not succeed with a specific objective and therefore opted to describe a vague objective for which neither success nor failure could be clearly demonstrated.

Strategies

The entire campaign here focuses on a classic pseudo-event. In this context, the action strategies are all actions intended to prepare and present the Ban Bus tour itself. The campaign does present an interesting mixture of mediated and direct publicity. Using presentations, photography exhibits, and speakers that are part of the tour is direct publicity. Securing media coverage of these events is mediated publicity.

In the context of action strategies, one should note the creation of alliances with local groups. The creation of such alliances could obviate the need for media research. Simply put, the local group should already know what local media would cover the Ban Bus events. By tapping their knowledge, the national planners of the event did not need to conduct their own media research for each tour stop.

Communication strategies included the incorporation of messages intended to personalize the landmine issue. From the campaign description is does not appear any communication theory or paradigm guided these decisions. It seems the campaign's organizers sought to make an emotional appeal to their target publics. Here again, the lack of pre-campaign research may have hurt the campaign's chances of success. To understand the weaknesses presented here it is essential to remember that most people in the target publics neither have any experience with landmines nor know anyone who has. In short, it is easy for them to avoid emotional appeals or appeals based on human cost by exercising their selective exposure, attention, perception, and retention. For example, the description of costs for landmine removal is only relevant to the target public if they see themselves as responsible for those costs. Since one of the campaign's goals was to encourage public support for international programs for mine clearance, we can assume that those in the target publics do not now support landmine clearance. Even if the public's members heard and paid attention to the message, they could have decided it did not apply to them or could have quickly forgotten the message without taking any action.

Another possibly powerful message was the description of human costs. This message was delivered through photographs of landmine victims and the testimonial of a severely wounded landmine survivor. Such appeals are only successful if audience members can see themselves or those they care about in similar situations. Without research on existing values and attitudes in the target public it is nearly impossible to know if these messages could be successful. One tactic used to present this message of human cost was the speech comparing U.S. and Afghanistan children's lives. Because their lives are so different, it is at least possible that parents in the United States do not see their own children as comparable to children in Afghanistan. If they cannot "translate" their concern for their own children to a concern for Afghani children, they will not be motivated by the plight of the Afghanis.

Tactics

Tactics that involved the publics in activities are an excellent way to overcome any tendency on the part of those publics to avoid attention or to distort perception. The demonstrations used in the Ban Bus tour, particularly the mock mine fields and mine clearance demonstrations, are excellent tools in this respect. The involvement of students at the Notre Dame v. West Virginia football game will make it very difficult for those students to forget the issues presented by the Ban Bus tour.

In particular the petition and pre-stamped post cards were excellent tools in this campaign. Much of the communication strategy was based on emotional appeals that used very unpleasant images. Photographs of landmine victims and the broken body of a landmine survivor are obviously repellent images, and these images spawn emotions such as guilt and sympathy. However, research shows that such emotional motivation is very short lived. If members of the public do not act on it quickly they will soon forget the unpleasant image that motivated their emotional state. Providing a petition to sign immediately or a post-card to mail quickly would allow the campaign planners to take advantage of even a soon-to-be-forgotten motivation.

Evaluation

Any campaign's evaluation depends entirely on whether the campaign met its public relations objective. Here the objectives are so vague and ambiguous it will be necessary to critique at least two.

If we assume the public relations objective was to secure endorsement of the Ottawa Treaty by the United States, then the campaign can only be described as a total failure. The U.S. government has not made any commitment to ban the use of anti-personnel landmines.

If we assume the public relations objective was to increase public awareness of the human and financial cost of landmines, then it is simply impossible to know if the campaign succeeded. The Ban Bus tour conducted more than 100 presentations and was covered in local media, but there is absolutely no evidence presented that there was any change in public awareness of the landmine issue. When evaluating a public relations objective to increase awareness, one must remember that the simple delivery of messages does not increase awareness. To demonstrate an increase of awareness we must show that the message was actually delivered to the target public, that members of the target public paid attention to the message, that member of the target public accurately perceived the message, and that members of the target public remember the message. Here we can only assert that one of these four steps might have been taken. Further, it appears the message was only delivered to a small part of the target public through some local media. We can only be sure of distribution in local media because there is no evidence the Ban Bus story was carried on national television news or in the *New York Times*. It seems unlikely that any significant increase in public awareness for a national campaign would not be accompanied by a report in these significant national news media.

There was, however, some action that suggests a limited public awareness. The cities of Milwaukee and Philadelphia and the state of Massachusetts did pass ordinances or decrees indicating their support for a ban on anti-personnel landmines. Obviously these actions suggest awareness. However, we do not know if these local governments supported a ban on landmines before the Ban Bus tour. Therefore, without some pre-campaign measure of awareness, we cannot know if the campaign created increased awareness.

DISCUSSION QUESTIONS

1. One approach to influencing government actions is called indirect or grassroots lobbying. In this approach the public relations campaign attempts to influence the opinions of constituents so that they will, in turn, influence their elected representatives. The Ban Bus tour may be seen as such a grassroots lobbying effort. The tour organizers hoped to influence people at sites they visited so those people would contact the President, senators, or congressmen and encourage those elected officials to vote for the Hagel-Leahy bill or to support the Ottawa Treaty. Describe some other indirect lobbying campaigns. Analyze those campaigns and describe what characteristics appear to coincide with success and what characteristics seem to coincide with failure for such campaigns.

2. A lack of good pre-campaign research may be one problem of the Ban Bus tour campaign. What research would you have conducted before deciding how to conduct the campaign?

3. Why do you believe the U.S. government did not support the treaty to ban anti-personnel landmines? Describe the secondary research sources you would use to answer this question.

4. What are the attitudes of the average U.S. citizen toward the use of landmines? What secondary research sources might you use to answer this question? If you could not find secondary sources, how would you design primary research to learn what the average U.S. citizen thinks about landmines?

5. What percentage of people in the United States think landmine use or a ban on landmine use is important? What are the demographics (age, geographic location, ethnic group, education level) of people most likely to work toward a ban on landmine use? Describe how you would conduct research to answer these questions.

6. Write a simple and operationalized public relations objective that would support an organizational goal to increase public awareness of the human and financial cost of anti-personnel landmines.

7. Write a simple and operationalized public relations objective that would support an organizational goal to have the U.S. government sign a treaty banning anti-personnel landmines.

8. What communication theories, models, or paradigms can you use to guide the identification of messages that will encourage college students in the United States to actively support a ban on anti-personnel landmines? Describe how each theory, model, or paradigm could be used in this context.

9. Describe how you could use face-to-face tactics like speeches and demonstrations to deliver the messages suggested by the theories, models, and paradigms you identified above. For each face-to-face tactic you describe, explain why you think it will be more effective or less effective than a tactic using mass media.

10. In a campaign to encourage support for a ban on anti-personnel landmines, describe how you would motivate reporters to cover face-to-face tactics like speeches and demonstrations.

11. If the objective of your campaign were only to raise awareness of the human cost of landmine use, how would you evaluate the success of your campaign?

REFERENCES AND SUGGESTED READINGS

American Friends Service Committee. (1997, Nov. 11). *Anti-landmines campaign arrives in Philadelphia Nov. 20.* [Press Release]. Retrieved from www.afsc.org/news/1997/nrmines.htm.

Cahill, Kevin. (1995). *Clearing the fields: Solutions to the global landmines crisis.* New York: Basic Books.

Cameron, M. A., Lawson, R. J., & Tomlin, B. W. (1998). *To walk without fear: The global movement to ban landmines.* Oxford: Oxford University Press.

Conklin, G. (1997, Nov. 11). *Anti-Landmines Campaign Arrives in Philadelphia Nov. 20, 1997.* Retrieved from http://www.wfn.org/1997/11/msg00110.html.

Eriksen, M. (1997, Nov. 14). Nobel Prize winners rally against mines. *The Michigan Daily.* Retrieved from www.pub.umich.edu/daily/1997/nov/11-14-97/news/news5.html.

Fuentes, C. (2003, Aug. 11). International campaign to ban landmines begins. *Daily Bruin.* Retrieved from www.dailybruin.ucla.edu/DB/issues/97/10.21/news.landmines.html.

Greenberg, Jill. (1997, October). *(Mines) ban bus update.* Retrieved from http://www.bonuslevel.de/mgm/archiv/1997/0206.html.

Iowa City Foreign Relations Council. (1997, Oct. 30). *Group opposing landmines to speak in Iowa City.* Retrieved from www.uiowa.edu/~ournews/1997/october/1030mines.html.

McNew, J. G. (1997, Nov. 21). Facing landmine "Danger Zones" everyday. *Disaster Relief.* Retrieved from www.disasterrelief.org/Disasters/971121landmines.

University of Notre Dame Public Relations and Information. (1997, Nov. 10). *The ban bus, a project organized by the U.S. Campaign to ban land mines, will visit the Notre Dame campus.* [Press Release]. Retrieved from www.nd.edu/~prinfo/news/1997/11-10e.html.

Vietnam Veterans of America. (1998). *Get on the ban bus, San Francisco to Ottawa, October 23–December 1, 1997, Report.* United States: Vietnam Veterans of America.

Wareham, M. (1997). *Ban bus tour updates.* Retrieved from http://members.iinet.net.au/~pictim/p17.html.

Wareham, M. (1997, Oct. 17). *Get on the ban bus.* Retrieved from www.bonuslevel.de/mgm/archiv/1997/0212.html.

4 Internal Public Relations in the Post-War Balkans

VIRGINIA KREIMEYER

The author of this case study was the U.S. Air Force officer who participated in the events discussed herein. Therefore, the majority of this case is derived from her experiences.

Executive Summary

In 1991, two years after the destruction of the Berlin Wall, the Federal Republic of Yugoslavia began dissolving as members of the federation seceded. Intense fighting ensued for the next two and a half years, destroying lives, property, and the governmental infrastructure. Finally, in 1995 the warring factions signed a peace treaty and U.S.-led troops, known as the Implementation Forces (IFOR) were deployed to the Balkans to establish and maintain peace. While the mission of IFOR was peacekeeping, communication with a multinational force, comprised of 40 nations and represented by dozens of languages, encompassed a unique challenge for the IFOR public relations team. New rules of engagement were spelled out, in detailed contingency plans for operations within the area of responsibility. However, for the cadre of public relations professionals congregated in Naples, Italy, in December 1995, a new chapter in military public relations emerged from a contingency plan that simply stated, "There will be an internal information program." In addition, when multinational troops had been deployed in previous operations, the internal information program was delegated to the individual nations, rather than to the authority of the coalition forces. This case study explains how the internal information program for IFOR was conceived, the research conducted for creating an internal program, the plan developed from and during the research, the execution of the program, and finally an evaluation of the program. The policies developed and the plans that were written became a blueprint for future operations, not just for the military but for those involved in international commerce.

Based on the experiences of a U.S. Air Force officer, an initial member of the IFOR team, and the division's first chief, this case examines the process of instituting the multinational internal information division and enumerates lessons learned as well as their application to many aspects of conducting public relations in an international arena. The key publics for the internal audience are explained, as well as the key participants in the process.

The process of public relations, from research to evaluation, is used to explicate the progression of public relations operations for IFOR's internal information program. With each step, examples are provided of how that process was accomplished or roadblocks that affected the process. Although the evaluation does not employ a scientific tool, follow-up contact with personnel involved with IFOR until its deactivation provided insight into its effectiveness. The conclusions and lessons learned from this effort reflect the successes and failures of the overall communication process of IFOR and its effectiveness in a multicultural environment.

Research

Research is a vital function for the process of public relations, and should always be the first consideration in designing a program. However, research in the public relations field is not limited to terms such as content analysis, public opinion polls, or surveys. As in this case study, the researcher employed secondary and informal techniques based on available data and the experience of a U.S. Air Force public affairs officer. It is tantamount to the situation that when no paradigms exist, research is limited. The challenge was to assess the situation and conduct research in a foreign country, without knowledge of the indigenous language, while responding to a myriad of volatile conditions. Therefore, the research phase and the planning stage of the program blurred as the international public information team came together. For example, the search for logistical information and recruitment of staff members coincided with the development of strategies and tactics for a novice program spanning several countries. These efforts laid the groundwork for an internal information program that produced the *IFOR Informer,* a newspaper for the 60,000 troops temporarily stationed in Bosnia, Croatia, and Hungary, as well those supporting the mission in Italy and Germany.

In this case, the research began with a perusal of various documents for guidance of an internal information program. When no documents provided substantive guidance, the researchers relocated from Naples, Italy, to Zagreb, Croatia, to conduct field research at the temporary headquarters of IFOR. Co-existing with the United Nations Protection Force (UNPROFOR) allowed researchers to rely on the corporate memory of UN Protection Forces' key personnel, who provided information and recommendations for the future IFOR Public Information Offices (PIO). Two public information officers, one British and one U.S., the plans officer and new division chief, respectively, moved to Zagreb, where initial operations and research continued simultaneously.

According to Martha Maznevski and Mark F. Peterson, "Multicultural management requires creativity and breath of experience" (Granrose, p. 87). In conducting an internal public relations program for the newly organized IFOR's Public Information Office, the division chief faced diverse cultural considerations. The first cultural obstacle was also a logistical concern: how to reach the primary audience, the 60,000 troops, representing 40 cultural identities, scattered over five countries. Secondly, language barriers presented a challenge of how to communicate, and in what language or languages. Although many languages were represented by the troops, English was the most common language. In many cases it was the second language, but was understood well enough to be the conduit of vital information. Third, to find a staff to meet the needs of a neophyte organization would require diplomatic negotiations as well as contending with the various work ethics and cultural clashes.

Not only were there cultural considerations for the public information officer's staff and the internal audience, but also, by virtue of the location, a mountain of cultural barriers existed. For more than 500 years war has persisted in an ebbing and flowing manner in the Balkans. Armies from the Ottoman Empire, the Deutschland, the crown of England, and many twentieth century countries occupied, fought, bled, and died in battles on the real estate know as the former Yugoslavia. Peace had been intermittent, with the longest period being 50 years during the middle 1700s. But in the fall of 1995, representatives of three of the warring factions of Bosnia-Herzegovina, the U.S. negotiating team, and other diplomatic peacemakers met in Dayton, Ohio, to seek peace once again. The "Dayton Peace Agreement" became the impetus establishing the peace with IFOR's deployment to the Balkans.

International laws and rules of engagement governed the policies established for IFOR, which had been outlined by the North Atlantic Treaty Organization (NATO). Under the auspices of NATO, the U.S.-led IFOR established a formidable foe for any government opposition, especially within the former Yugoslavia. However, because maintaining peace in the Balkans had worldwide attention, some non-NATO countries, including former Warsaw Pact nations, volunteered their troops. NATO, a 16-nation organization established in 1949, touted a "one for all and all for one" defense against its adversaries, comprised mainly from the Warsaw Pact. Thus, the mission of keeping the peace, by deadly force if necessary, juxtaposed troops from more than 40 nations, both NATO and non-NATO, in a precariously small area—slightly larger than a third of the size of Arkansas. Additionally, as will be discussed in more detail later, Italian law necessitated that a registered Italian journalist be a member of the staff to legally publish a newspaper in Italy.

The United States took the primary leadership role for IFOR because of established hierarchy within NATO. Since World War II, the commander for Supreme Headquarters for Allied Personnel in Europe (SHAPE), the military arm of NATO, has been a U.S. commander. In December of 1995, the commander was Gen. George A. Joulwan, a dual-hatted position with his SHAPE office in Bonn, Belgium, and his U.S. European Command (EUCOM) headquarters in Stuttgart, Germany. However, the mission for IFOR was delegated to Admiral Leighton "Snuffy" Smith, the commander for Allied Forces Southern Command (AF-SOUTH) in Naples, Italy. Although Admiral Smith directed his Allied Forces Southern Command operations from Naples, as commander for IFOR he originally planned to have his headquarters in Zagreb, Croatia, but moved them to Sarajevo, Bosnia-Herzegovina, for political reasons. Additionally, the peacekeeping mission was divided into three sectors, with U.S., French, and British commanders reporting to Admiral Smith.

By virtue of his position as the Chief of Public Information for AFSOUTH, Navy Captain Mark VanDyke became the director for IFOR public relations. Again, the United States took the lead for defining and directing public relations programs. VanDyke's multinational staff in Naples, composed of Italian, Greek, Turkish, British, French, German, and U.S. military and civilians, set the stage for IFOR's operations. Like that of Admiral Smith, VanDyke's IFOR office was eventually moved to Sarajevo, where the mission was broader in scope and required additional manpower from additional countries. By drawing from the manpower of NATO PIOs at bases throughout Europe, including those at SHAPE and the

European Command headquarters, VanDyke established a system of Combined Public Information Centers (CPICs) in Bosnia, Hungary, and Croatia. As non-NATO countries responded with their own public information officers, they were integrated into the CPICs. The complexion of the CPICs varied, with organizational policies that ensured the Russian troops were assigned to the U.S. sector, rather than aligning them with former U.S.S.R. states.

For two years, the UN headquarters at Zagreb had produced a biweekly magazine, ran a 24-hour radio station, and a weekly television production. If IFOR absorbed these facilities and their manning, then IFOR would have a ready-made internal information program. However, the cost of the operation, including the salaries of the UN personnel, was so exorbitant that it far surpassed IFOR's proposed budget. With the UN Protection Forces Public Information Officer still occupying the office space at the UN compound in downtown Zagreb, necessary facilities were extremely limited. Additionally, telephones, computers, and desks belonged to the UN Public Information Officer, who graciously shared his meager accommodations with the incoming IFOR contingent. Until the mission transferred from the UN Protection Forces to IFOR, there were no funds available to commit to any supplies. The situation was exacerbated by the lack of documents allocating money, manning, and equipment to an internal program.

Further investigations revealed that when U.S. military arrived in Tuzla, Bosnia, the Armed Forces Network (AFN), the U.S. military broadcasting network overseas, established a satellite radio station there, and began installing repeaters and an antenna system throughout the northeast sector of Bosnia. Television sets were later delivered and placed in communal areas of bases, where troops could watch the AFN and CNN broadcasts. Radio broadcasts were picked up by the troops' transistor radios anywhere within range of the repeaters, which included one in Sarajevo and others in the British sector or northwest Bosnia. The French military set up a radio station at Mostar, Bosnia, where they broadcast on low levels in French. Each nation operated its own facilities, but carried IFOR's messages as well as news from the homefront when IFOR became operational.

Reaching an internal audience with diverse identities, cultures, and ideologies produced an unprecedented challenge. During the Gulf War the coalition forces established joint information bureaus where they conducted media relations, but internal information programs were left to the individual nations. With more than 40 nationalities, communicating in a politically sensitive environment and meeting the diverse needs of the audience posed a dilemma. The responsibility of solving this problem was delegated to an Air Force major, who was the deputy chief of internal information for the Air Force at the Pentagon.

For the internal information program of IFOR, the primary target publics were the IFOR troops, but through the media, the world viewed IFOR vicariously. Although the world, including families of deployed military, watched events unfold in the Balkans, many of the troops did not have access to this information because of their remote locations. Compounding the situation was the need for the troops to understand and articulate the messages and policies of IFOR, because they were often interviewed by the media and became undesignated IFOR spokespersons. Keeping them informed about changes in the operation was as essential as updating them on the Commander of IFOR's policies and ensuring each member knew how as an individual he or she contributed to the mission's success. But as most military, they were hungry for information and wanted to keep in touch with the world beyond the Balkans. They wanted to know how their favorite sport's team was faring. They wanted to know what the other IFOR units were doing and where they were. Relevant and concise information was crucial to keeping these troops efficient performers.

A primary goal for the internal program was creating an internal publication for IFOR troops and for the Commander of IFOR to communicate with them. When the headquarters for IFOR planned to move to Sarajevo, moving the internal program to Sarajevo would have seemed logical. With the entire staff for IFOR located at President Tito's former residence in Sarajevo, space was the greatest concern. Even with temporary trailers placed within the compound, there was no room, nor equipment, for producing a newspaper. The Bosnian newspaper office in Sarajevo had been bombed during the war and was producing its daily paper from austere presses in the building's basement. As the only printing facility with limited operations, it had no capacity for producing an additional paper for IFOR. Facilities for a staff or newspaper production did not exist in Sarajevo; however, there were civilian newspapers being published in Croatia. Nonetheless, neither of these countries had facilities that could be used by IFOR's official newspaper. It is noteworthy to mention that the psychological operations cadre were able to use local publishers for their publications, which were printed in Serbo-Croatian and Cyrillic.

Finally, the research led to the Navy's Support Facility back in Naples. In addition to AFSOUTH headquarters, Naples housed the support facility for the Navy's Sixth Fleet. An Italian publisher, Stampa Generale, rented facilities at the Navy base and published a weekly newspaper for the U.S. military stationed there. Stampa Generale was interested in printing and delivering the newspaper for IFOR. However, the actual distribution to the bases throughout the former Yugoslavia was accomplished via IFOR's C-130 transport aircraft that made regular trips throughout the theater of operations. The newspapers were delivered to various airfields, where a member of the local CPIC would pick up the bundles and distribute them throughout the camps. With Naples being the best place to publish the newspaper, the internal program, which consisted of only two people, moved back to Naples.

Objective

For most military or international organizations, regulations, plans, or other documents provide specific guidelines and directives. However, IFOR's operational plan did not provide goals or guidelines beyond a statement that said, "There will be an internal information program."

The European Command in Stuttgart, Germany, published a plan in November, but according to it, the public information plan was to:

> Inform American and international public, and gain their support, for the role and activities of U.S. forces involved. Support U.S. and international media coverage of U.S. operations. Support NATO Public Information operations. Support combined U.S.–nonNATO public affairs operations. Establish Combined Information Bureaus.

None of these guidelines specifically applied to IFOR's internal information program, which needed to expand the European Command's goals. However, as previously stated, the primary goal for the IFOR internal information program was to create and maintain a medium for two-way communication up and down the chain of command. Keeping the troops informed about the mission and encouraging feedback from the field were essential to good morale and discipline for the international forces.

While IFOR's "corporate image" was important for other publics, the target public for the internal information program was the "corporation's employees." Much like a multinational company, IFOR consisted of 40 nationalities, but its "employees" were not indigenous to the region. They had been deployed before or after the entity was established on December 20, 1995. The quandary for the internal information program was to coalesce the multinational forces into a cohesive unit that understood and articulated the mission, the goals, and the purpose of IFOR. Additionally, the internal program had to provide two-way communication up and down the chain of command. A specific tool for meeting these needs and overcoming language barriers was found in the *IFOR Informer.*

Once a publisher for the *IFOR Informer* had been located, the process for the first edition was established. The next step was the allocation of funds, which required approval from the IFOR comptroller, an Italian civilian employed by AFSOUTH. However, with the Commander of IFOR's approval, it was mere paperwork, including the contract with the publisher. The primary objective was to distribute a top quality, bi-monthly newspaper, with the first edition a stellar example. Therefore, the first edition entailed a rigorous review process, but still hit the streets, from inception to publication and distribution, within a mere six weeks. Initially the target date of publication was the first of February, but due to the review process, the first printing was delayed until Wednesday, February 14, 1995. Figure 1 shows the cover of the second issue. The newspaper was published for the duration of IFOR, and its successor, the *SFOR Informer,* continued to provide information to the Stabilization Forces (SFOR) in the Balkans.

Strategies

Developing a plan for communicating within a multinational, multicultural, and newly constructed organization while conforming to and remaining consistent with the political sensitivities embedded within the relationships involved, was the challenge. A formal plan was written and submitted through IFOR's PIO to the commander for approval. In a military unit, as in corporations, without top management endorsement, no plan will be funded. The plan included building a team, procuring equipment, determining the location for the operation, and creating documents needed to facilitate the process.

The first order of business required that current strategic planning documents be modified to reflect the provisions of the new internal information program, which included manning slots for journalists and clerks to support the newspaper staff. Secondly, the internal information program's basic strategy relied heavily on the *IFOR Informer* as a communication tool:

- To provide an avenue for the commanders to communicate with their troops, through articles and editorials
- For the troops to learn about other units and the countries they represented

FIGURE 1   Masthead from the IFOR Informer

- To entertain the troops
- To provide valid information of interest to IFOR for the duration of the mission

Face-to-face communication, the most efficient and effective way of communicating, is a method often used by U.S. military commanders, especially in deployments. Admiral Smith and other commanders, such as British General Sir Michael Walker, visited various bases and remote sites on a regular basis to boost morale. In special instances, heads of state such as U.S. President Bill Clinton and Crown Prince Charles of England made special trips to address troops. While the newspaper covered these historic moments, the real value was demonstrated in the face-to-face communication with the troops. The visits proved to be morale boosters for the leadership as well as the thousands of men and women in attendance.

Coalescing a multinational entity like IFOR into specific messages for its target publics conjured a diplomatic dance. However, IFOR solidified its identity and mission by developing the following themes and messages:

IFOR is here to help, the right tool for the right mission, an example of NATO's new attributes and abilities, impartial and even-handed in treatment of all people, and in favor of cooperation by all involved.

These messages were integrated into the *IFOR Informer,* which communicated vital information to the troops and promulgated its themes and messages until IFOR ceased to exist.

Tactics

Since the *IFOR Informer* was a formative tool for communicating the commander's messages and themes, specific tactics for making it efficient were employed. Tactics used in the communication process included:

- Developing themes into stories. For example, since mine safety was paramount, a series of articles addressed different aspects of mine safety.
- To ensure equal treatment, a corporate policy stated that photos of heads of state would not be used on the front page, because it would be reserved for the troops.
- Writing stories was the responsibility of each staff member who traveled to remote sites and chronicled events.
- Photographs for the newspaper were contributed by various staff members, the Commander of IFOR's official photographer, and the U.S. military's Joint Combat Camera team.
- Meeting the requests of the troops was not always the politically correct decision for the newspaper. For example, in a survey the Scandinavians responded that a "pin-up" girl should be a regular part of the newspaper. American culture and Department of Defense sexual harassment policy prevented this item from being a part of the organization's flagship publication.
- A request to the European Associated Press allowed the newspaper to use stories and photos free of charge. AP became the primary source for sports and international news.
- As a military publication, all copy had to be approved by VanDyke before it could be published. This review ensured that politically sensitive material met the most stringent requirements.
- To keep the people informed and to promote even-handedness by IFOR-deployed troops patrolling Bosnia and meeting with government officials and international media, the newspaper focused on troop activities.
- To ensure that policies and procedures for the internal program were followed, all communication was conducted in English, the common language of the staff.

- The newspaper was printed in English and French, because those were the official languages of NATO.
- A *Letters to the Commander* column promoted two-way communication by allowing the troops in the field to call or write questions and comments.

Stampa Generale published the newspaper in Naples and the contract, written in both English and Italian, stated that:

- 15,000 copies would be published for six months with a renewable option (which was renewed every year)
- The biweekly newspaper would be printed in two colors with an optional four-color separation issue
- Each issue would be printed in English and French, the official languages of NATO. Additionally, the peacekeeping troops were divided into three sectors of Bosnia—one with the U.S.-led forces, one with British-led forces, and one with French-led forces—so with English and French were the two dominant languages of the troops, as well.
- Stampa Generale, the publisher, would deliver the newspapers, separated into bundles for specified destinations, to Allied Forces Southern Command's headquarters the morning of publication

With no manning requirements in the basic IFOR plan, there were no authorizations specifying journalistic skills. Unlike in the corporate world, where positions can be created as needed, the bureaucracy of the military prohibited a unit from arbitrarily assigning people without a manning document. The first member of the staff was the chief of the division, who recruited a Norwegian conscript and trained journalist. The Norwegian lieutenant had been working in media relations at the Zagreb office. Both the lieutenant and the major moved from Zagreb to Naples, where two U.S. Navy lieutenants concluding their summer reserve training in Naples were added to the staff. To comply with Italian law, any newspaper distributed in Italy must have a registered Italian journalist as the "responsible editor." The Italian special assistant to VanDyke, Mr. Franco Veltri, met these requirements, and became the next *IFOR Informer* staff member. Another Allied Forces Southern Command staff member was a British ex-patriot who was fluent in Italian and had previously edited Allied Forces Southern Command's monthly magazine. Before even one issue was published, it was inherently obvious that the paper required bilingual French journalists to report, write, and translate for the newspaper. As stated previously, the official languages of NATO are English and French, which became the official languages of IFOR. Therefore, a telephone call to the French military headquarters in Paris produced two military journalists within two weeks. The French Navy lieutenant and the French Army sergeant arrived about the same time as the German clerk, who set up the office. In addition to the staff in Naples, public information officers and enlisted personnel at Combined Public Information Centers throughout Europe contributed stories, photographs, and ideas for the newspaper. A small cadre of public information personnel at Sarajevo assisted with editing and rewriting articles.

Evaluation

From 1995 to 1997, the *IFOR Informer* was published bi-monthly and was recognized as a valuable tool by the IFOR commander. In an unconfirmed comment by Admiral Smith, he said he was so pleased with the internal tool that he wanted to continue publishing a newspaper when IFOR was deactivated. Therefore, in 1997 when the military forces in Bosnia morphed into the Stabilization Forces and were given a new mission, the newspaper continued to be published, but with its name changed from *IFOR Informer* to *SFOR Informer.*

IFOR's Public Information Officers established a new model for an internal information program to meet the needs of international public relations. From the international staff to the publics, this operation established the identity of IFOR in the hearts and minds of the troops, the countries where they were stationed, and the world, its publics. The military has had a long history of conducting successful public relations campaigns with diverse publics in the international arena, but this was the first undertaking for internal publics. In the history books, IFOR will be remembered for what it did—maintained peace in a volatile, war-torn country through even-handiness and impartiality. This was the image the Commander of IFOR wanted to portray and the *IFOR Informer* conveyed these messages to its publics. The success of a program can be measure by its readership. Although no scientific methods were employed for this purpose, many Combined Public Information Centers reported the popularity of the newspapers with the troops.

Additionally, the measurement of success can be found in the completion of a task. After six weeks of research, planning, and communicating, the first newspaper rolled off the presses and was distributed throughout the theater. This was completion of a major objective for the program—to provide a communication tool for the Commander of IFOR. To obtain feedback from the troops, after the first two issues a survey was distributed unscientifically throughout the area of responsibility. The troops returned only a few surveys, but some recommended additions to the newspaper, such as having monthly pin-up girls, while others indicated that the readers found it informative. Story contributions from the field were another indication of the positive reception of the newspapers and the effects of two-way communication. Public Information Officers at the Combined Public Information Centers penned articles about their sectors, while others explained their experiences. The *Letters to the Commander* column provided an avenue for everyone to be heard by allowing anyone to voice his or her opinion.

Finally, initiated as a tool for communicating with the troops, the newspaper became a souvenir for many of those serving their time in Bosnia. It was a way of remembering their part in a special mission and the cohesiveness of a diverse organization. Thus, the program built new roads in an international environment and developed policy and procedures for successors to compare their programs, which is an indication of success.

Although the UN had deployed troops (UN Protection Forces) and conducted public relations in the Balkans prior to IFOR, the concepts and missions differed. U.S. involvement had been extremely limited and under IFOR the U.S. assumed the lead. While boilerplate plans to facilitate how the military from various nations work in unison emerged from this operation, it is imperative that one realize that the U.S. does not have a monopoly on successful endeavors such as this. The success of working in an international environment to conduct public relations activities takes determination, sensitivity, tenacity, and savvy. It isn't enough to know how to conduct your business or programs, but to make them effective in a fluid situation.

Critique

While this campaign demonstrated some very significant successes, it did have weaknesses. The primary weakness of the campaign came from its hurried beginnings. Initial research was, at best, serendipitous and the objective was never operationalized.

Research

Initially, the campaign administrators tried to answer what Newson has called basic public relations questions—Who are our publics? What is our action/message? What channels of communication reach our publics? What is the reaction to our efforts? What should we do to keep in touch? Because, as in most public relations programs, time was short, empirical research was not used until after the campaign tactics were begun. A readership survey was distributed after the second issue of the newspaper; its returns were limited in scope and information. However, more extensive research could have determined specific demographics about the target audience.

Before the campaign began, secondary research was done, but it could have been more systematic. For example, there was no need to rely on the organizational memory of those in the CIPC and those with experience in the geographic area. Extensive records of prior NATO joint operations could have been referenced, as could the extensive library of historic material on Bosnia, Croatia, and Hungary.

Strengths of the research included the identification of existing resources, such as military aircraft for delivery of a newspaper, and printing facilities in Italy.

Objective

From both the operational plan and the public relations plan, it seems the only objective was to create a medium of communication. However, there was also an implied objective—to establish a corporate identity. Both objectives present problems both for campaign implementation and for evaluation. An objective to create a medium of communication does not provide any guidance for message selection or strategies, and an objective to create a corporate identity is both vague and without operational definition. Because there was no way to measure "corporate identity" it was difficult, if not impossible, to determine what actions and messages would best accomplish the objective. Further, because the objective was not measurable there was no way, at the end of the campaign, to determine if that objective was met.

Strategies

Military organizations are known for detailed planning documents, but in this case the internal information program was omitted. Creating a program from the vague statement,

"There will be an internal information program," created a significant challenge to be overcome by the chief of the internal information division. However, this is how new ground is broken and how IFOR adapted to the changing environment. The organization's messages proclaimed the mission of IFOR and the newspaper advocated these messages through its stories. Effective public relations meant effective communication, whether communicating face-to-face, through the *IFOR Informer* to the troops, or through the news media to the world.

Action Strategies. The actions implemented here seem appropriate, under the circumstances. Those running this campaign established media of communication that were essential to communicate with the public. Other actions might have included some measure of the success of the peacekeeping efforts and modification of the client's actions to facilitate success. Such actions on the part of the client (CIPC) would have provided message content that would have supported the secondary objectives.

Communication Strategies. In this case, those administering had to create their own media of communication. Since only the media they created were available, the choice of media had to be correct. This, of course, assumes that the media (newspaper and radio) created were the most effective that could have been created. It is possible that another medium such as meetings, special events, or word-of-mouth could have been more effective. From the report it appears these options were never considered.

While the messages provided (news from home and local survival information) did secure the interest and attention of the soldiers who made up the target public, there is no way to determine if these were the most effective messages. More specific research on the interaction between information and the sense of "corporate identity" in the soldiers would have made it easier to defend the messages provided.

Another strategic success is the modification of messages to include two-way communication. Although a publication like the *IFOR Informer* is often considered a one-way communication tool, creating the *Letters to the Commander* column facilitated two-way communication. Additionally, it was recognized that the commanders—Commander of IFOR, the U.S. President, and the Crown Prince of England—sought to communicate face-to-face with the troops. How well this process worked can only be measured in the readership of the newspaper and the attendance of the troops at the commanders' gatherings. This last measure is complicated by the conflicting facts that most commanders' meetings are mandatory, and the U.S. President was not always well received by the military.

Tactics

The tactics for creation and distribution of the *Informer* seem more than appropriate—they were essential. Perhaps a tactical lesson-learned for this case study would be "how to steal manpower, in one easy lesson." As noted in the Tactics section, there were no authorizations for a staff in any of the operational documents. It is difficult, if not impossible, to create a staff function without manpower. The chief of the division wrote a plan including manning authorizations, then filled the positions with people slotted against other positions until additional troops were assigned. Just as the Commander of IFOR and the IFOR Public Information Officer were dual-hatted, so were many of the newspaper's staff, including the "responsible editor," who served on the Allied Forces Southern Command staff. Secondly, stringers from the Combined Public Information Centers were used in collecting, editing, and contributing stories, as well as distributing the newspapers after publication. Finally, two major entities augmented the newspaper staff—Associated Press wire service granted permission to use international sports stories, and the U.S. military's Joint Combat Camera supplied high-quality photographs. From all indications, the tactics used to initiate a plan and deliver the messages to target publics were successful.

Evaluation

In any program there are successes and failures, but with this case the successes can be explained by the support of management. The leadership of IFOR recognized the need for an internal program and the *IFOR Informer* emerged as the flagship of the program. Unofficial surveys of the privates in the field and the commanders of IFOR revealed that this newspaper was more than a communication tool. It became an icon for IFOR and the Bosnian peacekeeping mission. On the other hand, the biggest failure was not having an internal information program in original operations plans. This is the most important lesson to be learned from this case study.

As was said in the critique of the objectives, without an operationalized objective it is impossible to measure success of this campaign. Although it is apparent the client was pleased with the campaign and the target public was interested and attentive to the newspapers and broadcasts, there is no measure of whether there was an increased "corporate identity" or whether the medium created really did inform the target publics. In effect, we know the campaign successfully delivered information—we simply do not know if it communicated with the desired effect.

DISCUSSION QUESTIONS

1. Is there other information you would want to know before you decided how best to create a "corporate identity" among the soldiers who made up the target public?

2. Remembering that this campaign had a very limited budget, how could you conduct research to gather the information you identified in 1, above?

3. What is meant by "corporate identity?"

4. How could "corporate identity" be measured or operationalized?

5. What actions could have been recommended by CPIC to the commander of IFOR that might have contributed to the establishment of a "corporate identity" among his soldiers? For example, would the commander visiting the troops (particularly those not of his or her nationality) have assisted the public relations objective?

6. The CPIC staff was obviously literate and well educated. How sure are you that English was an acceptable language of communication for most soldiers in the target public? How would you make that determination?

7. What media of communication could have been used to reach soldiers in remote areas? (Be sure not to limit yourself to traditional media of mass communication.)

8. Are there media that are more effective, more efficient, or more appropriate to some cultures than are newspapers or broadcast? Consider, for example, messages incorporated into media such as religious services, social events, entertainment, or story telling.

9. Were there soldiers in the target public for whom the age, nationality, race, gender, military rank, or language of the information source was an important part of the message? Why is it important to know this before attributing information to a source?

10. Is there any historic, political, or social conflict between different groups within the target public or between groups in the target public and the populations in Bosnia, Croatia, or Hungary? Why is it important to know this? How would you identify any such conflicts?

REFERENCES AND SUGGESTED READINGS

Culbertson, H. M., & Chen, N. (1996). *International public relations.* Mahwah, NJ: Lawrence Erlbaum Associates.

Cutlip, S. M., Center, A. H., & Broom, G. M. (1994). *Effective public relations* (7th ed.). Upper Saddle River, NJ: Prentice-Hall, Inc.

Dilenschneider, R. L. (1996). *Dartnell's public relations handbook* (4th ed.). Chicago: The Dartnell Corporation.

Downey, S. M. (1986–1987). The relationship between corporate culture and corporate identity. *Public Relations Quarterly,* Winter, 7–12.

Granrose, C. S., & Oskamp, S. (1997). *Cross-cultural work groups.* Thousand Oaks, CA: Sage Publications, Inc.

Hunt, T., & Grunig, J. E. (1994). *Public relations techniques.* Fort Worth, Texas: Holt, Rinehart and Winston, Inc.

Kruckeberg, D. (1995–1996). The challenge for public relations in the era of globalization. *Public Relations Quarterly.* Winter, 36–39.

Neuman, J. (1996). *Lights, camera, war.* New York: St. Martin's Press.

Newsom, D., Turk, J. V., & Kruckeberg, D. (1996). *This is PR: The realities of public relations* (6th ed.). Belmont, CA: Wadsworth Publishing Co.

Seelye, N., & Seelye-James, A. (1995). *Culture class: Managing in a multicultural world.* Chicago: NTC Business Books.

5 Protecting Drug Patents in Africa

MICHAEL PARKINSON

This case report was completed from public records without the cooperation or input of pharmaceutical companies.

Executive Summary

Four large U.S. pharmaceutical companies (Bristol-Meyers Squibb, Merck, Abbott Laboratories, and Pfizer) and the U.S. government spent literally billions of dollars researching cures and treatments for Acquired Immune Deficiency Syndrome (AIDS) and Human Immunodeficiency Virus (HIV). When successful, the U.S. pharmaceutical companies protected their discoveries with patents. These drugs were then sold for prices that allowed the pharmaceutical companies to recover the cost of manufacturing the drugs, the cost of the research, and a profit for the shareholders who had funded the research. These AIDS treatments can cost more than most people in the developing world earn.

Both consumer groups in the United States and government representatives from developing countries accused U.S. and European pharmaceutical companies of profiting from the AIDS epidemic. This criticism reached a peak in late 2001. Some developing countries responded to this pressure by acquiring "copy-cat" drugs and circumventing the patents of the pharmaceutical companies who developed the drugs. Others threatened to create laws that would void the patents.

This case describes and explores actions by the pharmaceutical companies to protect both their existing patents and the patent laws that they believe provide the motivation for future medical research.

Research

Although the major pharmaceutical companies involved are in the business of medical and market research, they conducted virtually no research into public opinion and seem to have ignored two emerging latent publics. They had established favorable relations with both their

160

regulators and legislators who had the power to change or amend patent laws. For example, in 1999 drug companies spent 90.6 million dollars to lobby U.S. politicians.

The latent publics the drug companies failed to adequately research were consumer groups in the United States and health officials in developing countries. Early in the Clinton administration (1992), public interest in universal health care was encouraged. Since that time, groups like the Gray Panthers and Ralph Nader's Consumer Protection on Technology have advocated public licensing of pharmaceuticals. Public licensing would give the U.S. government authority to permit manufacturers to make and sell generic versions of patented drugs. Such licensing would make drugs significantly less expensive but would not allow the companies that conducted the development research to recover their costs.

Many public officials in the developing world were dealing with problems that motivated them to fight U.S. drug patents. While many countries in the world have significant AIDS/HIV problems, two areas had a particular impact on attitudes toward and treatment of U.S. pharmaceutical companies. These two areas are the country of India and the continent of Africa. In 2001, South Africa reported 4.7 million citizens with HIV/AIDS. This number, which many believe may be less than half of the actual cases, is still 11% of the countries' entire population. The South African Health Ministry estimates that there are 1,700 new AIDS/HIV cases in that country every day. Other countries in Africa have even more significant problems (Figure 1). Kenya and Nigeria, for example, estimate that one in eight citizens between 15 and 49 are HIV positive. India has an estimated AIDS population of 3.7 million. While there are no accurate measures, some Indian health officials fear the actual number may be ten times that. Some international health officials suggest that Thailand and China may have even larger numbers of AIDS sufferers than do India and South Africa. Regardless of the actual numbers, even cursory research indicates AIDS/HIV is a massive epidemic in some of the poorest countries in the world.

Health officials in India and Africa also are dealing with overwhelming poverty. In India, for example, a survey of family values and income indicates that the maximum an average family would spend to "save the life of a daughter" is 50 cents per day. When the cost is raised to one dollar per day, most families indicate they could not afford to save her life. Fifty cents per day is particularly significant when placed in context of the actual cost of treatment. The cost of AIDS/HIV treatment in the United States is $30 to 40 per day. Numbers in Kenya are even more telling. Purchasing drugs to treat all its AIDS/HIV patients would cost $141 to 167 million per year. The entire annual budget of Kenya is $115 million per year.

One last characteristic of the publics in Africa is their resentment of U.S. wealth and power. In April of 2001, an article in *Time Africa* pointed out that it would cost the United States two cents of every $100 in GNP to provide AIDS drugs to Africans for free. This article, which reflected views held by many citizens and health officials in Africa, made it appear that only callousness and greed in the United States was costing 5 million African lives. The fact that drug companies in the United States made a profit from the sale of AIDS treatment only exacerbated the impression that greed was the primary cause of the epidemic in Africa.

In short, the AIDS epidemic in Africa is overwhelming the governments and the societies. In South Africa, for example, an animal welfare group (Community Led Animal Welfare) has begun picking up AIDS patients along with starving cats and dogs.

The pharmaceutical companies have conducted excellent marketing and medical development research. This research supports a need for strong patent protection and conflicts

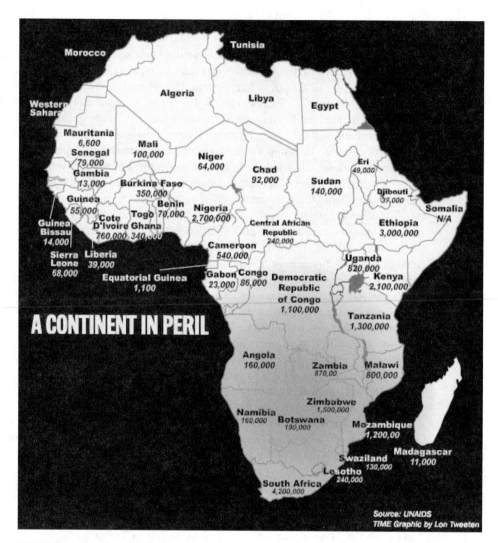

FIGURE 1 Continent in Peril

© 2000 TIME, Inc. Reprinted with permission.

diametrically with the perceptions of consumer groups and developing country health officials. They find, for example, that there is very little support from charities or governments of developed countries for providing AIDS/HIV treatment in the developing world.

The U.S. government budgets $23 billion for research annually. U.S. pharmaceutical companies spend 50 times more on research than do companies outside the United States. The U.S. pharmaceutical companies also produce the majority of new treatments and drugs. Also, U.S. law provides 20 years of protection for a patent. However, because of stringent U.S. drug protections it usually takes 8 to 9 years for a drug to be approved for marketing.

Therefore, on average, a drug company has 11 years of sales during which to recover its research costs. Analysts of the U.S. drug industry argue that it is the patent protections that motivate U.S. pharmaceutical companies to spend so heavily on research and that it is the spending by the drug companies that leads to medical discoveries. Serendipitous support for this idea can be seen in the actions of other governments. Canada had a law that allowed the government to license production of generic drugs. When that law was repealed in 1993, spending on pharmaceutical research in Canada increased from $167 million to $900 million per year. When the European Union countries began to impose government controlled drug-pricing, funding for pharmaceutical research in those countries was reduced. (It should be noted that British, Dutch, and German pharmaceutical companies do make major contributions to medical research, but they are also located in countries that still have some significant patent protections.)

The U.S. government and the governments of most world nations see the need to protect patents as important. They codified this belief in the World Trade Organization (WTO) and treaties like the General Agreement on Tariffs and Trade that protect patents internationally. These treaties do include provisions that permit nations to void patent protections in times of national health emergencies.

Simply put, research shows two very different perspectives on drug pricing and patent protections. The groups that pharmaceutical companies treated as their primary publics—medical professionals, investors, and government—recognize the need to protect patents and profits in order to motivate future medical research. The latent publics that were not researched or seen as primary by the pharmaceutical companies—consumer groups and developing world health officials—do not recognize a need to protect patents and are motivated by the immediate need for cheap and large-scale AIDS treatment.

Objective

The goal for the pharmaceutical companies is simply to stay in business. To do this they must maintain the profitability that allows them to recruit investors and to fund research. To accomplish this goal the companies have to keep the patent protections that allow them to market their drugs at much higher prices than the simple cost of production.

The public relations objective of the pharmaceutical companies, in this context, is to persuade government officials both in the United States and the developing world to protect their patents. Secondary objectives include:

- Motivating government officials in developing countries not to permit the manufacture or sale of generic or copy-cat versions of patented drugs.
- Countering messages from consumer groups and health care officials who advocated compulsory licensing or other legal means of voiding patent protections.

To meet their objectives, the pharmaceutical companies were compelled to explain a very complicated and abstract justification for high drug prices while countering the very basic and appealing argument that high drug prices were unfair, greedy, or discriminatory.

Strategies

In part because the pharmaceutical companies had not researched or had underestimated the impact of AIDS crisis in developing countries, the first round of strategic action was taken by those opposed to patent protections and the drug companies were forced to respond, rather than to act proactively. The most important action taken by those opposed to patent protections began in India. The Indian government does not enforce pharmaceutical patents and a lucrative drug industry has grown there. This drug industry, in part, takes patented drugs developed in the United States and Europe and simply copies those drugs. Since these Indian companies do not have to bear any research costs, they are able to sell their versions of the patented drugs at significantly lower prices.

The third largest generic drug manufacturer in India is Cipla. Although it is the third largest generic manufacturer in India, its specialization in copying patented AIDS drugs has made it the most profitable of the generic manufacturers. Forty-four percent of Cipla stock, valued at $530 million, is owned by Yusuf Hamied. In 2000, Cipla was exporting its generic AIDS drugs to countries in Africa. While Cipla's practice of copying patented drugs may have been legal in India, the sale of these drugs in Africa clearly violated the international agreements on patent protection. However, the AIDS crisis in Africa was so severe that the Nigerian government refused to take any action against Cipla, the Kenyan government legalized the import of generic drugs, and the South African government publicly declined to take any action against Cipla or the humanitarian aid groups purchasing Cipla products for use in South Africa.

Action Strategies

Initially, 39 pharmaceutical companies primarily from the United States and Europe initiated legal action against the governments and aid agencies importing the Cipla drugs. The defendants in these actions included many church-related not-for-profit groups that were purchasing AIDS/HIV drugs for their patients. One defendant was Father D'Agostino, who used the drugs to treat patients in his poverty clinic. Another defendant named in one action was Nelson Mandela. Initially, the U.S. government supported the pharmaceutical companies in these efforts to use legal channels to enforce their patent rights.

Defendants in these legal actions did not respond within the traditional international legal system. Many took their case directly to the media. Father D'Agostino, for example, made public statements both in Kenya and the United States that he would not honor any legal decision that "forced him to simply watch his parishioners die." Public sympathy and respect for Nelson Mandela was also used by several consumer groups to make the drug companies appear to be racist, greedy, or indifferent to suffering. Fairly quickly, the Bush administration in the United States withdrew it support for the lawsuits, and in April of 2001 the drug companies themselves dropped the actions.

The drug companies also began to enter into negotiations to lower prices to countries that would agree not to import Cipla's products or other generic versions of patented drugs. In May of 2000, five drug companies began these price negotiations. As late as March of 2001, Bristol-Meyers Squibb reduced the price of its drugs Videx and Zerit to one dollar per day in Africa. They also made the patent for Zerit available at no cost to treat AIDS in South Africa.

Bristol-Meyers Squibb, Abbott Laboratories, and Merck offered AIDS drugs and HIV diagnostic kits in Africa at no profit, and Pfizer began to offer Diflucan (an AIDS/HIV treatment) for free in sub-Saharan Africa. Despite these offers, only four African countries—Rowanda, Ivory Coast, Uganda, and Senegal—agreed to stop importing copies of the patented medicines.

Communication Strategies

To support each action taken by the pharmaceutical companies they offered explanations of their actions. These explanations were often made in statements to western media and responses to inquiries from English language newspapers. Many of these included statements affirming the drug companies' commitment to improving health care and their dedication to their patients. For example, John McGoldrick, Vice President of Bristol-Meyers Squibb, in March of 2001 released a statement that included the phrase, "We seek no profit on AIDS drugs in Africa and we will not let our patents be an obstacle [to medical care in Africa]." However, most of the messages also addressed the complex relationship between motivation for medical research, profits, and patent protections. Also in March of 2001 a pharmaceutical group in South Africa, in response to a press inquiry about dropping patent enforcement actions, said "[they feared] the multinational pharmaceutical industry would exit South Africa, and South Africa would be the poorer for it." Many of these messages also tried to explain that dropping drug prices would not realistically improve AIDS care in Africa. Pfizer, also in March of 2001, included the following phrase in a response to an inquiry about its decision to give away AIDS medication in Africa: "There is no better price than zero. For patients in sub-Saharan Africa, the difference between a medication that costs $5,000 and a medication that costs $500 a year is not material. Most Africans can't afford it at any price."

These messages, while factually accurate, presented ideas that are complicated and based on an economic perspective that was not shared by most people in Africa.

Tactics

Because this case has been prepared without input from the pharmaceutical companies themselves, any description of tactics is limited to what is apparent from the results of those tactics. From public records and media coverage it appears the tactics of the pharmaceutical companies that addressed the consumer groups and African health community were limited to reporting price negotiations and responses to the actions of Cipla and African governments. Simply put, the tactics were reactive rather than proactive. At each significant change in public opinion about the price of AIDS drugs and the importance of patent protection, the pharmaceutical companies appear to have been reacting to criticism or threatened action against them.

Evaluation

With no empirical measure of public opinions about patent protection, we must rely on serendipitous measures of success. Unfortunately, all of these suggest that any attempt to strengthen patent protections or to prevent compulsory licensing of drug production failed. Under pressure from the United States and the drug companies, the WTO did vote to require India to put strong pharmaceutical patent protections in place by 2005, but this action was taken in March of 2001—early in this campaign. In June of 2001, a World Bank economist proposed an alternative that would permit patent enforcement only in wealthy nations. According to Nick Stern, the World Bank's chief economist, "What we're looking for is to get prices down in developing countries for basic medicines, while recognizing that you need an incentive to actually create new medicines." This proposal suggests the world economic community was already moving to permit licensing or to void drug patent laws in developing countries, like those in Africa. Even in the United States the Hatch-Waxman Act that would encourage the faster availability of generic drugs was supported by groups as diverse as the United Auto Workers, General Motors, and the Gray Panthers. In the European Union Germany adopted "reference pricing," which forced drug companies to sell patented pharmaceuticals at a rate based on the cost of generic production. In December of 2002, France was considering similar legislation. Walter Koebele of Pfizer said the price controls would wipe out $61.6 million in sales and Lehman Brothers investment analysts say the European measures will cut revenue for drug research by $2.2 billion per year.

Perhaps the most powerful evidence that patent protections are expected to fail is the economic impact on the drug companies themselves. In August of 2002, Bristol-Meyers Squibb announced that it had the worst financial period in its 100-year history. Other drug companies have announced significant cuts in research and new product launches, and drug profits are down as investors move out of the industry.

Other evidence of the campaign's failure is the apparent move of drug research from AIDS and into more discretionary medical areas. In the past few years the most profitable patent drugs have addressed such discretionary health problems as toe nail fungus (Lamisil) and erectile dysfunction (Viagra). These are health arenas where the pharmaceutical companies are more confident that governments will not compel nonprofit sales. When announcing FDA approval of its most recent entry into AIDS treatments, Reyataz, the head of research at Bristol-Meyers said, "We're kind of worrying about stuff at the margin and losing track of what kills people."

Critique

Research

Although it may be impossible to anticipate a new public or a significant change in attitudes, the pharmaceutical companies here limited their research to traditional publics. That limitation and the failure to anticipate trends left them reacting to changes rather than anticipating changes and acting proactively.

Latent publics are those groups that are neither active in the client's business nor completely passive. They are people who, if they received the right information, would become active. Public relations campaigns and strategies usually focus on latent publics who can be made active supporters of the campaign objective with the right information. However, a latent public who will become an active opponent cannot be ignored.

In this situation, if the pharmaceutical companies had more aggressively monitored news media and political trends, they should have anticipated that consumer groups and health officials in developing countries could become very active opponents of patent protection. Further, analysis of political trends should have predicted that once consumer groups became active opponents, that political support would evaporate.

Objective

Here the objective of securing support for enforcement of patent protections was a simple and operationalizable objective. The major problem was the focus on the primary public—legislators. Failure to anticipate the need to address secondary publics was the major weakness.

Strategies

Action Strategies. The decision to take legal action against churches, charities, and Nelson Mandela was obviously ill advised. Those who recommended this action failed to anticipate the very negative public reaction to an apparent attack on groups and people who have significant public sympathy. The decision to reduce drug prices in developing countries also seems to have come too late to have significantly improved public opinion or support for patent protections.

Communication Strategies. The most important problem with the message supporting patent protection was its complexity. Trying to explain the complex interaction of motivation, profits, research costs, and future benefits may have been just too much to do. Opponents of patent protections have the extraordinary advantage of delivering a very simple and emotionally attractive message—drugs cost too much and people die.

Tactics

The pharmaceutical companies and their public relations representatives were forced into a reactive position and simply never recovered. As a result, their tactics were always rushed and appeared disjointed.

Evaluation

The campaign's objective makes evaluation relatively simple. In this context evaluation is good. We only need look at the profitability of the companies and the extent to which patents are being protected to determine if the campaign was successful. Unfortunately, these simple measures indicate that the campaign failed.

DISCUSSION QUESTIONS

1. Hindsight is 20–20. Now that you know latent publics can become active opponents of a corporation's goals, how would you suggest that a corporation identify and monitor latent publics?

2. Research in developing countries often presents unidentified problems. How would you conduct research to determine what messages would convince people in South Africa to support patent enforcement?

3. Can you suggest any action strategy the pharmaceutical companies could have taken to secure public support for patent protection? Or, can you suggest any action strategy the pharmaceutical companies could have taken to ameliorate public opposition to patent protections?

4. How would you suggest the drug companies explain the need for patent protections to generate profits so they can secure investor funding for future research?

5. Is there any way to explain the need for future research to people in a country where more than 10 percent of the population is dying now?

6. Are there long-term strategies the drug companies can use to regain public support for patent protections in the United States? Are there long-term strategies they can use to gain public support for patent protections in the developing world?

7. Are there cultural values or beliefs in different parts of Africa that will make campaigns to prevent AIDS difficult to implement? In particular, are there existing attitudes toward the United States or Caucasians that will make it difficult for U.S. companies to deliver messages in sub-Saharan Africa?

8. What medium or media should be explored for delivering messages about preventing AIDS/HIV in sub-Saharan Africa?

REFERENCES AND SUGGESTED READINGS

Abbott laboratories to offer AIDS drugs and rapid diagnostic test at no profit in Africa. (2003, December 30). Retrieved December 30, 2003, from http://abbott.com/news/press_release.cfm?id=248

Block, R. (2001, July 9). Spring dogs and cats, Cora Bailey is finding people to rescue too. *The Wall Street Journal,* p. A1.

Fuhrmans, V. (2003, January 8). Italy's pharmacists still concoct drugs, even better Viagra. *The Wall Street Journal,* p. A1.

Fuhrmans, V., & Zimmerman, R. (2002, May 7). Swiss drug giant joins exodus to the U.S. with new global lab. *The Wall Street Journal,* p. A1.

Harris, G. (2002, March 14). Judge permits cheap knockoff of Bristol drug. *The Wall Street Journal,* p. B1.

Harris, G., & Adams, C. (2001, July 12). Drug manufacturers step up legal attacks that slow generics. *The Wall Street Journal,* p. A1.

Harris, G., & Fuhrmans, V. (2002, August 23). Its rivals in funk, Novartis finds way to thrive. *The Wall Street Journal,* p. A1.

Harris, G., & McGinley, L. (2001, April 23). AIDS gaffs in Africa come back to haunt drug industry at home. *The Wall Street Journal,* p. A1.

Hensley, S. (2003, January 24). Pharmacia nears generics deal on AIDS drugs for poor nations. *The Wall Street Journal,* p. A1.

Hensley, S. (2001, March 2). AIDS epidemic traps drug firms in a vise: Treatment or profit. *The Wall Street Journal,* p. A1.

Hilsenrath, Jon. (2001, December 11). Globalization persists in precarious New Age. *The Wall Street Journal,* p. A1.

Landers, P. (2003, June 23). Bristol-Meyers AIDS Drug cleared. *The Wall Street Journal,* p. A10.

Landri, L. (2002, July 29). FDA is urged to hasten efforts to require bar codes on drugs. *The Wall Street Journal,* p. B5.

Manning, J., & Fauber, J. (2001, April 1). Drug makers depend on lobbying to protect patents. Retrieved April 1, 2001, from www.jsonline.com/bym/news/apr01/scripsid02040101a.asp.

McGirley, L., & Adams, C. (2002, July 29). Generic drugs find potent new formula: Friends in Congress. *The Wall Street Journal,* p. A1.

Murry, A. (2001, March 19). Drug makers battle is one over ideas. *The Wall Street Journal,* p. A1.

Naik, G. (2002, September 6). Glaxo to cut prices in poor countries. *The Wall Street Journal,* p. B5.

Naik, G., & Fuhrmans, V. (2002, December 26). How Americans may subsidize Euro-health care. *The Wall Street Journal,* p. A8.

Pearl, D. (2001, February, 16). Companies weigh offer of royalties for AIDS drugs aimed at Africa. *The Wall Street Journal.* p. A1.

Pearl, D., & Freedman, A. (2001, March 12). Behind Cipla's offer of cheap AIDS drugs: Potent mix of motives. *The Wall Street Journal,* p. A1.

Pearl, D., & Stecklow, S. Drug firms incentives to pharmacists in India fuel widespread abuse. *The Wall Street Journal,* p. A1.

Pharmaceutical companies lose battle in court of public opinion. (2001, May 2). *Power Lines.* p. 31.

Phillips, M. (2001, June 13). AIDS drug plan envisions two markets for firms patents. *The Wall Street Journal,* pp. A2, A10.

Pollack, A. (2002, April 21). Defensive drug industry fuels fight over patents. Retrieved April 21, 2002, from www.nytimes.com.

Quenqua, D. (2002, July 29). Rand hopes global healthcare initiative will help perceptions of U.S. *PR Week,* p. 1.

Schroeder, M. (2002, August 15). Under gun from SEC, Bristol, others divulge accounting issues. *The Wall Street Journal,* p. A1.

Shoops, M. (2001, July 19). Overseas tests of AIDS drug skirt regulations. *The Wall Street Journal,* p. B1.

Tomlinson, C. (2002, February 21). Priest to import AIDS drugs to Kenya. Retrieved December 30, from www.africast.com/article.php?newsID=9470&strRegion=East.

Waldholz, M., & Zimmerman, R. (2001, March 15). Bristol-Meyers offers to sell two AIDS drugs in Africa at below cost. *The Wall Street Journal,* p. B1.

Competing Community Relations Campaigns in Australia: Public Relations Efforts for and against a Biosolids Production Facility

STEVE MACKEY

This case is based on interviews with an Australian state government environmental protection officer, a spokesperson for a water authority, and a campaigner who led a fight to stop one of the water authority's biosolids projects. The chief executive officer of the water authority broke off contact with the researcher after seeing an initial draft of his interview. The CEO did not try to stop the case study investigation or invoke the university ethics procedures to withdraw from the study. However, it has been thought prudent not to use any comment from the water authority or to identify the organization or its location.

Executive Summary

This case involves something with which we all have an intimate, life-long familiarity. But the subject is also something that many communities find difficult to address both as a public engineering problem and as an emotional or psychological issue. The subject is human waste. The vast majority of us do not think about the disposal of human waste as soon as the substance enters the sewerage system. However, what happens then is becoming increasingly prominent in discussions about disposal, public health, and environmental sustainability. The water industry globally has devised the term "biosolids" as arguably a more accurate (some would say euphemistic) term for sewage sludge that has been made safe and solid. It may be stored for years or disposed of as landfill or burned. Some grades of biosolids are deemed safe enough to be used for agricultural purposes after harmful organisms and industrial and domestic chemicals have been removed, neutralized, or reduced to specified levels.

The case description begins with background on the general issue of biosolids. It then describes an Australian water authority's initially rejected effort to gain public acceptance of a biosolids production facility. In the first proposal, liquid sludge would be trucked to a location approximately five kilometers (three miles) from a town of 800 people. There the sludge would be placed in open troughs or pits and dried until solid. A small opposition group used very simple public relations techniques to stop this proposal. Later, the water authority succeeded in obtaining public acceptance to open a similar plant near a larger town in the same region.

Because the water authority withdrew cooperation in this study, most of the material in this case study is written from the perspective of a group that protested against the first proposal. The case study can be seen as relevant to all points of view, however, because it paints a picture of the sorts of difficulties such public authorities and private organizations may come up against when they encounter a group of dedicated neighborhood protesters.

Research

The protest organizers gathered their research to defeat the biosolids proposal largely from secondary sources. They used libraries, the Internet, and the public documents made available by the water authority. They also kept a cuttings file as their campaign started to be reported by local newspapers. Primary research was confined to drawing on local knowledge and talking to neighbors, public servants, and townsfolk. Here is some of the information that was available to them:

The subject of biosolids is tinged with controversy. The name biosolids was coined in 1991 after a competition among members of the Water Pollution Control Federation that was later renamed the Water Environment Federation (WEF) (Stauber & Rampton, 1995; Blatt, 2000). On its website the WEF describes itself as:

> An international not-for-profit educational and technical organization of more than 40,000 water quality experts. Members include environmental, civil, and chemical engineers, biologists, chemists, government officials, students, treatment plant managers and operators, laboratory analysts, and equipment manufacturers and distributors. WEF's mission is to preserve and enhance the global water environment. (Water Environment Federation website accessed 11 August 2000)

WEF is based in the United States but has affiliate organizations from many countries, including the Australian Water Association (AWA). According to Stauber and Rampton (1995), the word biosolids was coined to break some of the connotations of the expression "sewage sludge." The WEF naming competition was organized by a federation member, Peter Machno, who wanted a name that would make it easier to convince the public at large that sludge could be made safe for spreading on tree farms near Seattle. Other names entered in the competition included: all growth, purenutri, biolife, bioslurp, black gold, geoslime, sca-doo, the end product, humanure, hu-doo, organic residuals, bioresidue, urban biomass, powergro, organite, recyclite, nuti-cake, and ROSE—short for recycling of organics environmentally (Stauber & Rampton, 1995, p. 106). The National Biosolids Partnership (NBP) describes itself in the following way:

> The goal of the National Biosolids Partnership (NBP), a not-for-profit alliance formed in 1997 with the Association of Metropolitan Sewerage Agencies (AMSA), Water Environment Federation (WEF), and US Environmental Protection Agency (EPA), is to advance environmentally sound and accepted biosolids management practices. . . . (National Biosolids Partnership, 2000)

The National Biosolids Partnership and the Water Environment Federation lobby policy makers and deal with news media and other groups to defend and advocate biosolids use. The WEF issues an electronic newsletter that discusses good biosolids practice and responds to criticism from other agencies and groups that have concerns or that campaign against biosolids—often via the medium of other websites. The comments on biosolids from the U.S. Environmental Protection Agency and the U.S. Center for Disease Control and Prevention discussed below were made available on their respective websites.

In Australia the term biosolids seems to have won general acceptance and support among water authorities, water engineers, academics, and scientists as an appropriate term. Dr. Geoffrey J. Syme is a scientist and researcher at the (Australian) Commonwealth Scientific and Industrial Research Organization (CSIRO). He, together with Katrina D. Williams and Mark A. Lee, made an important study of public attitudes to sludge in Australia in 1990 and says he supports the term "biosolids" (personal communication, August 11, 2000). The study published by Williams, Lee, and Syme does not use the term biosolids. It was published in 1990 before the term biosolids was coined. Instead, it uses the term "domestic sludge." The study examined "public perceptions and concerns in relation to domestic sludge management with a view to deriving preliminary recommendation for public education and involvement in sludge management."

It is clear that Syme and his colleagues are concerned with how the topic is perceived and interpreted in the minds of the public in general. One of the three issues their research report addresses is public perception. According to them, " . . . in areas of risk or uncertainty in sludge management, subjective perceptions of risk need to be incorporated in the design of the public involvement program" (Williams et al., 1990, p. 2). Elsewhere the paper suggests (rather contradictorily) that:

> . . . there is no need for the public to fully understand all technical issues. Public involvement should be about input into the criteria for planning (e.g., a health-preserving sludge policy or one which involves the maximum recycling) rather than the technicalities of the solution. People need either to know enough about the technicalities to understand what is impossible or to trust the relevant authorities sufficiently to believe that there is an honest attempt to incorporate their views. Technical information flow should be designed with this point in mind. (Williams et al., p. 4)

In August 2000, Syme said he thought public attitudes toward the issue of domestic sludge were "very similar" to those at the time the 1990 paper was written. He continued the 1990 paper's criticism of the professionals in the field who had: ". . . a reluctance to actively pursue reforms." These were reforms aimed at involving the public in planning domestic sludge or biosolids projects, albeit on the basis of limited public understanding of the technological issues involved. The 1990 paper justifies limitation of understanding because ". . . it is evident that too much, or the wrong kind of information, can result in risk (or uncertainty) amplification in the community, which may lead to over-concern about issues." (Williams et al., p. 4).

It appears that many sewage disposal professionals see the term biosolids as a useful "know-enough" term that provides target publics with a euphemism for sewage sludge, without stimulating either interest in details about the material or concern for its safety. The Williams, Lee, and Syme report concurs with literature suggesting it would defeat the interests of the sewage disposal industry to provide the public with full information about a biosolids project. They prefer omission of much of the scientific information about risks associated with its use. For example, Williams, Lee, and Syme said "All parties should understand that public involvement programs do not require technical expertise from 'amateurs' but a contribution to setting planning criteria" (Williams et al., p. 18).

By the twenty-first century the term biosolids had been routinely adopted in Australia. For instance, the Sydney Water Authority and the Melbourne Water Authority have both carried out public consultation on this subject using the term biosolids. There was, however, still some uncertainty about the term within the industry, as revealed in the industry's important publication *A Global Atlas of Wastewater Sludge and Biosolids Use and Disposal* (1997):

> The language used for discussion is in itself critical. So 'sludge dumped on land' sends out a different message than does 'biosolids used in agriculture'! There is still no agreement on how far the word 'biosolids' should be extended but for the time being there is agreement that when wastewater solids are used, particularly in agriculture, the word is highly suitable. (Matthews, 1997, p. 1)

Whatever the terminology, continuing disagreement about the use of biosolids was highlighted in an August 2000 news release from the U.S. Environmental Protection Agency that said:

> (U.S. EPA) Headquarters Press Release. Washington, DC
>
> NATIONAL ACADEMY OF SCIENCES TO STUDY SLUDGE
>
> To ensure that government standards for land applications of sewage sludge are fully protective of human health and the environment, EPA has asked the National Academy of Sciences to review the science and methodology behind the standards and to provide the agency with recommendations that will strengthen the sludge program. The Academy's definitive review and its recommendations will strengthen existing programs for protecting public health and the environment. The US Center for Disease Control—National Institute of Occupational Safety and Health has agreed to work with EPA and NAS on this review . . . U.S. Environmental Protection Agency. (August 3, 2000)

This release followed one in July of 2000 from the National Institute for Occupational Safety and Health that published a message on its website as follows:

> ***Workers Exposed to Class B Biosolids During and After Field Application***
> Workers may be exposed to disease-causing organisms while handling, applying or disturbing Class B biosolids on agricultural lands or mine reclamation sites.

Class B biosolids are sewage sludge that has undergone treatment by processes that significantly reduce pathogen concentrations. These processes include aerobic and anaerobic digestion, air-drying, composting, and lime stabilization. According to the US Environmental Protection Agency (EPA), Class B biosolids may contain pathogens in sufficient quantity to warrant restricted public access and special precautions for exposed workers. . . . (US) National Institute for Occupational Safety and Health (27 August 2000)

Three years later, WEF issued a press release (Figure 1) that addressed some of these earlier concerns and, at the same time, illustrated some of the difficulty in writing both accurately and clearly about biosolids.

In short, there is contradictory information available from secondary sources about the risks associated with the use of biosolids. Some highly qualified organizations and individuals say it is safe and well tested. Others suggest there may be risks and that further testing is needed. There is some evidence that those who seek to dispose of biosolids or to manufacture biosolids may be using euphemisms and omitting information in order to avoid public opposition to the placement or production of these materials near homes or businesses and there is some evidence that it is difficult, maybe impossible, to accurately describe biosolids without stimulating fear and opposition.

Research

In the late 1990s, a small Australian water authority proposed to produce biosolids. The project would involve trucking treated liquid sewage residue to a series of open pits or troughs five kilometers from a town of 800 people. Once in these troughs the sludge was to be further treated to eliminate disease-causing pathogens and to detoxify the material, then left to dry. The project required land use planning approval from the local council. The small group who opposed the biosolids project used secondary research methods. This initially very small group of protesters found that the test project was not initially opposed by the town inhabitants. Little community consultation had been organized by the water authority. The authority's primary mode of consulting the local community was to leave leaflets in the local post office to tell people a biosolids project was being proposed near the town.

In these leaflets there was no mention of the word "sewage." The townsperson who became the lead protest organizer read the leaflet, saw the word biosolids, and did not understand it. When she found out what it meant she became alarmed. She spoke to other people in the town and found that they did not understand the term either and that they became concerned when they learned what the leaflet was actually about.

As alarm grew in the town, the lead protester and three other concerned townsfolk spent two weeks gathering information about the proposed biosolids project. They looked at websites about the topic. They researched worrying examples of biosolids use and case studies of disasters caused by toxic materials in the vicinity of homes. The examples they found on the Internet were mostly in the United States. In addition, the protesters requested detailed official documents on the proposal that had been compiled by the water authority. They also questioned water authority and council officials by phone and personal visit. The protesters made a breakthrough when they discovered what they claimed to be an error in

FIGURE 1   WEF News Release. The Water Environmental Federation issued this press release. It is presented here to show the difficulties of both accurately and clearly writing about biosolids. The release is used with permission of the WEF.

FOR IMMEDIATE RELEASE

Public Education Is Needed on the Science and Benefits of Biosolids Recycling

WEF Comments on EPA's Response to the NRC Biosolids (Sewage Sludge) Report

ALEXANDRIA, VA – April 17, 2003. The Water Environment Federation (WEF) has issued an editorial authored by WEF Executive Director **Bill Bertera** entitled, **"Biosolids Recycling . . . A Safe Practice and Sound Science in the Public Interest"**. The piece was prompted by the U.S. Environmental Protection Agency's proposed strategy, filed in the Federal Register on April 9, to respond to the recommendations in the National Research Council's National Academy of Sciences July 2002 report, "Biosolids Applied to Land: Advancing Standards and Practices".

The NAS report concluded, "there is no documented scientific evidence to indicate that the Part 503 sewage sludge regulation has failed to protect human health." However, according to Bertera, this same report was "couched in terms that could, by dint of its ambiguity and lack of clarity, raise scientifically unwarranted doubts about the land application of biosolids. The EPA has now definitively responded to the NRC report and reiterated the scientific conclusions of the NRC committee, that the land application of biosolids, based on what we know scientifically, remains a viable and beneficial management option."

The science of biosolids and land application has continued to evolve over the past ten years since the regulation was issued and the Federation supports EPA's commitment of further inquiry into the process to avoid any uncertainty that could result in confusion among local communities. While WEF is confident that current evidence points toward positive benefits of biosolids recycling, the primary goal of the Federation and the water quality community is to protect public health and ensure good environmental stewardship.

WEF, a not-for-profit technical and educational organization, supports EPA's commitment to further inquiry, "not out of concern that there is evidence that such an inquiry is needed, but because there are areas in which our knowledge needs enhancing and because the public is better served by more comprehensive information," concluded Bertera.

To view the editorial in its entirety, visit http://www.wef.org/PublicInfo/editorial03.jhtml. To learn more about the activities of the Water Environment Federation, please visit www.wef.org.

# # # #

Founded in 1928, **the Water Environment Federation (WEF)** is a not-for-profit technical and educational organization with members from varied disciplines who work toward the WEF vision of preservation and enhancement of the global water environment. The WEF network includes water quality professionals from 79 Member Associations in more than 30 countries.

the report of a scientist hired by the water authority to prove the suitability of the sludge-processing site. The scientist's report said the existing quality of underground water throughout the site was poor—meaning that there was no danger of further contaminating it. But the same report showed that underground water samples at one point of the site were of good quality. Protesters said this was a contradiction that placed a question mark over all of the water authority's scientific research and thus the case for this use of the land. The volunteers had no technical training in water science or geology. Commenting on the scientific research in official documents, the lead protester said:

> I don't think you need to go to school for three years to read a consultant's report and an EPA report on surface water and catchments. We read these reports from cover to cover. When we found that the [water] classification was wrong we realized that this called into question a lot of other information.

Objectives

The initial goal of the protesters was to question the proposal, but this goal was quickly changed to one of completely stopping the biosolids plant. The goals were approached through a number of input and output objectives involving various targeted publics. After the new goal of total opposition was decided, the primary target public of the protesters was seen to be the local council, which would have to give planning permission for the land use to enabled the project to go ahead. The other publics targeted included:

- the wider range of townspeople, whom campaign leaders wanted to motivate to swell the protest
- the water authority. Protesters wanted to undermine the confidence of officials and the advisory board of this authority in order to make them rethink their proposal.
- citizens in the surrounding region, including a 28,000-population city where most of the sludge originated
- other relevant opinion leaders, such as state and federal politicians whose future polling returns might be influenced by their public statements on this issue

The local news media were seen as channels for reaching the more dispersed publics. Local publics in the town were reached via word of mouth, posters, leaflets, and occasional meetings. The protest group's goal was exactly contrary to the goal of the water authority, which was seeking to secure approval for the biosolids project.

Strategies

Action Strategies

The only actions required of the opposition group involved gathering and disseminating information. Since they had not existed before this campaign and existed only for the purpose of communication about the water authority's proposed project, their actions were limited to careful preparation for their acts of communication. This preparation was accomplished by conducting thorough research.

Communication Strategies

The communication strategies were very simple. The opposition group gathered and disseminated information. The techniques used to gather the information were already described. The delivery of the information was accomplished through word of mouth in the town, news releases to local newspapers, planning meetings by the protesters' inner circle, meetings organized by the protesters for townsfolk, and attendance at meetings organized by the local council and water authority. At these latter, officially organized meetings, the protesters raised questions and revealed information that was not being shared by the water authority. The protesters' set-piece and knowledgeable performances at officially organized meetings was always planned in the protesters' own pre-meetings. Their carefully researched questions put the water authority and council officials on the defensive. This embarrassment of officialdom stimulated press interest.

The opposition group knew that press coverage would get the attention of the residents who elected the members of the council. Through the media they could use the council members' constituents to put pressure on the council to oppose the biosolids project in their community. Seeds of distrust were planted by the poor performance of both council and water authority representatives under expert questioning by protesters at public meetings. The main objective of creating this distrust and embarrassment was to make it difficult for the council to give land use go-ahead to the water authority. Publicly elected councilors, now clearly spotlighted in the public arena over this issue, would invoke the ire of their electorate if they gave permission for a project that was so riddled with inconsistencies and suspicion.

Tactics

The protesters' primary tactics were to intelligently challenge the water authority's proposals at public meetings in front of large home-crowd audiences. The crucial meeting was in April 1998. It was organized by the local council as a public consultation meeting for the concerned residents. Of the 800 town residents, 350 attended. Journalists from local newspapers, radio, and television were present. Councilors and water authority representatives were on the platform. From the point of view of the water authority, the meeting had been called to put residents' minds at rest, to quell their fears about the proposals. Instead the protest organizers took advantage of the water authority's assumption that the community was ignorant. They accused the authority of holding a paternalistic view about how information should be shared with the community. The depth of technical knowledge displayed in protesters' questions contrasted with an inability or reluctance on the part of the water authority representatives to answer. These representatives did not sufficiently engage with difficult questions about the dangers that campaigners had discovered in their Internet research. Instead, they asked to be given time to come back with answers on another date.

In this unbalanced dialogue, campaigners appeared far more eloquent and knowledgeable than the water authority administrators and technicians present. The protesters quoted the authority's own information about the biosolids project back to them and asked probing and tricky questions. The protest group had made themselves expert in much of the subject under discussion. They accurately used terminology and asked about rules and concepts that the council members present were not familiar with. Although the campaigners' vocabulary and scientific knowledge was not superior to that of the water authority representatives, it was superior to that of the council members. This made the organized opposition group appear credible in the eyes of the bulk of the townspeople at the meeting. The councilors, by contrast, were made to seem as if they did not understand what they were dealing with. The mood of the meeting became angry as people lost faith in their apparently bumbling council representatives who seemed to be deferring to the (now discredited) expertise of the water authority. By the end of the meeting, most of the 350 audience members were of the opinion that they were not being given the whole story and that the truth was being manipulated by the water authority. This creation of suspicion was exactly the objective that the protest leaders had planned.

The meeting was chaired by the councilor for that district and the room was arranged so that representatives of the water authority were on a platform in front of the assembled citizens. The room layout implied control and authority by those on the platform, as well as unity between the water officials and the council representatives. But this format played into the hands of the protest organizers. The opposition group spokeswoman, speaking from the body of the hall, was able to present herself as the representative of the assembled citizens. Her questions thus appeared to be on their behalf. The water authority representatives' request to write down the questions and return with answers at a later date looked at best like stalling or at the worst like incompetence. Even the television journalist who reported proceedings said that this was no way to win the confidence of 350 concerned citizens who had turned out to get some answers to their fears. The way the event was reported on television and in the press thus added to the public's perception that the water authority was not completely honest in their description of the project and its risks.

In June of 1998 the protesters called another public meeting and unanimously passed a motion that said:

> This meeting declares that we are offended by the over simplistic presentation and lack of supporting evidence to date in the response given by [the water authority] to the questions raised [at the April meeting] and request that an open public meeting be convened by an independent body to discuss the proposals.

This resolution was reproduced in the local newspaper and the report gave the impression that the resolution represented the opinions of the all local citizens.

Evaluation

This protest campaign can be most simply evaluated by noting that the water authority scrapped their proposal. A few months after the meetings on the biosolids project a local newspaper reported that:

The plan was abandoned after the authority failed to take up an option on the land which would have housed the facility. The authority's [spokesperson] said the decision to abandon the plan came after his authority failed to acquire the proposed site . . . five kilometres north of [the town] before the . . . deadline. "With the option expiring [the water authority] had no choice but to withdraw its . . . applications for biosolids storage approvals which are currently before the . . . Shire Council and the EPA," [the spokesman] said. The planning application was to have been decided upon by the . . . Shire Council at a special meeting to be held at . . . tomorrow. . . . Chief executive officer . . . said the council had agreed at a meeting earlier this week to recommend refusing the biosolids application based on insufficient information.

Another local newspaper reported, [The decision] "was greeted with enthusiasm by residents and active members of the [opposition group] who had spent much time in researching the outcomes of the proposal."

Other evidence of success can be seen in the local treatment of those who opposed the biosolids project and in campaigns by the water authority in other communities. In the next council election the chairwoman of the protest group was elected to the position which had been held by the local councilor member who had chaired the pivotal April, 1998 meeting. Other evidence of the quality of the opposition group's campaign can be found in later campaigns to establish biosolids production facilities. Following the campaign reported here, the same opposition group worked with citizens in another more remote town and, using nearly identical tactics, successfully stopped another biosolids project.

In 2003, however, the water authority was successful in its third attempt to establish a biosolids production facility. The water authority secured approval for its facility near this third town after holding meetings with local residents and farmers and after a considerable amount of media relations work. A local newspaper reporter confirmed in 2003 that she had not heard of any local protest in the town that became the final host of the biosolids project. The facility was some distance outside this town. The reporter confirmed that there had been consultation meetings organized by the authority and that there was farmer acceptance of the scheme. She said the water authority's CEO had dealt with her personally to keep the media informed of the course of the project. It would appear the opposition group not only succeeded in preventing the location of the biosolids project near the first community, but that they also taught the water authority how to be successful elsewhere—the hard way!

Critique

This case study demonstrates what a small group of people can accomplish in campaigning terms if they are well motivated and willing to work hard. It also illustrates the dangers that established organizations may get themselves into if they have an overblown impression of their own ability to set the public agenda. It is clear that at least some sections of society are well educated, very able to communicate among themselves as communities, able to use the Internet to good advantage, and assured of their rights as citizens—even in the face of the intentions of well-resourced organizations. As a consequence, any organization that assumes public opinion is not important, or can be manipulated by spin or euphemism, may be heading for trouble. The grassroots opposition group's successful campaign was aided by their good planning and accomplished choice of strategies and tactics. By contrast, the methods used by the water authority to get their proposal up were inappropriate and showed a misunderstanding of how to gauge and carry public opinion. The critique of this campaign will include comments about both sides' actions and communications.

Research

The dedicated oppositional volunteers combed available reports and Internet sources. They phoned up the council, the water authority, and the state environment protection authority. They also spoke to their neighbors and paid attention to "parish pump" and "in the pub" conversations of townsfolk on this subject. If they had been better resourced, some scientific sampling of attitudes might have added to their planning. But given the limited resources, they did what research they could.

The water authority, on the other hand, had significant resources but failed to commission reliable and valid research into the opinion of the relevant publics. One significant error was a failure to incorporate issues management into their approach.

> Issues management is a means of linking the public relations function and the management function of the organization in ways that foster the organization's efforts to be outer-directed and to have a participative organizational culture. (Heath, 1997, p. 6)

Organizations that carry out issues management scan the future for social, cultural, economic, and technological changes that the organization has to understand and adapt to, or perhaps influence, in order to maintain its reputation and the sympathetic understanding of the groups of people who are important to it. The organization has to maintain this high esteem with important sections of its audience or risk clashing with public opinion—with the risk of negative political effects and, possibly, eventual policy difficulties. The case of this water authority presents a classic study of a failure to see ahead to the controversies and consequent policy difficulties surrounding the advent of biosolids.

Another significant error on the part of the water authority was a failure to appropriately address risk management. In discussing risk management, Lerbinger (1997) noted:

> Being aware of the existence of risk in transactions with nature, technology, people and organized groups is a fundamental necessity of being a manager. . . . Organizations should provide sufficient information and background knowledge to members of the public affected by a risk situation to enable them to engage in dialogue and directly to share risk decision making with them. Interested parties must exchange information and views about risks so that everyone feels adequately informed about the limits of available knowledge. (pp. 267–282)

In the first campaign, the water authority failed to conduct research to gauge the opinions of the interested parties in the community near where they proposed placing the biosolids project. The failure to conduct this research meant they were not prepared for the target public's need for information about the risks. It also meant they did not anticipate the creation of the organized group that opposed the proposal. In their later campaign that succeeded with another town in 2003, the water authority deliberately set about getting to know their target publics. They had access to the people who would be affected and probed their thoughts through meetings that were conducted in a far more friendly, informal, and consultative-style than had been the approach at the first town. The water authority took a much more proactive stance toward informing these people, and they also worked with the news media to this end. These successful efforts are evidence of better, more thorough research.

Objectives

The opposition group began with one goal—to gather information. The failure of the water authority to provide information forced them to adopt a new goal—to prevent approval of the biosolids project. One could interpret these changing goals as a weakness of the group. However, many authors would describe public relations campaigning as a process, and the ability to adapt or change could be viewed positively. On the other hand, the inability of the water authority to change its primary target public from the local council to the opposition group and vocal citizens may have contributed to its failure.

Strategies

The opposition group's action strategy was simply to gather information and to attend meetings where their questions and concerns could be heard. Their communications strategy was equally simple. It was to create doubt and damage credibility by claiming and demonstrating misinformation and omission in the water authority's messages. These simple strategies might not have been successful against a well-organized and well-administered campaign from the water authority. However, the water authority's campaign was poorly researched and their poor decisions about action and communications strategies seem to have helped the opposition group's campaign.

A contemporary theory of society that might have helped the water authority to realize the problem it was confronting is Ulrich Beck's theoretical notion of "The Risk Society." Beck's central thesis is that for much of the developed world, the politics of the poor versus the rich is becoming less important than the politics of the whole lot of us surviving or being destroyed by the dangers that relative affluence has brought. For Beck the formerly, more clearly separated social classes are now tending to be blurred with, or recast into, interest groups that oppose our environmental annihilation. In the more affluent parts of the world we are all in the same boat or class when it comes to risks from, for example, car crashes, pollution, cancer-causing diets, global warming, and so on. For Beck in his "risk society," class politics has not disappeared but it has this added dimension:

> Risk societies are not class societies. . . . They contain within themselves a grass roots developmental dynamics that destroys boundaries, through which the people are forced together in the uniform position of civilization's self-endangering. . . . The place of eliminating scarcity is taken by eliminating risk. Even if the consciousness and the forms of political organization for this are still lacking, one can say that risk society, through the dynamic of endangerment it sets in motion, undermines the borders of nation states as much as those of military alliances and economic blocs. (Beck, 1996, p. 47)

For Beck, the age in which we live is entering a stage of "reflexive modernity," where people are now becoming far more conscious of the way their world works and, as a consequence, the pathologies of the way their world works. These pathologies include the administrative pathologies. In other words people are now reasonably well informed about how they might be deceived by organizations about the dangers the organizations might be causing (p. 41).

In "risk society" terms, the water authority failed to recognize the contemporary need to involve all citizens in a combined strategy based on shared information and shared concerns about the environment everyone shares. The water authority overlooked the reflexive consciousness—the heightened awareness that many groups and individuals now possess in relation to environmental matters. As a consequence, instead of obtaining cooperation with the relevant publics, the water authority allowed a situation to develop where they were in competition for the leadership of public opinion over environmental concerns. A considerable opportunity was missed, because Beck's thesis implies there might well have been considerable sympathy for an argument about the sustainable reuse of effluent if the authority had approach this subject in the right way. At the final town where agreement was eventually obtained, considerable effort went into explaining to farmers how the processing of sewage sludge could be seen as environmentally advantageous, as well as advantageous in various economic and logistical ways. Sustainable, safe re-use of sewage sludge, as opposed to sea dumping, land dumping, or incineration has many attractions in terms of Beck's 'risk society' thesis.

Tactics

Once they had identified the strategy of creating suspicion of the water authority, the opposition group's tactics were simple and singular. They concentrated on probing and exposing the inaccuracies of the water authority. They also highlighted the authority's inability to satisfy the informed and justified questions that they asked in public. They delivered that message primarily through the medium of public meetings. Campaigners received an unexpected bonus when this exposé was repeated in the media coverage of the public meetings.

The water authority officials attempted to deliver their information in one-way media that did not allow any adjustment or modification. Their documents, mostly leaflets, could not, or did not, respond to citizen concerns. Further, their performance at two crucial public meetings added to the impression that they were withholding information on the project's risks.

Applying social science and management concepts, one can see a conflict between Beck's idea of a risk society and the naive tactics relied on by the water authority. The water authority's tactics presumed the community would believe and trust in scientific and administrative "authority." The water authority did not want to go into the full detail of the risk-laden proposals. Public relations author Lerbinger and cultural theorist Beck both imply that it is dangerous to impose any restriction on the flow of information, because with self-reflexivity, society no longer goes along with a straightforward trust in modernity—in progress—in the power of science and "the administration." Risk-society consciousness no longer goes along with pronouncements when the authorities (in this case a water "authority") tell people what is good for them in a paternalistic manner. Recall that what spurred the opposition group into action most was the feeling that they had only been given half the picture. They were initially told that the scheme was about "biosolids," but it was not clear what this mysterious new term meant.

The risk society opposition group also proved themselves quite capable of reading a thick consultant's report from cover to cover. When they were not sure of the scientific implications they quickly found scientifically competent risk society allies who could back them up. This, arguably, is the nature of the risk society. It is a society that has gone far further than the need for authorities to provide polite consultation and an appeal for trust on plans that involve environmental risks.

The very notion of authority in the risk society is, in fact, under attack. This sort of authority is a concept from the time of rather different economic-, national-, and class-based politics—not risk society–based politics. Issues management or public relations people should not today presume that any organization carries authority where it comes to considering putting people at risk in some way. The best an organization involved with introducing risk can do, it if wishes to garner public support, is to be perfectly open and communicative about what the risks are and why there is a need to take them.

Evaluation

The opposition group successfully met the goal of preventing location of the biosolids project in their community. This was clearly the most important achievement. There were, however, additional spin-off benefits such as heightened community group identity and self-esteem. There remains to this day a good community spirit in this small town. This spirit has been fostered in a number of ways, such as through community festivals and fund-raising projects for civic amenities. However, the story of how the town 'saw-off' the water authority has a firm place in its community-spirit building history. Another side effect was the launching of a temporary local political career for the main protest leader. She withdrew from this role at a subsequent election, however. Another postscript to this campaign was, however, that another town *did* accept the biosolids project to be implemented nearby. Was it because of improved public relations by the water authority, learned by the hard lessons in the first town? This would seem to be impossible to determine in view of the break in cooperation by the authority. A fair view of the situation, however, might include the fact that the town that accepted biosolids in 2003, although larger than the protest town, is a fairly remote, low wage-earning locality that had recently lost many jobs. The first town where the opposition group was successful was in a more prosperous area with a more mixed economy. It is in easy commuting distance of a flourishing rural city with a university campus. For these reasons one might expect to find people with better financial and educational resources in the protest town than in the town that eventually accepted the project. This socio-economic analysis is relevant to Grunig's (1984) situational theory of publics which lists: (a) problem recognition; (b) constraint recognition; and (c) level of involvement as the independent variables that influence whether people protest (p. 149). Of course, the water authority's better campaign may have met and reduced the concerns of variable *a,* problem recognition, by the accepting townsfolk. However, one might speculate that the potentially better educated and relatively economically sound townsfolk of the protest town were less "constrained" (variable *b*) than the townsfolk near where the plant was eventually built. The protest townsfolk may have been educationally better able to launch a protest campaign and they may have had less to lose in terms of jobs.

DISCUSSION QUESTIONS AND STUDENT EXERCISES

1. An inoculation campaign is one designed to provide information to a target public so that they will not be influenced by another competing campaign. Was the campaign by the opposition group here an inoculation campaign? If you think it was an inoculation campaign explain why and how the campaign reacted to or prevented the success of the water authority campaign. If you think it was not an inoculation campaign, explain why it was not and describe the relationship between the campaigns by the opposition group and the water authority.

2. Please familiarize yourself with the issues discussed in this case study by exploring the websites in the reference list. If the websites have moved, please "Google search" for these and other water authorities and related organizations.

3. After visiting the websites, please put yourself in the position of the water authority chief executive officer in this case study. Assume that a version of this case study, naming the water authority, has been published as an exposé in a local newspaper in its geographical area of operation. Write a 500-word letter for a future edition of that newspaper to restore any damage to reputations that may have been perpetrated.

4. From reading this case study, as well as from your website research and common knowledge, list words that clearly, accurately, and technically describe the original materials that go into the production of biosolids. Then assume you are the public relations officer for a water authority. Write the text of a leaflet for circulation to a community near where your authority is proposing to create a biosolids plant. Be sure to accurately describe what is being proposed. Then do either exercise 5 or 6.

5. Make a second list of the euphemisms that you have used in this leaflet, then quiz people who are unaware of this case study. Read them your euphemisms and ask them to translate those euphemisms back into words that clearly, accurately, and technically describe biosolids raw materials. You are looking to see if what you have written in the leaflet accurately and ethically describes the project, or whether your leaflet is likely to confuse or rhetorically color the issue.

6. If you have not used any euphemisms in this section of your leaflet, convene a focus group of family or friends and ask them how they would feel about a biosolids project in their neighborhood. In outlining the project use the explicit language that you used in your leaflet. *Do not* tell participants that the purpose of the focus group is to judge their emotional reaction to the use of blunt language in your leaflet, rather than to gauge their views on biosolids. Record if there is any uneasiness in this discussion. Uneasiness is often betrayed by attempts at humor. Observe if there is a tendency by you or any group member to resort to euphemism. Reflect on how any emotional reactions to particular use of language affect public relations campaigning in this matter. Are you dealing with emotional factors that get in the way of your program? If so, what is the best way to overcome these difficulties?

7. Review Grunig's situational theory of publics and write a 500-word essay discussing the three independent variables of that theory as they may apply to the township that rejected the biosolids plant and the town that accepted it. In your essay speculate on how socioeconomic and educational factors may have been involved in these independent variables.

8. Locate yourself in time before the start of the whole story discussed in the case study. Making reasonable assumptions, design a public relations program that you think might have had a better chance of getting the biosolids plant accepted and built near the first town that rejected it.

9. As part of your answer in question 8, write a 5-minute speech for the chief executive to use to introduce the biosolids proposal at the first public meeting in the first town in this case study. Also write a confidential memo to the CEO on how to deal with the local press, radio, and television stations that are currently completely unaware of the project. Draft a suggested news release to go along with this media relations advice.

10. Now analyze the language that you have used in the speech, memo, and draft news release in terms of clarity and euphemism in a similar way as suggested in exercises above.

11. Assume you are a poor, unemployed single parent who lives in the town that accepted the biosolids project two years ago. You have just read Stauber and Rampton (1995) *Toxic Sludge Is Good for You* (see reference above) and you have seen the health warnings in this case study after a version of the study was carried as a feature article by a local newspaper. Your house is near the biosolids project site and your three young children have suffered from mysterious illnesses over the last two years. Some neighbors' children have suffered similarly. You are now convinced that pathogens are being carried on the wind from the plant into the back garden where your children play and into the playground of the nearby junior school. You are determined to get the plant shut by the force of public opinion. Describe how you would go about this. Remember you have no personal money for this campaign. (Note: Exercise 11 is purely fictitious and is an invention for the purposes of public relations education only.)

12. Now please put yourself in the shoes of the water authority CEO. It is six months into the very effective community protest campaign that you have designed in exercise 11. The planning committee of the local council for the area has recommended retrospectively rescinding planning permission for the plant. The plant directly and indirectly employs 50 local people and is making a big profit selling biosolids to local farmers and grazers. This is reducing water bills for everyone in the water authority area. The local council's lawyers say that at present there are no legal powers for going back on a previously agreed planning decision. The council is taking legal advice on its next move. State and federal politicians and news media are taking an interest in the row. Over the last two months your water authority has commissioned exhaustive testing by international experts who have concluded that no pathogens or toxic chemicals are escaping from the plant. As CEO you are convinced that any illnesses are not the fault of your organization. You are considering challenging the protesters to produce sound medical evidence about their children's ailments. Making reasonable and plausible assumptions in line with this (fictitious) scenario, please outline the full detail of all aspects of the counter-campaign that you are now running.

13. There is a local council-arranged town meeting of all local citizens to discuss this issue at a public hall in the town next week. The water authority has been invited by the council to outline its safety testing results by international experts. Many news media representatives,

including from national television, and dozens of placard-waving rowdy protesters are expected to attend. In relation to this meeting, assuming you decided to attend and speak:

   a. What would you be saying to the council this week about how this council-organized town meeting should be structured?

   b. Show us a draft of the 5-minute speech you, as CEO, expect to be making to start off your contribution to that meeting.

   c. Show us the sort of confidential media relations advice that you expect your media relations people will have given you for the present situation and in view of next week's meeting.

   d. Also draft the news release you will be issuing in conjunction with the meeting.

REFERENCES AND SUGGESTED READINGS

Beck, U. (1996). *Risk society: Toward a new modernity.* Thousand Oaks, CA: Sage.

Environmental Protection Agency (U.S.). (2000, August 3). News Release, National Academy of Sciences to Study Sludge.

Environmental Protection Authority. (2000). *Environmental guidelines for biosolids management* (draft). Victorian Government.

Grunig, J., & Hunt, T. (1984). *Managing public relations.* New York: Rinehart and Winston.

Heath, R. (1997). *Strategic issues management organizations and public policy challenges.* Thousand Oaks, CA: Sage.

Lerbinger, O. (1997). *The crisis manager: Facing risk and responsibility.* Mahwah, NJ: Lawrence Erlbaum Associates.

Matthews, P. (ed.). (1997). *A global atlas of wastewater sludge and biosolids use and disposal.* London: International Association of Water Quality.

Melbourne Water. (2000). Retrieved from www.melbournewater.com.au/default.asp?bhcp=1.

National Biosolids Partnership. (2000). Retrieved from http://biosolids.policy.net/about.

National Institute for Occupational Safety and Health (US). (2000, August 27). News Release, Workers Exposed to Class B Biosolids During and After Field Application.

Stauber, J., & Rampton, S. (1995). *Toxic sludge is good for you: Lies, damn lies and the public relations industry.* Monroe, ME: Common Courage Press.

Sydney Water. (2000). Retrieved from www.sydneywater.com.au/.

Water Environment Federation. (2000). Fact Sheet. Retrieved from www.wef.org/PublicInfo/Fact Sheets/wqexperts.htm.

Williams, K., Lee, M., & Syme, G. (1990). *Public attitudes to and knowledge of sludge management and disposal: "Winning the Pooh."* Canberra: Commonwealth Scientific and Industrial Research Organization.

7 Global Public Relations in South Korea: A Case Study of a Multinational Corporation

MINJUNG SUNG

The case study was prepared based on public records and cooperation from General Motors Daewoo Auto & Technology, such as internal documents and interviews with its public relations professionals.

Executive Summary

On October 17, 2002, General Motors Daewoo Auto & Technology Co. (GM Daewoo) publicly launched in South Korea, as General Motors (GM) took over Daewoo Motors, Ltd. (Daewoo Motors). Daewoo Motors, once South Korea's second largest automobile manufacturer with its own worldwide operations and thousands of employees, had been put on sale as its parent company Daewoo Group bankrupted in the late 1990s because of the financial crisis in Asia. It was a major driving force in the development of Korea's automotive industry and national economy throughout its history before it crumbled. After more than four years of negotiation, GM, a leading global automobile manufacturer based in Detroit, finally took over the company, but only the profitable parts. The sale negotiation was a hot issue in South Korea because of its impact on Korean economy and the society.

South Korea provides a unique environment in terms of culture, consumer perceptions, and the media system. Since the negotiation period, GM had faced negative public opinions and publicity, because Koreans viewed the sale of the national brand as an invasion of foreigners. The company's public relations effort mainly focused on the media, the government, and the publics to obtain support for GM. According to one public relations executive, "Keeping the media and the public neutral to positive was a bit of challenge." Activist groups and Daewoo Motors' labor union were against the sale and held aggressive campaigns, worrying that the U.S. company would exploit the country's economy and technology. General Motors had to deal with much negative public opinion and attitude from the employees of Daewoo Motor, the media, activist publics, and the general public.

This study examines GM Daewoo's public relations strategies and activities to successfully launch a new company in South Korea. It also deals with issues regarding the communication problems the company is facing, such as the loss of consumer trust and negative perception toward the Daewoo brand from the public, mistrust from the employees, cultural clashes between people from different cultures, language differences, and the shortfall of understanding about the local situation. The company hopes to (1) build a new corporate image as a technology-driven global company based in South Korea, (2) obtain consumer trust, and (3) gain employees' confidence and understanding.

Research

GM Daewoo's public relations campaign had two stages: before and after the launch. Its post-launch programs are still in progress. Before the takeover deal was finalized, GM's research focused on public opinions and attitudes. GM conducted a survey regarding South Korean audiences' attitude and overall public opinion for foreign ownership through a Gallup poll. The company also monitored media coverage to evaluate the tone of articles regarding the issue. However, it did not conduct formal research in its employees or other categories of publics.

Cultural Considerations

To examine the success of public relations practices and the characteristics of the publics in South Korea, it is important to understand the core cultural values of the country. Culture was a critical factor for the public relations campaign of GM Daewoo internally and externally.

South Koreans tend to get together when they have something in common such as a school, a hometown, an organization, or a job. This results in in-groups and strong cohesive power among the members, while excluding out-group people (Yi, 1994). Because of this tendency, newcomers to South Korea often face difficulties. For example, multinational corporations that make inroads into South Korea often have to deal with negative attitudes from their publics because they are "foreign." Sometimes the native South Korean workers of those companies are hostile to and keep some distance from their foreign management; Korean workers refer themselves as "woo-ri" (we, us), a big family or an in-group, whereas foreign managers are referred as they or them. The emphasis on hierarchy and order in South Korea corresponds to what Hofstede (1997) called "large power distance" (p. 14). Power distance is defined as the extent to which the less powerful people in organizations or societies expect and recognize that power is distributed unequally; it offers different levels of status to members of different layers. For example, the boss–subordinate pair at work places also has unequal relationships; people in lower positions are expected to obey and respect those who are on higher levels. There is unspoken consensus among the members that the hierarchical system is based on this inequality, which enables centralization of power.

The bankruptcy of the Daewoo Group shocked South Koreans. As the country signed the International Monetary Fund (IMF) agreement for $58 billion in loans in 1997, the country had to undergo stringent restructuring in economic policies and the financial sector; various public movements occurred based on patriotism. One example was *Gold Collecting*

Campaign to Save the Country, a public campaign to help the country pay the debt to circumvent the IMF supervision. A total of 225 tons of gold that households had kept was collected to increase the country's foreign exchange holding. More than three million Koreans participated, which is 23 percent of the nation's population.

Because of Daewoo Motors' symbolic meaning as one of the representative national brands, many people regarded GM's takeover as an invasion and economic exploitation by outsiders. Consequently, GM faced much negative publicity and public opinion during and after the sales negotiation. For example, the president of the state-run Korean Institute for International Economics and Trade argued, "The sale of Daewoo Motor to foreigners will result in the death of auto parts suppliers and the weakening of Korea's auto research and development ability." The mistrust emerged as GM bought only the profitable assets of Daewoo Motors; in the final agreement, the company purchased only some facilities but decided not to buy Daewoo Motors' largest manufacturing facility in Bupyung. As one public relations executive pointed out, there was a perception of being a loser in the negotiation; some people had resentment and disappointment that the company has been swallowed by GM.

At the company, both the management from GM and the employees, almost all of whom were from Daewoo Motor, were experiencing rapid changes and gaps in terms of corporate culture and national culture; the new management system and culture were viewed as *Western* or *American,* whereas the old system and culture were considered *Korean.* Consequently, the employees still have mistrust in and feel distance with the new management.

In addition, language was a big problem. Most executives of GM Daewoo were English-speaking Westerners from GM headquarters, whereas most employees are native Koreans. Since everyday conversations with these high-level managers were based in English, a majority of employees, mostly from Daewoo, did not feel confident about their language skills. A large number of employees took English classes privately or through the company's training programs. Yet, most of them did not have confidence and considered language a big burden. Non-Korean executives have also experienced frustration from misunderstanding and miscommunication due to the language barriers. One manager said, "[It is a] huge issue. There's just no diminishing how big the issue is. And it may be *the* issue."

Despite the company's effort to send a message that GM Daewoo is committed to the development of local economy and R&D, the company was often viewed as American. Negative perceptions remained among the publics because they believed the company would only exploit the country's economy and leave them when it becomes not profitable. Local competitors, such as Hyundai and Kia Motors, used this issue and appealed to consumers' patriotism by identifying themselves as national brands while referring GM Daewoo as "invasion into the nation." Moreover, the anti-American sentiment and boycott campaigns against U.S. brand products have increasingly spread among Koreans since 2002.

Government Considerations

During the time of launching, the South Korean government did not have any particular regulations or laws that would influence the campaign. Rather, since the government itself was involved in the sale of Daewoo and wanted to finish it to regain the country's credibility, it was supportive of GM and its actions.

Description of Client

GM Daewoo, headquartered in Bupyung, South Korea, has manufacturing facilities in Changwon and Kunsan, South Korea, and in Hanoi, Vietnam, with nine overseas subsidiaries. GM Daewoo recently unveiled a new corporate identity and logo, which was designed to represent a "company that's modern, on the move and at the same time recognizes its roots," according to the company's executive. As part of GM's global network, GM Daewoo shares GM's resources and is strategically related to its global business. Most of GM Daewoo's top executives are from GM, whereas most employees are the former employees of Daewoo Motors.

Daewoo Motors.   Daewoo Group's history reflected the history of modern South Korea's economy: a shift from being a poor agricultural economy to a country with great prosperity. Founded in 1967, Daewoo Group became one of the largest conglomerates in South Korea until the financial crisis hit South Korea in late 1990s. As the parent company Daewoo Group crumpled in 1999, Daewoo Motors, once Korea's second-largest carmaker and a major driving force in the development of South Korea's automotive industry, collapsed.

GM's Daewoo Takeover.   As the parent company Daewoo Group became bankrupt, Daewoo Motors was put up for sale as a way to redeem the debt. In October 2000, it signed an initial agreement with GM, but they did not reach the final agreement for two years. During the negotiation, GM had to face much negative publicity and public opinion in South Korea, because Korean people considered the takeover as an invasion of foreigners into their national economy. Many Koreans had negative sentiment toward the deal; some people formed an active public and ran a campaign to prevent Daewoo Motors from being sold to a foreign company. Daewoo's labor union, which traditionally held strong power, also protested against GM's takeover.

The acquisition of Daewoo provides GM with an opportunity to establish a presence in Asia. In his address to the Federation of Korean Industries and U.S. Chamber of Commerce, GM's Chairman Rick Waggoner said that the partnership was an important move for GM, because "No automaker can win in the global race without a serious strategy for Asia-Pacific, and no strategy for Asia-Pacific is complete without Korea" (Smith, 2000). Daewoo was seen as a strategic ally and a key source of low-cost vehicle platforms for export in key markets around the world—especially the developing countries where Daewoo was already strong.

GM Daewoo.   GM Daewoo belongs to GM Asia-Pacific (GMAP), along with other 13 countries, as part of GM's worldwide communication network. As a global company, it is also in the process of establishing a global communication network to maintain timeliness and consistency of information and message distribution. GM Daewoo's senior management consists of executives mostly from GM.

The company's public affairs department consists of approximately 30 public relations professionals spread out over four offices—Seoul, Bupyung, Kunsan, and Changwon. The largest team is located in the main office in Bupyung, where the company is headquartered, and is responsible for public relations programs in general, product public relations, and internal communication. The teams in Kunsan and Changwon play similar roles in their respective communities. The main office also includes the Communication Center, which deals with employee communication, labor union management, government relations, and protocol. Given that 25% of the country's population resides in Seoul and a majority of the national media offices are located there, the team in Seoul is the contact point for most media inquiries and is mainly in charge of media relations, including press release production and distribution, face-to-face communication with journalists, interview arrangements, and crisis management. The company established a new function called the Product Communication Team to focus on product-related publicity and media relations worldwide. The team, with one or two "brand managers," provides journalists with in-depth information based on their extensive product and industry knowledge.

Publics

GM Daewoo had several groups of publics. Its primary publics included the employees and the labor union of Daewoo Motors, government officers, the media, and the activist public. The secondary publics were consumers, opinion leaders, and the general population.

Among them, the active publics included the Daewoo Motors union labor and activists who ran a Daewoo reviving campaign. The sales of Daewoo Motors and giving up the ownership of the country's national brand to a foreign company upset South Korean people. Some of them identified themselves as *Daewoo Supporters,* and ran a public campaign, *Surviving Daewoo Motor,* to turn Daewoo Motor into a public enterprise. These *Supporters* had outdoor gatherings or did fundraising to purchase the company. Although the leaders of the campaign explained that it was not about opposing inroads of GM in South Korea but about reviving Daewoo as a public enterprise with public power, the campaign still showed negative sentiment of South Koreans toward foreign influence.

Another critical group of an active public was the employees and the labor union of Daewoo Motors. Specifically the labor union viewed GM's takeover as a foreign invasion to exploit the company as a "subcontractor" and protested against the sale; its biggest concern was the reduction of the number of jobs if the U.S. company attempted restructuring. Figure 1 is a statement against GM's acquisition, from the Korean Confederation of Trade Unions.

In July 2001, the Daewoo employees, including both plant and clerical workers, formed the "Pan-Daewoo Emergency Committee" and urged GM to take over Daewoo in a package deal. It finally endorsed the merger only after the management agreed to keep all 13,000 Korean workers on the payroll after the deal. The union opposed the deal based on the following reasons:

- Research and development will rely on GM's headquarters in the United States or Opel facilities. As a result, Daewoo will become nothing more than a subcontractor assembly plant.
- GM will attempt to introduce an aggressive work regime aimed at establishing a dominant control over the labor in the workplace.
- This will give sow the seeds of aggravated industrial dispute.
- Once the decision is made by the government (and the creditor banks) to accept the GM bid for takeover, it will generate massive resistance opposing the takeover (Korean Federation).

FIGURE 1   Statement Against GM's Acquisition, from Korean Confederation of Trade Unions

The Negative Impact of the Foreign Take-Over of the Daewoo Motors

The disruption and collapse of the entire Korean automobile industry will result from the crippling control of the domestic market

If the two major automobile companies are sold to a foreign operator

- It will reduce the cost of tariff and transportation cost compared to bringing the cars from overseas
- The low cost of quality labor will reduce the overall production cost
- The adoption of models designed and developed centrally from the heart of the global network will reduce the research and development cost
  - As a result, the foreign operator will take control of luxury car market where quality and brand name—rather than price difference—are more important
  - Domestic makers will find more difficult to change out of the small lower price range cars
  - Domestic makers will find even more difficult to finance the necessary research and development programs.

The Daewoo Motors under the control of a foreign operator will become simple assembly line and subcontract production plant

- The research and development function of the Daewoo Motors will be scaled down, eventually to be abandoned all together.
- High value-added core components will be brought in from overseas
  - Daewoo will become merely a assembly subcontractor producing models and core parts produced and brought in from other overseas operations.

Massive structural adjustment and retrenchment will ensue

- If the foreign operator faces—in future or any time—a need to shed its over-capacity, reduce production level, or reduce employment level, the overseas operations, such as that in Daewoo Motors will become the first target
- The foreign operator will dismantle the overseas sales network it had built up as it has its own global sales network
- The foreign operator enters with pre-established and consolidated network of components and parts suppliers. The resultant global outsourcing will drive the local parts makers into extinction.
  - The example of the GM's closure of its Mexican operation and the recent case of the Rover in the United Kingdom are eloquent demonstration of the consequence of giant foreign operator behavior.

Weakening of national autonomy will undermine policy capacity

- The government and even the civil society, including the trade union movement, will lose any kind of influence on the strategic decision making of the transnational corporation. Social policy priorities, industrial policy priorities, or employment policy priorities will become powerless and ineffective.
- An oppressive and severely unbalanced and asymmetric industrial relations will be established to the detriment of the rights and welfare of workers and trade unions.

FIGURE 1   Continued

It will alienate the society and people

■ The various opinion polls undertaken by independent agencies indicate that majority of the people oppose the sale of the Daewoo Motors to a foreign operator.
  • a survey conducted in December 1999 found that only 31.3% of the respondents agreed with the plan to sell the Daewoo Motors to the General Motors; 59.3% of the respondents found that Hyundai Motors should take over the Daewoo Motors
  • a survey by SBS television network in March 2000 found that 67% of the people opposed the sale of the Daewoo Motors to a foreign operator and 68% supported the KCTU proposal for making it into a public enterprise.
  • a survey by Hangil Research on April 8, 2000 found that 64% of the people opposed the sale of the Daewoo Motors to a foreign multinational corporation (23.4% strongly oppose, 40.6% oppose) while only 30.7% supported the plan to sell it to foreign operator (strongly support 9.6% and support 21.1%).
  • a survey of automobile industry specialists by the Korea Economic Newspaper found that 50–52% of the industry specialists felt that the Daewoo Motors would be allowed to be taken over by the General Motors
    • The prevailing feeling among people and specialists is that the Daewoo Motors will be made to be taken over by the General Motors while the people remain opposed to it.
    • This indicates that the government will push ahead with an action which the majority of the people oppose. This will create an even more hostile lack of confidence in the government policy and action.

Source: Korean Confederation of Trade Unions website, www.kctu.org/arguments/daewoo-02.htm

The concerned publics included some Korean consumers and nonunion Daewoo Motor employees. Since 2002, U.S. companies operating in South Korea had been concerned about the possible negative impacts of prolonged anti-American sentiment in the country (Figure 2). Young South Koreans have called for a boycott campaign against U.S. brands such as McDonald's and Coca-Cola as part of the protest against the United States. The boycott campaign initially began during the 2002 Salt Lake City Winter Olympic Games. Protesters believed the U.S. skater Apolo Ono snatched the gold medal from South Korean skater Kim Dong-sung in the men's short track skating. The campaign prolonged as a U.S. court-martial acquitted the two servicemen who manned a vehicle that killed two schoolgirls in June 2002. South Koreans continue to protest against the United States, asking for an apology as well as appropriate punishment for the two men. McDonald's sales has fallen by 15 percent because of the boycotts. The U.S. automakers, including Daimler-Chrysler, Ford, and GM, became sensitive to the changes in the consumers' perception of American vehicles and tried to diminish the negative perception that imported cars were luxury goods for the rich.

Media

GM Daewoo used both external and internal media. Before using external media, mostly news media, and planning a public relations campaign, it is necessary to understand the

FIGURE 2   Korean Newspaper Article on Anti-American Movement

[KOREA TIMES] December 11, 2002

Anti-U.S. Goods Campaign Alerts American Cos.

By Seo Jee-yeon Staff Reporter

U.S. companies operating in South Korea are concerned about the possible negative impacts of prolonged anti-American sentiment on their sales. Young Internet users have called for a boycott of U.S. icons McDonald's and Coca-Cola in protest against the U.S. court-martial acquittals of the two servicemen who manned a vehicle that killed two schoolgirls last June.

U.S. brand businesses such as fast food chains and family restaurants are particularly worried about possible boycotts as their main customers are young people, who are the most critical of the U.S. McDonald's, the world's biggest hamburger chain, has seen its South Korean sales slip further after a 15 percent sales reduction in the first quarter on the back of boycotts in protest against the U.S. short-track skater Apolo Anton Ono. Protesters believe Ono snatched the gold medal from South Korean skater Kim Dong-sung in this year's Winter Olympics.

"I am sorry our company has become a subject of anti-U.S. sentiment again. Although McDonald's is a U.S. brand, we are a Korean company that was set up as a joint venture with a local partner in 1988 and has been run 100 percent by Koreans," McDonald's Korea team manager Song Hyun-jeong said. Song said he was striving to promote the understanding of the company among locals. T.G.I. Friday's and Pizza Hut also said they are monitoring the movement of anti-American protests online and offline, although they have yet to see the impact on their sales of netizens' campaign. Ahead of Christmas and the year-end bargain season, Lee Sun-kyung, spokesperson for another target brand Coca-cola was worried that the anti-American sentiment may have an impact on its promotional and marketing activities.

U.S. carmakers, including DaimlerChrysler Korea, Ford Sales & Service Korea and General Motors (GM) Korea, are also sensitive to changes in the perception of American vehicles by consumers and have made efforts to reduce the negative perception that imported cars are luxury goods for the rich. "Companies doing business on the globe are global companies, not just U.S. companies or French companies. Even though our parent company is General Motors, after the takeover deal we became a Korean company," said Kim Sung-su, spokesperson of the newly launched GM Daewoo Auto & Technology Company (GM Daewoo).

Business leaders are also showing concern over the possibility that the anti-American sentiment and potential anti-U.S. goods campaign may backfire. It may ignite anti-Korean sentiment and an anti-Korean goods drive in the U.S., they said. Korea Chamber of Commerce and Industry (KCCI) chairman Park Yong-sung told a radio program yesterday, "I am so sad because of the death of our two schoolgirls but, given the Korea-U.S. relations, we have to consider the economic losses and gains. The U.S. is the biggest export market for Korea."

Outgoing president of the American Chamber of Commerce (AmCham) in Korea Jeffrey Jones also warned last week that the ongoing anti-American sentiment here could lead to an anti-Korean movement in the U.S. Jones noted that Korea's anti-American activities have received extensive coverage in the U.S. from nationwide media outlets like the New York Times, which will create a negative image about South Korea and our export products among U.S. citizens. The U.S. is also the biggest foreign investor in Korea. According to the Ministry of Commerce, Industry and Energy, the number of foreign companies was estimated at 12,000 last June, out of which 2,620 were U.S. Americans accounted for 54 percent of the cumulative foreign investment in Korea at the end of September.

overall background about the media environment of the country as well as the company's available internal communication media.

South Korea has a unique media system. First, the country has a large number of news media; there are 17 general daily newspapers and six broadcasting companies, to name only the major organizations. All of these media are nationwide, which is unusual; for example, in the United States, even the major newspapers such as *The Washington Post* and the *New York Times* are local or regional. What is more unusual about the media environment is that almost every major news organization is headquartered in Seoul, the country's capital city. Therefore, even companies that are headquartered outside Seoul have media relations offices in Seoul. All business in South Korea is centrally located in Seoul and the media have immediate access to corporate executives and operations, whereas in the U.S. national media offices are located in major cities, many of them in New York, hundreds of miles away from the corporate offices.

Media relations in South Korea are heavily based on face-to-face communication and personal relationships with journalists. Many Korean companies have a press room, which is office space exclusively offered for journalists, in their public relations offices, and provide journalists with all necessary facilities and space to work. In addition, journalists often visit companies (and their public relations practitioners) or ask to meet outside of offices occasionally. During frequent face-to-face meetings with journalists, public relations practitioners try to provide as much correct information as possible, to prevent unfavorable coverage. In South Korea, it is common for public relations practitioners to cultivate favorable relationships so that journalists will not generate negative stories that are not necessarily true. In contrast, in the United States, much of the communicating is done via telephone and electronic mail. In almost every major public relations program in Korea, reporters physically visit the public relations offices, while press kits and collateral material play a more important function in the United States.

The large number of media outlets in Korea results in intensive competition in terms of circulation and advertising sales. Because of the limited advertising budget of private corporations, news organizations lack advertising revenue, which limits the number of journalists and employees. Therefore, journalists must cover a wide range of areas and industries and produce ten or more articles a day. As a result, they often fail to collect enough in-depth data for stories; they are too busy to produce comprehensive stories. Journalists depend on the information provided by organizations and their public relations representatives. In that situation, the best way for public relations practitioners to induce favorable stories is maintaining favorable relationship with journalists through face-to-face, personal contact. Most times, since public relations people are major sources of stories, personal contacts and meetings are the main channels for providing information. In addition, since journalists are rotated frequently, they do not have in-depth understanding or knowledge about a particular industry; they are not able to "digest" in-depth knowledge, nor they need to. They often ask very basic questions, such as the products, the company's executives, and general management strategy, which do not need professional knowledge or expertise. In other words, there are not many journalists who are specialized in a particular industry.

Internally, GM Daewoo had several communication channels, such as a bi-monthly corporate magazine, a weekly newsletter, letters from the company to the employees' families, and the intranet; all of these reach the employees quite effectively. The internal publications, especially the newsletter, have high circulation rate among employees. "Word of mouth" is another way of sending out messages, especially to the plant workers.

Objective

GM Daewoo's public relations campaign was programmed to support and reinforce the company's management strategy: To become a Korean automaker that offers the best value to customers by creating "must have" new and unique products. The company also hoped to build a strong presence in the Korean market and integrate the two corporate cultures, GM and Daewoo, through continuing communication efforts based on trust and openness.

Before the takeover was finalized, the goal of the public relations programs was to inform various audiences—government officials, opinion leaders, general audiences, and the media—of the company's intentions in the Korean market in order to lessen negative perceptions and attitudes. Since the company was publicly launched, the goal of GM Daewoo's public relations programs was to make GM Daewoo the most respected company in South Korea and the world. Internally, its goal was to build up an innovative corporate culture and to solidify the corporate culture.

The public relations objective of GM Daewoo was to build a completely new corporate reputation: an auto company with world-class technology and quality. Its secondary objectives were as follows:

- To generate a positive corporate image and public trust during the first few years
- To support product marketing and sales by generating a favorable product reputation
- To change negative employee attitudes to positive ones and to improve employee morale by facilitating communication both top-down and bottom-up.

Strategies

To understand GM Daewoo's public relations strategies and tactics, it is important to know that the campaign consists of two phases: before and after the takeover. During the negotiation process, GM's public relations efforts were made to inform diverse groups of publics of the positive aspects of the takeover. After the company publicly launched, GM Daewoo's main public relations strategy was to create a favorable reputation and positive public opinions by highlighting the company's interest in the Korean market and commitment to the society as a responsible Korean corporate citizen. It also hoped to build a new, positive image by differentiating itself from Daewoo Motor. At the same time, the company wanted to separate itself from GM and be positioned as an independent Korean automobile company.

Action Strategies

Before the company was officially launched, much of the company's public relations efforts were made in media relations; it attempted to eliminate negative perceptions among the publics by reinforcing positive aspects and benefits that GM would bring to the country.

As a way of distributing those messages to consumers and the general audience, the company hired a public relations agency for media relations and event planning. However, it was not yet a legal business entity in South Korea, so the new company could not take many official actions. Rather, the company worked on contacting opinion leaders and creating positive public opinions in the country, including identifying who were the most influential and appropriate opinion leaders, how it would approach them, and when it would meet them.

After GM Daewoo was established, it generated several public relations strategies in the following areas: corporate public relations, product public relations, and employee relations. As part of its initial step, the company identified 23 influencers, such as product quality, service, and CEO image, which were critical for its corporate image. Those 23 points were assigned to members of the public relations department to develop appropriate communication strategies.

On September 17, 2002, GM Daewoo unveiled its new corporate identity, including a company logo and a brand slogan, *Driving Innovation,* during its company launching ceremony. It also moved all offices and functions, except the media relations team, into Bupyung Headquarters to show unity. A few months later, the company introduced new employee uniforms. One of the strategies was to run a corporate advertising campaign through mass media; a series of corporate public relations advertising, which was different from product advertising managed by the marketing department, was aired in 2003.

The media were one of the major targets of the public relations plan; GM Daewoo invited the journalists from each major news organization to its official events or held special events for them. For example, the company hosted media tours and events so that journalists could get familiar to the company and its products. It also invited journalists to several motor shows, such as the Detroit Motor Show or Busan Motor Show, and sponsored their trip and helped them with data collection by providing detailed information and arranging interviews or visits. In addition, the company decided to keep the press room in its Seoul office like other Korean companies; usually three to five journalists visited and stayed in the office.

To reinforce its reputation as a good corporate citizen and a technology company, GM Daewoo generated R&D projects that involved major universities in South Korea. The company announced that it would support and cooperate with those selected universities by providing funds and facilities.

The strategies for employee relations included generating communication channels between management and the employees and supporting a new relationship with the labor union; face-to-face communication was used as a key method of communication. The company decided to maintain Daewoo Motor's internal publications, such as the weekly newsletter and the bi-monthly corporate magazine; the name of the magazine was changed to "Driving Innovation." In addition, internal communication channels such as publications and the intranet were employed to reach the employees who were not included in the meetings or events.

GM Daewoo established a new function called the product communication team within the public affairs department to reinforce sales increases and actively promote its products from a public relations aspect. The team, consisting of "brand managers" who had extensive knowledge of the company's products and the industry, focused on product-related publicity and media relations worldwide.

Another important action the company took was a new project called "Buy from Korea." In September 2002, GM Daewoo announced that GM and the company would purchase automobile parts from South Korean manufacturers through this project; GM selected 19 parts and components manufacturers and contracted with them. Those parts would be used for automobile products for both domestic sales and export. The company also joined South Korean trade associations and organizations as a member.

Communication Strategies

The most significant point of the communication strategy was sending messages to the right people. The message each action contained was often in speeches and statements of the management executives, interviews with the media, and press releases. During the negotiation, the main message was that GM's takeover was to revive the bankrupt Daewoo Motor and the brand name by implementing a long-term program. Since there was a rumor that GM would withdraw from Korea if the business did not go as planned, the company also made it clear that it was in the business of making long-term investments with a strong commitment. At the official launching of GM Daewoo, the new company's CEO and president Nick Reilly stated, "Our company is absolutely committed to reclaiming and securing a place of prominence in the Korean and global markets."

The company's new corporate identity and the brand slogan, *Driving Innovation,* were designed to represent a "company that's modern, on the move and at the same time recognizes its roots." In November 2002, Mr. Reilly said the company would invest in its product and image, and planned to enlarge its long-term investment in South Korea rather than focus on short-term gains. Consequently, GM Daewoo's public relations practices intended to convey the following messages: (1) GM Daewoo is an innovative company based on technology advancement; and (2) GM Daewoo is a new Korean automobile company, not just combination of old Daewoo and American GM. The company positioned itself as a "Korean" company, and highly emphasized its commitment to the country and its market as response to the public skepticism. Mr. Reilly underscored it by saying that more than 98% of GM Daewoo's employees were Koreans and its operation was based in South Korea. To demonstrate its local characteristics to the media, employees, and consumers, the company often introduced the localization efforts of foreign management, including the CEO. The media were chosen as a primary channel to communicate these messages to the publics such as consumers and the general population. These stories were covered by many major South Korean newspapers and journals.

Immediately after the final contract, the management team from GM made an effort to have its employees, who were former employees of Daewoo, understand the goal and background of GM's acquisition as well as the future management strategy. The focus of the message was "We are here to help" and "This is your company, not mine"; these messages were delivered to the employees through management briefings or the speeches by the top management. At the meetings, Mr. Reilly presented his management principles, such as the emphasis on the value of the company, human resources, and products, and the possibility of re-hiring the employees who were laid off for restructuring. The internal media were used as an alternative channel. In addition, the management's effort to communicate with the labor union and rehiring of former employees demonstrated the company's willingness to talk and its interest in its people.

Tactics

To deliver the changes in the working environment and the corporate culture and the characteristic of GM Daewoo as a Korean company to the media, and hopefully their readers, the company employed various media relations tactics. Media-related writing was the responsibility of public relations team members in the Seoul office.

- *Feature stories:* Themes and topics were developed for feature stories. For example, during the 2002 Korea–Japan World Cup Soccer Games, some major Korean newspapers put a photo of Nick Reilly cheering for the Korean soccer team with Korean people on the street.
- *Interviews:* The public relations professionals arranged interviews with the company's executives, such as the CEO and vice presidents, for major newspapers and journals.
- *Press releases:* It frequently distributed press releases to the media. The releases covered quite a broad range of subjects, such as corporate culture, a new management system, and the company's business plan.
- *Articles and special editions of internal publications:* Interesting stories on GM Daewoo's management, such as the managerial style, management philosophy, and personality, were developed and distributed to the employees through word of mouth as well as internal print media. The staff members of the Communication Center were in charge of planning and writing.
- *Weekly newsletter articles:* After the takeover contract, the message from management was delivered as part of an introduction.
- *Bi-monthly Corporate Magazine:* In its first issue after the takeover in October, the magazine ran an interview with Nick Reilly, with emphasizing his management philosophy and long-term business plans for the new company.
- *Management briefings and special meetings:* After the final contract, the management teams from GM participated in several face-to-face meetings with the employees. Larry Zahner, vice president at that time, had management briefings in each local plant, and Mr. Reilly had management briefings for department heads and supervisors at plant sites in Bupyung, Changwon, and Kunsan.
- *Soccer tournament:* The company held a company-wide "GM Daewoo Auto & Technology soccer tournament" in October 2002. The event aimed to reinforce unity among employees and stir up the employee morale and cooperative spirit through employee participation. This tournament, the first athletic event for employees since 1997, is expected to continue as an annual employee event.
- *Family event:* In August 2003, GM Daewoo invited 1,000 children of its employees to the Bupyung plant for a tour. Through this event, the children saw where their parents work; at the end, they wrote letters to their parents.
- *Language training program:* To help the employees have English proficiency, the company offered language education for its staff and employees with an investment of US $ 600,000. The program was designed to meet the needs of the employees for language training; 5,200 employees would take the course annually.

Evaluation

It is somewhat early to evaluate the success of GM Daewoo's public relations campaign in South Korea, since the company is still trying to implement communication programs. So far, the company's efforts have been partially successful for certain groups of publics. For example, the campaign against the takeover by an activist group ceased as the sale was finalized. The negative public opinions regarding GM's entrance in South Korea has also decreased. GM Daewoo's business in general has been successful in the short-term; it was the second largest automobile exporter in August 2003. Sales in South Korea remained stable although the domestic market shrank.

However, the company has not conducted any formal evaluation of its public relations program to this point; current evaluation relies on informal measures, such as individual public relations managers' experiential evaluation and comments, and the employees' feedback through word of mouth, without empirical measures of public opinion. Consequently, no concrete evidence has been found to measure the success of GM Daewoo's corporate image advertising campaign or other consumer-related public relations programs, either.

Conceivably, one of the available evidences of the success of the public relations program is positive publicity in major media; the company's effort to build relationships with the labor union, a new corporate culture based on participation, and the revitalization of the bankrupt Korean company were some examples of positive articles. These stories, appearing in many newspapers and journals, delineated GM Daewoo's new corporate culture as rational, whereas Daewoo Motor's culture was authoritarian and hierarchical. On the other hand, some issues had been left unsolved and were pointed as problems for the company by the media. For example, wages were frozen without increase since the late 1990s; the plant in Bupyung was still left out in the takeover despite public opinion and the employees' wish to be included.

Some public relations staff members, who had extensive media relations experience in South Korea, were skeptical about the company's new product public relations system; they said that such in-depth information about specific products would be not necessary for South Korean journalists. However, by maintaining the press room in its Seoul office, the company adopted some extent of media relations convention in South Korea, which helped the company retain the network and connection with the media.

The company's employee relations can be considered successful to this point. It successfully resolved wage bargaining and avoided a strike, as the union conceded. In return, the management promised transparent management, continuous investment, and betterment of welfare for the employees. This was evaluated as an achievement for both the company and the employees through understanding and communication.

Critique

Research

The weakness of this case is the lack of formal research in the beginning. Although the company was aware of the characteristics of South Korean culture to some extent, its public relations activities were relatively reactive to those issues. While information was collected through diverse sources, such as professionals from the public relations firm and staff members of the public relations department, it was not empirical and not thoroughly explored. If the company had conducted formal research and analysis of the South Korean culture and understood its uniqueness, such as the emphasis on networks and in-groups before designing its public relations programs, it could have approached its publics more proactively and effectively.

The need for more research on culture is reflected in the company's lack of understanding of the South Korean media environment. As some public relations professionals pointed out, the company may need to consider more localization in its media relations, at least for now. The comment from one media relations expert is worth noting: "GM has an advanced, well-developed public relations system, which is good. But it may not be appropriate for our situation, at least for now." Similarly, the different perception and practice of public relations was noteworthy. Korean public relations managers explained that maintaining favorable relationships with journalists through face-to-face, personal contact was inevitable to get positive coverage in South Korea, although it could be viewed as unethical or unreasonable from a Western perspective. Meanwhile, the strengths of the research include identifying various groups of publics and effective communication channels for each of them.

In fact, after several months passed since the company launched, both the management and the local employees pointed out some problems and issues stemming from the differences between values as well as corporate cultures. For example, some Korean employees felt the company's decision-making process based on GM culture was slow and complicated, and was not appropriate for the Korean situation, which often required prompt actions or on-spot responses to journalist inquiries. At GM Daewoo, final decisions involved several steps, because issues had to be circulated to all executives to obtain everyone's approval. On the other hand, in many Korean companies, managers directly report to the executives and the CEO to obtain their prompt approvals.

Objectives

The communication programs had quite clear goals and objectives—to generate a positive reputation and public trust and to establish a positive corporate culture by improving employee morale. However, the company's public relations program had a few problems. As seen from the objective and goal statement, they were not time- or sequence-specific and not operationalized. Consequently, the results and effect of the campaign were not measurable. For example, the company did not conduct employee-related research before it planned and implemented employee-related communication programs; although the goal of the program was enhancing employee morale and understanding, it would be difficult to know how exactly the employees attitude was changed because of the public relations program.

Strategies

The public relations strategies were reactive rather than proactive, in general; the campaign could have been more effective if the company had generated programs that involved the members of publics other than the employees. Most of its strategies for the publics outside of the company are based on the news media. Besides, the public relations function does not have a sophisticated monitoring and environmental scanning system. Although the public relations staff regularly monitored major news media and received clipping service from the public relations firm, the company was not very proactive in detecting and identifying issues and problems.

Action Strategies.   The company took appropriate actions that fit the situation. Many programs were designed to show its commitment to the local market as well as the community, which in return resulted in positive media attention. However, it seems that GM Daewoo has some issues within the public relations department; it had not obtained understanding from those who execute these programs. Some public relations managers were not supportive about the new public relations function or programs, but mostly focused more on media relations and publicity. More communication and education, such as workshops, would help achieve internal consistency and efficiency.

Communication Strategies.   The choice and use of communication channels were appropriate; a variety of media was employed to maximize effectiveness. Nevertheless, it is possible that other media such as meetings or special events could have been more effective. Although the management visited the plants and met with supervisors several times, there still were employees excluded from those meetings. Face-to-face meetings with them could have more impact than communication through internal publications. The messages were also well crafted in that they clearly communicated what the company hoped to achieve through actions.

Tactics

The tactics used to create and disseminate messages were appropriate. However, as previously mentioned, GM Daewoo's public relations activities for the publics other than its employees were heavily based on publicity and media relations.

Evaluation

As was pointed out in the objectives, GM Daewoo's public relations campaign did not have operationalized objectives, which made it impossible to measure its success or failure. Although the company had received a great deal of media attention and was successful in gaining much positive coverage, no empirical research was conducted to measure the implementation and the outcome of the public relations programs. It is possible that the company will evaluate its campaign in the future; nevertheless, it will be difficult to measure the outcome rigorously without previous research.

DISCUSSION QUESTIONS

   1. Is there any information you would need more to design and evaluate the public relations program in this case?

2. Did GM Daewoo establish an appropriate communication system and structure for public relations?

3. What are the specific market situation and environmental issues of South Korea that GM Daewoo needs to keep in mind in its public relations planning?

4. What will be the most effective way of using the media in South Korea?

5. Who do you think would be the publics that the company failed to identify?

6. If you should be a public relations professional of the case organization, how would you measure and operationalize each program?

7. What can be possible strategies and tactics from a public relations perspective to overcome the cultural and language challenges and cultivate positive corporate culture?

REFERENCES AND SUGGESTED READINGS

Grunig, J. E., & Hunt, T. (1984). *Managing public relations.* New York: Holt, Rinehart and Winston.

Hofstede, G. (1997). *Cultures and organizations: Software of the mind.* New York: McGraw-Hill.

Korean Confederation of Trade Unions, www.kctu.org/arguments/daewoo-04.htm

Smith, John F., Jr. (2000). Chairman and Chief Executive Officer, General Motors Corporation. Remarks to the Federation of Korean Industries and U.S. Chamber of Commerce (May 11, 2000).

Yi, J. (1994). Negative effect of nepotism on the development of Korean society and an exploration of an alternative. *Korean Journal of Psychology: Social Issues, 1*(1), 83–94.

8 The Latvian Naturalization Project

VIRGINIA KREIMEYER

Executive Summary

By definition, public relations engages in relationship building and advocates a position for an organization or entity. Baskin et al. define public relations as "a management function that helps achieve organizational objectives, define philosophy, and facilitate organizational change. Public relations practitioners develop, execute, and evaluate organizational programs that promote the exchange of influence and understanding among an organization's constituent parts and publics." In emerging democracies, ethical public relations practices can facilitate the process whereby a country moves from authoritarian government to a democracy. As the country's political structure changes, the influence levied by public relations practitioners directly impacts the process within specific organizations. For a nation to move from oppression to freedom, those in government positions must make a concerted effort to provide transparency to society.

This case study discusses how public relations enhanced and facilitated the processes for Latvia, an emerging democracy, through the Latvian Naturalization Board's promotion of the naturalization process, citizenship, and social integration issues.

Research

With an expansive coastline along the Baltic Sea, Latvians fished and farmed their fertile waters and land for centuries, but the Soviet era crowded the country's strategic location with electronic factories and military bases. Since its re-independence in 1991, Latvia, like many Eastern European countries, has launched its economy in the information age with more than 20 desktop publishing companies, about 40 advertising firms, and nearly 50 web services. Riga, the capital, bustles with nearly 900,000 people jammed into a variety of mass transit conveyers and an ever-increasing number of private autos.

While the pay from U.S. and European businesses located in Latvia is generally higher than indigenous firms, there are many Latvians who struggle to keep their meager salaries at government agencies. The average monthly gross salary of the highest level of civil servant is 350 lats ($US 595), the mid-level salary is 170 lats ($US 289), and the lowest level is 140 lats ($US 238). The civil servants of the mid- and higher level may receive additional bonuses, which allows them to have a reasonable standard of living. Still, the average monthly salary is about 380 lats ($US 650). Salaries for most positions in the private sector begin at $800 a month and are frequently paid in foreign currency, despite the reliability of the lat.

Although the official language is Latvian, many educated people speak English or Russian, or both. Heavily influenced by its neighbors throughout the centuries, Latvia continues to be a multicultural society. The strong Latvian ethnic identity has resisted oppression and preserved the Latvian language—a derivative of the Livs', which is known as the Lettgalean language and is used in a certain area of the country today.

Cultural Considerations

Ethnic Latvians have been oppressed by other cultural groups dating back to the 12th century, when the Germanic aristocracy lorded over the Livs, the Latvian peasants. But in 1991 when the Latvians joined in the efforts of other former Soviet states to emerge as a free and democratic society, the forced emigration during the years of oppression had taken its toll on the population. By the end of the 50 years, the ethnic Latvian population dwindled to about 30 percent of the residents. Additionally, many ethnic Russians—approximately a third of the country's population—chose to reside in Latvia even after it became an independent state. Therefore, with the new democracy, the rights of citizenship became a key issue for Latvia in 1991. At first, citizenship was accorded only to those persons who were citizens of the independent Latvian Republic in 1940 and their descendants. As a result, approximately 700,000 people who had been citizens of the Soviet Union became "noncitizen residents" of Latvia. However, because the government allowed former Latvians to return and reclaim family land, many repatriated in the 1990s.

In the 2000 issue of the annual Human Rights Committee Report, Nils Muiznieks wrote:

> In Latvia the primary human rights concerns in 1999 were the lengthy pre-trial detention of minors, encroachments on freedom of expression, as well as the government's failure to allocate sufficient funding to ensure smooth implementation of social integration policy, thereby threatening recent progress in the realm of minority rights. On the positive side, 1999 saw the abolition of the death penalty, the opening of a new involuntary commitment facility for mental patients who have committed serious crimes, and a significant increase in the naturalization rate of Latvia's large population of stateless 'non-citizens.'

The diversity of Latvian ethnic groups is another major obstacle to any communication campaign. There are more than a dozen recognized ethic groups, and ethnic Latvians make up less than three percent of the population (Table 1).

Government Considerations

A 1994 citizenship law provided that various categories of noncitizens would be eligible to apply for naturalization, as long as they met Latvian language and residency requirements.

TABLE 1 Latvian Citizenship by Ethnicity in 2002

	Citizens	% of citizens	Non-citizens	% of non-citizens	Others	%	Total	%	% of ethnicity with citizenship
Latvians	1369042	77.21	4647	0.79	748	2.83	1374437	57.58	99.6
Russians	297792	16.80	392941	66.86	16108	61.04	706841	29.61	42.1
Belarussians	22580	1.27	74091	12.61	1300	4.93	97971	4.10	23.0
Ukrainians	6382	0.36	54679	19.30	2875	10.89	63936	2.68	10.0
Poles	39600	2.23	20106	3.42	343	1.30	60049	2.52	65.9
Lithuanians	15496	0.87	17081	2.91	1009	3.82	33586	1.41	46.1
Jews	5770	0.33	4510	0.77	292	1.11	10572	0.44	54.6
Roma (Gypsies)	7470	0.42	665	0.11	14	0.05	8149	0.34	91.7
Germans	1320	0.07	1997	0.34	229	0.87	3546	0.15	37.2
Tartars	229	0.01	2791	0.47	168	0.64	3188	0.13	7.2
Estonians	1440	0.08	1012	0.17	224	0.85	2676	0.11	53.8
Armenians	407	0.02	1977	0.34	231	0.88	2615	0.11	15.6
Moldavans	207	0.01	1591	0.27	98	0.37	1896	0.08	10.9
Azerbaijanis	232	0.01	1366	0.23	99	0.38	1697	0.07	13.7
Georgians	241	0.01	718	0.12	79	0.30	1038	0.04	23.2
Others	4844	0.27	7553	1.29	2572	9.75	14969	0.63	32.4
Total	1773052		587725		26389		2387166		74.3

Some groups, such as former Soviet intelligence and military officers, were still excluded. Additional requirements stipulated that applicants possess knowledge of the Latvian constitution and history and take an oath of loyalty to the Latvian State. When Latvia held a referendum on the amendments to the citizenship law in October 1998, 53% of the voters supported the law, which abolished age and birthplace restrictions for citizenship candidates. The new law also granted citizenship to children born in Latvia after August 21, 1991. As a result, practically all noncitizens became eligible to apply for naturalization. Again in 1999 the naturalization procedure was eased and the fee for specific groups, mainly indigent people, was reduced so that only about 50 percent of applicants paid full fees. To further alleviate a barrier to citizenship, the naturalization tests were revised in 2000, resulting in a 95 percent or better pass rate for applicants' first try. As a result, Max van der Stoel, High Commissioner on National Minorities of the Organization for the Security and Cooperation of Europe (OSCE), confirmed the progress in the field of naturalization and congratulated Latvia for its successes in a January 1999 statement.

One of the key factors in the significant increase in the naturalization rate of Latvia's stateless people was the government's relaxing of the laws, but additionally, it was the leadership of the Naturalization Board. Elizenija Aldermane, the head of the Naturalization Board, recognized the need to inform the residents of these new procedures as well as to provide the manpower necessary to process the applications. As with any new government, funding was a major problem, but Aldermane approached the U.S. Aid for International Development's (USAID) chief of mission to Latvia for assistance. Through a USAID-funded project called the Latvian Naturalization Project, Freedom House, a nonprofit organization based in Washington, D.C., managed several public relations campaigns for the Naturalization Board.

Description of Client

The Latvian Naturalization Board, located in the historic area of Riga, was established in 1995. With a very restrictive policy that prevented many residents, especially ethnic Russians, from applying for citizenship from 1991 to 1998, the board functioned in a limited manner as the agency to implement the citizenship and naturalization process. Unlike the other Baltic States with the majority of their residents being Lithuanian and Estonian, respectively, only 33 percent of Latvia's population was ethnic Latvian. This imbalance was a major concern for the international communities that supported the wave of democracy spreading across Eastern Europe. The United States and the European Union were vitally interested in Latvia's future. Additionally, since many residents of Latvia wanted to join the European Union, which would help sever ties with the former USSR and solidify its independence, Latvia sought ways to increase its potential for EU membership.

Therefore, when Aldermane approached the USAID mission chief and the former U.S. Ambassador to Latvia for them to work with her agency, the Americans agreed to fund the $500,000 Latvian Naturalization Project, through the State Department. At the time of the arrival of Freedom House's Resident Advisor, 28 percent of Latvia's residents were noncitizens, and the major focus was to increase the number of citizens through the naturalization process.

Freedom House submitted a project work-plan based on data collected and analyzed by the Baltic Data House in a national, comprehensive research project. Baltic Data House, an independent company, had spent a year interviewing several thousands of residents of Latvia in 1997–98 about the naturalization process, their attitude toward the government in regard to citizenship issues and social integration, and their ethnicity. As a result, a three-volume report called "Toward A Civic Society" was published and disseminated in three languages—Latvian, Russian, and English. The report stated the main reasons people were not applying for citizenship as, lack of knowledge of the Latvian language, difficulty of the process, and fear or lack of trust in the government.

As a new government agency, the Naturalization Board was still growing in responsibility and attempting to keep up with the ever-increasing workload. By May 1999 the Board had more than 1,400 employees in its offices in Riga and in the 12 regional branches throughout Latvia. A staff of five worked in the Information Center (IC) or public relations department, which had not yet been authorized by the Cabinet of Ministers. In her effort to promote the Board and its activities, Aldermane had assembled a young, highly motivated staff. Although motivated, the staff did not have much public relations training. Gunta Line, the head of the IC, had been a historian. A trained librarian filled the librarian/receptionist position; a former newspaper reporter was the Board's press secretary. The functional deputy, who had a graduate degree in sociology, had the title of "senior desk officer." The two regional public relations representatives were former schoolteachers. They worked in offices in Daugvapils and Liepiaja. With only four people in the main office and one in each of the largest two regions, the Information Center had a tremendous and daunting task before it.

Publics

By the new millennium Latvian NGOs (nongovernmental organizations which contribute to the success or failure of a nation's ability to sustain a democratic state because they become the backbone for promoting democratic ideals and human rights issues) had exercised influence in the content and passage of three NGO-related laws: the Law on Social Organizations and their Associations, the Law on State Guardianship, and the Law on Charity. The NGOs relied heavily on public relations activities such as lobbying and public debates, which resulted in the government's willingness to engage in dialogue with such organizations. The Cabinet of Ministers worked with NGOs to adopt the National Program on the Protection and Promotion of Human Rights in Latvia. Although the Latvian National Human Rights Office receives its basic financial support from the state and is run by a state-appointed director, it has been widely supported by human rights NGOs in Latvia. According to a 1997 report by the NGO Center in Riga, 82 percent of NGOs cooperate with national and local governments and 31 percent include representatives of national and local governments in management structures.

Other obvious publics considered in this project were the stateless or noncitizens of Latvia and third-party support systems like the European Union's Organization for the Security and Cooperation of Europe, as well as the governments of the United States and European countries.

Media

Throughout Latvia there were 14 major newspapers, which published in Latvian, Russian, and English. Additionally, there were national and regional television and radio stations, which had previously been owned by the government but were privatized and became independently operated. In Riga, the Russian language television and radio stations became key factors in reaching the noncitizens with the Naturalization Board's messages. A more thorough discussion of the relationship between the Latvian Naturalization Board and the media is presented in the evaluation section of this case study.

Objective

Organizational Goal

In 1998 the head of the Latvian Naturalization Board recognized the need for assistance in informing the board's publics about the purpose and operations of this controversial government agency. Therefore, the Latvian government requested that the U.S. government provide an expert public relations consultant to meet the needs and objectives of the Board.

PR Objective

In May 1999 a public relations practitioner was engaged to assist the Latvian Naturalization Board in promoting human rights issues of citizenship, naturalization, and social integration in Latvia. To reach these goals, the three areas of emphasis for the project were to provide institutional capacity building, manage a $60,000 subgrant program to NGOs, and assist with the Latvian language pilot project.

Strategies

Action Strategies

To ensure the changes were optimized, the Latvian Naturalization Board (LNB) requested a long-term expert to work with and train its own people in this new—two-way symmetrical—approach to public relations. The LNB and Freedom House hired a public relations expert to serve as the resident advisor, with a contract of one year, to help plan and execute public relations campaigns aimed at promoting citizenship, naturalization, and social integration issues throughout Latvia.

Communication Strategies

As Latvia moved from an authoritarian government to a democracy, citizenship issues required a major overhaul. New ways of approaching the rights and privileges of citizenship was a key factor, and how to inform the noncitizens of these new opportunities. While under

Soviet rule, Latvia's public relations practices were the epitome of the propaganda or press agentry model, expounded by James Grunig. Grunig's four models of public relations begin with the press agentry, which was essentially propaganda as espoused in the Soviet era—a one-way communication of information from the government to the people. There was no necessity of truth telling, because the government was in control. The next model of public relations, according to Grunig, is the public information model, which stresses the need to provide factual information to the organization's (in this case, the government's) publics. In his third model, which Grunig calls the two-way asymmetrical, the organization actually gathers information through the social sciences and uses the information to plan its programs.

In 1998 Latvia moved to this third model when the government authorized Baltic Data House to conduct extensive research to determine the attitudes of the country's residents toward naturalization, citizenship, and social integration issues. However, it was how the country used the data that demonstrates Latvia's progress to Grunig's fourth model of public relations, the two-way symmetrical model, which is considered the best in the practice of public relations. As often happens in Eastern European countries that are emerging democracies, the movement from the first model to the fourth in an effort to democratize the government was accelerated. A case in point is the referendum of the Law on Citizenship in October of 1998, which resulted in the government radically changing its policies about citizenship and naturalization. When the voters overwhelmingly passed the referendum, the government took heed. By responding to the people, the government had entered the mutual understanding and adaptation phase, which is indicative of the two-way symmetrical model. Simply stated, the people spoke and the government not only listened, but also responded.

Tactics

To meet the goals of the project, the first priority was training for the Institutional Capacity Building program—an essential element of the project to make it sustainable. Within the first month a retreat/training seminar was arranged at an off-site hotel to ensure seclusion and prevent job distractions. Aldermane kicked off the four-day seminar, once again demonstrating her leadership and support for meeting the needs of the Naturalization Board's customers. Providing top management support for any public relations endeavor is essential for its success, as Grunig and his associates noted in *Manager's Guide to Excellence in Public Relations and Communication Management*. Training, however, was not limited to public relations, although this was an area of emphasis; team building, time management, and strategic planning accounted for the majority of the week's activities. These seminars included writing vision and mission statements, as well as a strategic plan for the Information Center.

Using the retreat to jump-start the Institutional Capacity Building program and an ongoing mentoring effort, the resident advisor, a seasoned public relations practitioner, was augmented by three short-term advisors, who spent four to five weeks in Latvia. One was a public relations consultant from South Carolina, one a citizenship drive expert from Boston, and the other a language-training instructor from the University of California-Davis. With the assistance of the short-term advisors, additional seminars consisted of media training for the management of the Board, team building, and time management for the managers of the Latvian language-teaching program. The resident advisor worked with other government agencies to promote third-party support for the Information Center by conducting seminars in crisis communication for businesses and government agencies, basic public relations for the Ministry of Foreign Affairs, an international panel discussion at the Goethe Institute, and a mini lesson on the public relations four-step process for OSCE's seminar with the Prime Minister of Norway.

The USAID grant for the Latvian Naturalization Project included not only the training component, but also a multifaceted public relations campaign, which aimed at increasing the awareness of the naturalization process and citizenship issues. The project included a yearlong national student competition called "Toward A Civic Society," which was co-funded by Freedom House and the EU's PHARE program. Other community outreach programs ranged from special events commemorating the 20,000th new citizen and the fifth anniversary of the Naturalization Board, to a special naturalization ceremony as part of the closing of the USAID mission in Latvia.

Although some of the smaller Naturalization Board branches had new citizen ceremonies on a regular basis, the publicity and magnitude of each event was dependent on the heads of the regional branches and their involvement with local government officials. Two months after the resident advisor arrived, the USAID mission closed in Latvia. As with most USAID closings, there were several activities to commemorate the work that had been completed. The city of Jelagva, which was about an hour's drive from Riga, became the site of a citizenship ceremony and an emotional highlight for the U.S. Ambassador and the USAID Washington Office representative, as well the Latvian staff.

The next big event included a special ceremony in Riga for the 20,000th person to be naturalized. The ceremony included special presentations by Aldermane and the mayor of Riga. A commemorative certificate for the 20,000th citizen was a new concept that had nearly been rejected, but proved to delight the new citizen, Aldermane, and the mayor. By scheduling activities that included third-party supporters of the Naturalization Board, the board's fifth anniversary in February 2000 served as another component of the public relations campaign. More than 20 media attended the board's reception and launching of the website. An anniversary book highlighting the board's first five years was presented to key attendees, including representatives from the U.S., Swedish, and Danish embassies in Riga.

No public relations program is complete without considering the internal/employee communication component, which was one of the major problem areas for the Naturalization Board and the Information Center. Even though the Riga office had e-mail capabilities, not all the branches did. Therefore, a monthly newsletter called "Good Ideas," which would provide an opportunity to share ideas that worked in one region with the others, was suggested. Unfortunately the newsletter never made it past the prototype because the press secretary was not ambitious enough to initiate such a project. However, the librarian provided a monthly update on publications available in the resource library. E-mail became the main mode of communication throughout the board, but once a month all the regional branch heads, the two regional representatives, and key headquarters staff met with the top management in Riga.

Face-to-face communication also enhanced the Information Center staff's relationship with the communities at the regional branches outside of Riga. After the head of the Board set up the initial visit to one of the branches, these trips became a monthly or bimonthly excursion for the center's staff to meet with the other Board people as well as the local government, news media, and key members of the NGO community. The site visits provided valuable insight in understanding the attitudes and reactions of the communities to the naturalization process, and how the board's operations were perceived in these areas. Often the contacts with the NGOs established excellent resources for future projects such as the subgrant program, a major component of the project.

One of the most successful aspects of the LNP was the subgrant program. With the assistance of Freedom House's Regional grant director from Budapest, the resident advisor organized an expert review committee to select the grant proposals, defined the criteria for the proposals, set up a tracking system for the proposals, and wrote letters to the committee and the respondents as well as advertising for the program. Nearly 60 submissions were reviewed and seven grants were awarded to promote naturalization, social integration, and citizenship through community outreach efforts as well as partnering with the media. After the review process was completed and approved by both the USAID representative and Freedom House's Washington office, Aldermane and the Resident Advisor called a press conference to announce the awardees. Both Freedom House and the Naturalization Board received excellent coverage in both Latvian and Russian language press, as did the NGOs in subsequent media reports, as noted in the evaluation section's report of the content analysis. The grants ranged from the printed word in newspaper inserts and brochures, to radio and television productions. The messages contained elements of informing the target audiences of the process, how easy it was to attain citizenship, and the importance of being a citizen in an emerging democracy. While some NGOs focused on learning the language, other NGOs capitalized on Latvia's pursuit of membership in the EU. Nonetheless, each of these grants had a component for using the mass media to reach target audiences—to help with the overall public relations campaign for the project.

The following is a synopsis of the NGOs receiving grants:

- The Daugavpils Center for Human Rights was awarded $12,000 to conduct a radio program and create a brochure on naturalization called "Naturalization—Step to Integration."
- The Democracy Advancement Center was awarded $10,700 to translate into Russian and print a U.S. university-developed manual called "Project Citizen." This project has been implemented in several cities in Latvia.
- Latgales Television Company was awarded $12,400 to conduct a televised competition between families to promote naturalization by testing their knowledge of Latvia's varied culture, history, and language. The competition, called "Latvia in My Family" required each family to have at least one noncitizen and one citizen to qualify for participation. It received positive grassroots publicity.
- The Latvian Human Rights Committee was awarded $12,400 to produce a series of radio programs called "Saprast" on Super FM. These programs aired twice a week and discussed the naturalization process and helped people to learn the Latvian language.

■ A special insert for Russian language newspapers was created by the NGO European Latvia with a grant of $2,800. This colorful insert in Russian provided information about the naturalization process as well as stories about key people discussing citizenship and naturalization.

■ One NGO submitted two proposals that were funded under the subgrant program. The Open Society Fund was awarded $10,400 for a television production called "My Choice" and $2,300 for a youth discussion club named "Pro ET Contra." "My Choice" aired a series of interviews with key people in Latvia who chose to be naturalized. "Pro ET Contra" was a series of Saturday discussions by 30 to 50 young people who listened to experts and voiced their opinions of issues related to naturalization and citizenship.

Since Latvian was the official language and a large group of residents' native language was Russian, language posed a formidable barrier. Many of these people were at least middle-aged, and learning a new language presented too much of a challenge for them. Although there were several Latvian language-training programs in place, some of them targeted professions such as law enforcement and teaching. The USAID headquarters in Washington responded to a request from the Naturalization Board and Freedom House was awarded an $80,000-plus grant to conduct a pilot program for teaching Latvian for free. Before signing up for the program, a person must have applied for citizenship. There were more people who wanted the courses than there were spaces space available in the classrooms. After the grant was awarded to the Latvian Folk School, Freedom House set up a training and evaluation process to ensure the project's efforts were maximized. A final evaluation of the language project was made in July 2000, and other similar projects have been considered as joint ventures with the Danish and Swedish governments. At a seminar outside of Riga, the Prime Minister of Denmark stated his support of the language-training program as a part of what Latvia calls their "Social Integration Program." The social integration program includes the naturalization process but further looks at ways to improve Latvia's cultural, political, and economic situation.

Evaluation

In evaluating a comprehensive program, there are many intangible benefits. Perhaps the most conclusive is that the number of citizens doubled during the project's timeframe. However, a measurement of the media coverage would also indicate how the project was viewed by one of PR's powerful publics. Therefore, a content analysis of media coverage of Freedom House for the period of May 1999–April 2000 assessed articles in a variety of publications on Freedom House and the Latvian Naturalization Board.

The extent and prominence of news coverage in local newspapers gives some measure of the campaign's success. Not only were a large number of articles carried (Figure 1), but they also were prominently featured. Most appeared on page two, suggesting they were seen as important (Figure 2).

In addition to newspaper coverage, there was coverage by the Baltic News Service and LETA, the two Latvian news service agencies (Figure 3). Many of the articles discussed the

FIGURE 1 Number of Articles in Newspapers

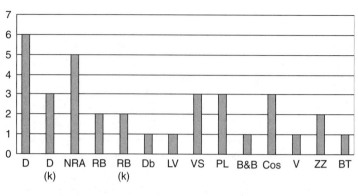

D   Diena
D(K) Diena Business
NRA Neatkariga Rita Avize
RB   Baltische Rundschau
RB(K) Baltische Rundschau Business
Db   Datoru Avize
LV   Latvietis Latvija
VS   Latvijas Vestnesis
PL   Plesums
B&B Business and the Baltics
Cos Chas
V   Ventspils Zenas
ZZ   Zemgales Zinas
BT   Baltic Times

FIGURE 2 Number of Articles by Newspaper Page

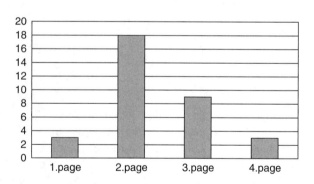

resident advisor's site visits, the subgrant program, and the language-training program. Since the articles were used by newspapers and posted to the news wires' websites, it can be inferred that the project also received international coverage.

An analysis of the slant or orientation of the coverage (Figure 4) shows that the majority of the articles were either "very positive" or "positively informing," which indicates

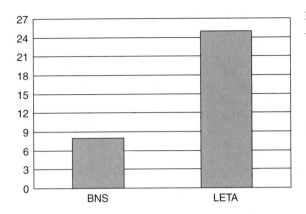

FIGURE 3   Number of Related Articles in BNS and LETA

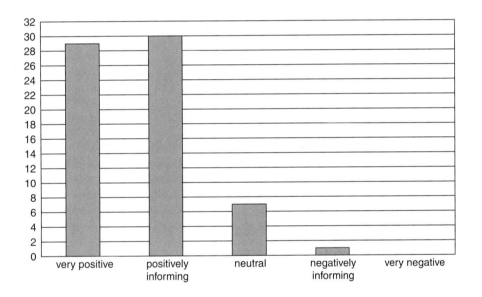

FIGURE 4   Distribution Frequency of Coverage by "Slant"

not only that there was a plethora of articles, but they were also favorable. The one article that was negatively informing resulted from one of the subgrant projects, which was an insert for the Russian language newspapers. The insert contained graphic artwork depicting the naturalization "window system," which was abolished in 1998. The "window system" had been established shortly after independence in 1991 to slow down the process for ethnic Russians, thus preventing them from gaining political and government positions. Although this artwork was not previewed on the proof sheet, it was included on the first run of this insert. As soon as the mistake was discovered, distribution stopped, but 200 had already gone out. Of those 200 were five that went to the Russian Embassy in Riga. The Russian Ambassador called Aldermane and demanded an explanation. The mistake nearly caused an international incident, but with the advice of the resident advisor Aldermane wrote "Letters to the Editor" of the Russian newspapers explaining the mistake in the insert. Only one newspaper printed an article discussing the letter and the mistake. By telling the truth, a major crisis between Latvia and Russia was averted.

Practicing public relations in a foreign country has indicative barriers such as culture, language, and technology. However, the same basic principles employed in the four-step process of research, action/planning, communication, and evaluation, worked for this project.

Critique

In March 1999, Freedom House was awarded a contract by the US Agency for International Development that would promote citizenship and social integration, raise public awareness of legal rights and responsibilities, and instill confidence in the naturalization process. Once the contract was signed, Freedom House established a presence in Latvia and worked with the Latvian Naturalization Board. This was a close and productive relationship in terms of accomplishing the goals of the Latvian Naturalization Project.

There were three main areas in which this relationship has prospered. They are (1) strengthening the institutional capacity of the LNB, specifically the Information Center, (2) promoting the naturalization process with a major emphasis carried out through the subgrant program, and (3) establishing a pilot project for teaching the Latvian language to people who desire citizenship through naturalization. Each of these main goals was intimately tied to the promotion of human rights through public relations campaigns.

First, Freedom House had outstanding success in strengthening the institutional capacity of the LNB. Six LNB staff members participated in Freedom House's Visiting Fellows Program, where they spent 6–10 weeks in the U.S. working side by side with professional counterparts after a brief orientation in Washington, DC. In addition, Freedom House provided a resident advisor, who mentored and trained the staff, as well as two short-term public relations advisors to conduct intense training in Riga, Daugavpils, and Liepaja. During the year the Information Center and staff developed a five-year strategic plan, a communications plan, partnered with NGOs to conduct media and community relations programs, and found innovative ways to communicate with its target audiences. With financing by Freedom House, the board created a new website to provide information in both Latvian and English with the click of a mouse. Freedom House also provided $17,000 for three special projects coordinated by the Information Center. One project was a seminar co-sponsored by the Council of Europe to discuss Information and Integration in Daugavpils. The second project consisted of two television programs aimed at young people, with teams from Riga and Liepaja who debated citizenship and the naturalization process, respectively. Working with the LNB's branches throughout Latvia, the Information Center conducted the national students' contests, "On the Way to a Civic Society." These contests resulted in excellent media coverage, grassroots support, and an overall success story for Latvia in international supporters' eyes.

Second, Freedom House conducted a subgrant program that awarded $60,600 for seven projects conducted by NGOs, which reached target audiences throughout Latvia. By forming an expert committee, Freedom House and the LNB jointly worked to select seven of the nearly 60 project proposals to fund. The successes of these projects were reflected in the positive media coverage, detailed in the content analysis section of this case study.

The third area of emphasis by Freedom House was the Latvian language Fast-Track pilot project. Freedom House brought in a language specialist to coordinate the grant of $79,600 for language training to the Latvian Folk School. Recognizing that one of the basic needs of noncitizens wanting to become citizens was free Latvian language training, Freedom House coordinated with LNB and USAID for this ongoing project. More than 300 people received free language classes, with 98 percent passing the language portion of the naturalization tests.

One of the main goals of the project was to increase the number of noncitizens to citizens through the naturalization process. Through various means of educating the public, conducting community outreach programs, and media campaigns, the numbers of naturalized citizens increased dramatically. From March 1999 until March 2000, the number of noncitizens who became naturalized grew from 13,898 to 27,569, or doubled in one year's time. Another goal, to increase the general public's awareness of the naturalization process, was reached through the subgrant program and the special projects conducted by the Information Center. In addition to the publicity about Freedom House, Aldermane made the media campaign much more successful, because of her television and radio appearances on a regular basis as well as newspaper coverage, and she continued to promote a positive image of the board. The successes of the Latvian Naturalization Project can be best demonstrated by the number of applications for naturalization (Figure 5). By 2002, more than 35,000 applications had been made.

Cutlip, Center, and Broom, in *Effective Public Relations,* defined the practice of public relations as "the management function that identifies, establishes, and maintains mutually beneficial relationships between an organization and the various publics on whom its success or failure depends." In emerging democracies, human rights issues are critical to the success of the new government. Therefore, the management of government agencies of a country must promote human rights, especially those of citizenship, to its people—both citizens and noncitizens. In the case of Latvia, a public relations campaign was launched

**FIGURE 5   Naturalizations
Granted as of March 4, 2000**

Year	Applications	Granted
1995	4543	984
1996	2627	3016
1997	3075	2993
1998	5607	4439
1999	15179	12427
2000	4259	5375

using the four-step process and successfully raised awareness as well as changed the behavior of the country's people. From the public relations practitioners' standpoint, the campaign required aligning the goals of the campaign with the goals of promoting human rights, especially the basic right of citizenship in the country. In the end the success is not only measured by the numbers—that is the increase in the number of people naturalized—but also, in improving the quality of life through the promotion of basic human rights. Conducting public relations in an emerging democracy requires a basic understanding of the rights of people as well as the ethical principles of public relations.

DISCUSSION QUESTIONS

1. If Latvians have a strong ethnic identity and pride, will they resist any public relations campaign organized or planned by foreigners?
   a. What research would you conduct to answer question 1?
   b. If you believe Latvians are suspicious of, or resent, U.S. or other foreign involvement in their country, how would you design a pro-Latvian campaign to overcome their resistance?

2. Why do you believe so many non-ethnic Latvians remain in Latvia?
   a. How would you design and implement research to answer question 2?
   b. Would you use different research methods to ask this question of different ethnic groups? For example, how would you ask Russians in Latvia as opposed to ethnic Latvians in Latvia?

3. How would you make the Latvian Naturalization Board's public relations objective more specific and operationalized?
   a. Would you specify a target public or publics? If so, what public(s) would you target?
   b. How would you operationalize "promoting the human rights issue of citizenship"?
   c. How would you operationalize "promoting the human rights issue of naturalization"?
   d. How would you operationalize "promoting the human rights issue of social integration"?

4. Can you suggest an action strategy for the Latvian government that would help a public relations campaign to promote social integration? For example, what could the government do to integrate the ethnic Latvians and Russians?

5. Is a two-way communication strategy helped or harmed by a government policy that includes a Latvian language requirement for citizenship?
   a. Do the requirements for U.S. citizenship include a language test?
   b. Should a test in one language be required for citizenship in the U.S.? Why or why not?
   c. Should a test in one language be required for citizenship in Latvia? Why or why not?

7. If a retreat or isolated workshop is a good tactic for building a public relations team, why is it not used more often to establish client teams in U.S. public relations agencies? In the United States, how many newspapers would you expect to find serving a population of 250,000?
   a. Why do you believe Latvia has 14 major newspapers?
   b. Does the number of newspapers make public relations easier or more difficult in Latvia than it would be in the United States?

8. When dealing with potential ethnic and nationalistic conflicts, one must be careful not to offend any subgroup in the target public. What procedures or requirements would you put in

place to prevent a recurrence of the distribution of the graphic artwork depicting the "window system" of naturalization that offended the Russians in Latvia?

9. Was this campaign successful? If you believe it was successful, how would you demonstrate its success to those who funded the campaign?
   a. Would you make any changes in the objective statement to facilitate your "proof of success"?
   b. What measures or evidence would you present to the funding agencies to demonstrate your accountability?

REFERENCES AND SUGGESTED READINGS

Baltic Data House. (1998). *The programme for studies and activities: Towards a civic society report.* Baltic Data House, Riga, Latvia.

Baskin, O., Aronoff, C., & Lattimore, D. (1997). *Public relations: The profession and the practice* (4th ed.). Dubuque, IA.: Brown & Benchmark Publishers.

Cutlip, S., Center, A., & Broom, G. (1985). *Effective public relations* (6th ed.). Englewood Cliffs, NJ: Prentice-Hall, Inc.

Dozier, D. M., Grunig, L. A., & Grunig, J. E. (1995). *Manager's guide to excellence in public relations and communication management.* Mahwah, NJ: Lawrence Erlbaum Associates.

Heath, R. L. (Ed.). (2001). *Handbook of public relations.* Thousand Oaks, CA: Sage.

Indans, I. (2001). *Nations in transit.* Washington, DC: Freedom House.

Plakans, A. (1995). *The Latvians: A short history.* Stanford, CA: Hoover Institution Press.

Muiznieks, N., Kamenska, A., Leimane, I., & Garsvane, S. (2000). *Human rights in Latvia in 1999.* Riga, Latvia: Latvian Center for Human Rights and Ethnic Studies.

The Bhopal Carbide Disaster: A Lesson in International Crisis Communication

PADMINI PATWARDHAN and
NILANJANA BARDHAN

On the night of December 3–4, 1984, water used to flush pipes at U.S. multinational Union Carbide's Indian subsidiary (Union Carbide India Limited, or UCIL) pesticide plant in Bhopal, India, leaked into a methyl isocyanate (MIC) storage tank through several open valves. There it combined with the highly volatile MIC to form a toxic mixture of gases, foam, and liquid. Forty-five tons of this toxic gas escaped from the plant's stack at a temperature in excess of 200° C (about 400° F). The lethal gas spread rapidly through the densely populated city, causing catastrophic suffering and loss of human and animal life. Estimates placed the immediate death toll at more than 2,000; eventually it rose to over 4,000 (*Time Atlantic*, 2002). Even today, thousands of surviving victims are still battling the effects of the toxic gas, and suffering chronic, debilitating health problems (*Chemical Week*, 1996).

Initially set up to formulate pesticides for the Indian market using raw materials imported from Union Carbide USA, the Bhopal unit had begun to manufacture hazardous pesticide components like MIC to exploit economies of scale as well as save on transportation costs (Shrivastava, 1989). However, the plant's continued unprofitability had resulted in the adoption of numerous cost-cutting measures including poor safety and emergency procedures (Mitroff, 1994). Due to its low strategic importance on the MNC's global radar, the Indian subsidiary was subjected to neglect. Thus, as a leading Indian business magazine commented, Bhopal was a result of total quality failure "of product . . . process . . . system . . . management . . . [and] individuals" (*Business India*, 2002).

The magnitude of the environmental and human devastation resulting from the leak confronted Carbide with a challenge that severely tested the mettle of its crisis communication expertise. Although two decades have elapsed since the disaster, Bhopal is still evoked as an example of "what not to do" in the case of a crisis of global proportions. As one of the world's worst industrial disasters, the Bhopal tragedy devastated an entire city (and country) both physically and emotionally. Carbide's ignoring of vital local publics resulted in widespread anti-Carbide sentiments in India and beyond. Its single major failure was in

220

communications and public relations at the local level. With no spokesperson at the scene, and with the Indian subsidiary UCIL completely muzzled, the glaring lack of corporate representation reinforced the myth of callous multinational corporation exploitation of local communities in developing nations.

The disaster had far-reaching ethical, social, environmental, legal, and financial consequences for Union Carbide and UCIL. After a protracted and acrimonious legal battle, Carbide reached a $470 million out-of-court settlement with the Indian government in 1989. As part of the deal, it sold its shares in the Indian subsidiary and established a trust to fund construction of a hospital in Bhopal. However, the corporation was unable to recover fully from this debacle. In the 20 years since Bhopal, as Carbide stock plummeted due to loss of shareholder and public confidence, the corporation aggressively pursued class action litigation in both U.S. and Indian courts, fought a hostile takeover, sold off several profitable ventures, and finally merged with Dow Chemical, the world's largest chemical company (Devin, 2000; *New York Times,* 1997; *Occupational Hazards,* 1996; *Business Week,* 1984).

Multinational corporations (MNCs) such as Union Carbide face major challenges when dealing with crises simultaneously at both local and global levels. As senior Carbide spokespersons observed: "the problems raised by the tragedy spanned two companies, two governments, two continents, and two cultures" (Browning, 1993). An event of this magnitude severely tests the mettle of a company's crisis strategies. Many commentators (for example, Shrivastava, 1989; Sen & Egelhoff, 1991) have linked the decline of Union Carbide with the negative impact of its crisis management strategies in the aftermath of the disaster.

This case study focuses on Carbide's handling of crisis communication at global and local levels following Bhopal. It investigates how Carbide prioritized its publics and stakeholders and developed strategies and tactics to address their information needs. The chapter concludes with a critique of Carbide's crisis communication planning and execution in the post-Bhopal scenario.

Research

Unlike planned public relations campaigns, crisis communication efforts, unless backed by pre-emptive risk communication (Heath & Palenchar, 2000), tend to be reactive in nature. Hence, although it is advisable for all companies to engage in constant issues tracking and have a general crisis communication plan in place, no formative research (Kendall, 1996) in a formal sense is possible. Crisis management and communication get even more complex when subsidiaries located in different cultures are involved (Sen & Egelhoff, 1991). Most MNCs exercise greater (or total) control in managing crises, since the essential goal of crisis management is to bring the situation under control as quickly as possible (Heath, 1997). This was the context for Union Carbide's reputation management efforts in the aftermath of the Bhopal incident.

In the confusion following the disaster, the immediate cause of the leak could not be ascertained. Conflicting theories about how water entered the MIC tank were advanced. An investigation by the Indian government found that water used to flush pipes gushed through valves into the tank due to safety failures, thus positioning Carbide and UCIL as culpable for safety violations and negligence. Several months after the incident, Carbide released its own report based on an independent investigation and claimed that sabotage, initiated by a disgruntled employee who deliberately introduced water directly into the tank, was the cause of the disaster (Browning, 1993; Kalelkar, 1988).

Despite these conflicting positions and Carbide's rhetorical attempts to partially dissociate itself (Benoit, 1995) from the cause of the leak, it is evident that the Bhopal pesticide unit was beset by problems prior to the disaster. In fact, Bhopal was not an isolated accident for Union Carbide. Many such incidents, including gas leaks, had occurred at Carbide locations around the world, as well as in the United States (Heath, 1997). However, none of these received much publicity, with minimal repercussions for Carbide's reputation and policies. Bhopal changed all that. The struggle for justice by the victims of the gas leak, supported by activist and legal groups, continues to this day (Laughlin, 1996).

For Carbide, immediate research consisted of gathering information about the disaster and its possible causes, as well as gauging the impact of the disaster both locally and globally. The first reports of the disaster reached Carbide headquarters in Danbury more than 12 hours after the incident. In those early hours, Carbide relied on information through sources in other major Indian cities, namely New Delhi and Bombay (now Mumbai), since overloading of telephone lines out of Bhopal hampered access to information on the ground (Browning, 1993). Carbide's lack of knowledge of what was unfolding in Bhopal was a key factor in how the crisis was handled in the days immediately following the leak. Its initial press statements were fuzzy (Heath, 1997), and there was an overall impression of delay in addressing the local situation, an impression that thoroughly destroyed trust in the wake of the disaster (Hearth & Palenchar, 2000; Morley, 1998).

The publics of an MNC are spread around the globe. A stone dropped into the pond has a ripple effect; similarly, reputation management efforts by an MNC have to take into consideration the global ramifications of crisis events. In the absence of information from Bhopal, Carbide crisis managers quickly focused on containing the U.S. and global fallout of the crisis. Apart from the immediate humanitarian aid to Bhopal victims, Carbide primarily addressed its global (particularly U.S.) stakeholders (Benoit, 1995). The United States headquarters in Danbury, Connecticut, was transformed into a "command center to gather information and mobilize resources," and it was clear that Carbide took complete control of both crisis management and communication activities (Browning, 1993). This ethnocentric (Botan, 1992) approach was a major mistake.

Overall, Bhopal had a devastating impact on Carbide's global image. Global media coverage further exacerbated the situation with graphic images and stories from the scene of the disaster (Heath, 1997; Benoit, 1995). Carbide's public safety record, corporate credibility, and financial stability as a global MNC were at stake. These concerns set the stage for the communication initiatives that Carbide adopted after Bhopal. They defined the corporation's identification of significant publics and objectives, as well as the strategies and tactics devised to target crisis communication messages to these publics.

Cultural Considerations

It is advisable for MNCs operating in diverse global regions to be attuned to local cultures and adjust their operations (including public relations) to suit local environments (Morley, 1998). According to Botan (1992), most corporations engaging in international or multinational public relations tend to be ethnocentric in their approach, which means that the public relations culture of the country in which the corporation is headquartered is imposed on local conditions. The opposite of this stance is the polycentric approach, wherein much strategic and cultural power is handed over to the local unit. Public relations scholar Laurie Wilson (1990) argues that local involvement and contributions, mutual understanding, and committed relationship building need to be the top priorities for MNCs.

With a presence in India spanning several decades, Carbide was well integrated into the Indian environment, and thus could have utilized knowledge of the local scene for developing effective crisis communication strategies for its various Indian stakeholders in the aftermath of the crisis. However, routine communication channels between Carbide and UCIL appear to have been limited, perhaps due to Carbide's stated hands-off policy regarding management of routine operations at global subsidiaries (Shrivastava, 1989). Thus, when Carbide USA took control of Bhopal's crisis management, its approach was mostly ethnocentric with little consideration or understanding of the local environmental, social, and cultural concerns that UCIL would have been more familiar with. The following sections briefly describe the environment in which Carbide operated in India.

Social Characteristics

Bhopal, the capital of the state of Madhya Pradesh, was a center of burgeoning industrial activity. It was chosen to set up Carbide's new pesticide unit because it had adequate infrastructure (water, electricity, and labor) to sustain large-scale industrial chemical plants. Its central location also ensured ease of distribution, since it was particularly well connected by rail and road to the rest of the country. However, Bhopal's rapid growth as an urban industrial center came at a price. In 1985, its population had swelled to about 700,000, up from 400,000 a decade earlier. Most of this was due to the influx of migrant workers from surrounding rural areas, drawn by the economic lure of the big industrial units. These migrants, the majority of whom were illiterate, provided a pool of cheap labor for many of the industries in the city (Shrivastava, 1989).

The migrant influx also created a chronic housing shortage in the city. Slums and shanty towns sprang up illegally near the industrial units as local and state governments turned a blind eye. The Carbide plant was set up in the northern part of the city in a heavily populated commercial area (Shrivastava, 1989).

Historical Considerations

The ideological position of Carbide in Bhopal, an MNC representing a world superpower, is a point worth noting. India is a postcolonial nation that achieved independence from the British in 1947. In the aftermath of independence there grew a fierce tendency to protect national sovereignty both materially and symbolically. In the business sector, this tendency translated into an anti-foreign investment fervor, fueled by the socialist stance of successive governments (Bardhan & Patwardhan, 2003). Several MNCs had been driven out of India by the late 1970s, and this was the rhetorical reality in which Carbide operated—a reality held together by the tension between the economic and developmental benefits of foreign investment and the nationalistic aversion to "foreign exploitation." Given this context, an ethnocentric approach to crisis communication in the wake of the Bhopal disaster was a serious mistake.

Organizational Culture

With an established presence in India since the 1930s, Carbide was part of the Indian industrial landscape (Shrivastava, 1989). Its foray into pesticides was an attempt to profit from the Indian government's "green revolution" promotion of pesticides to boost the agrarian economy (Shrivastava, 1989). Before the Bhopal disaster, UCIL (and, by extension, Carbide) was generally respected in India, and considered a good employer and corporate citizen. The community also benefited from various social welfare drives initiated by the company that helped it integrate into the local environment.

Gradually, the unit became a financial setback for Carbide. The pesticide market in India became highly competitive, forcing many companies, including Carbide, to assess their options. Carbide's response to market pressures was to begin manufacturing its pesticides in India rather than merely formulating them using raw materials imported from the parent company. This contributed to a decision to "backward integrate" into the domestic production of components (including the hazardous MIC) at Bhopal, to achieve economies of scale. When this move failed, the company adopted various cost-cutting measures, including layoffs, which undermined Carbide's position in the local community (Shrivastava 1989; Sen & Egelhoff, 1991).

Governmental Considerations

According to Kent and Taylor (1999), in many countries, the government is a prime stakeholder when it comes to public relations operations. Such is the case in India (Bardhan & Sriramesh, 2003). Before the disaster, UCIL enjoyed a good relationship with state and central government agencies in India (Shrivastava, 1989). Since pesticides were an important part of the government's drive to boost agricultural production, it was a mutually beneficial relationship. MNCs such as Carbide were considered partners in achieving national development goals. In turn, Carbide won several concessions from the government, including a license to manufacture rather than merely formulate pesticides at Bhopal. In addition, UCIL worked closely with local, state, and central government authorities to promote social welfare programs.

The company thus developed strong contacts in government to its considerable advantage, benefiting from several profitable decisions. However, its decision to manufacture the hazardous MIC was met with stiff resistance from local authorities, since the unit was located in a densely populated area meant for commercial and light industry use. Leveraging its affiliate's clout with state and central government agencies, Carbide managed to override local pressures and began to manufacture MIC in 1979. Thus, even though Carbide's relationship with higher government decision makers was one of collusion and mutual benefit, its relationship with local government had already begun to sour before the disaster (Shrivastava, 1989).

The alliance ended with the disaster. Carbide and the Indian government positioned themselves on the opposite sides of the legal and ethical divide, and adopted increasingly adversarial stances. As global Carbide managers took control of crisis management, local

UCIL managers were rendered almost invisible. The stage was thus set for a major confrontation between a global multinational entity and the government of a developing host country in which it operated.

The Company

At the time of the disaster, Union Carbide was the seventh largest chemical company in the United States, with sales of about $10 billion. It pursued goals, values, products, and strategies typical of traditional chemical companies and produced heavy chemicals, pesticides, batteries, carbon products, consumer products, and plastics. Many inherently hazardous materials were involved in its production processes (Shrivastava, 1989; Paul, 1995). As a chemical company, despite a stated policy of worldwide safety and environmental standards, Union Carbide's environmental policies were aimed at regulatory compliance, driven by legal and economic rather than ecocentric and humanitarian concerns (Shrivastava, 1995).

Union Carbide was also a major global player, employing more than 33,000 people in businesses across 40 countries. It held a 51 percent controlling stake in its subsidiary UCIL. UCIL was the 21st largest company in India, employing more than 10,000 people at its 13 manufacturing units, making products as diverse as batteries and pesticides. Initially incorporated as Eveready Company (India) Limited to manufacture dry cell batteries, its name was changed to Union Carbide India Limited (UCIL) in 1959. The Bhopal plant was a key facility of its Agricultural Products Division, one of five UCIL divisions, each of which functioned as a separate profit center. However, the division was a financial liability and was often headed by managers with nonchemical backgrounds. A high turnover in division leadership and the departure of several key managers trained to operate the MIC plant at Bhopal had severely compromised the internal systems and procedures of the division and its operations (Shrivastava, 1996). UCIL represented less than 2 percent of the parent company's worldwide sales and under 3 percent of its profits (Sen & Egelhoff, 1991). Thus the Indian affiliate and its Bhopal unit were, presumably, of low strategic importance for the multinational corporation.

According to Carbide spokespersons, the Indian subsidiary operated as an independent entity. It is probable that day-to-day operational decisions were left to local management; however, it is highly unlikely that strategic business decisions (e.g., to sell off the failed Bhopal unit) would have been made independent of United States headquarters. Despite Carbide's repeated insistence that all its worldwide operations met the highest safety standards, it is evident that these standards were missing at Bhopal (Shrivastava, 1989). With regard to process standards, it is apparent that Union Carbide had double standards when operating its two MIC plants in India and in Institute, West Virginia. The Bhopal plant was on the verge of being closed down. Trained personnel had not been replaced, and safety procedures were fairly lax (Mitroff, 1994). An investigation of both the UCIL plant and its counterpart in Institute revealed that "while the latter plant had a computerized warning and monitoring system, the former relied on manual gauges and the human senses to detect gas leaks. The capacity of the storage tanks, gas scrubbers, and flare tower was greater at the Institute plant. Finally, emergency evacuation plans were in place in Institute, but nonexistent in Bhopal" (Cassels, 1993, p. 19).

After the exodus of trained managers, novice plant managers were largely ignorant of the hazards of operating an MIC unit. Many of the Indian operators at Bhopal at the time of the disaster were either illiterate or knew only the local language, Hindi, but Carbide continued to provide safety manuals printed in English (Laughlin, 1996). Thus, at the time of the disaster, the Bhopal plant comprised a staff that was ill-trained, ignorant of the dangers of MIC, and lax in safety procedures. No efforts had been made to engage in risk communication, a process that high-risk companies invest in to keep their publics informed and prepared to act in case of a crisis. Such confidence-building measures tend to create a more forgiving public, mitigate the impact of a crisis, and contribute toward post-crisis image restoration (Seeger, Sellnow & Ulmer, 2001; Heath & Palenchar, 2000).

At the time of the disaster, a communication breakdown was evident at the local level. Effective risk communication (internal as well as external) would have alerted Carbide to communication problems with several local publics. For example, employees were unhappy at being downsized and thrust into jobs they were not trained to perform. Civic authorities were unhappy with Carbide's decision to make hazardous MIC at a plant located in a heavily populated area reserved for light industry. Negative news coverage, highly critical of the dangers posed by the unit, had also appeared in the local press in the year preceding the gas leak (Shrivastava, 1989).

One of the major criteria that should determine the selection of a crisis response narrative or "apologia" (Heath, 1997; Benoit, 1995) aimed at clearing the name of the company is the company's performance history, which is a combination of that company's crisis as well as relationship histories. Of the two, the latter is a stronger predictor of success (Coombs & Holladay, 2001). Although no previous crises had occurred at the Bhopal unit, Carbide had experienced problems with smaller leaks at other plants, incidents that had not received much media attention (Heath, 1997). Moreover, its souring relationships with publics in India and other related conflicts that had been repressed up until the leak were thrust into the foreground once the trigger incident occurred (Seeger, Sellnow, & Ulmer, 2001).

Publics

The crisis managers at Carbide were faced with the unenviable task of addressing the fears and uncertainties of multiple publics and stakeholders at both local and global levels. Based on Esman (1972), Grunig and Hunt (1984) distinguished corporate relationships into four types: enabling, functional, normative, and diffused. *Enabling publics* represent authorities that both allocate resources and regulate the organization's activities. *Functional publics* constitute those who both supply inputs and receive outputs. *Normative publics* represent bodies that share similar values and set shared standards. And *diffused publics* include the community at large as well as other general publics that may be impacted by the organization's actions. As described by Ice (1991), Carbide's crisis communication publics included enabling (government, stockholders), functional (employees, suppliers and distributors, consumers), normative (chemical industry), and diffused (media, public at large, victims) publics.

However, Carbide's own reports provide clear evidence that there was a disconnect between global and local publics in its crisis communication planning (Browning, 1993). Under the parent company's control of crisis communications, vital publics appear to have been prioritized using a global rather than local approach (Benoit, 1995). Thus, U.S. and global publics identified by Carbide for its crisis communications included the U.S. government and Congress, stockholders, the chemical industry, Carbide employees, and global industrial consumers of Carbide products, as well as the U.S. media (a vital conduit to the U.S. public at large). Personal communication and contacts were used to target members of Congress and regulatory agencies, with senior executives also testifying before Congressional subcommittees (Browning, 1993).

The Indian subsidiary, UCIL, did take some initial steps in reaching out to its Indian stakeholders. For example, top management reopened established channels with government bodies, UCIL employees, and shareholders (Sardana, 1999). Subsequently, as communication control passed to the parent company, the Indian publics (media, victims, and the public at large) assumed secondary importance. The only Indian public that Carbide chose to deal (or battle) with was the enabling Indian authority—the government of India.

Media

To communicate with various external publics, Carbide extensively used the mass media to present its side of the story to United States and global audiences. Frequent media updates were provided through press conferences and press releases out of its headquarters in Danbury, Connecticut, in the United States. Industry publications were used to target the chemical industry. For Carbide employees, internal print and electronic media and personal meetings were utilized. These included news bulletins, employee publications, and specially prepared company videos (Browning, 1993).

UCIL employed its own channels for targeted communication in the initial days. However, despite contentions that UCIL had an open door media policy (Sardana, 1999), no local spokesperson was appointed at ground zero as a contact point for media, and UCIL held no press conferences. Another factor that posed a hurdle in media relations was the fact that the broadcast media at that time were government controlled (Bardhan & Sriramesh, 2003). When control of the crisis passed to Danbury, UCIL's external communications all but ceased, even though it continued to utilize some regular internal communication media for its employees.

Objectives

One of the main all-time public relations objectives of any company is to maintain and enhance reputation and protect the same from harm (Benoit, 1995). For an MNC, this is a tough challenge, since its reputation depends on the performance of many widely dispersed units, all in a position to impact reputation. The financial objective of Carbide, as it would be for any MNC, was to profit through its diverse global operations, and its specific goal in setting up the Bhopal pesticide plant was to produce fertilizers to capitalize on India's green revolution. Carbide's failure in attaining this latter objective severely impacted subsequent decisions regarding the Bhopal unit, including decisions about public relations and reputation management strategies.

At the time of a crisis, there is an expectation of an immediate response. Various publics demand answers, and overall there is a need for certainty in the face of ambiguity

(Seeger, Sellnow, & Ulmer, 2001; Heath, 1997). During and after the crisis, Carbide's primary objective was to attain containment, correction, and image restoration. Carbide's management adopted task-oriented short-term and long-term objectives. Short-term objectives focused on:

- containing or neutralizing the danger at the scene of the disaster
- taking pre-emptive steps to prevent recurrence at other Carbide locations
- providing immediate medical aid and relief to victims
- providing financial support to orphanages
- maintaining shareholder confidence
- attempting to establish control over crisis communication activities

It is important to note that there were no clear short-term objectives regarding media relations and crisis communication at ground zero.

Long-term objectives included:

- efforts to provide vocational training to victims
- engagement in urban renewal programs
- reputation management to restore credibility and public image
- addressing crucial legal, financial, and business implications of the crisis

Carbide did not publicize any long-term rehabilitation or compensation objectives for the victims as an important objective. This was probably its most costly mistake, in terms of image restoration.

No information is available regarding the timeline or measurability of these objectives. Overall, the glaring mistake from a public relations perspective was that no specific crisis communication objectives and goals appear to have been defined to address the specific needs of Indian publics, especially the victims and their families and the local media (Benoit, 1995). Carbide was thinking global and communicating global (Morley, 1998).

Strategies

Action Strategies

Carbide officially claimed that it simultaneously addressed important technical, humanitarian, legal, and business implications of the disaster (Browning, 1993). However, as the following section indicates, many of the strategies that were adopted in the days and months following the disaster served the legal and business aspects of the issue rather than technical, communication, or humanitarian concerns.

Adaptation or Change Strategies

- *Operational:* A centralized task force, headed by then Carbide Chairman Warren Anderson, was set up to direct crisis management from U.S. headquarters. (This was a deviation from Carbide's self professed hands-off approach in overseas operations.)

- *Informational:* It was decided that media communications would also be centralized. Danbury was identified as the media contact point, allowing Carbide to control the overall flow of information. Plant managers in India and elsewhere were directed not to speak to the media.
- *Ethical:* Carbide proclaimed grief for the victims but shied away from accepting full moral responsibility for the disaster, especially in the light of its evolving legal strategy of dissociation and shifting of blame.
- *Legal:* Carbide's legal strategy was orchestrated to limit liability and defend itself aggressively against all charges. The corporation began distancing itself from its subsidiary, localizing blame to minimize both the global impact and its financial culpability from a legal standpoint. A decision was made to continue the battle in the courts as long as possible (Shrivastava, 1987)
- *Humanitarian:* Carbide expressed its grief and humanitarian concern for victims and their families, announcing that it would do everything in its power to alleviate the suffering.

Audience Participation (Involvement of Target Publics). It appears that Carbide's involvement of external local publics in either defining or executing strategy decisions was minimal. However, internal publics, namely Carbide employees, were more involved. In order to boost the morale of a devastated work force, internal communication strategies sought to involve employees through reassurance, information, and participation.

- *Reassurance:* Employees were reassured by senior company officials about the safety measures in their plants and Carbide's commitment to its employees. A similar approach was adopted by UCIL for its Indian employees.
- *Information:* Employees were kept informed about developments at the same time as the media. Though UCIL was not permitted to directly release information to the media in India, it was allowed to keep its own employees informed about events.
- *Participation:* Both Carbide and UCIL employees were encouraged to establish a Carbide Employees Relief Fund that collected more than $100,000 to aid the victims.

Special Events. No special events appear to have been scheduled by the company during the crisis management period.

Communication Strategies

According to Benoit (1995), crisis response rhetoric can assume five forms: denial, evasion of responsibility, reducing offensiveness of the event through bolstering, transcendence or differentiation, correction and mortification or acceptance of blame, and asking for forgiveness.

Carbide's crisis communication strategies were largely reactive and restorative. These dealt with the corporation's relationships with (1) enabling publics represented by the U.S. and Indian governments and U.S. stockholders, (2) functional publics that included employees, suppliers, distributors, and consumers, (3) normative publics consisting of the chemical industry, and (4) diffused publics in terms of the global and U.S. public at large, the media, and victims. As discussed by Ice (1991) and others (Heath, 1997; Benoit, 1995), the primary strategies adopted for each of these publics were as follows.

Enabling Publics.   Communication strategies directed at the U.S. government and other regulatory government agencies like the Environmental Protection Agency aimed to reduce offensiveness by bolstering (Benoit, 1995) or stressing the safety factors in Carbide's U.S. operations and repeatedly attempting to allay fears that "it could happen here."

For the Indian government and regulatory agencies, Carbide's communication strategies changed as the relationship changed. Before the disaster, the relationship was cordial and collusive. Immediately after the disaster Carbide emphasized its willingness to cooperate in relief operations as well as reach an early settlement (Ice, 1991). However, as the Indian government moved from a regulatory role to one representing the victims, the relationship turned adversarial. As the Indian government distanced itself from blame, ostensibly for reasons of political expediency, Carbide also became increasingly concerned with limiting its financial liability. Guided by its legal defense team, the initial cooperative stance was increasingly replaced by aggressive strategies of confrontation, attack, and some amount of denial (Benoit, 1995).

For its third enabling public, shareholders, Carbide once again adopted a bolstering strategy of reassurance by emphasizing the corporation's financial stability, as well as positively reinforcing the contributions made by the chemical industry as a whole (Ice, 1991).

Functional Publics.   Communication strategies utilized for Carbide employees aimed at restoring morale by bolstering the company as safe, stable, and concerned about the disaster. Another functional public that needed to be reached was Carbide consumers. The main concern was primary industrial consumers of Carbide products who were directly impacted by the crisis. For example, several countries, including France and Brazil, suspended the import of MIC due to safety concerns. Once again Carbide responded to these concerns by bolstering the corporation's safety record. No communication strategy seems to have been adopted for general consumers of Carbide's highly profitable consumer products division, since most of the products had different trade names, were not perceived as being associated with Carbide, and suffered no adverse fallout (Ice, 1991).

Normative Publics.   Carbide adopted a strategy of transcendence (Benoit, 1995) when it came to its normative public, the chemical industry. This served three purposes: to expand, through transcendence, the discourse from a Carbide problem to an industry issue, thereby shifting the context of the disaster; to develop a support group within the chemical industry; and to apportion collective responsibility for the disaster.

Diffused Publics.   The public at large was mostly unaware of Carbide before the disaster, except as a leading MNC with diverse global interests. As much a result of the extensive media coverage as the tragic aftermath of the disaster, Bhopal served to irrevocably associate Carbide with the worst industrial disaster in history in the minds of general publics.

Carbide had to devise both short-term (containment) strategies, as well as long-term (corrective) image restoration strategies. Its primary conduit for relaying image restoration messages to the public was the media. Browning (1993) states that media relations played an important role in conducting external public relations. Carbide's media strategy was two-pronged: to provide a centralized access point for company information, and to provide "open and early release of factual information" (Browning, 1993). A decision was also made not to offer speculative comments.

The victims of the tragedy (the ones most directly impacted by the disaster) and the extended Indian public formed an essential diffused public. Carbide did take several immediate steps in response to their medical needs. Its initial strategy was to neutralize the disaster and dispense aid as quickly as possible (Sardana, 1999). However, Carbide did not have a strategy for dealing with the local (Indian) media that directly influenced the anti-Carbide framing of the disaster. Carbide distanced itself from the press in India in the initial stages of the crisis. It had no local spokesperson, since in order to enable top-down control over crisis communication operations, UCIL managers were instructed not to talk to media (Sardana, 1999).

Tactics

Enabling Publics

U.S. Government.   Initially Carbide sought to reassure the U.S. government and regulatory agencies of its high technological safety and emergency standards at all global operations. Carbide also crafted its message to create dissociation between the Indian plant and its U.S. counterpart, suggesting that the disaster was a result of local ineptitude. Senior executives also testified before Congressional subcommittees and used their personal contacts to influence target members of Congress and regulatory agencies.

Indian Government.   Carbide eventually took an adversarial stance with the Indian government. Public messages accused the Indian government of noncooperation and opportunism, preventing Carbide officers from conducting investigations, providing conflicting and inadequate information, and generally preventing the corporation from discharging its humanitarian obligations.

U.S. and Global Shareholders.   Efforts included publishing damage control messages in the corporation's annual reports. These included messages from financial and legal consultants detailing financial stability to withstand a payout, reports extolling Carbide's contribution to the Indian green revolution, as well as commentaries on the chemical industry's value to society. Subsequent messages included presentation of the Indian government as the major stumbling block in the way of Carbide's humanitarian goals.

Functional Publics

U.S. Employees.   Internal communication messages focused on allaying safety fears, building morale, and emphasizing a proactive employee-oriented approach. Repeatedly, in communication with U.S. employees, safety at the U.S. plants was stressed, while the incident at Bhopal was presented as a "local" issue. The internal magazine *UC World* dedicated the front cover of its January 1985 issue to Bhopal. A company videotape series "What's

Going On" was shown in company cafeterias and at employee meetings to respond to the media coverage of the tragedy. Then-Chairman Warren Anderson made a personal visit to Charleston, West Virginia, to address employee concerns. This was videotaped and distributed to company and affiliated sites throughout the world (Ice, 1991; Sardana, 1999). Employees were also encouraged to get involved by setting up relief funds for the victims on their own initiative.

Indian Employees.   In India, UCIL published a special issue of its house magazine *Hexagon,* highlighting the facts and relief measures at Bhopal. This was followed by serialized features and articles detailing the company's positive actions (Sardana, 1999). However, as Carbide began to withdraw support to its subsidiary as it shifted to a dissociation strategy, these efforts ceased to have much impact.

Consumers.   No specific information was available regarding communication messages directly disseminated to this group, especially industrial consumers of Carbide products.

Normative Publics

Meta messages aimed at the chemical industry included placement of articles in leading industry journals emphasizing the linkages and lessons to be learned from Bhopal (Ice, 1991).

Diffused Publics

United States.   Activities included a formal Carbide statement on the Bhopal tragedy (Benoit, 1995), regularly scheduled press conferences, frequent distribution of press releases, strategic release of favorable information, withholding of negative information, and publicizing results of Carbide's own investigation. Official releases for global and U.S. media detailed steps taken in Bhopal and at other facilities and emphasized Carbide's determination to find the cause of the tragedy and apply the lessons learned. Carbide also used the media to advance its strategy of dissociation.

Indian.   Activities included dispatching a medical team to Bhopal to provide immediate relief to victims, announcing interim relief contributions to the State Chief Minister's and Prime Minister's Relief Fund, dispatching Chairman Anderson to India, and sending a technical team to Bhopal within 24 hours to assist in the safe disposal of the remaining MIC at the plant. No media relations or other communication tactics at the local level were in operation, except that UCIL had specific orders, due to legal concerns, not to communicate with the local media.

Evaluation

Carbide officials contended that their campaign was successful in meeting stated objectives (Browning, 1993), though no specific measurements of success were provided. However, independent evaluation by external commentators based on events after the disaster suggest that Carbide's crisis communication strategies were, in most cases, unsuccessful in meeting their objectives (Ice, 1991). The following are summaries of how each public was affected by the campaign.

Enabling Publics

U.S. Government. A gas leak at the Institute, West Virginia, plant eight months after Bhopal contradicted Carbide's insistence that U.S. plants had the highest standards of safety (Benoit, 1995). Media reports of other accidents prior to Bhopal at various Carbide facilities (including in the United States) further undermined the credibility of Carbide's safety assertions.

Indian Government. Carbide's confrontationist attack and denial strategies served to alienate this crucial public. As a result, the bitter litigation dragged on for years, keeping the disaster alive in the press and among diffused publics. Justice for the victims was badly served due to the effects of this soured relationship, thus further eroding Carbide's public image.

Shareholders. Investor confidence in Carbide was never really restored. Carbide stock continued to fall. Carbide's financial credibility also suffered due to the protracted litigation. Carbide had to sell off profitable units, fight a hostile takeover attempt, and it finally bailed out to Dow Chemicals.

Functional Publics

U.S. and Indian Employees. Carbide was partially successful in restoring morale in the initial days after the disaster. However, overall and ongoing negative media coverage, the subsequent leakage in West Virginia, and Carbide's aggressive legal maneuvers affected morale and led to employee attrition. In India, as a result of its dissociation strategy, Indian employees felt betrayed and were no longer proud "Carbiders" (Sardana, 1999).

Consumers. Though no specific information is available, Carbide's communication with industrial clients were not completely successful. The disaster did affect industrial sales of Carbide products. In addition, more and more host countries began to take a harder look at Carbide facilities in their backyards.

Normative Publics

The communication strategy aimed at the chemical industry appears to have been successful. The chemical industry did close ranks ("it could happen to us"), and rallied around Carbide to avoid government legislation. An important outcome was the industry's voluntary creation of a system of emergency management for its members. For example, the Chemical Manufacturers' Association (CMA) developed the Community Awareness and Emergency Response (CAER) program in 1985, less than half a year after Bhopal(Begley & Coeyman, 1994). Furthermore, federal U.S. legislators, afraid of similar disasters at home, created the Emergency Planning and Right-to-Know Act of 1986 (Sara Title III) (Heath, 1997).

Diffused Publics

United States.   Carbide's media strategy was not successful. Immediately after the disaster, media spokespersons were not well prepared to answer questions. This was mostly due to the fact that the MNC did not have a good grip on all the facts, did not have an emergency evacuation plan in place in Bhopal, and did not understand the context of the disaster accurately. In addition, its total communication plan to address the situation was slowed down by continued confusion about how to best address the post-crisis scenario (Health, 1997). The centralization of communications, absence of spokespersons at ground zero, initial silence due to lack of information, and refusal to speculate all led to perceptions that Carbide was stonewalling the media, especially in India. Also, despite the company's efforts, the evidence of suffering on the ground was graphic and overwhelming. Thus media coverage, which in the initial days was highly event-centered, placed Carbide in an unfavorable light. Over time, coverage of the gas leak at Institute, as well as Carbide's delaying legal tactics, also were negatively framed by the media. Thus, public opinion about Carbide as a corporate citizen continued to erode.

Indian.   Though company officials maintained that Carbide was able to neutralize the danger posed by the remaining MIC in the tanks at Bhopal (Browning 1993), reports circulated that the MIC inventory was neutralized by an Indian government task force in an operation labeled "Operation Faith" (Shrivastava, 1995). Subsequently, Carbide's confrontation with the Indian government, its ban on Indian media, and the legal delays in disbursing aid to victims all served to fuel the growing anger against the MNC. Indian publics were also enraged at its legal attempts to limit liability by undervaluing human life in a developing country (Laughlin, 1996), its abandonment of UCIL, and the assertion that Carbide was more concerned with saving its skin than providing meaningful aid to the victims gained support. The stories of the aid it did provide got backgrounded amidst the fury and outrage of the Indian public and government as well as the censure of U.S. and global dispersed publics. Resentment and anger continue to this day. Two very different views of the status of the Bhopal disaster can be seen on the Internet at www.bhopal.com and www.bhopal.org. The website www.bhopal.com is used by Union Carbide to explain its environmental commitment and the status of its Bhopal-related obligations. The other website, www.bhopal.org, is the website of the Sambhavana Trust. Eighteen years after the Bhopal disaster, this site still actively pursues Union Carbide and Dow Chemical.

Critique

Shrivastava (1989) outlines several communication failures at different stages in the Bhopal crisis.

- In the pre-crisis phase, people living in the vicinity were not informed about the dangers, local authorities were not informed about emergency procedures, employees were not issued adequate safety and emergency information in a language they understood, and safety violations were not communicated to higher management. No risk communication program or emergency evacuation plans were in place.

- During the crisis, lack of communication between Carbide, UCIL and the Indian authorities, medical personnel treating victims, and the affected public hampered the transmission of medical and toxicological data.
- After the crisis, Carbide's evasive communication strategies and fuzzy press statements sent poor image messages and led to loss of stakeholder and stockholder confidence.

Research

In the pre-crisis stage, Carbide failed to conduct the research that was necessary to keep it informed of the local public relations problems UCIL was facing. It also failed to monitor the environment and research the need for risk communication in a high-risk situation. After the crisis, although Carbide put in much effort to identify the cause of the leak, it failed to research all relevant local publics, understand the Indian media and political culture, and include the cultural knowledge that UCIL could have provided in forming post-crisis strategy. Doing the above might have avoided later errors in planning an effective and culturally attuned crisis response and image restoration campaign.

Objectives

Although Carbide seemed to have short- as well as long-term objectives in place, these objectives failed to address two crucial aspects—specific communication and media relations goals at the local level, and a clear rehabilitation and compensation statement to victims and their families. It is true that legal concerns may have hampered such specific commitments in the latter case; however, given the magnitude of the disaster and the human suffering involved, clear communication of intent was necessary.

Strategies

The first mistake was that the crisis management and communication efforts were ethnocentric. The global was prioritized over the local, with no or minimal involvement of local publics. This initial approach alienated the victims and other crucial Indian publics, thus paving the way for an acrimonious rhetorical and legal battle. According to Robert Berzok, director of Corporate Communications at Union Carbide in 1996 (Occupational Hazards, 1996), Carbide would have been better served by designating plant-level spokespersons who knew the situation well and could have dealt with local media. This was the first failure in strategy. The lack of a clear media relations and communication plan at the local level was a mistake which allowed Carbide no control whatsoever in the local framing of the crisis. The little bit of control that it had was at its headquarters in the United States. Overall, the top-down communication approach did not serve well in controlling the bottom-up surge of the ground reality.

Second, the priority that was given to the legal rather than public relations concerns was a myopic move. Constrained by liability concerns, Carbide's participation in the relief operation was haphazard, thus further reinforcing the image of it being a callous MNC resisting payout to victims of a horrific disaster in a third-world country.

Third, adopting an unequivocal position on safety standards left little room for possible future failure and shot Carbide's credibility further when a leakage occurred at the

Institute plant eight months after Bhopal ("Credibility, planning keys," 1996). The bolstering strategies used with U.S. and global publics and with stockholders did not work out. Strategies adopted to restore image in the eyes of U.S. and global publics backfired, since denial and distancing only served to highlight the MNC's self-preservation motivations.

On the positive side, immediate expression of grief was a good bolstering move, as was the corrective rhetoric. But the gradual denial as the battle continued, and the attack and distancing strategies adopted with the Indian government and other publics, backfired. Another wise strategy was to involve the chemical industry and gain the support of allies with similar concerns. Leaving everyday consumers of its commercial products out of the picture was also a good move, since there was no need to inflame publics that did not directly associate the products they used with the Carbide name.

Tactics

Once again, Carbide's tactics did not communicate well in local languages or with local publics. They also failed to conduct ground-level media relations. It did not adequately publicize the aid it was providing at ground zero. Reliable emergency communication networks should have been established with all stakeholders, immediately following the crisis.

Evaluation

Effective evaluation was not possible since no pre-crisis benchmarks of public opinion were available. In addition, the haphazard nature of the post-crisis efforts did not make thorough evaluation in the areas of public opinion and media relations possible. A Harris poll after the crisis (Benoit, 1995) indicated that U.S. publics largely held Carbide's management (U.S. and Indian) responsible, rather than the Indian employees and the Indian government.

Measuring components of its crisis communication efforts, however haphazard, would have helped Carbide better track shifting public opinion among its various global as well as local publics. Ongoing monitoring and survey of employees, shareholders, local groups, and victims as well as press coverage might have provided the crisis management team with a better understanding of the situation as the narrative of the disaster unfolded.

To conclude in the words of Benoit (1995), the refusal to take full moral responsibility for the disaster was Carbide's key mistake. Mortification was necessary, since no amount of rationalizing rhetoric can correct a crisis that caused and continues to cause such intense human suffering. Also, from an international public relations standpoint, we would like to add that an MNC with diverse cultural publics can never afford to bypass the local in a crisis situation, since it is the local that provides sense-making data to the global.

DISCUSSION QUESTIONS

1. Any company that manufactures herbicides and pesticides should anticipate some kind of industrial accident. Imagine you are the public relations officer for Union Carbide's plant in Bhopal prior to the accident. What research would you have conducted to prepare for an industrial accident? What information would you need? How would you have gathered that information?

2. Again imagine you are the public relations officer for the Union Carbide plant in Bhopal prior to the accident. What information or materials would you have available to use in the event of an accident?

3. Many people in the United States who heard about the toxic leak in Bhopal assumed the city was a small and rural village. Why do you think that is true? Did that impression have anything to do with Union Carbide's initial response?

4. On what public did Union Carbide focus its initial efforts? Why do you think they selected that public?

5. Why do you believe Carbide had a good reputation prior to the accident? What research would you conduct to determine the reason for this reputation?

6. Was the public relations objective of Carbide identified in this case report a good objective? Why or why not?

7. Did Carbide have multiple public relations objectives? Did it have different and unique target publics?

8. Is it possible that Carbide did not fail to consider the needs of Indian publics but rather consciously decided not to target those publics? What reasons do you think Carbide might have for consciously focusing on publics outside India?

9. What conflicts do you see between the legal objectives and public relations objectives of Carbide? How can these conflicts be rationalized, given the organizational goals of Carbide?

10. Are humanitarian and relationship-oriented objectives consistent with an organizational goal focused on profit and business success?

11. In a case like this one, is victim compensation a legitimate public relations objective? Is it a strategy or tactic that can be used to meet some other more appropriate public relations objective?

12. In this case, is evaluation really impossible? Assume you have been assigned to create an evaluation plan. What objective would you use? What research would you do to determine if your objective has been met?

REFERENCES AND SUGGESTED READINGS

Bardhan, N., & Patwardhan, P. (2003, November). *Striking a niche between reaching out and reaching in: Multinational corporations and public relations in a historically resistant host culture.* Paper presented at the National Communication Association Convention, Public Relations Division, Miami Beach, Fla.

Bardhan, N., & Sriramesh, K. (2004). Public relations in India: A profession in transition. In K. Sriramesh (Ed.), *Public relations in Asia* (pp. 62–95). Singapore: Thomson Press.

Begley, R., & Coeyman, M. (1994). After Bhopal: A CMA 'war room,' new programs, and changed habits. *Chemical Week, 155*(22), 32–34.

Benoit, W. (1995). Accounts, excuses and apologies: A theory of image restoration strategies. Albany, NY: SUNY Press.

Botan, C. (1992). International public relations: Critique and reformulation. *Public Relations Review, 18*(2), 149–159.

Browning, J. B. (1993). Union Carbide: Disaster at Bhopal. In J. A. Gottschalk (Ed.), *Crisis response: Inside stories on managing under siege.* Detroit, MI: Visible Ink Press. Retrieved from www.bhopal.com.

Cassels, J. (1993). *The uncertain promise of law: Lessons from Bhopal.* Canada: University of Toronto Press Inc.

Coombs, T., & Holladay, S. (2001). An extended examination of the crisis situations: A fusion of the relational management and symbolic approaches. *Journal of Public Relations Research, 13*(4), 321–340.

Credibility, planning keys to crisis communications. (1996). *Occupational Hazards, 58*(5), 98–99.

Esman, M. J. (1972). The elements in institution building. In J. W. Eaton (Ed.), *Institution building and development* (pp. 19–40.). Beverly Hills, CA: Sage.

Sen, F., & Egelhoff, W. G. (1991). Six years and counting: Learning from crisis management at Bhopal. *Public Relations Review, 17*(1), 69–83.

Grunig, J. E., & Hunt, C. (1984). *Managing public relations.* New York: Holt, Rinehart & Winston.

Heath, R. (1997). *Strategic issues management.* Thousand Oaks, CA: Sage.

Heath, R., & Palenchar, M. (2000). Community relations and risk communication: A longitudinal study of the impact of emergency response messages. *Journal of Public Relations Research, 12*(2), 131–161.

Ice, R. (1991). Corporate politics and rhetorical strategies: The case of Union Carbide's Bhopal crisis. *Management Communications Quarterly, 4*(3), 341–362.

Kalelkar, A. S. (1998, May). *Investigation of large-magnitude incidents: Bhopal as a case study.* Paper presented at The Institution of Chemical Engineers Conference on Preventing Major Chemical Accidents, London, England.

Kendall, R. (1996). *Public relations campaign strategies* (2nd ed.). New York: Harper Collins College Publishers.

Laughlin, K. (1996). Representing Bhopal. In G. Marcus (Ed.), *Connected engagements with the media* (pp. 221–246). Chicago, IL: University of Chicago Press.

Mitroff, I. I. (1994). Crisis Management and environmentalism: A natural fit. *California Management Review, Winter,* 101–113.

Morley, M. (1998). *How to manage your global reputation.* New York: New York University Press.

Sardana, C. K. (Ed.). (1999). *Applied public relations in the Indian context.* New Delhi: Har-Anand Publications Pvt. Ltd.

Seeger, M., Sellnow, T., & Ulmer, R. (2001). Public relations and crisis communication: Organizing and chaos. In R. Heath (Ed.), *Handbook of public relations* (pp. 155–165). Thousand Oaks, CA: Sage.

Shrivastava, P. (1987). *Bhopal: Anatomy of a crisis.* Cambrige, MA: Ballinger Publishing Company.

Shirvastava, P. (1989). Managing the crisis at Bhopal. In U. Rosenthal et al. (Eds.), *Coping with crises: The management of disasters, riots and terrorism.* New York: Industrial Crisis Institute Inc.

Shirvastava, P. (1995). Industrial/Environmental crises and corporate social responsibility. *Journal of Socio-Economics, 24*(1), 211–227.

The reason for disasters. (2002, February). *Business India.* EBSCO Publishing item number 2W81132942916.

Union Carbide's name takes a beating. (1984, December). *Business Week,* 2875, pp. 40.

Wilson, L. (1990). Corporate issues management: An international view. *Public Relations Review, 16*(1), 40–51.

10 Developing and Maintaining the Aljazeera Websites

PHILIP J. AUTER

Executive Summary

Established in 1996, Aljazeera's Arabic satellite news service has had a short, but meteoric history. Although initially fully funded by the government of Qatar, the channel differentiated itself from state-run news services in that it followed a Western journalism model by covering stories of interest to Arab viewers in a way that attempted to represent all sides of an issue. This objective approach, along with faster paced video and programming style, resulted in Aljazeera quickly becoming one of the most popular channels in the Arab world and with Arab-speaking people worldwide.

Five years after its inception, Aljazeera created a companion Arabic website (www.aljazeera.net), effectively increasing its reach to any reader of Arabic with Internet access worldwide. In addition to stories and photos, the website initially attempted to provide free streaming video of the TV channel, briefly abandoned that service, and now has gone to a subscription video streaming service. There have also been several abortive attempts to launch an English version of the website that would thus expand the Aljazeera audience beyond the realm of Arab-speaking peoples. Several of these attempts were sabotaged by hackers, while others never quite got off the ground. Finally, in the autumn of 2003, the English website (http://english.aljazeera.net) was born, but to less than critical acclaim.

While a fairly stable entity, Aljazeera.net has faced a number of challenges over its short history. Some mirror those of the parent organization, such as criticisms from many governments about its reporting as well as struggles to move to an advertiser-funded model. Other problems have been unique to the web experience, including difficulties with video streaming, hacker attacks, and the challenges of developing a foreign language (English) version of the site.

This case study will review the past, current status, and future prospects of Aljazeera's companion websites from a public relations perspective. It will deal with the website's startup, its link to Aljazeera TV, the difficulties with video streaming, and the challenges with the English website.

Research

What is commonly known as the "Arab World" is a region that stretches from the shores of the Atlantic to the Persian Gulf and consists of 22 nations. Broadcast media came to the region relatively late, with many Arab countries about 20 years behind the West in the development and distribution of broadcast radio and television. In the 1970s, television systems in the Arab world were constrained by three major problems. First, the insufficient local program production led to external program importation, mainly from the United States and Western Europe. Second, close government scrutiny and control led to prohibitive working environments. Finally, shortages in human and financial resources led to dull and low-quality local programming.

News on these predominantly state-run TV channels has been until recently characterized as particularly lackluster and consisting of "protocol news" heavily laden with government propaganda. News gathering and reporting—as defined in the Western sense—were not central to the government-run newscast model. The primary purposes of such news organizations were to improve dissemination of information about national government, and to control access to and formatting of incoming foreign news. Newscast formats were bland and monolithic in both content and delivery. Political news dealing with leadership speeches, official visits, and protocol activities was always topping Arab world TV news agendas. In many cases, video of state events essentially unedited with no commentary or detailed moment-by-moment breakdowns of a ruler's event schedule would be the primary focus of such "news." Anchors were essentially readers, and a newscast generally consisted of long items dealing with leadership news and short items dealing with regional and international developments. TV's visual potential was used in a very limited fashion and news "packages" were not used at all.

In the 1980s, however, advances in satellite and telecommunication technologies gave rise to a direct broadcast satellite revolution in the region. Arabs both rich and poor obtained satellite dishes (even in countries where they were banned), and used them to tap into global media satellite broadcasts that were beyond the direct control of their countries' governments. Faced with the competition of international television news that had been so carefully censored in the past, Arab governments determined that it would be better for them to compete by creating their own satellite channels or bringing their broadcast operations over to direct broadcast satellite. This created the added benefit—and challenge—of most state-run Arab media that have become transnational: crossing regional borders. This created an interesting phenomenon that promised to disturb power dynamics and public opinion in the region. Although government-run TV had now achieved the technology to get their message on the same dish as their global competitors, their television news was still predominantly used for propaganda. Most investment was in technologies, but some channels began to establish networks of reporters and correspondents.

As a result, many Arab viewers began to see several types of direct broadcast channels available on their satellite dishes: those that belonged directly to their home government, broadcasts from other governments, and ones considered to be privately controlled. The face of Arab television news was changing, and at the forefront of this change was Aljazeera Television.

The home of Aljazeera is the small Gulf State of Qatar. Although Qatar is a member of the Gulf Cooperation Council (GCC), its constitutional monarchy has a more liberal political system than other countries in the Gulf States. Government control of media has varied since the establishment of the monarchy. The Department of Information was created in 1969. It was replaced by the Ministry of Information and Culture in 1972. In 1975, a separate department was added to the ministry, the Qatar News Agency. The Press and Publication Law, which is considered the first official censorship from the government to control the media and population, was issued in Qatar in 1979. It was aimed at regulating the relationship between the state and press establishment, printing, publishing and distributing houses, libraries, bookshops, artistic production sales outlets, and publicity and advertisement agencies. For example, the law banned many newspapers and books from access to the country because they did not agree with the government's political, economic, or religious perspective.

In 1995, while the Emir of Qatar, Shaykh Khalifa bin Hamad ath-Thani, was visiting Geneva, he was deposed by his 45-year-old son, Shaykh Hamadi bin Khalifa ath-Thani, in a bloodless coup. The new emir ushered in a wave of liberalizations in government and society. Censorship was essentially lifted in 1995 when a new, much more liberal, Press and Publications Law was enacted, a law that is periodically reviewed and updated even today.

Aljazeera satellite TV was started in 1996 with an initial government grant (the equivalent of $U.S. 137 million) and the mission to speak out to Arab people and provide the many sides of stories that affect the Arab World. Despite its government funding, Aljazeera worked under a clear mandate of freedom of speech. The climate in which it worked became even more favorable when Qatar abolished the Ministry of Information and Culture in 1998. The nation now has both government-sponsored and privately owned newspapers, radio, and TV.

In November 1996, Aljazeera was introduced in Qatar as the first Arab all-news and public affairs satellite channel. Although initially funded by the Qatari government, with only a small amount of revenue coming from advertisers and subscribers, the network has grown by leaps and bounds. Aljazeera quickly became the most popular TV news channel of Arab people in the region and world-wide, stealing Arab television audiences from every one of the big television powers in the region. Few in the West had heard of Aljazeera, which operates from cramped and heavily fortified studios in the outskirts of Doha. But when the station started broadcasting video statements by Osama bin Laden and became the only foreign network to broadcast from inside the Taliban, who controlled Afghanistan, its name became familiar throughout the world. In 2001, the network had an estimated 40 million viewers, including 150,000 Americans. After the start of the U.S.-led war with Iraq, Aljazeera saw its European subscriber numbers double almost overnight.

Aljazeera's popularity was due in part to several major breaks from the formatting of traditional Arab TV news programming: a more objective, dual-sided approach to news coverage; more video of events and the people that were affected; and a much greater reliance on regularly featured anchors and reporters—all characteristics of the BBC and other Western media on which it was modeled. Western-trained newscasters and producers use video and slick graphics and emphasize fast-paced, sleek deliveries on the part of anchors and regularly featured correspondents. Whenever possible, video—often live—of events and the people they happen to are emphasized. The network also features many talk shows, hosted by regular personalities, that cover controversial topics and invite guests of varying opinions. News and programs such as these have led Aljazeera to captivate a growing number of viewers. The network has soared in popularity in a region accustomed to state-controlled news.

Aljazeera has become very popular by modeling much of its format on Western news outlets such as BBC and CNN. Viewers cannot seem to get enough of the channel. In understanding how and why viewers use the channel, it is important to first review studies of Arab audience use of, and gratifications from, television.

As the network continues to replace government funding with advertiser sponsorship, it has faced several governmental challenges. First, despite claims of its hard-hitting, investigative approach to issues that affect the Arab World, critics have complained that Aljazeera rarely if ever trains its eye on the government and social structure of Qatar. While perhaps considering the sensibilities of its host/owner, as many Western media have also been accused of doing with their own, it has indeed angered many governments in the Middle East, considering the needs of its viewers above maintaining good relations with regional leaders. Leaders and governments that often have significant persuasive pull on Arab businesses that may—or may not—advertise on Aljazeera.

In many respects, Aljazeera seems to have taken into consideration the cultural sensitivities of the "Arab Street"—the average person in most of these nations with access (often in coffee houses) to satellite TV news. A diverse tapestry of cultures and beliefs with several common threads running throughout, the Arab world is a mixture of beliefs, religions, and political positions. One of Aljazeera's catch phrases, to present "the opinion and the opposite opinion," addresses a common theme among viewers in different nations. Many had to rely in the past on state-run censored media that would only present the government opinion— supplemented by news from the West that seemed to take a decidedly Western spin on stories even when presenting both sides. Aljazeera's controversial style, which at times raised concerns with almost every Arab nation, was precisely its strongest tool in attracting its target audience.

Aljazeera was clearly addressing the needs and gratifications of its primary public— the Arab person in the street, hungry for uncensored news from the Arab point of view. Like most news organizations, it had been less successful in pleasing another one of its "publics," the governments and corporations that could affect significant sway over the company's profitability and even its very existence. Still, poised as it was at the crest of a successful satellite television run, Aljazeera was now prepared to extend its reach and influence through a companion news site on the World Wide Web (Figure 1).

Objective

From its inception, Aljazeera's organizational goal has been to provide the Arab world with an informative alternative to censored state-run media and also the news as provided by dominant western global players such as CNN and the BBC. Aljazeera's approach has at times angered governments in the Middle East and throughout the world. While this in many cases has impressed its core audience, it has often dissuaded secondary audiences, called into question the network's objectivity, and initially affected its ability to obtain support from Arab governments and advertising revenue from Arab businesses.

FIGURE 1   Aljazeera's Arabic Website

Source: Used with permission from Aljazeera.

Several complementary, but in some cases competing, issues surround Aljazeera's entry into the World Wide Web and its more recent attempt to expand from only an Arabic audience site to an English site as well. Its goal is to provide Arabic audiences worldwide greater access to news content developed by and for the network. It would also like to expand its advertiser base. The English version of the website is meant to expand their base further, bringing their brand of journalism to non-Arabic-speaking people around the world, but particularly those who speak English as their primary language, in the West.

From a news editorial perspective, these are challenging, worthwhile goals. From a public relations perspective, several conflicts arise with secondary objectives. The primary PR objective is to expand the reach of Aljazeera via the Arabic and later English websites, to provide Aljazeera's particular "take" on the news to a larger global audience as a supplement to the globally distributed satellite television news network.

Secondary objectives included (1) to provide a companion website to the TV network that would both enhance audience experiences and drive traffic to the station, (2) make a live video stream of Aljazeera's television programming freely available via the Internet, increasing overall program audience, (3) develop a new medium in which to expand their advertising revenue opportunities, and (4) branch out into English content to further expand their audience base beyond Arabic-speaking people (Figure 2).

Strategies

Aljazeera launched a companion website (www.aljazeera.net) in Arabic in January of 2001 with almost immediate plans to launch a companion English site. More than 25 people were hired from a number of reputable regional media institutions to staff the website. They were trained to work online and put to work in five different departments: editorial, research and studies, monitoring and analysis, multimedia, and e-marketing. The original staff of the Aljazeera website grew to 60 persons independent of the television news personnel. Of these, 36 were editors, journalists, and researchers. Over the past two years, the organization has grown to about 150 professionals—including the news staff of the English website.

Aljazeera partnered with iHorizons (www.ihorizons.com), an Internet and e-business content manager founded in Qatar in 1994 to build its Arabic news site. The company's server software is designed to allow businesses to easily take existing content and modify it for the web and also to create new content for a site such as user chat rooms and polling. iHorizons personnel trained Aljazeera's website news staff on the Arabic-language-based interface, and the website team began building a rich, multimedia news portal.

As an internal department of the Aljazeera Satellite Channel, advertising on the website is separate from that on the news service and is handled by the E-Marketing Department. In addition to advertising packages, which include banner ads, sponsorship banners, and newsletter ads, the department offers clients other services: (1) syndication of Aljazeera content, (2) Aljazeera.net short messages service (SMS) to cell phones, (3) Aljazeera news via phone, (4) streaming video, (5) interactive financial services, and (6) a tourism page.

Although it was popular with Arabic reading audiences from its inception, the website's popularity doubled after September 11—jumping from about 700,000 page views a day to about 1.2 million page views, with more than 40 percent of them from the United States. Popularity of the site increased, from 3 million hits per day during the initial phases of the Afghanistan war to over 10 million hits per day by late 2002. Aljazeera.net ranks top in the Arab World and as tensions in the Middle East mount and the website's reputation grows, its popularity has skyrocketed to more than 811 million page views and 161 million visits in 2002 alone.

One of the popular features of the original website was the live streaming video of the channels' programs. This service was initially offered for free, but was limited to a relatively

FIGURE 2   Aljazeera's English-Language Website

Source: Used with permission from Aljazeera.

small number of simultaneous viewers. Particularly in times of great news interest, potential web-based viewers of the streaming video were almost never able to connect. To improve the quality and allow more people to enjoy the service, an external company (www.jumptv.com) was appointed to develop and present it to the online audience worldwide, on a subscription basis. In addition to program scripts, the station still offers many free streaming audio and a few video clips of stories that previously aired on the channel.

The English Website

In part due to the enormous number of requests that began to come in after the network and website's coverage of the war in Afghanistan, management decided to launch an English website, often the only alternative look at news shaping the world for non-Arabic readers, particularly in the West.

Initially, English.aljazeera.net was supposed to launch in late March of 2003, and hosted by the U.S. company DataPipe (www.datapipe.com). The site, which was very streamlined in content, was almost immediately shut down by intense hacking attacks. Some were in the form of "denial of service," which blocked users from accessing the site since its host had been inundated with so much junk e-mail and partial computing code that the system overloaded. Additionally, their domain name (along with that of the Arabic site) were "hijacked" so that users would be redirected to U.S. patriotic slogan pages or to porn sites.

While Aljazeera worked to alleviate these problems, many of their Western partners dropped out of the venture—some claim due to political pressure from the U.S. government and some American citizens. DataPipe gave notice as the website's host. Later, U.S.- based Akamai Technologies (www.akamai.com), a company that claims its servers can stand up to unprecedented traffic, signed on to host the English site—but promptly pulled out of the deal for unspecified reasons. Additionally, some companies like "Yahoo!" declined to carry ads for the Aljazeera programming and websites, citing concerns about sensitivities over the war in Iraq.

The site was up and down several times, in great part due to an aggressive attack by hackers. Eventually, the site found a new host, but until the situation was resolved, it stayed offline until the fall of 2003 when it reappeared to little fanfare and some criticism.

With the establishment of the English website, and at some time in the future possibly an English audio translation with the satellite news feed, Aljazeera faces a challenge in trying to attract a new target audience without disenfranchising its existing audience. News from the Arab perspective, if considered too inflammatory by Western readers, will result in the site being ignored by many English-reading individuals. Truly angry groups may attempt to hack the site, an approach that has been successful in the past. On the other hand, when the site debuted again in the fall of 2003, it was criticized by many who like the original Aljazeera site; they feel it was watered down and is lackluster—not a true representation of news from the Arab perspective. For a comparison, see the sites listed in Figure 3.

FIGURE 3   Compare These International News Websites

The Aljazeera websites in English and Arabic are said to mirror the reporting style of the United Kingdom's BBC. Compare them to BBC coverage and CNN coverage from the United States.

    Aljazeera (Arabic)   www.aljazeera.net

    Aljazeera (English)   http://english.aljazeera.net

    BBC   www.bbc.co.uk/

    CNN   www.cnn.com

Tactics

The Arabic Website

The Arabic Aljazeera website covers news, sports, entertainment, technology, health, arts, and culture throughout the Middle East and around the world. Content is available as text, still images, audio files, and video clips. Live streaming audio fed from the network— once freely available on the website—is now a pay service available through Jump TV (www. jumptv.com). This change was made because the original free service was unable to handle the crush of interested viewers and Aljazeera could not afford to put more resources into this free service.

The website presents in-depth analysis, special coverage, book reviews, marketing, and advertising. It also offers user interactivity options, such as quick vote and discussion forums where users can express their opinions directly without censorship. The website originally provided the full script of Aljazeera Satellite Channel's main programs, attached with its audio file within 24 to 36 hours from the time of the first broadcasting. While much of the content on the web is the same as the TV programming, as with most TV news websites, the service provides somewhat different and sometimes additional content to the satellite channel. Like its parent television channel, Aljazeera.net's focus on war has increased with the increased fighting in the Middle East. Also like the satellite news channel, it has often angered governments and "secondary audiences" with its graphic representations as well as a journalistic approach that its detractors claim is unbalanced.

Like the satellite news channel, Aljazeera.net has often angered Arab country leaders with the type of content that it published on the website. Initially praised by the United States as a beacon of free expression in the Arab World, its reputation with U.S. government officials changed when the network began airing tapes of Osama Bin Laden and the website printed graphic pictures of the negative effects of the U.S.-lead wars in Afghanistan and Iraq on citizens of the region.

The English Website

The initial content of the English website—the first time it was launched—was very rudimentary. The level of news coverage and content was nowhere near the amount available on the Arabic site because English.aljazeera.net was a new venture and the organization's resources were already stretched due to its increasing popularity as a result of interest in the Iraq war. Consequently, during the site's brief history, it limited itself to limited text and still photo coverage of the Iraq war.

The focus of the site was somewhat unclear at first. There was a stated goal to "bridge the gap" between news as presented in the Arab world and in the West. It was not destined to be a site, however, that offered full English translations of all stories on the Aljazeera.net website or satellite news channel. Although the amount of content carried was dramatically less that the Arabic site, the graphic photos of wounded civilians and wounded and captured U.S. soldiers displayed on both sites resulted in a hacker backlash against the Aljazeera sites.

When the site returned, first abortively in March of 2003 and then later in the autumn of the same year, it was greeted with lukewarm praise. With hacker and server problems settled, the staff was able to focus on increasing the quantity and quality of the content. Complaints were raised by critics because its initial second launch consisted mostly of wire stories obtained from other services and a few in-house stories that were not well received by reviewers. Still, the site has slowly built up and now provides a significant amount of original news and opinion—though much less that the Arabic site does. A polling feature exists, and some of the Arabic site content is translated and used, but stories featured on the site do differ in many cases from the Arabic content. Multimedia content has yet to be incorporated. Stories tend to focus or frame events in a perspective that differs from most Western news media and often times english.aljazeera.net carries stories that Western media do not. The site walks a difficult line between presenting the news from an Arab perspective and alienating much of its English-reading potential audience with its particular editorial slant.

Evaluation

The Arabic Website

Despite difficulties branching out into the English reading audience, Aljazeera has clearly established a strong following among Arabic reading people worldwide. Many new findings about Aljazeera's primary audience have been revealed as a result of an online Arabic survey conduced in the fall of 2002. The management of Aljazeera's website allowed for an 80-item Arabic survey developed by a Qatari masters student and his professors in the United States to be made available through Aljazeera.net's homepage. The original intent was to leave the survey up for at least a month, but response was so great that over 5,300 useable responses were obtained in a two-week period from August 20, 2002, to September 4, 2002. At that point, the survey was pulled down and the data analyzed. It is important to note that while this information can help to provide valuable insight into the Aljazeera online audience, it was a one-time sample and was taken prior to the war in Iraq.

    Findings were in some cases confirmatory of expectations about the audience and in some cases quite surprising. Respondents hailed from over 120 individual countries around the world; however, the majority, nearly 25 percent of the sample, lived in Saudi Arabia ($n = 1,215$, 22.6%) at the time they responded to the survey. The next largest groups of respondents lived in the United States ($n = 386$, 7.2%), the United Arab Emirates ($n = 356$, 6.6%), Jordan ($n = 304$, 5.7%), Syria ($n = 265$, 5%), Egypt ($n = 238$, 4.4%), and the Palestinian territories ($n = 206$, 3.8%). Interestingly, only 106 respondents (2%) resided in Qatar, Al-Jazeera TV's home. Slightly over half ($n = 2,879$, 53.5%) of the sample lived in the country they were originally from, while the remainder lived abroad ($n = 2,500$, 46.5%). The vast majority of the sample ($n = 4,972$, 92.4%) were originally from one of the 22 Arab world countries. Of those originally from an Arabian nation, 3,690 (74.2%) were still living in the Arab world at the time of the survey. At the time of the study, 70.3 percent ($n = 3,782$) of the entire sample lived in the Arab world—nations where the predominant language is Arabic (Hejleh, 2001)—regardless of where they were originally from.

    Although ages ranged from 18 to 65 plus, the vast majority ranged between 18 and 35, with male respondents surpassing females by 10 to one. They were about equally split between single and married, with almost none widowed or divorced. The overwhelming majority of the sample was Muslim (96.5%), with only a very limited number of Christians,

Jewish, and other faiths and belief systems. Half of the group surveyed considered themselves to be politically and socially moderate, with only a few considering themselves to be extremely liberal or conservative within the context of their culture. Most had an advanced education, with at least the equivalent of a bachelor's. Many had pursued advanced degrees as well. The majority of the participants (35.9%) had an annual household income equivalent to less than $U.S. 15,000 although another 30.4% made between $U.S. 15,000 and $U.S. 35,000 per year. Income varies widely in the Arab world and with the Arab Diaspora, depending greatly on the country in which they live.

The survey found that the amount of time spent with the Aljazeera website was directly related to fulfilling socialization as well as news-gathering needs. Web users consider the site to be extremely credible. Interestingly, users living inside the Arab World—but not necessarily within their own nation of origin—developed stronger socialization feelings for the service than did those living outside the Middle East.

Aljazeera.net has clearly met its objectives in developing and maintaining a rich, multimedia website offering news and opinion from an Arab perspective, but free of regional governmental censorship restrictions. Its success can be seen in the large and demographically diverse pool of Arabic users as well as the many satellite channels and companion websites that have begun to imitate Aljazeera's style.

The English Website

While the Arabic Aljazeera website seems to be a stunning success, the jury is still out on the English Aljazeera website. The site faces unique challenges in trying to speak to an English-language public about news and information from an Arab world perspective. If the quality and quantity of content continue to expand to match that of the parent website, the audience may continue to grow. However the overarching question that remains is, will English-language audiences accept this non-Western perspective to news and information? And if not, will english.aljazeera.net be subsidized by the parent company and the Qatari government, or will it simply become an interesting but failed experiment in cross-cultural journalism?

Critique

While reading this critique of this campaign, keep in mind that the campaign to expand the reach of Aljazeera targets multiple publics in several very different cultures. Because of this diversity, both campaign planning research and evaluation research are very difficult.

Research

The research presented is limited to descriptions of the history of broadcasting in the Arab world and the development of Aljazeera. Questions that should have been asked and answered before developing a campaign include:

1. Who are the potential target publics for this campaign? Specifically, what group of people now watches Aljazeera and what groups might be motivated to watch Aljazeera?

What businesses now advertise on Aljazeera and what businesses might be induced to advertise there?

2. What are the demographics of Aljazeera's existing and potential audiences? Where do they live? What language(s) do they speak? How well educated are they? Are they literate in English, Arabic, or both?

3. What are the existing attitudes in the target publics toward news coverage? Are they really "hungry for uncensored news" or do they only want news consistent with their worldview? What is their worldview?

4. Do members of the target publics have Internet access? Where do they access the Internet—in schools, offices, homes, or cyber cafes?

5. What media reach the target publics? Will those media carry messages encouraging people to visit the Aljazeera websites or to view Aljazeera broadcasts? What media do members of the target public evaluate as credible?

6. Finally, who watched Aljazeera before the introduction of the website? How large was its audience and what were the audience demographics and psychographics?

Reliable and valid measurement of the existing and potential audiences was essential to designing a potentially successful campaign to expand the reach of Aljazeera. Further, identification and analysis of existing media should have preceded any selection of strategies or tactics.

Objective

The organizational goals were to "provide the Arab World with alternative media and to provide Arab audiences with access to news content developed by and for the network." These goals are too broad and vague to provide much campaign guidance. The lack of specificity in the goals also makes it difficult to judge whether any particular public relations objective can advance those goals.

The public relations objective here is to expand the reach of Aljazeera via the Arabic and English websites. This objective could be met if only one additional member of the target public viewed Aljazeera because of its websites. In short, it provides too little guidance to help those planning the campaign and it lacks the detail needed to facilitate evaluation of the campaign.

Strategies

The action strategies reported here focus on the launching of the Arabic website in 2001 and the English website in 2003. These are completely appropriate. Unless the client takes the action of launching the websites, it obviously will be impossible to exercise communication strategies to use those websites to expand the reach of Aljazeera.

The communication strategies, on the other hand, are limited to describing problems associated with the action strategies. Communication strategies should include some description of what messages can be delivered to what publics in order to accomplish the campaign's objectives. Here we simply are not told how members of the target public were informed of the websites. This weakness may be the result of the lack of research on what media are available to the target publics and what messages might motivate those publics. It is also possible the campaign planners simply had no communication strategy. In other words, the campaign planners may never have adopted any strategy to tell the target publics about the websites.

Tactics

The campaign's tactics, like its communication strategies, focus on the content of the website. Of course it is critical that the content of a website keep visitors returning. But a new audience cannot be motivated to attend to a medium by the content of that medium. People in the target public must hear of the website from another source, and something in that other source must motivate them to visit the Aljazeera website.

This campaign failed to adopt any procedure for motivating members of its publics to make their first visit the Aljazeera website.

Evaluation

The survey presented as evaluation shows that Aljazeera has a large audience and identifies some demographics of that audience. The fact that the survey respondents in the evaluation research are all self-selected volunteers raises serious questions about the reliability and validity of the results, but this is not the major problem with the evaluation. The most significant problem with the evaluation research is that it does not evaluate whether the public relations objective was met. The public relations objective was "to expand the reach of Aljazeera via the Arabic and English websites." To measure whether the reach of Aljazeera has expanded, one would need a baseline measure of its reach prior to the introduction of the websites. To prove the campaign expanded the reach, a second survey or measure would be needed to show that the number of viewers had actually increased. The evaluation here lacks such a measurement of increased audience. Further, the survey was administered only through the Arabic website. It does not provide any measure at all of the audience or effect of the English website.

DISCUSSION QUESTIONS

1. In the research section of the critique, several research questions are listed. Describe how research could be designed to answer each of those questions.

2. There are several nations, cultures, and governments in the Arab world. Pick one of those cultures or countries and research its values and attitudes toward news coverage. Based on your research, describe what messages you believe would motivate citizens there to watch Aljazeera.

3. In many parts of the Arab world, individual communication or word-of-mouth is the major source of information. Describe some tactics that could be used in such a culture to disseminate information about Aljazeera.

4. Assuming that the objective of a public relations campaign is to increase the audience for Aljazeera in the United States, write a complete public relations objective that could be used to guide the planning and evaluation of such a campaign.

5. Visit the English language Aljazeera website and the BBC website. Does it appear to you that the Aljazeera coverage and the BBC coverage are based on the same model of a "dual-sided" approach to news coverage? If you agree, describe the similarities in the two site's approach to coverage. If you do not agree, describe the differences in the two sites' approach to coverage.

6. Describe how you would evaluate the success of a campaign whose public relations objective was to use the Aljazeera websites to expand the reach of Aljazeera broadcasting. Be sure to operationalize all the variables you would use in any evaluation research.

REFERENCES AND SUGGESTED READINGS

Aljazeera Web site. (2002, December). *Aljazeera Net celebrates its first year.* Retrieved from www.aljazeera.net.

Al-Jaber, Khaled (2002). *The uses and gratifications and media credibility theories applied to Arab broadcasting: The case of Aljazeera.* Unpublished master's thesis. Pensacola, FL: The University of West Florida.

Al-Makaty, S., Boyd, D., & Van Tubergen, N. (1994). Source credibility during the Gulf War: A Q-study of rural and urban Saudi Arabian citizens. *Journalism Quarterly, 71,* 55–63.

Al-Tamimi, E. (1995). *Mass media and development in the state of Qatar.* Unpublished doctoral dissertation, Boston University.

Alterman, J. (1998). *New media, new politics: From satellite television to the Internet in the Arab world.* The Washington Institute for Near East policy.

Al Wakeel, D. (2002, July 3). Arab world must work together to achieve self-sufficiency. *Jordan Times.* Retrieved from www.jordanembassyus.org/07032002003.htm.

Arafa, M., Auter, P. J., & Al-Jaber, K. (2003, August). *Instrumental vs. ritualized use of Arab satellite television.* Paper presented at the Association of Educations in Journalism and Mass Communication convention, Kansas City, MO.

Arafa, M., & Auter, P. J. (2003, August). *Audience perceptions of Aljazeera TV.* Panel presentation at the Association for Educators in Journalism and Mass Communication annual convention, Kansas City, MO.

Auter, P. J., & Al-Jaber, K. (2003). Qatar media/Aljazeera TV. In D. DesJardins (Ed.), *World press encyclopedia, 2nd ed.* Farmington Hills, MI: Gale Group.

Auter, P. J., Arafa, M., & Al-Jaber, K. (2003). *Identifying with Arabic journalists: How Aljazeera tapped parasocial interaction gratifications in the Arab World.* Paper presented at the Arab-USA Communication Education (AUSACE) conference, Dubai, United Arab Emirates, October 12–15.

Ayish, M. I. (2002). Political communication on Arab world television: Evolving patterns. *Political Communication, 19*(2), 137–154.

Ayish, M. I. (2001, Spring). American-style journalism and Arab World television: An exploratory study of news selection at six Arab World satellite television channels. *Transnational Broadcasting Studies.* Retrieved from www.tbsjournal.com/Archives/Spring01/Ayish.html.

Boyd, D. (1972). *An historical and descriptive analysis of the evolution and development of Saudi Arabian television, 1963–1972.* Unpublished doctoral dissertation, University of Minnesota, Minneapolis.

Boyd, D. (1999). *Broadcasting in the Arab World: A survey of the electronic media in the Middle East.* Ames: Iowa State University Press.

Cable News Network. (2001, November 6). *Aljazeera presents Arabic view of war.* Retrieved from www.cnn.com.

Campagna, J. (2001). *Between two worlds: Qatar Aljazeera satellite channel faces conflicting expectation.* Retrieved from www.cpj.org/Briefings/2001/Al-Jazeera_oct01/Al-Jazeera_oct01.html.

Cozens, C. (2003, March 25). Europeans flock to Aljazeera. *MediaGuardian.co.uk.* Retrieved from http://media.guardian.co.uk/broadcast/story/0,7493,921693,00.html.

el'Nawawy, M., & Iskandar, A. (2002). *Al Jazeera: How the free Arab news network scooped the world and changed the Middle East.* Westview Press.

Ghareeb, E. (2000, Summer). New media and the information revolution in the Arab World: An assessment. *Middle East Journal, 54,* 395–418.

Hejleh, M. (2003). The countries and people of Arabia. Retrieved from www.hejleh.com/countries/.

Higgins, J. (2002). Aljazeera media pariah or pioneer? *Satellite Broadband.* Retrieved from http://the broadbandeconomy.com/ar/broadband_aljazeera_media_pariah.

Jones, B. (2003, March 1). All that Aljazeera voice for freedom. *World on the Web, 18*(8). Retrieved from www.worldmag.com/world/issue/03-01-03/cover_2.asp.

Kawach, N. (2002, January 27). UAE becomes second richest in the Arab world. *Gulf News Online Edition.* Retrieved from www.gulfnews.com/Articles/print.asp?ArticleID=39103.

Sakr, N. (2000, Fall). Optical illusions: Television and censorship in the Arab World. Transnational Broadcasting Studies, 5. Retrieved from www.tbsjournal.com/Archives/Fall00/sakr1.htm.

Sampedro, V. (1998). Grounding the displaced: Local media reception in a transnational context. *Journal of Communication, 48*(2), 125–143.

Williams, D. (2001, October 13). Aljazeera ascends to world stage. *The Washington Post,* p. A22.

11

Improved Internal Communications in a Large South African Financial Services Organization

DERINA R. HOLTZHAUSEN

Executive Summary

The ABSA Group was created in South Africa by the merger of four banks. The name ABSA started out as an acronym for Amalgamated Banks of South Africa, but eventually was adopted as the full name for the organization. Following the merger, a communications audit of ABSA found poor internal communications and an autocratic corporate culture. The organization's executive consultant for internal communication used a general theory of public relations to develop an internal communications program. The strategies and tactics adopted in that program were designed to improve relationships between management and employees.

Research

Client

The ABSA Group, with its head office in Johannesburg, South Africa, is Africa's largest financial services organization with about 35,000 employees. The group came about after four commercial banks amalgamated at the beginning of the 1990s. This resulted in a complicated organizational structure, which consisted of 32 divisions, organized according to product, service, or region. Internal communication was made difficult not only because of the different cultures the respective banks brought to the group, but also because of geographic dispersion. Most of the divisions had their own head offices in Johannesburg, geographically separate from the corporate head office. In addition, each of the nine provinces of the country had a regional head office under the management of a regional CEO.

Communications Audit

A communications audit conducted in the organization during the first half of 1995 pointed to a number of communication problems typical of large, complex organizations (Miller,

1999). It was clear that a power distance existed between employees and managers, trust levels were low, and employees relied heavily on the grapevine for information.

The communication audit further indicated that the organization was using an asymmetrical model of public relations when communicating with its internal publics. The audit pointed to an autocratic, nonparticipative organizational culture, consistent with an asymmetric organizational worldview. Several other factors also attested to this worldview. For instance, the dominant coalition of the organization consisted of only men, with asymmetric, masculine worldviews, which resulted in a single, dominant cultural and gender perspective. As a result, fewer than 10 women were appointed to executive management level, despite the fact that women represented 70 percent of the work force. Press agentry was the dominant public relations model. Communication with employees emphasized media content, which resulted in the employment of technical public relations staff who had very little management input. Public relations was not part of the dominant coalition.

However, the highly threatening external environment of the organization, brought about by the political changes in the country, created the desire within the dominant coalition to change organizational behavior. A department responsible for transformation and process innovation was in place in the human resources division and was to work closely with a newly restructured internal communication department, created in 1995. The internal communication department also formed part of the group's human resources division, and the executive consultant appointed to head up the internal communication function was one of the executives who reported to the executive director responsible for group human resources. It was felt that such a senior position would be the only way to ensure real change in organizational culture and internal communication processes.

Available Resources

The internal communication department itself was very small, with only six staff members. However, each staff member was an expert in her field and had an adequate budget to make use of outside services such as production and design houses. The flagship of the department was *Abacus,* the internal bi-weekly newspaper. It was a full-color publication that was not afraid to take on sensitive issues. It also had a policy of publishing the results of internal surveys, such as the communication audit, even when it was not favorable to management. Another very powerful communications tool was the internal television news broadcast. The ABSA Group had its own internal television broadcasting facility and was able to use this for news and other information broadcasts, as well as for the group's continuous training needs. Banking halls and offices provided space for employees where they could watch television broadcasts.

However, as the communication audit indicated, the group had serious communication and information flow problems, despite these very progressive communication tools. Through focus group research it became apparent that middle management posed a huge problem. They viewed communication as a waste of time and would not allow employees to watch the television broadcasts because it took them away from their desks. Some managers even prohibited their employees from reading the *Abacus* at work. The newly appointed executive consultant for internal communication (an experienced public relations practitioner with a Ph.D.) had only two months to put a new internal communication policy on the table for it to be included in the corporate strategy for the 1996/97 financial year. She decided to use a general theory of public relations as proposed by Holtzhausen (1995) and Holtzhausen and Verwey (1996) as a diagnostic tool to determine the status of communication management in ABSA and as the basis for a new, more strategic internal communication design for the group (Figure 1).

Objectives

Following the research and based on the general theory of public relations, four objectives were identified. They were:

Objective 1: To establish and maintain a two-way symmetric communication process in ABSA to improve the relationship between management and employees by an improvement of communication levels from 55 percent to 75 percent.

Objective 2: To coordinate information in ABSA to ensure that all employees have access to the organizational media by improving viewership patterns from 27 percent to 50 percent.

Objective 3: To improve communication skills and communication management skills in the ABSA Group by training 100 percent of all consultants and champions and 50 percent of employees.

Objective 4: To establish and maintain communication as a transformation process in the group.

Strategy

As suggested in the Excellence model of the general theory (Figure 1), an internal communication strategy based on a symmetrical communication philosophy was proposed. This approach emphasized interpersonal and small group communication and equality in the communication relationship between all employees. A first draft of the strategy proposed three levels of design.

Macro-Level Design

This level of design included the following features:

- Group acceptance of an internal communication policy, based on symmetrical communication, and a three-year strategy
- Confirmation of internal communication roles and plans for each of the executive committee members (the highest management body in the organization) and the CEO
- Specific communication plans for other executive managers to help with the roll-out of the strategy and to gain support from middle management

FIGURE 1   General Theory of Public Relations

A general theory of public relations holds that public relations takes place at three levels in the organization and across the spectrum of persuasive to two-way symmetrical communication. The three levels are the following:

- the *macro* level, which involves strategic environmental management and particularly focuses on the communication role of executive managers
- the *meso* level, which involves strategic organizational management of the group communication function and focuses on how the function is organized
- the *micro* level, which involves strategic communication management and focuses in particular on communication and information flow between employees and their superiors

Three communication models are included in the general theory. They are:

1. An *excellence* model (as adopted from J. Grunig, 1992) that focuses on creating an environment conducive to two-way symmetrical public relations
2. a *persuasion* model that is practiced when organizations have asymmetric communication cultures and view public relations as a marketing function
3. a *mixed* model that is indicative of poor practitioner skills and education and is typified by confusing public relations practices

Holtzhausen (1995) argued that the excellence model was the most effective of the three models, particularly for internal communication, and as a result this model was adopted for the practice of internal communication in the ABSA Group.

Excellence Model

To briefly summarize, the excellence model, explained through its three levels, holds the following:

The Macro Level.   At the macro level it is important that the most senior managers in the organization support communication symmetry. This would be reflected through respect and tolerance for differences in culture and gender, support for a participative organizational culture, and a willingness to change. If senior managers did not support symmetrical communication at this level, the public relations practitioners would not be able to implement symmetrical communication practices in the organization.

The Meso Level.   The meso level refers to the management of the public relations function itself. The most senior public relations practitioner should strive for communication symmetry in every aspect of practice. This would mean less dependence on communication through media, and inclusion of interpersonal and small-group communication practices. This manager should also be well educated in public relations and communication management, should be part of the top management team, and should be group-goal oriented. The communication function should be practiced strategically and the practitioners should be boundary spanners who bring the opinions and needs of the organization's publics to the attention of organizational decision makers.

The Micro Level.   At the micro level the actual communication activities take place. Communication should be strategically focused on specific, key publics. Practitioners should have symmetric worldviews whereby communication leads to understanding and conflict resolution. Feedback from publics should always be used to change the organization and help it to adapt to its environment.

- Research to re-evaluate the role and use of the organizational media and their ability to assist with information dissemination. They should not be used to replace the communication responsibility of individuals.
- Internal communication should form part of specific organizational change processes, called *En Route to 2005* and *ABSA2,* and these processes should have their own internal communication strategies.
- A Strategic Communicators' Forum should be established to coordinate cross-functional information flow.
- Training courses in organizational communication management for strategic communicators and communication skills training for all employees should be designed and implemented.

Meso-Level Design

In addition to ensuring proper skills and management of the internal communication function, the meso-level design focused on creating a communication infrastructure that could roll out and implement the communication philosophy and strategy to the lowest levels of 'he organization. The design stressed the importance of a decentralized communication function for the organization and proposed the following:

- Each of the 31 divisions should appoint a communication consultant. Each cost center should democratically elect a person to act as the communication champion.
- The consultants and champions should coordinate information flow and implement programs to improve face-to-face communication through actions such as workplace forums, representation at management meetings, facilitation of higher visibility of managers, and conducting communication skills training. They also should address workplace-specific communication problems.
- There would be no formal job specifications for the consultants and champions because they needed to respond to the communication needs of their immediate work environment.
- Consultants and champions would be provided with training and should be offered many opportunities to network and discuss issues, problems, and solutions of mutual concern.

Micro-Level Design

In the spirit of the two-way symmetrical approach, the communication strategy was distributed as a draft document. For eight months the strategy was extensively communicated in management and employee forums, through work sessions and seminars with communication consultants, in the organization's print media, and through the interactive use of the in-house television network.

Inputs from all sessions and forums were used to adapt the strategy and accommodate feedback. After the eight-month consultation process, a final strategy based on the many inputs from employees at all levels was adopted.

After 10 months the process was adopted by 28 of the 31 divisions in the group, and communication consultants were in place in these divisions. In addition, the executive committee recognized the importance of the function and promoted the senior consultant responsible for internal communication to executive management level.

Tactics

The adoption of a group communication policy and three-year strategy was only the first step in the implementation process. The internal communication department had to ensure that the process remained high on the organization's agenda and was implemented correctly. At a special planning retreat the internal communication team decided on the first year's tactics. These were to be evaluated after a year for realignment or redesign. Each set of tactics is presented following a restatement of the objective those tactics were designed to support.

Objective 1: To establish and maintain a two-way symmetric communication process in ABSA to improve the relationship between management and employees by an improvement of communication levels from 55% to 75%. The following tactics supported this objective:

- Staff breakfasts and electronic seminars were set up with the members of the executive committee and the CEO. Each executive manager had his own strategic internal communication plan. The overall aim was to break down the power distance between these executives and employees at all levels. Small-group meetings were held in the regions and divisions for which these executives were responsible. Employees had the opportunity to give direct feedback and executives were often astounded with the perspectives of these employees. This frequently resulted in changes in corporate strategy and immediate response to employees' opinions.
- The development of regional and divisional communication strategies fostered through training of divisional and regional internal communication consultants. A well-known academic designed and delivered a special training course for this purpose. This improved the strategic planning skills of consultants and allow them to support the corporate internal communication strategy through regional and local strategies that address the needs of each region and division.
- Employees' key performance areas should include the proper management of communication. In this regard it was particularly conducive for the group internal communication function to be part of the corporate human resources division. This allowed direct access to and communication with the human resources consultants in regions and divisions, so they could assist with disseminating the relevant information to all people in supervisory positions. Key performance areas, or KPAs as they are popularly called, are the specific areas of responsibility negotiated between each employee and her or his supervisor. Supervisors had to discuss progress on these performance areas with each employee at the end of every quarter, allowing employees to get feedback on their performance. Including "communication" in these key performance areas proved to employees that management was serious about communication in the organization and that communication was viewed as a formal organizational

process, at the same level of importance as marketing, human resources, financial management, and other support functions.

- A booklet containing the ABSA internal communication policy was distributed to every employee. The booklet explained why internal communication was important for the future of the organization. The policy (ABSA, 1996) also stated and explained in detail what is meant by the following:
  - The ABSA group adopts a two-way symmetrical communication process as the group model for internal communication, which emphasizes interpersonal and small-group communication between management and staff.
  - Group internal communication media are mass media that support the two-way symmetrical process by supplying timely, accurate, and essential information to all employees to assist managers in their communication role.
  - Executive management members serve as communication role models and champions of the internal communication process within their own environment.
  - Business unit managers accept their own communication responsibility to employees.
  - The group internal communication department acts as a facilitator to bring about information flow in the group, create awareness of the importance of communication, and improve communication skills of management and employees, in cooperation with divisions and regions.
  - The group internal communication department reports to the group general manager: human resources with informal (dotted) communication lines where necessary, within the framework of the full acceptance by all managers of their communication responsibility.
  - Each division or region has a dedicated person responsible for the transformation and change process, with special emphasis on internal communication and "buy-in" of staff.
  - Each business unit has a communication champion to assist the business unit manager with managing his/her communication function.
  - The effectiveness of the communication process is measured through a 360° questionnaire, involving employees, colleagues, superiors and other stakeholders.
- A communication awareness campaign that was launched in different ways. All internal communication materials were branded with a specially designed logo consisting of two African masks, showing the African roots of the organization (Figure 2). The masks, in contrasting hues of brown to symbolize communication across racial and ethnic barriers, were not gender specific. The slogan, *The Visible Voice,* was part of the design and its aim was to make employees aware that people not only communicate in words but also through their actions. To illustrate printed materials such as the policy booklet and the training manual, a mime artist was photographed in different poses to further illustrate the importance of nonverbal communication. In addition to the policy booklet, all employees received leather key holders with the logo in full color and a computer "wobbler," a logo on a soft spring that could be attached to the frame of the computer screen and moved around. These were inexpensive but effective tools to launch the campaign and to remind employees of the importance of communication.

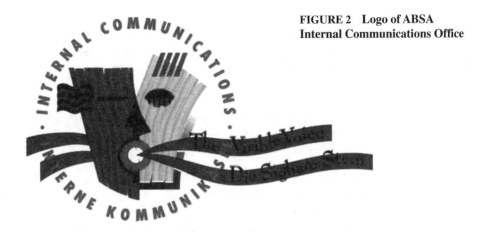

FIGURE 2 **Logo of ABSA**
Internal Communications Office

Objective 2: To coordinate information in ABSA to ensure that all employees have access to the organizational media by improving viewership patterns from 27% to 50%. The tactics supporting this objective were:

■ Involvement of internal communication practitioners with all key organizational transformation processes. Because this was a time of major political and social transformation for South Africa, many change initiatives were launched through the human resources division. This allowed the group internal communication department to be part of all major change initiatives and to involve regional and divisional communication consultants and champions in change processes.

■ Clarification of the role of consultants and champions regarding information flow. Because the group internal communication function was involved in all major corporate decisions pertaining to important group initiatives, it could provide the necessary knowledge and information to internal communication consultants and champions. Consultants had to participate in regional or divisional management meetings and had to brief these management teams on major decisions and processes. They also had to provide this information to the champions in the business units, who in their turn had to attend cost center management meetings and facilitate dissemination of information to employees at cost center level.

■ Maintenance and evaluation of membership of the Strategic Communicator's Forum. This was one of the most difficult and least successful initiatives. Communication practitioners of the different head office units attended these meetings irregularly, and turf battles were common. This did help, however, to keep some information flowing across divisions, or silos.

■ Evaluation of all the media in the organization. Initial research indicated that the *Abacus* (the bi-weekly newsletter) was the most preferred way for employees to gain information about the organization. They preferred this medium to their own supervisors. However, only 25 percent of employees regularly watched the television broadcasts, which was the most expensive of the communication media used.

■ Promotion of the electronic media. As a result of the poor viewership, promotion of the times and contents of the different television broadcasts was part of the campaign. Supervisors and managers were targeted in particular because they often prohibited employees from watching television broadcasts. They viewed time spent on these activities as a waste of time.

Objective 3: To improve communication skills and communication management skills in the ABSA Group by training 100 percent of all consultants and champions and 50 percent of employees. This took place through:

■ The creation of a communication skills training course, workbook, and video
■ Training the communication consultants and champions to conduct the training through a Train the Trainer program
■ Developing a Communication Star Grading Scheme for all cost centers and a process to name an Internal Communication Consultant of the Year and a Communication Champion of the Year
■ Research to evaluate the effectiveness of the program

Objective 4: To establish and maintain communication as a transformation process in the group. This took place through:

■ Effective functioning, positioning, and image building of the group internal communication department. The internal communication department itself adopted two-way symmetrical communication and operated as a team. All team members participated in strategic planning and in important departmental decisions. Special attention was given to management of their key performance areas and the development of skills. The head of the internal communication department regularly met with executives to discuss the process and get feedback.
■ Upgrading of equipment and technology use to ensure the effective and productive use of resources. All internal communication practitioners had to acquire the necessary computer skills, which was quite a challenge in 1996 South Africa.
■ Maintenance of the internal communication consultant and champion network. An internal communication consultant was appointed in the group function to specifically work with consultants and champions to improve their communication skills through training, to schedule regular get-togethers, and disseminate information to this network.

Evaluation

The internal communication process was comprehensively evaluated in July 1998 through both qualitative and quantitative research.[1]

The quantitative research was conducted through three separate surveys among senior executives, cost center managers, and employees. Of the senior executives, 23.4 percent ($n = 68$) participated. Cost center managers participated at a rate of 42.1 percent ($n = 632$). Of the 10,000 employees randomly sampled to participate, 27 percent ($n = 2,709$), returned responses. The decision to have three different surveys was taken because the communication responsibilities of the three populations were slightly different. Nonetheless, in broad terms the three surveys measured the same five constructs. The survey instruments were delivered electronically and were limited to 24 items each because of the computer platform used.

The qualitative research consisted of in-depth interviews of one to one-and-a-half hours each with 18 senior executives and 21 regional and divisional communication consultants. Nineteen focus groups involving 148 champions in total were conducted across the country. The five constructs and their results were:

1. *To determine the extent to which the internal communication process has been implemented.* Measurements both from employees (72.5%) and cost center managers (79.2%) indicated a high level of process implementation. The fact that only 62.9 percent of senior managers thought the process was implemented indicated that they were much less involved in the process implementation than required. Only 45.6 percent of these senior executives invited their communication consultants to attend management meetings, as was required in the policy. This explained why some divisional head offices were less successful with the implementation process. These results were confirmed through the qualitative research. Consultants said they were often not involved in management meetings, and talked about the power distance between them and their senior executives.

2. *To determine the credibility and success of the communication champions or consultants.* There was a considerable discrepancy between employees' (69%) and managers' (80.1%) overall credibility rating of champions. Although the employees rated champions relatively high after only 18 months, the results concurred with a previous measurement that indicated that 30 percent of champions were felt not to be the right people for the job. Qualitative results indicated that this occurred particularly in environments where managers and supervisors did not want champions elected democratically but rather appointed champions whom they could manipulate and who were often too junior to execute such a difficult function. Further statistical analysis indicated that where the champions were elected democratically, employees perceived that the communication climate improved dramatically. Again, the qualitative results provided more insight. Champions who were not elected but rather appointed said they lacked credibility and trust from employees.

3. *To determine if, and what, benefits were derived from the process.* All three populations who participated in this research viewed the communication process as beneficial (84.7% of cost center managers, 70.3% of employees, and 72.1% of senior executives). These improvements were "more information" (71.4% of employees, 84.7% of cost center managers, and 66.2% of senior managers) and "a better team spirit" (69% of employees, 84% of cost center managers, and 73.5% of senior executives). Qualitative research indicated that one of the problems that prevented champions from being more effective in building team spirit was their inability to organize regular team meetings or workplace forums. Again, supervisors stood in the way of these communication practices.

4. *To determine whether the process has addressed certain communication problems, as indicated in the previous communication audit.* Of those who felt the process addressed specific communication problems, 66.7 percent were employees, 75.2 percent were cost center managers, and 76.1 percent were senior executives. Because the communication skills training was only at that time starting to filter through the organization, this measurement was low at 38.2 percent, about 12 percent below the set target. However, other results showed a dramatic improvement: 82.1 percent of employees now felt free to make use of the organizational media, and 70.8 percent of employees and 80.9 percent of cost center managers now said they received more information through formal communication channels than through the grapevine. This was in stark contrast with the communication audit conducted in 1995, which indicated that only 48 percent of employees received more formal information than information through the grapevine. About 76 percent of employees now also felt freer to speak their mind, an improvement of 15 percent over previous research. Again, qualitative research provided numerous examples of how the communication climate and culture in the workplace were rapidly changing as a result of the process.

5. *To determine whether the process has improved communication between employees and their superiors.* The perception that communication between employees and managers had improved was overwhelmingly positive, with 78.5 percent of employees and 87 percent of cost center managers agreeing. This question was not asked of senior executives. Some problems remained, however. Although cost center managers were viewed as having an open door policy, they were not equally keen to venture out of their offices and do floor walking.

Critique

Research

The research that was conducted in 1995 and that started the organization on this road was a rather standard communication audit. Although comprehensive, it did not try new ways of looking at the communication problems of the organization. An outside research provider conducted this research but did not know the organization well enough to always ask the right questions. The communications audit did reveal that middle management viewed communication as a waste of time and even prohibited employees from watching the internally produced broadcasts or reading the internal newsletter. However, it did not appear to measure employee confidence in the available internal media. Even if middle managers permitted or encouraged consumption of the internal media, the media can only be as effective as the employees' perception of its credibility.

Even if practitioners do not conduct their own research they should know enough about research to guide contractors through this process. Research did not stop with the investigation of communication problems and attitudes toward internal media. In ABSA the effectiveness of media and the link between communication behavior and productivity were also researched during the time the campaign was launched.

Objectives

Usually having four objectives in a single public relations campaign would be viewed as a weakness. Here, however, each objective targets a specific problem identified by research. Also, there are strategies and tactics developed to target each objective. While the large number of objectives make this campaign more complex than some, they do not appear to weaken the campaign's potential for success.

Internal communication practice is complex and needs to be practiced at the highest level of the organization. To facilitate real systems change, internal communication practice should address organizational issues such as organizational philosophy and worldview, structure, and transformation processes, which is what the objectives in this campaign set out to do. However, changing a system is a long and tedious process and can take years, not months. It is important to let everyone know this so that expectations are not too high.

Strategy

The strategies used in the campaign were unusual because they addressed the problem by changing the structure of the whole communication function. Decentralizing the internal communication function and making it a core organizational process through the use of formal and informal internal communication practitioners is perhaps the only way to really improve the communication climate in organizations. Another very important strategy was incorporating democratic principles into the organizations. In this case it took the form of electing communication champions. The research results indicated that this made an important contribution to the improvement of internal communication climates. A third important strategy was to make communication in the organization everyone's responsibility. Communication change in organizations can only take place if all employees at all levels take responsibility for their own communication behavior. Communication is not only the responsibility of communication practitioners or managers. These strategies were only possible because of the high level of education of the communication practitioners involved. Public relations practitioners can make significant contributions to their organizations if they are educated and have the ability to apply the theories they learned through formal public relations education.

Tactics

Communicating through media will never change any communication climate or culture. That happens through behavior change. Behavior change only happens through two-way symmetrical communication, which is best facilitated through interpersonal and small-group communication practices. Also, the normal way of practicing internal communication through newsletters, memos, social functions, intranets, or other mediated forms of communication is ineffective if these practices do not take place under the umbrella of a corporate internal communication policy and philosophy that direct message design and actions.

Evaluation

Although the system of evaluation implemented here was extraordinarily thorough, it did have some significant weaknesses. Primary among these was the selection of the five constructs to be measured. Some of those constructs measured the apparent success of elements of the internal communication process and some sought to determine if problems identified in the earlier audit had been corrected. However, not directly and specifically measured were whether the four public relations objectives had been met. Proof of campaign success would have been easier with a more direct relation between evaluation research and the objectives.

Another problem with evaluating the progress made was that the communication audit conducted in 1995 did not necessarily measure the same outcomes as the audit done in 1998. It is much easier to measure progress if the same questions are asked during evaluation as those asked before the campaigns phase. The fact that a new communication process was adopted and implemented made this direct comparison more difficult.

ENDNOTE

1. This research was discussed comprehensively in two articles published in 2002 by D. R. Holtzhausen.

DISCUSSION QUESTIONS

1. Throughout the campaign report there are references to the "highly threatening external environment of the organization" and to "political changes in the country." What are these changes and threats?

2. The internal communication department of ABSA Group is described as very small. It had six staff members. Compared to the internal communication department in other similar sized organizations is a staff of six small?

3. The campaign described here began with a communication audit. Describe a communication audit. What research methods are typically used in such an audit and how is the data gathered analyzed?

4. One component tool in most communication audits is a focus group. Are there problems with either the reliability or the validity of focus groups? If so, what are those problems and how can they be controlled to maximize reliability and validity?

5. This campaign had four public relations objectives. Is that good or bad? What problems, if any, does having multiple public relations objectives create? How can a public relations practitioner compensate for those problems?

6. Several theories and models of public relations practice are incorporated in this campaign. Pick one of those models or theories and explain it. Was the model you selected used appropriately in this campaign?

7. Can you identify tactics that were not used here that might have been implemented to help this campaign? If so what were they and how would you have used them?

8. Were there tactics used in this campaign that could not have been used in a similar organization in the United States (or any other country)? If so, what were they and why would they not work in the United States (or the other country)?

9. Describe how you would have evaluated the success (or failure) of each of the four public relations objectives in this campaign.

REFERENCES AND SUGGESTED READINGS

ABSA Group. (1996). *ABSA Internal Communication Policy.* Johannesburg, South Africa.

Grunig, J. E. (Ed.). (1992). *Excellence in public relations and communication management.* Hillsdale, NJ: Lawrence Erlbaum.

Holtzhausen, D. R. (1995). *The role of public relations theory and research in a postmodern approach to communication management in the organization.* Unpublished doctoral dissertation. Johannesburg: Rand Afrikaans University.

Holtzhausen, D. R., & Verwey, S. (1996). Toward a general theory of public relations. *Communicare, 15*(2), 25–56.

Holtzhausen, D. R. (2002). The effects of workplace democracy on employee communication: Implications for competitive advantage. *Competitiveness Review, 12*(2), 30–48.

Holtzhausen, D. R. (2002). The effects of a divisionalized and decentralized organizational structure on a formal internal communication function in a South African organization. *Journal of Communication Management, 6*(4), 323–339.

Miller, K. I. (1999). *Organizational communication. Approaches and processes.* Belmont, CA: Wadsworth.

Image Building in the International Media: A Case Study of the Finlandia Communications Program in Russia

KATERINA TSETSURA

Case study materials were prepared by Sergey Chumin and Elena Groznaya of Maslov, Sokur and Associates. The author would like to especially thank the senior partner of the Moscow public relations agency "Maslov, Sokur and Associates," Mr. Maslov, whose genuine help and amazing dedication to promote and practice more sophisticated, ethical public relations practices in Russia are greatly appreciated.

Executive Summary

Nation Image Building

The process of image construction is one traditional focus of public relations (Benoit, 1997; Cheney & Christensen, 2001; Cutlip, 1994). In the past decade several studies of image creation and restoration strategies have added a great deal of depth and complexity to the conception of image (Benoit, 1997; Kunczik, 2003; Moffitt, 2001). The construction and maintenance of images are equally important for companies (Cutlip, 1994; Hearit, 2001; Heath, 1997), individuals (Shishkina, 1999), and countries (Kunczik, 1997, 2003).

Using public relations tools to help build their nation's image has become a common and acceptable practice for many countries. The cultivation of the image of the country is usually associated with political and economic goals that are part of the international relations policies of the nation (Kunczik, 1997). For instance, the national and international image of Romania was seriously hurt during the propaganda era of Ceausescu. Because of this, a specific image-restoration media campaign was developed to restore the nation's image in the eyes of the European community (Jackel, 2001).

As in the case of Romania, often the client asking for such image-restoration or image development campaigns is the nation–state itself. Public relations and advertising campaigns sponsored by nation–states often aim to improve tourism, trade, investment, and image cultivation (Kunczik, & Weber, 1994; Kunczik, 1997). Economic and trade issues are often the driving force behind nation image building campaigns sponsored by countries. The following case study illustrates an international public relations campaign furnished by the Finnish government. The campaign was implemented to stimulate trade relations between Finland and Russia by cultivating the image of Finland and Finnish products.

2001–2003 Finlandia Communications Program

In 2001 a Moscow public relations agency, Maslov, Sokur & Associates (the "agency") was hired to work on Finlandia Communications Program (FCP). The program was initiated by the Finnish government, established by the Finnish Association of Foreign Trade (Finpro), and partly sponsored by a group of Finnish companies that represent several industries. The three-year program was launched in the Russian market in 2001.

FCP was a two-level program that included both country image building (country PR) and corporate image building (corporate PR) in Russia. It focused on the promotion of the image of Finland and on improvement of the image of products produced by individual Finnish companies participating in the program. This approach allowed the agency to combine corporate and national campaign goals, providing specific target audiences with more developed, comprehensive views of what stands behind the word "Finnish."

The program was advantageous for companies, which participated in the program under a national "Finnish" brand (they could choose specific public relations services in accordance with their own budget, and the nation of Finland. Finland's national image was presented vividly and comprehensively through the companies' activities and their products. Small and middle-size companies were given an opportunity to market their products in Russia without having massive advertising and public relations budgets. All Finish companies were represented under one national brand—"Finland."

To manage the wide variety of services provided for each company by the agency, Finpro suggested the annual so-called eight-point system. Each company had eight points to use for public relations activities throughout a year. Each activity was equal to a set number of points. For example: one point equaled a press release; two points were an interview or a joint press conference; three points equaled a media tour, a site location visit, a press-conference, or any special event. In the beginning of each year every company, together with the agency managers, chose their eight activities for the year. As long as they used the official Finland Campaign logo in their ads, the Finnish companies were also partially reimbursed by the government for their advertising expenses in the Russian market.

Research

History of the Problem

In the year 2000, before the launch of the program, Finpro turned to a St. Petersburg marketing research company "Toy-Opinion" to find out how Russian people (specifically, residents of St. Petersburg and the Leningrad region, which are closest to Finland) perceived the overall image of Finland and its economy and industries.

During the time Russia was part of the Soviet Union, the trade between Finland and the Soviet Union was very active. Soviet people considered Finnish products to be of high quality, but those products were very hard to get. After the fall of the Soviet Union, Russian boarders opened to many foreign goods from different countries and many of those imports were as good as Finnish products. Then in 1998, due to the economic crisis in Russia, a great many Finnish companies had to leave the Russian market. Many of them believed the Russian economic crisis caused considerable economic and image damage in Finland during 1998 and 1999.

In 2000, marketing research showed that most Russians remembered Finland and its goods, but those memories were associated only with the Soviet times. For many Russians, Finland was still a land of "Viola" butter, warm winter boots, and "Rosenlew" refrigerators. This was a very outdated image of Finland's leading products. This image, for example, failed to consider the fact that Finland's Nokia was the world leader in mobile technologies and the country itself was extraordinarily advanced technologically. Finland had the largest number of mobile phones and Internet connections per person in the world.

However, when Russian people saw Finnish products such as furniture, sanitary ware, and kitchen fixtures in shops, supermarkets, and salons, they did not realize those products were Finnish. For example, "IDO" and "Oras" sanitary ware and faucets were usually thought to be produced in Italy, and "Fazer" chocolate—quite well known in Russia—was thought to be German. Not surprisingly, Russians were not at all familiar with some smaller Finnish companies.

Finnish media publications concentrated on the beauty of Finnish nature and encouraged tourism. They did not promote the Finnish economy and industry, nor did they feature the high quality of Finnish products.

Target Market Determination

By the year 2001 the economic situation in Russia was more stable. The economy had begun a recovery after the 1998 crisis that forced many small and middle-sized foreign companies (including many Finnish companies) to leave. By the year 2001 they were back in Russia restarting business, setting up new representative offices and showrooms, and trying to increase sales.

In 2001 the Russian population also experienced a significant increase in disposable income. This income growth continued in 2002 and was higher yet in 2003. More and more people in Moscow and other big industrial centers, whose income had improved to the middle and upper-middle level and were between 25 and 60 years old, had permanent jobs, and owned apartments or country houses—or both. These middle-income Russian families are characteristically the ones who redecorate homes in accordance with the latest European design trends, regularly travel abroad for vacations (at least once a year), buy goods in supermarkets and big stores, go to the cinema, theatres, restaurants and bars, and choose "high quality" products over "cheaper" ones. This group, with specific demographic and psychographic characteristics, became a target public for FCP. The target public was slightly varied for each sphere of industry, represented by a participating company.

Cultural Considerations

One of the most important factors affecting the cooperation between the agency and the client was the difference in their cultures. These differences were particularly obvious when their attitudes toward organizational matters were compared. The way of life and procedures for doing business in Finland and in Russia differ greatly. Life in Finland moves more slowly, so every activity is planned well in advance, while in Russia the speed of life and business is much faster, plans change more quickly, and there is little advance planning.

Initially, the agency managers were unprepared to deal with these differences. The Finnish companies' representatives were not able to quickly react to the Moscow's agency's suggestions and requests, or to inquiries from the media. The agency had to adapt to the client's slower pace of work and had to be more proactive at every step, anticipating the client in order to avoid delays that could affect positive perceptions of the client by the media. This was a surprise, because most of the participating companies had been conducting business in Russia for several years.

Description of Client

General Description. Finpro is the Finnish Association of foreign trade. Its clients are Finnish companies that are in different stages of internationalization. Finpro provides Finnish companies, especially small and medium ones, access to comprehensive internationalization services that help them in markets all over the world. It supports Finnish companies by helping them find effective operational models to compete in international markets. Finpro operates in 40 countries around the world with 52 Finland Trade Centers. Two of these centers are located in Moscow and St. Petersburg. In the program described here, Finpro united a number of Finnish companies that have or were about to launch activities in the Russian market. Although Finpro is referred to as the client in this case, it acted more like a financial coordinator on the Finnish side of FCP. The number of real clients, companies that participated in the project, changed from year to year. In 2001 there were 15 companies. In 2002 there were 22, and in 2003 the program united 14 companies. Thus, in reality, the agency had between 14 and 22 separate clients that represented seven different Finnish industries. To consolidate the interests of all participating companies, the public relations strategies were concentrated on building the national image of Finland.

Financial Resources of Client. Although Finpro bore the majority of the financial expenses, some of the costs were to be covered by the companies themselves. The expenses covered by individual companies included the cost of entertainment programs and meals for journalists during media tours to Finland and site location visits in Russia and the cost of press conferences, seminars, and special events. Financial resources of each separate company differ, but on average their budgets for this campaign were very moderate.

Past Communication Efforts of the Clients. Some of the participating companies did have a system of cooperation with a relevant sector of the media, but those were, for the most part, limited to cooperation with advertising departments. Several companies participated in specialized exhibitions in Russia.

In Soviet times some Finnish products, such as butter, some sport clothes for children, warm winter jackets, and boots were regularly imported to Russia, but they were expensive or difficult for Russians to buy. At that time "Made in Finland" meant the highest quality available, because consumers had no access to any other goods produced abroad and Soviet products were far less competitive. Thus, Finnish companies did not have much competition and, as a result, did not invest in communication campaigns oriented toward consumers.

Publics

For most companies, their primary target public was upper-middle income consumers, both male and female, aged 25 to 60, who live in Moscow and St. Petersburg. Target publics were more limited for each company or industry. For example, for the construction and interior design companies, the target public was described as private owners of country houses and apartments who were building or redecorating those homes. Their publics also included large construction companies, architectural bureaus, design studios, private schools and hospitals, big retail stores, supermarkets, and boutiques. Local authorities were also included in the target public.

For the producers of women's and children's hygiene products, the agency specified as end users women between the ages of 13 and 50, future mothers, and the mothers of babies. Strategies for automobile companies were directed toward male and female drivers in the middle- to high-income bracket.

Both the corporate public relations and country public relations programs included in the Finlandia program were designed to promote the overall image of the country. That is why the program targeted not only specific publics for each company or industry but also the general Russian audience. Tactics that were used to spread information about Finland included: (1) an information bulletin "What's new in Finland," issued on the website www.finpro.ru, (2) a series of contests "Do you know Finland," that ran in consumer magazines and, (3) other national and product image-building activities. Each of these will be discussed in detail later.

Media

Available Media.   At the initial stage of the campaign the agency created media directories for each industry. These directories were constantly updated and expanded. Each database contained in-depth information. There were directories for media categories such as business, general interest, trade, consumer-oriented, and lifestyle. These directories listed the media outlets that were relevant to each of the industries the agency represented. They included all contact information, spheres of media interest, and the names of key editors. The total number of media contacts established and supported for the program exceeded 150 people in more than 100 periodicals.

Limitations on Media Use.   One limitation was that the agency refused to cooperate with any medium that required payment to review or use public relations releases. Russian media, like media in many other countries, have a history of requesting payment for publishing public relations releases as news (IPR, 2003; Tsetsura, 2003; Tsetsura & Kruckeberg, 2004a, 2004b). The "Maslov, Sokur and Associates agency" that worked on this campaign strongly opposed such practices. After some preliminary research it was learned that the refusal to pay for the review or use of public relations materials made it impossible to set up cooperation with several general-interest and lifestyle Russian publications.

Objective

Organizational Goal. The overall organizational goal was reputation management for the State of Finland and relationship management for both the state of Finland and for each participating company.

Public Relations Objectives. The primary public relations objective was to create and strengthen media awareness of Finland and its industries. More specifically, the campaign sought to create the impression of Finland as a modern European country with highly developed industry, breakthrough innovation technologies, and rich traditions. It also sought to position the participating Finnish companies as active elements of the economic relations between Russia and Finland. Most importantly, the focus had to be made not only on the products of the companies and their features, but also on the "nationality" of these products and a positive impression of all goods labeled as "Finnish." The following secondary objectives were also identified:

- To change the existing outdated stereotypes of Finland
- To ensure permanent presence of Finpro and FCP participants in a variety of target media
- To broaden the media audience to include business and consumer or lifestyle publications while continuing to work with trade media
- To coordinate public relations communications with marketing programs and advertising activities

Strategies

Action Strategies

To achieve the objectives of the FCP the agency worked out a public relations plan that included media relations, special events, and strategic communication consulting. Media relations included constant contact with journalists and reaction to their inquiries, media database maintenance, monitoring media coverage and collecting clippings, and proactive contacts with the media. Special events covered media events and different promotional activities. Finally, strategic communication consulting focused on several key issues, the most important of which was internal media training.

To lower costs and raise efficiency of the campaign, it was decided to split the FCP participants into several major divisions or industry sectors based on their scope of interests. These divisions were construction, interior design, food, automobile, telecommunications, publishing, and women's and children's hygiene products.

Communication Strategies

The FCP campaign aimed to remove the existing stereotypes of Finland held by the Russian people and to position Finland as a modern European country with a highly developed economy and with industries characterized by breakthrough innovation policies and the most sophisticated technologies. The campaign also needed to demonstrate the modern and high-quality products and services of the participating companies of every industry.

Several general key messages were identified for the campaign to reflect the interests of the state of Finland and each participating company. The main idea was to gain a "Positive attitude toward the word Finnish" in the media and among the target publics and to prove that if a product is "Made in Finland" it means "the highest quality and complete trust." Other messages varied for each company, depending on its industry. For instance, products of the so-called interior design companies (furniture for home, kitchens, and bathrooms; sanitary ware, faucets, and accessories) were positioned as an integral part of Scandinavian design.

Benefon, the leading provider of GSM- and GPS-based mobile telematics instruments, was positioned as "the innovator in the sphere of mobile telematics that provides unique services in Russia." Three food industry companies, producing milk products, chocolate, and confectionery, were positioned as manufacturers of "high quality, healthy ecological products made only from natural ingredients." Later, due to a high interest from specific consumer-oriented medium, the concept was changed to focus on "functionality of foods"— the most important component of a healthy person's daily ration.

Tactics

The work within the FCP was mainly focused on media relations. The agency created media databases for each industry and updated them frequently. The total number of established and supported media contacts exceeded 150 people in more than 100 periodicals. Throughout the program, the agency maintained routine relations with the media by providing journalists with information and comments from Finpro and participating companies. The agency also adapted press materials from the participating companies and distributed those press releases to the media.

The agency organized and carried out several special projects and distributed editorials to key media. The special projects included a contest, "Do you know Finland" that featured questions about Finnish history, traditions, and famous Finnish people. The editorials included a series of theme supplements to key business daily and weekly print media. Those supplements were fully dedicated to Finland and included political and cultural news and descriptions of major trends in economic development.

Several interviews with heads of the participating companies were organized for leading Russian business and general interest media. Interviews with participating company officials were also provided for representatives of the specialized and trade media relevant to the company's industry.

In addition, the agency organized a series of media tours in Finland for Russian journalists. On these tours the journalists were able to see offices and production capacities of the participating companies. All the visits were directly related to the major divisions of the program, including construction, design, food, and automobile. The agency identified journalists from appropriate publications, negotiated terms of the visits, and coordinated visa applications and logistics inside Russia. A representative of the agency always accompanied every group during such tours. This representative could provide the agency with updated information on what about the visit was most or least interesting to the media representatives. This information was used to schedule and improve future activities.

There also were several site location visits for journalists, during which the participating companies' products were installed or services were used. This was done to show the journalists how the products worked in a natural setting. One of the most vivid and unusual examples of such site location visits was the one carried out for Harvia, the leading Finnish producer of saunas, stoves, and accessories. The agency organized a real sauna day in one of Moscow's saunas equipped by Harvia. The media representatives were invited there, together with the company's top management, who answered journalists' questions and showed the equipment in an informal atmosphere of a famous Finnish sauna. Beer and snacks were served.

Among media events the agency regularly organized were press conferences, press briefings, and press lunches. These events were sometimes sponsored by an individual company and sometimes jointly sponsored by all the companies of an industry division. Joint press conferences were best for those companies that had no new products to present at the time of the conference but who wanted to deliver a message to the media. For example, three Finnish companies Valio (milk products), Leaf (confectionery), and Raisio (margarine, porridge flakes, etc.) participated in a joint press conference for the food industry. The topic of the conference was "Food products' quality control policy in Finland compared to Russia."

Several special events were carried out within the framework of FCP. For instance:

- Educational and informative seminars were created for clients and partners, to which journalists were also invited.
- Representative office or salon opening ceremonies were organized quite often for the companies within the interior design industry. Journalists from relevant media were invited to these ceremonies and were given a chance to talk to the companies' leading architects and designers.
- Also, exhibition events took place at a company's exhibition stand. At these events journalists were specially invited to meet and interview company representatives.

Another instrument of promotion was a website www.finpro.ru that was created after the campaign started. This website, in the Russian language, was dedicated to the participants of the program, to the State of Finland, and Finpro and its activities in Russia. The target public for the website was the journalists, who were able to quickly find all necessary information about Finland, its economy, political system, geography, traditions, and climate on the website. They could also use the website to view all the press releases issued during the campaign, and to check the news of the companies. The website had a feedback option that was widely used by journalists and businesspeople from Russia and by consumers from Moscow, St. Petersburg, and some other regions. For the companies that were not interested in media relations, the agency organized sales promotion activities such as product samplings and premiums.

In addition, every year the agency organized and carried out media welcome events to improve the journalists' loyalty to the companies and to Finland in general. All the FCP companies participated in those meetings. The meetings were organized at the Embassy of Finland in Moscow twice a year. The meetings were held in spring and late autumn and were tied to Finnish traditional holidays such as Harvest Day in August and Pikkujoulu (the annual Christmas celebration at the Finnish Embassy) near the end of November. Although these events took place in an informal atmosphere with traditional Finnish live music, national food, and drinks, they provided a good opportunity for the company representatives to meet and talk about their businesses to the Russian media representatives and government officials.

Among the general activities carried out in order to raise the efficiency of the FCP at every level, the agency also organized media training for companies' representatives. During this training the representatives were taught how to communicate with Russian journalists efficiently and effectively.

Evaluation

The agency and the client evaluated the campaign as having met both the primary and secondary objectives. Continuous work with the media allowed the companies to establish contacts with Russian journalists and to continue communication with the media after the campaign was officially over.

The success of the campaign was measured by the number of publications about Finland, Finpro, and the participating companies that appeared in Russian media during the period of the campaign. From March 2001 to June 2003, more than 500 publications appeared, with more to be published at the end of 2003 and the beginning of 2004. This is an exceptionally large number of publications, according to the agency managers. The success is particularly impressive when one recognizes the problems faced by those who planned and implemented the campaign. These problems include:

- Some of the companies operated in a very narrow niche of the market sector, and sometimes it was rather difficult to find any relevant media for them (for example, "Labko" is a producer of oil and grease tanks and separators). This concern was especially relevant for business-to-business companies because most of the trade business-to-business publications in Russia are, unfortunately, extremely corrupt.
- Most of the companies had a very moderate public relations budget and, for that reason, had to reject many interesting promotion ideas. Alternative and less expensive methods for delivering their messages to the media were substituted. The most common alternative was a simple press release.
- Several companies were not interested in media relations at all and planned to have only promotional activities. Companies in this category included "Fazer" (chocolate) products, and "Delipap" (women's hygiene products). Other companies not interested

in media relations focused exclusively on marketing activities such as seminars for existing and potential clients. One company in this category was "Quebecer World Nordic" which specializes in print communication services.

The most important measure of success emphasized in the agency report is that not a single of these 500 publications was paid for. Cooperation with the media was based only on the interest of a source in the message delivered by a company. Getting publicity materials into the Russian media for free was considered a major success because of the Russian media's history of requesting payment for such materials. An IPR research study of countries where journalists demand payment for publicity ranked Russia 16th (out of 33 places available) (IPR, 2003). The preliminary analysis of this campaign and personal communication with the agency management suggest that this problem may be much bigger in Russia than even the IPR study demonstrates.

According to the agency, the success in forming and projecting a favorable image of Finnish products as well as the country of Finland in the Russian media is illustrated by some article headlines. Again, the goal was to create and maintain a positive image of Finland and Finnish goods. Here are some examples of such headlines:

"Made in Finland—means you can trust it"
"Finnish quality means the best"
"NORDIC oatmeal flakes: quick and healthy"
"Asahikawa design contest: Finnish design appreciated by Japanese architects"
"Goods transportation through Finland: quick and reliable"

The number of materials appearing in the Russian media indicates that the campaign attracted attention and influenced media opinions about the country of Finland and Finnish products. The extent of this change, however, is hard to evaluate. In addition, changes in perceptions of Finland and Finnish products by Russian publics were not measured at the end of the campaign and thus cannot be discussed in appropriate fashion.

The feedback on the website www.finpro.ru also indicated a level of interest expressed by different target groups of the campaign. The agency managers received many e-mail inquiries from end-users from different Russian regions. People were eager to buy the companies' products shown on the website. Thus, the website helped to create an informed consumer environment and to generate a demand for Finnish products.

There were also e-mails and calls to the agency offices as a result of promotional business-to-business activities. These came from business people interested in business contacts with companies, both in Russia and Finland.

Because of the continuous contacts with the media, journalists became used to getting news from the participating companies on a regular basis by the end of the first year of the campaign. Strong media relation contacts were established through this campaign. Later, journalists often initiated contacts with the agency managers and sought new or unique information about Finnish companies. Thus the country of Finland and Finnish companies became well known to the leading Russian media and their representatives, and as a result this met the primary objective of the campaign.

Critique

The Finlandia public relations campaign is a typical example of a national economic image development campaign. Usually, the primary goal of such campaigns is to facilitate the entry or maintenance of products and services from the client country's companies in the markets of a target country or countries. However, this campaign goes well beyond simplistic company promotions. The reason this campaign is appropriately described as a public relations campaign is that its goal was to create a unified image of the country and to improve the perception of products or services labeled Finnish.

Historically, Finland experienced national image problems (Arter, 1989; Jakobson, 1998, also see media publications, such as *the Economist,* 2003). As late as in the middle of the 19th century, some claimed that even though Finland has a rich history and distinct literature, it was not a nation (Kare, as cited in Arter). Thus, a crucial strategy for the state of Finland in the age of globalization and the growing influence of the European Union is to strive for "the right balance between . . . commitments on the international stage and the protection and promotion" of the traditions of the state as a nation (Arter, 1989, p. 243). This campaign was designed to support this balance through Finnish companies present in the Russian market. This strategy should not come as a surprise to those who study the process of construction of national images in the international arena. Particularly for small countries, cultivating their national images abroad is "often crucial to their economy" (Kunczik, 1997, p. 65).

National image is defined as the cognitive perceptions that the publics hold of a given country. National image is "a person's beliefs about a nation and its people" (Kunczik, 2003, p. 412). There are numerous examples of campaigns to develop national images that are directed at the mass media (Albritton & Manheim, 1985; Avraham, 2003; Kunczik, 1997, 2003). Media relations often become a focus of such a campaign for the creation of a national image.

Nation economic image is one of the building blocks of any national image and it is often cultivated by public relations professionals. This campaign showed how the politically driven, theorized goal of constructing or correcting the national image can be emphasized throughout the campaign and achieved through the use of the media.

The national image building goal of this media campaign was suitable and appropriate. The agency understood the importance of changing images of Finland and Finnish products in the media. The results of another study demonstrated how images and perceptions of China have changed in print media in the United States over the years (Liss, 2003). Even though Liss did not focus this research on the nation building or public diplomacy strategies that may have influenced the changing images of China, he seems to argue that the change in perception may have caused changes in diplomacy and trade relations. Thus, Liss' work does provide some evidence that public relations or public diplomacy efforts could exist.

Research

Pre-campaign research provided some good background information for the agency that helped to formulate specific objectives of the campaign and to highlight potential obstacles.

The agency used the information to its advantage. The public relations plan that was ultimately implemented was based on research findings. Most importantly, the agency correctly identified the objective of national image building and stressed this objective at all stages of the campaign. Correction of Finland's national image was the main goal of this campaign, and the public relations plan was designed to achieve this goal.

The "Toy-Opinion" pre-campaign research could be a major strength of this campaign. The existence of that research should have made it possible to compare the image of Finland and its products before and after the campaign. However, to really take advantage of this pre-campaign research would have required repetition of the research after the campaign. No such post-campaign measure of the image of Finland or Finnish products is reported. Further, the "Toy-Opinion" research is not described in enough detail to assess its reliability or validity. Therefore, it is not possible to evaluate the effectiveness of the campaign in changing attitudes of Russian consumers toward the image of Finland and Finnish products.

Strategies

From the perspective of the agency, the main problems of the campaign were associated with a lack of agreement between participating companies about how to implement media plans and promotional activities. This problem was exacerbated by the reluctance of some companies that joined the FCP. Some of the companies that participated in the program changed their goals and objectives several times. While the campaign was in the process, some companies that had initially agreed to the agency media plan refused to follow the plan. Instead, they requested promotional activities. The lack of agreement on implementation through publicity and promotion plans was frustrating for the agency. They had to change strategic plans for the some companies while the original program was already in action.

Reluctance of some companies to participate in the media relations can be explained by the mismatch between the goals of the overall campaign that was sponsored by the country of Finland and the goals of individual participating companies. Several companies joined the FCP just to get the governmental reimbursement. Many felt they really did not need public relations activities in Russia or did not have newsworthy messages to deliver to the media and the target publics. For some companies, the reimbursement was the only stimulus to be in the program. Such reluctance generated potential problems in achieving the ultimate goal of this national image building campaign. Ultimately, not only were the images of those companies hurt in the eyes of the agency, but also the image of Finland and Finnish companies as a whole could have been damaged by the actions of these companies. Any company that engages in similar national image campaigns, whether those campaigns focus on politics or the economy, needs to realize the potential positive or negative outcomes of its behavior. National image building begins by working with public relations specialists from a different country. They are the ones who must be trusted to transport the desired image to international publics.

Another big problem for this campaign was its length. The program was launched for three years, but most companies were not ready to participate in the campaign for that long. The first year had a good and interesting start, and the second year was the most fruitful and exciting in terms of the number of companies participated and activities completed. In the third year the agency saw a decrease in the companies' desire to participate in the program, so the agency had to invest more energy and time keeping the companies active in media relations. The most difficult task was to make sure that journalists did not tire of the campaign's publicity. Publicity redundancy was a potential problem, since most of the media events had to focus on a limited number of Finnish companies. A more ideal time period for such a campaign would probably be a year and a half or two years.

Certainly, there was adequate research, and a number of creative communication strategies had been designed for the campaign. The campaign might have been improved if its strategies had been explained to the participating companies in terms of a consolidating theory of communication with clearly identified end goals. Finland is a well-educated country and the companies' representatives might have been more easily inspired to participate in the media campaign if they had been shown its importance in terms of the image-building process as it relates to communication theories.

Tactics

Among the tactics used, one in particular was very productive and generated great interest. Partner seminars were an efficient instrument to get third parties together and create potentially newsworthy situations in times when a company had no actual news to present. These partner seminars served to provide mutual enrichment for all parties. A company generated novel messages by supporting its partners, and the partners received some media coverage.

Media training initiated by the companies and organized by the agency for all the companies' representatives was also very useful because most of the representatives had difficulty communicating with journalists and lacked the skills needed to make effective public presentations during press conferences or seminars. As a result of the media training, companies reported a higher level of effectiveness in media relations and public speaking. However, there were no data provided to support this claim.

Evaluation

Although the agency presented good evidence of an increase in the number of publications about Finland and Finnish products, this was not sufficient to conclude that the national image of Finland was transformed in some way. Additional post-campaign research needs to be done to evaluate any real influence of this campaign on the media and the publics. A formal study, similar to the one conducted before the campaign was launched, will help to answer questions about image cultivation and image repositioning for Finnish products and the country of Finland.

DISCUSSION QUESTIONS

1. A pre-campaign measure of the image of Finland and Finnish products was brought up in the description of this campaign. If you wanted to measure how Russians perceived Finland and Finnish products, how would you design that research? What population or publics

would you measure? How would you draw a sample from those publics? Exactly what would you ask the subjects?

2. The primary strategy here was to convey the message that Finland was technologically advanced and that Finnish products were of high quality. What theory or model of communication can you use to explain or predict how that message will impact the perceptions of the target publics in Russia?

3. In the campaign's background research you were told that at the time when Russia was a part of the Soviet Union, Finnish products were thought of as exceptionally good, but in 2000 Finnish products were not as positively perceived. What would have caused that change in perception? If you wanted to be sure about the cause of the change in perception, how would you conduct research to determine the cause?

4. Describe how you would determine what publics within Russia are most likely to consume Finnish products. How would you determine what they value or perceive as attractive? Describe your study population and sample and how you would gather information from your sample.

5. In this case you were that told that journalists in many countries may request or even demand payment for reviewing or using public relations materials in the publications they represent. If you represented a client doing business in a country where this is a common practice, would you make such a payment if a journalist requested it? Explain why such a payment might be appropriate and proper. Explain why such a payment might be improper. If you were conducting a press tour for Russian journalists in Finland and one of the reporters could not afford to pay for travel to Finland, would you provide transportation? Is this different than paying for review of a press release? Why or why not? Do you think such payments and/or services are provided to journalists in the United States? Is this considered appropriate among U.S. journalists? Consult special literature and suggested readings to answer this question.

6. In this campaign you were told that the image of Finnish products shifted from Soviet times to the present. There was a time in the United States from about 1950 to the 1970s when the phrase "made in Japan" was synonymous with cheap and inferior goods. What does the phrase "made in Japan" mean to you today? If there has been a change, is that because of a public relations campaign by the Japanese? Considering what has happened to the perception of Japanese products in the United States, do you believe it is possible to change the perception of Finnish goods in Russia without a public relations campaign?

7. In this campaign there is only cursory mention of costs. What do you think would be an appropriate budget for a campaign to change the image of a nation in a country as large as Russia? Explain how you decided on the budget.

8. One of the tactics employed here was communication training for the participating companies' representatives. Could the agency have more cheaply and effectively just provided one of its own public relations staff to deal directly with the media and end-users? Why or why not?

9. Describe how you would evaluate the success of this campaign. How would you demonstrate with reliable and valid research that the campaign actually caused a change in the perception of Finland held by Russian publics?

REFERENCES AND SUGGESTED READINGS

Albritton, R. B., & Manheim, J. B. (1985). Public relations efforts in the Third World: Images in the news. *Journal of Communication, 35,* 43–59.

Arter, D. (1989). Finland: A typical post-industrial state? In M. Engman, & D. Kirby (Eds.), *Finland: People, nation, state* (pp. 226–243). London/Indianapolis, IN: Hurst & Company/Indiana University Press.

Avraham, E., & First, A. (2003). "I Buy American": The American image as reflected in Israeli advertising. *Journal of Communication, 53,* 282–240.

Benoit, W. L. (1997). Image repair discourse and crisis communication. *Public Relations Review, 23,* 177–186.

Cheney, G., & Christensen, L. T. (2001). Public relations as contested terrain: A critical response. In R. L. Heath (Ed.), *Handbook of public relations* (pp. 167–182). Thousand Oaks, CA: Sage.

Cutlip, S. M. (1994). *The unseen power: Public relations, a history.* Hillsdale, NJ: Lawrence Erlbaum.

De Cillia, R., Reisigl, M., & Wodak, R. (1999). The discursive construction of national identities. *Discourse and Society, 10,* 149–173.

From Vikings to peacemongers (2003, June 14). *The Economist, 367* (8328), 13–15.

Hearit, K. M. (2001). Corporate apologia: When an organization speaks in defense of itself. In R. L. Heath (Ed.), *Handbook of public relations* (pp. 501–511). Thousand Oaks, CA: Sage.

Heath, R. L. (1997). *Strategic issue management: Organizations and public policy changes.* Thousand Oaks, CA: Sage.

Heath, R. L. (2001). Learning best practices from experience and research. In R. L. Heath (Ed.), *Handbook of public relations* (pp. 441–444). Thousand Oaks, CA: Sage.

IPR (Institute for Public Relations) (2003). *A Composite Index by Country (66 countries) of Variables Related to the Likelihood of the Existence of "Cash for News Coverage," developed by Kruckeberg and Tsetsura.* Retrieved from www.instituteforpr.com/international.phtml?article_id=bribbery_index

Jackel, A. (2001). Romania: From tele-revolution to public service broadcasting, national images and international image. *Canadian Journal of Communication, 26,* 131–141.

Jackobson, M. (1998). *Finland in the new Europe.* Westport, CT: Praeger.

Kunczik, M. (1997). *Images of nations and international public relations.* Mahwah, NJ: Lawrence Erlbaum.

Kunczik, M. (2003). Transnational public relations by foreign governments. In K. Sriramesh, & D. Vercic (Eds.), *The global public relations handbook: Theory, research, and practice* (pp. 399–424). Mahwah, NJ: Lawrence Erlbaum.

Kunczik, M., & Weber, U. (1994). Public diplomacy and public relations advertisements of foreign countries in Germany. *The Journal of International Communication, 1,* 18–40.

Lavery, J. (1997). Finland at eighty: A more confident and open nation. *Scandinavian Review, 85,* 13–18.

Liss, A. (2003). Images of China in the American print media: A survey from 2000 to 2002. *Journal of Contemporary China, 12,* 299–318.

Moffitt, M. A. (2001). Using the collapse model of corporate image for campaign message design. In R. L. Heath (Ed.), *Handbook of public relations* (pp. 347–355). Thousand Oaks, CA: Sage.

Shishkina, M. A. (1999). *Public relations v sisteme sotsialnogo upravleniya* (Public relations in the system of social management). St. Petersburg, Russia: St. Petersburg State University Press.

Tsetsura, K. (2003). The development of public relations in Russia: A geopolitical approach. In K. Sriramesh, & D. Vercic (Eds.), *A handbook of International Public relations* (pp. 301–319). Mahwah, NJ: Lawrence Erlbaum Assoc. Inc.

Tsetsura, K., & Kruckeberg, D. (2004a). Theoretical development of public relations in Russia. In D. J. Tilson (Ed.), *Toward the common good: Perspectives in international public relations* (pp. 176–192). Boston: Allyn & Bacon.

Tsetsura, K., & Kruckeberg, D. (2004b). Contemporary Russian journalism's problems and opportunities (pp. 242–256), a part of the chapter "Eastern Europe, the newly independent states of Eurasia and Russia." In A. S. deBeer and J. C. Merrill (Eds.), *Global Journalism,* 4th ed. (pp. 212–256). Boston: Allyn & Bacon.

13 Avon's "Kiss Goodbye to Breast Cancer" Campaign in the Philippines

ZENAIDA SARABIA-PANOL

Executive Summary

True to its corporate mantra as the champion of women's health, beauty, and empowerment, Avon launched a global program called "Kiss Goodbye to Breast Cancer" in 2001. The goals of the campaign were to create awareness and raise funds to improve access to medical care, especially by underserved and uninsured women, as well as to support research for a breast cancer cure.

A year later this worldwide campaign debuted in the Philippines. In partnership with the Philippine Cancer Society, Avon Philippines launched its own Kiss Goodbye to Breast Cancer program in March 2002. The campaign underscored the importance of awareness and early detection as the best cure for the disease. Through media relations and the use of Filipino women celebrities in government, education, the corporate world, and entertainment.

The fundraising part of the campaign featured the sale of special-edition lipsticks in March through April 2002. A five-peso donation for every lipstick sold was earmarked for (1) the establishment of a Breast Care Center at the Philippine General Hospital Cancer Institute, and (2) the purchase of a new mammography machine for the Center. In October 2002, the Breast Care Center was inaugurated (Public Relations Society of the Philippines, 2003). The choice of the Philippine General Hospital, a publicly-funded health facility known for research as well as reasonably-priced expert medical treatment, is noteworthy. It signaled that Avon wanted to benefit the less privileged among Filipino women, perhaps the larger market segment of its products as well.

Research

Since the Kiss Goodbye to Breast Cancer campaign is a global project started in the United Kingdom, Avon Philippines was not aware of any primary research done specifically for the program. From media reports, it was evident that secondary research on the general status of breast cancer in the Philippines may have been undertaken and shared with the media. News stories cited the following statistics/facts: a) that breast cancer is the most common form of cancer among women and is the leading cause of cancer death in women aged 40–55 (Jimenez-David, 2002); b) that the incidence of the disease among poor Filipino women is increasing; c) that one out of 28 women in the Philippines who reach 64 years, and one out of 19 who live up to 74 years, will have breast cancer; d) that every year cancer claims the lives of 4,000 Filipino women (DeLeon-Matsude & Defensor, 2002); and e) that the Philippines has the highest incidence of breast cancer in Asia and the 10th-highest in the world (The Philippine Breast Cancer Network, 2003; Mugas, 2003).

Cultural Considerations

Anecdotal evidence showing that Filipino women, or women in general, defer their own healthcare in favor of other concerns seems to have guided the campaign. Attitudes of women in the Philippines, such as finding it easier to discuss beauty rather than sensitive health issues like breast cancer, may have driven the decision to emphasize improving awareness of the disease. Older Filipinas consider health matters private and are therefore not inclined to discuss problems, particularly those involving their private anatomy.

Aside from cultural factors, there are other psychological and economic impediments to early detection of breast cancer or other diseases. Louie Migne, senior public relations manager of Avon Philippines, said in an interview that Filipinas, especially those who are indigent, would rather not go to the doctor for fear of finding out that they are sick (Migne, personal communications, Oct. 28, 2003). She quoted a very familiar refrain: "*Ayoko na lang pumunta sa doctor, baka malaman ko pa na may sakit ako.*" (I don't want to see the doctor; I might know that I am sick.)

This general fear among the poor of knowing about their illness is very much an economic issue. Being sick is an added financial burden for many who confront the daily pressure of making ends meet. Many female daily wage earners don't want to go to the hospital and lose a day's wage. Often, they go to the Philippine General Hospital Breast Care Center only when they are already in the late stages of breast cancer, Migne noted. In a country where there is no universal health-care system and health insurance provided by either large corporations or the government to their employees is, at best, limited in coverage, getting sick becomes a battle over putting food on the table or buying medicine.

Faced with conflicting priorities, many Filipinos often resort to fatalism (*bahala na* mentality), religion, or the cheaper neighborhood *albolario* (quack doctor). About 85 percent of Filipinos are Roman Catholics, primarily women, in general. It is a country where churches are still packed on Sundays and other religious days. Like other women in many parts of the world, Filipinas are considered the primary caregivers. As a result, their own health care is given lower priority than other family needs. But unlike women in other Asian countries, Filipinas enjoy a special and rather powerful place in the home. For traditional Filipino families, it's the wife who manages and controls the purse strings. Opportunities such as education and employment are made available to women the same as they are for men. In fact, remnants of a long history of chivalry shaped by centuries of Spanish rule are still apparent, albeit to a lesser extent now, in Filipino men's behavior. Philippine men still can be seen relinquishing a seat on the bus for a woman. Also, Filipino men are generally protective and possessive of their women.

Avon's Organizational Culture

Operating in 143 countries, this "company for women" established its presence in the Philippines in 1978. Avon is known for its advocacy of women's health, particularly breast cancer education and treatment. The company seems to have a decentralized structure. Avon agreed to the general strategies and the execution tactics proposed by the Philippine office (Migne, personal communications, Oct. 29, 2003).

There are about 300,000 "Avon ladies" in the Philippines. They do not just sell company products but they also help to spread the life-saving gospel of early detection and better education in the fight against breast cancer.

Past Communication Efforts.   In 1993, Avon Philippines conducted the *Bigay Alam ay Bigay Buhay* (Give Knowledge, Give Life) Women's Cancer Information Crusade. With the help of the Philippine Cancer Society's volunteer doctors, Avon organized seminars nationwide to teach Filipinas how to detect breast cancer in its early stages and how to develop good preventive health habits among women. Many of the women targeted and reached by the campaign belong to poorer communities. Since the start of the crusade, Avon averaged 180 seminars a year and reached approximately 7,200 women annually (Migne, personal communications, Oct. 29, 2003).

Complementing this effort is the information on how to do a breast self-examination contained in the packaging of Avon brassieres sold in the country by Avon ladies or through department stores. The company sells at least half a million bras each year.

Marking the tenth anniversary of the Avon Breast Cancer Crusade, Andrea Jung, Avon chairperson and chief executive officer, reported that the goal of raising $250,000 worldwide had been reached in 2002. The funds were appropriated to support the breast cancer cause in the following areas: medical research, clinical care, support services, education and advocacy training, and early detection and awareness programs, with a focus on reaching medically underserved women (Avon website, www.avon.com). The Avon Breast Cancer Crusade benefits 50 countries, including the Philippines. The Avon Crusade in the United States was the largest program in the worldwide campaign. In 10 years of the crusade, some 2,000 educational sessions have been conducted in the Philippines, reaching about 70,000 Filipino women (Avon website).

Publics

The primary audience of the Kiss Goodbye to Breast Cancer campaign are Filipino women age 19 and older who can have breast cancer. Priority was given to reaching indigent or medically underserved Filipinas. Targeting this age group means reaching roughly 21.8 million Filipinas. In 2002, the number of Philippine residents was placed at 79.5 million, with women comprising 49.6 percent of the population (Philippine Department of Health, 2003). About 48 percent of the nation's population is urbanized, indicating that slightly more than half live in rural areas. The Kiss Goodbye to Breast Cancer campaign also targeted the local media and cancer support groups. The Philippine Cancer Society (2003) estimated that in 1998 there were close to 10,000 new cases of breast cancer in the country. The disease ranked third among the leading cancer deaths in the Philippines. About 3, 057 women died of breast cancer in 1998.

Objectives

The Philippine Kiss Goodbye to Breast Cancer program's objectives were twofold: (1) to increase breast cancer awareness among Filipino women, and (2) to raise funds for the establishment of a Breast Care Center at the Philippine General Hospital Cancer Institute and to equip the Center with a new mammography unit. The two-month fundraising project started in March 2002. The timeline for the fundraising effort included turning over funds to the Philippine General Hospital Cancer Institute in May 2002. The Center's inauguration was scheduled for October 2002.

The Kiss Goodbye to Breast Cancer project is a multi-year campaign. The project is part of the overall positioning of Avon as a "socially responsible corporate citizen that actively supports women's health issues."

Strategies

For optimal impact of the awareness part of the campaign, Avon Philippines targeted opinion leaders in the media, used celebrity women, and allied with breast cancer support groups and the Philippine Cancer Society. It also strategically utilized its Avon ladies, who in addition to the Philippine Cancer Society's medical volunteers, had direct face-to-face interaction with the target audience.

Action Strategies

Although Avon did not start as an advocate for women's issues during the company's inception, no change in the corporate culture was needed specifically for the Kiss Goodbye to Breast Cancer program. The company was already cultivating a reputation for social responsibility in the early 1990s. It has successfully positioned itself as an advocate of women's health and other issues such as leadership and empowerment. Perhaps it is not too far-fetched to say that Avon's advocacy role crescendoed with the Kiss Goodbye to Breast Cancer campaign.

Definitely not a do-it-alone kind of corporation, Avon formed special coalitions and alliances. It developed good partnerships with the media, celebrities, cancer support networks, and the Philippine Cancer Society. By establishing these alliances, Avon earned added legitimacy for its cause.

Special project launches were scheduled for each of these partner groups. During these launch events, invited guests were asked to commit their support to the breast cancer cause with the purchase of the lipsticks. The commitment is "sealed" with their lip prints on specially made Kiss GoodBye to Breast Cancer Pledge Cards. These special events and media relations formed the core of the high public visibility aspects of the awareness campaign. To generate maximum media buzz, Avon solicited celebrity support. Unique Kiss Goodbye to Breast Cancer cards were sent to well-known Filipina movie and television personalities as well as women leaders in business, academic, public service, and government sectors. Many Filipina celebrities donated their "kiss prints" free to the cause.

Communication Strategies

The country's broadsheets and women's magazines were the targeted media outlets. Because the Kiss Goodbye to Breast Cancer campaign is a public service aimed to raise awareness of a devastating disease, three of the nation's top dailies (*Philippine Daily Enquirer, Philippine Star,* and the *Manila Bulletin*) donated a spread each to help publicize the project. In addition to print ads and public service announcements, news stories and feature articles found their way in the news media.

Avon's use of women celebrity endorsements is a classic application of a propaganda/persuasion technique. In a country where celebrities have such a magnetic hold of a vast segment of the target public, it would be folly not to harness the potency of their following. Another strategy was the involvement of the Philippine Cancer Society, with its corps of medical experts and volunteers. The Society's participation provided credibility needed for the project to accomplish its intended persuasive impact. This is another definitive application of the Elaboration Likelihood Model (Petty & Cacioppo, 1986), where expert sources, as exemplified by the doctors and cancer specialists of the Society, dispensed information to Filipino women about the disease and how to detect it in its early stages.

In the fundraising effort the main strategic forces were: a) the already established Avon brochures with estimated nationwide circulation of 600,000, and b) the Avon sales associates spread all over the country. Avon supported the fundraising drive by providing front-cover promotion of the lipsticks in their brochures. For every Kiss Goodbye to Breast Cancer lipstick sold, five Philippine pesos were appropriated for the construction of the Breast Care Center and the acquisition of a new mammography machine installed at the Philippine General Hospital Cancer Institute's Breast Care Center.

Raising funds for the establishment of the Center became a significant component of the project because past experiences pointed to the urgent need for such a facility. During Avon's breast cancer advocacy campaign in the early 1990s, for instance, a growing number of women exposed to the company's message at their seminars asked where they could go when a lump was detected. These women were referred to provincial or government hospitals that woefully lacked the facilities to address their concerns.

Diffusion of ideas and innovations theory had important lessons in developing countries to which Avon, through its Kiss Goodbye to Breast Cancer project, wisely paid attention. The lesson is that communication without the supporting infrastructure is not sufficient to bring about change in attitudes and behavior of target publics. By providing the means and equipment support such as those of the Breast Care Center, Avon's call for vigilance in the fight against breast cancer has the potential to gain more success among Filipinos.

While media relations and celebrity participation were certain attention-grabbing devices that started the campaign with a big bang and added glitter, for the project to make an impact where it is needed, it has to put a face to the campaign that the ordinary Filipino woman can identity with. Persuasion research has found that "communicators are more likely to change attitudes if they are perceived to be similar rather than dissimilar to those they seek to influence" (Perloff, 1993). Because similarity between message source and receiver enhances persuasion, Avon rightly involved its female sales force. The 300,000-strong Avon ladies literally became the foot soldiers of the campaign as they zealously brought the crusade door-to-door, selling the Kiss Goodbye to Breast Cancer lipsticks and the idea that the best cure for breast cancer is education and early detection. Planning and preparation for the campaign took nine months. All planning was done internally. An outside public relations firm handled media relations, and production of collateral materials was likewise outsourced.

The total budget for the first year (2002) of the Kiss Goodbye to Breast Cancer campaign was 1.5 million Philippine pesos. U.S. dollar-peso exchange rate at the time of the campaign ranged from 50 to 55 pesos to a dollar.

Tactics

The key messages sent through multiple channels were: a) that breast cancer is a threat to ALL women regardless of age, race, and social or economic status, and that b) awareness and early detection are the best weapons to control the disease.

Associated messages were also included, such as that having breast cancer is not a death sentence and that Filipinas must have yearly medical checkups. The campaign stressed that Filipino women must take care of themselves. It is an obligation to themselves and to their families if they truly love them. These messages were crafted out of the client's understanding of the cultural and socioeconomic realities of the target public discussed earlier. The Kiss Goodbye to Breast Cancer campaign emphasized that cancer is a survivable disease, if detected early. The message was that prevention and early detection are much less traumatic and expensive than a full-blown treatment regimen or surgery.

These messages were repeated in several controlled and uncontrolled communication channels such as the mass media; corporate collateral materials that included product packaging, promotional brochures, and pledge cards; small-group communication in the form of campaign launch events; community seminars; and the direct interpersonal communication done by Avon ladies and medical volunteers of the Philippine Cancer Society.

All of the Avon information materials were written in English. The Philippines has a large English-speaking population. The country also has a literacy rate of 95 percent, one of the highest in Asia.

Evaluation

No formal evaluation research was conducted for the public awareness phase of the Kiss Goodbye to Breast Cancer campaign. However, the Avon Philippines senior public relations manager indicated, "if you will consider combined readership of all newspapers and television programs that broadcast the event, we easily reached over two million people. To add to this the reach of 550,000 Avon brochures that included the program, that would make it at least three million people reached" (Migne, personal communications, Oct. 29, 2003).

The Kiss Goodbye to Breast Cancer campaign also received critical approval from the nation's public relations industry. Avon Philippines received the 38th Anvil Award of excellence given annually by the Public Relations Society of the Philippines. In the project description submitted for the Silver Anvil Award, Avon wrote, "Through press releases and feature articles in major broadsheets and women's magazines, "Kiss Goodbye to Breast Cancer" gained high publicity mileage and strengthened Avon's image as the company committed to women's health" (PRSP, 2003).

The fundraising part of the program had more measurable results. Some 700,000 lipsticks were sold by April 2002. The funds generated led to the construction of the Breast Care Center at the Philippine General Hospital Cancer Institute. The Center was inaugurated October 8, 2002, and was attended by several luminaries. Senator Loren Legarda-Leviste, also a popular television personality, was the guest of honor at the inauguration. The Center was fully operational in November. Based on the latest reports, the Center is serving an average of 150 women daily four times a week. Wednesday is chemotherapy day. Before the Center was built, the Philippine General Hospital Outpatient Department was open to women with breast cancer concerns one day a week only.

Critique

Research

By local and perhaps many other standards, the Kiss Goodbye to Breast Cancer Philippine campaign was a resounding success despite one obvious weakness: the lack of primary research to guide the program. The campaign could have made use of research that empirically established prior knowledge of and attitudes toward breast cancer in the Philippines, especially because the Kiss Goodbye to Breast Cancer campaign followed a decade-long breast cancer information crusade that started in the early 1990s. Anecdotal evidence was useful in strategic communication planning, but the choice of media and the language used in information materials and related message elements reveal the common pitfalls of implementing global campaigns without adequate localization.

Also, whatever secondary research was done could have been more systematic. The program could have benefited from simple audience research that largely drew from existing census records and other studies as well as observations. This audience research, along with past experiences with similar campaigns, could have been used to create a profile of the target public in terms of demographic information, such as age, income, education, marital status, media habits, etc. The campaign planners could also have used statistical information and other existing secondary data on the extent of the problem in order to identify at-risk groups. Research could have been helpful in scientifically understanding the communication behavior as well as information sources of the target audience across different economic, age, educational, or even geographical strata. Database information on their customers as well as their women sales associates could have generated a wealth of knowledge vital to the planning and strategic decision making for the campaign.

The use of English-language broadsheets, for instance, reveals an urban economic and educational bias. While Manila and other big cities, such as Cebu, Davao, Naga, and Tuguegarao, have indeed several pockets of medically underserved women, the vast majority of at-risk women are outside the metropolitan areas, some in far-flung rural places not reached by newspapers and television. Radio and local-dialect publications are most likely the more accessible media for the poverty-stricken, less educated, and non-urban members of target women populations in the Philippines.

Defining the audience as women 19 years or older is a good start, but begs for more substantive information. For instance, how many and where are they? What's their educational background and prior knowledge about breast cancer? These are legitimate questions to ask, but in a country where it is often a choice between using scarce resources for research or actual information dissemination as well as the purchase of medical equipment, the questions may be rendered moot and academic. It can be argued that having a program like Avon's is better than none at all. Besides, doing primary research in the Philippines has its inherent difficulties as well.

To the credit of local program organizers, they appeared to have a general sense of the prevailing attitudinal/behavioral framework of the target audience, particularly in relation to health issues. Culled from experiences in their previous breast cancer crusade project in the 1990s, Avon Philippines made the best use of what information they had to offset the absence of real, systematic primary research data.

Objective

The first objective, "to raise awareness . . ." was not stated in measurable terms. Raise from what to what level? This lack of specifics is understandable, though, as no rigorous research was done on prior awareness levels. It is therefore difficult to empirically determine if this objective was satisfactorily met. For instance, did the campaign increase awareness of those that had some knowledge of the threat posed by the disease? Or did the campaign mean to reach those who have never heard of breast cancer? If the campaign aimed to increase awareness of particular aspects of the disease, what message, media, and information materials were chosen to accomplish this?

By deduction, however, it can be said that since the information crusade in the early 1990s reached approximately 700,000 Filipinas, the estimated three-million reach for the Kiss Goodbye to Breast Cancer represents an increase of some 2.3 million more Philippine women.

The fundraising part of the program was better defined. It was straightforward in the sense that it set aside a fixed amount of money for the establishment of the Breast Care Center and to equip the facility with a mammography unit. It could have been better, however, to explicitly state what was the goal in actual pesos or the total number of lipsticks that needed to be sold at the start of the fundraising campaign. The reader is left to conclude that what was raised was what was needed to completely fund the Center's construction and equipment purchase. But was this the case?

Moreover, the underlying objective, which was "to enhance Avon's image as a socially responsible corporate citizen that actively supports women's health issues," assumes that in the first place Filipinos already perceive the company as socially responsible. Again, without scientifically finding out how the company is actually perceived, it is rather difficult to ascertain if the perception is to be "enhanced" or to be created.

Strategies

Action Strategies.   Given that the corporation has for a decade developed a reputation as a champion of women's causes, it is not hard to imagine that this value or the corporation's advocacy role permeated the organization at all levels in the various countries where it operates. It would seem that the actions implemented in the Philippines were appropriate. The building of alliances was an exceptionally clever strategy.

Communication Strategies.   Cognizant of the project constraints due to a lack of primary research, the communication strategies used created the high visibility and media attention it wanted. However, creating age-specific information and selection of media channels that accounted for critical differences in education, language, and geographic location would have tremendously improved the campaign. Even if English is widely spoken in the Philippines and the country has one of the highest literacy levels in the region, it is still better to reflect the diverse demographic characteristics of the target audience in the communication materials used, particularly if the primary public is underserved women. It must be recognized that functional literacy does not necessarily mean medical literacy. Scientific and technical terms or medical jargon often need more explanation and are therefore not readily accessible to the ordinary Pepe and Pilar in the Philippines.

Fortunately, what Avon lacked in this area may have been offset by the use of its women sales associates, the Philippine Cancer Society, and other cancer support groups. However, it was not clear if the company provided special training or communication strategies for its sales force in relation to the Kiss Goodbye to Breast Cancer program.

Tactics

The creative approach used is an undeniable strength of the campaign. The kiss-prints in pledge cards were unique and relevant, since the sale of lipsticks was the primary fundraising mechanism. The celebrity kiss-prints were instant and sure-fire media attention-getting placements. Special events also generated excellent media coverage.

However, the campaign basically used a formulaic technique that had the built-in ease of translating or exporting the Kiss Goodbye to Breast Cancer campaign to destination countries. Just change the celebrities and you have a local angle. The messages, such as how to do a self-breast examination, can be sent without change, as the steps are the same. What is different is the language used. Here, Avon could have taken that extra step to really localize the campaign materials. Fortunately, they have the local volunteers and health workers who can do, and must have done, the translating.

Evaluation

Evidently, the campaign used media impressions to gauge success of the awareness campaign. Many public relations programs use this method, including award-winning ones, and it is generally seen in the industry as an acceptable measure. The fact that others use this strategy does not make it a valid measure of campaign success. The Kiss Goodbye to Breast Cancer campaign could have used a more systematic procedure, for example, a before-and-after comparison of the media coverage of breast cancer in the Philippines. This kind of information would establish, beyond a doubt, the impact of the campaign in terms of media exposure.

The problem is that the stated objective was to "raise awareness," so without a benchmark, it is hard to evaluate if this was indeed accomplished. Creating the messages and publishing them does not automatically mean that people paid attention, became aware of, or understood the message. Walt Seifert, public relations emeritus professor at Ohio State University, wrote: "Dissemination does not equal publication, and publication does not equal absorption and action. All who receive it won't publish it, and all who read or hear won't understand or act upon it" (Wilcox et al., 2003, p. 168).

The Kiss Goodbye to Breast Cancer campaign, by organizer's estimates, reached at least three million people. This is a high media penetration figure and is quite impressive, regardless of what Seifert said. But if you compare this with the total population of women age 19 and above, the number accounts only for 14 percent of the target population. If the program was clear with their targeted number or if Avon Philippines simply wanted to reach three million or so and stated this in the objective, it would have been far more easy to judge whether or not the goal was met.

Obviously, the fundraising achieved what it intended because the Breast Care Center is up and running. It is a facility that can serve more and more Filipinas that need medical attention and treatment for cancer. This part of the campaign unequivocally illustrates Avon's success in cause-oriented marketing.

DISCUSSION QUESTIONS

1. What is cause-oriented marketing? Is this what was done in this campaign? What ethical questions does cause-oriented marketing raise?

2. What types of research could be done for health-related information campaigns such as Kiss Goodbye to Breast Cancer? How would you design such research?

3. How can the research be done more cost-effectively?

4. How important is the need to consider local conditions in implementing health campaigns that are part of a global initiative? What local conditions do you think are important for implementing a campaign in the rural Philippines?

5. In what ways can the Kiss Goodbye to Breast Cancer program be made more relevant and better attuned to Philippine conditions?

6. What information do you want to have about the country, the disease, the target audience, and the media when implementing a campaign like the Kiss Goodbye to Breast Cancer campaign?

7. Why is responsible corporate citizenship important for a global company such as Avon?

8. What were the strengths and weaknesses of the Avon campaign?

9. What other possible groups and institutions can Avon tap as possible partners in their crusade against breast cancer in the Philippines?

10. Does it create an "elitist" perception for Avon Philippines because of its use of well-known Filipino women in their campaign? If it does, what can be done to reconcile its declared effort to reach medically underserved or otherwise ordinary but disadvantaged women populations?

REFERENCES AND SUGGESTED READINGS

Avon website (2003). Retrieved from www.avon.com/women/avoncrusade/services/.

DeLeon-Matsude, M. L., & Defensor, T. (2002, February 11). Kissing breast cancer goodbye. *Business World (Philippines)*.

Department of Health, Philippines. (2003). Retrieved from www.doh.gov.ph.

Jimenez-David, R. (2002, February 10). A life-saving lipstick story. *Philippine Daily Enquirer.*

Mugas, N. V. (2003, February 24). Breast cancer patients pin hope on new drug. *The Manila Times.*

Perloff, R. M. (1993). *The Dynamics of persuasion.* Hillsdale, NJ: Lawrence Erlbaum Associates.

Petty, R. E., & Cacioppo, J. T. (1986). The elaboration likelihood model of persuasion. In L. Berkowitz (Ed.), *Advances in experimental social psychology* (pp. 123–205). New York: Academic Press.

The Philippine Breast Cancer Network (2003). A government's role in the rise of breast cancer. Retrieved from www.pbcn.org.

Philippine Cancer Society (2003). Retrieved from www.philcancer.org.

Public Relations Society of the Philippines (2003). Retrieved from www.prsponline.org/programs/38th_anvil_winners/kiss_goodbye_to_breast_cancer.html.

Wilcox, D., Cameron, G., Ault, P., & Agee, W. (2003). *Public relations strategies and tactics* (7th ed.). Boston, MA: Allyn & Bacon.

14 One Tambon, One Product: Part of the War against Poverty in Thailand

ROSECHONGPORN KOMOLSEVIN

Executive Summary

The "One Tambon, One Product" project, or OTOP, was initiated in 2001 by the Prime Minister of Thailand, Thaksin Shinawatra, as one of the urgent policies to "wage war against poverty" among farmers and the rural poor. The project derived from the success of a similar project in Oita, a Japanese village, and was designed to create income for each tambon's (sub-district of a province) farmers, merchants, and artisans through the continuous promotion for national consumption of the local products as well as market expansion to include international distribution. The project had three basic principles:

1. Local yet global—producing products from local talents and resources, yet achieving global standard and acceptance.
2. Self-reliance and creativity—focusing on local potentials, skills, and independence.
3. Human resource development—enhancing abilities and potentials among villagers.

Project Goals

The project aimed to help villagers to be self-reliant in the long run; therefore, the government provided only necessary financial support and helped in research, product development, manufacturing, and marketing strategies. The project's goals were to achieve:

1. Products with global standards—the manufactured products have to attain the acceptable quality standards in the international markets.
2. Uniqueness—the products should be regarded as one-of-a-kind, incomparable and irreplaceable.
3. Human resource development and technological improvement—to develop human quality with planning vision, knowledge, and skills.

Involved Parties

The following parties were involved in the OTOP project.

1. Government agencies acted as a liaison and supportive function for community initiatives.
2. Local businesses participated in developing products and solving any problems arising within the community.
3. Community leaders served as leaders and addressed the community's needs.
4. Public/civic groups (such as agricultural cooperative groups, chambers of commerce, and women groups) represented the public interests and initiated marketing strategies and operations.

Research

Before the project was introduced to the whole nation, it had been piloted in Chiang Mai, the largest province in the northern part of Thailand. This province has long been famous for its exotic handicrafts, agricultural products, and several tourist attractions. Other than the pilot project, there was no systematic study investigating the possibility of launching the local products in the international markets. The OTOP products were launched and promoted only on the assumption that hand-made and environmentally friendly products have been highly valued in the global market.

Although exporting OTOP products to international markets is a goal of this project, no market-oriented studies were conducted, unfortunately. The government focused mainly on restructuring the production base in the industrial and services sectors to meet the needs of modern-day markets. Further, a great deal of effort was invested in strengthening local cooperatives, businesses, and organizations to prepare them for upcoming new business ventures.

Government Considerations

The OTOP project was initiated by the Prime Minister as an urgent and long-term program to eliminate poverty, to improve community self-reliance, and to strengthen the grassroots economy. It therefore received unanimous support from every party concerned in both public and private sectors. In addition, the project was allocated a generous budget from the government. In 2003, 800 million baht (or about $U.S. 20 million) was appropriated to continue the project.

Description of the Project

OTOP products can be categorized according to the regions in which they were implemented.

1. Northern region—ceramics and Chinaware
2. Central and Southern regions—hand-woven products
3. Northeastern region—hand-woven cloth and garments

The varieties of OTOP products also included all aspects of the four vital elements in daily life: food, clothing, medicine, and housing.

Problem Identification

No matter how well local products were showcased, some OTOP products were still perceived as low quality. Some consumers thought poor hygiene was used in their processing and manufacturing. This perception may have resulted from the fact that some villages still lacked knowledge in production, planning, and marketing strategies.

Another problem was that not all communities were committed to the project. This was probably because they were used to receiving handouts from the government, and never had to make an effort to initiate an income-generating project.

Further, despite the government's arduous promotion efforts, the public awareness of OTOP products was fairly limited. The government's Public Relations Department (PRD) was responsible for promoting OTOP products nationally, while the Ministry of Commerce and private groups were in charge of marketing, promotion, and product distribution internationally. Only 24 million baht (or about $U.S. 600,000) was appropriated for the domestic PR efforts, while 160 million baht (or about $U.S. 4 million) was spent for marketing and promotion tasks.

Publics

The government's goal was to market products of the OTOP project throughout the country and to the rest of the world. The Ministry of Commerce and the Department of Export Promotion (DEP) were responsible for introducing and distributing the products to the international markets. As mentioned earlier, there were no data on the foreign customers' needs for or interests in these products. However, with their extensive experiences on export promotion, along with information about foreign markets and needs supplied by Thai embassies worldwide, the DEP was able to market the OTOP products to the overseas markets without much difficulty.

Communication Vehicles

To reach the predetermined goal of international acceptance of locally made Thai products, a number of communication projects were implemented. The Prime Minister himself, for example, has served as a main spokesperson for the project. He has made numerous speeches to both local and international audiences to promote the acceptance of OTOP products. He also urged Thai embassies worldwide to do the same.

OTOP products have been exhibited and distributed via numerous channels. The main traditional venues are the OTOP fairs, regularly held in big cities to introduce the products to international traders. In addition, Thai Airways International has served OTOP snacks and drinks and sold them as duty-free goods on board. Hotels and restaurants put them on their menus. Foreign-backed supermarkets (e.g., Big C, Tesco, Carrefours) dedicated a portion of their space to display and sell the OTOP products. Exhibitions and displays of OTOP products at some international seminars and conferences were also held.

Objectives

Since this project's concept is relatively new to the public, the government primarily wanted to make the international public aware of the project and to encourage support for OTOP products. Hence, extensive efforts in marketing and promotion activities were used to penetrate the international markets.

PR Objectives for International Public

1. To build awareness, knowledge, understanding, and positive attitudes among foreign customers in and out of Thailand toward OTOP project and products.
2. To distribute information about OTOP products to the international markets in both public and private sectors.

The OTOP publicity activities were planned on a yearly basis, usually from January to September. The Planners expected 70 percent awareness among the domestic public. However, no exact percentage for measuring international outputs and outcomes was mentioned.

Strategies

Action Strategies

The promotion of OTOP products to international markets was implemented by the Department of Export Promotion (DEP), Ministry of Commerce (with the support of the private sectors), Ministry of Foreign Affairs, Tourism Authority of Thailand, National Electronics and Computer Center (NECTEC), Ministry of Industry, and Ministry of Transportation. Those efforts were focused on marketing rather than public relations.

To push the products to the overseas markets, DEP asked manufacturers from 75 provinces throughout the country to display their products in the "Made in Thailand" fairs. Additional OTOP trade fairs were scheduled in other countries, as well. OTOP products were also carried at several department stores, foreign-owned retail stores, and local community stores.

Communication Strategies

Use of Communication Technology in OTOP Promotion.   An Internet network was established for every tambon (estimated 7,000 sites), called "Internet Tambon" or Thaitambon.com, as a center for information and e-commerce service for local products from all districts nationwide. Technology was used to facilitate transactions between the villagers and international customers.

Interpersonal Channel.   The Prime Minister stated in his policy that Thai ambassadors worldwide should perform the "salesman" role because they have extensive contacts with and knowledge about the people in their assigned country. Thai delegates and representatives in international trade meetings were expected to play the salesman role as well. Further, besides pitching OTOP products, they were also expected to use those products.

Print Media. Feature articles about OTOP products often appeared in the flight magazine of Thai Airways International, which is owned by a state agency.

Tactics

Product Display. Exhibitions and displays of OTOP products have been regularly held at tourist attraction sites, shopping malls, international seminars, and conferences (Figure 1). Moreover, Thai embassies worldwide were expected to display OTOP products.

OTOP Gifts. The government recommended that OTOP products be promoted as New Year gifts. Consequently, all governmental agencies, central and local, joined hands with the private sectors to promote and sell the products. The policy has been extended to subsequent years.

FIGURE 1   A vendor displays Thai drums at a One Tambon, One Product Fair.
Source: Photo by R. Komolsevin

OTOP Fairs.   Fairs displaying OTOP products have been held in Thailand and in other countries such as in Japan, Malaysia, Brunei, South Korea, and Switzerland. These fairs are usually held at a famous trade exhibition center in a big city. The fairs featured numerous activities, including stalls selling products from several tambons in all the regions, and seminars to enable the local and international wholesalers and distributors to meet with the producers face-to-face. Thai and foreign export-import agents, along with foreign tourists were invited to attend the fairs (Figure 2).

FIGURE 2   OTOP Exhibit Plan

In Search of Excellence: OTOP Thailand

Venue	Convention Hall, Chiang Mai University, Chiang Mai, Thailand
Duration	7–8 August 2003 (10.00–18.00 hrs.) for trade negotiation only 9–10 August 2003 (10.00–21.00 hrs.) for retail sale
Organizer	Department of Export Promotion, Ministry of Commerce, Royal Thai Government
Exhibited Products	The showcase display of approximately 300 OTOP (One Tambon One Products) products that are best-selected from the villages all over Thailand and are ready to export to the world market. Product categories in this fair include:

    1. food and beverage products and herbs
    2. garments, jewelry and other fashion products
    3. gift, decorative items and household products

Exhibitor Profile	1. The manufacturers of OTOP products that are selected as the best of One Tambon One Products from every regions in Thailand 2. The Thai manufacturers/exporters who sell high-quality export products
Visitor Profile	1. approximately 400 businessmen who participate in APEC Business Forum 2. importers/buyers from all over the world, invited by Department of Export Promotion 3. buying agents in Thailand 4. Thai exporters/buyers/wholesalers
Special Activities	1. The gala dinner in Thai, northern style, on 6 August 2003 2. Field trip of cultural heritage and cottage craft makers in northern region
Contact Point	Ms. Nuanchawee Sintuchao/Ms. Natiya Suchinda Office of Thailand International Trade Fair Activities Thailand Export Mart Building, Department of Export Promotion 22/77 Rachadapisek Rd., Bangkok 10900 Tel. 0 2511 6020-30 ext. 706, 733 Fax. 0 25116008-10 email: hbs@depthai.go.th website: www.depthai.go.th

One Tambon One Product is the government project to enhance grass root movement and SMEs, especially the local producers, in order to present Thai-applied ingenuity, from nature to extraordinarily skilled hands and cultural heritage, together with local inspiration. Now, products from the project are ready to be presented to the world market.

Internet Tambon. In 2003, there were more than 1,200 OTOP items available on www. thaitambon.com. This represented an increase of more than 100 percent from the 585 items available in 2002 when the website started to offer information and sell local products on-line. The website received cooperation from each tambon in providing information about its specific products. Thaitambon worked closely with the Community Development Department, under the Ministry of Interior, to complete its information database and product details for every tambon nationwide. In addition, the website, in cooperation with several government agencies, will work on upgrading and standardizing local product quality and packaging, as part of a 5-year program initiated by the government to increase Thai products' competitiveness.

Evaluation

A formal evaluation of the project's success was to be conducted at the end of 2003. This case report was written before that evaluation was complete. So far, the government claimed that this project has been a big success because it has built awareness, favorable attitudes, and interest within overseas markets. Sales of OTOP products to foreign sellers were said to be abundant. However, this claim lacks substantive proofs from related authoritative agencies.

Critique

The OTOP project is an attempt by the government to decentralize its administrative efforts and development initiatives at the grassroots level. This project encourages rural people to be self-reliant and self-supporting.

Most villagers have readily welcomed the project, and most villages in every province seemed to be ready to start this project. They already had their own products before the implementation of the OTOP project, but they operated on a small scale and only for daily and limited local use.

This project aims not only to generate adoption of the products among domestic consumers, but also to introduce them to overseas markets as well. Consequently, extensive marketing and promotion efforts have been conducted to achieve the intended goal. Public relations, however, has played a less significant role than marketing in this project. Public relations has been limited to generating publicity about the products in Thailand. Drawbacks in the OTOP promotion may be summarized as follows:

Research

There has been no systematic research on the physical and psychological characteristics of the overseas publics who are different from one another in terms of their needs, values, and norms. Further, there was no research on existing attitudes toward, or awareness of, Thai products. DEP, with supports from other related agencies, relied heavily on previous experiences in international trading. Lack of formal research will deprive DEP of clear visions about the true nature of the overseas markets, and of their capability to place the "right products in the right markets."

Objectives

The objective of the project is clear—that is, to promote OTOP products to international markets. However, there was no clear public relations objective. For example, the stated objective included increased awareness and information distribution, but it did not specify any change in a target public. Further, there was no timeframe for this project. The one reasonable public relations objective indicated the project would increase domestic awareness of OTOP by 75 percent. However, with no pre-campaign measure of awareness, it would be impossible to measure success of even that objective. This project relies mostly on marketing and promotion, not public relations. However, there were not even marketing objectives with specific timeframes or specified marketing outcomes.

Strategies

This project relies on the "push" strategies of marketing and product promotion rather than the "pull" approach of public relations. Marketing or push strategies are suitable for "maturity-stage" products that already have a stable image, but not for new competitors who are trying to grasp the public's attention. To build a favorable image of the new products, the pull strategies of public relations may be a better choice. This is the approach aimed at generating the public's demands of the products first, and the public will seek for the products later. With the unique characteristics of OTOP products, they should not be treated like other common goods competing in the marketplace. Rather, they should be guided into a particular niche where consumers have specific demands for unique or unusual products. The unique image of the OTOP products, once that has been created successfully, may better generate interest and favorable attitudes among overseas customers.

The marketing approach, in this case, focused mainly on the desired customers in oversees markets. By and large, it ignored other stakeholders who may provide fruitful inputs and benefits to the products. These people include, for example, the press, the general publics of respective countries, or other interest groups. If the Thai government could stimulate needs or desire for OTOP products within those publics they would, in turn, force the marketers to acquire the products for them. In this matter, only public relations can successfully fulfill the said tasks.

The strategy also lacked a theoretic foundation. While several activities were conducted to ensure display or availability of the products, there was no consistent theme or message about those products. Applying communication theory may have facilitated identification of messages and media that would more readily establish a favorable image of the OTOP products.

Tactics

In accordance with the marketing approach, information has been regularly supplied to potential foreign marketers, in hopes they will make an order for OTOP products to sell in their respective countries. Marketing information is available on the OTOP website and at a number of product exhibitions held both in and outside Thailand. However, not many Thai people are aware of the website. Foreign tourists and traders are even less likely to know of the website. Likewise, product exhibitions should target more specific publics with common interests. Therefore, we cannot and should not expect those product exhibitions to provide thorough information to appropriate publics.

Evaluation

The stated objectives of the OTOP project were quite vague and there was no pre-campaign research. Therefore, it is impossible to evaluate the campaign's success. Claims of the project's success made by several government and private sectors were superficial and without substantiated and valid evidence. In this matter, formal evaluation is required in three areas. First, how far have OTOP products been penetrating into the particular overseas markets? Second, how are the customers in those respective countries satisfied with OTOP products? Third, what are the target publics' future needs for the products? Information generated from responses to the above questions will shed more light on the effectiveness of the OTOP project.

DISCUSSION QUESTIONS

1. If you were responsible for designing a campaign to create a demand for Thai products in the international market, what information would you need before you began to plan the campaign?
   a. What questions could you answer with secondary research? What questions would require primary research?
   b. Describe the sources you would use for secondary research. Describe how you would design any primary research you would use.

2. Who are the target publics for this campaign? Define them in as much detail as possible.

3. Are all the stakeholders in the campaign target publics? Who are other stakeholders?

4. Do you agree with the marketing approach used to promote the OTOP products to overseas markets? Why or why not?

5. If you wanted to market Thai products in the United States, how would you do that? How did you select these marketing techniques? What makes you think they will be successful?

6. How does public relations differ from marketing? Which is a better approach to creating demand for Thai products? Explain why you made your selection.

7. Assume your client is the Thai government and their organizational goal for OTOP is to increase sales of Thai products outside of Thailand. Write a public relations objective that supports this goal.

8. What theory or theories can be used to help develop a strategy to support a campaign to increase demand for Thai products in the United States? Explain both the theory or theories and the strategy you would create based on the theory or theories.

9. What tactics would you use to distribute the message or theme of this campaign? Explain why you think those tactics will be successful in delivering the campaign message to the target publics.

10. How would you evaluate the success of this campaign? Explain in detail any pre-campaign measurement and post-campaign testing you would do.

REFERENCES AND SUGGESTED READINGS

Anongkapongpun, C., & Ing-am, A. (2001). *The study of feasibility in establishing One Tambon One Product shop, Prachinburi province.* Retrieved on October 9, 2003 from http://library. kmitnb.ac.th/projects/itm/IM/im0002e.html.

ASIA Travel Tips.com. (2002, Oct. 2). *THAI signs agreement for sales of duty free goods on board to ensure good procurement governance. Latest Travel News.* Retrieved Oct. 9, 2003 from www. asiatraveltips.com/print.cgi?file=20ct02Thai.shtml.

Botbat/parakit khong nuay ngan tee keong kong [Roles/missions of related agencies]. (2003). Retrieved from www.cdfundnet.com/otopeight.htm.

Chiangmai is selected as the first province to launch the pilot One Tambon, One Product project. (2001, Aug. 13). *PRD On Line: National News Bureau.* Retrieved from http://thaimain.org/ cgi-bin/newsdesk_perspect.cgi?a=321&t=index_2 html.

Department of Business Development, Ministry of Commerce. (2003). *Promotion and development of markets for community products: The One Tambon-One Product (OTOP) concept.* Retrieved from www.thairegistration.com/eng/develop/mission3.phtml.

Department of Export Promotion, Ministry of Commerce, Thailand. (2002). *One Tambon-One Product Project: A report* [in Thai].

Department of International Economics, Ministry of Foreign Affairs, Thailand. (2003). *One Tambon-One Product Project: A report* [in Thai].

Internet Thailand. (2002, Aug. 14). *INET'S payment gateway helps Thai Tambon.com increase transaction efficiency and security.* [Press Release]. Retrieved from www.inet.co.th/newsflash/ 140802-eng.html.

One Tambon, One Product Program and APEC. (2003). *Thailand Board of Investment Bulletin.* Retrieved from www.boi.go.th/chinese/focus/foc_one_tambon_apec2003.html.

Paiboonrat, P. (2002, January 23). *IT for rural development: Internet villages, One Product One Tambon.* Retrieved from www.affrc.go.jp:8001/agwg/2002Phuket?papers/ab_nr4-1.htm.

Public Relations Department. (n.d.) *One Tambon, One Product: Promoting local* creations for global consumption. *Thailand Illustrated Magazine.* Retrieved from www.prd.go.th/ebook/ story.php?idmag=13&idstory=112.

Public Relations Department. (2002, June 2). One Tambon, One Product Project in Suphanburi. (2002). *Focus on Thailand.* Retrieved Oct. 9, 2003 from www.prd.go.th/ebook/focus/june02_ 03.html.

Public Relations Department. (2002, December). *Policy and public relations plan: First meeting agenda of the sub-committee on public relations for OTOP project.* Bangkok: Thailand: Ministry of Interior.

Public Relations Department. (2003, Aug. 13). *The Government will hold a grand exhibition on One Tambon One Product project at Sanam Luang Grounds. PRD On Line: National News Bureau.* Retrieved from http://thaimain.org/cgibin/newsdesk_local.cgi?a=1091&t=index_eng_ local.html.

Rungfapaisarn, K. (2002, December 8). One-Tambon, One-Product: Big chains eye Thai goods. *The Nation.* Retrieved from www.siamfuture.com/ThaiNews/ThNewsTxt.asp?tid=1427.

Shinawatra, T. (2003, August 7). *In Search of Excellence: One Tambon, One Product.* Speech presented at the opening ceremony of One Tambon, One Product fair. Chiangmai University, Thailand. Retrieved Oct. 9, 2003 from www.boi.go.th/thai/focus/foc_pm_opening_one_tambon.htm.

15

Engaging Colombian Coffee Growers in Dialogue: Social Reports Campaign of the Departmental Committee of Antioquia

**JUAN-CARLOS MOLLEDA
and ANA-MARÍA SUÁREZ**

The case was developed from a review of corporate publications and an in-depth interview with Berenice García, Chair of the Department of Communications and Public Relations of the Departmental Committee of Coffee Growers of Antioquia (Medellín, Colombia).

Executive Summary

This case study describes the development of a public relations campaign carried out in Colombia by the Departmental Committee of Antioquia Coffee Growers to produce and promote its "Annual Social Report." A social report is a measure of effectiveness for public relations professionals when the philanthropic activities, sponsorships, or outreach projects presented in the report were encouraged, planned, or implemented by the professionals as an essential or secondary part of their responsibilities within their organizations. Both outputs and outcomes are evaluated in social reports of Colombian organizations. Outputs are the actions or community projects, and outcomes are reported by including feedback or reactions of those benefited or involved in those actions or projects.

Relationships are identified and nurtured through partnerships with employees, government agencies, and community organizations. Finally, the ultimate goal of social reports should be a tool of relationship maintenance, which includes the following strategies: access, positivity, openness, assurances, networking, and sharing of tasks (Hon & Grunig, 1999). Transparency and disclosure can be added to this set of indicators.

Before presenting the specific elements of the campaign program we will summarize research that provides background for the campaign. This background includes a brief history of the coffee industry in Colombia as well as the nature and administrative structure of the national and departmental (state) trade associations. An overview of the concept and promoters of "social balances" or "social reports" in Colombia is also introduced as a trend in the business sector of this South American nation.

Research

Coffee Industry

Coffee has been known in the American Continent since 1690; specifically, the Arabica variety was introduced in the Dutch Indies (Federación Nacional de Cafeteros, 1999). Later, coffee was introduced in French Guyana and Brazil. The French, through other routes, transported coffee to Guadalupe and Martinique. In Colombia, coffee entered via Cúcuta, Northern Santander Department, coming from the Venezuelan Andes in 1830. In the same year, the first plantation was harvested in Valdivia (city of the Antioquia Department).

The National Federation of Coffee Growers of Colombia, founded June 27, 1927, is an private trade association with not-for-profit status. The federation is integrated by coffee producers of the various regions of the country (Federación Nacional de Cafeteros, n.d.).

According to the federation's Statutes, reformed in 2002, permanent coffee growers are only considered for institutional membership; similarly, membership can be granted to producers that cultivate coffee crops with an annual production above 500 kilograms (a little over half a ton) and the cultivated area is a half-hectare (about 1.25 acres) or more (Federación Nacional de Cafeteros, 2002 Statutes). The federation assists all coffee growers, whether or not they are registered members, with technical and extension assistance for cultivating and improving coffee production and sales. It also provides educational and health programs and infrastructure.

The federation has a functional structure that facilitates its activities in defense of the country's coffee growers. Thus, the federation negotiates agreements with the national, departmental (state), and municipal governments to support the betterment of the industry, the interest of coffee growers, and to advance scientific research in every field related to cultivation, storage, and industrialization of coffee and its derivative products. These activities are carried out following principles of environmental protection. Additionally, the federation develops extension programs and informs its members of advances in cultivation techniques, better pest control, and commerce.

The administrative structure of the federation is complex, but guarantees democratic participation. Coffee growers and Municipal Committees are the base of the structure. This organizational level represents the countryside producers and facilitates their participation in the federation at both regional and national levels. The second level is the Departmental Committees that coordinate the activities and representation of the individual producers and the Municipal Committees. The third level belongs to General Administration, which is headquartered at the main office of the National Federation of Coffee Growers of Colombia. In the highest layer of the structure are the Executive Committee, the National Committee of Coffee Growers, and the National Congress of Coffee Growers; the latter is the political body of the Colombian coffee sector.

Social Reports

"Social balances" or "social reports" are publications produced by some public relations practitioners in Colombia and other parts of the world. They include information on the establishment of goals, performance indicators, evaluation parameters and, most important, the definition of corporate social policies of an organization. More specifically, "a social report is a performance instrument for planning, organizing, conducting, recording, controlling, and evaluating in qualitative and quantitative terms the social performance of an organization in a specific period of time and according to stated [organizational] goals" (Organización International del Trabajo, 2001, p. 16).

In Colombia, the social balance or report was introduced as an instrument for measuring social responsibility in the 1970s (Organización International del Trabajo, 2001). At that time and still today, there is confusion between social balance and social report. The social report is an instrument in which the social performance of an organization is recorded in qualitative and quantitative terms for a specific period of time. The social balance is an instrument for measuring goals, performance indicators, and a parameter of social performance. Since the first publications of social balances, they were understood as a way to comprehend the demands imposed by business ethics in organizations. The ideology arrived in Colombia in the late 1970s. Organizations were pressured to review their economic and political actions and assume responsibility before the society for their actions.

Professional associations organized encounters and documents concerning the status of corporate social responsibility in Colombia. In 1960s, social foundations such as CONDESARROLLO (Medellín, 1960), Carvajal Foundation (Cali, 1962), and Corona Foundation (Medellín, 1963), represented the entrepreneurs' and the national government's explicit commitment to respond to a felt need: to attend to the demands of publics related to or influenced by an institution and take advantage of a governmental initiative that considered social investment for a tax credit (Cámara de Comercio de Medellín, 2001).

In 1977, two organizations—INCOLDA and Foundation for Higher Education (FES)—sponsored the study *Toward a New Commitment of the Colombian Entrepreneur* (ANDI, 1985).The study found a need for a unified criterion to define social responsibility and socially responsible action. The first formal manual to guide the development of social reports was produced by ANDI with the support of OIL in 1987.

Communication Policy of the Departmental Committee

The Departmental Committee of Antioquia was founded in 1927 when the federation started its operations in Medellín, capital of the Antioquia Department (geopolitical administration of Colombia). This committee oversees an area of 125,000 hectares of coffee out of 869,157 hectares nationally cultivated (National survey of the coffee industry, 1993/1997). They represent some 96,000 coffee growers organized in 71 Municipal Committees. The Departmental Committee has 148 administrative personnel that, among other functions, coordinate four Coffee Cooperatives. The staff also supervises the work of 850 community leaders from the coffee plantations who know, thanks to their daily work, the most felt needs of "campesinos." The leaders live with the rural communities and their duty is to stimulate and coordinate the work of coffee growers and their families.

The Federation of Coffee Growers was created to fulfill an education mission. In 1975, its communication policy was institutionalized with the creation of a National Communication Office under the Technical Management of the Federation. The informative and information diffusion function of the Communication Office has been included in the Federation statutes, which states the need to carry out a more effective education program for coffee growers to increase their identification with the sector and their lands and, therefore, motivate them to remain in their plantations.

The Departmental Committee of Antioquia does not plan or conduct formal research before the publication and promotion of the annual social report. The public relations professionals base their objectives, strategies, and tactics on past experiences and results. Procedures for the publication's production are replicated over the years with constant improvement. The diffusion of the report is included as an essential part of the public relations function of the committee. The informal evaluation presented later in the case is used as benchmark for future social report programs.

Objectives

The objectives sought by the Coffee Growers Federation with the publication and promotion of its social report are to provide information about the service and social actions carried out by the Departmental Committee of Antioquia and the federation on behalf of their communities of coffee growers. The public relations campaign seeks to engage some 96,000 coffee producers and employees, mass media representatives, university communities, and public opinion in general through the diffusion and discussion of the information contained in the social report. As an instrument of mediation, the social report allows the qualitative and quantitative evaluation of the organization's social performance according to its established annual goals. The publication is used to generate debate among the aforementioned publics, which contributes to the consideration of corrective actions for future social programs and activities in support of the welfare of the coffee growers' communities.

Strategies

Action Strategies

The federation also promotes economic development and diversification in coffee zones, the promotion and support for cooperatives, and financial assistance for producers. The federation considers among its functions the promotion of development and improvement of infrastructure of rural areas, which is indispensable for the social and economic well-being of coffee growers and their families.

Communication Strategies

To achieve its goal, the National Federation of Coffee Growers of Colombia has clearly defined objectives and functions so the national coffee sector can control the development of its activity. For instance, the federation is aware of and monitors macroeconomic variables and the sector's policies to benefit the coffee trade. In the face of fluctuations in coffee prices and differences in offered and demanded prices, they intervene in domestic and international markets seeking fair and stable prices. The national and international promotion of Colombian Coffee is achieved with the use of a popular character named "Juan Valdez" who is the ambassador of the federation (Figure 1).

The federation does not produce a social report; this is developed, published, and promoted by the Departmental Committees. The Departmental Committee of Antioquia (Medellín) is the oldest and the first to develop a social report, which has being published periodically. This case study focuses on the public relations activities of this committee to engage coffee growers (primary public) and other secondary publics in a dialogue centered on its annual social report (Figure 2).

FIGURE 1   Juan Valdez, Ambassador of the Columbian Coffee Growers Association

FIGURE 2   Examples of Social Reports

Beginning in 1990, the Departmental Committee structured a Department of Communications and Public Relations, which became in charge of internal and external communications with a main focus on supporting the work of coffee growers. The communication team has a director, a social communicator, a university intern, a radio editor, and an administrative assistant. Graphic design and publication services are outsourced.

The communication policy includes the production and diffusion of the social report to document and promote the activities of the federation in favor of the coffee sector. Following the guidelines of the ANDI/OIL *Manual of Social Reports,* the Departmental Committee initiated the publication of its first Annual Social Report in 1990. The report includes information on the Technical Division, Social Development, Coordination of Municipal Committees, and the Educative Foundation of Coffee. The Communications and Public Relations Department gathers information, sets the editorial tone with the active participation of the Executive Director of the Committee (highest authority in the organization), writes, coordinates the design and layout of the publication, and coordinates the distribution of the document to all the institutional publics (some 1,000 copies are distributed).

Tactics

As soon as the social report is published, the Departmental Committee initiates its diffusion through a news conference, media news releases, and personalized invitations to attend introduction and discussion meetings for various publics. The social report is available for the following publics: coffee growers (most important group), community leaders, coffee cooperatives, employees of the Departmental Committee and their families, retirees, suppliers, government officials from local to national levels, leaders of the private sector, university administrators, mass media editors and reporters, and finally, involved consumers. Tailored tactics are planned and implemented for each public. Coffee growers are the primary public of the campaign.

Tactics for Coffee Growers/Producers

This public represents the base of the coffee industry. Each coffee grower is an agent who diffuses information and public positions on issues concerning the coffee industry to family and relatives. Coffee growers need to be reassured of the importance of their contributions to the regional and national economies. They also must understand that their contribution to the economy justifies government action to improve their social welfare. The social report presents the projects and programs the federation and the Departmental Committee developed in the previous year for the benefit of coffee growers and their families.

The organization of the encounter between the Executive Director of the Committee and the coffee growers requires well-orchestrated logistics of transportation and must be carefully planned and implemented because participants come from many locations to a strategically selected meeting place. In years past, the meetings took place in each municipality, which required the transportation of the coffee growers within each territory. Today, the encounter is hosted eight times at the same location because of the critical situation Colombia faces resulting from a civil war the government fights against guerrillas, paramilitaries, and drug traffickers. As a consequence, transportation to the meeting location for the committee's representatives and the individual coffee growers could last between two and eight hours. Participants are members of each Municipal Committee. They are selected as representatives of the municipality in annual democratic elections.

According to the Director of Communications and Public Relations of the Departmental Committee, it is important to distribute the reports before scheduling the encounters. This allows coffee growers to process the information and think about their questions and concerns. The coffee growers have a high rate of illiteracy and low levels of reading comprehension; therefore, an executive summary sent with a letter on behalf of the Executive Director helps to highlight the most significant indicators concerning the support of the federation and committees for agricultural activities, productivity, and programs of education extension. The ultimate purpose of the letter is to present the report that is published in March to the different communities and ask each Municipal Committee to assist coffee growers in its diffusion, review, analysis, and evaluation. Greater emphasis is put on the diffusion of this key information through a group of Municipal Community leaders who are somewhat better educated that the average coffee grower.

Written forms to record the reception and evaluation of the report are used as a control mechanism. The completed forms are returned to the Departmental Committee before the first meeting between the Executive Director and the groups of producers. The forms also contain a section to provide a brief evaluation of the report's content. These evaluations are compiled to provide the Executive Director with talking points to be addressed during the sequence of meetings. The Executive Director is prepared to address all kinds or questions and concerns, having a fairly good idea what the common topics are likely to be.

The next tactic is to announce the date of public introduction of the report to the Municipal Committees. The public introduction is begun a month after initial publication and is made at eight presentations between April and August. The objectives of the presentations are to hand the publication out directly to the coffee growers and establish a two-way forum to address concerns, answer questions, and expand explanations of complex issues. Each presentation is organized to host an average of 120 people representing the 13 Municipal Committees and the potential leaders of the community (in total, some 1,000 attendees). These are all influential people who represent their individual regions and offer legitimate community engagement.

In the presentations, the Executive Director of the Departmental Committee summarizes the report and opens the dialogue, during which any participant is allowed to express concerns, opinions, and suggestions regarding the information presented and contained in the social report that has been read in advance. The content of the written and oral reports does not contain technical language and is logically structured to facilitate comprehension. It is written and presented to help the growers understand the relationship between the documented indicators and the original social policies of the federation and the committees. Furthermore, the publication of Antioquia is one of the very few social reports that, instead of mainly presenting several statistical tables and graphs, includes more photographs illustrating the social impact of the programs. It includes visually attractive scenes of the work and life of coffee-producing communities. The social report is produced with the coffee growers in mind, yet its editorial content and production also consider other publics, such as government officials and the federation's top management.

Tactics for Employees of the Departmental Committee

Informative meetings are conducted in the various administrative offices of the Departmental Committee. The employees, like coffee growers, receive the report in advance so they have time to read and discuss the document with their peers and supervisors. Employees receive personalized letters with the report attached. The ultimate objective is to boost employee morale, group identification, and satisfaction.

The focus of the employee meetings is different from the encounters with coffee growers. Employees are asked to critically evaluate the participation of each administrative unit in the social programs planned and implemented by the committee to benefit the coffee growers and their loved ones. They are also asked to evaluate the way their efforts are portrayed in the report and, if needed, suggest refinements to the programs and the communication strategy.

Tactics for University Communities

The report is mailed to the colleges or schools of economics and communications of every university and college in the Department of Antioquia. According to the Director of Communications and Public Relations, administrators, faculty, staff, and students of economics and communications appear to be most interested in the content of the publication and its positive or negative impact for the coffee growers' communities. The Departmental Committee believes the two groups serve as a network that further diffuses information about the social actions that impact the lives of producers of this vital commodity in Colombia.

Tactics for the Retirees of the Departmental Committee

As of December of 2002 there were a total of 116 people in the retiree community of the Departmental Committee. They also receive a personalized letter with the hard copy of the social report. This is strategy to maintain contact with this group of individuals who are highly identified with the sector. They often provide quality feedback concerning the social programs or specific aspects of the publication itself.

Tactics for the Media

Reporters from local and national media outlets are invited for a special introduction of the report (Figure 3). In a news conference staged as a gathering of friends to share a cup of coffee, journalists receive the publication and an explanation of its main features given by the Executive Director. A news release is provided to the reporters in which the emphasis is placed on the benefits of the social programs for the involved communities instead of emphasizing the main indicators as an impersonal set of statistics. The numbers are illustrated with personal success stories and testimonials.

FIGURE 3   **Press Conference Describing Coffee Growers' Social Report**

Evaluation

In general, the indicators used to assess the effectiveness of the public relations strategies are not sophisticated. Basically, the assessment focuses on outputs and limited outcomes as evidence of the reception of the text and its readership:

- Number of reports published and distributed, including number of personalized letters introducing and debriefing the publication
- Number of news releases sent and published by the mass media
- Number of stories resulting from interviews with representatives of the Departmental Committee, the National Federation, Municipal Committee, community leaders or coffee growers, as well as independent reporting produced by print and broadcast journalists
- E-mail messages received by the Communication Office from different levels of the coffee sector, including management, coordinators, and coffee producers
- Written forms used by the Municipal Committees to document and report that the publication was received and distributed and read in their meetings
- Number of participants of the meetings and encounters of coffee growers where the social report is distributed and read
- Informal, qualitative feedback received from coffee growers and community leaders during the meetings. This feedback is not systematically recorded, summarized, cataloged, nor filed for future use.

The Department of Communications and Public Relations of the Departmental Committee of Antioquia organizes meetings to analyze the evaluation data and, according to these indicators, considers modifications of the publication design and the methods of its diffusion. The committee also takes into consideration the comments and suggestions expressed by the participants at the different activities organized for the introduction and discussion of the report. This information is used to show the various publics that the organization values their feedback for the improvement of both the social report and the social policies and programs sponsored by the Departmental Committee of Antioquia.

Critique

The critiques presented here focus on the campaign's success in meeting the needs of the coffee growers. The campaign's ability to meet those needs is somewhat restricted by constraints imposed both by the government that supports it and the past practices of the Federation of Coffee Growers. It is also somewhat limited by the motivation for social reports. Social reports were created as a means of monitoring an organization's progress in meeting social responsibility. The reader of this critique should keep in mind that the comments address the campaign's consistency with the ROSTE model and are not intended as criticism of the federation or its organizational goals.

Research

By its own admission, the federation does not plan or conduct formal research. Their public relations professionals base their decisions regarding objectives, strategies, and tactics on past experiences. Without such formal research it is impossible to gather the specific information needed to design and implement a successful public relations campaign. One glaring omission is research on competing industries and interests. For example, we know the Colombian government fights a civil war against guerillas, paramilitaries, and drug traffickers because we were told that war makes transportation to meetings on the social reports difficult. Research identifying the motivation of the guerillas and drug traffickers would help identify problems of the coffee growers and facilitate the selection of messages that would appeal to growers who may be trying to decide whether to back the guerillas or convert their coffee production efforts to drug production.

Other helpful research could be designed to identify the specific interests of the coffee growers. Since the social report is intended to describe the federation's success in meeting its social responsibilities, knowing what is important to its members and what actions they would view as attractive would help the goals for a program of social responsibility. Other research addressing the existing attitudes and values of the growers would help identify what information they see as attractive and what media they find most useful for receiving that information.

Finally, some pre-campaign measure of the knowledge and opinions of the target public would permit comparison with post-campaign measures of the same variables. The difference between these two measures would provide a more reliable and valid measure of campaign success than the existing qualitative measures that are made only after the social reports are delivered.

Objectives

The objectives are really too vague and unspecific to guide campaign strategy selection or campaign evaluation. In the objective statement the reader is told the social report is intended to "provide information" to the community of coffee growers. Later in the statement it says the campaign "seeks to engage" coffee producers. One could provide information with even the most simplistic and inconsequential campaign and one could engage the producers if the only campaign activity offended those producers. In short, the objective should identify some specific change in the knowledge, beliefs, or behavior of the target public, specify some means of measuring that change, and specify a time for accomplishing that change. Without these concrete elements of an objective there is no way to know if the campaign actually has any positive impact on the target public.

Strategies

The action strategies of promoting economic development and providing financial assistance are admirable and the creation of an icon like Juan Valdez certainly helps identification of the federation and the product "Colombian Coffee." Most weaknesses in the strategies arise because of the absence of any theoretic basis for strategy selection. Without knowing why strategies are selected and what principle, paradigm, or theory predicts their success, it is difficult or impossible to know whether the strategy selected is, in fact, the best for this campaign.

Another potential limitation of the strategies is the fact that the Communications and Public Relations Department sets the editorial tone of the social report with the active participation of the highest authority in the organization. The members of the target public will be very different from these individuals in literacy, sophistication, and social needs. Therefore it seems advisable to consult representatives of the target public, or research about those individuals, when deciding on message construction and "editorial tone."

Tactics

There are a great many tactics, all of which have a significant potential to help deliver messages to the target public. In particular, the meetings designed to describe the content of the social report and to invite discussion of the report seem very well tailored to the coffee growers as a public. Even content, structure, and language for the social report itself was adjusted to meet the needs of the public, which is described as having a high rate of illiteracy, and often low levels of reading comprehension.

The tactics targeted to the employees and retirees of the Departmental Committee and to university economics and communication programs do require more justification. If we assume the public relations objective of this campaign is to reach the coffee growers, then the employees, retirees, and university audiences must be treated as secondary publics. Some measure of how efficiently these publics can relay information to the primary public of coffee growers should be included in the analysis and planning. Further, part of the message to these secondary publics should be information on how to present the messages to the primary public.

Evaluation

By their own description, the evaluation used for this campaign is not sophisticated. It includes measures of information dissemination and informal qualitative feedback. Further, the information on feedback from the coffee growers is ". . . not systematically recorded, summarized, cataloged, nor filed for future use." This may be the best possible evaluation given the lack of a concrete and operationalized objective, but it does mean that one cannot determine if the campaign has any actual impact on the target public. In order to effectively evaluate the campaign it would have to include a more concrete objective and some pre-campaign measure of the target public characteristic it seeks to change.

DISCUSSION QUESTIONS

1. In the campaign description here, the coffee growers who are the primary target public of the campaign are described as having "a high rate of illiteracy and low levels of reading comprehension." What problems does this characteristic of the target public pose for research and communication?
   a. Describe how you would gather information about the target public. How would you identify their media consumption habits and gather information on what they valued or viewed as important?

b. How would you communicate with this target public? For example, do you agree with the campaign tactic of sending the social reports to the growers in advance of the meetings so that they can be prepared with questions?

2. In the United States there have been several criticisms of the ethics of large corporations. Some of these criticisms have motivated changes in SEC reporting requirements. Review the recent changes in U.S. corporation reporting requirements and compare them to the practice of developing a social report. Do you believe requiring U.S. corporations to prepare and defend social reports would improve their ethics and social responsibility?

3. In the critique, the objective of this campaign was described as too vague. Based on what you believe the Coffee Growers' Federation hopes to accomplish with their social report, write a public relations objective that identifies a target public, that specifies some change in that public, and that operationalizes the terms in the objective statement.

4. Colombian coffee growers face several problems associated with their government's war against guerillas and drug traffickers. From sources outside this case report, please research the current Colombian conflict. Explain how the conflict impacts the coffee growers. Is there anything a public relations campaign can do to help ameliorate the problems created by the civil war?

5. Have you seen or heard of Juan Valdez, the icon of the Colombian Coffee Growers' Federation? For audiences in the United States, what does this symbol represent? Are there any problems with using Juan Valdez as a symbol of Colombian coffee? Would you recommend any changes in the symbol or would you recommend a new symbol? Why?

6. Some of the action strategies mentioned are financial assistance and infrastructure improvement. How would you decide if the coffee growers actually value these activities? In other words, how would you do evaluation research to determine the success of these strategies?

7. Some of the tactics deliver information about the social report to publics who are not coffee growers. These publics include university departments. Can university students, faculty, staffs, and administrators help deliver the campaign's message to the primary public of coffee growers? What would you do to insure that the secondary publics like university students, faculty, staffs and administrators actually helped communicate with the coffee growers?

8. When evaluating this campaign's success, how would you improve on the techniques described? For example, do you believe pre-campaign and post-campaign surveys of the coffee growers are practical? If so, how would you conduct such evaluation research? Are there alternative systems of evaluation?

REFERENCES AND SUGGESTED READINGS

ANDI [National Association of Industrialists]. (1985). *Hacia un Nuevo compromiso del empresario colombiano [Toward a new commitment of the Colombian entrepreneur].* [catalog]. Medellín, Colombia.

Cámara de Comercio de Medellín [Chamber of Commerce of Medellín]. (2001). ¿*Cómo asumir la responsabilidad social en las empresas*? [How to assume social responsibility of enterprises]. [catalog]. Medellín, Colombia.

Federación Nacional de Cafeteros de Colombia [National Federation of Coffee Growers of Colombia]. (2002). *Estatutos* [Statutes]. [Brochure]. Medellín, Colombia.

Federación Nacional de Cafeteros de Colombia, Comité Departamental de Cafeteros de Antioquia [National Federation of Coffee Growers of Colombia, Departmental Committee of Coffee Growers of Antioquia]. (2002). *Informe Social* [Social Report]. Medellín, Colombia.

Federación Nacional de Cafeteros de Colombia [National Federation of Coffee Growers of Colombia]. (1999). *El café en el desarrollo de Antioquia, visión histórica y acción gremial* [Coffee in the development of Antioquia, historical vision and trade union's action]. [Brochure]. Medellín, Colombia.

Federación Nacional de Cafeteros de Colombia [National Federation of Coffee Growers of Colombia]. (n.d.) *Conocimientos Básicos de su Organización* [Basic knowledge of its organization]. [Brochure]. Medellín, Colombia.

Hon, L. C., & Grunig, J. E. (1999). *Guidelines for measuring relationships in public relations.* Retrieved from www.instituteforpr.com.

López-Aragón, W. (2002). *Café, técnica y tradición* [Coffee, technique and tradition]. Cali, Colombia: Editorial Universidad Santiago de Cali.

Organización Internacional del Trabajo (OIT), Asociación Nacional de Industriales (ANDI), & Cámara Junior de Colombia (JCI) Capítulo Antioquia [International Labor Organization, National Association of Industrialists, & Junior Chamber International of Colombia]. (2001). *Manual de balance social; versión actualizada* [Manual of social balance; updated version]. Medellín, Colombia: Gráficas Pajón.

Palacios, M. (2002). *El café en Colombia, 1850–1970: Una historia económica, social y política* [Coffee in Colombia, 1850–1970: An economic, social and political history]. Bogotá, Colombia: Planeta.

Pizano-Salazar, D. (2001). El café en la encrucijada: Evolución y perspectivas [Coffee on the crossroad: Evolution and perspectives]. Bogotá, Colombia: Alfaomega.

16 Protecting the Environment and People's Well-Being in the Nigerian Ogoni Land

BOLANLE A. OLANIRAN and DAVID E. WILLIAMS

This case was prepared from public records without the cooperation of any of the oil companies or environmental groups described herein. Much of it represents the views of those who oppose the oil companies' actions and who support charges against them by the Nigerian Ogoni people.

Executive Summary

For four decades, multinational oil companies like Shell, Texaco, BP, Agip, and Chevron have drilled for oil in the West African country of Nigeria. Although there is significantly contradictory information, many in Nigeria and elsewhere believe these oil companies acted in collusion with a corrupt government, ignoring the rights of the indigenous Ogoni people and damaging the environment on their lands. This case focuses on the actions and messages of a group called The Movement for the Survival of the Ogoni People, which identifies itself with the acronym MOSOP, that specifically targeted Shell Oil in an attempt to improve the lot of the Ogoni. The actions described here all took place between 1980 and 1999. During that time Nigeria was under a military regime that was world-famous for it corruption and for the financial mismanagement of Nigeria's natural resources.

There have been reports of frequent oil spills and the oil companies' responses have been called dismal or worse. Other alleged problems include gas flaring, explosions, oil spills, and waste. Accusations of agricultural land destruction and heightened health problems also dogged the Nigerian oil operations. Both environmental groups and people who live in these oil lands have called attention to the growing concern in the region. Accusations of environmental abuse and collusion with the government are rampant. Those who oppose the oil operations particularly note that the oil companies provided ammunition to the government and allege this was done in an attempt to silence the local people's complaints.

Tactics employed by MOSOP or those acting on its behalf included partnering with international environmental and human rights groups like Greenpeace and Amnesty International and an extensive Internet communication campaign. Their tactics also included more aggressive actions such as kidnapping oil workers, and demonstrations that were occasionally violent.

The crisis in the Ogoni land reached its height in 1996. At that time the Nigerian government imprisoned and eventually executed Ken Saro-Wiwa and six other people who were leaders of MOSOP. The execution of Saro-Wiwa generated extensive criticism from groups such as Amnesty International and Greenpeace. This criticism specifically targeted Shell Oil, which was the largest oil company doing business in Nigeria. It was alleged that Shell was in collusion with the government and was responsible for the arrest of individuals who made claims against the company.

Research

Before one can properly evaluate the actions of MOSOP and the oil companies it opposed, one must understand the structure of Nigerian society and the country's economic dependence on oil.

Nigeria and Its Oil Industry

The Federal Republic of Nigeria lies on the West Coast of Africa south of Niger and northwest of Cameroon. It is Africa's most populous nation, with a total population of nearly 134 million. The Niger River flows through Nigeria and forms a delta on the Gulf of Guinea. Extensive oil deposits are found in the Niger Delta and further west toward the Bakasi Peninsula. The economy is heavily dependent on this oil. Oil provides 20 percent of the total revenue produced in the country and 95 percent of its foreign exchange earnings. Oil also pays 65 percent of the entire national government's budget (World Factbook, 2003).

Nigeria's first oil refinery, near Port Harcourt, began operations in 1965 and a second refinery was opened in 1978. These plants were constructed and run by the Nigerian National Petroleum Company (NNPC), that owned between 80 and 100 percent of the oil production. Because of technical problems and internal conflicts these plants were not able to produce adequate oil to meet Nigeria's economic needs. Beginning in the early 1980s NNPC had substantial amounts of oil refined abroad, primarily by Shell Oil, which is headquartered in Great Britain (Library of Congress, 2003). Between 1980 and 1999, the interests of foreign oil companies grew. By the 1990s, about 96 percent of Nigerian oil was produced by foreign companies. In descending order of importance these companies were: Shell, Chevron, Mobil, Agip, Elf Aquitaine, Phillips, Texaco, and Ashland. However, the NNPC retained a 60 percent interest in all of these operations. In short, although there is a significant presence of foreign oil companies in Nigeria, the Nigerian government, through NNPC, has always retained a controlling interest in the production and refining of Nigerian oil (Library of Congress, 2003).

In addition to oil, Nigeria has one of the largest reserves of natural gas in the world. This gas accounts for approximately 20 percent of Nigeria's energy needs but is expensive and difficult to transport to other consuming countries. Until the early 1990s the majority of natural gas was "flared" or simply burned off at oil well heads. In May of 1989 a joint project by NNPC (60%), Shell Oil (20%), Agip (10%), and Elf (10%) began to liquify natural gas for export. The first liquid natural gas tanker was launched in October of 1990. That tanker was a joint project of Nigeria and Japan (Library of Congress, 2003).

Despite its oil wealth, Nigeria has some of the poorest people in the world. In 1988 Nigeria's per capita gross national product was U.S. $290. The country also has a very high rate of income concentration. What little income is available in the country is concentrated in the hands of a very small group of people, primarily high-ranking government administrators (Library of Congress, 2003). Rural subsistence farmers, including the Ogoni, are politically weak and even poorer than the average Nigerian. This disparity is exacerbated by what the U.S. Central Intelligence Agency calls the worst government corruption in the world (World Factbook, 2003). In short, the Ogoni live on land that is extraordinarily rich but they do not benefit from that wealth.

The Ogoni are further disadvantaged because of religious and ethnic divisions of Nigeria. The country is 50 percent Muslim, 40 percent Christian, and 10 percent of its people practice indigenous beliefs. Islamic Shariah law governs some northern states (World Factbook, 2003). The U.S. Library of Congress says that "Ethnicity is one of the keys to understanding Nigeria's pluralistic society." It estimates there are between 250 and 400 distinct ethnic groups living in Nigeria. In many cases, these groups are identified with distinct languages or are viewed by themselves and others in Nigeria as a unique culture. There are frequent disagreements between these ethnic groups over land holdings and control of business dealings. These disagreements often erupt into violence (Library of Congress, 2003).

The most populous and politically influential groups are the Hausa, Fulani, Yoruba, and Igbo. No other ethic group makes up more than 10 percent of the population and no ethic group in the rural Niger Delta and Bakasi peninsula makes up more than three percent of the population. These small and rural ethnic groups like the Ogoni are often powerless and disenfranchised. Evidence of the interethnic friction over land and revenue rights can be seen in the fact that the people of the Bakasi Peninsula seceded from Nigeria because of disagreements over allocation of oil revenue. Thereafter, both Cameroon and Nigeria claimed the oil-rich region. In 2002, the International Court of Justice awarded the peninsula to Cameroon. As of this writing Nigeria has not ratified that decision (World Factbook, 2003).

In order to understand this case, one should also note that Nigeria is a party to several international environmental agreements but that because of poor funding or other problems has not taken steps to enforce those agreements (World Factbook, 2003).

The Ogoni and Shell Oil

While Shell controls less than 20 percent of the oil production in Nigeria, it is the most visible symbol of the oil industry and is often the target of any complaint against oil production, refining, or transporting practices. Further, Shell is the major purchaser of NNPC's exported petroleum so it can be seen as the major source of capital for all oil activities in Nigeria.

In spite of nearly constant criticism from several groups, including the Nigerian Ogoni people, Shell apparently has not conducted any research to assess public opinion of its operations or its involvement with NNPC. As a matter of fact, there is some evidence that Shell specifically decided not to pay attention to any publicity generated on behalf of the Ogoni people. Apparently Shell instead concentrated on creating a favorable relationship with the Nigerian military government, which controlled NNPC. There are allegations that this relationship was so cordial that the military often responded with Mobile Police and the Nigerian Army to stop any demonstrations against Shell in the drilling region (Greenpeace, 2003).

The United States has significant interests in Nigerian oil production. Between 8 and 10 percent of U.S. oil supplies come from Nigeria and the United States has expressed interest in increasing imports from Nigeria to reduce its dependence on oil from Arab states. In fact, the Clinton administration condemned the executions of Ken Saro-Wiwa and other Ogoni leaders. That administration also condemned other repression of the people in Nigeria's oil-producing regions (Shell, 2001). Despite public pronouncements endorsing human rights for the Ogoni, the U.S. government has not taken any action to assist the Nigerian oil communities or to communicate directly with Shell or other oil companies doing business in Nigeria.

Oil drilling and pipeline construction on Ogoni land have resulted in significant environmental degradation. Agricultural land has been lost to oil spills and clearing for drilling and pipelines. There are also allegations that the health of people in the oil-producing region has suffered. MOSOP and some environmental groups report that the oil companies always respond to environmental complaints as though they were unwarranted, and any accidents such as fire, explosions, or oil spillage are always treated as acts of sabotage even where there is evidence to the contrary (Greenpeace, 2003).

One of the major environmental concerns is constant gas flaring (at times, 24 hours a day) from oil wells. This flaring is alleged to cover oil communities with thick soot and results in acid rain that ultimately renders agricultural land and crops useless and poisons water supplies (White, 1998). The oil companies respond to complaints about gas flaring by explaining that their flares are located away from the communities and that there is no evidence to suggest that gas flares hinder crops and yields (Tookey, 1992). It should also be noted that gas flaring is a common and legal practice in all oil-producing countries, including the United States (*Zink v. National Airoil,* 1980).

Many of the oil communities and their leaders resent the oil companies' practices and operating procedures in Nigeria. The people believe the oil companies use different standards in developing countries than they do in developed countries. For example, a comparison was made with a pipeline project at Stantlow, Scotland, where it was reported that 17 different environmental surveys were commissioned before any drilling began and that the Stantlow community was consulted throughout the process (Ryder, 1992). This is different from what the company did in Nigeria, where no environmental study was conducted and none of the community leaders were asked for input regarding environmental impact or concern. The Ogoni leaders, along with Greenpeace, claimed that Shell did not respond or provide any of the environmental impact studies that the company claims to have conducted from 1982 onward (Nigeria and Shell, 1993).

Finally, the Ogoni people have not benefited financially from the exploitation of their land. A British Petroleum engineer working in Nigeria was quoted as saying that he had explored for oil in other developing countries including Venezuela and Kuwait and that he had never seen an oil-rich town as completely impoverished as the Ogoni community of Oloibiri in the Niger Delta (Oloibiri: In Limbo, 1990).

To summarize, there is no doubt the Ogoni people have been exploited and their land damaged. Further, the Ogoni people view Shell and its subsidiary Shell Petroleum Development Company as a contributor to their exploitation. They also note that Shell is primarily concerned with the protection of its investments in, and revenue from, Nigeria. There is also the perception that because Shell's payments to the Nigerian government account for 80 percent of Nigeria's export revenue, the government is at the mercy of Shell (Bassey, 1997). Ledum Mttee, President of MOSOP, at the Oputa Commission (a panel investigating human rights violations in Ogoni land) said that Shell constantly blackmailed the government by reminding it of the "dire economic consequences" that would result if Shell withdrew its capital support for operations in Nigeria (Ogbu and Akunna, 2001).

Objective

While The Movement for the Survival of the Ogoni People (MOSOP) has not issued a single clear objective statement, it appears from their name that their organizational goal was to improve the environment of their land and to seek some restitution for the damage done to their homes and their health. Some communications from MOSOP indicated they also wanted to condemn both the Nigerian government and the oil companies; however, their actions suggest the primary goal of their campaign was condemnation of Shell Oil. One statement made by the group comes close to a public relations objective. That statement indicated they wanted to insure no more oil drilling took place until their concerns were addressed.

Strategies

Obviously the goals of MOSOP conflicted with those of Shell and the other oil companies, including NNPC, who were predominantly concerned with revenue production. Many of the actions of the government compelled MOSOP to create new objectives and strategies. Also, many actions, particularly the execution of Ken Saro-Wiwa after trial by what many called a "kangaroo court," actually assisted the efforts of MOSOP. Exploiting the misconduct of the government or oil companies was also a strategy used successfully by MOSOP.

Action Strategies

Ken Saro-Wiwa was involved in the first major action strategy of MOSOP. He, and others, engaged in active protests against the practice of gas flaring in villages such as Dere in the Bomu oilfield. In 1996, Saro-Wiwa and six other leaders of MOSOP who had been involved in the protests against gas flaring were arrested by the Nigerian government. Later that year they were tried, convicted, and executed by hanging. In other protests, Ogoni youths shut down oil flow stations and some, who may not have been associated with MOSOP, kidnapped oilfield workers.

The most successful action strategy of MOSOP was creating partnerships or alliances with international environmental and human rights organizations. In particular, the aid of the environmental group Greenpeace was enlisted. Greenpeace representatives might not be able to enter the country to obtain incriminating evidence, but they possessed the communication network needed to advise other groups and individuals about the events on the Ogoni land. Amnesty International joined MOSOP in their cause after Saro-Wiwa was hanged. Amnesty International eventually condemned not only the Nigerian government but also the oil companies and the practices against which Saro-Wiwa had protested.

Communication Strategies

One of the major communication goals of the campaign was to destroy the complacent relationship that existed between Shell Oil and the Nigerian military government. In order to do this, several messages were delivered. Outside of Nigeria Shell was labeled as a murderer and the campaign attempted to create the image that every ounce of oil Shell produced was tainted with innocent blood. After the execution of Saro-Wiwa this message was easier to deliver because of the cooperation of Amnesty International.

In particular, MOSOP and its allies described the purchase of weapons by Shell for the Nigerian military and police forces. It was alleged these weapons were used to crush protests against oil companies through mobilization of the Nigerian military (Duodu, 1996). By connecting the information that Shell had provided weapons to the Nigerian Government and that the Nigerian government has executed Saro-Wiwa, they were able to imply Shell was responsible for the execution.

Another strategy involved responses to Shell's explanation of the allegations against it. For example, Shell, Chevron, and other oil companies described many of the claims against them as attempts by poor people to extort money from rich companies from the Western World. The oil companies often argued that whenever they attempted to pay damages in case of oil spillage, the people always claimed more than fair market value for any property damaged by oil production projects. Responding to descriptions of gas flaring, the oil companies alleged that any damage was the fault of the community because they expanded into the vicinity of oil operations. Furthermore, Shell maintained that once flares are found to be in close proximity to the people, flares are relocated away from populated areas (Nigeria and Shell, 1993). The MOSOP strategy involved simply denying the accuracy of the defenses raised by Shell.

Tactics

The pivotal tactic by the Ogoni people in their protest against the oil companies was bypassing traditional media like newspapers, radio, and television. In Nigeria those media are controlled by the government. MOSOP and its allies relied almost exclusively on alternate media, including e-mail, the Internet, chat rooms, and facsimile to deliver their messages outside the country. For instance, pictures of human rights abuses, environmental destruction, and protests that would never have made it into newspapers and other traditional media were placed on the Internet for anyone with access to a computer to see.

Because of the involvement of activist groups like Greenpeace and Amnesty International, those groups were also able to use their existing communication networks to reach latent publics like environmentalists and human rights advocates. These latent publics were made active by the information. They, in turn, exercised their access to alternate media including word-of-mouth to create new, active populations of Ogoni sympathizers.

Using their newfound supporters and alternative media, the Ogoni sought to deliver their message beyond the boundaries of Nigeria. It was once true that a crisis or image problem could be contained within a country's geographical boundary. However, with modern technology this is no longer the case. The Ogoni people and environmental activists were able to use the Internet to publicize their complaints around the world and to call for broad boycott of Shell and its products (Greenpeace, 2003b).

Evaluation

The absence of a single clear public relations objective makes concrete evaluation of this campaign impossible. However, there are some measures of success. These measures include the large number of Internet contacts and news placements about the predicament of the Ogoni people.

Perhaps the most dramatic measure of success for MOSOP and its allies was the total change in the Nigerian government. Following 16 years of military rule, Nigeria adopted a new constitution in 1999 and a peaceful transition to civilian government followed. After democratic elections in 1999, the first democratic transition of power under this new government occurred in April of 2003. As of this writing the president of Nigeria is General Obasanjo who was a senior officer in the military regime that is largely responsible for the oppression of the Ogoni people (World Factbook, 2003; Starr, 1999). The new government of Nigeria, with support from environmental groups and The World Commission on Development and Culture, organized the Oputa Panel. This panel is a human rights commission established to reconcile differences between the peoples of Nigeria and the oil companies. Shell and other companies have testified before the panel and submitted to its review (Ogbu and Akunna, 2001).

Countering these measures of success is an unfortunate observation indicating the campaign failed. Simply put, no significant improvement in their lot has been acknowledged by the Ogoni people since the 1996 arrest of Saro-Wiwa.

Critique

It is impossible to completely evaluate or analyze the MOSOP campaign without also looking at the actions and strategies of Shell and the other oil companies. The critique here will consider those actions as well as the actions of MOSOP and its allies.

Research

Neither MOSOP nor the oil companies conducted any real research into public awareness or opinion. Because of this it is frankly impossible to know if the MOSOP campaign created any real change in the world's view of either the Ogoni or Shell Oil. The publics most likely to effectively change the conduct of Shell are investors and consumers in developed countries. These individuals are notoriously ignorant of and indifferent to the plight of publics in developing countries. Whether one identifies with the Ogoni or with Shell in this conflict, the campaign would have benefited had there been some measure of public awareness of the events in the Ogoni land. Further, these measures should have been made for publics both in Nigeria and in the oil-consuming countries of Europe and the Americas. Also, a measure of the pre-campaign reputation of Shell in developed countries would have been useful. If Shell had a good reputation for environmental responsibility and corporate citizenship prior to the campaign, this fact would make the task of MOSOP much more difficult. Under these circumstances, MOSOP might have been better advised to focus their campaign either on another oil company or on the Nigerian government itself.

Other research which might have benefited Shell or been used by MOSOP was some measure of the stability of the Nigerian military government. Shell obviously relied on its ability to maintain a solid financial relationship with that government. Such reliance seems ill advised, given the instability of many governments in developing countries. Had the Ogoni known the military government was susceptible to collapse they might have focused on either encouraging that collapse or forming favorable relations with those who would come to power in the new democratic government. Of course, this strategy would have posed significant risks for the Ogoni. It may have been safer for them to focus their opposition on Shell, a British company, than on the military government that had the power to execute Ogoni leaders. Had Shell anticipated the collapse they may have found it more efficient to secure the support and sympathy of those in the oil-producing communities than to continue payment to and cooperation with the military regime.

Objective

Because this campaign report was prepared without direct input from either MOSOP or Shell, it is impossible to know whether they had a clear public relations objective in mind. However, it seems reasonable to assume MOSOP sought to improve the lives of the Ogoni people.

Strategies

One of the most successful strategies for MOSOP was also one of the most problematic. The decision to ally with Greenpeace did provide the Ogoni access to an extensive network of environmental activists. Greenpeace also had access to extensive e-mail and Internet media. All of these resources were used to help communicate the Ogoni's description of environmental exploitation and human rights violations. However, the alliance with Greenpeace brought with it an association with prior friction between Greenpeace and many industries in developed countries. The change in government and creation of the Oputa panel certainly indicate some success, but without specific research it is impossible to know whether the alliance with Greenpeace helped or hurt the Ogoni cause with any specific public. It is at least possible that perceptions of Greenpeace among Shell investors were so negative that any group allied with Greenpeace could be viewed by that particular public as environmental extremists whose concerns were not worthy of consideration.

Further challenge to MOSOP's credibility came from the decision to focus on gas flaring and the charge that Shell assisted the Nigerian military junta to import arms. Gas flaring is a common practice in oil production and most significant investors in the petroleum industry have seen gas flares that are safe and nontoxic. There are no international laws prohibiting gas flaring and the United States National Acid Precipitation Assessment Project found that such flares do not pose a noteworthy environmental hazard (Easton, 1997; National Acid Project, 1990). Furthermore, in the United States gas flaring is not only legal but many states require flaring and insist that such flares burn constantly to improve their safety (*Zink v. National Airoil,* 1980). When Shell claimed that they did not flare wells in populated areas and that the flares were not environmentally harmful, MOSOP's response was to deny the accuracy of this information. They might have been more successful in influencing Shell's investors and customers by explaining that the gas flaring operation in the Niger Delta was extraordinarily large and may have been potentially harmful, but without extensive explanation and evidence, many investors and consumers in the petroleum industry could interpret the Ogoni claims as exaggerated.

Another criticism of Shell targeted the involvement of the company in supplying arms to the Nigerian military. After initial denials, Shell admitted that it in fact imported guns for the Nigerian military and for its own security guards, in a story by the *London Observer* (Adabanwi, 2001). Even this involvement with the Nigerian government would have benefited from more extensive explanation. At the time Shell provided the weapons to the Nigerian military regime, that regime was the internationally recognized government of Nigeria. Supplying arms to the legitimate military of a sovereign nation is not illegal and is an accepted practice engaged in by virtually every industrialized nation. In 1976, Great Britain repealed all sanctions against supplying arms to Nigeria (Eaton, 1997). To some, the information about arms imports destroyed the image of Shell, but to members of other significant publics this information may have done no harm at all. The pro Ogoni campaign would have benefited from more detail about how the arms were used and more credible evidence, if such evidence existed.

When selecting strategic messages it is essential to identify the target public and to use both knowledge of the existing values of that target public and some theory or paradigm to predict how the public's members will react to the information. Certainly, active environmentalists and human rights advocates may have been motivated to support the Ogoni cause after receiving information about gas flaring and arms imports. However, major investors and consumers may not have been inspired by this information to support the Ogoni or to oppose Shell.

Tactics

MOSOP's goals were actively opposed by the Nigerian military regime, which controlled access to the traditional media. Therefore, the use of the Internet as a medium of communication was, no doubt, essential to MOSOP's campaign. Evidence of the significance of the Internet source of information about Shell's practices in Nigeria can be found on Shell Oil's own web page. The first thing one sees when browsing the website for Shell Nigeria is the following statement.

> During the 1990s we were heavily criticized for our lack of commitment to human rights, for our environmental track record and for failing to address the needs of the communities of the Niger Delta. There have been accusations of corrupt practices in relation to our community development projects. Some of these issues are in the past, but many continue to be debated in the world press. You can read our current stand on these topics in this section.

It seems apparent the Internet was and is a successful medium. This fact is made even more apparent when one notes that even Shell has recognized the importance of the Internet and has been motivated to use its website to respond to the allegations against it. Shell has also chosen to use the Internet to deliver its own messages. For example, their corporate website includes statements describing environmental practices and charitable contributions to developing countries and their people, including a scholarship program for Nigerian students. The Shell website also includes a forum for the discussion of concerns and a place to post opinions about Shell's practices. The forum and posted opinions allow Shell to monitor people's concern and to identify those that warrant response.

Evaluations

There is no doubt there have been significant changes since the MOSOP campaign. Nigeria has a new government and Shell has been both a target of and a participant in investigations of environmental damage and human rights violations. However, there is no reliable or valid research to suggest the MOSOP campaign actually caused these changes. In addition, if the Ogoni sought to remove Shell from Nigeria or to alter the oil extraction program, there simply is no way to argue they succeeded. The new democratic government under President Obasanjo has, in fact, kept the contracts with Shell and other international oil companies (World Factbook, 2003). Shell itself has been quite successful financially. Neither its stock prices nor its retail sales appear to have suffered because of the allegations against it or the attempted boycott of its products.

DISCUSSION QUESTIONS

1. From this campaign it is obvious that even small and relatively powerless groups can reach large international publics through the Internet, and that such information can motivate otherwise latent publics to action. Given the importance of Internet communications, how would you advise a corporation to monitor activity on the Internet? How would you suggest they use the information gained by monitoring the Internet to stay proactive rather than simply reacting to allegations against them?

2. If you were the public relations representative for the Ogoni people, what medium of communication would you use to deliver messages intended to motivate latent publics outside of

Nigeria? What medium or media would you use to communicate messages intended to motivate the more active publics in Nigeria? What medium or media would you use to communicate with the Ogoni people themselves?

3. If you were a public relations representative for Shell Oil and were aware of the allegations of exploitation in the Ogoni lands of Nigeria, how would you recommend Shell respond to those allegations? Consider both actions and communications. What would you recommend that Shell do and how would you tell significant publics what they had done?
   a. Given the relative wealth of Shell and relative poverty of the Ogoni, do you believe that Shell could simply pay the Ogoni for their claims? Why or why not?
   b. There are allegations that Shell did make substantial payments for injuries and damage in the Ogoni land, but that these payments were usurped by Nigerian officials and never reached the Ogoni who were injured. How could Shell have ensured that payments they made actually reached the injured parties?

4. Multinational companies often operate in developing countries with unstable or corrupt governments. Under these circumstances, is it appropriate for the company to become involved in the political governance of the country in which they do business?
   a. Does such a multinational company have an obligation to encourage democracy?
   b. Does such a multinational company have an obligation to ensure that payments it makes are used to assist the needy or poor in the country in which it does business?
   c. Does such a multinational company have an obligation to respect the recognized government of a sovereign nation even if that government is dictatorial, unethical, or exploitive?

5. Shell Oil is a British company that was doing business in Nigeria. Did Shell Oil have an obligation to honor British standards of environmental protection or occupational safety while operating in Nigeria? If the laws or regulations of Nigeria and Great Britain conflicted, what law or rules should Shell have followed?

6. Since the United States, Mexico, and Canada signed the North American Free Trade Agreement, many U.S. companies have moved manufacturing operations into Mexico. Do you see similarities between these companies and Shell Oil in Nigeria?
   a. Many people allege these plants were moved to escape U.S. environmental protection regulations. Do U.S. companies operating in Mexico have a legal or an ethical obligation to follow U.S. environmental regulations?
   b. Labor costs in Mexico are significantly lower than in the United States. Do U.S. companies moving to Mexico have a legal or ethical obligation to pay workers U.S. minimum wages or to provide health and retirement benefits that would be required in the United States?

7. Describe exactly how you would have conducted research to identify the pre-campaign reputation of Shell Oil. Also, describe how you would have measured the reputation of Shell Oil after the campaign to evaluate any change. Be sure to specify what publics you would measure and to explain why you selected those publics.

8. Both Shell and MOSOP have offered very different descriptions of the events in Ogoni land. Shell alleges that many of the oil spills, fires, and explosions for which they are blamed are the result of sabotage or protest by the Ogoni. MOSOP alleges the spills, fires, and explosions are the result of poor quality equipment and indifference to the Nigerian environment. From secondary research, how would you decide which version is true? As you explain how you would make this decision, be sure to include the concepts of reliability and validity. In other words how do you know when the assertions made in a secondary source are reliable and/or valid?

9. One of the most famous early U.S. public relations practitioners was Ivy Lee. He represented John D. Rockefeller after the famous Ludlow Massacre, in which armed force was used to suppress strikes and protests by laborers. What similarities do you see between the actions of Shell and Rockefeller? How could Shell have benefited from the advice of Ivy Lee?

REFERENCES AND SUGGESTED READINGS

Adabanwi, W. (2001). Nigeria: Shell of a state. *Dollar and Sense*. Retrieved from www.thirdworld traveler.com/Africa/Nigeria_Shell_State.html.

Alcorn, B. (1996, March 1). Blood and oil: Executions in Nigeria spark global boycott of Shell. Retrieved from www.webcom.com/hrin/magazine/july96/nigeria.html.

Bassey, N. (1997, November 27). Back to Shell game. Retrieved from www.moles.org/ProjectUnder ground/motherlode/shell/nig.html.

Benson, J. A. (1988). Crisis revisited: An analysis of strategies used by Tylenol in the second tempering episode, *Central States Speech Journal, 39,* 49–66.

Brooks, G. (1994, May 6). Slick alliance: Shell's Nigerian fields produce few benefits for region's villagers, *The Wall Street Journal*, p. 1.

Duodu, C. (1996, January 28). Shell admits importing guns for Nigerian police, *Observer.* Retrieved from www.archive.greenpeace.org/comms.ken/observer.html.

Eaton, Joshua P. (1997). The Nigerian tragedy, environmental regulation of transnational corporations and the human right to a healthy environment, *Boston University International Law Journal,* 15, 261–255.

Greenpeace (2003a) The environmental and social costs of living next door to Shell. Retrieved May 30, 2003, from www.greenpeace.org/~comms/ken/enviro.html.

Greenpeace (2003b) References. Retrieved December 26, 2003, from http://archive.greenpeace.org/ ~comms/ken/refer.html.

John Zink Company v. National Airoil Burner Company, Inc. 613 F.2d 547 (5th Cir., 1980).

Library of Congress-Nigeria (2003) Retrieved December 27, 2003, from http://lcweb2.loc.gov/ frd/cs/ngtoc.html.

Lubbers, E. (1998, September 29). Counterstrategies against online activism—The Brent Spar syndrome. Retrieved from www.infoshop.org/news3/corpspys.html.

National Acid Precipitation Assessment Project (1990), The causes and effects of acidic deposition. Washington, DC: U.S. Government Printing Office.

Nigeria and Shell: Partners in progress (1993). Shell Petroleum Development Company. Retrieved from archive.greenpeace.org/comms/ken/27.

Ogbu, A., & Akunna, C. (2001, January 25). Nigeria: Ogonis say arms were sponsored by Shell. Retrieved from www.corpwatch.org/news/PND.jsp?articleid=186.

Ogwuda, A. (1998, November 30). Fresh disaster looms in Jesse, *Guardian News*. Retrieved from www.mgrguardiannews.com/.

Oil Spill Intelligence Report. (1992). Custom oil spill data—Shell's ten-year spill record. Cutter Information Corporation, Arlington. Retrieved from http://archive.greenpeace.org/~comms/ken/ refer.html#42.

Okafor, C. (1998, November 30). Former Shell director absolves Jesse people of sabotage. *Guardian News.* Retrieved from www.mgrguardiannews.com/.

Olaniran, B. A., & Williams, D. E. (2001). Anticipatory model of crisis management: A vigilant response to technological crises. In R. L. Heath (Ed.), *Handbook of Public Relations* (pp. 487–500). Thousand Oaks, CA: Sage.

Oloibiri: In limbo (1990, December 3). *African Concord*, p. 29.

Oyekan, A. J. (1991). The Nigerian experience in health, safety and environmental matters during oil and gas exploration and production operations. Ministry of Petroleum, *Proceedings of First International Conference on Health, Safety and Environment in Oil and Gas Exploration and Production.* Vol.2, p. 74. Hague, The Netherlands.

Ryder A, (1992), The Last of the Line, *Shell UK Review,* No.2, p. 9.

Shell acknowledges arms purchase (2001, February). [Msg 1699]. Message posted to http://groups. yahoo.com/group/corporations/messages/1699.

Starr, Joel E. (1999). What do you have for me today? Observing the 1999 Nigerian Presidential Election, *Stanford Journal of International Law,* 35, 389–398.

Tookey, R. W. (1992, December 9). Letter to Shelley Braithwaite, London Rainforest Action Group, Shell International Petroleum Company Limited. Retrieved from http://archive.greenpeace. org/~comms/ken/refer.html#21.

White, J. (1998, October 21). Who is responsible for the oil explosion in Nigeria? Retrieved from www.wsws.org/news/1998/oct1998/nig-o21.shtml.

The World Factbook. (2003). Retrieved December 27, 2003, from www.cia.gov/cia/publications/ factbook/geos/ni.html.

17 St. Jude's Health Outreach Project in Brazil

JUDY B. OSKAM

In late 1998, the administrative director of St. Jude's International Outreach Program contacted the author to examine the role communications might play in early diagnosis and treatment of childhood cancer in the city of Recife, Brazil. This case description was developed from the personal experiences of the author who received a grant from St. Jude Children's Research Hospital's International Outreach Program to visit and consult with St. Jude representatives both in the United States and Brazil.

Executive Summary

This case describes a health communication outreach project in Brazil. The campaign described involves a comprehensive outreach plan with the objective of encouraging earlier diagnosis and treatment of pediatric oncology patients in northeastern Brazil, particularly in the city of Recife, and the state of Pernambuco. Physicians there were faced with the problem of trying to treat children with cancer in advanced stages. Earlier detection would provide a greater opportunity for an increased cure rate. Major challenges to improving treatment included a significant number of patients presenting with advanced-stage disease, lack of facilities to support critically ill patients, inadequate staff, and lack of advanced diagnostic laboratories.

A grant from the St. Jude Children's Research Hospital's International Outreach Program provided funds for the author of this case and a graduate assistant to visit key medical and media professionals in Brazil from January 5 to 15, 1999. During this site visit they developed some understanding of the organizations involved and their challenges. A communication outreach plan was developed and submitted to St. Jude Children's Hospital in July 1999. The campaign described here is based on that outreach campaign.

The outreach campaign used very limited resources to both encourage early diagnosis and treatment of childhood cancer and to raise funds to improve facilities for treating childhood cancer. Although the campaign did include tours for representatives of mass media, most of the campaign's tactics employed informal communication systems, including interpersonal communication from rural health workers and media. Post-campaign evaluation suggests that both objectives were met. There was an increase in the survival rates for curable cancer and funds were raised to construct a new treatment facility.

Research

As is the case with many outreach campaigns, here it was necessary to consider a wide range of issues including the relationship between St. Jude Children's Research Hospital and international partner sites, the unique characteristics of diagnosing and treating pediatric cancer, the administrative structure of the health system, and the communications network in Recife, Brazil.

Various research methods were used in this project, including site visits to medical facilities in Recife; in-person interviews with key medical, education, media, and communications professionals; structured interviews with parents of cancer patients and medical personnel; and telephone and electronic mail interviews with health communication specialists. Prior to visiting Brazil, several fact-finding meetings were held with various university faculty and local professionals. In addition, a review of available resources (via the Internet and a U.S. university library system) supplied basic information for the project.

Before the project team traveled to Brazil in January 1999, e-mail and telephone communication with St. Jude International Outreach Program Associate Director Lynne Jordan Bowers and Recife contact Arli Melo Pedrosa provided the opportunity to coordinate meetings and research activities. The stay in Brazil, during which this campaign was designed, lasted only 10 days. Therefore, it was important to maximize the time in Brazil and to take advantage of all available resources in order to gain an understanding of the challenges facing the client. Arli Melo Pedrosa is the president of Núcleo de Apoio às Crianças com Câncer (NACC) and an administrator at Centro de Hematologia e Oncologia Pediátricia (CE-HOPE). NACC is the local foundation and the shelter facility for childhood cancer patients in Recife. CEHOPE is the outpatient clinic for childhood cancer patients in Recife. Because of her connection with CEHOPE and NACC and her good standing in the community, Pedrosa was able to schedule meetings and interviews with media professionals, medical experts, and opinion leaders in Brazil. This entrée provided access to important experts who could provide insight into the client institution's problems and possible solutions for those problems.

Client Description

The client for this project was the St. Jude Children's Research Hospital International Outreach Program, based in Memphis, Tennessee. St. Jude Children's Research Hospital, founded by entertainer Danny Thomas, opened in 1962. Since then, St. Jude has treated more than 19,000 children from the United States and 60 foreign countries. "The mission of St. Jude Children's Research Hospital is to find cures for children with catastrophic illnesses through research and treatment" (St. Jude Children's Research Hospital, 2003).

The International Outreach Program at St. Jude Children's Research Hospital strives to improve survival rates of children with tragic illnesses around the world. According to St. Jude officials, fewer than 30 percent of children with cancer have access to modern treatment. The International Outreach Program uses transfer of knowledge, technology, and organizational skills to accomplish its goals (St. Jude Children's Research Hospital, 2003). The International Outreach Program, led by Dr. Raul Ribeiro, includes a dedicated team of medical, education, and administrative professionals.

A statement on the St. Jude Children's Research Hospital International Outreach Program website describes how the organization works with partner sites in countries around the world:

A basic health care infrastructure is needed to support pediatric oncology programs, which in turn further improve the development of basic health care. At the local level, International Outreach develops partnerships with medical institutions and fund-raising organizations and facilitates the involvement of other agencies and organizations to support key programs and the education of local personnel; at the regional level, International Outreach develops programs through the use of technology. The primary goal is to promote local and regional self-sufficiency. This model results in significant overall improvement in health care facilities, the level of practice, the self-confidence of health care providers, and local community involvement. (St. Jude Children's Hospital International Outreach Program, 2003)

The St. Jude Children's Research Hospital International Outreach Program serves pediatric cancer patients through partner sites in Guatemala, Mexico, Costa Rica, Ecuador, El Salvador, Brazil, Honduras, Venezuela, Ireland, Morocco, Russia, China, Chile, Jordan, Lebanon, and Syria (Figure 1).

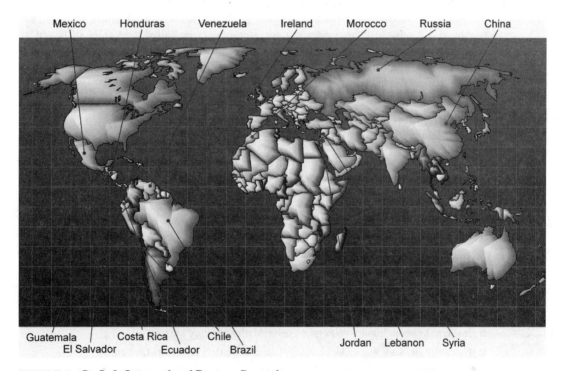

FIGURE 1   St. Jude International Partner Countries

Source: Yuri Quintana, Ph.D., Education Director, International Outreach Program—St. Jude Children's Research Hospital.

An understanding of the relationship between the medical organizations was an important step in this project. While the client was the St. Jude International Outreach Program, the project was developed specifically for the Recife, Brazil, partner site. The primary hospital for treating childhood cancer in and around Recife is the Instituto Materno Infantil de Pernambuco (IMIP). The outpatient clinic is Centro de Hematologia e Oncologia Pediátrica (CEHOPE). CEHOPE treats pediatric oncology patients from Recife and the surrounding area. Núcleo de Apoio às Crianças com Câncer (NACC) is the foundation that provides short-term housing for families who come to Recife for cancer treatment. NACC was founded in 1985 by a group of health professionals, parents, and community members committed to helping children with cancer and their families. The facility is a home away from home that provides food, shelter, treatment, and psychosocial support. More than 70 percent of the patients at NACC come from rural areas, 15 percent are from the city of Recife, and the remaining 15 percent come from elsewhere (Figure 2).

Program medical director Dr. Francisco Pedrosa, Arli Melo Pedrosa, and their staff have dedicated their lives to providing high-quality medical care to the children of northeastern Brazil. They work tirelessly to bring the latest technology, medical training, and facilities to those in need. While they realize the importance of and value public relations, more pressing medical matters take priority. It was clear that all funds were allocated to serve patients and no resources could be diverted to an outreach campaign.

Recife, located on northeastern coast of Brazil, is the capital of the state of Pernambuco. Because of its many waterways, Recife is often called the Venice of Brazil. It is one of the poorest areas of the country, and NACC officials estimate that half of Recife's inhabitants are children. In 1996, the city of Recife had a population of 1,346,045. The nearby city of Olinda had a population of 349,380 (State of Pernambuco, 2003).

Media Professionals

Meetings with the editors of the three leading Pernambuco newspapers and a journalist with the state television network presented an overview of the local media system. These interviews also proved very beneficial in providing information and garnering support for CEHOPE and NACC. In fact, these scheduled meetings resulted in an informal media tour that was successful in promoting local efforts to fight childhood cancer. Three newspaper arti-

FIGURE 2   Key Organizations for St. Jude in Brazil

Key Organizations

- St. Jude Children's Hospital International Outreach Program
- Instituto Materno Infantil de Pernambuco (IMIP)—primary hospital
- Centro de Hematologia e Oncologia Pediátrica (CEHOPE)—outpatient clinic
- Núcleo de Apoio às Crianças com Câncer (NACC)—foundation and shelter facility

cles, two accompanied by photographs, and an on-camera television interview segment were generated. All media coverage explained the problem of late diagnosis and the importance of identifying pediatric cancer in the early stages. Two newspapers and the television network expressed an interest in routine health coverage with an emphasis on childhood cancer.

Opinion Leaders

In addition to interviews with influential media professionals, meetings with significant health, education, and communication officials helped shape the communications plan. In January 1999, interviews were conducted with the Secretary of Education of Pernambuco, the Director of the Health Agent Program, a professor of sociology and communication from the Catholic University in Recife, an accomplished public relations consultant, and key medical professionals.

One of the best sources of information was Teresa Cristina Alves Bezerra, director of the health agent program for the state of Pernambuco. The health agent program in Brazil, supported by the government since 1993, is similar to a health agent model in Africa. In the state of Pernambuco, 8,800 health agents service families in rural and urban areas. Health agents are scheduled to visit each family one time a month to provide basic health care information. Health agents keep a "report card" for each child that documents the child's health and welfare. The health agents are also required to attend educational workshops and seminars to keep up to date on health issues (Personal communication, Jan. 11, 1999).

A meeting with Recife public relations consultant Anna Queiroz provided a greater understanding of the communications system in Brazil. She confirmed perceptions about the needs of the organization and provided local support for campaign efforts. During a meeting with Queiroz, she contacted the office of the newly elected vice president of Brazil to arrange a meeting to discuss the project with him and his wife. This personal connection is invaluable to a successful public relations program. It was clear that a credible, competent public relations professional in Recife could facilitate the implementation of a comprehensive outreach plan (Personal communication, Jan. 11, 1999).

Professor Ana Azevedo is on the faculty of the Universidad Catolica in Recife. Her connection with students and young journalists presented opportunities for developing and disseminating cancer awareness messages. For example, one of Professor Azevedo's former students has a weekly radio program targeting women that airs in 14 cities in Brazil (Personal communication, Jan. 7, 1999).

Dr. Silvia Rissin is the president of the hospital foundation for IMIP. She offered useful recommendations about how to reach the public with childhood cancer messages. According to Dr. Rissin, community leaders would be the key to reaching the public. She also recommended that factories and companies be involved in outreach activities. Rissin believed women, as the primary caregivers, are a significant target audience. She mentioned a yearly workshop event sponsored by a large supermarket chain that attracts 2,000 housewives (personal communication, Jan. 7, 1999). A colleague of Dr. Rissin's, Maria Aurea Bittencourt Da Silvia, discussed a model health agent program that promoted a Down Syndrome project in a neighboring state. The UNICEF-funded program created public awareness about Down syndrome using television public service announcements (personal communication, Jan. 7, 1999).

Parents of Cancer Patients

In an effort to learn more about how and why pediatric cancer patients come to visit a clinic or physician, a study of parents was conducted. A convenience sample of 31 parents with children in the CEHOPE clinic provided insight about the target population. A survey instrument was developed in collaboration with St. Jude International Outreach officials, Recife medical professionals, and Texas Tech University mass communications faculty. The questionnaire included sections about socioeconomic situation, literacy, home environment, media access and use, education, resources for health information, doctor visits and diagnosis, and symptoms leading to contact with a medical professional. Participation by parents was voluntary and they were interviewed during their child's clinic visit. The parent interviews were conducted in Portuguese by Luiz Andre, the recreation director at CEHOPE and Spencer Miller, a volunteer, undergraduate intern at St. Jude Children's Research Hospital. Andre is fluent in Portuguese and was familiar with both the parents and their children. Miller, who speaks conversational Portuguese, compiled the questions and coordinated the interviews during the last two weeks of 1998 and the first two weeks of January 1999.

Medical Personnel

In addition to input from the parents of cancer patients, it was important to gain an understanding of the situation from medical professionals. A survey instrument, consisting of 15 open-ended questions, was administered by Miller during the last two weeks of December 1998 and first two weeks of January 1999. Three nurses, one administrator, two social workers, one psychologist and seven physicians participated in the study. They were interviewed at either the IMIP hospital or at the CEHOPE clinic. The medical personnel interviews were primarily conducted in English, although sometimes Portuguese was spoken.

The medical personnel who were interviewed said that doctors who work in the rural areas in the interior of Brazil lack the ability and equipment to diagnose disease properly. Medical professionals recommended educating interior and city doctors, health agents, and nurses about childhood cancer.

Key Findings

The qualitative and quantitative research outlined above provided a framework for campaign recommendations. Key findings included:

- Medical personnel are a significant internal target audience for training and education about childhood cancer. This group includes health agents, physicians, nurses, and medical students. Health agents and physicians are seen as credible sources of health information.
- The media in Recife are receptive to participating in childhood cancer awareness campaigns.

- Television, radio, and outdoor (billboard and bus) signage are the primary mass media used to reach the general population in Brazil.
- Women should be a key target audience for health communication messages, as they are the primary caretakers of children.

Objectives

The client's goal was to improve the survival chances for children with cancer. In order to meet this goal, their secondary goals were to get the patients to the clinic sooner and to raise money for improved treatment. Early diagnosis would certainly improve survival rates for curable cancers in Northern Brazil, and improved treatment facilities would obviously help patient survival.

In order to meet these goals it was necessary to develop a comprehensive communication outreach plan to address late diagnosis of pediatric oncology patients. In developing a plan it was important to consider both the internal audience (medical professionals) and external audience (media, education, government, and community organizations). It was also crucial to provide recommendations that would enhance and maximize the limited financial and human resources at NACC and CEHOPE.

Simply put, the public relations objectives were to (1) raise funds for improved treatment facilities, and (2) increase the survival rate of children with cancer by encouraging earlier diagnosis.

Strategies

The following recommendations were designed to provide administrators with the St. Jude International Outreach Program, CEHOPE, and NACC with a blueprint for action. With this campaign, it was important to consider not only what communication methods would be effective for the target audiences, but also how they would be managed and implemented.

Action Strategies

In this campaign it is difficult to separate actions from communications because most of the actions were made simply to facilitate communication. However, several specific actions were recommended to the client. These included hiring competent and local public relations counsel, taking advantage of the local university by involving a student intern and faculty mentor, and developing specific educational materials for use by health agents and other opinion leaders.

Communication Strategies

The communication messages selected for this campaign were straightforward and simple. First, target publics, particularly parents, had to be provided information about the importance of early diagnosis, and be motivated to seek medical treatment. Second, those target publics able to provide support had to be told of the importance of childhood cancer diagnosis and treatment and motivated to support the efforts of IMIP, CEHOPE, and NACC.

Media were selected for the campaign based on research results that predicted that medical personnel, media, and women would be best able to deliver the campaign's messages.

Tactics

Based on the research and strategies identified, several specific tactics were recommended. Although limitations on resources made it impossible to implement all of the recommended tactics, they are all listed here.

1. A local Recife public relations consultant, such as Anna Queiroz, should be hired to provide PR coordination for the outreach program. Queiroz is already knowledgeable and supportive of CEHOPE and NACC.

2. A journalism/communications student should be assigned as an intern or hired as a part-time employee in coordination with Professor Ana Azevedo. This student could provide support for PR efforts at a low cost.

3. In coordination with clinic administrators, develop childhood cancer educational print and video materials for medical professionals and medical students. Arli Pedrosa has developed some excellent resources that could be used as the basis for this educational unit.

4. Provide educational materials about childhood cancer for health agents. Each child has a report card that charts various health statistics (immunizations, childhood diseases, growth, etc.). During monthly visits, health agents review the cards and fill in the appropriate information. Provide a cancer checklist sticker for health agents to affix to existing health cards

5. Coordinate and sponsor a yearly workshop for health agents, to educate them about childhood cancer. The workshop should include presentations by medical professionals, parents and, if possible, children with cancer.

6. Provide educational sessions about childhood cancer for women who attend the BomPreco yearly event. BomPreco grocery stores could also serve as a distribution point for posters and educational material.

7. Coordinate with the Secretary of Education and other health organizations to implement a new health education curriculum for the public schools. The American Cancer Society's Comprehensive School Health Education program could serve as a model for this long-term effort.

8. Use the network of churches to disseminate cancer prevention/detection information. CEHOPE and IMIP (hospital) could host educational workshops for church leaders and give a tour of the clinic and NACC. The church community is a well-established source of information.

9. Coordinate a public relations campaign for childhood cancer awareness. The campaign should include the following:

    a. Media tour. A media tour should be conducted to promote the warning signs of childhood cancer with an emphasis on the importance of early detection.

    b. Spokesperson. A high-profile celebrity or official should serve as spokesperson for the campaign. Brazilian soccer legend Pele and his wife Xuxu would generate media coverage. Xuxu hosts a popular children's television program in Brazil.

    c. Speaker's Bureau. Coordinate with other cancer/health organizations in Recife to organize a Childhood Cancer Speaker's Bureau.

    d. TV and radio public service announcements

    e. Outdoor billboards and bus signage

    f. Brochures & pamphlets (simple, conversational language with minimal text)

    g. Special events and community activities

    h. Special appearances (on Telenovelas, for example)

    i. Educational videos on early detection of childhood cancer

    j. Routine health columns. Monthly or weekly newspaper columns could present various issues related to childhood cancer.

  10. Conduct additional research to determine how rural health professionals in Brazil prefer to receive information about children's health issues.

Fortunately, St. Jude's International Outreach Program was able to provide a marketing/public relations professional to live and work in Recife as a St. Jude volunteer. Heidi Huang was in Brazil from January to March 2002 assisting the St. Jude International Outreach Program with fundraising and development activities for CEHOPE and NACC. Through telephone and e-mail communication, Huang was given the recommended campaign tactics before leaving for Brazil. In February 2002, Huang collected valuable data on implementation through in-person interviews with Arli Melo Pedrosa. Huang was also able to observe the status of the communications efforts during her stay in Brazil.

As mentioned earlier, the outreach campaign recommendations were developed with full consideration of the tight budget and human resource limitations of the Recife facilities. It was no surprise then, that some recommendations could not be implemented. While public relations professional Anna Queiroz has not been hired to facilitate outreach efforts, she has volunteered her time to assist NACC. NACC did hire a professional journalist to edit a monthly newsletter that is being distributed to donors, schoolteachers, and medical professionals. NACC has also reserved a budget to hire a full-time PR professional and plans to start an internship program in coordination with local universities.

NACC has developed and provided childhood cancer information to medical professionals in Northeastern Brazil. Each year, a group of doctors and medical professionals from IMIP, CEHOPE, and NACC offer two-day weekend seminars to health agents, nurses, and schools. Seminars have been held for nurses and medical professionals. Educational pamphlets have been provided to the health agents, and handbook and video materials are in the development stage due to budget constraints. NACC has suggested that the government include a "cancer checklist" in each child's health report card. Along with the checklist, NACC officials have recommended appropriate training for health agents so they are familiar with the information and the process. Arli Pedrosa developed an implementation plan for the health agent training curriculum and approached the government to secure support for the plan.

While NACC officials have not secured one specific high-profile celebrity or spokesperson to represent the organization, they have adopted a one-campaign one-celebrity approach. For example, a famous artist originally from Recife donated 100 pieces of art as a fundraiser. A famous national volleyball player who had cancer made a one-time visit to NACC and generated positive media coverage.

In addition to maintaining good media relations with the top newspapers and electronic media, NACC officials have also built a strong relationship with leading advertising agencies. One agency produced a television public service announcement for NACC for grassroots fundraising purposes. The PSA aired on all local TV stations during November and December 2001. Another large local agency placed NACC information on unoccupied billboards throughout Recife. In November 2001, an exclusive 7-minute presentation of the significant accomplishments of IMIP and NACC was broadcast during prime time on a national television program. NACC has also established a professional web presence at www.nace.org.br.

NACC officials have participated in various community outreach events and activities. The BomPreco grocery store sponsored NACC at its yearly community event in 2000. While the recommendation to connect with the church network has not been implemented, officials have given educational speeches at churches, when invited. Arli Pedrosa said that using the church to distribute information requires members and patients to be involved on a regular basis.

Additional brand recognition and fundraising efforts have included fashion shows and musical concerts. NACC has also developed a corporate sponsorship certificate program to recognize donors and organizations.

Evaluation

The client was pleased with the initial plan and subsequent results addressing late diagnosis of pediatric oncology patients in Recife. Since 1999, the author of this campaign has been invited to work with the International Outreach Program on other projects in Guatemala and Honduras.

Arli Pedrosa understands the importance of and is successful at blending fundraising and public relations. She has held two large conferences for fundraising foundations across Brazil that support children with cancer. St. Jude International Outreach Program Director, Dr. Raul Ribeiro, and Associate Director Lynne Jordan Bowers addressed an audience of 700 participants at a 2002 meeting. The pre-meeting workshop included information about public relations and fundraising strategies. St. Jude International Outreach Program officials recognize that an increased awareness of public relations activities helped Pedrosa raise the funds for the NACC facility.

More specific evaluations of the campaign's success can be seen in fundraising and treatment records. Within 2 years of the beginning of the public relations campaign, the NACC had raised enough money to build a 7-story building which houses the domiciliary care facility and the NACC offices.

A new pediatric oncology unit was opened at IMIP in 2002. The 37-bed unit also contains a new auditorium with teleconference capabilities and a modern laboratory. The NACC foundation has also raised more than $500,000 in donations to support the pediatric oncology program in Recife.

Probably the most significant indicator of the success of this project is whether pediatric patients were coming to treatment at an earlier stage in the disease. According to St. Jude, survival rates for most curable cancers improved on average from 30% to 60% in Recife since the International Outreach program began there in 1993. Patients would abandon treatment in Recife at a rate of more than 12 percent in 1994. In 2003, the abandonment rate was less than 1 percent. Public relations is just one of many factors that may have contributed to these positive results.

Critique

Research

Pre-campaign research for this program was extensive. Particularly when one considers the limited resources and time available, a great deal of information was gathered. The combination of formal surveys and interviews produced significant insights that were used to identify both potentially useful messages and secondary publics. The meetings with opinion leaders provided a foundation for visits to medical and outreach facilities. While the language was a hindrance, it was possible to communicate both in English and in Portuguese with Pedrosa translating. The availability of the St. Jude intern, Spencer Miller, also helped bridge the language barrier.

In hindsight, more time to prepare appropriate research tools would have improved this project. Also, access to greater resources could have improved the research. For example, limited time, money, and translation expertise compelled the use of a convenience sample of patients' parents. It would have been useful to be able to survey parents of children who were not already patients. Those subjects could have provided greater insight into why some children never sought diagnosis or treatment.

Objective

The client, the St. Jude International Outreach Program, had a clear goal. However, it was necessary to adapt that goal to the needs of the Recife partner site. Despite any possible problems, the public relations objectives selected supported both the organizational goals of the International Outreach Program and the Recife partner site. Further, both the objective of securing funding for an expanded treatment facility and the goal of increasing the number of children seeking early diagnosis were easily measurable. In short, the objectives for this campaign were one of its real strengths.

Strategies

This campaign's primary strengths are its thorough research and clear objectives, and it is impossible to argue with its success. Its strategies were, however, weak. Here the campaign planners appear to have moved directly from research to specific tactics for delivering information. Had the strategies been more clearly separated from tactics, it might have been possible to identify either some theory or communication model that would facilitate identification of messages or media to even more effectively assist Brazilian children with cancer.

Tactics

The list of proposed tactics seems well supported by the research and they appear to have been successful. It should be noted, however, that budget constraints made it impossible to implement some tactics. For example, there is every reason to believe that using the network of churches as a point of contact and a distribution system for cancer detection and prevention would have been effective.

Evaluation

Some of the measures of success, like the report of client satisfaction and the number of people attending meetings, are frankly irrelevant. However, it is impossible to argue with both the fundraising and treatment success of the program. The campaign met its objective to improve treatment facilities by securing funding for both a new shelter and pediatric care facility. Further, evidence that the campaign met its objective to improve the survival rate for children with cancer is overwhelming.

DISCUSSION QUESTIONS

1. Keeping in mind that funds were limited, what other research would have been beneficial for this project? Describe how you would have conducted this research with limited resources while maximizing the reliability and validity of the research.
   a. Are there secondary research sources you would have used?
   b. What publics or subjects would you have asked for information?
   c. How would you have drawn samples from those publics? Keeping in mind that some of your subjects may be from rural Brazil, what problems do you anticipate with identifying subjects and encouraging their participation in your research?

2. At the time of the project, the Recife partner site had no paid professional public relations support. What impact did this have on strategies and tactics?

3. Today the Internet is a standard communication medium. Why do you suppose it was not a main focus of this project?

4. How would you evaluate the success of this project? What evaluation methods would you use to illustrate accomplishments for the Recife partner site and the St. Jude International Program office?

5. Assuming you decided that your public relations objective is to encourage mothers from the rural areas of the State of Pernambuco to bring their children to the clinic in Recife, what strategies would you adopt? Is there a theory, model, or principle of communication that would help you pick messages and media to reach that public?

REFERENCES AND SUGGESTED READINGS

Brazilian Embassy, Washington, DC. Retrieved from November, 2003 www.brasilemb.org.

Centro de Hematologia e Oncologia Pediátricia (CEHOPE). Retrieved from November, 2003 www.cehope.com.br/.

Instituto Materno Infantil de Pernambuco (IMIP). Retrieved December, 2003 from www.imip.org.br/.

Núcleo de Apoio às Crianças com Câncer (NACC). Retrieved from November, 2003 www.nacc.org.br .

St. Jude Children's Research Hospital (2003). Retrieved November, 1999 and September, 2003 from www.stjude.org ; and December, 2003 from www.stjude.org/about-st-jude.

St. Jude Children's Research Hospital International Outreach Program (2003). Retrieved November, 1999 and August, 2003 from www.stjude.org/international-outreach.

State of Pernambuco, Brazil. Government information (2003). Retrieved from December, 2003 www.pernambuco.gov.br.

18 Burson-Marsteller's Depression Awareness Campaign in Thailand

PEERAYA HANPONGPANDH

The critique and discussion question portions of this case summary were prepared by the text authors and may not reflect the views or opinions of Peeraya Hanpongpandh.

Executive Summary

The U.S. manufacturer, Eli Lilly and Company, is a world leader in the pharmaceutical industry. In 1996 Lilly agreed to join three Thai institutions in co-sponsoring a program to increase awareness of depression. The program's objectives were to increase public awareness of the danger of the illness. The ultimate goal was to reduce the rate of suicides, especially among teenagers and children. Lilly and its cosponsors hired the Burson-Marsteller Company to design and implement the program.

Campaign development began with a situation analysis intended to determine how best to apply public relations to mitigating depression disorder. The situation analysis produced a large number of findings. One such finding was that the Thai suicide rate has been increasing for 20 years and that depression disorder is the root cause of this increase. Three plausible causes of Depression Disorder were identified. They were social stress, economic competition, and psychosocial problems. Of the three, psychosocial problems was the most significant cause of depression. Social stress and economic competition were identified as causes of depression primarily in citizens of larger cities. While depression was most common in people who were about 40 years old, the rate among Thai teenagers and children was found to be increasing.

The study's results also suggest that depression disorder is a clinical illness, not a personal weakness. It is therefore curable, either with medication, electro-convulsive or shock therapy, and psychosocial treatment. Interpersonal therapy encourages the patients to adjust themselves to the affliction through developing good relation with others. Behavior therapy, on the other hand, helps those suffering from distorted ideas causing the depression disorder through changing their attitude, using appropriate behavior.

It was learned that that most people perceived depression disorder to be the same as mental disease. Further, many people in Thailand thought depression disorder was incurable. There was also significant social stigma associated with the disease, and many people were unwilling to reveal the fact that they suffered from depression. Obviously, these people did not seek any form of treatment.

In light of these problems, a campaign was designed to encourage people suffering from depression to seek treatment from medical doctors. Toward this end the campaign sought to educate target publics that the disease was curable, and to enlighten medical doctors so they could facilitate treatment.

The target publics for the campaign were current patients, doctors, nurses and the media. Techniques used to reach these publics included organizing a seminar, publishing a bi-monthly magazine as advertorials, issuing press releases, testing documents and feature stories, interviews with selected experts, and providing a post office box for public comments.

Research

Before describing a campaign to increase awareness of depressive disorder it is necessary to explain the illness and why it is important in Thailand. Depressive disorder is one of the three major causes of suicide attempts. The other two are imbalance of neurotransmitters in the brain and social environment. Studies suggest that 50 to 70 percent of all suicides are caused by depressive disorder. In Thailand, the illness is particularly widespread among teenagers and children, and Thailand has an exceptionally high rate of childhood and teenage suicide.

Symptoms of depressive disorder include increased sadness, loss of interest in life events, dullness of mind, chronic headaches, stomachache, constipation, irritation, insomnia or oversleeping, lack of appetite or overeating, and a lack of work efficiency. In children, the symptoms include social withdrawal, lack of concentration, disinterest in companionship, and poor educational performance.

Situation Analysis of Depression in Thailand

The campaign's research started with a situation analysis. The goal of this analysis was to determine how best to apply the tools of public relations in mitigating depressive disorder. It also included documentary research and interviews with health experts and key persons from Thailand's Royal College of Psychiatrists, the Psychiatric Association of Thailand, and the Department of Mental Health. These interviews sought information about the major causes of depressive disorder. The situation analysis has unveiled a large number of findings, summarized below.

Cultural Considerations.   In the Thai society, speaking about one's sense of inner turmoil or emotional problems is considered taboo. A typical Thai would never admit if he or she had experienced depression because of fear of ridicule or fear of not being accepted in society. In many cases, Thais go to temples to be cured of their depression. It is said that Thais seek help at temples because it is the easiest way out and they do not have to reveal their fears and frustrations. The second refuge for most Thais when dealing with depression is to go to local faith healers or fortunetellers who use superstition as their medium for healing. The last thing they would do is to see a doctor. They avoid physicians because they are afraid of losing face by exposing some weakness. These practices are the result of the importance of self-face in Thai culture. Self-face is the concern for one's own image that is found in most Asian cultures (Ting-Toomey & Kurogi, 1998).

Because of the motivation to preserve self-face, depression has been a silent killer for many Thais. In extreme cases, depression can lead to suicide. Around the world, 15 percent of all suicides are caused by depression, but in Thailand 50 to 70 percet of suicides are caused by depression. Further, the suicide rate in Thailand is increasing dramatically. According to statistics from the Information Center of the Planning and Budget Office of the Royal Thai Police Department, the suicide rate in Thailand has increased dramatically since 1992, when there were 1,113 self-inflicted deaths. In 1993, there were 1,259 reported suicides, and in 1994 the number jumped to 1,451. The increase continues.

Causes and Treatment of Depression Disorder.   The situational analysis performed prior to this campaign also found three usual causes of depression. Of these three, psychosocial illness is the most common cause. Social stress and economic competition are the two other major causes of depression. These are found primarily among people in large cities. Depression occurs most often among middle-aged people. Forty is the median age for depression. However, the rate of depression among the Thai teenagers and children is increasing alarmingly.

The psychological illness that causes depressive disorder comes from three main sources: genetics, biochemical factors, and psychosocial factors. The genetic link was identified by correlating occurrence of the disease with family relationships, particularly through studies using twins. The other major cause of depression—biomedical factors—can be caused by an imbalance of neurotransmitters in the brain. This imbalance can induce feelings of sorrow and guilt that increase the probability of depressive disorder.

Most often, depressive disorder is the result of psychosocial factors, including experiences with parents or one's childhood guardian, negative experiences in life, unemployment, lack of a satisfying relationship or marriage, and an unpleasant work environment. Tension and loss, and perhaps some cultural customs and beliefs can also contribute to depression. Symptoms of the disease are emergence of sadness, loss of interest, dullness of mind, chronic headaches, stomachache, constipation, irritation, insomnia or oversleeping, lack of appetite or overeating, and lack of work efficiency. In children, the symptoms include social withdrawal, lack of concentration, disinterest in companionship, and poor educational performance.

In the medical field it is generally accepted that depressive disorder is a clinical illness, not a personal weakness. It is therefore curable, either with medicines, electro-convulsive or shock therapy, and psychosocial treatment. Interpersonal therapy encourages the patients to adjust themselves to the affliction through developing good relation with others. Cognitive-behavior therapy, on the other hand, helps those suffering from distorted ideas causing the depression disorder through changing their attitude using appropriate behavior. Short-term psychodynamic psychotherapy helps rehabilitate patients who have psychological conflicts causing a distorted personality structure. Psychotherapy can help find the origins of conflicts and thus help treat them.

One reason few Thais sought treatment for their depressive disorder was that many of them stigmatized depressive disorder as a mental disease. In addition, many Thais regarded depression disorder as incurable. Of equal importance was that most people in Thai society were very reluctant to reveal their depressive disorder. Nongpanga Limsuwan, President of the Thai Academic Affairs at the Royal College of Psychiatrists, said:

> . . . every year we cure a great many people who suffer from this dangerous illness, and we find out that those who come for treatment are not aware that they have this illness at all, perhaps because the public has not been educated about it.

She suggested that to avoid the agony of depressive disorder, one has to study and understand the episodes of depression that make up the disease. Knowledge of what depressive disorder is and an understanding of the individual's own self-consciousness can help diagnose the disease. This information can also be used to identify the disease in time for successful treatment.

The Client

Eli Lilly, a world leader in the pharmaceutical industry, is a global research-based corporation headquartered in Indianapolis, Indiana. One of the company's goals is to provide information on technological advances in medical treatment and health care concerns. Because Eli Lilly is a global company, this goal includes informing people in virtually every country around the world.

Recognizing the dreadful effects of depression in Thailand, Eli Lilly joined with the Thai Department of Mental Health, the Thai Royal College Psychiatrists, and the Psychiatric Association of Thailand to provide information that might motivate Thais to seek treatment for depression and therefore mitigate the suicide rate. In 1996 they hired Burson-Marsteller to design and implement a depression communication program to support those goals.

Objectives

The overall objective of the campaign was to raise public awareness of the danger of depression. A component objective was to motivate more people in Thailand to acknowledge their own personal symptoms of or susceptibility to depression, to openly discuss depression, and to consult with doctors about any emerging symptoms of depression. The following information or output objectives were set to accomplish the general purpose:

1. To directly educate the public about the effect of depression on individual families and Thai society as a whole
2. To encourage people to consult their doctors about depression and to seek treatment and medical cures

3. To enlighten the people about the symptoms of depression and inform then that depression can be cured
4. To increase the awareness of medical doctors and nurses in different fields about the effects of depression so that they could encourage diagnosis and treatment of the disease

Strategies

The campaign strategy rests on a series of interconnected assumptions. First, the campaign planners believed that if people in Thailand were given information about depression disorder they would be more likely to consult with medical doctors. Second, it was envisioned that providing doctors and nurses with information about depression disorder would increase their ability to treat the disease. Finally, it was hoped that increasing the number of people treated for depression would decrease the suicide rate.

Burson-Marsteller used a combination of one-way and two-way communication strategies to educate the target publics. The target publics included current patients, doctors and nurses, and the media. Most campaign messages used third party endorsements and direct involvement of the target publics to strip away the social stigma of depression.

Tactics

To deliver the strategic message that depression is a disease and should not be socially stigmatized, six general tactics were employed. These were feature stories, one-on-one interviews, press releases, advertorials, a world mental health day seminar, and the establishment of a post office box. Each of these tactics is described below.

Feature Stories

Each feature story was developed after close coordination with doctors who were familiar with depression disease and its treatment. After the articles were written and edited by the public relations staff, they were pitched to appropriate media. Following discussions with the media representatives, follow-up articles were also produced. Some of the topics for these articles are listed below.

1. Depression: An illness not a weakness. An article on depression detailing how it is nothing to be ashamed of but rather is a disease that can be treated and, in most cases, cured.
2. Depression—Symptoms and Treatments. This article included a list of hospitals that treat depression.
3. Doctors can help. An article on depression and case studies that encouraged readers to see doctors.
4. Depression: Disease of a changing life style. This article included statistics on annual increases in the numbers of depression patients in Thailand and other developed countries.

5. Women and depression. An article on why women are more prone to depression.
6. Fighting depression. The article described techniques for preventing and handling depression.
7. Yes or No: Are you depressed? A self test
8. Depression: Background and history. An article on the history of depression, how it has been investigated, the myths and the facts about the often-misunderstood disease.
9. The Mind—Our body's most sensitive part. This article looked at the mind as a part of the body with an emphasis on how it can become ill.
10. Changing Attitudes. An article on how attitudes, particularly attitudes toward depression, are changing.

Many of these articles were placed successfully in Thai magazines. For example, one was placed in *Dichan,* a leading women's magazine with a circulation of 160,000 copies. Articles were also placed in other women's magazines including *Delite,* which has a circulation of 60,000, and *Chandra,* which has a circulation of 59,000.

Interviews

Five one-on-one interviews were arranged between prominent medical authorities and Thai media representatives. The first was one with Dr. Chutitaya Panpreedcha, Director General of the Department of Mental Health. He met with a writer for *Priew Magazine,* a popular bi-monthly women's magazine with a circulation of 100,000. Another interview was conducted by representatives of *Wattachak,* a daily newspaper with a circulation of 200,000. The *Wattachak* representatives met with Dr. Nongpanga Limsuwan, President of the Academic Affairs of the Royal College of Psychiatrists of Thailand. Three other interviews were conducted at Pra Mongkutklao Army Hospital with Dr. Aroon Chawanasai, President of the Royal College of Psychiatrists of Thailand. Dr. Chawanasai met with reporters from *Thai Rath,* the highest circulated daily newspaper in Thailand, *Kulalstree,* a leading bi-monthly women's magazine with a circulation of 230,000 copies, and *Wongkarn Phat,* a weekly publication for healthcare professionals with a circulation of 25,000.

For each of these interviews the public relations staff recruited media representatives and pitched the interviews. They also prepared and distributed materials for the reporters prior to the interviews and suggested topics for discussion. The topics that were suggested for discussion are listed below.

1. How does the Mental Health Department plan to deal with the increasing incidence of depression in Thailand?
2. What are the effects of depression on patients, their families, society, and the country?
3. What are the causes of depression and how is it treated?
4. How does one recognize the symptoms and signs of depression?
5. Why is it harder to seek help for depression in Asia?
6. What are some ways to encourage people to learn that they are sick and to get help?

Press Releases and Media Queries

Two general circulation press releases were issued. The first was on the topic of "Psychiatrists Say Depression Is on the Rise with a Resulting Increase in Suicides." This release was printed in 14 publications with a total circulation of over 2 million. The second release was titled "Psychiatrist says Depression Sufferers Should Avoid Liquor and See a Doctor." It resulted in six articles in publications with a total circulation of over 50,000 copies.

Not only were the press releases published, they also stimulated press inquiries. These queries were answered by the public relations staff and were used as an additional vehicle to provide information on depression to the media. The media were also offered interviews with psychiatrists and other experts on depression.

Advertorials

Advertorials were placed in two famous women's magazines—*Dichan* and *Kullastree*. The advertorials were written and placed by the public relations staff. The magazines in which they were placed were distributed to the campaign's target publics.

World Mental Health Day Seminar

More than 100 people attended a seminar on October 16, 1999, which was World Mental Health Day. Attendees represented several nongovernment organizations including nursing and teaching institutions. Other participants included representatives of newspapers, magazines, radio, and television. Not only did media representatives attend the seminar, but its messages were also covered in news reports.

Post Office Box

The public relations staff arranged to rent a post office box in Bangkok under the name of the Royal College of Psychiatrists of Thailand and the Psychiatric Association of Thailand. This box was used to collect responses to the depression awareness campaign and to provide a vehicle for people to ask questions about depression and its treatment. Nearly 700 requests for more information were collected.

Evaluation

Evaluation of the campaign shows that there was extensive media coverage of depression. Coverage included three feature articles, five one-on-one interviews between health experts and media, 14 published articles from the press releases, placement of two advertorials, a large audience at the World Health Day Seminar, and nearly 700 responses to the post office box.

Critique

This campaign's greatest strengths are the involvement of very credible and knowledgeable experts in depression disorder and the detailed attention to media placement. Its most significant weakness is the lack of any measure of its impact on depression or the suicide rate.

Research

Research for a public relations campaign must meet two criteria. It must ask the right questions and it must provide reliable and valid answers to those questions. Here, many very important questions were not asked. Also there were some problems with research gathering methods that make the reliability and validity of the research results suspect.

Questions That Were Not Asked.   The situational analysis began with a very detailed description of depression disorder and some information about why Thais do not seek medical attention. However, some very important information was omitted. Important research questions that were not asked dealt with available media options, existing attitudes toward and knowledge about depression, and resources available to the campaign planners.

Selecting appropriate media from all available media is central to any public relations campaign that seeks to reach a large audience. In this case there was no analysis of available media. The research could have been improved by first identifying a list of all media that could reach the target publics. From this list media could have been selected to reach the target publics. It would also have been helpful to have research on the media consumption habits of those people in the target publics. For example, information about what newspapers or magazines are read by physicians and nurses could be used to guide decisions about which print media to target with the campaign's news releases.

It would have been very helpful for the campaign planners to know more about existing attitudes toward and knowledge about depression. The objectives and tactics that were ultimately selected were based on the assumption that the Thai public thought of depression as a stigmatized mental disease. Without some systematic research it is impossible to know whether this assumption is accurate. If the assumption was not accurate and Thais already knew that depression was treatable, then all the campaign's tactics would simply be wasted. Another advantage of pre-campaign research into the target public's knowledge and attitudes is that the results of that research could be compared to the results of post-campaign research to measure the campaign's impact or success. Such research could also be used to identify alternate media. Such alternate media might even include passing information though Buddhist monks if the research showed monks were willing to assist the campaign and that those in the target public found the monks credible sources of information.

In addition to media research, some research into resource availability should have been conducted. From the reported research we do not know how much money was available to spend or what size staff was available. Other resource questions could include some determination of the enthusiasm or commitment of the campaign's cosponsors. For example, it would be useful to know the size and budget of Thailand's Royal College of Psychiatrists, the Psychiatric Association of Thailand, and the Department of Mental Health.

Validity and Reliability.   The technique used to develop the situational analysis was not described in any detail. Without some description of the research method it is impossible to judge the reliability or validity of the research. One example of this weakness is the assertion that "Thais go to temples to be cured of their depression." Given the absence of any description for how this information was gathered we do not know if this refers only to some segment of the population or if it only represents the opinion of one author or that author's source. Before making such a blanket assertion it is important to insure that the information is based on a valid measure of the behavior of Thais and on a reliable observation or that behavior.

Objectives

All public relations objectives must advance the organizational goal of the client. In this case the client's organizational goal is never specified so it is impossible to judge whether any public relations objective helped achieve the goal. After reading the research and objective statement it is not clear whether the goal was to reduce suicides, to increase the number of people who sought medical treatment for depression, or to simply provide information.

The overall public relations objective that is specified is "to increase public awareness of the danger of depression." While this is not an unreasonable objective, it is not operationalized well enough to guide campaign decisions. It does not, for example, specify what publics are to be changed nor does it indicate how change in awareness will be measured.

Following this "overall objective," several component or alternative objectives are listed. Limiting the number of objectives and making them as specific as possible generally helps guide campaign decisions. Here the selection of tactics, in particular, could have been improved had there been one or two very specific objectives.

Strategies

The strategies seem to rest on the assumption that informing Thais about depression will motivate them to seek treatment. No theory or communication principle is provided that would support that assumption. Using some theory might have helped guide the selection of media or spokespeople. For example, if the campaign were based on a simple theory of credibility we would know that we must select spokespersons who are perceived as credible by the target audience. Taking this example further, if our target public includes Thais who seek a cure at a temple rather than through medical treatment, then the decision to use physicians as sources of information was ill advised.

Tactics

The tactics seem to be a "catch all" of typical media campaign components. We are never told, for example, why the feature stories went primarily to women's magazines. Was this narrow medium chosen because women were an important target public, because Thais typically seek health information in these media, or only because they were the media willing to publish the features?

The World Health Day Seminar seems a good idea for dissemination of information to medical professionals who may already be motivated to improve their knowledge about depression. Further, the establishment of a post office box for soliciting requests for information may help potential depression patients. However, it is at least possible that neither tactic was fully exploited. The relatively small attendance at the seminar (100 people) and the small number of inquiries directed to the post office box suggest these campaign components either were not well publicized or were not seen as attractive to many in the target publics. In particular, it should be noted that securing information through a post office box requires the inquirer to give his name and return address. If there is a social stigma associated with depression, people in the target public may have been reluctant to seek information in such a public venue.

Evaluation

This campaign did succeed in securing significant media coverage. The placement of multiple feature articles in high circulation magazines and several news releases are enviable. There was, however, no measurement of any change in the target public. One simple measurement of success would be to survey physicians to see if the number of depression patients increased.

Another even easier system of evaluation would be to compare the suicide rate prior to the campaign to the suicide rate after the campaign. The pre-campaign research used suicide statistics from the Information Center of the Planning and Budget Office of the Royal Thai Police Department. It would have been a simple matter to gather the same information for a time period after the campaign.

DISCUSSION QUESTIONS

1. How significant is the problem of suicide in Thailand? In order to answer this question consider the following:
    a. What is the population of Thailand?
    b. Is 1,451 suicides a high rate for a country that size?
    c. What is the suicide rate in other countries? Compare Thailand's suicide rate to that in the United States and in Sweden.

2. Since the situation analysis says that many people suffering from depression in Thailand prefer going to a temple to going to a doctor, would it be possible to involve the Buddhist monks at the temple in the campaign?
    a. From secondary research can you identify any example of the clergy in other countries assisting in health care campaigns?
    b. Can you find any example of Buddhist monks helping with a health care program?

3. Since depression may be a taboo subject, it may be difficult to get research subjects to talk about it. How would you conduct research into attitudes toward a taboo subject like depression?

4. Do you think depression is a taboo subject in the United States? Find out how medical associations, health care organizations, and pharmaceutical companies conveyed their messages

to destigmatize clinical depression. Do you think the same messages and tactics could be applied in Thailand?

5. How are products that are thought of as taboo sold or described in the United States? Consider, for example, Viagra or condoms.
   a. Will the same tools work for disseminating information about a taboo subject in Thailand?
   b. How would you decide how such techniques would be received in Thailand?

6. What is the real objective of this campaign? In other words, what do you think the campaign planners really wanted to accomplish? Is there an easy way to decide if this objective was met?

7. The Executive Summary and the Situation Analysis discussed concern for childhood and teenage depression. What media should have been used to reach that public? How would you identify popular media for children and teenagers in Thailand?

8. What theory or theories could you use to predict what messages would be most successful in motivating Thais to seek medical treatment for depression?

9. What theory or theories could be used to predict what spokespeople would be most credible with a Thai public?

10. Is it reasonable to conceptualize all Thais as one public? What subgroups or separate publics might you expect to find in Thailand? How would you identify those groups, their media consumption habits, and their attitudes toward medical treatment of depression?

11. The tactics used in this campaign seemed to focus on women's magazines. Why do you think the feature articles and advertorials were placed in women's magazines?
    a. How would you decide if women in Thailand are more susceptible to depression than men?
    b. If women are not more susceptible to depression is there any other reason to target women with information about depression?

12. Why do you believe the campaign's planners decided to use a post office box as a tool for two-way communication with their publics?
    a. Why do you think they did not use an Internet site?
    b. How would you decide which is better?

REFERENCES AND SUGGESTED READINGS

Aktawan. (April, 1996). Depression. *Priew.* p. 183.

Burson-Marsteller (Thailand) Co., Ltd. (1996). *Healthcare Department, Burson-Marsteller: Case studies.* Bangkok, Thailand: Burson-Marsteller (Thailand) Co., Ltd.

Burson-Marsteller (Thailand) Co., Ltd. (1996). *Final report of 1996 depression communication program.* Bangkok, Thailand: Burson-Marsteller (Thailand).

Clinic depression: A danger near you. (November 9, 1996). *Daily News,* pp. 3–4.

Down in the dumps. (November 25, 1996). *The Nation,* p. 3.

More suicides from depression. (April 3, 1996). *Bangkok Post,* p. 4.

Pannawadee. (October, 1996). *Sam-paat Khun-morr Arun Chaowanasai* [Interview with Dr. Arun Chaowanasai]. *Kulastree,* p. 73.

Teng, P. (1997). *Burson-Marsteller's public relations case study: The 1996 depression communications program.* Unpublished manuscript. Public Relations Department, School of Communication Arts, Bangkok University, Thailand.

Ting-Toomey, S., & Kurogi, A. (1998). Facework competence in intercultural conflict: An updated face-negotiation theory. *International Journal of Intercultural Relations, 22,* 187–225.

19 Public Television in the United States and Croatia: A Comparison of Two Campaigns

BONITA DOSTAL NEFF and VLADO SUSAC

This article describes two related campaigns. One campaign sought to improve support for a public broadcasting station in the United States. The other campaign's goal was the creation of a public broadcasting system in Croatia. The two campaigns are presented together to emphasize the differences that culture and the stage of national development can impose on what would otherwise be similar campaigns.

Executive Summary

Two campaigns are presented here. The first is a community relations program for a Public Broadcasting System (PBS) television station in the Midwestern United States. The second is a government relations or lobbying campaign, the goal of which was to develop a public broadcasting system in Croatia. This second campaign was a joint effort by communication practitioners and university faculty. These two campaigns are presented to illustrate the importance of dialogic relations or the communication exchanges between publics.

The planners of the U.S. campaign based their strategic decisions on dialogic and co-orientation perspectives. In other words, they focused on the relationship between a PBS station and the community it served. Their goal was to secure support, primarily financial support, for the station.

The Croatian campaign emphasized the role of professional communicators in monitoring, scanning, and interpreting the behavior of governmental bodies. The campaign by these professionals used interpersonal and electronic communication and its goal was to develop a television system that is free of government control and can assist the country in its move toward democracy.

Research

Significant research preceded each campaign. For the PBS campaign in the United States the research began with a survey used to identify topics for focus groups. The focus groups were made up of representatives of the community to be targeted for the station's outreach program. Research for the Croatian public television campaign used secondary sources, including analysis of media coverage and direct communication with key stakeholders in the legislature.

Results of these two research programs are presented below in five sections. The sections cover: research techniques, client needs, target publics, history and image of the subject television systems, and legal and financial limitations.

Research Techniques and Initial Findings

PBS in the United States.   A regional Midwest PBS station developed its constituency profile using research that began with telephone interviews. Later research using focus groups provided more in-depth information. The populations studied were PBS subscribers and others within the broadcast reach of the station. The entire study population is located within a two-state region with high population density.

Initially, it was difficult to convince the client organization that research was needed. After the research was completed it was also difficult to make the opinion leaders within the client organization understand the importance of the research as a basis for ongoing decision making.

The first stage of the research was designed to measure the audience size for the evening local news program. Knowing the audience size was important because news programs and their audience size have a significant impact on the station's budget. The research to measure the viewing audience covered two states. The sample of subjects for the study was 10 percent of the station's subscribers (a total of 500 subjects). Demographic analysis of these subscribers showed that 50 percent came from each of the two states.

The results of this research showed that the evening news program had a significant following. This fact was further substantiated by Nielsen data. The data established the station had a one-share Nielsen rating. Each Nielsen share represents thousands of viewers. Prior to this research, the station management was not aware of this significant audience because the cost of subscribing to the Nielsen data service was financially prohibitive. The Nielsen Company, however, was willing to share their data to confirm the research results. This first research established the value of the local news program. It served as the basis of a longitudinal study and provided a needed confirmation of the worth of this station to the local community.

The second study of the station's membership and viewing audience was designed to address the potential for expanding the viewing audience. As part of this second study, interviews were conducted with 303 PBS subscribers in the two-state area. One goal of this study was to determine how subscribers received the PBS station. Reception means included antenna, cable, satellite, or some combination of these. Results showed a high penetration for cable (66%) for the home state and 82 percent for the neighboring state. A large number of viewers received the station by satellite. The survey established that the audience was investing in cable and satellite, which were necessary for digital reception.

Another component of the research was assessment of diversity in the station's audience. The results in this area showed differences between the subscribers in the two states. Many subscribers in the station's home state identified their ethnic origins as Central European and complained about the lack of ethnic or Polish programming. Many subscribers in the neighboring state also lamented the "lack of ethnic programs." They, however, stated, "there is not Hispanic programming to point to with pride." Obviously, there are very different ethnic viewing audiences for this station.

Other research results suggested that many of the station's subscribers were really not committed to supporting the station. Many of these individuals became members or subscribers simply to receive some premium during a pledge drive. These premiums included CDs and videos given to individuals who became station subscribers. Although those working at these pledge drives stressed the opportunities of membership such as a program guide and special mailings, many subscribers simply did not identify themselves as a member or supporter of the station. This "soft membership" seemed to concern the station CEO, who was reluctant to invest station resources in efforts to increase subscriber membership. The CEO's decision could create a problem for station support, because subscribers are "renewable" and can be contacted for future support.

Croatian Public Television.   The Croatian campaign focused on efforts to pass legislation to support a public broadcasting system. The intent was to develop a television system with private management to help Croatia's evolution toward democracy.

Data for this campaign's research came primarily from media publications and legislative documents that describe developments in Croatian Public Television (HRT). The focus on HRT was selected because HRT is seen by many as a model for using visual communication to support efforts by countries that are transitioning to democracy.

Client Needs

PBS in the United States.   The public broadcasting systems in the United States depend on government support. PBS legislation has given life to a broadcasting system that is critical to the public needs. However, financial support from the government has eroded over the years. Today PBS receives less government money than does, for example, the British Broadcasting Corporation (BBC). This loss of government support has forced PBS systems to scramble for other sources of revenue. Fortunately, the station that is the focus of this campaign is located in a state that provides some support. The state's support included the purchase of all digital equipment in 2003. This equipment was installed at the time of this campaign. The digital equipment was broadcasting a basic test pattern because digital programming could not be broadcast until at least 80 percent of the public had a means of receiving digital signals.

Croatian Public Television.   The Croatian public television system is being created by legislative act but there is no legislative precedent for the system. Although three acts have been passed to create or modify broadcast infrastructure, the legislature does not see this project as a high priority. In fact, the latest legislative mandate, passed in 2003, has restructured the Croatian public television system under parliament control. Television journalists and communication academics are the people primarily motivated to see the system established. They want a broadcast system with private management or control. Efforts to establish a broadcast system with private control are often frustrated because Croatia does not have a well-established democratic structure. Many in Croatia are working toward establishing democracy and hope the television system, free from government control, will contribute to this movement.

Croatia has few newspapers and even fewer people reading their newspapers. The news from public broadcasting is their primary source of information. The void in print journalism, some say, is due to the lack of standards, with reporters leaving the profession for publication positions outside of journalism. Affecting these developments is the recent war in the Balkan area. The past conflict affecting parts of Croatia has hurt tourism, the country's main source of revenue, even if rebuilding is evident. The recovery has been even slower than expected with the turmoil around the world contributing to these perceptions.

Target Publics

PBS in the United States.   The target public for the PBS station is the people within the broadcast reach of the station. However, only a small percentage of people within the station's broadcast reach actually watch public television, and even fewer are subscribers or supporters of the station. The research results show an even more significant problem. Those results indicate that the subscribers often do not know they are members of PBS.

Throughout the United States there are generally held misconceptions about PBS. These misconceptions are also found in the local area affecting the station. For example, most people in the United States believe PBS is supported by advertising or the U.S. government. In fact, very little financing comes from the federal level and PBS cannot allow advertising from commercial organizations. Another major misconception is the belief that the cable bill's "must carry rule" provides income to PBS. While that rule does require cable systems to carry PBS, no revenues from the cable system go to support PBS.

In contrast to these misconceptions, most people in the United States are very familiar with PBS programming. For example, almost everyone in the United States can relate to *Sesame Street* and the character Big Bird. Familiarity with public television is pervasive on some levels, but needs to be expanded to encourage support for the system.

Croatian Public Television.   The Croatian public television campaign primarily targeted legislators in Croatia. Their support and understanding is key to passing the bills needed to establish the infrastructure of the television system. The primary concern at this stage is the establishment of private control over the television system. There is not yet much concern about programming and there is little need to involve the general public in the campaign. Legislative actions remain in flux and the public television organizational structure has been changed three times within the last six years. The most recent change was made in 2003.

History and Image of the Television Systems

PBS in the United States. The regional public broadcasting station that was the client for this campaign was originally founded as an educational station by a school. The station was later sold and the PBS designation came at that time. Under its current identification the station has one signal. After it becomes digital it will change its identification and call letters. Keeping the identity of the organization while moving to a different site on the signal band will create another challenge.

The PBS broadcaster has its own studio and tower. It now has digital equipment that was purchased by the state government. Twenty-five percent of the stations' programming comes from PBS. The remainder of the schedule is local programming. This mix of PBS and local programming is allowed under the PBS system.

As a regional public broadcasting station, always in the shadow of a larger PBS affiliate and commercial national broadcasting systems, survival depends on establishing a niche for viewers that no one else can clearly fulfill. This regional station has been officially recognized as one of the first and few PBS stations to have a local news program. The station established its local news program as the central key to the viewers' loyalty.

Although the station that is the client in this campaign is overshadowed by a larger PBS station and several major commercial broadcasting systems from a nearby state, the programming of this station is unique and helps establish the station as an important part of the local community. Competing stations in the bordering state rarely cover events in the station's home state. What little coverage is given the home state by the competitors is often negative and focuses on crime, environmental violations, and other problems. The client public broadcasting station has the opportunity to observe and cover positive events in its home state. This favorable coverage is a real advantage for the local community where the station is located.

As a regional public broadcasting station with a mission focused on the needs of the constituency located near the station site, the station's publics are very complex. Providing programming and appealing to the communities near the client station are particularly difficult because of the diversity of the community served by the station. The viewing audience in both states represents the full range of racial, age, and ethnic groups. The station's community also includes urban, suburban, and rural areas as well as a wide range of industrial and service businesses.

Croatian Public Television. Croatia is close to volatile countries like Serbia and Bosnia but is also just across the Adriatic Sea from Italy and it shares a border to the north with Slovenia. Slovenia is a stable country and as of May 2004 is the outer boundary of the European Economic Community. Croatia is also geographically complex. Significant distances separate population centers and part of the country is cut off at the Adriatic Sea by Bosnia. A successful public television system would improve communication and would contribute greatly to the feeling of unity in this country.

Croatia's population is very interested in a reliable news source. The combination of a desire for news and the need for training that could be provided by a public television system suggest the potential for success. Further, Croatia has a potentially very receptive television audience. Croatians have universities with doctoral programs and a population that is fluent in a number of languages.

In Croatia, the parliament, television journalists, and communication academics are working hard to create a public television system that supports both the sense of unity in the country and contributes to a sense of democracy by avoiding governmental control of programming and news content.

Croatian public television is a very young client. The system still must create an infrastructure and decide how to meet the needs of its relevant publics. This fledgling public television system and a few print newspapers do not give the Croatians much of a mass media system. Therefore, any public relations program must rely heavily on e-mail, personal communication, and other types of publications. The Internet is the major medium for mass distribution of information.

Croatia is still in the early stages of sorting out the relationship between government and private business. The television system that has evolved since 1998 is the product of a combined effort by the government, commercial broadcasting, television journalists, and the newly formed public broadcasting system. As these groups sort out their relationships, Croatian public television can begin to develop its own identity. For example, if the government would focus on standards and leave the operations to the private or commercial broadcasters, then concerns about interference from government could be resolved.

At this time the legislature seems more interested in creating laws or regulations to control the infrastructure than in encouraging the programming or technical facilities that will make a fine broadcast system. Since there is a great deal of interest from academics in Croatia and from supporters from other countries, there is significant pressure to create a democratic system free of government control.

Legal and Financial Limitations

PBS in the United States.   Financing and other legal requirements are major considerations. In the United States, PBS cannot have commercial advertisements from profit-making organizations. Instead of advertising, PBS is partially supported by underwriting. This means that businesses can be given credit for supporting a PBS announcement but cannot be allowed commercial airtime. However, groups that qualify as nonprofits can be given opportunities for presentations that are very similar to commercials. There are penalties if these guidelines are violated. Lately, because of reduced funding from the federal level, larger PBS stations have been pushing the envelope by creating more aggressive underwriting spots. Some people say these more aggressive spots are really advertisements.

Croatian Public Television.   Croatia does not have a democratic history. Therefore, its legislators often do not understand or see a need for a television system that can inform a democratic electorate. This legislature, without any experience with democracy, is charged with creating the organizational structure of Croatian public television.

Under these circumstances it is not surprising that the first impulse for a democratic system came from abroad. The Council of Europe and a small number of television journalists, known as Forum 21, were the first to argue for a Croatian television system with private control and democratic goals. Eventually, Forum 21 succeeded in motivating the Croatian legislature to pass laws in 2001 that laid a foundation for the development of a public television system free of government control. The 2001 laws took program control away from the Program Council that had been appointed by the Parliament. The law gave private organizations and institutions the opportunity to appoint their own representatives to the Program Council. However, this law, considered by the Council of Europe to be the most promising among transitional countries, has only been in place about a year and a half. During this short time, politicians and the government officials have done everything possible to prove that this kind of organizational structure does not work.

Objectives

The goal of public broadcasting systems is to provide programming to serve the communities in which they are located. In order to meet this organizational goal, each of these campaigns identified completely different public relations objectives.

PBS in the United States.   The organizational goal of the U.S. public television station was to determine and meet the needs of the subscribing public and the underwriters. In order to meet this goal the station had to both involve its publics in programming decisions and to secure support from those publics. In order to involve the publics in programming decisions, the campaign planners identified three community relations objectives. They were:

1. Reconnecting the viewing area public to their experience with public broadcasting
2. Involving the viewing area public in the development of programming
3. Empowering and engaging the viewing public to assist in the capital campaign effort to support the future of public television

Of course, this third community relations objective could also help raise funds to support the station. Public broadcasting survives in the United States on diminishing state and federal monies and membership subscriptions. Therefore, member subscriptions are essential to the station's survival and its ability to serve its community.

Responding to the need for funds, a more specific public relations objective was identified. Specifically, the campaign sought to double both membership and underwriting support within a three- to five-month period. The baseline measure of current subscribers and underwriting support was clearly established and served as the benchmark for the project.

Croatian Public Television.   For the Croatian public television campaign, the initial goal was to establish a public television system that had private leadership. Long-term organizational goals include building cultural and national identity and preserving the Croatian language. Language preservation is particularly important because it is the vehicle that will permit Croatian culture to survive and flourish. Of course, the organizational goals also include providing programming that is informative, entertaining, and educational. These umbrella goals are similar to those of PBS in the United States. In Croatia these goals are not universally supported.

For the present, public relations objectives to help meet the organizational goals focus on stabilizing Croatia's public television infrastructures by:

1. Designing a campaign addressing the publics' needs for public television
2. Developing strategies and tactics to establish standards for public television to assure the system will flourish in a young democracy
3. Establishing the role of public relations as a means for developing an organizational infrastructure both internally and externally

Obviously, any measurement of change is very complex when one is examining an infrastructure that should be supporting the ideals of educating, informing, and entertaining. The change will be incremental at best. Partly due to cultural traditions that do not emphasize deadlines or punctuality, it is not possible to specify a timeline for accomplishing the public relations objectives.

The only measurable public relations objectives may be the establishment and continuation of communication with the interest groups who support the public television system and maintaining progress toward a stable and privately controlled public broadcasting system that meets the needs of its viewers.

Strategies

Each campaign described here had a very different strategy. The U.S. PBS outlet adopted a community relations campaign, while the Croatian public television campaign was based on a government relations or lobbying approach.

PBS in the United States.   Research from two different studies guided strategy selection. The research identified a lack of community involvement. This lack of involvement affected awareness of PBS programming, membership levels, and financial contributions from underwriting and donations. However, it was obvious from the research that the station had the potential for becoming a very involved part of its community.

The client station is the only television outlet that has favorable local news. There are two significant regional newspapers, but these papers are zoned so greatly the result is the area is Balkanized and no one receives the news beyond a narrowly defined area. Therefore, the regional public television station is the sole source of news for the entire area that dedicates significant resources to local news. Recently the station was connected to the local alert system giving automatic news updates on serious situations. This is important, since broadcast stations are the primary source of news during crises in the United States. In short, the station's local news program can become the vehicle for integrating it into the local community. This integration can be used to motivate memberships, subscriptions, and financial support.

Based on these observations, the campaign's planners adopted a community relations approach designed to connect the community with its PBS station. The strategy was to establish relationships with select community organizations and to focus on viewership, membership, and fundraising.

Croatian Public Television.   The key players in public television development for Croatia are the parliament, a small number of television journalists, and the Council of Europe. The parliament was the primary target public for the campaign. The television journalists supported the campaign and were used as advocates. The Council of Europe is a group of academics that monitor, mentor, and report on relevant developments.

The television journalists and communication academics have united in an interpersonal campaign supported by written and electronic letters. Messages in this campaign are intended to stimulate a change in the television system. The decision to focus on interpersonal media was made because traditional mass media are not well developed in Croatia.

Other strategies include seeking intervention from the outside. Such intervention might come from countries adjoining Croatia to the north, like Slovenia, which has a rather well-developed sense of public relations. Academic ties in the area and close proximity to academic colleagues in other countries may facilitate a mutual and joint effort to be conducted on a broad communication project. The transitional countries in Southeast Europe already involved in projects to create public broadcasting systems include Romania, Bulgaria, Moldavia, Albania, Hungary, Poland, and Italy. These countries have joined Croatia in a project launched by Viadrina University in Frankfurt-Oder under the name 'The Process of Visual Media Transformation in Transitional Countries of Southeast Europe.'

Tactics

Tactics used in the two campaigns differ greatly due to the different target audiences, the different communications resources available, and the different strategies adopted.

PBS in the United States.   The campaign began with a meeting between the station staff and the board of director's community advisory committee in 2003. At that time the station was operating without a fully developed public relations program. The connection between their monthly schedule of programming, their pledge periods, their special mailings, and a few other outreach projects were not viewed or examined in terms of public relations standards. Consequently, opportunities were missed to connect these resources more closely with the station's primary mission of community relations. Even news releases had been stopped for a year until the lack of media presence was mentioned at a board meeting.

Once the campaign began, existing tactics and new communications efforts were integrated into the program. Tactics that were already in place included communication soliciting underwriting donations, and station tours. After the campaign began, new special events and competitions were begun. Special events involved the local library system and park and recreation sites. Business, government, and social groups such as chambers of commerce, Kiwanis, and Lions in 10 counties and two states were integrated into the outreach for a period of three months. The messages delivered to the target publics through special events and mailings emphasized that public broadcasting belonged to the community and stressed PBS as a community resource. Visual pieces developed for the campaign were designed with a multicultural audience in mind.

Specific messages included:

My favorite memory of Big Bird
Public Broadcasting is supported by you—the community
PBS programming of your flavor

In order to keep costs low, the junior- and senior-level students from a university public relations research class were recruited to donate most of the people power for this campaign. Other cost-saving techniques included using the station itself to disseminate information about programming and special events, and creating a new program of news releases. Use of the station included an increase in sports sponsorships and pledge opportunities. The station established a favorable relationship with two major newspapers and several weekly newspapers. News releases were favorably received by these papers because of the local perspective, because of the large numbers of people from the community who were involved, and because of the potential of digital television to deliver needed literacy and training programs to the area.

Croatian Public Television.   Tactics for this campaign were quite simple. They included e-mail and other forms of interpersonal communication directed to legislators by television journalists and communication academics. These communications sought to inform those managing the public television system in such basics as freedom of speech and the role of public figures, and to persuade them that public television, free from government control, is essential to a developing democracy.

Evaluation

PBS in the United States.   This campaign is making the client PBS station more interactive by involving the community in a significant way. As part of this increased community interaction the campaign has reached the population of school-aged children, the library system, and social groups like Kiwanis and Lions. Each of these groups is now involved with their public television outlet. One measure of improved involvement with the station is the increased number of children's requests for PBS club membership and the increase in membership subscriptions and underwriting. Most specific to the campaign's goal, both membership subscriptions and underwriting have both more than doubled, exceeding the original public relations objective.

Croatian Public Television.   The campaign has been successful in establishing a public broadcasting system with legislative acts in 1998, 2001, and 2003. However, the campaign has not been successful in establishing private control of the broadcasting system. The current act, passed in 2003, reestablished government control over the Croatian public broadcast system. The taint of the government-imposed control is reflected in the actions of television director, who terminated some programming editors because the former President Tudjman was mocked in a New Year's sketch. The status of the effort to establish a public television system remains fragile despite the quiet communication campaign of a few communication academics and TV journalists.

If the campaign's objective was to establish a privately controlled broadcast system in Croatia, it has, thus far, failed. However, the stated objective was only to ". . . continue communication with interest groups and to maintain progress toward a stable and privately controlled public broadcasting system that meets the needs of its viewers." The campaign has been successful in meeting this very limited objective.

Critique

Research

PBS in the United States. The research that preceded the PBS station's campaign was unusually thorough. Subjects covered included a description of the client and potential target publics. Further, both legal and cultural limitations were explored. Also, the combination of surveys and focus groups should provide information that is both reliable and valid. Because of the detailed and appropriate analysis, the campaign planners were able to identify a very specific objective and an appropriate strategy. If there was any weakness at all in the research it was the absence of information on available media.

Croatian Public Television. Data for the Croatian campaign came exclusively from media publications and legislative documents. This research omitted some critical questions. Information on the availability of supporters for privately controlled television would have been helpful, as would more information on loyalties in the Croatian Parliament. It would have been helpful, for example, to have some measure of how credible communications academics are with Croatian legislators. Information on the amount of popular support for privately controlled public television and the availability of Internet access would also help in trying to evaluate the campaign's potential for success.

Given that this campaign is in its very early stages and apparently does not have extensive resources with which to work, the research presented may be the best possible, but it is at least possibly influenced by the perceptions and commitment of the campaign's supporters. As soon as possible, the campaign could be improved with more detailed information gathered from more objective and reliable sources.

Objectives

PBS in the United States. The objectives presented do, in fact, support the articulated organizational goals. Those objectives that focused on involving the community around the client station would help improve programming and help meet the needs of the subscribing public.

The most specific objective was to double the number of subscribers within five months. The specificity of this objective lends itself to evaluation and provides ample guidance when evaluating the propriety of strategies or tactics. One might offer some criticism of the decision to adopt a very short timeline. The success of the campaign, however, suggests that five months was adequate time to meet the objective.

Croatian Public Television.   Cultural differences between Croatia and the United States may account for one weakness in the objective for the Croatian campaign. Simply put, the objective lacked any specific deadline and did not detail any change in the behavior of the target public. Within U.S. culture, people are fairly comfortable establishing timelines, deadlines, and specific behavioral objectives. Many other cultures are not as comfortable with deadlines and specific goals.

Here the objective was simply to continue communication and to maintain progress. While such an objective will frustrate specific evaluation, it may be the only kind of objective that is culturally appropriate.

Strategies

PBS in the United States.   The decisions to focus on community relations and to involve the publics within the station's broadcast reach are perfectly supported by the research and the organizational goal. Because of the relatively small and eclectic publics the station served and the station's commitment to a valuable local news program, it was perfectly positioned to establish itself as an important part of the community. This position as a community member could then be used to justify appeals for support.

Croatian Public Television.   Because they do not have a well-developed system of mass media, those supporting public television in Croatia had very few strategic choices. Relying on media like correspondence and e-mail and personal influence may be the only strategy available. Further, the target public for the campaign is very small. If only the legislators can decide the fate of Croatian public television, they are the primary public for the campaign. Traditional strategies involving mass media may be simply inappropriate in this case.

Tactics

PBS in the United States.   The tactics implemented here were traditional tools used in community relations programs. They included both activities to involve members of the target publics, and communications to insure people in the target publics were informed. It would have been helpful to have more detail about how the events were planned, who was involved, and how well the events were attended.

In particular, the decision to use students from a local university seems wise. The students' involvement reduces costs to the client and, if the students are from the community, it also increases the level of community involvement in the entire program.

Croatian Public Television.   It is very difficult to critique the tactics in the Croatian television campaign. The strategy was to use personal communication. Under these circumstances the tactics are individual personal messages. One might think it easy to critique such tactics, but each individual personal message can only be analyzed in the context of the relationship between its author and recipient. The critique would also require a detailed understanding of the exact content and timing of the message. In short, it is virtually impossible to critique or manage such tactics. The public relations practitioner who opts to use personal communications as a strategy must depend on the good judgment and skills of the campaign representatives who conduct each communication.

Evaluation

PBS in the United States.   The objective for the PBS station in the United States was operationalized and easily measured. The campaign succeeded in meeting the objective of doubling memberships and underwriting support. Criticism of such a simple numerical evaluation is difficult, but it might be suggested that the station consider adding an ongoing evaluation that might guide a longer campaign to create even more members and support.

Croatian Public Television.   On one hand, the fact that a transitional country like Croatia has officially established a public television system is viewed by many as a success. On the other hand, the imposition of government control over the Croatian television system in 2003 suggests the campaign may have failed.

Because the public relations objective focused on communication and ongoing progress rather than a specific accomplishment, evaluation must be ongoing. It will take a very long time to determine if the campaign is successful in supporting the organizational goal of establishing a stable and privately controlled television system.

DISCUSSION QUESTIONS

1. This campaign presentation is unusual because it describes campaigns for two similar clients in two different cultures. What elements of the two cultures make these campaigns different?
    a. Do you believe public relations is easier in the United States or in Croatia? Why?
    b. Does the absence of an extensive system of mass media make it easier or more difficult to communicate with a small target public? Explain at least one reason why it would be easier and one reason it would be more difficult.

2. One comment in the critique of the campaign in Croatia questioned the reliability of research based on media sources and legislative documents. If you wanted to research public opinion about government control of television systems in Croatia, how would you conduct the research?

3. Describe how you would design a study to measure how credible television journalists and communication academics are in Croatia. Describe how you would design that study if you only wanted to know how credible they are with members of the Croatian Parliament.

4. Do you agree with the decision by the PBS station in the United States to focus on community relations as a strategy? If the objective of the PBS campaign was only to raise money for the station, what other strategies might have been successful?

5. Why do boards of directors, CEOs, or government officials sometimes not welcome research?
    a. Describe why you think the people controlling the PBS station might not have wanted to support research about their station and its publics.
    b. Describe why you think the Parliament in Croatia might not support research about public attitudes toward public television.

   c. How would you convince each group to conduct research?

   d. How would you use the results of the research in a campaign effort?

6. When people operate from a U.S. perspective they may assume democracy is established in a country and often assume everyone in other countries values it. How do you think these assumptions affect your attitudes toward the campaign in Croatia?

7. How does the perception of public relations as a profession affect one's ability to conduct a campaign in the United States?

   a. How does the perception of public relations as a profession affect one's ability to conduct a campaign in other countries? Consider, for example, how you would relate to the local media or to your client.

   b. Would your sense of professional ethics or the concept of social responsibility be different if you were in a country where public relations expertise or skill was not valued?

8. What should public relations professionals know about cultures, society, demographics, geography, and organizational infrastructures before beginning a campaign? Is it important for you to know how your campaign might impact or change the culture or society in which you work? Explain.

9. Explain what the terms co-orientation and dialogic mean. How do these concepts relate to public relations, persuasion, and community relations?

REFERENCES AND SUGGESTED READINGS

Banks, S. (2000). *Multicultural public relations: A social-interpretive approach.* Ames, Iowa: Iowa State University Press.

Barker, J. R., & Tompkins, P. K. (1994). Identification in the self-managing organization: Characteristics of target and tenure. *Human Communication Research, 21,* 223–240.

Brownell, M., & Niebauer, W. (1989). Increasing professionalism in public relations: An [sic] system for categorizing practitioners. *Public Relations Review, 15*(3), 52.

Farmer, B., Slater, J., & Wright, K. (1998). The role of communication in achieving shared vision under new organizational leadership. *Journal of Public Relations Research, 10*(4), 219–236.

Grunig, L. A. (1990). Using focus group research in public relations. *Public Relations Review, 16*(2), 36–49.

Grunig, L. A. (1992). Matching public relations research to the problem: Conducting a special focus group, *Journal of Public Relations Research, 4*(1), 21–44.

Hansen-Horn. T., & Neff, B. D. (forthcoming in 2005). *Public relations theory.* Boston: Allyn & Bacon.

Heath, R., & Abel, D. (1996). Types of knowledge as predictors of company support: The role of information in risk communication. *Journal of Public Relations Research, 8*(1), 35–56.

Heath, R., Liao, S., & Douglas, W. (1995). Effects of perceived economic harms and benefits on issue involvement, use of information sources, and actions: A study in risk communication. *Journal of Public Relations Research, 7*(2), 89–110.

Johnson, M. (1997). Public relations and technology: Practitioner perspectives. *Journal of Public Relations Research, 9*(3), 213–235.

Lauzen, M., & Dozier, D. (1992). The missing link: The public relations manager role as mediator of organizational environments and power consequences for the function. *Journal of Public Relations Research, 4*(4), 205–220.

Lindenmann, W. K. (1990). Research, evaluation and measurement: A national perspective. *Public Relations Review, 16*(2), 8–16.

Neff, B. D. (1998). Harmonizing global relations: A speech act theory analysis of PRForum. *Public Relations Review, 24*(3), 351–376.

Neff, B. D. (2005). Community Relations. In Philip Lesly (Ed.), *Public Relations Encyclopedia,* Thousand Oaks, CA: Sage.

Neff, B. D., Walker, G., Smith, M., & Creedon, P. (1999). Outcomes desired by practitioners and academics. *Public Relations Review, 25*(1), 29–44.

Plowman, K. (1998). Power in conflict for public relations. *Journal of Public Relations Research, 10*(4), 237–262.

Rosser, C., Flora, J., Chaffee, S., & Farquhar, J. (1990). Using research to predict learning from a PR campaign. *Public Relations Review, 16*(2), 61–77.

Stacks, D. (2002). *Primer of public relations research.* New York: Guilford.

INDEX